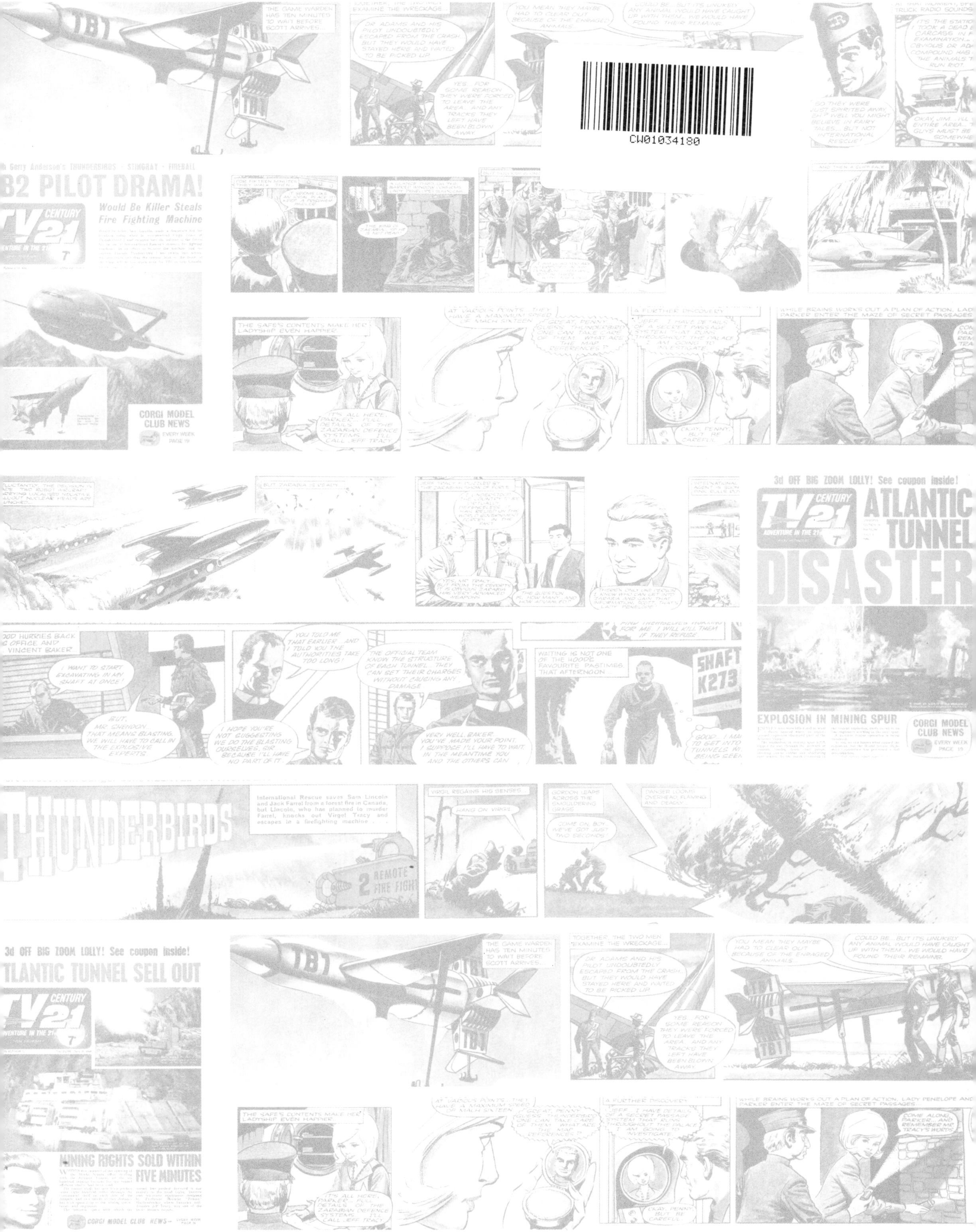
THE GAME WARDEN HAS TEN MINUTES TO WAIT BEFORE SCOTT ARRIVES...
DR. ADAMS AND HIS PILOT UNDOUBTEDLY ESCAPED FROM THE CRASH. BUT THEY WOULD HAVE STAYED HERE AND WAITED TO BE PICKED UP.
YES... FOR SOME REASON THEY WERE FORCED TO LEAVE THE AREA... AND ANY TRACKS THEY LEFT HAVE BEEN BLOWN AWAY.
YOU MEAN THEY MAYBE HAD TO CLEAR OUT BECAUSE OF THE ENRAGED ANIMALS.
B2 PILOT DRAMA!
Would Be Killer Steals Fire Fighting Machine
TV CENTURY 21
7d
CORGI MODEL CLUB NEWS
EVERY WEEK PAGE 19
THE SAFE'S CONTENTS MAKE HER LADYSHIP EVEN HAPPIER
IT'S ALL HERE, PARKER... FULL DETAILS OF THE ZARABAN DEFENCE SYSTEMS... CALL JEFF TRACY
OKAY, PENNY... BUT BE CAREFUL
3d OFF BIG ZOOM LOLLY! See coupon inside!
ATLANTIC TUNNEL DISASTER
EXPLOSION IN MINING SPUR
I WANT TO START EXCAVATING IN MY SHAFT AT ONCE!
BUT, MR. SHENDON ... THAT MEANS BLASTING. WE WILL HAVE TO CALL IN THE EXPLOSIVE EXPERTS.
YOU TOLD ME THAT EARLIER... AND I TOLD YOU THE AUTHORITIES TAKE TOO LONG!
THE OFFICIAL TEAM KNOW THE STRUCTURE OF EACH TUNNEL. THEY CAN SET THEIR CHARGES WITHOUT CAUSING ANY DAMAGE
I HOPE YOU'RE NOT SUGGESTING WE DO THE BLASTING OURSELVES, SIR. BECAUSE I'LL HAVE NO PART OF IT.
VERY WELL, BAKER. YOU'VE MADE YOUR POINT. I SUPPOSE I'LL HAVE TO WAIT. IN THE MEANTIME YOU AND THE OTHERS CAN
WAITING IS NOT ONE OF THE HOODS FAVOURITE PASTIMES THAT AFTERNOON
SHAFT K273
THUNDERBIRDS
International Rescue saves Sam Lincoln and Jack Farrel from a forest fire in Canada, but Lincoln, who has planned to murder Farrel, knocks out Virgil Tracy and escapes in a firefighting machine . . .
VIRGIL REGAINS HIS SENSES...
HANG ON VIRGIL
COME ON BOY WE'VE GOT JUST TWO SECONDS!
2 REMOTE FIRE FIGHT
ATLANTIC TUNNEL SELL OUT
MINING RIGHTS SOLD WITHIN FIVE MINUTES
CORGI MODEL CLUB NEWS
TOGETHER, THE TWO MEN EXAMINE THE WRECKAGE...
COULD BE... BUT IT'S UNLIKELY ANY ANIMAL WOULD HAVE CAUGHT UP WITH THEM... WE WOULD HAVE FOUND THEIR REMAINS.
A FURTHER DISCOVERY
JEFF... I HAVE DETAILS OF A SECRET PASSAGE SYSTEM THAT RUNS THROUGHOUT THE PALACE. I AM GOING TO INVESTIGATE.
WHILE BRAINS WORKS OUT A PLAN OF ACTION, LADY PENELOPE AND PARKER ENTER THE MAZE OF SECRET PASSAGES...
COME ALONG, PARKER... AND REMEMBER MR TRACY'S WORDS

THUNDERBIRDS™

OH, YOU POOR MAN. COME INTO THE DRAWING ROOM AND HAVE SOME TEA.
SUDDENLY FEELS IT LUCKY DAY...
I'LL JUST RING FOR PARKER
THAT MUST BE THE RAY TORCH. THIS IS GOING TO BE EASIER THAN I THOUGHT.
BY THE TIME THE TEA ARRIVES, THE TORCH IS IN STEEL'S POCKET...
WELL THANKS FOR YOUR KINDNESS, MA'AM... I'D BETTER BE ON MY WAY.
IT'S BEEN A PLEASURE... DROP IN ANY TIME YOU'RE PASSING... AND GOOD LUCK.
PARKER SHOWS STEEL OUT... AND HIS OLD SKILLS ARE SOON EMPLOYED...
SURPRISED AT WHAT HE HAS GAINED, PARKER REPORTS TO LADY PENELOPE...
PARKER! I'VE TOLD YOU BEFORE ABOUT BEING LIGHT FINGERED. BUT WHY SHOULD THAT NICE MAN HAVE TAKEN THE TORCH IN THE FIRST PLACE?
I FOUND YOUR INVISIBLE RAY IN HIS POCKET, M'LADY...
THEN ANOTHER VISITOR ARRIVES...
I WONDER IF THE LADY OF THE HOUSE WOULD BE INTERESTED IN THE NEW UNIVERSAL COOK BOOK?
EH? NOT ANOTHER ONE! OH, WELL... YOU'D BETTER COME INTO THE LIBRARY.
INTRIGUED, LADY PENELOPE REFUSES THE OFFER OF COOK BOOKS, AND AGAIN PARKER SERVES TEA.
IT WOULD APPEAR THERE ARE MORE SALESMEN THAN UNIVERSAL COOK BOOKS!
THERE IT IS! I WAS PREPARED TO KILL HER FOR THAT RAY... BUT I DON'T THINK THAT WILL BE NECESSARY NOW!
SUDDENLY, THE HOOD UPSETS HIS TEA...
I... I'M TERRIBLY SORRY... I'M SO CLUMSY.
AN ACCIDENT... PARKER WILL SOON CLEAN IT UP.
THE MISHAP HAS DISTRACTED ATTENTION...
NOW'S MY CHANCE!
MINUTES LATER, THE HOOD LEAVES...
COR! 'E'S A CAGEY ONE... DIDN'T LET ME GET NEAR HIS POCKETS...
THE INCORRIGIBLE BUTLER RETURNS TO THE DRAWING ROOM...
IS HE ONE OF YOUR FRIENDS, PARKER?
NO, M'LADY... WHY?
HE'S TAKEN THE TORCH!
I NOW HAVE THE POWER TO BECOME INVISIBLE. THE WORLD'S TOP SECRETS WILL BE MINE!

compiled and edited by

Graham Bleatham and Sam Denham

CARLTON BOOKS

Classic Comic Strips from

Edited and Compiled
by Graham Bleathman
and Sam Denham

Original Stories Edited
by Alan Fennell

Comic Strip Art
by Frank Bellamy, Eric Eden,
Frank Hampson and Don Harley
Cover by Graham Bleathman

Dedicated to the Memory
of Alan Fennell (1936-2001)
Editor of TV Century 21 and
Thunderbirds Screenwriter

This is a Carlton book

Published by Carlton Books Limited 2001
20 Mortimer Street
London W1T 3JW

"Tomorrow's News Today" and other intro-
ductory material, text and design © Carlton
Books Limited 2002

TM and © 1965 and 1999. THUNDER-
BIRDS is a trademark of Carlton
International Media Limited and is used
under licence.
THUNDERBIRDS is a Gerry
Anderson Production
Licensed by Carlton International
Media Limited
© 1999. The Carlton logotype deviceis a
trademark of Carlton International Media
Limited.

A CIP catalogue for this book is available
from the British Library

ISBN 1 84222 731 9

Project Editor: Lorna Russell
Design: Brian Flynn
Production: Janette Burgin

DATELINE 2066

Straight from the pages of classic 1960's comic *TV Century 21*, the *Thunderbirds* team and their fantastic machines blast into fantastic comic strip action.

Page 4
Tomorrow's News Today
How Gerry Anderson's famous Supermarionation TV shows inspired the creation of TV Century 21's amazing world of the future.

Page 14
Dateline 2065: Mansion at War!

Page 16
Mr Steelman - Robot Master!
In their first mission together, Lady Penelope and Parker face the robotic Mr Steelman.

Art: Eric Eden

Page 38
Danger in Unity City
Lady Penelope and Parker race to the rescue when they discover a plot to assassinate the World President.

Art : Frank Hampson

Adventure in the 21st century!

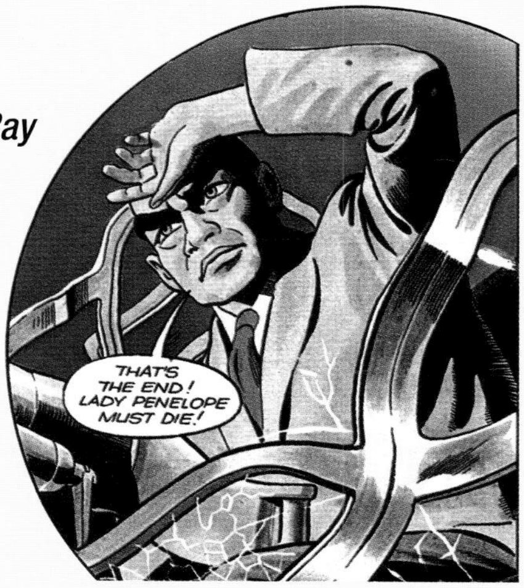

THAT'S THE END! LADY PENELOPE MUST DIE!

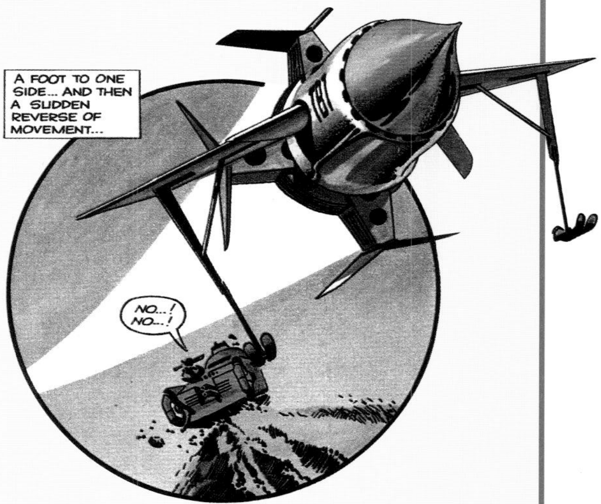

A FOOT TO ONE SIDE... AND THEN A SUDDEN REVERSE OF MOVEMENT...
NO...! NO...!

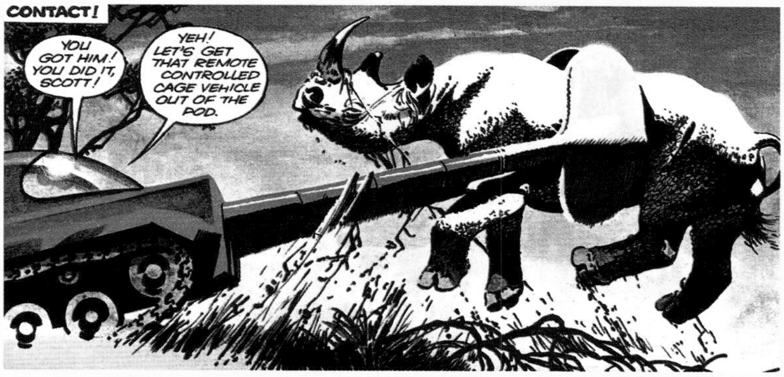

CONTACT!
YOU GOT HIM! YOU DID IT, SCOTT!
YEH! LET'S GET THAT REMOTE CONTROLLED CAGE VEHICLE OUT OF THE POD.

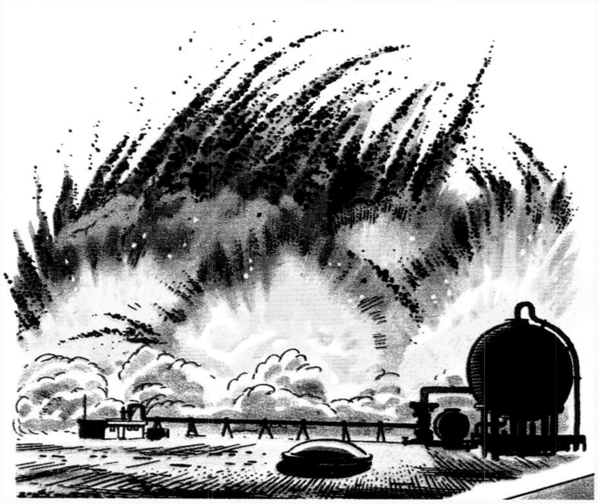

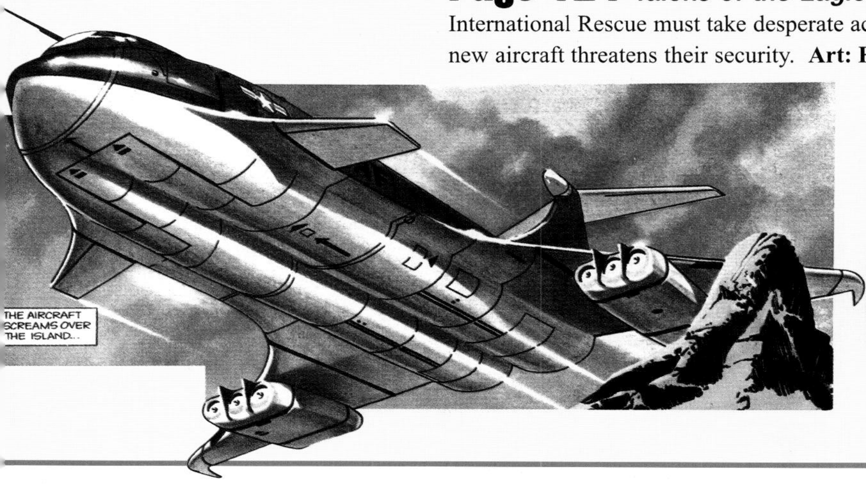

THE AIRCRAFT SCREAMS OVER THE ISLAND...

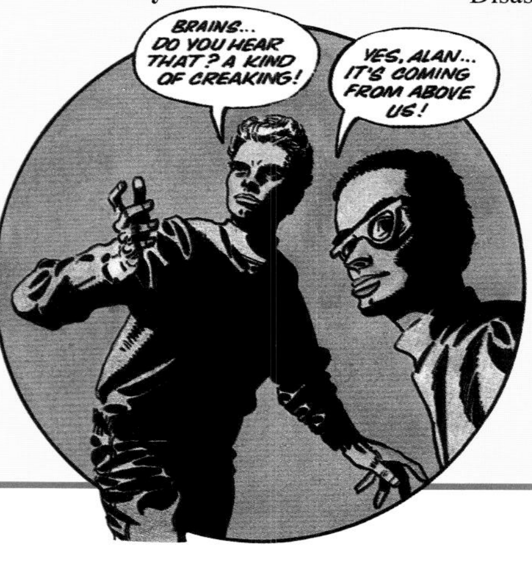

BRAINS... DO YOU HEAR THAT? A KIND OF CREAKING!
YES, ALAN... IT'S COMING FROM ABOVE US!

Tomorrow's news TODAY!

Creating the futuristic world of TV Century 21

Thunderbirds first blasted onto British TV screens in September 1965. Produced by space-age puppet master Gerry Anderson using a technique known as Supermarionation, the series was filmed in colour (or, as Anderson named it – Videcolor). However at the time, colour television was only available to viewers in America and Japan. British viewers had to make do with black and white TV. So while filming began on *Thunderbirds* during the summer of 1964, plans were put into action to launch the amazing adventures of International Rescue into another thrilling dimension. A new magazine featuring full colour comic strips would let the shows' British fans see just what they were missing!

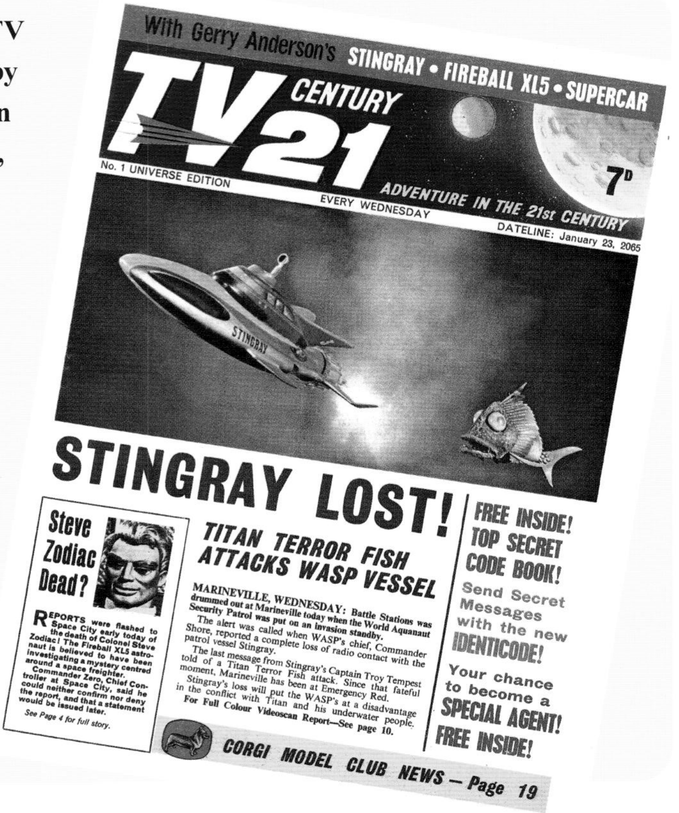
With Gerry Anderson's STINGRAY • FIREBALL XL5 • SUPERCAR

TV CENTURY 21

No. 1 UNIVERSE EDITION — EVERY WEDNESDAY — 7D

ADVENTURE IN THE 21st CENTURY

DATELINE: January 23, 2065

STINGRAY LOST!

Steve Zodiac Dead?

REPORTS were flashed to Space City early today of the death of Colonel Steve Zodiac! The Fireball XL5 astronaut is believed to have been investigating a mystery centred around a space freighter.

Commander Zero, Chief Controller at Space City, said he could neither confirm nor deny the report, and that a statement would be issued later.

See Page 4 for full story.

TITAN TERROR FISH ATTACKS WASP VESSEL

MARINEVILLE, WEDNESDAY: Battle Stations was drummed out at Marineville today when the World Aquanaut Security Patrol was put on an invasion standby.

The alert was called when WASP's chief, Commander Shore, reported a complete loss of radio contact with the patrol vessel Stingray.

The last message from Stingray's Captain Troy Tempest told of a Titan Terror Fish attack. Since that fateful moment, Marineville has been at Emergency Red.

Stingray's loss will put the WASP's at a disadvantage in the conflict with Titan and his underwater people.

For Full Colour Videoscan Report—See page 10.

FREE INSIDE! TOP SECRET CODE BOOK!

Send Secret Messages with the new IDENTICODE!

Your chance to become a SPECIAL AGENT! FREE INSIDE!

CORGI MODEL CLUB NEWS – Page 19

Right: *TV Century 21* – A new world of comic strip adventure

GERRY ANDERSON'S AP FILMS PRODUCTION COMPANY was in a fantastic position to create a comic featuring *Thunderbirds* and APF's earlier shows, such as the recently completed *Stingray*. The firm had already set up a licensing company headed by licensing manager Keith Shackleton to market toys, games and other spin-offs from the company's programmes. These spin-offs included successful comic strips in the magazine *TV Comic* based on *Fireball XL5* and *Supercar*. Shackleton realised APF could now create its own comic featuring its existing programmes that could also provide an extra launch pad for the eagerly awaited *Thunderbirds*. It was also obvious who should

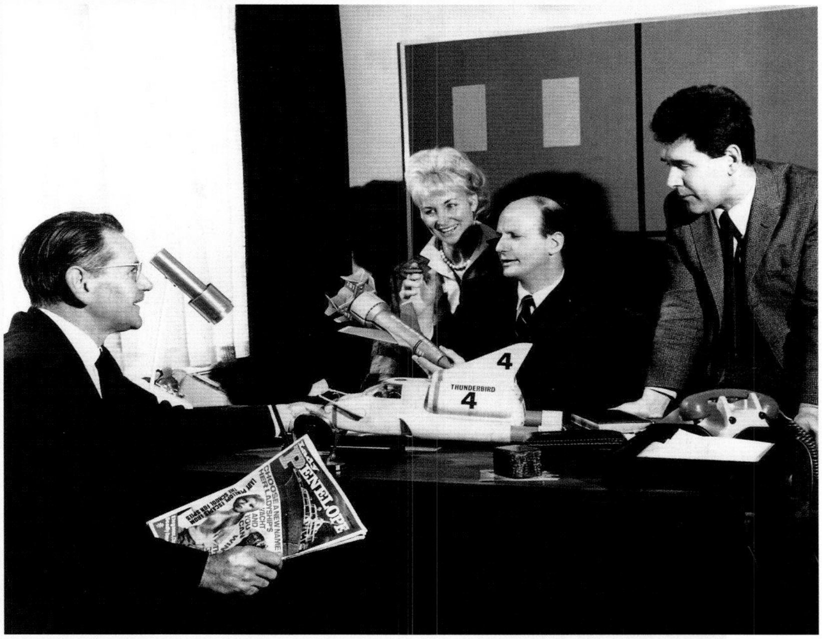
4
THUNDERBIRD
4

Right: **The creators of AP Films – Reg Hill, Sylvia Anderson, Gerry Anderson and John Read. Reg Hill is holding a copy of *TV21* spin-off comic "Lady Penelope".**

take charge of this ambitious new project. Scriptwriter Alan Fennell was responsible for writing the *TV Comic* Supermarionation strips, and had joined APF to write screenplays for the programmes themselves. Shackleton called a meeting with Fennell and Anderson to discuss the new publication. At Anderson's suggestion it would be based on a newspaper format, and while Fennell set to work creating a dummy first issue, Shackleton began contacting publishers who might be willing to take on the new venture.

An experienced comic strip writer, Alan Fennell had developed a special talent for writing action adventure stories. By 1963 he had become one of the major creative forces behind the Supermarionation programmes, so was perfectly qualified to edit a magazine based on AP Films' output. Born in 1936, Fennell started work in the publishing business as an office boy at Amalgamated Press in the early 1950s, but soon found more interesting work on the *TV Fun* and *Radio Fun* comics as a writer.

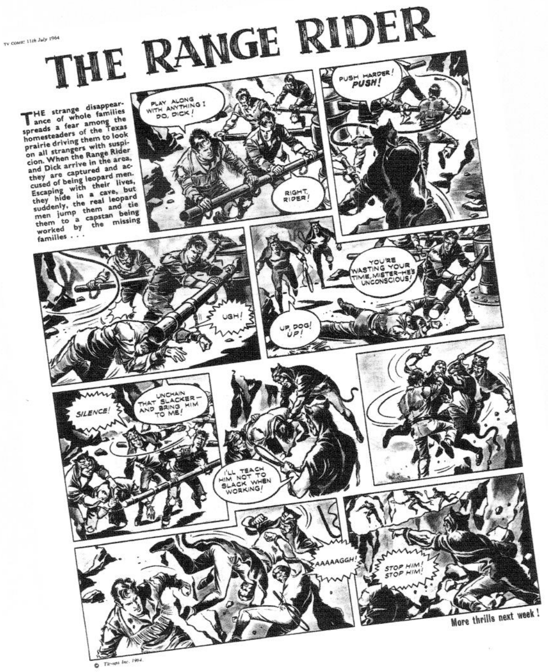
11
TV COMIC 11th July 1964
THE RANGE RIDER
THE strange disappearance of whole families spreads a fear among the homesteaders of the Texas prairie driving them to look on all strangers with suspicion. When the Range Rider and Dick arrive in the area, they are captured and accused of being leopard men. Escaping with their lives, they hide in a cave, but suddenly, the real leopard men jump them and tie them to a capstan being worked by the missing families . . .
PLAY ALONG WITH ANYTHING I DO, DICK!
RIGHT, RIDER!
PUSH HARDER! PUSH!
UGH!
YOU'RE WASTING YOUR TIME, MISTER—HE'S UNCONSCIOUS!
UP, DOG! UP!
SILENCE!
UNCHAIN THAT SLACKER—AND BRING HIM TO ME!
I'LL TEACH HIM NOT TO SLACK WHEN WORKING!
AAAAAGGH!
STOP HIM! STOP HIM!
More thrills next week!
© TV-ops Inc. 1964.

With fellow writer Angus Allan he then edited and produced the Cowboy Picture Library series of magazines, and before long he was working for TV Publications (TVP) as assistant editor on their new children's magazine *TV Comic*. TVP had already published comic strips based on APF's earlier productions, and with his experience of Western subjects Fennell negotiated a deal for *TV Comic* to feature AP Films' new puppet cowboy series, Four Feather Falls.

When APF launched its first science fantasy series *Supercar* in 1960, this too was added to *TV Comic*, and allowed Fennell to develop his skills as a comic strip writer even further.

At this time British comics were usually heavily captioned in a bid to please concerned parents that comics did not contain 'enough reading'. Moving away from this trend, Fennell created a balance between enough text to avoid confusion, with strong visuals that maintained the reader's attention. Impressed by Fennell's work, Gerry Anderson suggested he try writing a TV screenplay for a

Left: **Alan Fennell began his comic strip career writing cowboy stories. This is a strip drawn by future *TV21* artist Mike Noble.**

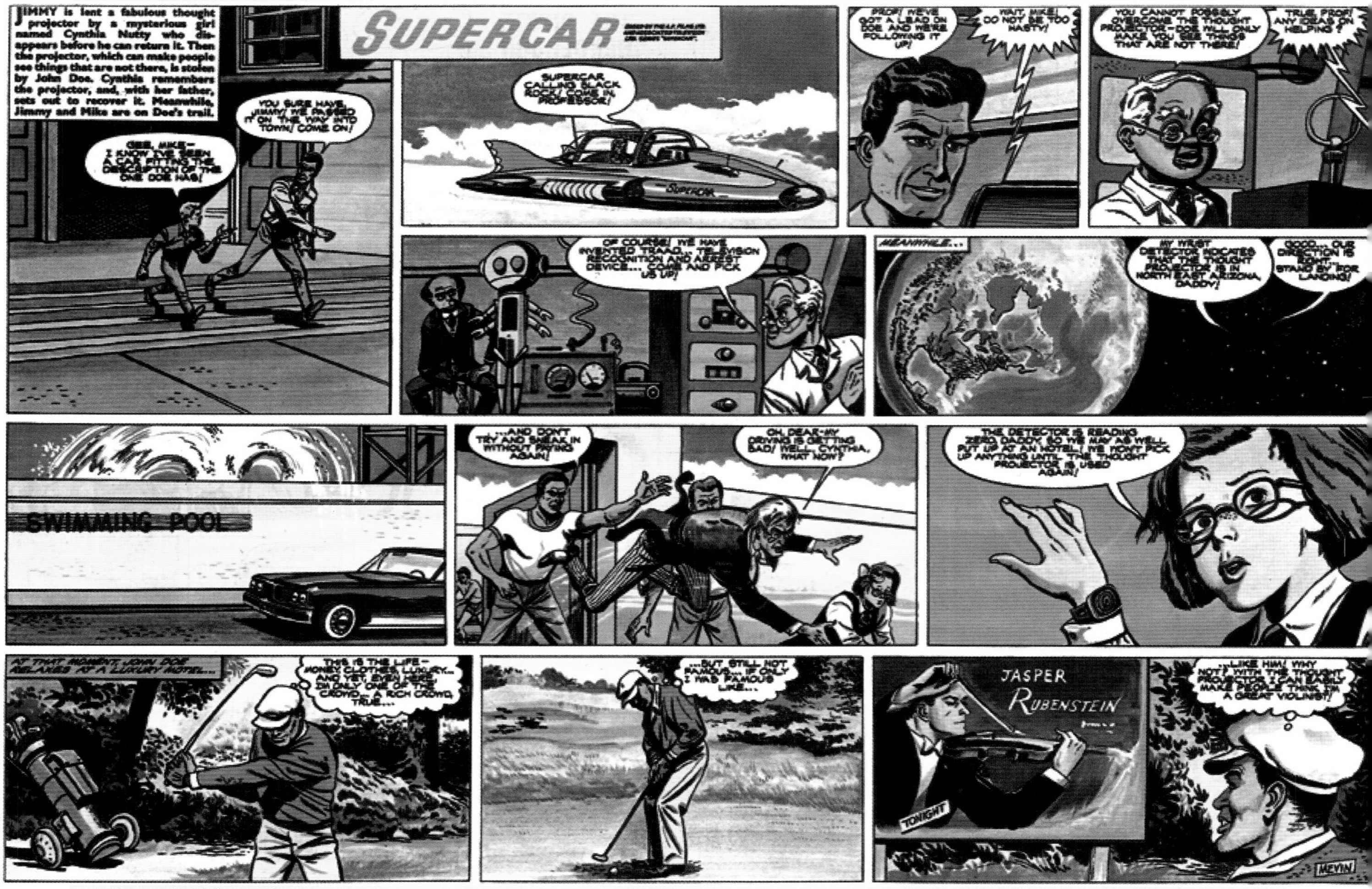
JIMMY is lent a fabulous thought projector by a mysterious girl named Cynthia Nutty who disappears before he can return it. Then the projector, which can make people see things that are not there, is stolen by John Doe. Cynthia remembers the projector, and, with her father, sets out to recover it. Meanwhile, Jimmy and Mike are on Doe's trail.
SUPERCAR
GEE, MIKE— I KNOW I'VE SEEN A CAR FITTING THE DESCRIPTION OF THE ONE DOE HAS!
YOU SURE HAVE, JIMMY! WE PASSED IT ON THE WAY INTO TOWN! COME ON!
SUPERCAR CALLING BLACK ROCK! COME IN, PROFESSOR!
PROF! WE'VE GOT A LEAD ON DOE AND WE'RE FOLLOWING IT UP!
WAIT, MIKE! DO NOT BE TOO HASTY!
YOU CANNOT POSSIBLY OVERCOME THE THOUGHT PROJECTOR—DOE WILL ONLY MAKE YOU SEE THINGS THAT ARE NOT THERE!
TRUE, PROF! ANY IDEAS ON HELPING ?
OF COURSE! WE HAVE INVENTED TRAAD... TELEVISION RECOGNITION AND ARREST DEVICE... COME AND PICK US UP!
MEANWHILE...
MY WRIST DETECTOR INDICATES THAT THE THOUGHT PROJECTOR IS IN NORTH EAST ARIZONA, DADDY!
GOOD... OUR DIRECTION IS RIGHT... STAND BY FOR LANDING!
SWIMMING POOL
...AND DON'T TRY AND SNEAK IN WITHOUT PAYING AGAIN!
OH, DEAR—MY DRIVING IS GETTING BAD! WELL, CYNTHIA, WHAT NOW?
THE DETECTOR IS READING ZERO, DADDY, SO WE MAY AS WELL PUT UP AT AN HOTEL! WE WON'T PICK UP ANYTHING UNTIL THE THOUGHT PROJECTOR IS USED AGAIN!
AT THAT MOMENT, JOHN DOE RELAXES AT A LUXURY MOTEL...
THIS IS THE LIFE— MONEY, CLOTHES, LUXURY... AND YET, EVEN HERE, I'M ONLY ONE OF THE CROWD... A RICH CROWD, TRUE...
...BUT STILL NOT FAMOUS... IF ONLY I WAS FAMOUS LIKE...
JASPER RUBENSTEIN
TONIGHT
...LIKE HIM! WHY NOT? WITH THE THOUGHT PROJECTOR I CAN EASILY MAKE PEOPLE THINK I'M A GREAT VIOLINIST!
MEVIN

Above: **Drawn by Bill Mevin, *Supercar* became a long running success in *TV Comic*.**

planned new series of *Supercar*. Although further episodes of *Supercar* were eventually abandoned in favour of an entirely new show, Anderson was pleased enough with the script to invite Fennell to join APF's scriptwriting team for the new production, *Fireball XL5*.

Produced from 1962 to 1963, *Fireball* was the most ambitious so far of the unique puppet film series that had become APF's speciality. Originally been established by Anderson and his partner Arthur Provis to film *The Adventures of Twizzle*, a simple children's puppet show devised by author Roberta Leigh, APF's success with this series led to a second Leigh creation, *Torchy the Battery Boy*. Both productions were financed by Associated Rediffusion Television, part of the British Electric Traction group. As BET also owned TV Publications, the appearance of APF's initial productions as comic strips in TVP's *TV Land* and *TV Comic* magazines was a natural development. However with Fennell's help the relationship between the comics and the TV programmes grew much closer. Having written almost half of the *Fireball XL5* screenplays while still writing for *TV Comic*, Fennell could now ensure even greater continuity was maintained when he adapted the series for its *TV Comic* appearances. He could also take advantage of the new opportunities for visual adventure inspired by the studio's inventive effects unit run by Derek Meddings and as a result, Fennell's comic strips became a major part of APF's growing merchandising operations.

With the support and backing of television mogul Lew Grade, under the control of Keith Shackleton, APF's merchandising arm had grown from strength to strength. Grade, head of Associated Television and its international sales division ITC, had successfully sold *Supercar* to the United States and then negotiated a US network screening for *Fireball XL5*. The resulting demand for APF merchandise was so enormous that Grade offered to buy out APF in return for a huge investment in the company. Realising that this would lead to even more spectacular programmes, Shackleton could see that the time was now right to think about publishing a comic that would exploit the growing interest in the company's shows and also advertise APF's merchandising spin-offs. Following his discussions with Anderson and Fennell Shackleton found a willing business partner in City Magazines, part of the News of the World group.

When APF began production on their new colour series Stingray, Fennell soon found himself busy writing TV screenplays for the new series and comic strips for Fireball XL5, while developing ideas for the yet to be produced Thunderbirds and creating the requested dummy issue of the new comic, at that time known simply as *Century 21*. Initially Fennell followed Anderson's suggestion that it should be a text based newspaper style magazine, but soon abandoned this approach in favour of a more traditional style format based on the classic *Eagle* comic. From its creation in 1950, *The Eagle*, featuring Britain's first space age comic strip hero Dan Dare, had quickly established itself with a reputation for high quality artwork and presentation, and Fennell would later admit he wanted to create something similar. *The Eagle's* influence can most clearly be seen in his choice of artists and the production techniques employed, such as the photogravure printing process. This process had been successfully used to produce *The Eagle* comic by Liverpool printers Eric Bemrose, and allowed the whiteness of ultra-smooth paper to shine through thin tuolene based inks. This resulted in superb quality reproduction that displayed artwork at its best.

FIREBALL XL5
THROUGH a fault in the gyros, Steve is forced to land Fireball on an unexplored planet. They carry out repairs, but then a giant snake wraps itself round XL5. Steve blasts off, but the snake starts to pull Fireball junior from the main body.
XL5
WE'VE ONLY ONE CHANCE TO SAVE FIREBALL! IF I CAN HIT THAT MARSH AT THE RIGHT ANGLE IT MIGHT STUN THE SNAKE ENOUGH TO MAKE IT RELAX ITS GRIP!
HOLD TIGHT EVERYBODY HERE WE GO!
IN THE NAVIGATION BAY VENUS, MAT AND ZOONIE PREPARE FOR THE CRASH...
CLING ON TIGHTLY, ZOONIE, AND DON'T LET GO, WHATEVER HAPPENS!

TV COMIC 11th July 1964
WITH SPLIT SECOND TIMING, STEVE FIRES THE MAIN BOOSTERS AND WITH TERRIFIC FORCE, SKIMS THE SURFACE OF THE MARSH...
YOUR PLAN HAS WORKED, STEVE. THAT MONSTER SURE HAS BEGUN TO LOSE ITS GRIP!
RIGHT! NOW TO MAKE IT LET GO ALTOGETHER!
ONCE FIREBALL IS OUT OF THE ATMOSPHERE THE MONSTER WILL HAVE TO LET GO THROUGH LACK OF AIR!
AND SO...
I BET THAT SNAKE WISHES HE'D GOT A LADDER RIGHT NOW, STEVE!
YEAH, MAT. HE'S GOING TO MAKE A BIG SPLASH WHEN HE LANDS IN THAT SWAMP!
WELL, STEVE, THAT'S THAT. NOW LET'S BEAT IT FOR HOME AND SEE WHAT OTHER ADVENTURES ARE IN STORE FOR US!
NEVILLE MAIN
A grand new adventure starts in next week's Fireball !

Right: ***Fireball XL5*** **first appeared in a black and white strip in** ***TV Comic*** **drawn by Neville Main.**

XL5
XL5
XL5

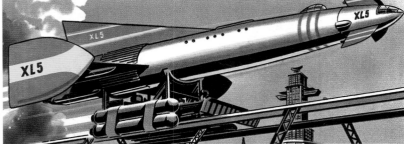

Left: ....But in ***TV21, Fireball*** **blasted off in full colour strips by Mike Noble.**

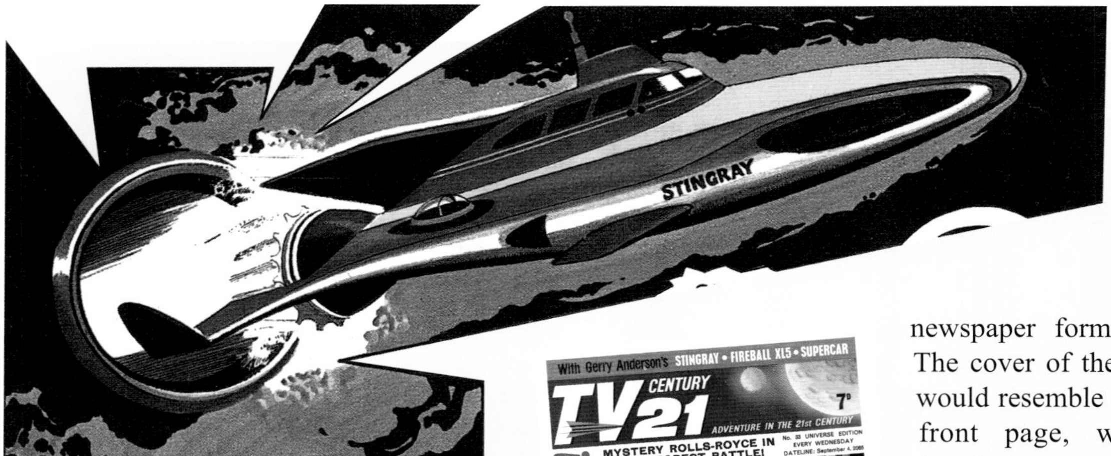
STINGRAY

Left: **Stingray is launched! A striking panel from *Stingray* artist Ron Embleton.**

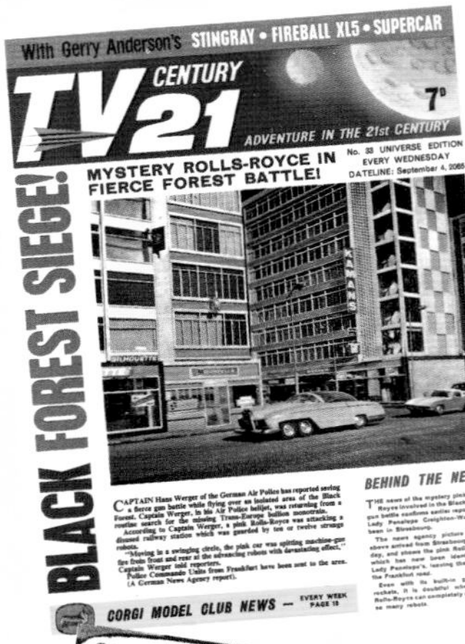
With Gerry Anderson's STINGRAY • FIREBALL XL5 • SUPERCAR

TV CENTURY 21

7d

ADVENTURE IN THE 21st CENTURY

No. 35 UNIVERSE EDITION EVERY WEDNESDAY DATELINE: September 4, 2065

BLACK FOREST SIEGE!

MYSTERY ROLLS-ROYCE IN FIERCE FOREST BATTLE!

BEHIND THE NEWS

CORGI MODEL CLUB NEWS — EVERY WEEK PAGE 15

Once the format and quality of the comic had been agreed, Fennell put together his editorial team. As art director, he recruited the talented Dennis Hooper, who had helped assemble the dummy presentation issue, with Peter Corri as designer. Old colleague Angus Allan was appointed as script editor, with Allan's wife Gillian employed as chief sub-editor. Together the team developed a comic that would base an entire fictional universe of the future around the programmes created by Gerry and Sylvia Anderson. To help maintain this illusion, Fennell kept one element of the original newspaper format proposal. The cover of the new comic would resemble a newspaper front page, with banner headlines, news reports and dramatic colour photographs. These would be created by Hooper, aided by office manager and additional scriptwriter Tod Sullivan. Only one further change would be made before production started on the comic in the autumn of 1964. At the request of City Magazines the comic was renamed *TV Century 21* to reflect the television origins of its contents, Fennell and Hooper then began selecting artists to create the comic's amazing vision of the 21st Century.

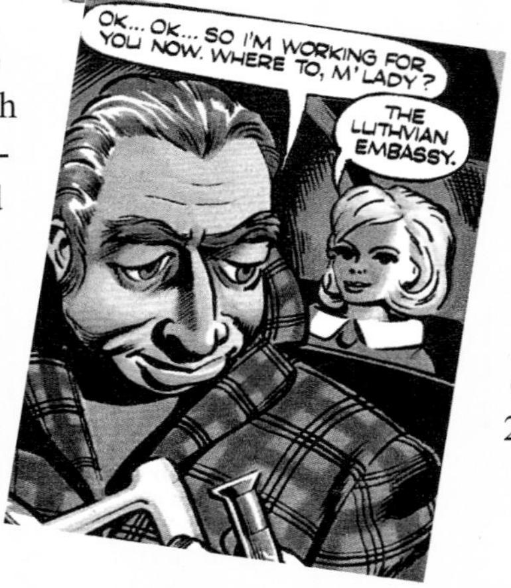
OK... OK... SO I'M WORKING FOR YOU NOW. WHERE TO, M'LADY?
THE LUTHVIAN EMBASSY.

Above: **Lady Penelope and Parker had their first adventures in TV21...**
Below and Right: **...Often foiling the schemes of robot master Mr. Steelman.**

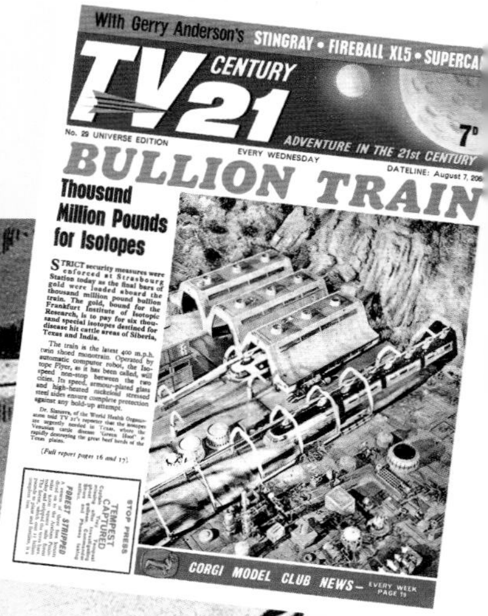
With Gerry Anderson's STINGRAY • FIREBALL XL5 • SUPERCA

TV CENTURY 21

7d

ADVENTURE IN THE 21st CENTURY

No. 29 UNIVERSE EDITION EVERY WEDNESDAY DATELINE: August 7, 206

BULLION TRAIN

Thousand Million Pounds for Isotopes

STOP PRESS

CORGI MODEL CLUB NEWS — EVERY WEEK PAGE 15

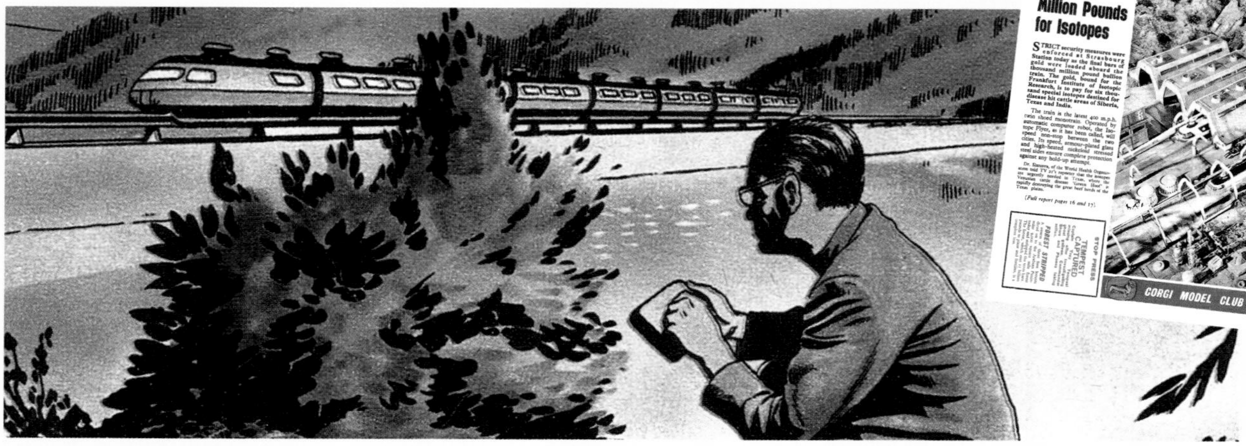

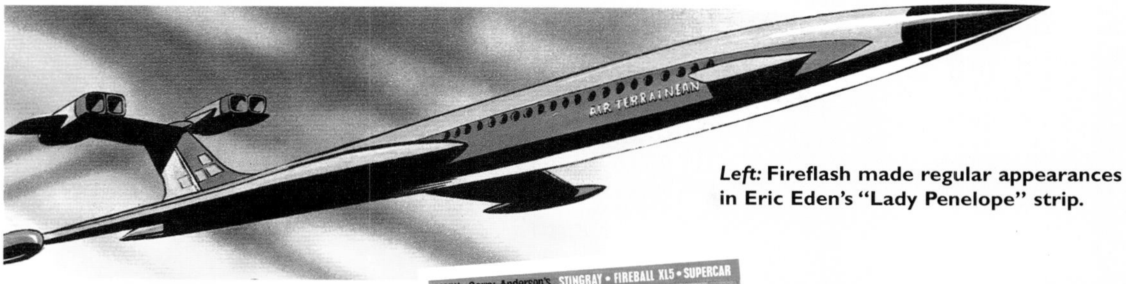
AIR TERRAINEAN

Left: **Fireflash made regular appearances in Eric Eden's "Lady Penelope" strip.**

Right and Below Right: **"Guest" machines from *Thunderbirds* featured in many *TV21* news stories before being seen on TV.**

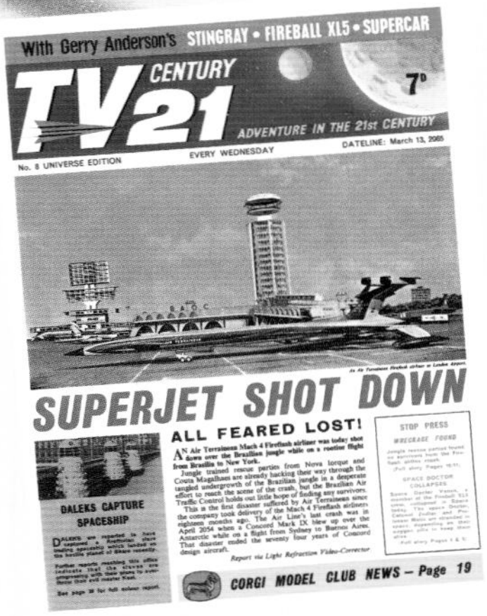
With Gerry Anderson's STINGRAY • FIREBALL XL5 • SUPERCAR

TV CENTURY 21 7d

ADVENTURE IN THE 21st CENTURY

EVERY WEDNESDAY

SUPERJET SHOT DOWN

ALL FEARED LOST!

DALEKS CAPTURE SPACESHIP

CORGI MODEL CLUB NEWS – Page 19

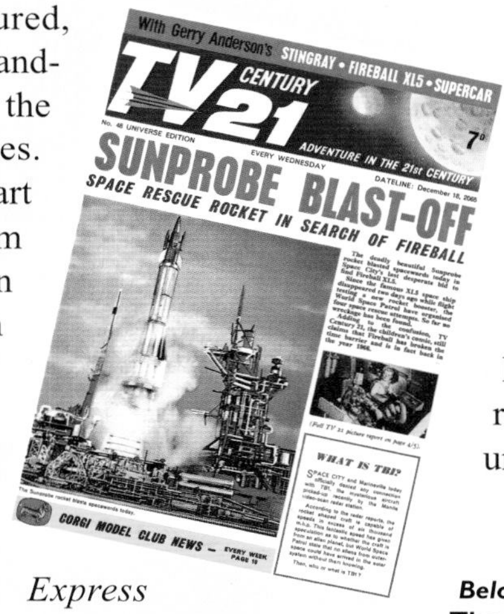
With Gerry Anderson's STINGRAY • FIREBALL XL5 • SUPERCAR

TV CENTURY 21 7d

ADVENTURE IN THE 21st CENTURY

EVERY WEDNESDAY

SUNPROBE BLAST-OFF

SPACE RESCUE ROCKET IN SEARCH OF FIREBALL

WHAT IS THIS?

CORGI MODEL CLUB NEWS –

This would be presented through news items and comic strips set a hundred years in future combined elements of existing programmes set against a unifying background. At first this new world would focus mainly around *Fireball XL5* and *Stingray*. *Supercar*, although featured, would only appear in a standalone strip that played on the show's cartoon qualities. After an unimpressive start with strips drawn by Graham Coton, *Fireball XL5* soon found its ideal visualiser in Mike Noble, an ex-*TV Comic* artist whose bold style fitted the serious tone of the show's comic strip scripts, while to illustrate *Stingray*, *TV Express Weekly*'s Ron Embleton was chosen. At first Embleton was asked to produce Stingray stories that combined artwork with colour film frames taken from the show's television episodes, but this approach was later abandoned in favour of 100% artwork. Adding to the comic's science fiction content, Fennell also secured the rights to Terry Nation's notorious *Dr Who* opponents, The Daleks, who appeared in a back page strip mainly drawn by Richard Jennings and Ron Turner.

The other main strip featured in *TV Century 21* formed part of Shackleton's original plan to prepare readers for the eagerly awaited *Thunderbirds*. In an inspired move, Fennell created a new strip based on twoof *Thunderbirds*'ini tially minor characters. The Adventures of Lady Penelope featured International Rescue's glamorous London Agent working as a James Bond-style spy assisted by her newly recruited manservant Parker. *Ex-Eagle* artist Eric Eden was selected to draw the undercover exploits of Her Ladyship as she battled against robot master Mr. Steelman and the unfriendly enemy state of Bereznik.

Below and Right: **The Sidewinder's appearance in an early *Stingray* story.**

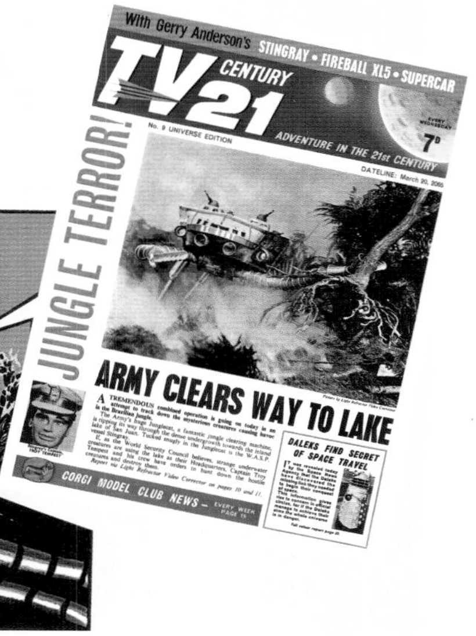
With Gerry Anderson's STINGRAY • FIREBALL XL5 • SUPERCAR

TV CENTURY 21 7d

ADVENTURE IN THE 21st CENTURY

JUNGLE TERROR!

ARMY CLEARS WAY TO LAKE

DALEKS FIND SECRET OF SPACE TRAVEL

CORGI MODEL CLUB NEWS –

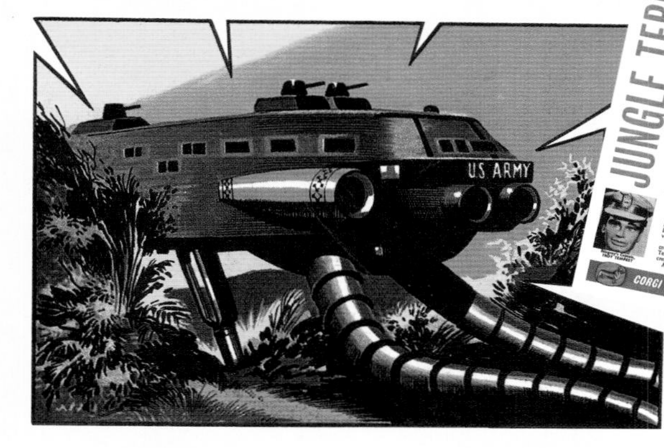
US ARMY

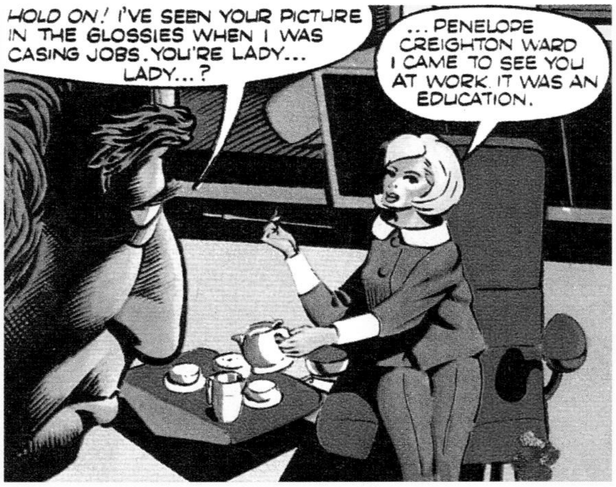
HOLD ON! I'VE SEEN YOUR PICTURE IN THE GLOSSIES WHEN I WAS CASING JOBS. YOU'RE LADY... LADY...?
...PENELOPE CREIGHTON WARD I CAME TO SEE YOU AT WORK. IT WAS AN EDUCATION.

Above: **Lady Penelope meets Parker for the first time.**

In addition to Penelope and Parker, various items of *Thunderbirds* technology would also be featured in *TV Century 21* stories. The Fireflash airliner, the Sidewinder junglecat and the transcontinental monorail system all appeared in comic strips before reaching the TV screen. These vehicles would also be featured on *TV Century 21*'s covers after Fennell had agreed, at Anderson's suggestion, to employ stills photographer Doug Luke at the studios. Anderson had been greatly impressed by promotional shots Luke had taken of earlier APF programmes and his fantastic colour photographs of the shows would now be used to dramatic effect in *TV Century 21's* "news" features.

By January 1965, *TV Century 21* was ready to be launched. With Stingray being screened on TV, hopes were riding high for the success of the new venture, and Fennell and his colleagues would not be disappointed. Within its first year *TV Century 21*'s circulation exceeded all expectations by sellling 600,000 copies a week. The comic's arrival had caught the imagination of a generation of readers for whom spies and science fiction were the latest trend. With its blend of action, adventure, scientific features and secret agent missions (set by the comic's "host" Secret Agent 21), *TV Century 21* soon created a loyal following. Fennell and his team were then able to introduce new strips, including Agent 21's own adventures scripted by Tod Sullivan and stylishly drawn by Rab Hamilton, and spin-off specials and annuals that further expanded the comic's futuristic world. Among these were a 1965 Summer Extra that fea-

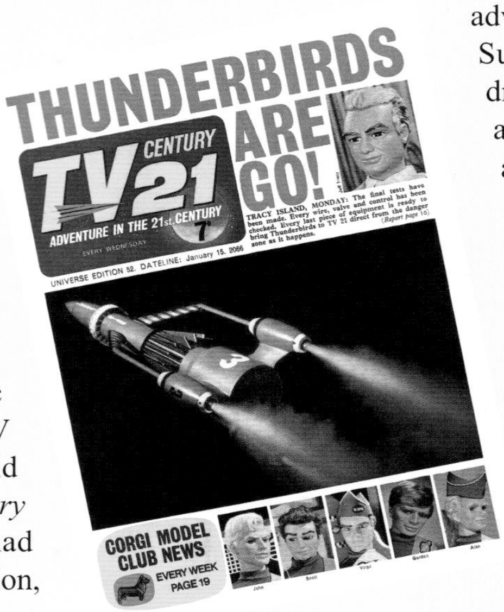
THUNDERBIRDS ARE GO!
TV CENTURY 21
ADVENTURE IN THE 21st CENTURY
CORGI MODEL CLUB NEWS
EVERY WEEK PAGE 19

Left: **In January 1966 *Thunderbirds* finally blasted from the pages of *TV21*.**

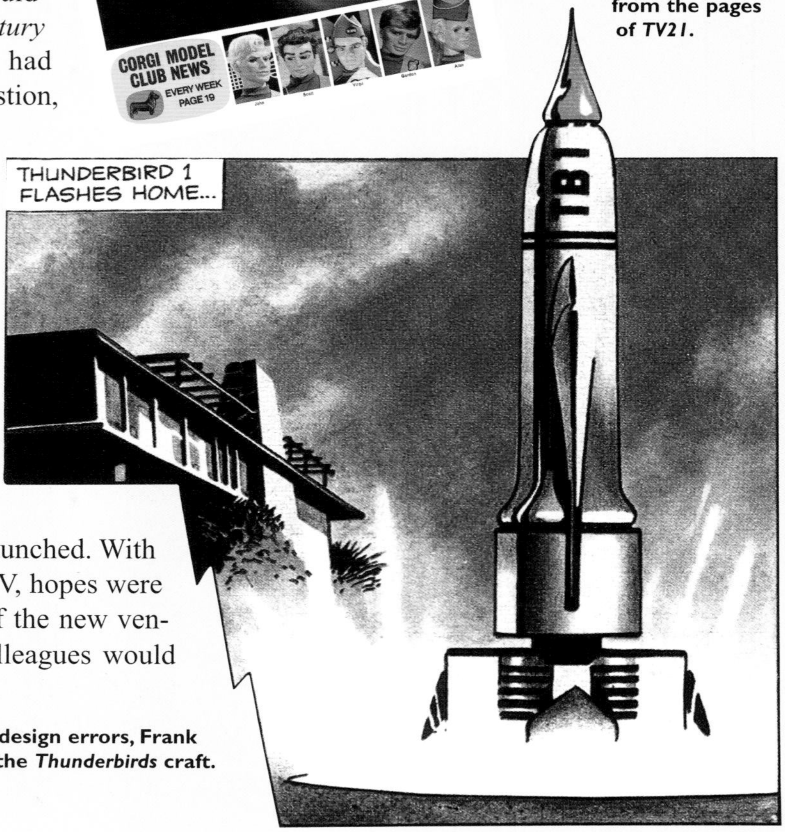
THUNDERBIRD 1 FLASHES HOME...
TB1

Right: **After correcting some early design errors, Frank Bellamy's strip perfectly captured the *Thunderbirds* craft.**

tured a rare contribution by Dan Dare's creator himself, when Frank Hampson was engaged to draw a one-off Lady Penelope story. By the autumn of 1965, plans were also being prepared to at last add *Thunderbirds* to the comic's pages.

Beginning in issue 44 an eight part story featured Lady Penelope's first encounters with Jeff Tracy, Brains and the Hood, while special features also prepared readers for Thunderbirds' long awaited arrival.

In issue 52, *Thunderbirds* finally blasted out of *TV Century 21*'s centre pages in a dazzling strip drawn by legendary comic strip artist Frank Bellamy.

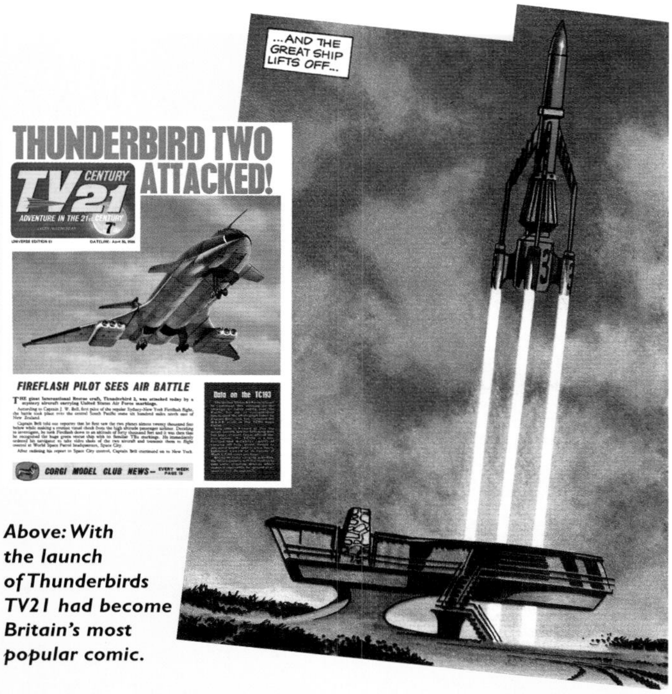
...AND THE GREAT SHIP LIFTS OFF...
THUNDERBIRD TWO ATTACKED!
TV CENTURY 21
ADVENTURE IN THE 21st CENTURY
FIREFLASH PILOT SEES AIR BATTLE
CORGI MODEL CLUB NEWS

Above: With the launch of Thunderbirds TV21 had become Britain's most popular comic.

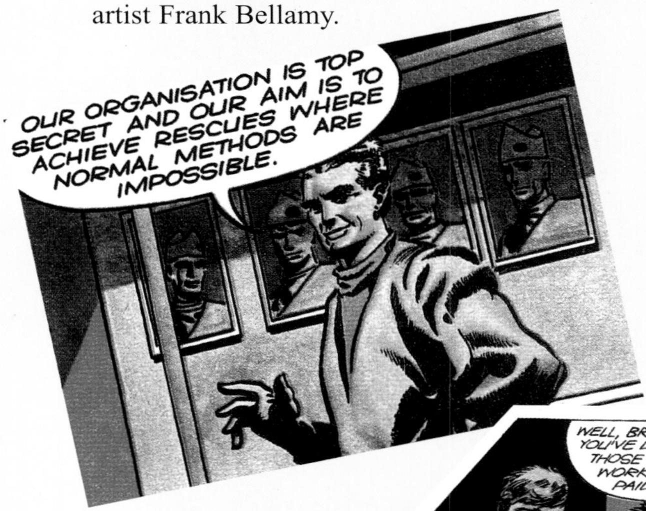
OUR ORGANISATION IS TOP SECRET AND OUR AIM IS TO ACHIEVE RESCUES WHERE NORMAL METHODS ARE IMPOSSIBLE.

Born in Kettering in 1917, Bellamy had worked as a graphic artist since leaving school at sixteen. His first comic strip "Commando Gibbs versus Dragon Decay" was an advertising cartoon created for Gibbs toothpaste in 1952. He was then offered work with *Mickey Mouse Weekly*, drawing a character called Monty Carstairs and a

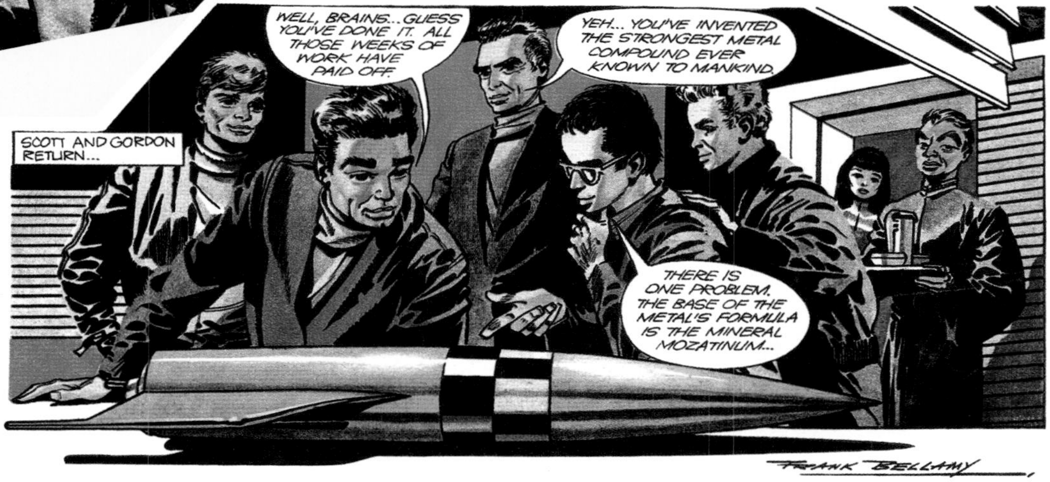
SCOTT AND GORDON RETURN...
WELL, BRAINS...GUESS YOU'VE DONE IT. ALL THOSE WEEKS OF WORK HAVE PAID OFF.
YEH... YOU'VE INVENTED THE STRONGEST METAL COMPOUND EVER KNOWN TO MANKIND.
THERE IS ONE PROBLEM. THE BASE OF THE METAL'S FORMULA IS THE MINERAL MOZATINUM...
FRANK BELLAMY

Above and Right: **To help create accurate images of the Thunderbirds characters, Bellamy worked from plaster casts of the puppets' heads.**

Fennell had originally planned to offer Bellamy the Stingray strip, but at the time Bellamy was under contract to the Eagle, and couldn't take up Fennell's invitation until the following year. The wait was worthwhile as Bellamy soon proved to be TV Century 21's star attraction.

Cornish set smuggling story "The Secrets of the Sands". This was followed by his first colour strip, based on the true-life Disney film "The Living Desert". After switching to Hulton Press (publishers of *The Eagle*), he drew several strips for *Swift* magazine, before joining *The Eagle* itself to draw his acclaimed

Winston Churchill strip "The Happy Warrior". Here Bellamy began to experiment with page layouts. He developed dynamic compositions using a combination of irregular or circular frames coupled with larger slash panels. In 1959, after cost-cutting measures forced Frank Hampson to resign from *The Eagle*, Bellamy was assigned to Hampson's creation Dan Dare, assisted by Don Harley and Keith Watson, both of whom would go on to work for *TV Century 21*. Harley would create several Thunderbirds strips for *TV Century 21* specials, and fill in for Bellamy on one weekly story during 1966. Although Bellamy didn't enjoy working on Dan Dare, the experience proved excellent preparation for working on *Thunderbirds*. His interest in Africa, vividly seen in his "Fraser of Africa" strip for *The Eagle*, also inspired an early *Thunderbirds* story.

VIRGIL TRACY IN CRASH

Charging Rhino Smashes International Rescue Machine

TV CENTURY 21 ADVENTURE IN THE 21st CENTURY EVERY WEDNESDAY 7°

UNIVERSE EDITION 64 DATELINE: April 9, 2066

FOUR tons of charging rhinoceros today nearly cost Virgil Tracy his life. The rhino, an albino black, smashed aside one of International Rescue's mighty machines as Virgil attempted to trap the animal in two giant clamps.

The impact crushed the machine's arms, tipping Virgil from the cab. Brother Scott immediately moved to the rescue in a second machine and protected Virgil from another charge.

It was in this desperate situation that the Tracys' courage and resourcefulness showed to the full, for after the near disaster, Scott immediately moved in on the rhino again.

The animal's capture is vital, for only a rare albino black will enable International Rescue to obtain the release of Dr. Adams from the Masai tribe and so save the life of Madagascar's great leader General N'Mobo. The general is at this moment fighting a losing battle against a deadly heart disease.

Full report and pictures page 10, 11, 12.

Pilot Virgil Tracy pictured at the controls of the captured vehicle only minutes before the crash.

MONSTER WEED MENACE

Shipping Attacked

THREE ships have been sunk and two others are missing as a strange, quick growing weed takes a hold in the Pacific and spreads its vines along the sea-ways.

The weed, part of a synthetic plant consignment bound for Venus, found its way into the Pacific when its metal container split after falling from space.

Wasp commander, Sam Shore, stated today that the weed menace is being tackled and will soon be brought under control.

CORGI MODEL CLUB NEWS EVERY WEEK PAGE 19

Above: Studio photographer Doug Luke provided hundreds of life-like shots for TV21.

THUNDERBIRD TWO WHERE IS IT?

TB 1 In Danger Zone

TV CENTURY 21 ADVENTURE IN THE 21st CENTURY EVERY WEDNESDAY 7°

UNIVERSE EDITION 62 DATELINE: March 26, 2066

HAS Thunderbird 2 crashed? This is the question that every correspondent has been asking himself since TB 1 arrived here in Kenya and joined the search for Doctor Adams.

According to our radio monitoring system, the pilot of Thunderbird 1 requested TB 2's assistance in the search, and the call was acknowledged by International Rescue's base—since then, nothing.

If, as is feared, the great rescue craft has crashed, then International Rescue will have suffered a severe blow, for although TB 3 could be used to transport the fabulous rescue machines to different operations it would not be as efficient or as flexible as Thunderbird 2.

STOP PRESS

TB 2 MODIFICATIONS

INTERNATIONAL Rescue report that modifications being made on pods carried by Thunderbird 2. It is understood that these modifications are to do with animal cages.

A World Press Report.

ROGUE PLANET THREATENS SKARO

OUR Dalek correspondent reports considerable activity on Skaro today as the planet is threatened by a rogue planet careering wildly through space.

The Dalek Emperor has ordered an emergency squad into space to intercept the planet and attempt to turn its course.

If this fails, Skaro is doomed.

Special Report page 20.

CORGI MODEL CLUB NEWS EVERY WEEK PAGE 19

Left and Below: **From photographic references Bellamy would often produce even more detailed artwork images.**

Having started work for *TV Century 21* in the autumn of 1965, Bellamy would illustrate *Thunderbirds* with only one break through to the middle of 1969, before leaving comics to work on magazine illustration and the Garth newspaper strip. His work for *TV Century 21* remains among his best work however, displaying a mastery of graphic tech-

BRAINS DRAWS UP A PLAN OF ACTION AND WORK IS BEGUN.
BY MODIFYING EXISTING EQUIPMENT WE CAN PRODUCE THE VEHICLES WE WANT IN THE TIME.
I SEE, BRAINS... I'M GLAD YOU'RE SO CONFIDENT...
HE'S NOT, MR. TRACY... IN FACT, TO COMPLETE THE JOB AND ALSO MAKE A CAGE IN TIME IS ALMOST AN IMPOSSIBILITY.

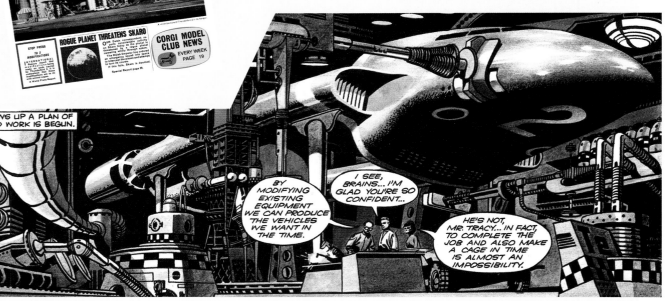

TV21
CAPTAIN SCARLET
WORLD PRESIDENT IN MYSTERON DRAMA!
WHITE AND PRESIDENT HEADING FOR DISASTER AREA
CORGI MODEL CLUB NEWS
INSIDE 19
SPECTRUM IS BLACK

Gerry Anderson's
JOE 90
TOP SECRET
JOE BECOMES A MOST SPECIAL AQUANAUT!
Collision Disaster
FREE GIFT INSIDE!
MAC'S JET CAR KIT! IT REALLY WORKS!
JOIN... WORLD INTELLIGENCE NETWORK
SUPER TV STRIPS
The CHAMPIONS
STAR TREK
LAND of the GIANTS

Later Bellamy work included TV21 covers for Captain Scarlet and the first issue of the Joe 90 comic.

nique that is breathtakingly dynamic and inventive. His layouts stretch comic strip conventions to their limits and his use of colour, tone and texture is inspired. His arrival in *TV Century 21* also appears to have had an influence on his fellow artists, their work becoming noticeably bolder and more imaginative. At first producing a three page strip, with the third page in black and white, from issue 66 to issue 140, Bellamy produced only a double page centre-spread. But in these issues he was able to give his imagination full reign, often basing his layouts around one main image. From issue 141 onwards his scope was limited when *Thunderbirds* was reformatted to two separate pages of art. By now the comic had begun to go into decline, but Bellamy stayed with the publication until a change of ownership in 1969, producing a further four-page story for the subsequent relaunch comic.

During his time with *TV Century 21* he also contributed a number of covers for *Captain Scarlet* when it was moved to the comic's front page, and the front cover to *City Magazine*'s spin-off *Joe 90* comic. He was also asked to produce a poster for the second *Thunderbirds* feature film *Thunderbird 6*, and found time in 1966 to work on a memorable episode of *The Avengers* TV series, featuring a murderous comic strip artist.

The last issues of the original *TV Century 21*, its name shortened to *TV 21*, were published in 1969 and marked the end of a golden age of British comics. Like Anderson's production company (itself renamed Century 21), Fennell's vision of the publishing future didn't survive the sixties dream. Since then, no comic publisher has been able to create a comic with such high standards of production and illustration, and although *Thunderbirds* and other Gerry Anderson inspired creations would return to comics, they would never enjoy such an imaginative showcase. Whenever the strips are reprinted however, readers can once again enjoy *TV Century 21*'s adventures in the 21st Century.

Below: **Bellamy's poster for *Thunderbird Six*.**

THUNDERING INTO YOUR SIGHTS
STAGGERING THE IMAGINATION
'BRAINS' GREATEST INSPIRATION!
GERRY ANDERSON'S
THUNDERBIRD 6
PRODUCED BY SYLVIA ANDERSON · DIRECTED BY DAVID LANE
SUPERMARIONATION

Below: **Mission completed – Bellamy's Thunderbirds head for home**

THE THUNDERBIRD MACHINES LEAVE...
FRANK BELLAMY
TB1

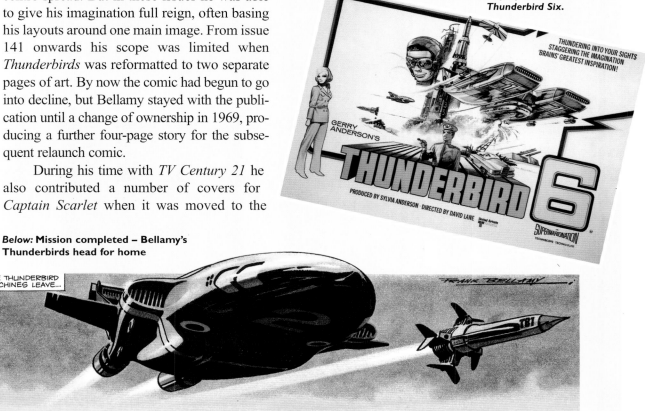

MANSION AT WAR!

Armed invasion of historic home

Above: The Creighton-Ward Mansion : beauty spot battleground

Shocked residents of Foxleyheath, England, rose the alarm when armed forces appeared to invade the historic mansion home of society super-model Lady Penelope Creighton-Ward. After armoured cars were seen approaching the building, the sounds of gunfire and explosive grenades were reported from the eighteenth century landscaped gardens.

Local Police called to the scene were met by an apologetic Lady Penelope. She informed officers that defence officials had failed to notify local authorities that she had allowed military manoeuvres to be carried out in her grounds. Pausing only to wave briefly at a small crowd gathered outside the mansion's gates, Her Ladyship then left for a modelling assignment in the Mediterranean.

WORLD PRESIDENT TO ADDRESS CONGRESS

Unity City announced that despite rumours of an assassination attempt by the independent state of Bereznik, the World President Nikita Bandranaik will make his annual address to the World Congress at four o'clock tomorrow.

Left: The World President Nikita Bandranaik

Above: Lady Penelope Creighton-Ward: "Sorry about the bangs."

NAPLES BAY BLAST!

By Peter Tracker in Naples

Explosion destroys luxury yacht

Air-sea rescue crews in the Naples area reported a minor atomic blast has completely destroyed Seabird I, the fabulous ocean-going yacht belonging to international beauty Lady Penelope Creighton-Ward.

Travelling to Pompeii at the time of the blast, Lady Penelope stopped to tell reporters : "What a pity - she was such a pretty yacht.' Her chauffeur Parker added, 'It must have been that faulty fuel rod in the h'atomic cooker."

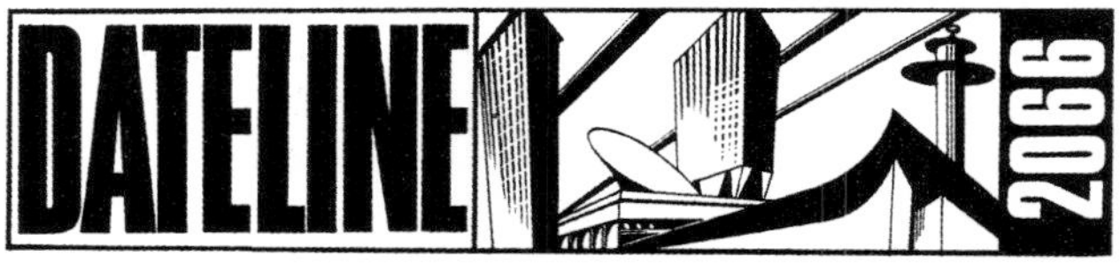

DATELINE
2066

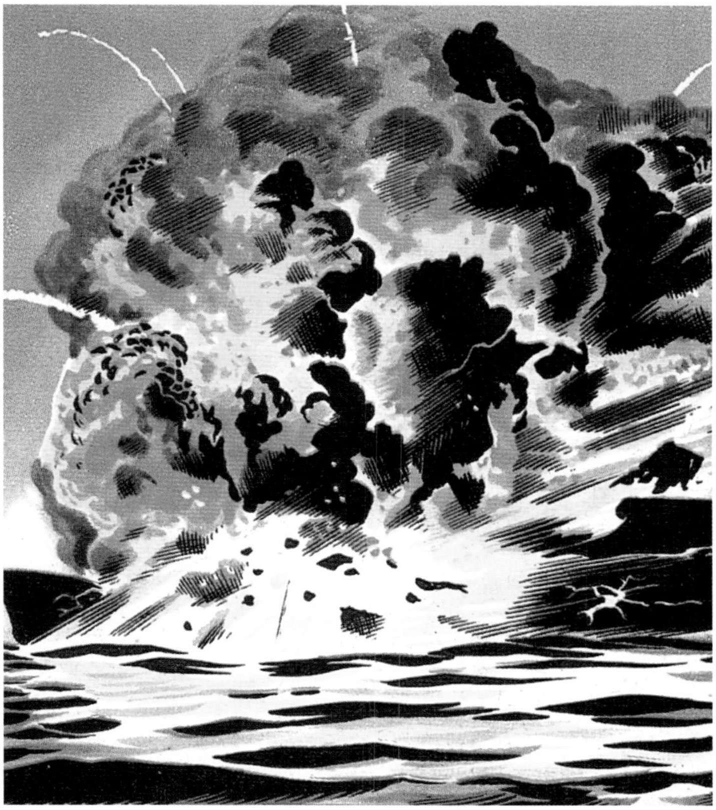

Above: **Local fisherman capture moment of destruction.**

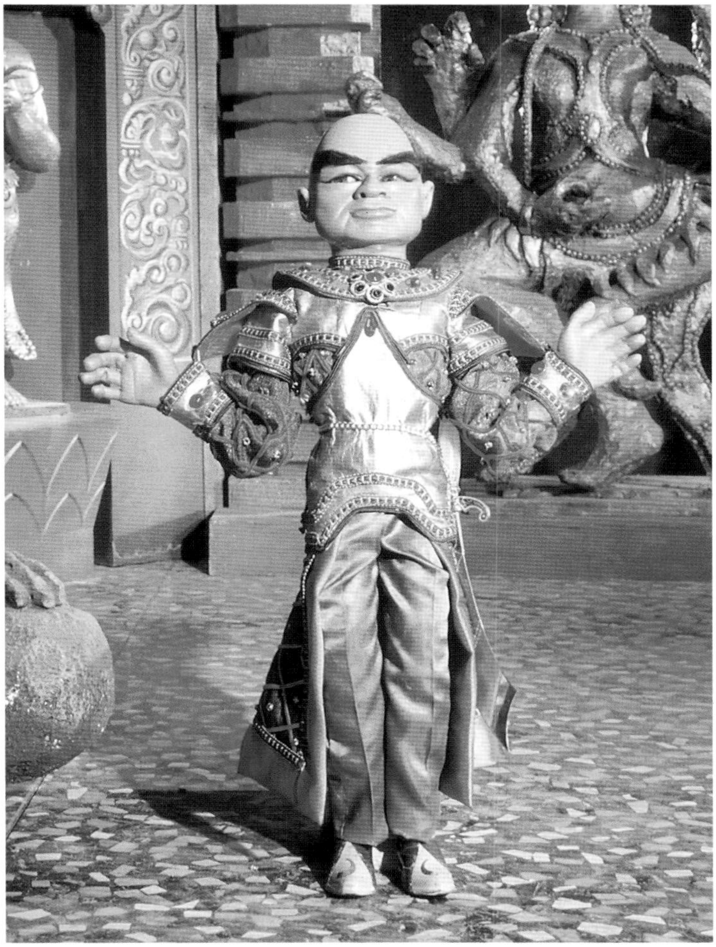

Who is public enemy number one?

By TV21's crime correspondent

World law enforcement agencies remain divided over which leading master criminal they should brand the greatest threat to global security.

Is mysterious robot mastermind Mr Steelman the most dangerous man on Earth? Or is shadowy master of disguise The Hood, the real enemy of the world? Only one thing is certain - nobody knows when either villain will make their next attempt to bring chaos to the planet.

Left: **Is this the true face of international evil?**

Right: **Artist's impression of the cybernetic Mr Steelman**

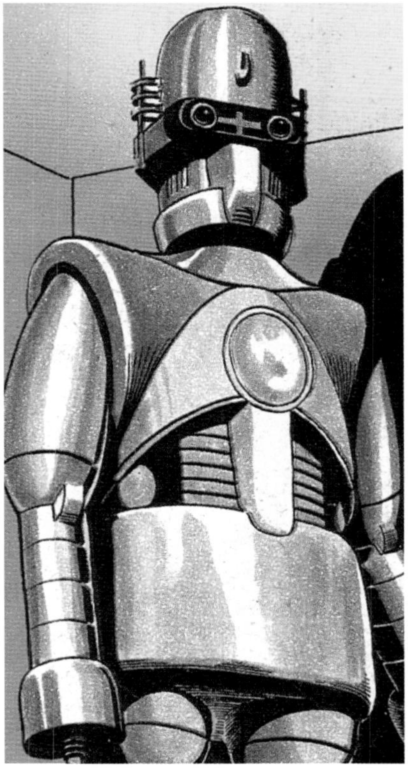

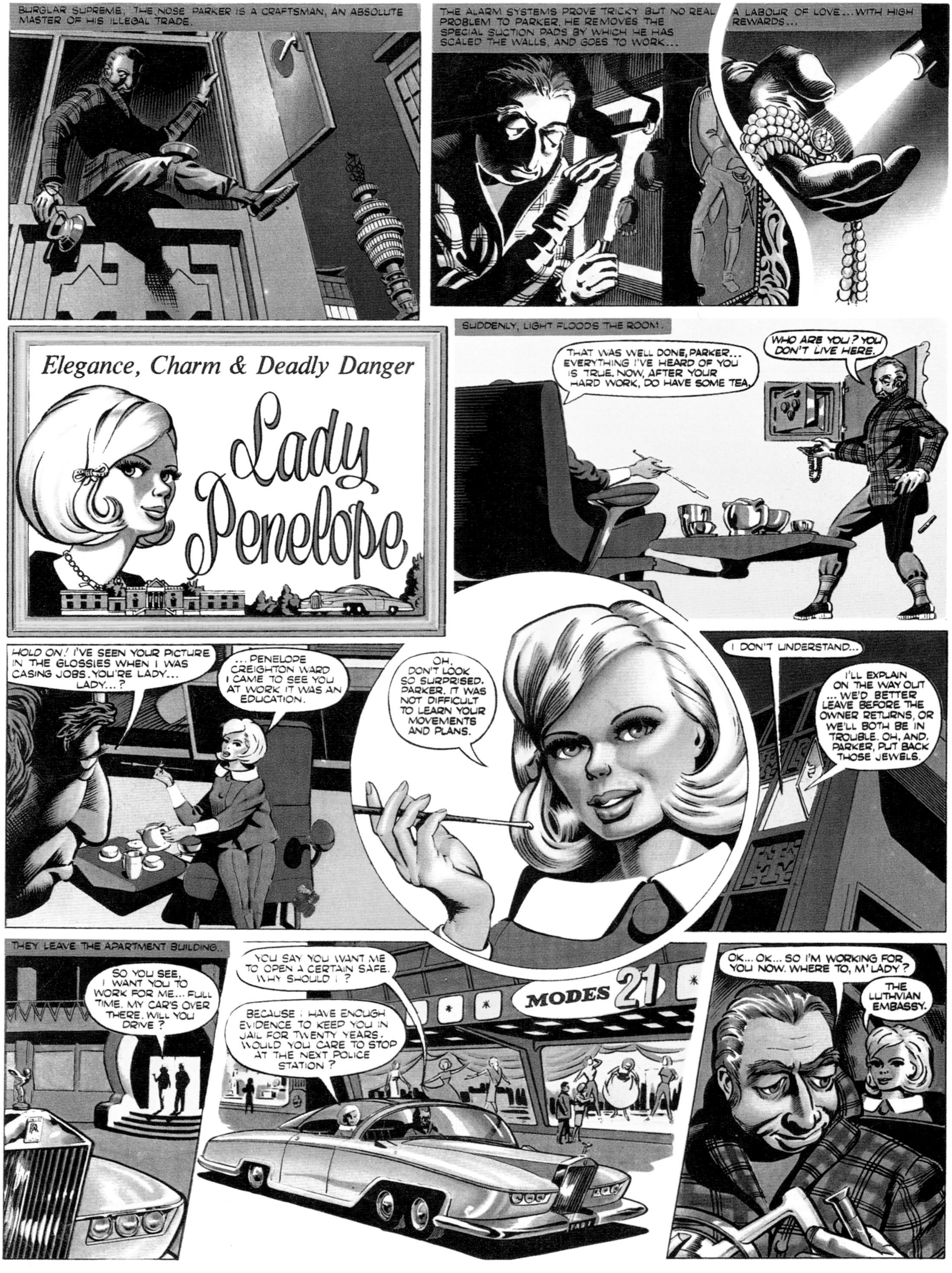
BURGLAR SUPREME, THE NOSE PARKER IS A CRAFTSMAN, AN ABSOLUTE MASTER OF HIS ILLEGAL TRADE.
THE ALARM SYSTEMS PROVE TRICKY BUT NO REAL PROBLEM TO PARKER. HE REMOVES THE SPECIAL SUCTION PADS BY WHICH HE HAS SCALED THE WALLS, AND GOES TO WORK...
A LABOUR OF LOVE... WITH HIGH REWARDS...
Elegance, Charm & Deadly Danger
Lady Penelope
SUDDENLY, LIGHT FLOODS THE ROOM.
THAT WAS WELL DONE, PARKER... EVERYTHING I'VE HEARD OF YOU IS TRUE. NOW, AFTER YOUR HARD WORK, DO HAVE SOME TEA.
WHO ARE YOU? YOU DON'T LIVE HERE.
HOLD ON! I'VE SEEN YOUR PICTURE IN THE GLOSSIES WHEN I WAS CASING JOBS. YOU'RE LADY... LADY...?
... PENELOPE CREIGHTON WARD. I CAME TO SEE YOU AT WORK. IT WAS AN EDUCATION.
OH, DON'T LOOK SO SURPRISED, PARKER. IT WAS NOT DIFFICULT TO LEARN YOUR MOVEMENTS AND PLANS.
I DON'T UNDERSTAND...
I'LL EXPLAIN ON THE WAY OUT ... WE'D BETTER LEAVE BEFORE THE OWNER RETURNS, OR WE'LL BOTH BE IN TROUBLE. OH, AND, PARKER, PUT BACK THOSE JEWELS.
THEY LEAVE THE APARTMENT BUILDING.
SO YOU SEE, I WANT YOU TO WORK FOR ME... FULL TIME. MY CAR'S OVER THERE. WILL YOU DRIVE?
YOU SAY YOU WANT ME TO OPEN A CERTAIN SAFE. WHY SHOULD I?
BECAUSE I HAVE ENOUGH EVIDENCE TO KEEP YOU IN JAIL FOR TWENTY YEARS. WOULD YOU CARE TO STOP AT THE NEXT POLICE STATION?
MODES 21
OK... OK... SO I'M WORKING FOR YOU NOW. WHERE TO, M'LADY?
THE LUTHVIAN EMBASSY.
FAB 1

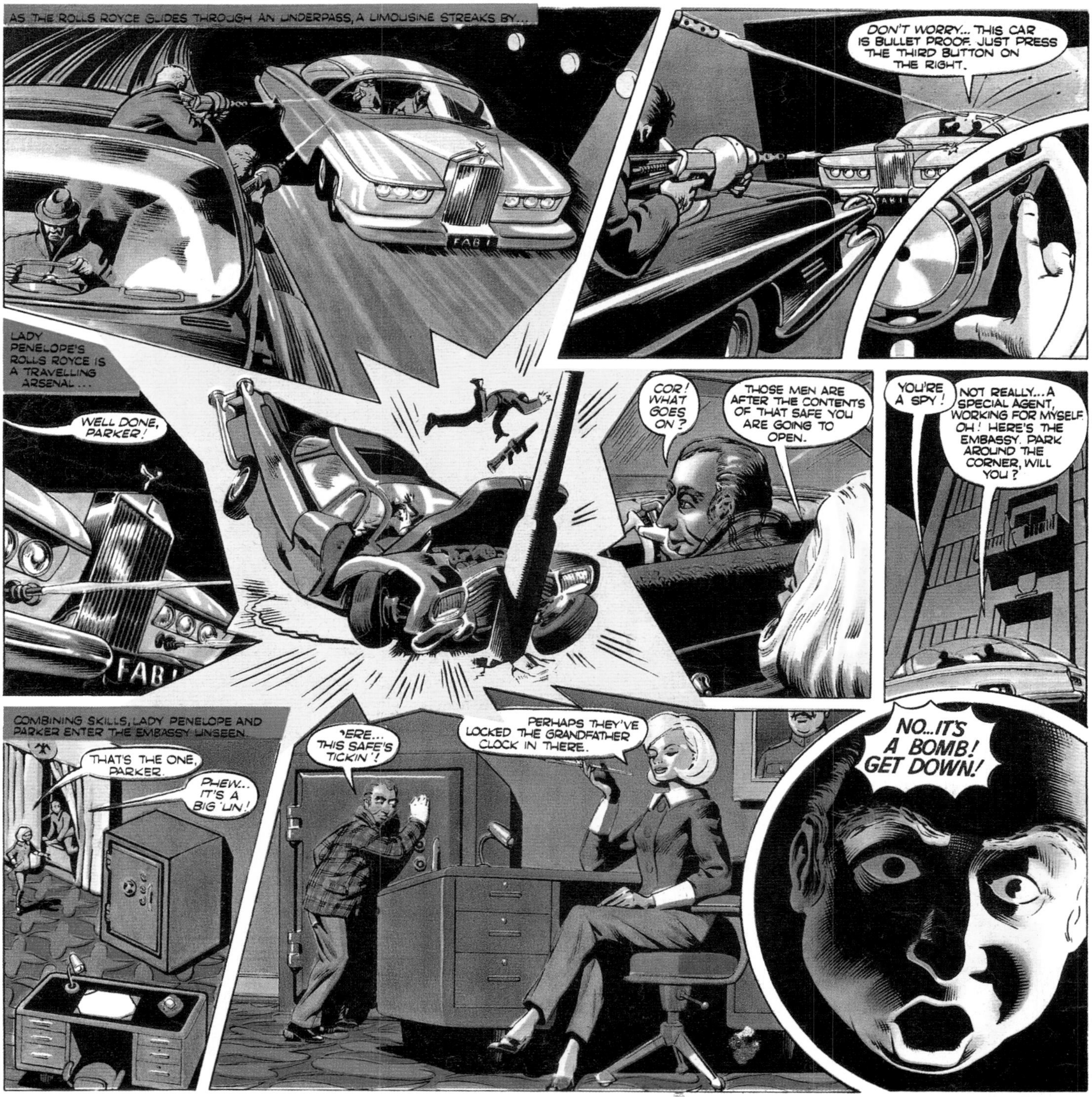

AS THE ROLLS ROYCE GLIDES THROUGH AN UNDERPASS, A LIMOUSINE STREAKS BY...
FAB 1
DON'T WORRY... THIS CAR IS BULLET PROOF. JUST PRESS THE THIRD BUTTON ON THE RIGHT.
LADY PENELOPE'S ROLLS ROYCE IS A TRAVELLING ARSENAL...
WELL DONE, PARKER!
FAB 1
COR! WHAT GOES ON?
THOSE MEN ARE AFTER THE CONTENTS OF THAT SAFE YOU ARE GOING TO OPEN.
YOU'RE A SPY!
NOT REALLY... A SPECIAL AGENT, WORKING FOR MYSELF. OH! HERE'S THE EMBASSY. PARK AROUND THE CORNER, WILL YOU?
COMBINING SKILLS, LADY PENELOPE AND PARKER ENTER THE EMBASSY UNSEEN.
THAT'S THE ONE, PARKER.
PHEW... IT'S A BIG 'UN!
'ERE... THIS SAFE'S TICKIN'!
PERHAPS THEY'VE LOCKED THE GRANDFATHER CLOCK IN THERE.
NO...IT'S A BOMB! GET DOWN!

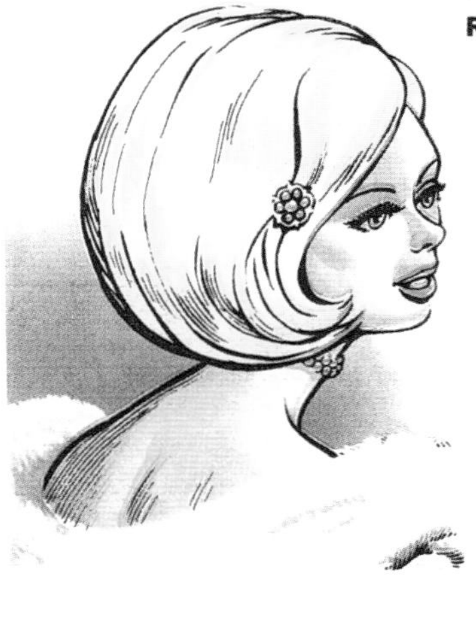

Pauline Harding of Gerrards Cross writes . . .

Roger Moore plays a SAINT on Television . . . was he a SAINT at School?

LADY PENELOPE INVESTIGATES

DISGUISED as a film extra—wig and dark glasses and my very largest hat—managed to smuggle myself into Studio for this week's assignment . . . Left Parker in Rolls Royce nearby for quick get away if discovered . . . Essential to get inside information.

Took opportunity of talking to Roger Moore on the film set between scenes—kept in shadows in case recognised . . . Noted he is even more handsome off screen.

"Of course I was a saint at school," he teased.

Managed to tear myself away to continue investigations . . . Rang school in Battersea, London . . . Yes—they remembered Roger Moore . . . A SAINT?!! That's not the word they would use . . . Still, boys will be boys!

Forced to the conclusion he was *not* a saint at school . . . Desperately trying to find reason to make return visit to Studio . . . Any more questions, readers?

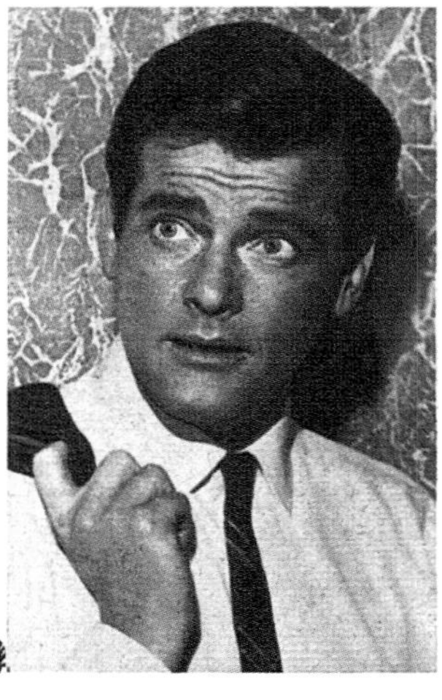

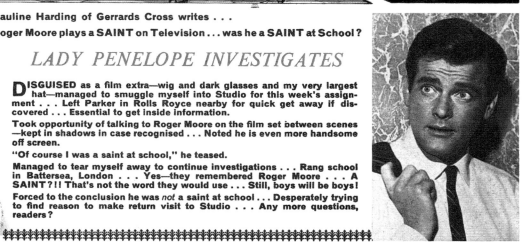

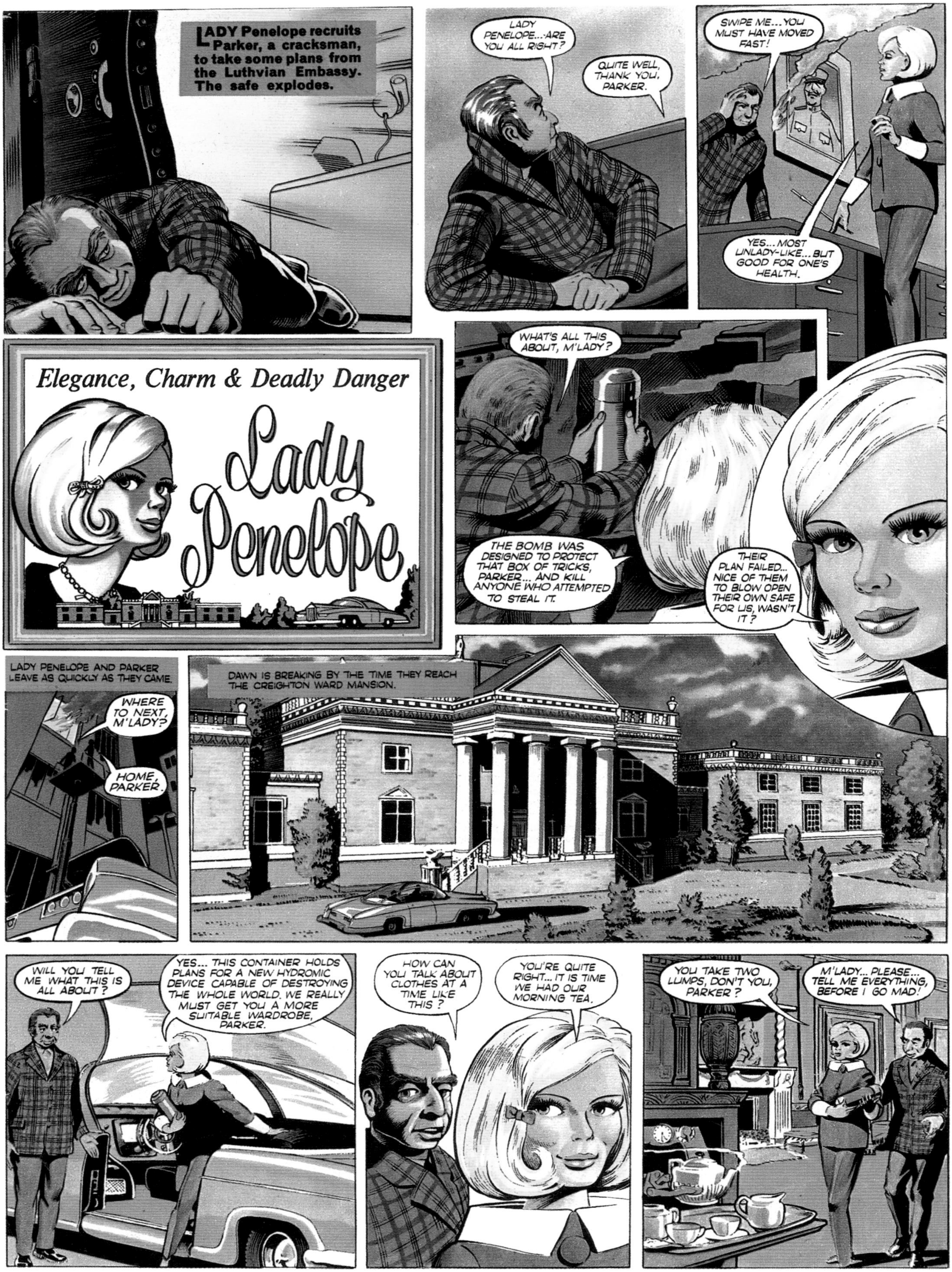
LADY Penelope recruits Parker, a cracksman, to take some plans from the Luthvian Embassy. The safe explodes.
LADY PENELOPE...ARE YOU ALL RIGHT?
QUITE WELL, THANK YOU, PARKER.
SWIPE ME...YOU MUST HAVE MOVED FAST!
YES... MOST UNLADY-LIKE... BUT GOOD FOR ONE'S HEALTH.
Elegance, Charm & Deadly Danger
Lady Penelope
WHAT'S ALL THIS ABOUT, M'LADY?
THE BOMB WAS DESIGNED TO PROTECT THAT BOX OF TRICKS, PARKER... AND KILL ANYONE WHO ATTEMPTED TO STEAL IT.
THEIR PLAN FAILED... NICE OF THEM TO BLOW OPEN THEIR OWN SAFE FOR US, WASN'T IT?
LADY PENELOPE AND PARKER LEAVE AS QUICKLY AS THEY CAME.
WHERE TO NEXT, M'LADY?
HOME, PARKER.
DAWN IS BREAKING BY THE TIME THEY REACH THE CREIGHTON WARD MANSION.
WILL YOU TELL ME WHAT THIS IS ALL ABOUT?
YES... THIS CONTAINER HOLDS PLANS FOR A NEW HYDROMIC DEVICE CAPABLE OF DESTROYING THE WHOLE WORLD. WE REALLY MUST GET YOU A MORE SUITABLE WARDROBE, PARKER.
HOW CAN YOU TALK ABOUT CLOTHES AT A TIME LIKE THIS?
YOU'RE QUITE RIGHT... IT IS TIME WE HAD OUR MORNING TEA.
YOU TAKE TWO LUMPS, DON'T YOU, PARKER?
M'LADY... PLEASE... TELL ME EVERYTHING, BEFORE I GO MAD!

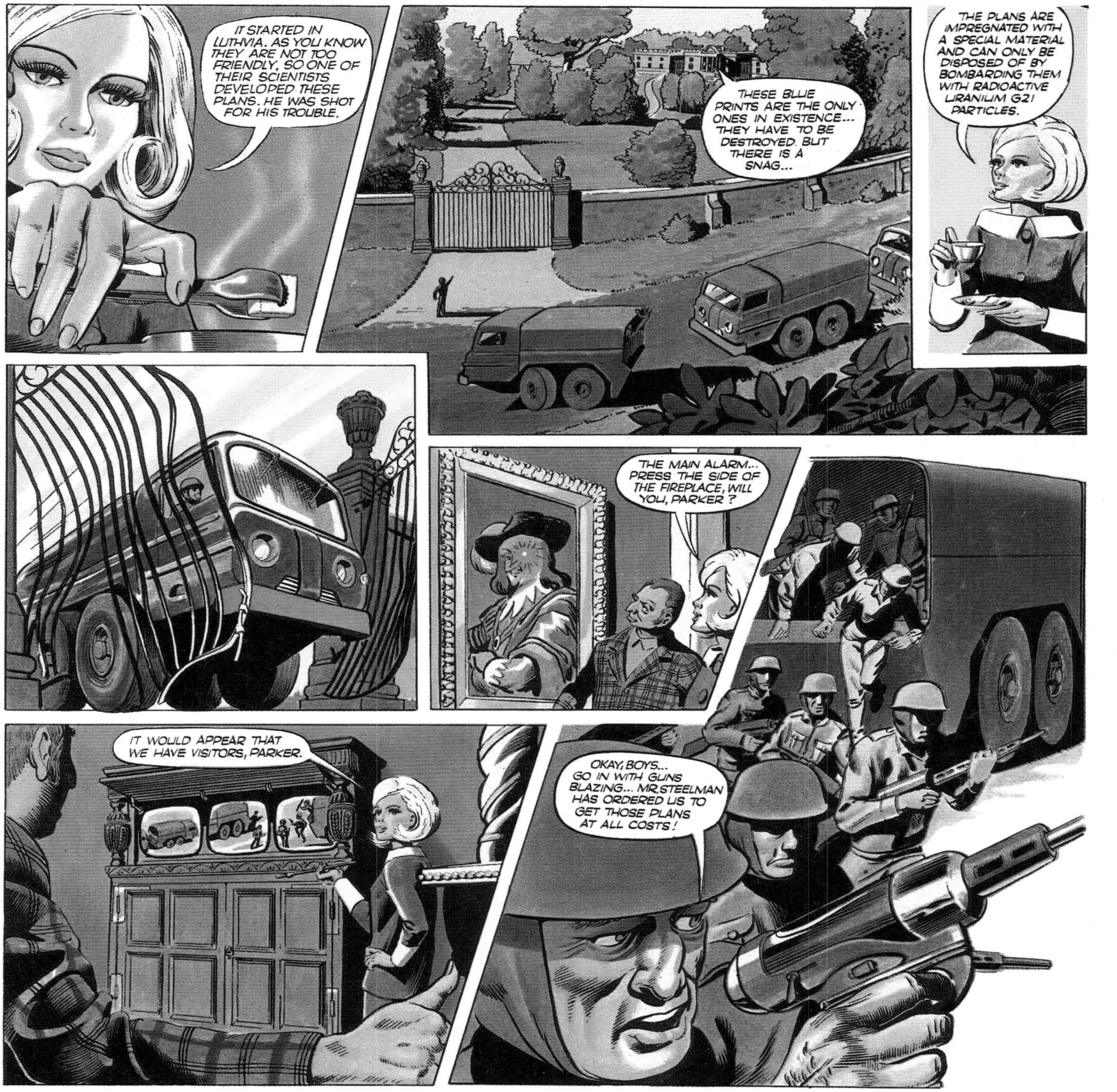
IT STARTED IN LUTHVIA. AS YOU KNOW THEY ARE NOT TOO FRIENDLY, SO ONE OF THEIR SCIENTISTS DEVELOPED THESE PLANS. HE WAS SHOT FOR HIS TROUBLE.
THESE BLUE PRINTS ARE THE ONLY ONES IN EXISTENCE... THEY HAVE TO BE DESTROYED. BUT THERE IS A SNAG...
THE PLANS ARE IMPREGNATED WITH A SPECIAL MATERIAL AND CAN ONLY BE DISPOSED OF BY BOMBARDING THEM WITH RADIOACTIVE URANIUM G21 PARTICLES.
THE MAIN ALARM... PRESS THE SIDE OF THE FIREPLACE, WILL YOU, PARKER?
IT WOULD APPEAR THAT WE HAVE VISITORS, PARKER.
OKAY, BOYS... GO IN WITH GUNS BLAZING... MR. STEELMAN HAS ORDERED US TO GET THOSE PLANS AT ALL COSTS!

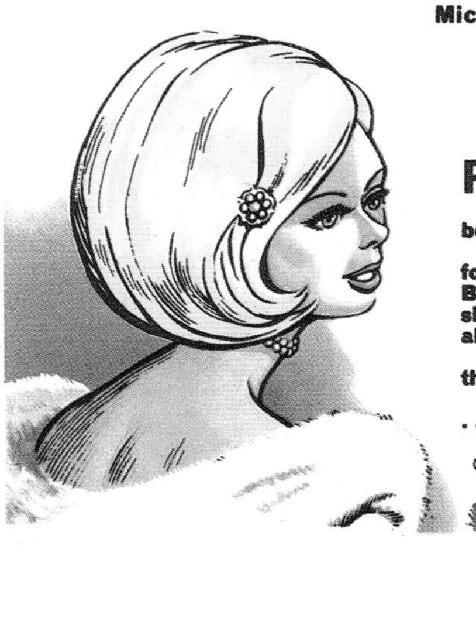

Michael Starkey of London, W.10. says . .

Is it true that Honor Blackman is a Judo expert?

LADY PENELOPE INVESTIGATES

PLOTTED with Parker the best course of action . . . Reminded of first rule of Secret Agent—always check the facts.

Honor Blackman of THE AVENGERS and GOLDFINGER fame—blonde, beautiful—known as Judo expert.

Decided to complete investigation by putting her to the test . . . Arranged for Parker to do a 'break in' job—waited in the Rolls Royce near Miss Blackman's flat—rigged so that Parker would be caught in the act—signalled she was on her way—checked watch—should be entering flat about now—soon know the answer.

Help!! . . . Crash! . . . Clonk! Poor Parker—I do believe he's fallen out of the third floor window!

What's that you're trying to say, Parker? . . . Honor Blackman . . . Yes? . . . I see . . . she *is* a Judo expert!

Well, Michael—there you are . . . it's true—and Parker has the bruises o prove it!

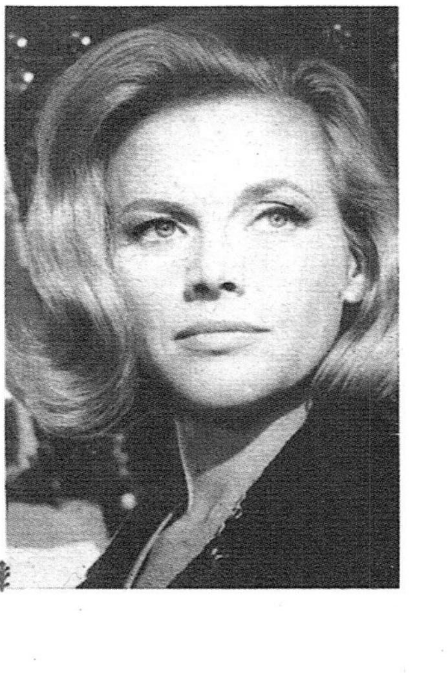

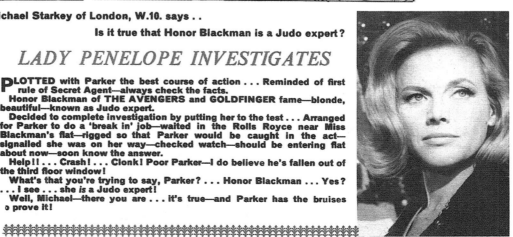

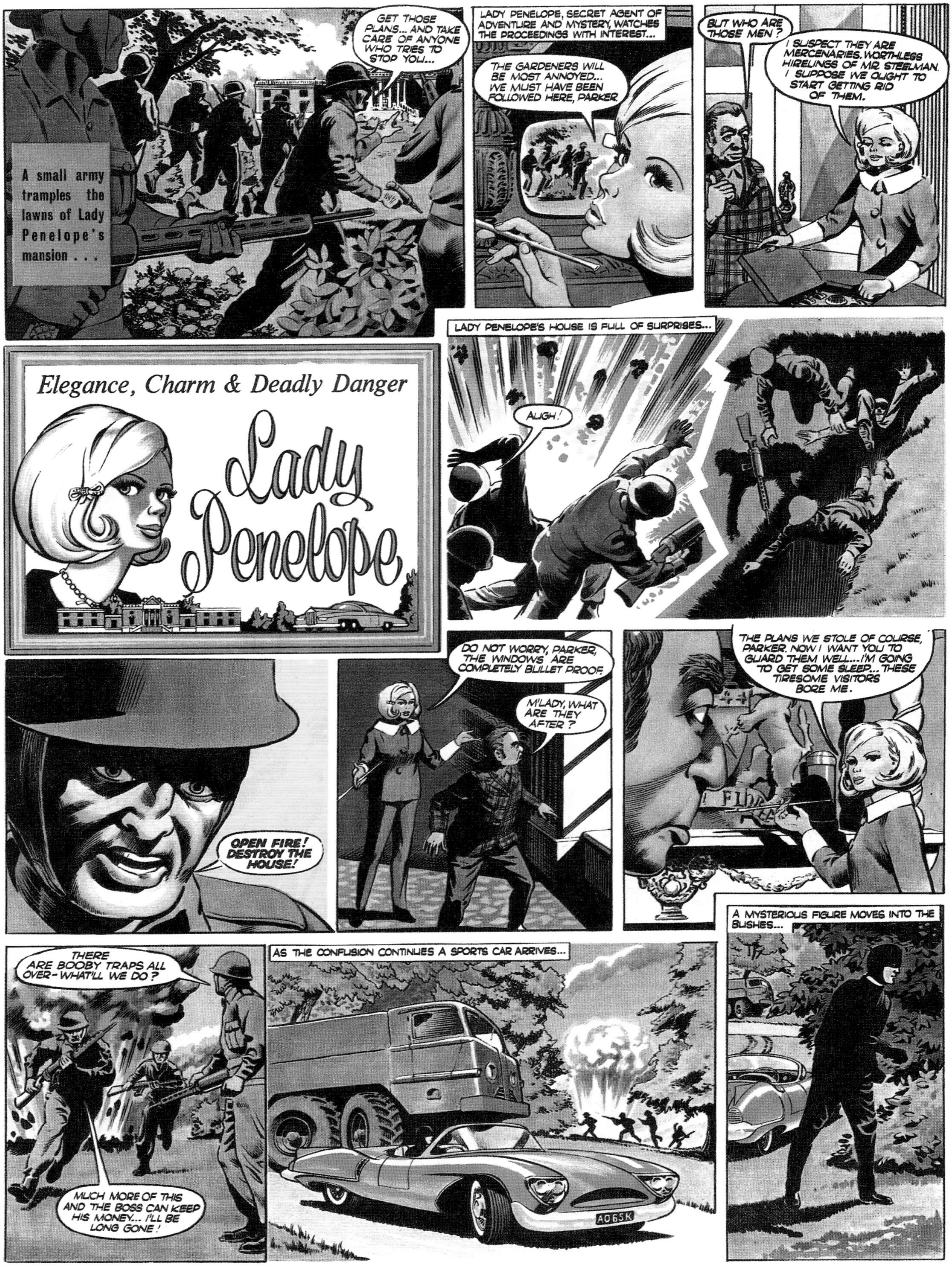

A small army tramples the lawns of Lady Penelope's mansion . . .
GET THOSE PLANS... AND TAKE CARE OF ANYONE WHO TRIES TO STOP YOU...
LADY PENELOPE, SECRET AGENT OF ADVENTURE AND MYSTERY, WATCHES THE PROCEEDINGS WITH INTEREST...
THE GARDENERS WILL BE MOST ANNOYED... WE MUST HAVE BEEN FOLLOWED HERE, PARKER.
BUT WHO ARE THOSE MEN ?
I SUSPECT THEY ARE MERCENARIES. WORTHLESS HIRELINGS OF MR. STEELMAN. I SUPPOSE WE OUGHT TO START GETTING RID OF THEM.
Elegance, Charm & Deadly Danger
Lady Penelope
LADY PENELOPE'S HOUSE IS FULL OF SURPRISES...
AUGH!
OPEN FIRE! DESTROY THE HOUSE!
DO NOT WORRY, PARKER, THE WINDOWS ARE COMPLETELY BULLET PROOF.
M'LADY, WHAT ARE THEY AFTER ?
THE PLANS WE STOLE OF COURSE, PARKER. NOW I WANT YOU TO GUARD THEM WELL... I'M GOING TO GET SOME SLEEP... THESE TIRESOME VISITORS BORE ME.
THERE ARE BOOBY TRAPS ALL OVER - WHAT'LL WE DO ?
MUCH MORE OF THIS AND THE BOSS CAN KEEP HIS MONEY... I'LL BE LONG GONE !
AS THE CONFUSION CONTINUES A SPORTS CAR ARRIVES...
AO 65K
A MYSTERIOUS FIGURE MOVES INTO THE BUSHES...

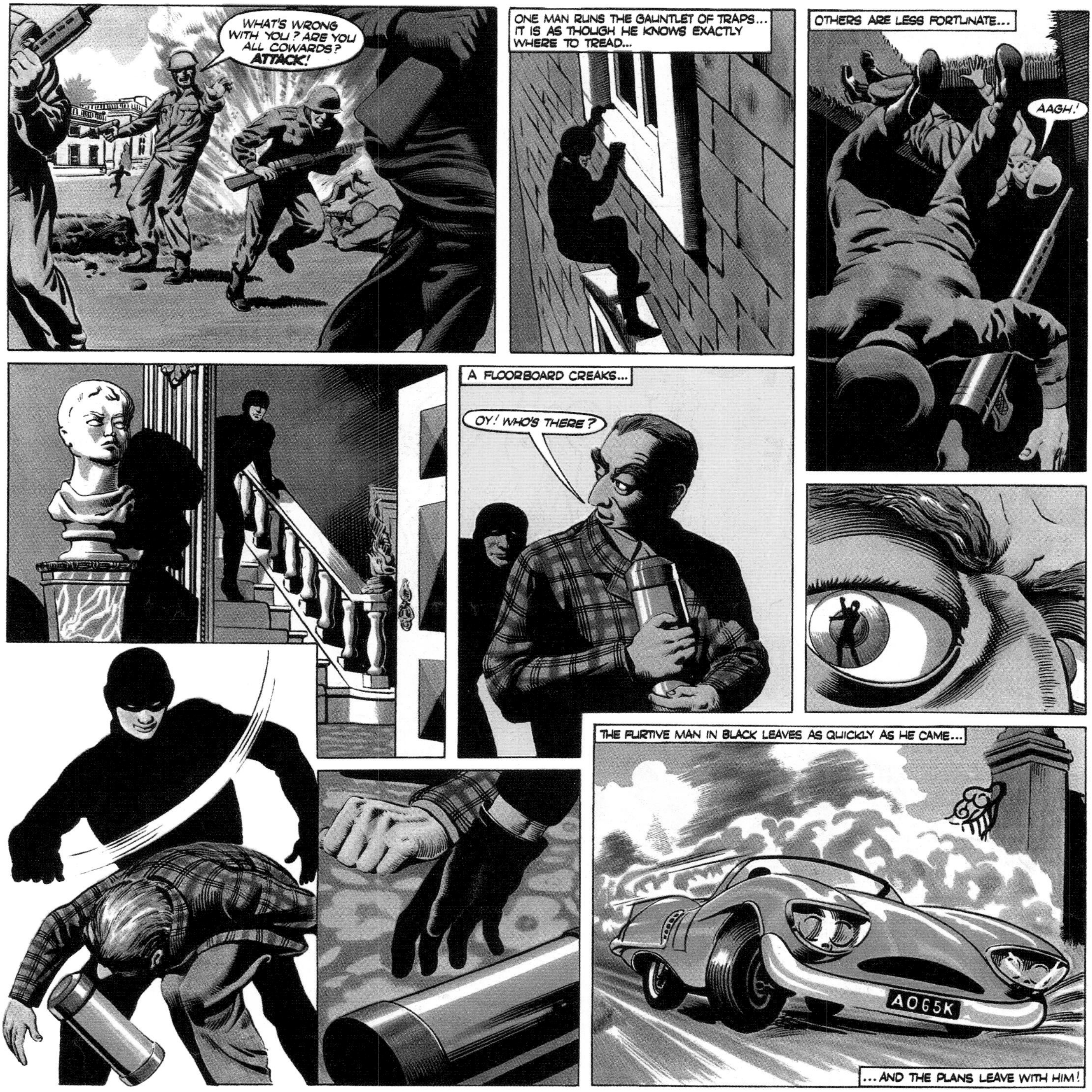
WHAT'S WRONG WITH YOU? ARE YOU ALL COWARDS? ATTACK!
ONE MAN RUNS THE GAUNTLET OF TRAPS... IT IS AS THOUGH HE KNOWS EXACTLY WHERE TO TREAD...
OTHERS ARE LESS FORTUNATE...
AAGH!
A FLOORBOARD CREAKS...
OY! WHO'S THERE?
THE FURTIVE MAN IN BLACK LEAVES AS QUICKLY AS HE CAME...
AO65K
...AND THE PLANS LEAVE WITH HIM!

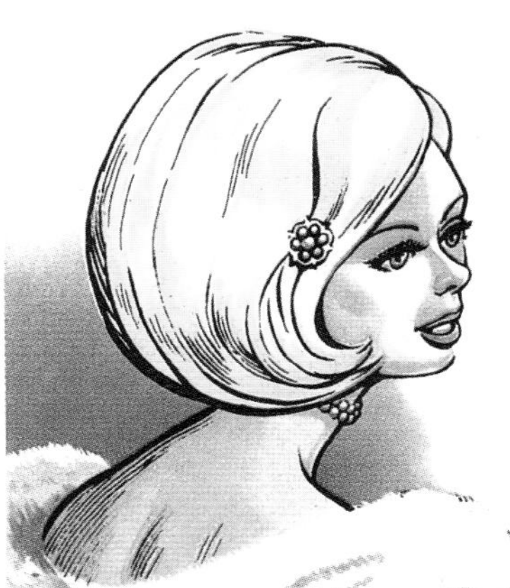

Ian Foster, of Blackwell Heath, Bucks., asks:
Did Graydon Gould, who is in The Forest Ranger, play the voice of Mike Mercury in Supercar?

LADY PENELOPE INVESTIGATES

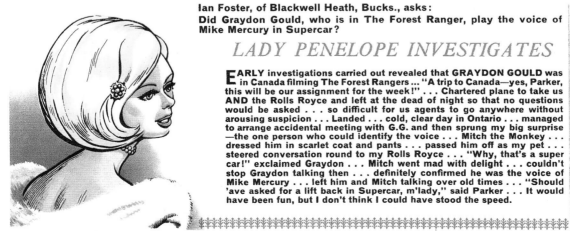

EARLY investigations carried out revealed that GRAYDON GOULD was in Canada filming The Forest Rangers ... "A trip to Canada—yes, Parker, this will be our assignment for the week!" . . . Chartered plane to take us AND the Rolls Royce and left at the dead of night so that no questions would be asked . . . so difficult for us agents to go anywhere without arousing suspicion . . . Landed . . . cold, clear day in Ontario . . . managed to arrange accidental meeting with G.G. and then sprung my big surprise —the one person who could identify the voice . . . Mitch the Monkey . . . dressed him in scarlet coat and pants . . . passed him off as my pet . . . steered conversation round to my Rolls Royce . . . "Why, that's a super car!" exclaimed Graydon . . . Mitch went mad with delight . . . couldn't stop Graydon talking then . . . definitely confirmed he was the voice of Mike Mercury . . . left him and Mitch talking over old times . . . "Should 'ave asked for a lift back in Supercar, m'lady," said Parker . . . It would have been fun, but I don't think I could have stood the speed.

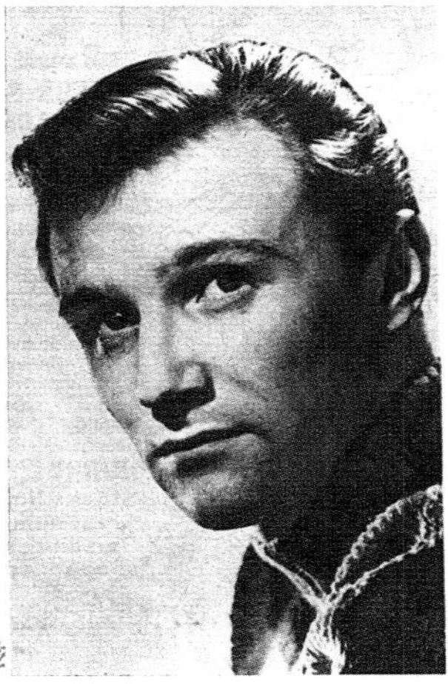

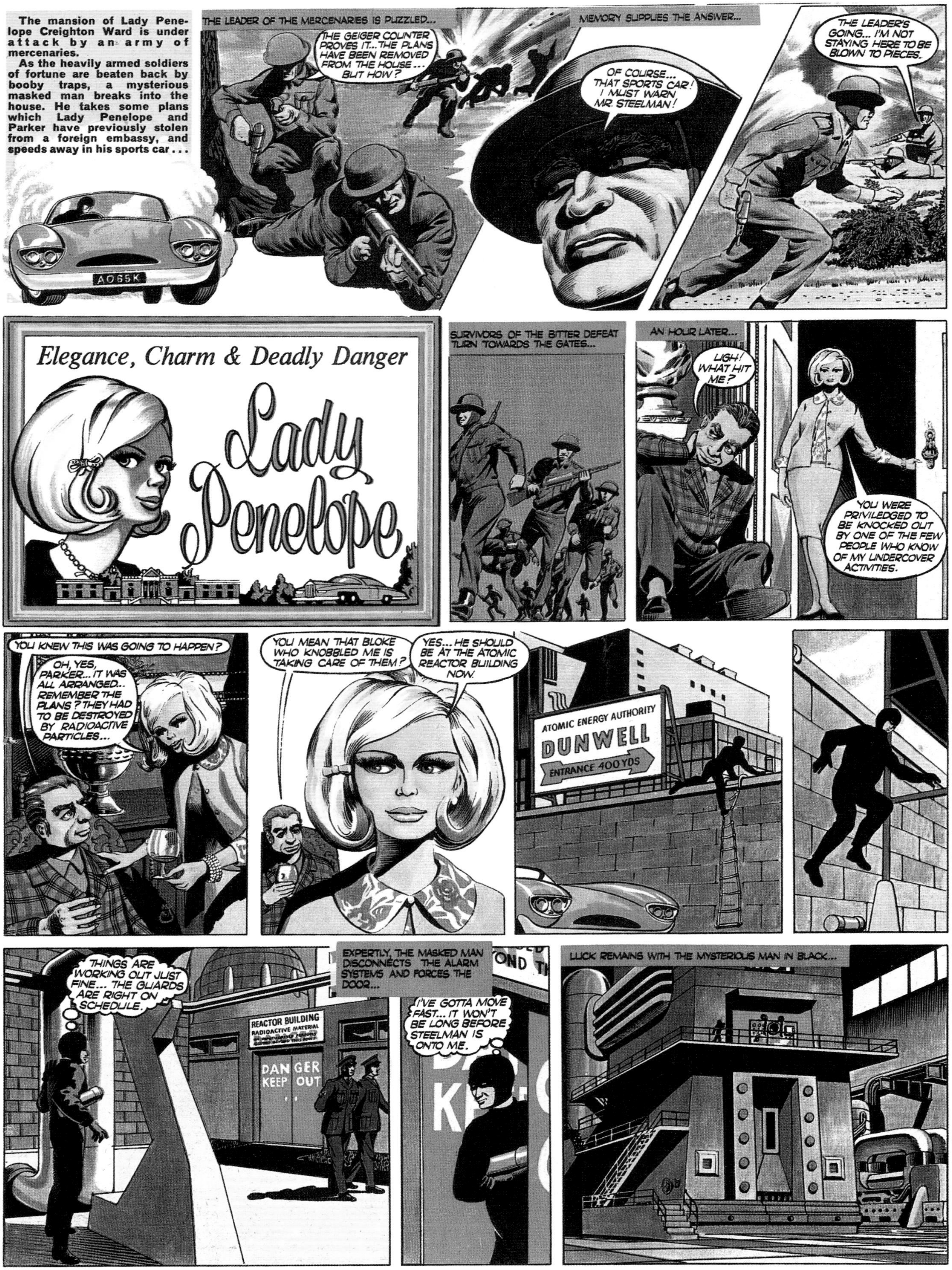
The mansion of Lady Penelope Creighton Ward is under attack by an army of mercenaries.
As the heavily armed soldiers of fortune are beaten back by booby traps, a mysterious masked man breaks into the house. He takes some plans which Lady Penelope and Parker have previously stolen from a foreign embassy, and speeds away in his sports car . . .
AO65K
THE LEADER OF THE MERCENARIES IS PUZZLED...
THE GEIGER COUNTER PROVES IT... THE PLANS HAVE BEEN REMOVED FROM THE HOUSE ... BUT HOW?
MEMORY SUPPLIES THE ANSWER...
OF COURSE... THAT SPORTS CAR! I MUST WARN MR. STEELMAN!
THE LEADER'S GOING... I'M NOT STAYING HERE TO BE BLOWN TO PIECES.
Elegance, Charm & Deadly Danger
Lady Penelope
SURVIVORS OF THE BITTER DEFEAT TURN TOWARDS THE GATES...
AN HOUR LATER...
UGH! WHAT HIT ME?
YOU WERE PRIVILEDGED TO BE KNOCKED OUT BY ONE OF THE FEW PEOPLE WHO KNOW OF MY UNDERCOVER ACTIVITIES.
YOU KNEW THIS WAS GOING TO HAPPEN?
OH, YES, PARKER... IT WAS ALL ARRANGED... REMEMBER THE PLANS? THEY HAD TO BE DESTROYED BY RADIOACTIVE PARTICLES...
YOU MEAN THAT BLOKE WHO KNOBBLED ME IS TAKING CARE OF THEM?
YES... HE SHOULD BE AT THE ATOMIC REACTOR BUILDING NOW.
ATOMIC ENERGY AUTHORITY
DUNWELL
ENTRANCE 400 YDS
THINGS ARE WORKING OUT JUST FINE... THE GUARDS ARE RIGHT ON SCHEDULE.
REACTOR BUILDING
RADIOACTIVE MATERIAL
DANGER KEEP OUT
EXPERTLY, THE MASKED MAN DISCONNECTS THE ALARM SYSTEMS AND FORCES THE DOOR...
I'VE GOTTA MOVE FAST... IT WON'T BE LONG BEFORE STEELMAN IS ONTO ME.
LUCK REMAINS WITH THE MYSTERIOUS MAN IN BLACK...

OPENING THE REACTOR CORE HATCH, HE INSERTS THE CANNISTER CONTAINING THE PLANS.

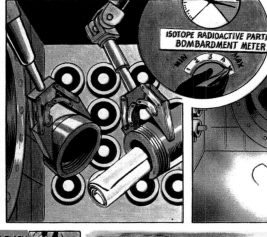

ISOTOPE RADIOACTIVE PARTI BOMBARDMENT METER

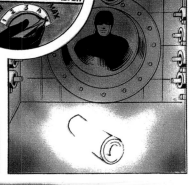

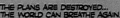

THE PLANS ARE DESTROYED... THE WORLD CAN BREATHE AGAIN.

NOW I CAN GET RID OF THIS MASK.

THE WORLD IS SAFE...BUT NOT THE MAN IN BLACK!

THAT'S HIM...

OKAY...LET'S GO!

THE LIMOUSINE QUICKLY OVERHAULS THE UNSUSPECTING MAN IN BLACK.

LADY PENELOPE INVESTIGATES

Michael Orme of Slough, Bucks., says: Amos Burke's car is super—can you tell me anything about it?

ALMOST before you could say 'Burke's Law,' Michael, Parker and I were on the aircraft bound for Hollywood . . .

Disguised as glamorous movie star—complete with very best mink and very long false eyelashes—managed to get part as one of Amos's girl friends in TV film.

Parker meanwhile investigated car ... Received following report... Car—Rolls Royce Silver Cloud II . . . Complete with Cocktail Cabinet . . . Telephone . . . Radio and Transistor TV . . . Record Player . . . Tape Recorder . . . Electric Windows . . . Air Conditioning . . .

A Rolls Royce Silver Cloud II

In case you're thinking of saving up for one, Michael—you'd better know the price . . . just a cool 24,000 dollars ! I must tell you about my Pink Rolls Royce sometime—even Amos Burke would be envious of that!

Lady Penelope and Parker have stolen plans of a bomb capable of blowing up the World. One of Lady Penelope's agents destroys the blueprints, but then his car is crashed.

THAT RAMMING BUSTED OUR DISGUISE SOME, BOSS.

GET RID OF IT. WE'LL ATTEND TO THE GUY DOWN THERE.

I MUST WARN LADY PENELOPE...

NO TRICKS, MISTER... OR YOU'RE DEAD. GET HIM UP HERE, LUIGI!...AND SEARCH THE CAR.

Elegance, Charm & Deadly Danger

Lady Penelope

DID YOU GET THE PLANS?

HE'S GOT RID OF THEM - BUT MR. STEELMAN WILL MAKE HIM TALK.

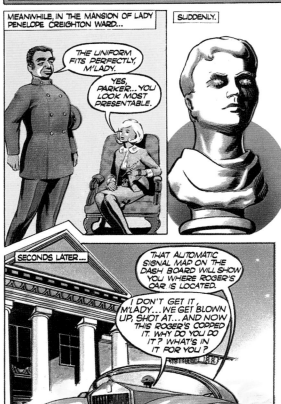

MEANWHILE, IN THE MANSION OF LADY PENELOPE CREIGHTON WARD...

THE UNIFORM FITS PERFECTLY, M'LADY.

YES, PARKER... YOU LOOK MOST PRESENTABLE.

SUDDENLY.

ONE OF YOUR GADGETS IS MAKING EYES AT ME... WHAT IS IT?

A SIGNAL... SOMETHING HAS HAPPENED TO ROGER LYON.

WHO'S HE?

THE YOUNG MAN WHO DESTROYED THE PLANS. HIS CAR IS FITTED WITH A DEVICE WHICH WARNS ME WHEN HE IS IN DANGER. HURRY... GET THE ROLLS ROYCE.

SECONDS LATER....

THAT AUTOMATIC SIGNAL MAP ON THE DASH BOARD WILL SHOW YOU WHERE ROGER'S CAR IS LOCATED.

I DON'T GET IT, M'LADY...WE GET BLOWN UP, SHOT AT... AND NOW THIS ROGER'S COPPED IT. WHY DO YOU DO IT? WHAT'S IN IT FOR YOU?

FAB 1

EXCITEMENT, PARKER. I ENJOY SKIRMISHING WITH THE CRIMINAL ELEMENT. IT'S CONVENIENT TO ALLOW PEOPLE TO THINK THAT I AM JUST ONE OF THE IDLE RICH, BUT AS A FEW TRUSTWORTHY FRIENDS KNOW, SUCH A LIFE WOULD THOROUGHLY BORE ME.

WHAT ABOUT THIS STEELMAN BLOKE...? HE KNOWS ABOUT YOU...

AH, YES... MR STEELMAN. HE IS EVIL... WITH ONE AMBITION... TO RULE THE EARTH. HE KNOWS OF MY WORK, IT'S TRUE... AND I'M NOT HAPPY ABOUT THE ARRANGEMENT.

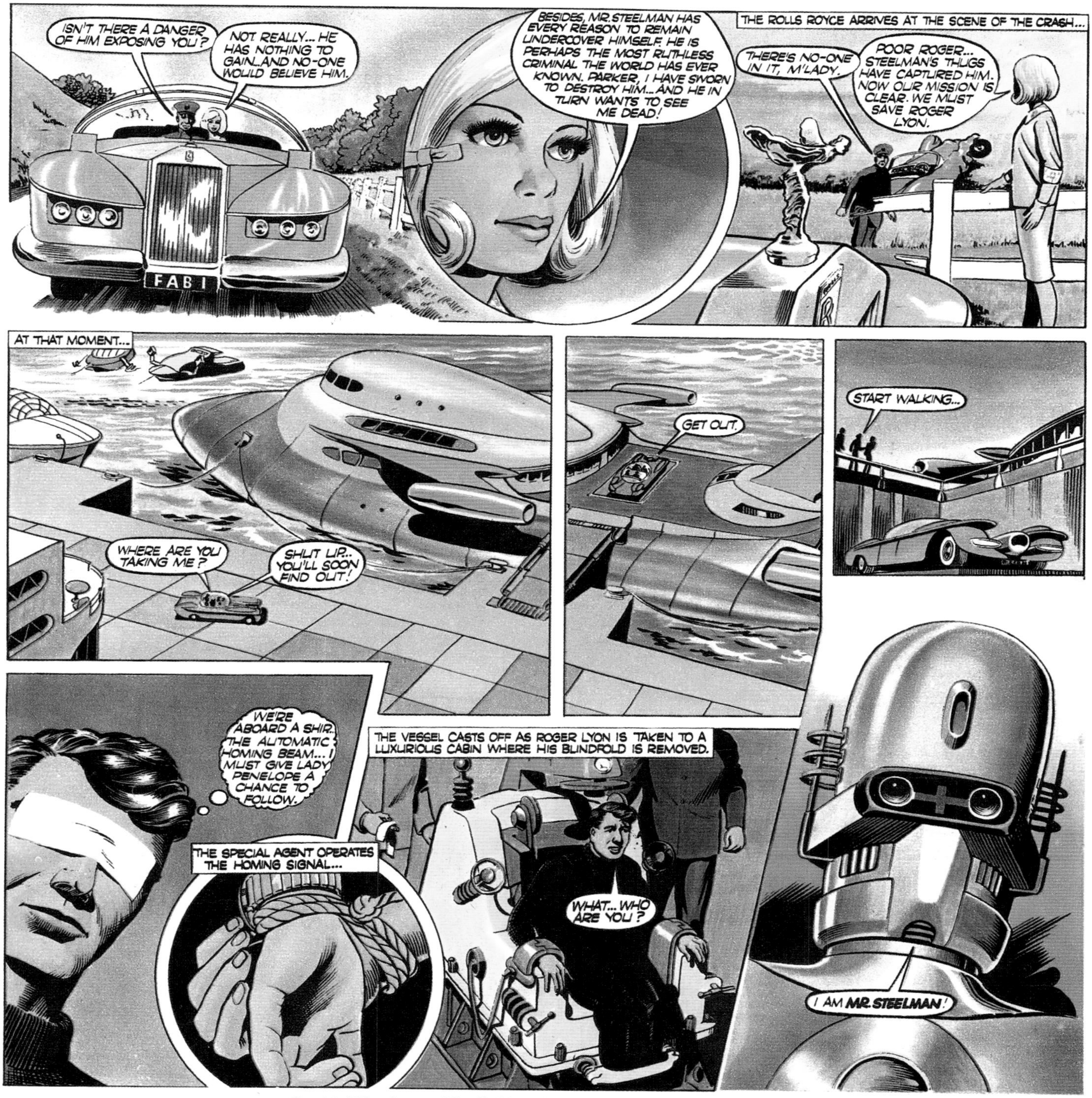
ISN'T THERE A DANGER OF HIM EXPOSING YOU?
NOT REALLY... HE HAS NOTHING TO GAIN...AND NO-ONE WOULD BELIEVE HIM.
FAB 1
BESIDES, MR. STEELMAN HAS EVERY REASON TO REMAIN UNDERCOVER HIMSELF. HE IS PERHAPS THE MOST RUTHLESS CRIMINAL THE WORLD HAS EVER KNOWN. PARKER, I HAVE SWORN TO DESTROY HIM...AND HE IN TURN WANTS TO SEE ME DEAD!
THE ROLLS ROYCE ARRIVES AT THE SCENE OF THE CRASH...
THERE'S NO-ONE IN IT, M'LADY.
POOR ROGER... STEELMAN'S THUGS HAVE CAPTURED HIM. NOW OUR MISSION IS CLEAR. WE MUST SAVE ROGER LYON.
AT THAT MOMENT...
WHERE ARE YOU TAKING ME?
SHUT UP.. YOU'LL SOON FIND OUT!
GET OUT.
START WALKING...
WE'RE ABOARD A SHIP. THE AUTOMATIC HOMING BEAM... I MUST GIVE LADY PENELOPE A CHANCE TO FOLLOW.
THE SPECIAL AGENT OPERATES THE HOMING SIGNAL...
THE VESSEL CASTS OFF AS ROGER LYON IS TAKEN TO A LUXURIOUS CABIN WHERE HIS BLINDFOLD IS REMOVED.
WHAT... WHO ARE YOU?
I AM MR. STEELMAN!

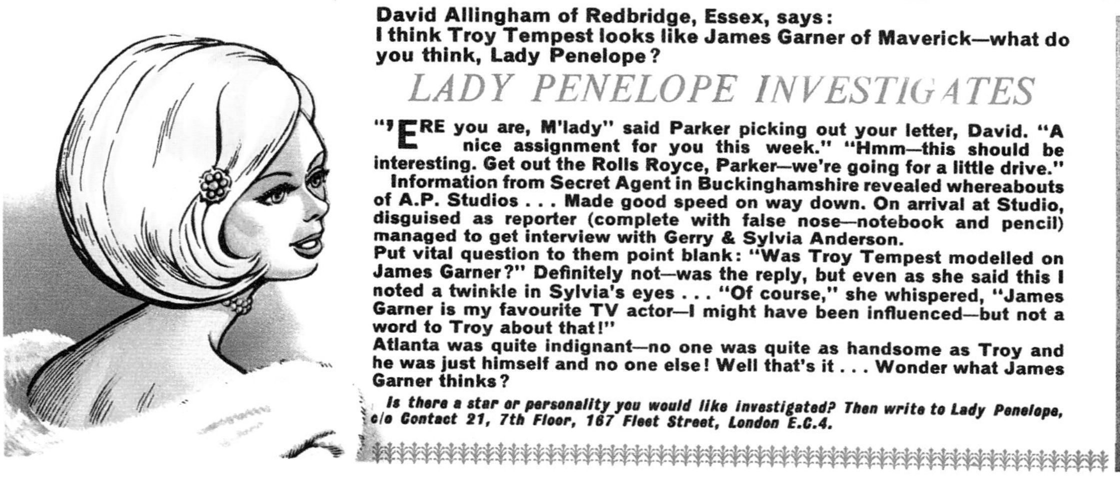

David Allingham of Redbridge, Essex, says:
I think Troy Tempest looks like James Garner of Maverick—what do you think, Lady Penelope?

LADY PENELOPE INVESTIGATES

"'ERE you are, M'lady" said Parker picking out your letter, David. "A nice assignment for you this week." "Hmm—this should be interesting. Get out the Rolls Royce, Parker—we're going for a little drive."

Information from Secret Agent in Buckinghamshire revealed whereabouts of A.P. Studios . . . Made good speed on way down. On arrival at Studio, disguised as reporter (complete with false nose—notebook and pencil) managed to get interview with Gerry & Sylvia Anderson.

Put vital question to them point blank: "Was Troy Tempest modelled on James Garner?" Definitely not—was the reply, but even as she said this I noted a twinkle in Sylvia's eyes . . . "Of course," she whispered, "James Garner is my favourite TV actor—I might have been influenced—but not a word to Troy about that!"

Atlanta was quite indignant—no one was quite as handsome as Troy and he was just himself and no one else! Well that's it . . . Wonder what James Garner thinks?

Is there a star or personality you would like investigated? Then write to Lady Penelope, c/o Contact 21, 7th Floor, 167 Fleet Street, London E.C.4.

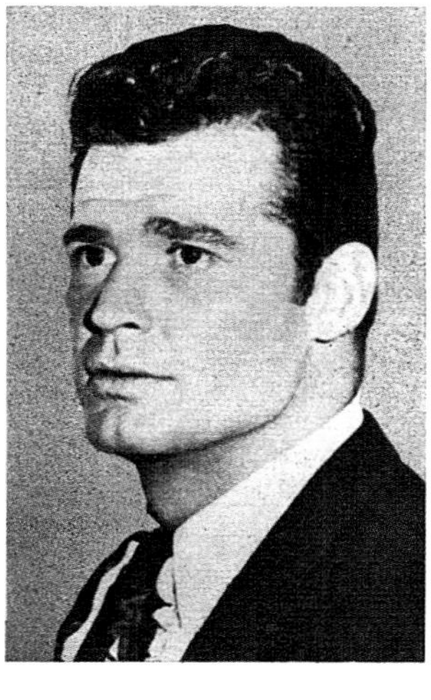

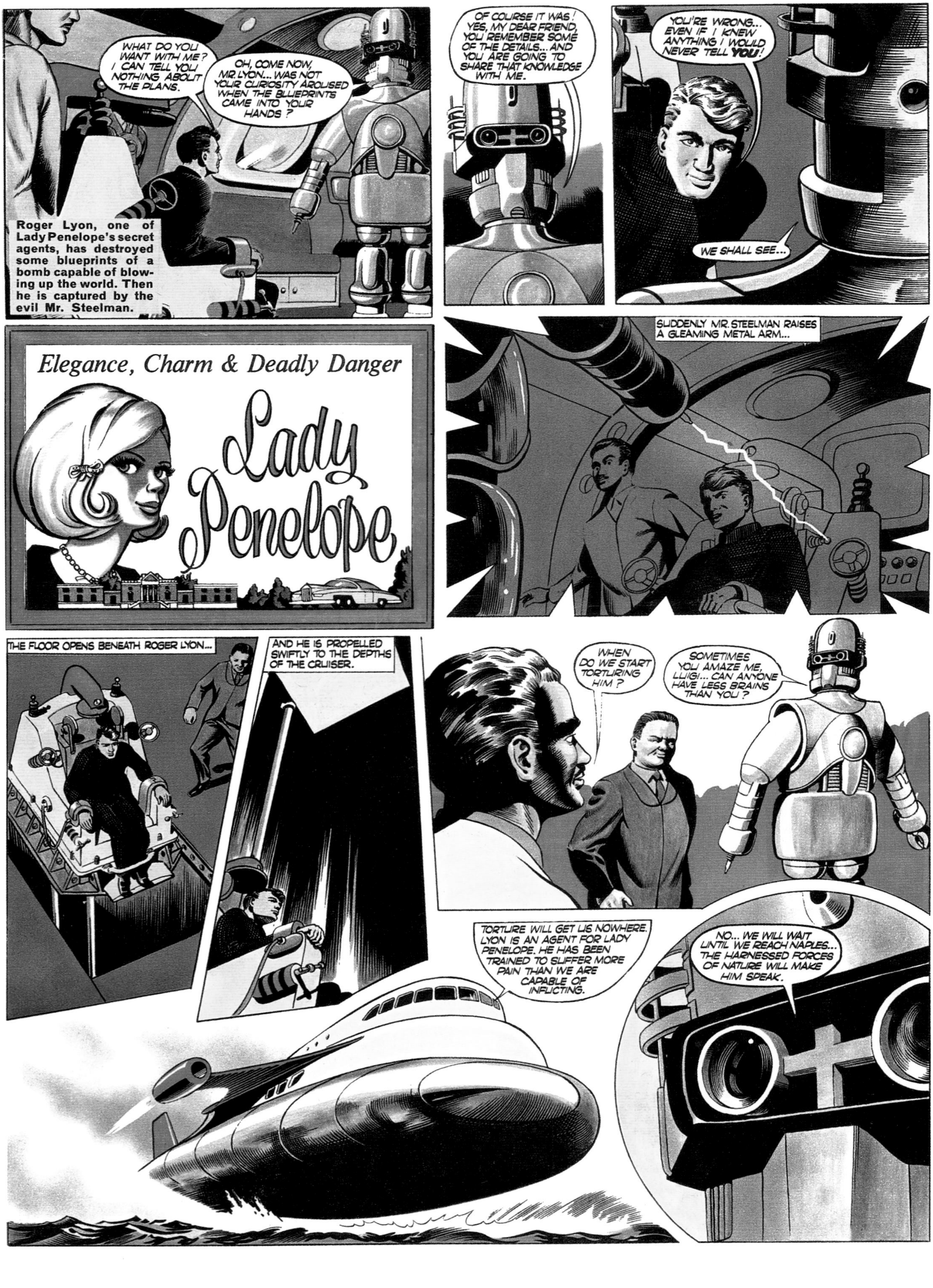

Roger Lyon, one of Lady Penelope's secret agents, has destroyed some blueprints of a bomb capable of blowing up the world. Then he is captured by the evil Mr. Steelman.
WHAT DO YOU WANT WITH ME? I CAN TELL YOU NOTHING ABOUT THE PLANS.
OH, COME NOW, MR LYON... WAS NOT YOUR CURIOSITY AROUSED WHEN THE BLUEPRINTS CAME INTO YOUR HANDS?
OF COURSE IT WAS! YES, MY DEAR FRIEND, YOU REMEMBER SOME OF THE DETAILS... AND YOU ARE GOING TO SHARE THAT KNOWLEDGE WITH ME.
YOU'RE WRONG... EVEN IF I KNEW ANYTHING I WOULD NEVER TELL YOU!
WE SHALL SEE...
Elegance, Charm & Deadly Danger
Lady Penelope
SUDDENLY MR. STEELMAN RAISES A GLEAMING METAL ARM...
THE FLOOR OPENS BENEATH ROGER LYON...
AND HE IS PROPELLED SWIFTLY TO THE DEPTHS OF THE CRUISER.
WHEN DO WE START TORTURING HIM?
SOMETIMES YOU AMAZE ME, LUIGI... CAN ANYONE HAVE LESS BRAINS THAN YOU?
TORTURE WILL GET US NOWHERE. LYON IS AN AGENT FOR LADY PENELOPE. HE HAS BEEN TRAINED TO SUFFER MORE PAIN THAN WE ARE CAPABLE OF INFLICTING.
NO... WE WILL WAIT UNTIL WE REACH NAPLES... THE HARNESSED FORCES OF NATURE WILL MAKE HIM SPEAK.

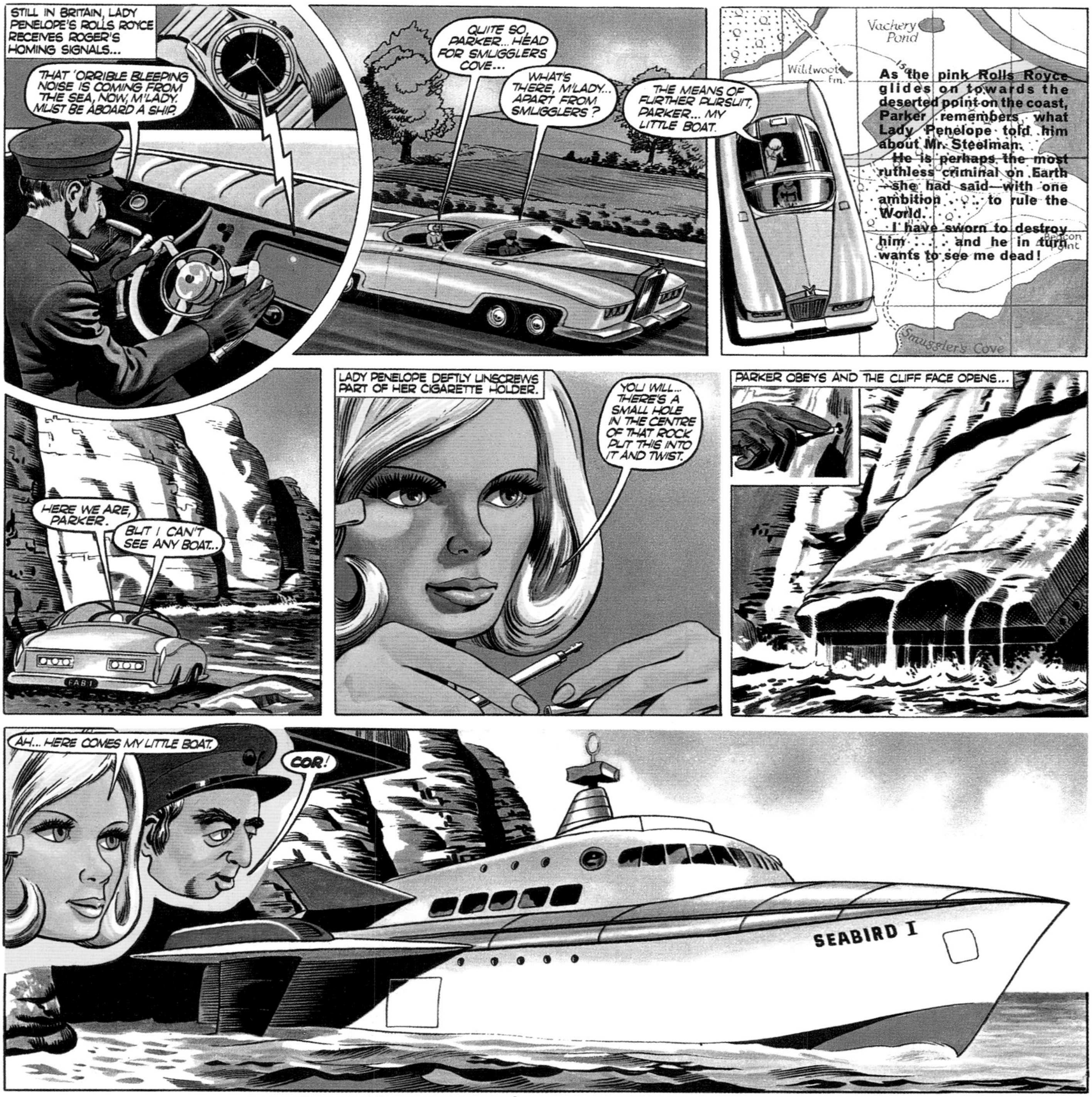
STILL IN BRITAIN, LADY PENELOPE'S ROLLS ROYCE RECEIVES ROGER'S HOMING SIGNALS...
THAT 'ORRIBLE BLEEPING NOISE IS COMING FROM THE SEA, NOW, M'LADY. MUST BE ABOARD A SHIP.
QUITE SO, PARKER... HEAD FOR SMUGGLERS COVE...
WHAT'S THERE, M'LADY... APART FROM SMUGGLERS?
THE MEANS OF FURTHER PURSUIT, PARKER... MY LITTLE BOAT.
Vachery Pond
As the pink Rolls Royce glides on towards the deserted point on the coast, Parker remembers what Lady Penelope told him about Mr. Steelman.
He is perhaps the most ruthless criminal on Earth—she had said—with one ambition . . . to rule the World.
I have sworn to destroy him . . . and he in turn wants to see me dead!
Smuggler's Cove
HERE WE ARE, PARKER.
BUT I CAN'T SEE ANY BOAT...
FAB 1
LADY PENELOPE DEFTLY UNSCREWS PART OF HER CIGARETTE HOLDER.
YOU WILL... THERE'S A SMALL HOLE IN THE CENTRE OF THAT ROCK. PUT THIS INTO IT AND TWIST.
PARKER OBEYS AND THE CLIFF FACE OPENS...
AH... HERE COMES MY LITTLE BOAT.
COR!
SEABIRD I

Mark Meddings of Addleston, Surrey, says:
I have read a lot about Charlie Drake's paintings—does he really paint them himself?

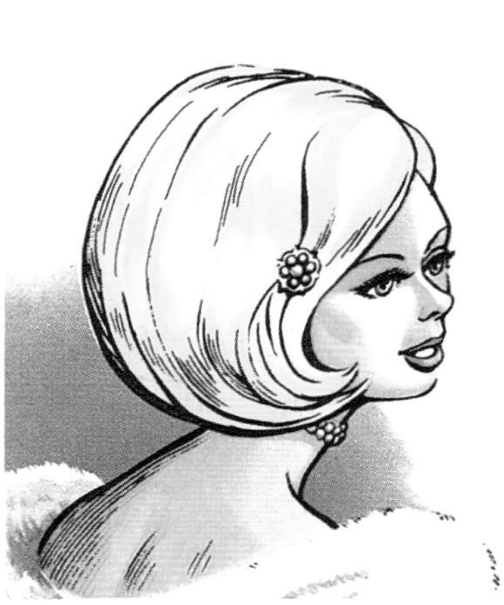

LADY PENELOPE INVESTIGATES

"YOU'RE a bit of an artist, aren't you, M'Lady?" enquired Parker. "This letter should interest you" . . . "I have a feeling this will interest you, too, Parker," I replied. "I happen to know that Charlie Drake is your favourite comedian . . ."

Before I could say another word Parker had whisked me off in the Rolls Royce heading for Surrey.

Opened box of disguises . . . decided this time to be travelling saleswoman selling Joke Books! Put on shabby raincoat, plain felt hat and sensible shoes . . .

"We're 'ere, M'Lady," announced Parker as we approached Weybridge. "Very well, park the car. I'll walk the rest of the way . . . and be ready to make a quick getaway," I instructed.

With Joke Books under my arm, I rang the bell at the Drake residence . . . then a voice said, "Hello my Darlings!" . . . Charlie Drake himself! . . . dressed in beret, smock and holding artist's brush and palette in his hand!

Well, Mark, that was proof enough—Charlie really does paint . . . and, incidentally, he didn't buy a Joke Book from me!

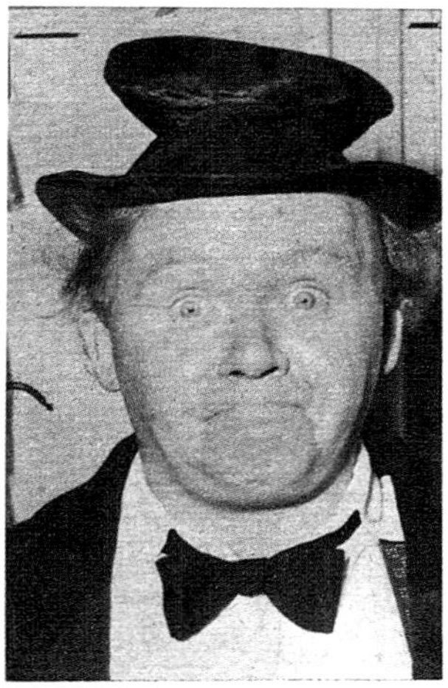

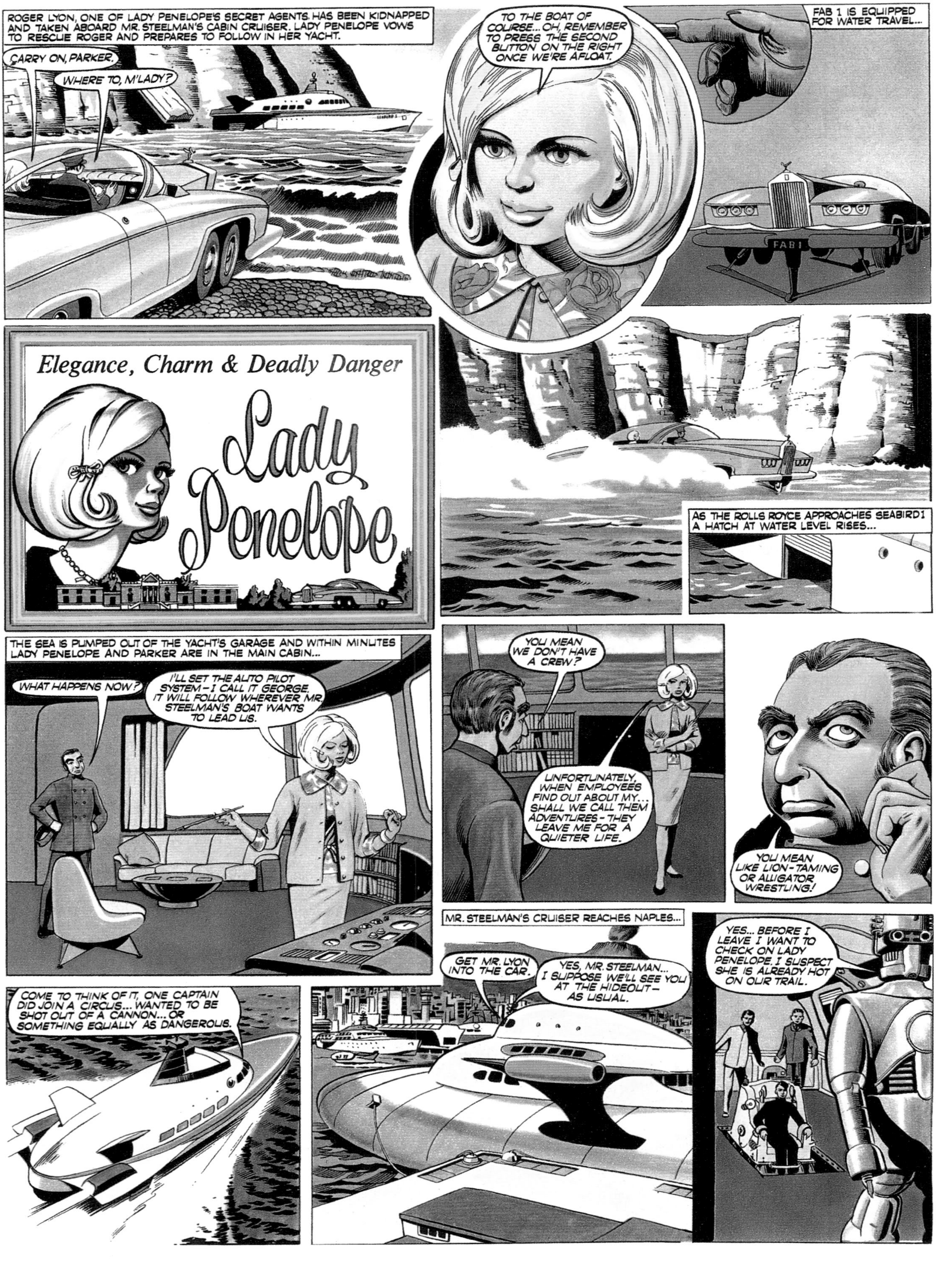
ROGER LYON, ONE OF LADY PENELOPE'S SECRET AGENTS, HAS BEEN KIDNAPPED AND TAKEN ABOARD MR. STEELMAN'S CABIN CRUISER. LADY PENELOPE VOWS TO RESCUE ROGER AND PREPARES TO FOLLOW IN HER YACHT.
CARRY ON, PARKER.
WHERE TO, M'LADY?
TO THE BOAT OF COURSE... OH, REMEMBER TO PRESS THE SECOND BUTTON ON THE RIGHT ONCE WE'RE AFLOAT.
FAB 1 IS EQUIPPED FOR WATER TRAVEL...
FAB 1
Elegance, Charm & Deadly Danger
Lady Penelope
AS THE ROLLS ROYCE APPROACHES SEABIRD1 A HATCH AT WATER LEVEL RISES...
THE SEA IS PUMPED OUT OF THE YACHT'S GARAGE AND WITHIN MINUTES LADY PENELOPE AND PARKER ARE IN THE MAIN CABIN...
WHAT HAPPENS NOW?
I'LL SET THE AUTO PILOT SYSTEM - I CALL IT GEORGE. IT WILL FOLLOW WHEREVER MR. STEELMAN'S BOAT WANTS TO LEAD US.
YOU MEAN WE DON'T HAVE A CREW?
UNFORTUNATELY, WHEN EMPLOYEES FIND OUT ABOUT MY... SHALL WE CALL THEM ADVENTURES - THEY LEAVE ME FOR A QUIETER LIFE.
YOU MEAN LIKE LION-TAMING OR ALLIGATOR WRESTLING!
COME TO THINK OF IT, ONE CAPTAIN DID JOIN A CIRCUS... WANTED TO BE SHOT OUT OF A CANNON... OR SOMETHING EQUALLY AS DANGEROUS.
MR. STEELMAN'S CRUISER REACHES NAPLES...
GET MR. LYON INTO THE CAR.
YES, MR. STEELMAN... I SUPPOSE WE'LL SEE YOU AT THE HIDEOUT - AS USUAL.
YES... BEFORE I LEAVE I WANT TO CHECK ON LADY PENELOPE. I SUSPECT SHE IS ALREADY HOT ON OUR TRAIL.

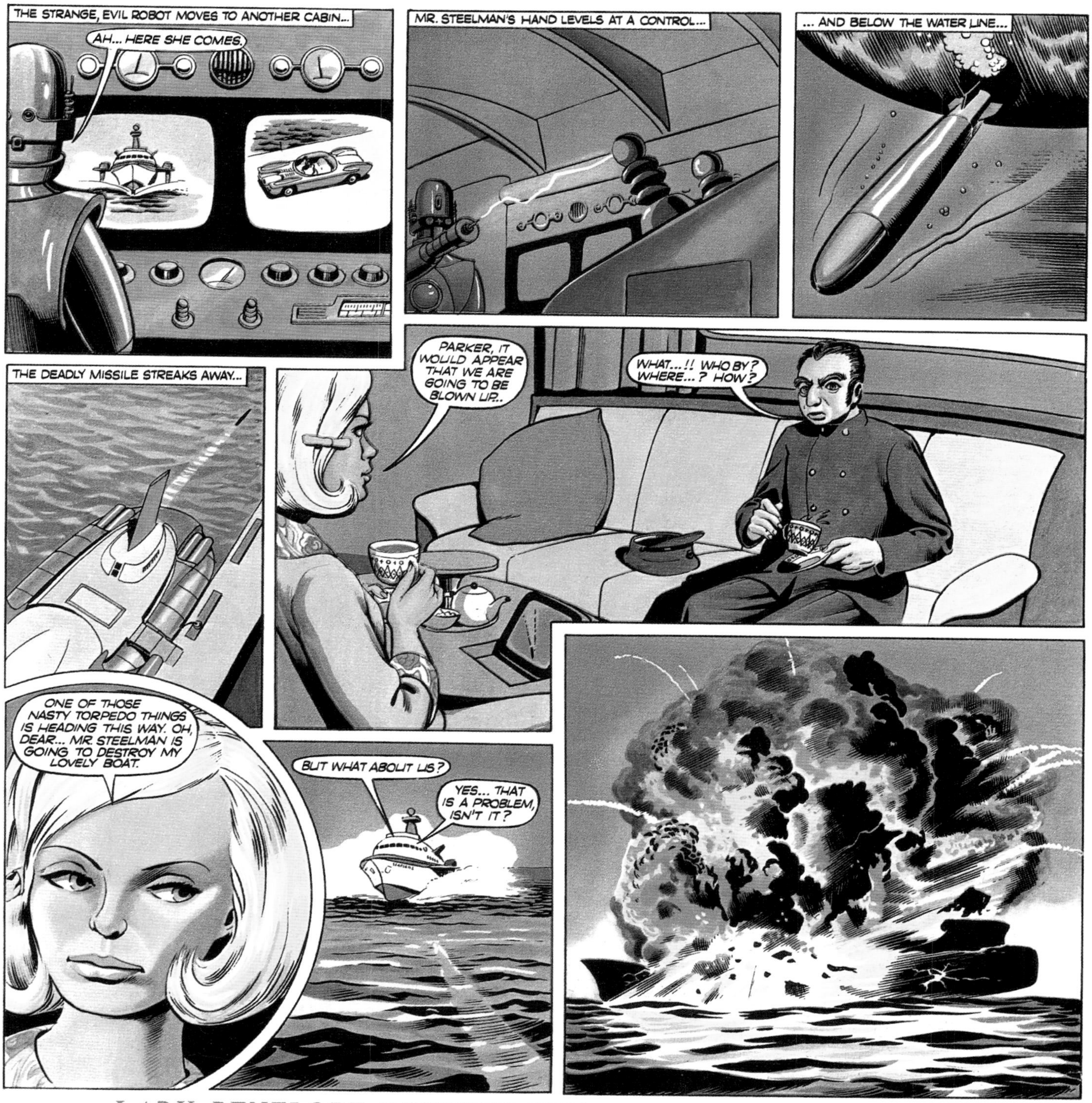
THE STRANGE, EVIL ROBOT MOVES TO ANOTHER CABIN...
AH... HERE SHE COMES.
MR. STEELMAN'S HAND LEVELS AT A CONTROL...
... AND BELOW THE WATER LINE...
THE DEADLY MISSILE STREAKS AWAY...
PARKER, IT WOULD APPEAR THAT WE ARE GOING TO BE BLOWN UP..
WHAT...!! WHO BY? WHERE...? HOW?
ONE OF THOSE NASTY TORPEDO THINGS IS HEADING THIS WAY. OH, DEAR... MR. STEELMAN IS GOING TO DESTROY MY LOVELY BOAT.
BUT WHAT ABOUT US?
YES... THAT IS A PROBLEM, ISN'T IT?

LADY PENELOPE INVESTIGATES

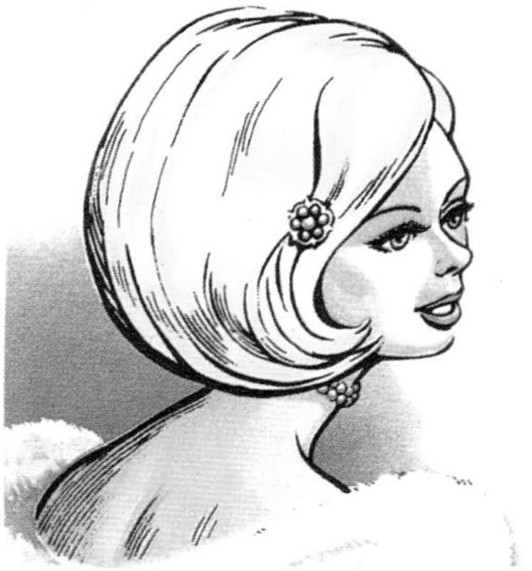

Philip Shutt of Berkhampstead asks, can you tell me anything about the test pilot of the T.S.R.2?

"NOW don't tell me I know anything about this subject, Parker, because I just don't," I commented as I opened your letter, Philip. "In fact I don't even know what T.S.R.2 means."

"Hmmph," snorted Parker. "It's an aircraft, M'Lady."

"Well, come on, Parker, let's take a look at it and find out all we can . . ."

Contacted X of the Secret Service and established that T.S.R.2 was short for Tactical Strike Reconnaissance. Chief Test Pilot R. P. Beaumont, D.S.O.,O.B.E., D.S.C., born August 10th, 1920, ex Battle of Britain pilot. At beginning of war shot down five enemy aircraft then took command of 609 Squadron . . . During flying bomb attack on London, destroyed 32 V1's and

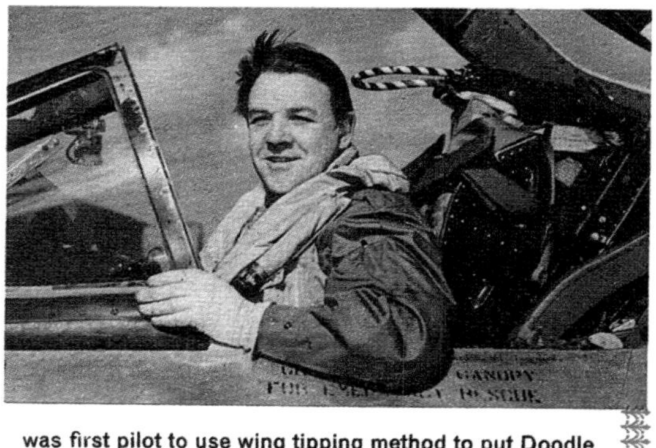

was first pilot to use wing tipping method to put Doodle Bugs off course! No time left to tell you about the trip I made in the T.S.R.2—some pilot and some flight!

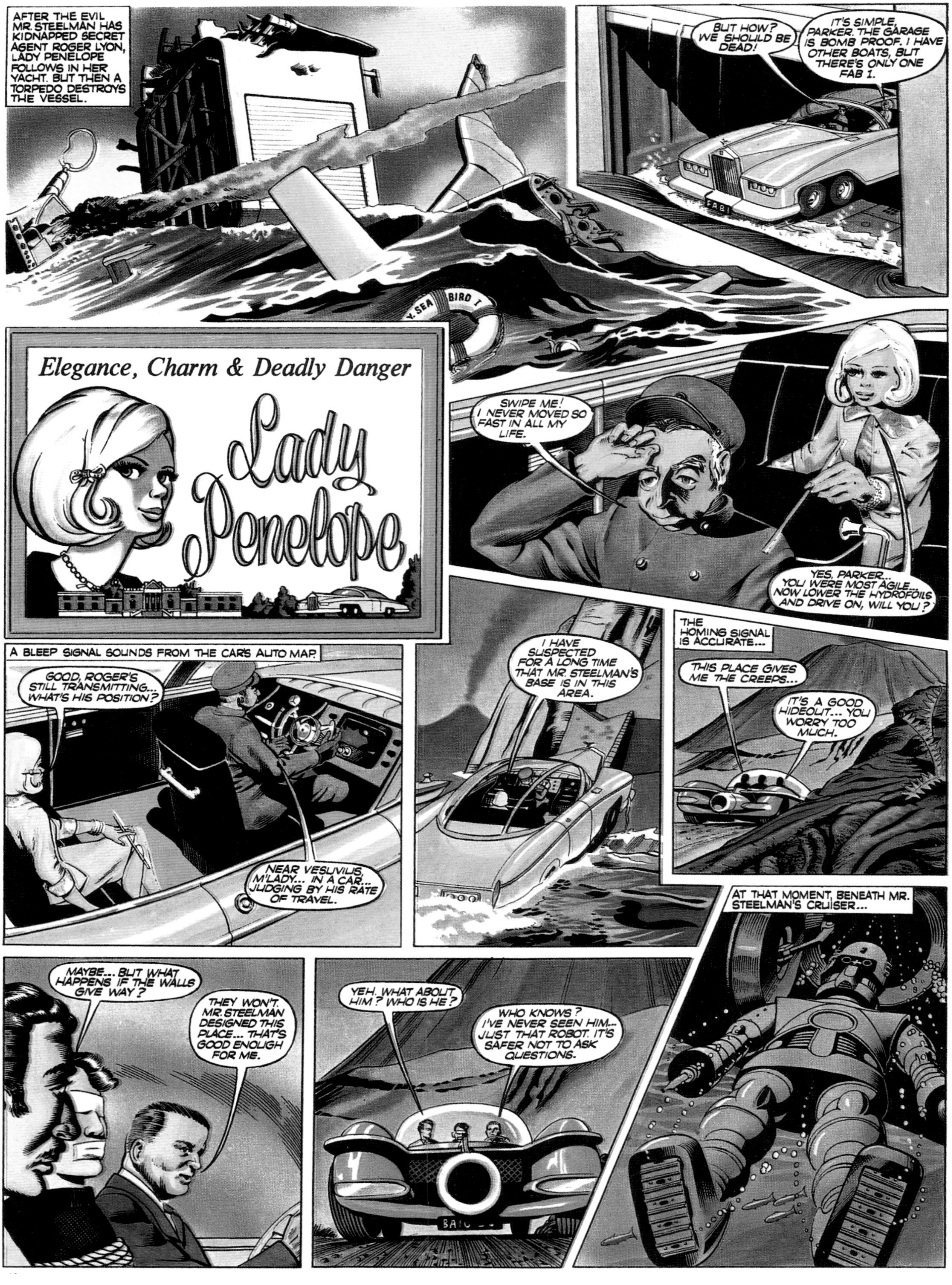
AFTER THE EVIL MR. STEELMAN HAS KIDNAPPED SECRET AGENT ROGER LYON, LADY PENELOPE FOLLOWS IN HER YACHT. BUT THEN A TORPEDO DESTROYS THE VESSEL.
BUT HOW? WE SHOULD BE DEAD!
IT'S SIMPLE, PARKER. THE GARAGE IS BOMB PROOF. I HAVE OTHER BOATS, BUT THERE'S ONLY ONE FAB 1.
FAB 1
Y. SEA BIRD I
Elegance, Charm & Deadly Danger
Lady Penelope
SWIPE ME! I NEVER MOVED SO FAST IN ALL MY LIFE.
YES, PARKER... YOU WERE MOST AGILE... NOW LOWER THE HYDROFOILS AND DRIVE ON, WILL YOU?
A BLEEP SIGNAL SOUNDS FROM THE CAR'S AUTO MAP.
GOOD, ROGER'S STILL TRANSMITTING... WHAT'S HIS POSITION?
NEAR VESUVIUS, M'LADY... IN A CAR... JUDGING BY HIS RATE OF TRAVEL.
I HAVE SUSPECTED FOR A LONG TIME THAT MR. STEELMAN'S BASE IS IN THIS AREA.
THE HOMING SIGNAL IS ACCURATE...
THIS PLACE GIVES ME THE CREEPS...
IT'S A GOOD HIDEOUT... YOU WORRY TOO MUCH.
MAYBE... BUT WHAT HAPPENS IF THE WALLS GIVE WAY?
THEY WON'T. MR. STEELMAN DESIGNED THIS PLACE... THAT'S GOOD ENOUGH FOR ME.
YEH. WHAT ABOUT HIM? WHO IS HE?
WHO KNOWS? I'VE NEVER SEEN HIM... JUST THAT ROBOT. IT'S SAFER NOT TO ASK QUESTIONS.
AT THAT MOMENT, BENEATH MR. STEELMAN'S CRUISER...

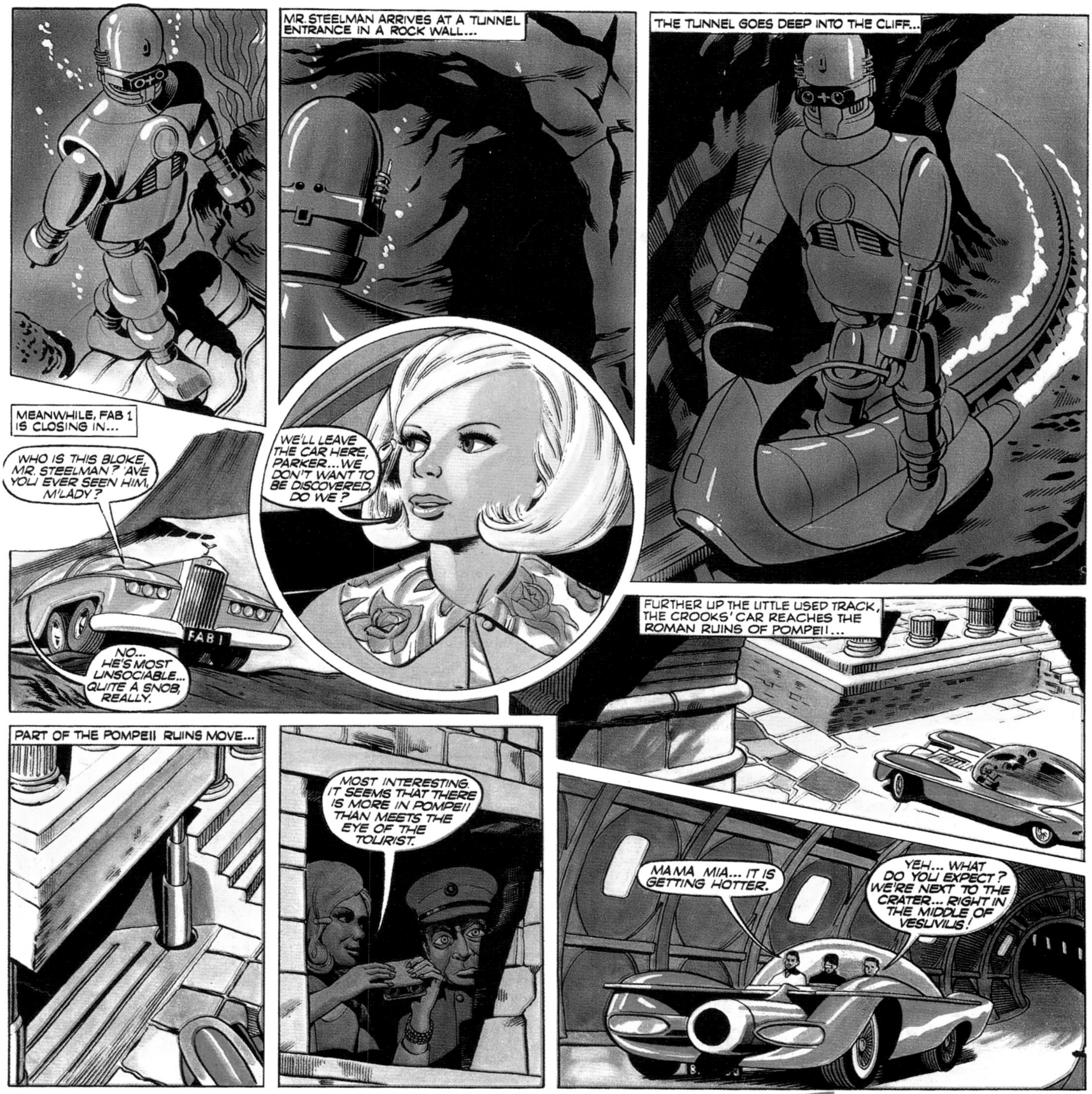
MR. STEELMAN ARRIVES AT A TUNNEL ENTRANCE IN A ROCK WALL...
THE TUNNEL GOES DEEP INTO THE CLIFF...
MEANWHILE, FAB 1 IS CLOSING IN...
WHO IS THIS BLOKE, MR. STEELMAN? 'AVE YOU EVER SEEN HIM, M'LADY?
NO... HE'S MOST UNSOCIABLE... QUITE A SNOB, REALLY.
WE'LL LEAVE THE CAR HERE, PARKER... WE DON'T WANT TO BE DISCOVERED, DO WE?
FAB 1
FURTHER UP THE LITTLE USED TRACK, THE CROOKS' CAR REACHES THE ROMAN RUINS OF POMPEII...
PART OF THE POMPEII RUINS MOVE...
MOST INTERESTING. IT SEEMS THAT THERE IS MORE IN POMPEII THAN MEETS THE EYE OF THE TOURIST.
MAMA MIA... IT IS GETTING HOTTER.
YEH... WHAT DO YOU EXPECT? WE'RE NEXT TO THE CRATER... RIGHT IN THE MIDDLE OF VESUVIUS!

LADY PENELOPE INVESTIGATES

'Could you please tell me the age of Sean Connery who plays James Bond in the films' says Tom Gennell, Agent No. 744959, from Greenock, Renfrewshire, Scotland.

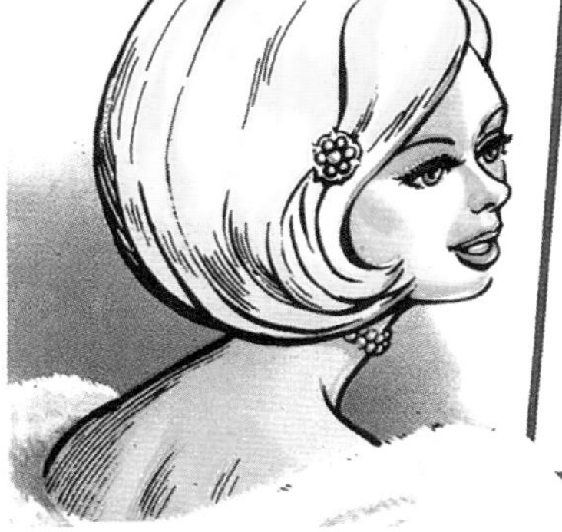

"NOW this really is my cup of tea, Parker—our assignment for the week."
"The Rolls is waiting in the driveway, M'lady," replied Parker with a superior smile. "I anticipated your reaction and I have tracked down the gentleman for you."
Sometimes Parker is so efficient he's downright irritating!
"What disguise this time, M'lady?"
"Something positively glam," I snapped as I put on my very prettiest wig and extra long false eyelashes!
Posing as a news photographer I approached the actor's home, Parker carrying all the heavy lighting and camera equipment . . . Putting on my very sweetest smile I rang doorbell . . . The smile froze on my lips as door opened by very glam blonde . . . This is Mrs. Sean Connery—actress Diane Cilento.
When I got over my disappointment managed to persuade her to let me take photograph of him and found out the following information!
Born Edinburgh 1930. Due to make another James Bond adventure this year called 'Thunderball' in Paris and Bahamas . . . Have already booked flight—more news then—meanwhile keep writing to me with your requests.

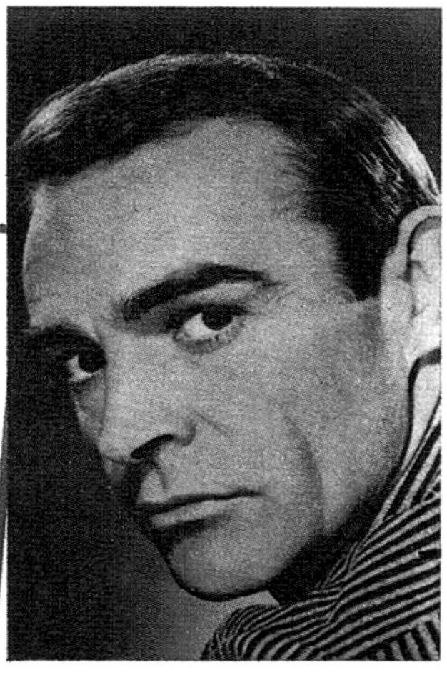

IN A BID TO SAVE ROGER LYON, ONE OF HER SECRET AGENTS, LADY PENELOPE TRAILS THE EVIL MR. STEELMAN TO MOUNT VESUVIUS.

LADY PENELOPE AND PARKER HAVE SEEN ROGER TAKEN TO THE RUINS OF POMPEII.

THE PERFECT HIDEOUT. I MUST CONGRATULATE MR. STEELMAN WHEN I MEET HIM.

YEH, BUT 'OW DO WE GET IN, M'LADY?

I SAW ONE OF THOSE GENTLEMEN PRESS THIS BRICK...

Elegance, Charm & Deadly Danger

Lady Penelope

THERE, PARKER... IT PAYS TO KEEP ONE'S EYES OPEN.

THEY ENTER THE TUNNEL...

THIS PLACE FAIR GIVES ME THE CREEPS. WHERE D'YOU RECKON IT LEADS TO?

I WOULD HAZARD A GUESS THAT WE SHALL BE VERY CLOSE TO THE CRATER OF MOUNT VESUVIUS WHEN WE REACH THE END OF THIS PASSAGE.

MR. STEELMAN'S HIDEOUT IS A MAGNIFICENT PIECE OF ENGINEERING SKILL...

OKAY, UNCOVER HIS EYES... MR. STEELMAN WILL BE HERE IN A MINUTE.

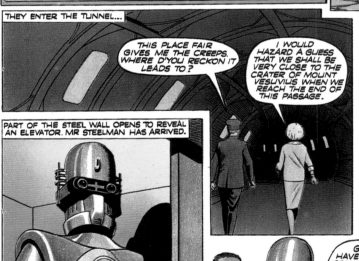

PART OF THE STEEL WALL OPENS TO REVEAL AN ELEVATOR. MR STEELMAN HAS ARRIVED.

GOOD, YOU HAVE MADE MR. LYON COMFORTABLE. NOW, MY FRIEND, YOU WILL TELL ME ALL YOU REMEMBER ABOUT THE PLANS OF THE DOOMSDAY BOMB.

I DESTROYED THEM... YOU'LL GET NOTHING OUT OF ME!

YOU ARE WRONG. YOU WILL TALK WITHOUT REALISING IT... SUCH ARE THE WONDERS OF SCIENCE AND TECHNOLOGY.

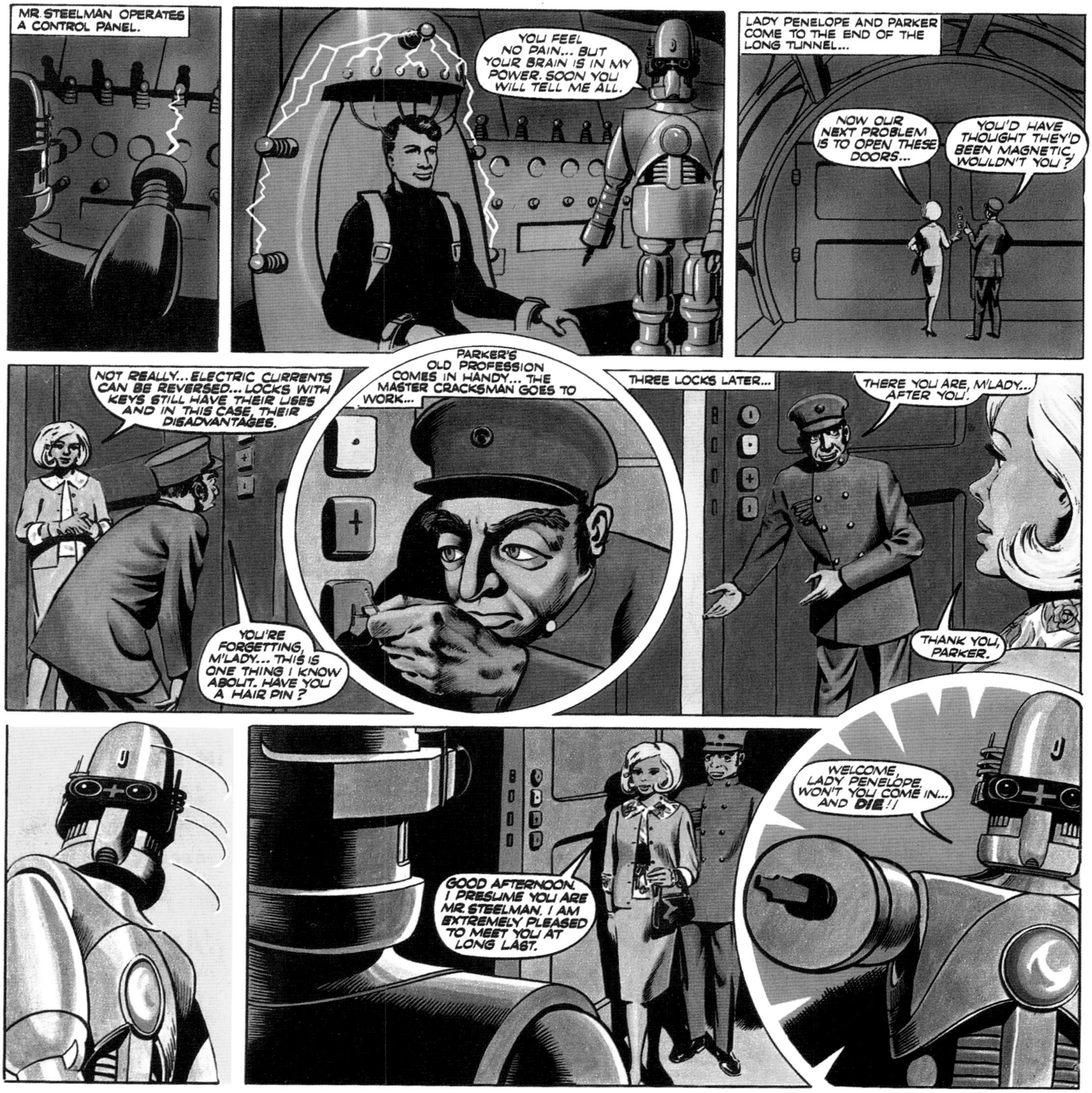
MR. STEELMAN OPERATES A CONTROL PANEL.
YOU FEEL NO PAIN... BUT YOUR BRAIN IS IN MY POWER. SOON YOU WILL TELL ME ALL.
LADY PENELOPE AND PARKER COME TO THE END OF THE LONG TUNNEL...
NOW OUR NEXT PROBLEM IS TO OPEN THESE DOORS...
YOU'D HAVE THOUGHT THEY'D BEEN MAGNETIC, WOULDN'T YOU?
NOT REALLY... ELECTRIC CURRENTS CAN BE REVERSED... LOCKS WITH KEYS STILL HAVE THEIR USES AND IN THIS CASE, THEIR DISADVANTAGES.
YOU'RE FORGETTING, M'LADY... THIS IS ONE THING I KNOW ABOUT. HAVE YOU A HAIR PIN?
PARKER'S OLD PROFESSION COMES IN HANDY... THE MASTER CRACKSMAN GOES TO WORK...
THREE LOCKS LATER...
THERE YOU ARE, M'LADY... AFTER YOU!
THANK YOU, PARKER.
GOOD AFTERNOON. I PRESUME YOU ARE MR. STEELMAN. I AM EXTREMELY PLEASED TO MEET YOU AT LONG LAST.
WELCOME, LADY PENELOPE. WON'T YOU COME IN... AND DIE!!

LADY PENELOPE INVESTIGATES

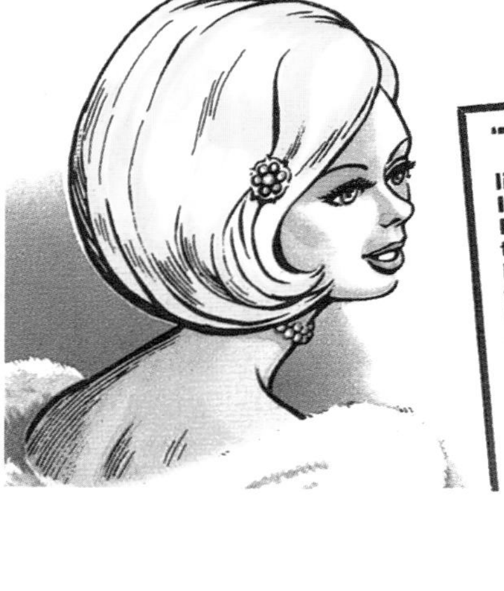

Ian Bacon, Agent No. 473241, of Broxbourne, Herts., asks: Are Patrick Macnee's parents Irish, Scottish or both?

'THERE you are, M'lady,' said Parker, 'another 'andsome gentleman you can meet this week—and one with a very aristocratic background like yourself.'

I never quite know with Parker whether he's getting at me or not! However, I chose to ignore the remark and selected your letter for my assignment this week, Ian.

Investigations revealed some very exciting facts—not only was Mr. Macnee the star of THE AVENGERS series but he was a descendant of ROBIN HOOD no less. Parents born in Scotland but of Irish descent . . . Grandfather Sir Daniel Macnee president of Scottish Royal Academy.

Arranged to be invited to Hunt Ball to meet him and found him delightful and amusing . . . amazed to learn his early ambition was to be jockey but became too tall . . .

Found we had a lot in common—invited him to my home for tea—sent Parker to collect him in the Rolls—shhh! Not a word to Cathy Gale about this! Must brush up on my Judo!

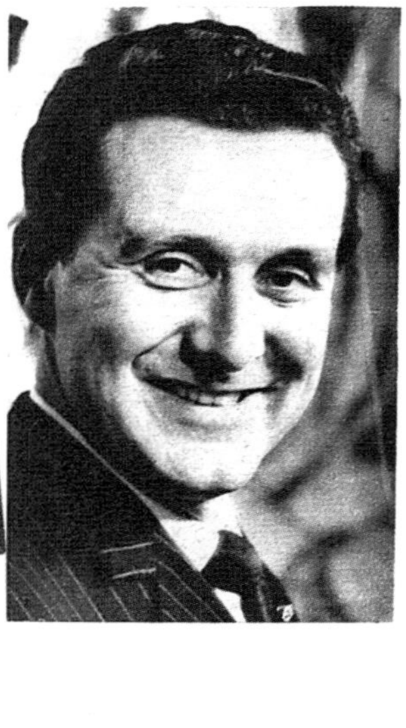

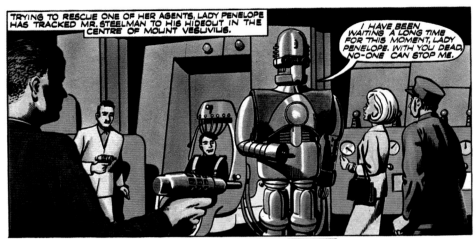

TRYING TO RESCUE ONE OF HER AGENTS, LADY PENELOPE HAS TRACKED MR. STEELMAN TO HIS HIDEOUT IN THE CENTRE OF MOUNT VESUVIUS.

I HAVE BEEN WAITING A LONG TIME FOR THIS MOMENT, LADY PENELOPE. WITH YOU DEAD, NO-ONE CAN STOP ME.

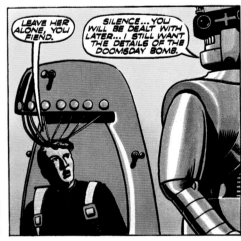

LEAVE HER ALONE, YOU FIEND.

SILENCE... YOU WILL BE DEALT WITH LATER... I STILL WANT THE DETAILS OF THE DOOMSDAY BOMB.

Elegance, Charm & Deadly Danger

Lady Penelope

MR. STEELMAN POINTS TOWARDS A CONTROL BUTTON...

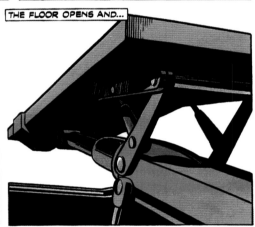

THE FLOOR OPENS AND...

NOW, MY LADY, WILL YOU TAKE A REST, PLEASE?

OKAY, BOSS... I'VE GOT HER!

WHAT ARE YOU GOING TO DO WITH HER?

IT IS SIMPLE... WATCH...

RAMP

DOORS

THE BOILING LAVA OF VESUVIUS LIES BELOW...

SECURE LADY PENELOPE TO THE RAMP, LUIGI.

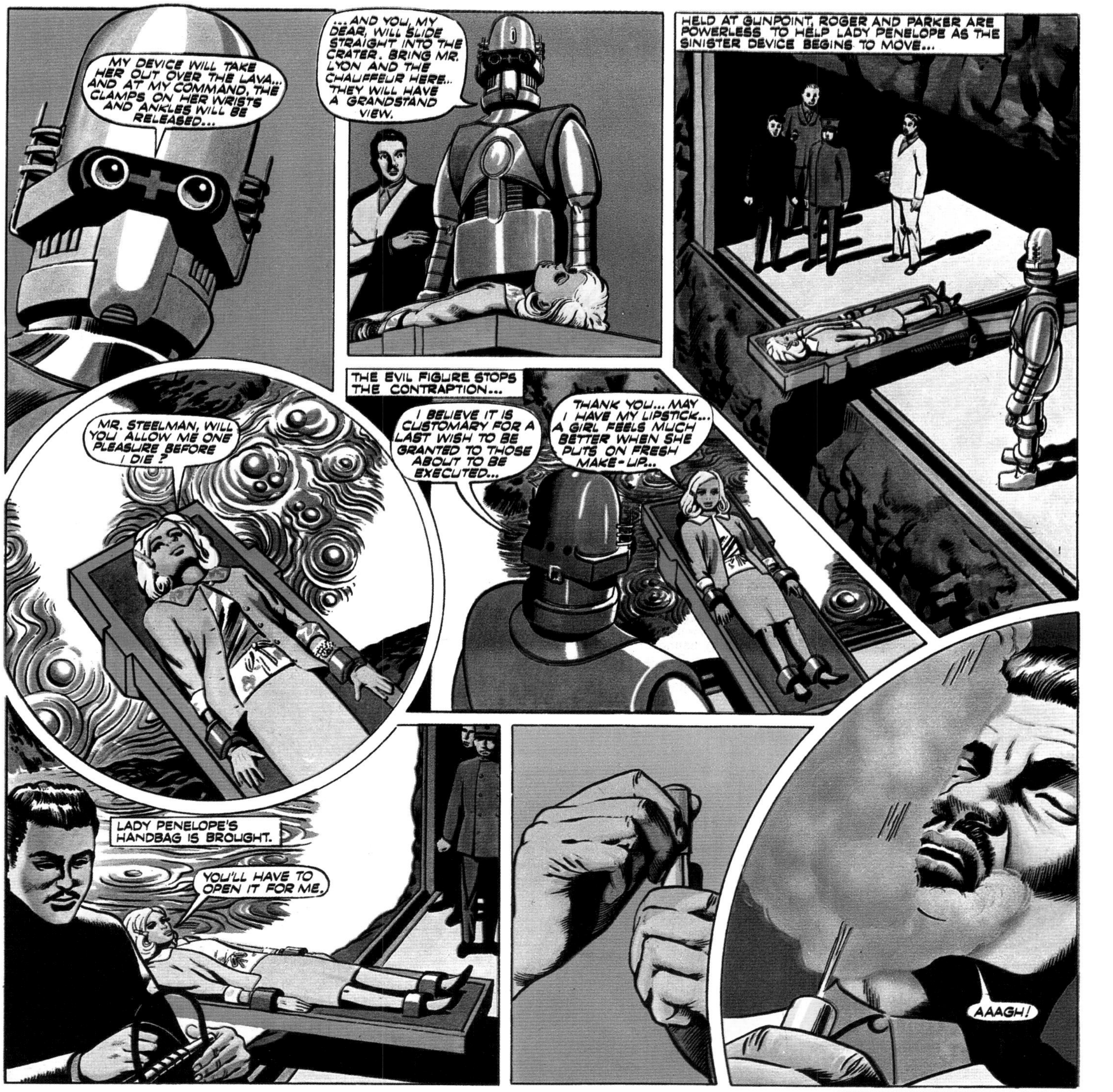
MY DEVICE WILL TAKE HER OUT OVER THE LAVA... AND AT MY COMMAND, THE CLAMPS ON HER WRISTS AND ANKLES WILL BE RELEASED...
...AND YOU, MY DEAR, WILL SLIDE STRAIGHT INTO THE CRATER. BRING MR. LYON AND THE CHAUFFEUR HERE.. THEY WILL HAVE A GRANDSTAND VIEW.
HELD AT GUNPOINT, ROGER AND PARKER ARE POWERLESS TO HELP LADY PENELOPE AS THE SINISTER DEVICE BEGINS TO MOVE...
MR. STEELMAN, WILL YOU ALLOW ME ONE PLEASURE BEFORE I DIE?
THE EVIL FIGURE STOPS THE CONTRAPTION...
I BELIEVE IT IS CUSTOMARY FOR A LAST WISH TO BE GRANTED TO THOSE ABOUT TO BE EXECUTED...
THANK YOU... MAY I HAVE MY LIPSTICK... A GIRL FEELS MUCH BETTER WHEN SHE PUTS ON FRESH MAKE-UP...
LADY PENELOPE'S HANDBAG IS BROUGHT.
YOU'LL HAVE TO OPEN IT FOR ME.
AAAGH!

LADY PENELOPE INVESTIGATES

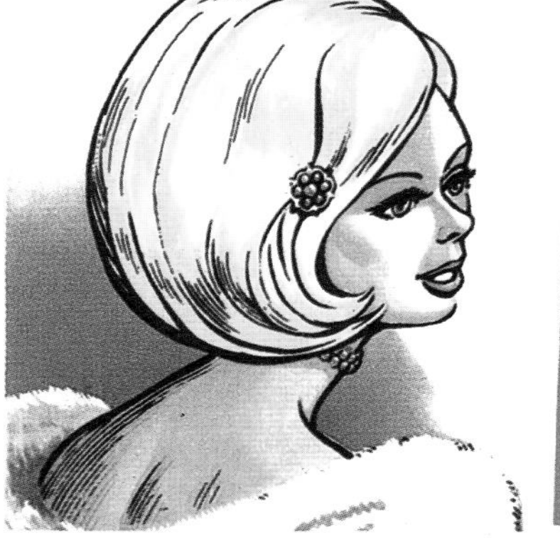

Paul Labrum of East Dulwich, S.E.22, asks . . . Can you tell me what Danger Man is like in real life? Perhaps you know him as you are both Secret Agents.

"THIS one is a bit of a challenge, M'Lady," announced Parker as he opened your letter, Paul. "From what I 'ear, 'e's a bit of a difficult one to track down." "Nonsense," I replied—deciding to take up the challenge—"he'll be our assignment for the week."

Looked up Secret Agent Dossier of Danger Man (alias Patrick McGoohan) born New York 1928, later lived in Ireland and England. Educated Sheffield and Leicester . . . etc. All very interesting but it did not tell us what he was really like. "Get out the Rolls, Parker, and head for Elstree Studios."

Arrived just in time to see his car speed out of the gate . . . "Follow him, Parker, and whatever happens don't let him give us the slip." "What about your disguise, M'Lady?" asked Parker as he skilfully slid the car round in hot pursuit. "He's a fellow agent," I snapped, "just dark glasses will do." By this time speedometer hovering on 110 m.p.h. mark. "Faster, Parker, faster." He obviously knew he was being tailed. "It's no good, M'Lady, he has given us the slip."

Sorry, Paul, but don't worry, I'll catch up with him one day . . . a good agent never gives up!

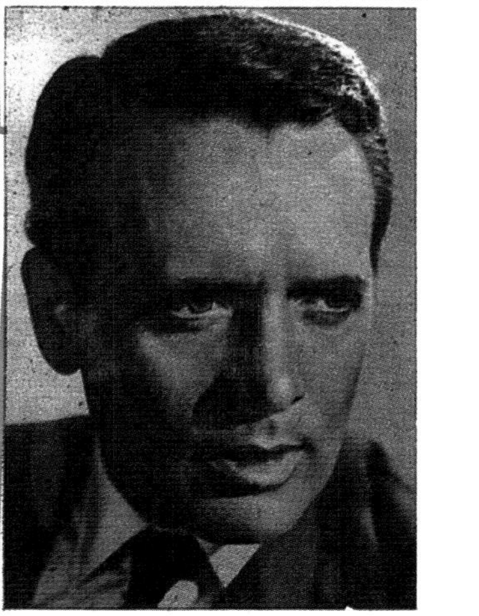

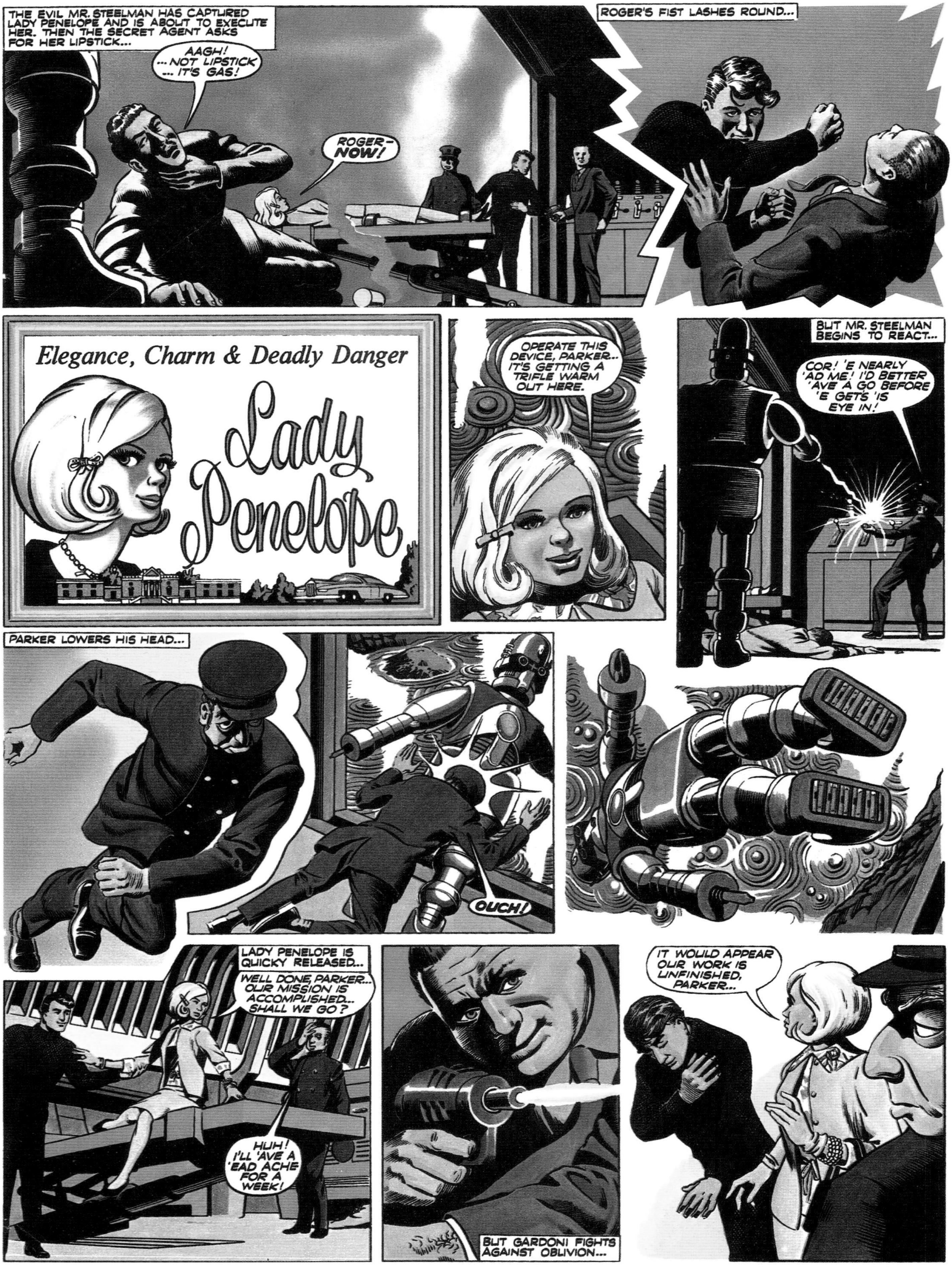
THE EVIL MR. STEELMAN HAS CAPTURED LADY PENELOPE AND IS ABOUT TO EXECUTE HER. THEN THE SECRET AGENT ASKS FOR HER LIPSTICK...
AAGH! ...NOT LIPSTICK ... IT'S GAS!
ROGER-NOW!
ROGER'S FIST LASHES ROUND...
Elegance, Charm & Deadly Danger
Lady Penelope
OPERATE THIS DEVICE, PARKER... IT'S GETTING A TRIFLE WARM OUT HERE.
BUT MR. STEELMAN BEGINS TO REACT...
COR! 'E NEARLY 'AD ME! I'D BETTER 'AVE A GO BEFORE 'E GETS 'IS EYE IN!
PARKER LOWERS HIS HEAD...
OUCH!
LADY PENELOPE IS QUICKY RELEASED...
WELL DONE, PARKER... OUR MISSION IS ACCOMPLISHED... SHALL WE GO?
HUH! I'LL 'AVE A 'EAD ACHE FOR A WEEK!
BUT GARDONI FIGHTS AGAINST OBLIVION...
IT WOULD APPEAR OUR WORK IS UNFINISHED, PARKER...

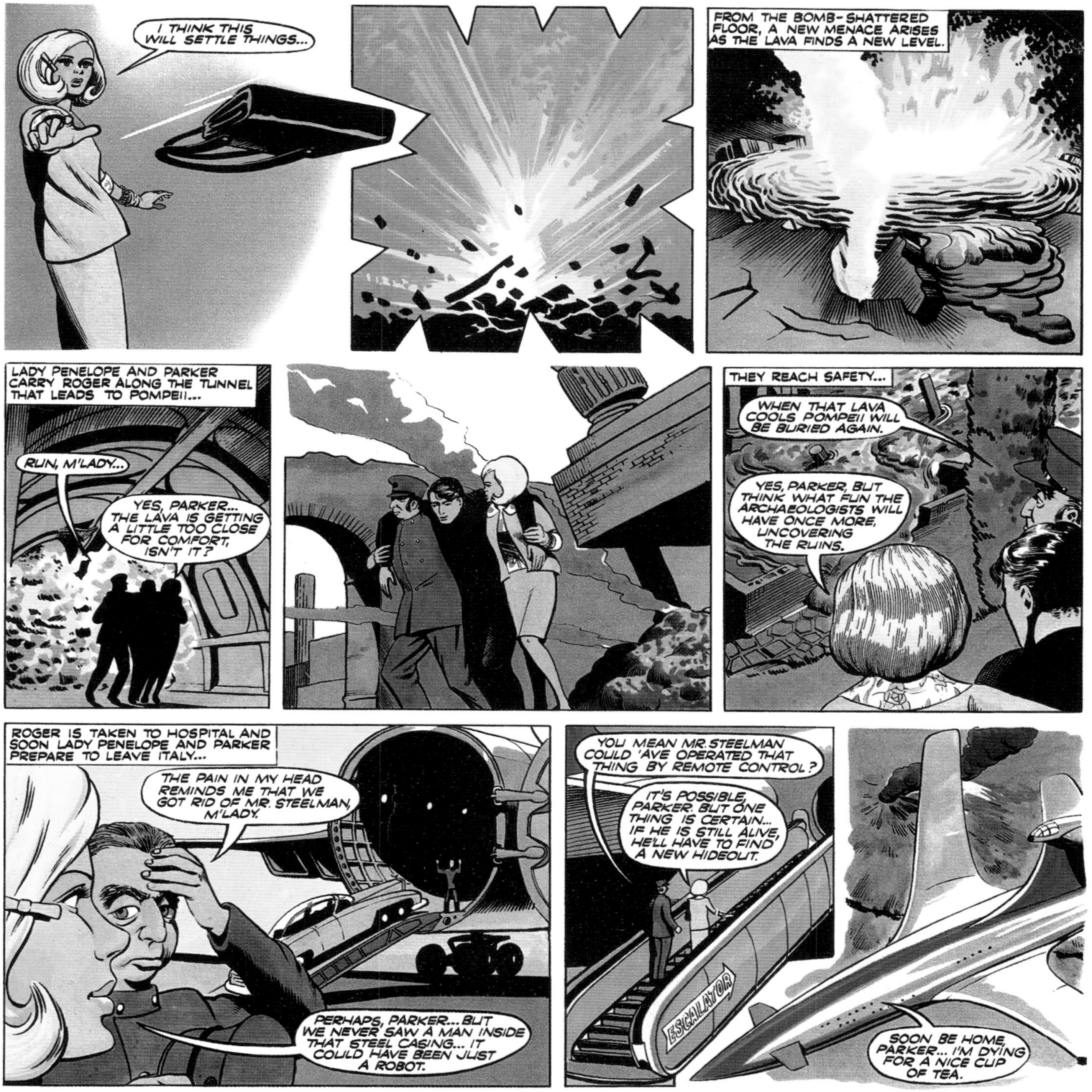
I THINK THIS WILL SETTLE THINGS...
FROM THE BOMB-SHATTERED FLOOR, A NEW MENACE ARISES AS THE LAVA FINDS A NEW LEVEL.
LADY PENELOPE AND PARKER CARRY ROGER ALONG THE TUNNEL THAT LEADS TO POMPEII...
RUN, M'LADY...
YES, PARKER... THE LAVA IS GETTING A LITTLE TOO CLOSE FOR COMFORT, ISN'T IT?
THEY REACH SAFETY...
WHEN THAT LAVA COOLS POMPEII WILL BE BURIED AGAIN.
YES, PARKER, BUT THINK WHAT FUN THE ARCHAEOLOGISTS WILL HAVE ONCE MORE, UNCOVERING THE RUINS.
ROGER IS TAKEN TO HOSPITAL AND SOON LADY PENELOPE AND PARKER PREPARE TO LEAVE ITALY...
THE PAIN IN MY HEAD REMINDS ME THAT WE GOT RID OF MR. STEELMAN, M'LADY.
PERHAPS, PARKER... BUT WE NEVER SAW A MAN INSIDE THAT STEEL CASING... IT COULD HAVE BEEN JUST A ROBOT.
YOU MEAN MR. STEELMAN COULD 'AVE OPERATED THAT THING BY REMOTE CONTROL?
IT'S POSSIBLE, PARKER. BUT ONE THING IS CERTAIN... IF HE IS STILL ALIVE, HE'LL HAVE TO FIND A NEW HIDEOUT.
ESCALATOR
SOON BE HOME, PARKER... I'M DYING FOR A NICE CUP OF TEA.

LADY PENELOPE INVESTIGATES

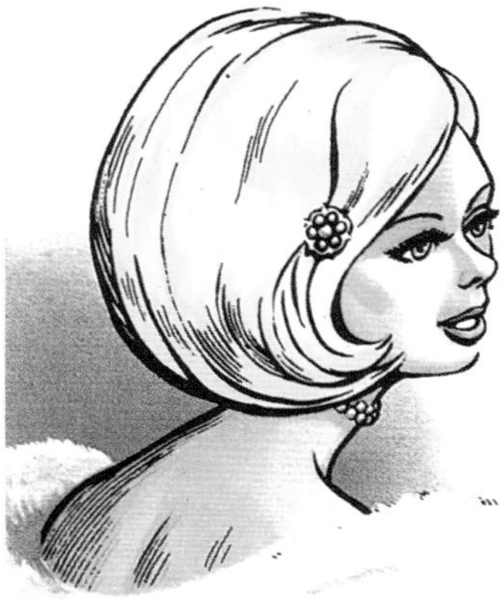

I have heard a record called RINGO sung by LORNE GREENE, says Robert Goode of Orpington, Kent, is that the same man who is in Bonanza?

THE only RINGO I had heard of was the BEATLE variety—so disguised as a very 'Way Out' teenager—wearing black leather jeans and jazzy sweater, went to local music shop and purchased disc . . . Caught PARKER redhanded furtively buying latest Pop recording. After hearing RINGO decided to proceed further with investigations and make it assignment for week . . . From usual sources obtained the following information . . . LORNE GREENE singer same man as actor who plays BEN CARTWRIGHT in BONANZA . . . Born Ottawa, Canada . . . studied to be chemical engineer . . . became interested in acting and worked on radio and stage . . . at present filming BONANZA series in Hollywood.

"Hmm—think it's time we went on a little trip, Parker—arrange for my private plane to be ready."

"Where to, M'Lady?" enquired PARKER.

"To Hollywood of course—to meet Hoss—Ben—Little Joe."

We'll be seeing them all—so watch out for my reports direct from Hollywood.

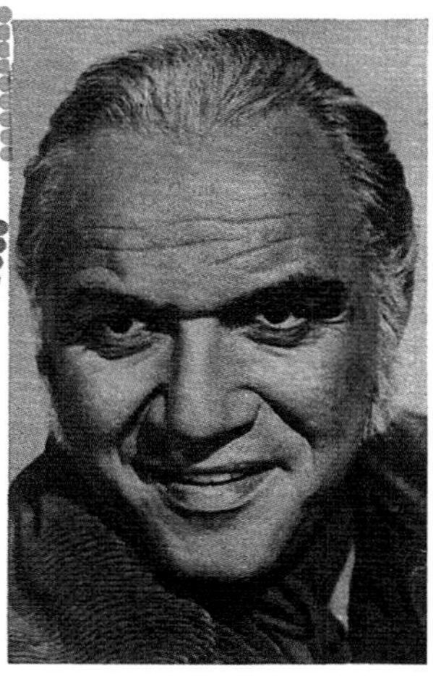

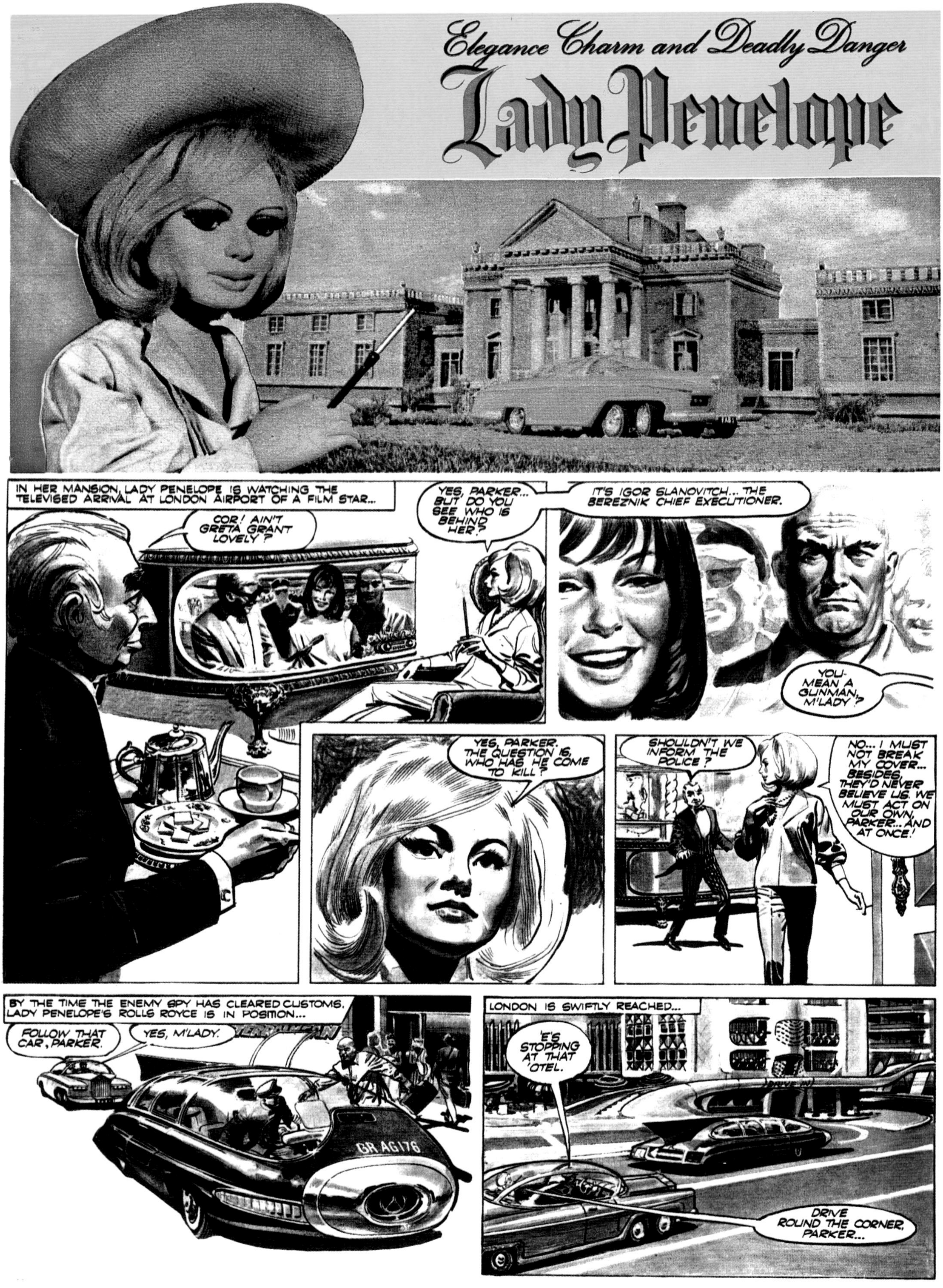
Elegance Charm and Deadly Danger
Lady Penelope
IN HER MANSION, LADY PENELOPE IS WATCHING THE TELEVISED ARRIVAL AT LONDON AIRPORT OF A FILM STAR...
COR! AIN'T GRETA GRANT LOVELY?
YES, PARKER... BUT DO YOU SEE WHO IS BEHIND HER?
IT'S IGOR SLANOVITCH... THE BEREZNIK CHIEF EXECUTIONER.
YOU-MEAN A GUNMAN, M'LADY?
YES, PARKER. THE QUESTION IS, WHO HAS HE COME TO KILL?
SHOULDN'T WE INFORM THE POLICE?
NO... I MUST NOT BREAK MY COVER... BESIDES, THEY'D NEVER BELIEVE US. WE MUST ACT ON OUR OWN, PARKER... AND AT ONCE!
BY THE TIME THE ENEMY SPY HAS CLEARED CUSTOMS, LADY PENELOPE'S ROLLS ROYCE IS IN POSITION...
FOLLOW THAT CAR, PARKER.
YES, M'LADY.
GR AG176
LONDON IS SWIFTLY REACHED...
'E'S STOPPING AT THAT 'OTEL.
DRIVE ROUND THE CORNER, PARKER...

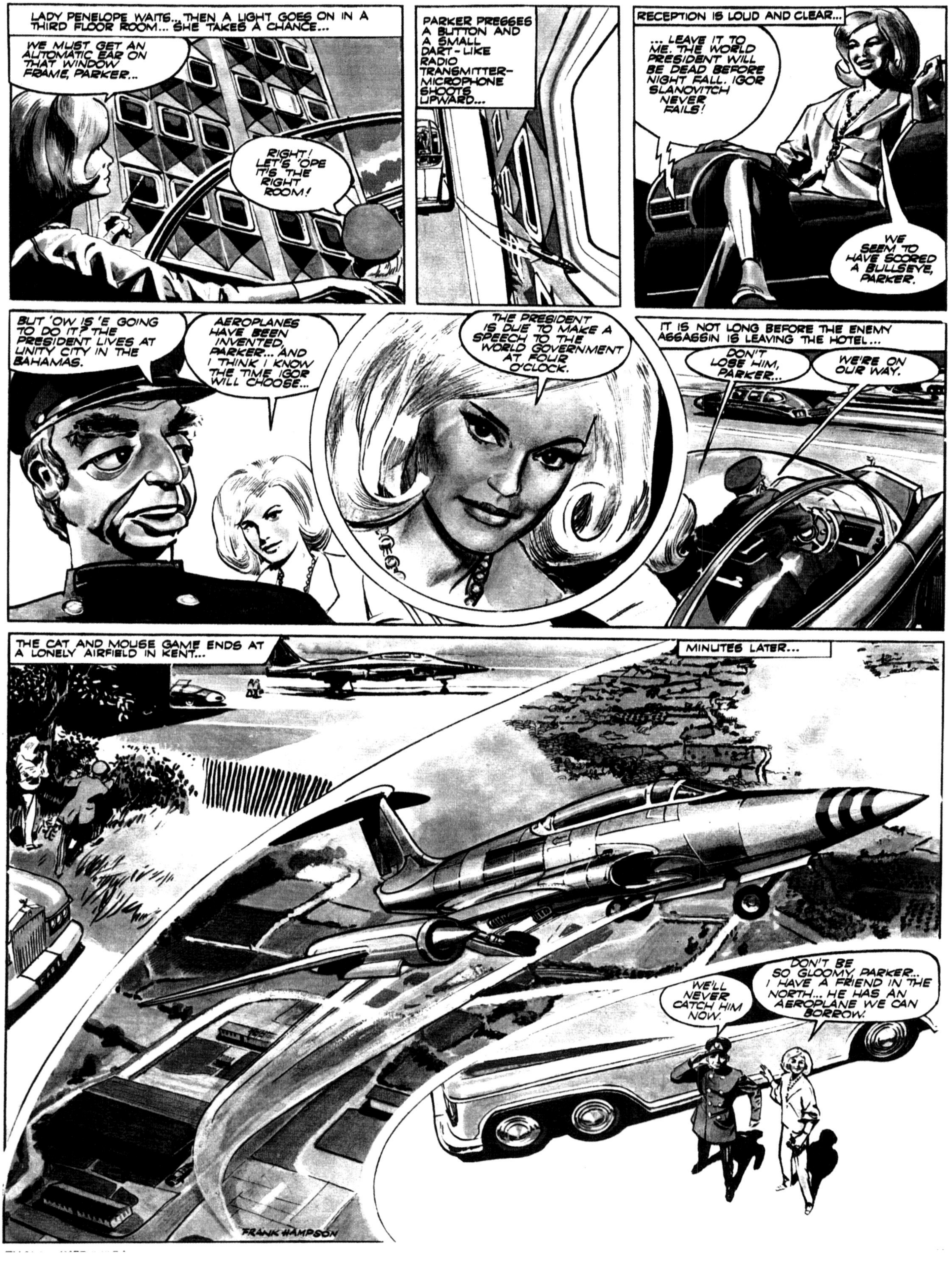
LADY PENELOPE WAITS... THEN A LIGHT GOES ON IN A THIRD FLOOR ROOM... SHE TAKES A CHANCE...
WE MUST GET AN AUTOMATIC EAR ON THAT WINDOW FRAME, PARKER...
RIGHT! LET'S 'OPE IT'S THE RIGHT ROOM!
PARKER PRESSES A BUTTON AND A SMALL DART-LIKE RADIO TRANSMITTER-MICROPHONE SHOOTS UPWARD...
RECEPTION IS LOUD AND CLEAR...
... LEAVE IT TO ME. THE WORLD PRESIDENT WILL BE DEAD BEFORE NIGHT FALL. IGOR SLANOVITCH NEVER FAILS!
WE SEEM TO HAVE SCORED A BULLSEYE, PARKER.
BUT 'OW IS 'E GOING TO DO IT? THE PRESIDENT LIVES AT UNITY CITY IN THE BAHAMAS.
AEROPLANES HAVE BEEN INVENTED, PARKER... AND I THINK I KNOW THE TIME IGOR WILL CHOOSE...
THE PRESIDENT IS DUE TO MAKE A SPEECH TO THE WORLD GOVERNMENT AT FOUR O'CLOCK.
IT IS NOT LONG BEFORE THE ENEMY ASSASSIN IS LEAVING THE HOTEL...
DON'T LOSE HIM, PARKER...
WE'RE ON OUR WAY.
THE CAT AND MOUSE GAME ENDS AT A LONELY AIRFIELD IN KENT...
MINUTES LATER...
WE'LL NEVER CATCH HIM NOW.
DON'T BE SO GLOOMY, PARKER... I HAVE A FRIEND IN THE NORTH... HE HAS AN AEROPLANE WE CAN BORROW.
FRANK HAMPSON

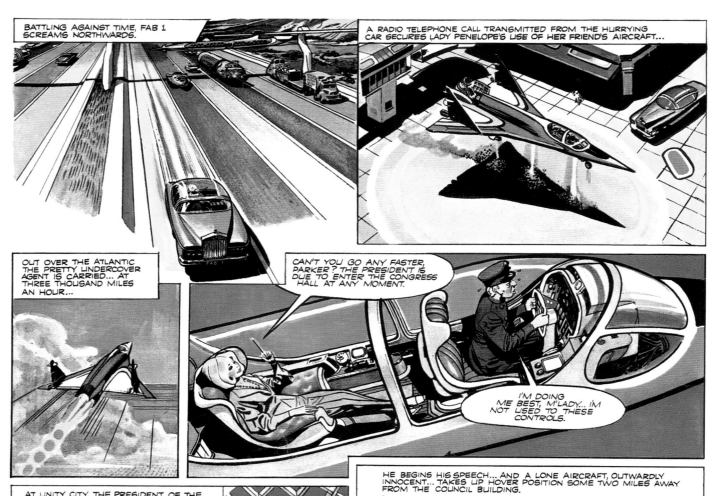

BATTLING AGAINST TIME, FAB 1 SCREAMS NORTHWARDS.

A RADIO TELEPHONE CALL TRANSMITTED FROM THE HURRYING CAR SECURES LADY PENELOPE'S USE OF HER FRIEND'S AIRCRAFT...

OUT OVER THE ATLANTIC THE PRETTY UNDERCOVER AGENT IS CARRIED... AT THREE THOUSAND MILES AN HOUR...

CAN'T YOU GO ANY FASTER, PARKER? THE PRESIDENT IS DUE TO ENTER THE CONGRESS HALL AT ANY MOMENT.

I'M DOING ME BEST, M'LADY... I'M NOT USED TO THESE CONTROLS.

AT UNITY CITY, THE PRESIDENT OF THE WORLD MAKES HIS APPEARANCE...

HE BEGINS HIS SPEECH... AND A LONE AIRCRAFT, OUTWARDLY INNOCENT... TAKES UP HOVER POSITION SOME TWO MILES AWAY FROM THE COUNCIL BUILDING.

USING THE LATEST LONG RANGE DETECTOR AND STRIKE FORCE EQUIPMENT, IGOR SLANOVITCH LINES UP THE HUMAN TARGET...

JUST TWO MORE MINUTES FOR THE SCREENS TO STEADY AND TAKE OVER THE SIGHTING...

TWO MINUTES... BARELY ENOUGH TIME FOR LADY PENELOPE TO LOCATE THE KILLER...

THERE, M'LADY... ON THE HUNTER SCREEN... THAT'S 'IM!

YES, PARKER... NOW WE HAVE TO MOVE EXCEPTIONALLY FAST.

WE DON'T WANT TO CAUSE A SCENE, PARKER, SO WE MUST ENTICE THEM AWAY FROM UNITY CITY. DO YOU UNDERSTAND?

YES, M'LADY.

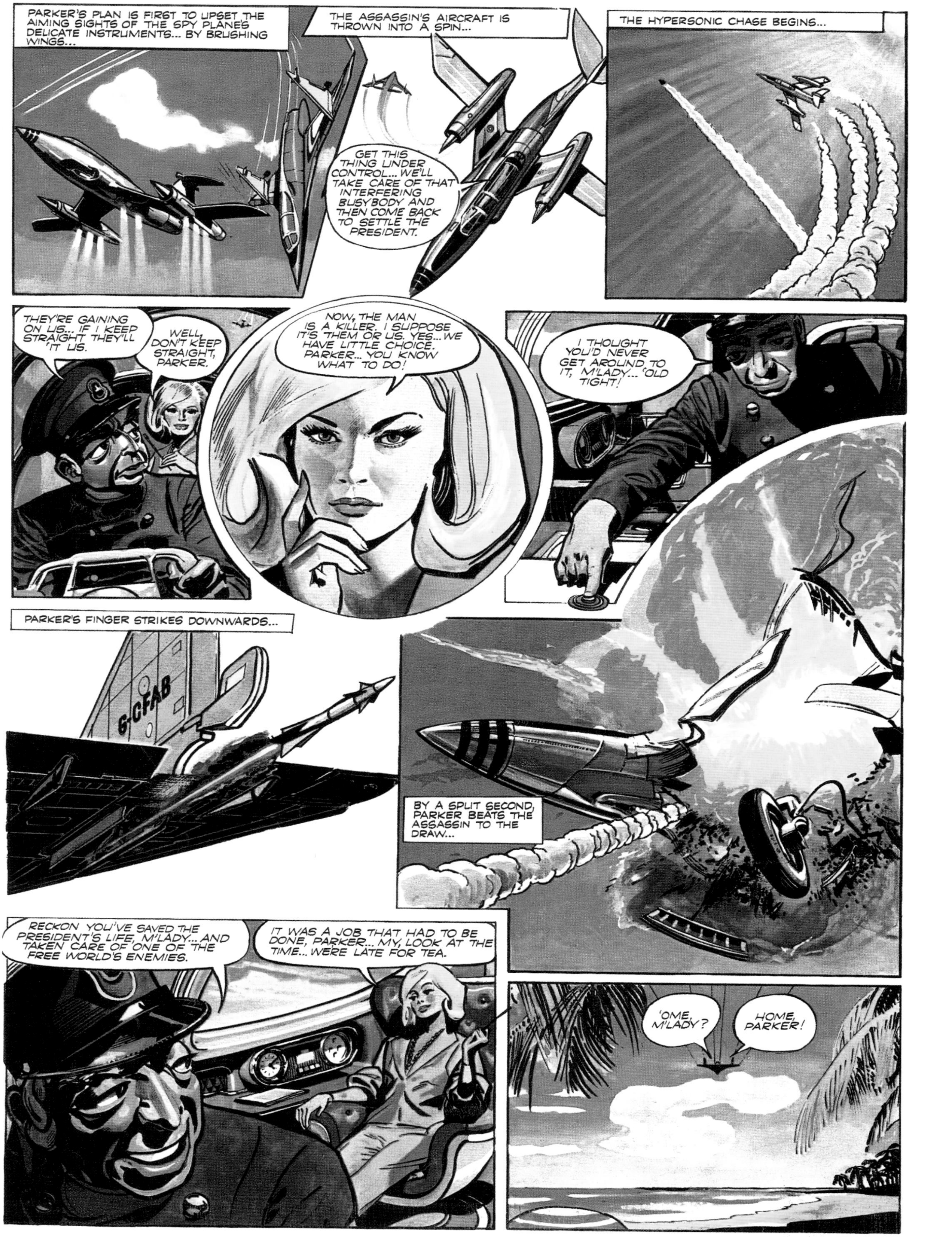
PARKER'S PLAN IS FIRST TO UPSET THE AIMING SIGHTS OF THE SPY PLANE'S DELICATE INSTRUMENTS... BY BRUSHING WINGS...
THE ASSASSIN'S AIRCRAFT IS THROWN INTO A SPIN...
GET THIS THING UNDER CONTROL... WE'LL TAKE CARE OF THAT INTERFERING BUSYBODY AND THEN COME BACK TO SETTLE THE PRESIDENT.
THE HYPERSONIC CHASE BEGINS...
THEY'RE GAINING ON US... IF I KEEP STRAIGHT THEY'LL 'IT US.
WELL, DON'T KEEP STRAIGHT, PARKER.
NOW, THE MAN IS A KILLER. I SUPPOSE IT'S THEM OR US. YES... WE HAVE LITTLE CHOICE. PARKER... YOU KNOW WHAT TO DO!
I THOUGHT YOU'D NEVER GET AROUND TO IT, M'LADY... 'OLD TIGHT!
PARKER'S FINGER STRIKES DOWNWARDS...
G-CFAB
BY A SPLIT SECOND, PARKER BEATS THE ASSASSIN TO THE DRAW...
RECKON YOU'VE SAVED THE PRESIDENT'S LIFE, M'LADY... AND TAKEN CARE OF ONE OF THE FREE WORLD'S ENEMIES.
IT WAS A JOB THAT HAD TO BE DONE, PARKER... MY, LOOK AT THE TIME... WE'RE LATE FOR TEA.
'OME, M'LADY?
HOME, PARKER!

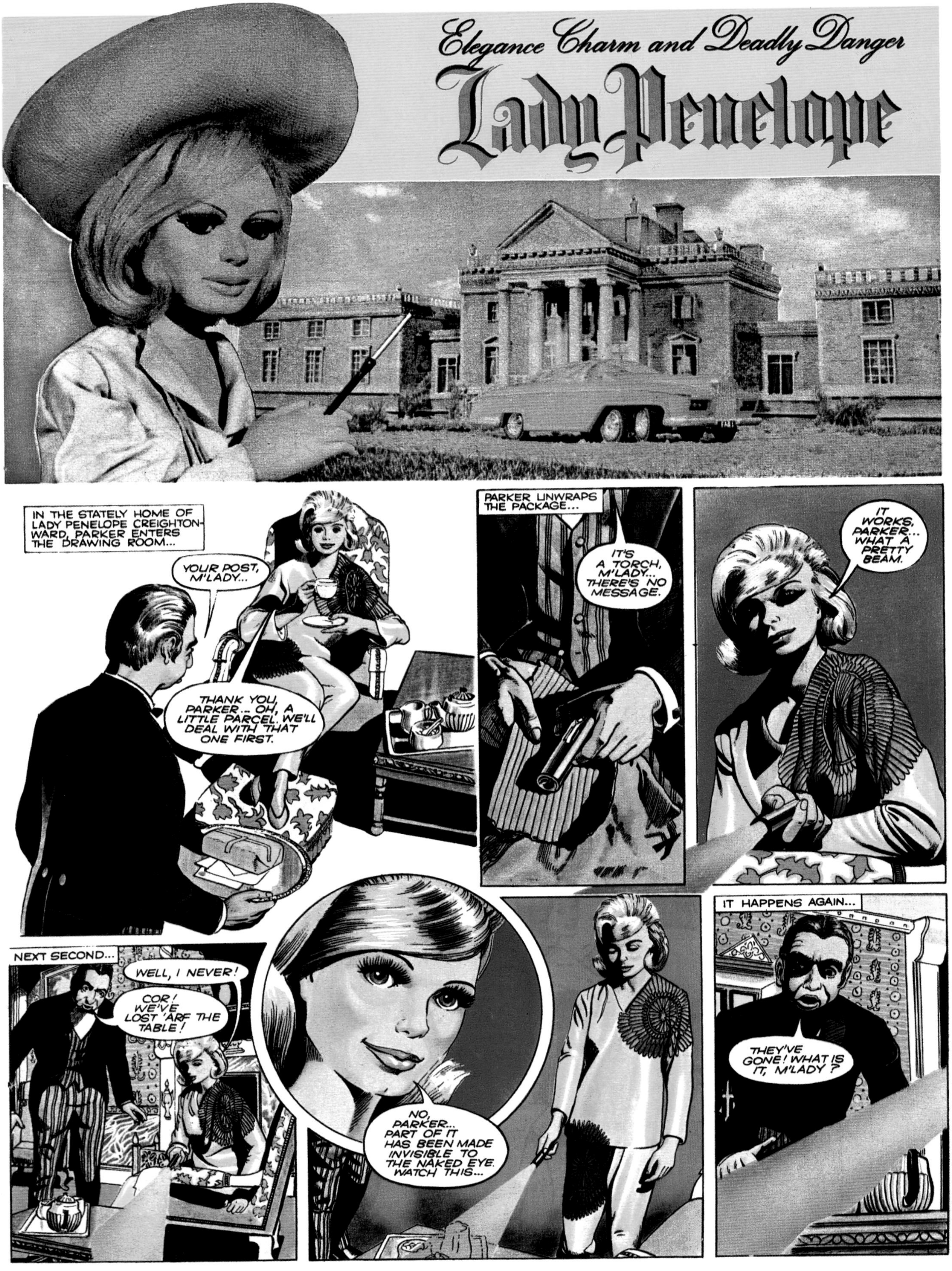

Elegance Charm and Deadly Danger
Lady Penelope
IN THE STATELY HOME OF LADY PENELOPE CREIGHTON-WARD, PARKER ENTERS THE DRAWING ROOM...
YOUR POST, M'LADY...
THANK YOU, PARKER... OH, A LITTLE PARCEL. WE'LL DEAL WITH THAT ONE FIRST.
PARKER UNWRAPS THE PACKAGE...
IT'S A TORCH, M'LADY... THERE'S NO MESSAGE.
IT WORKS, PARKER... WHAT A PRETTY BEAM.
NEXT SECOND...
WELL, I NEVER!
COR! WE'VE LOST 'ARF THE TABLE!
NO, PARKER... PART OF IT HAS BEEN MADE INVISIBLE TO THE NAKED EYE. WATCH THIS...
IT HAPPENS AGAIN...
THEY'VE GONE! WHAT IS IT, M'LADY?

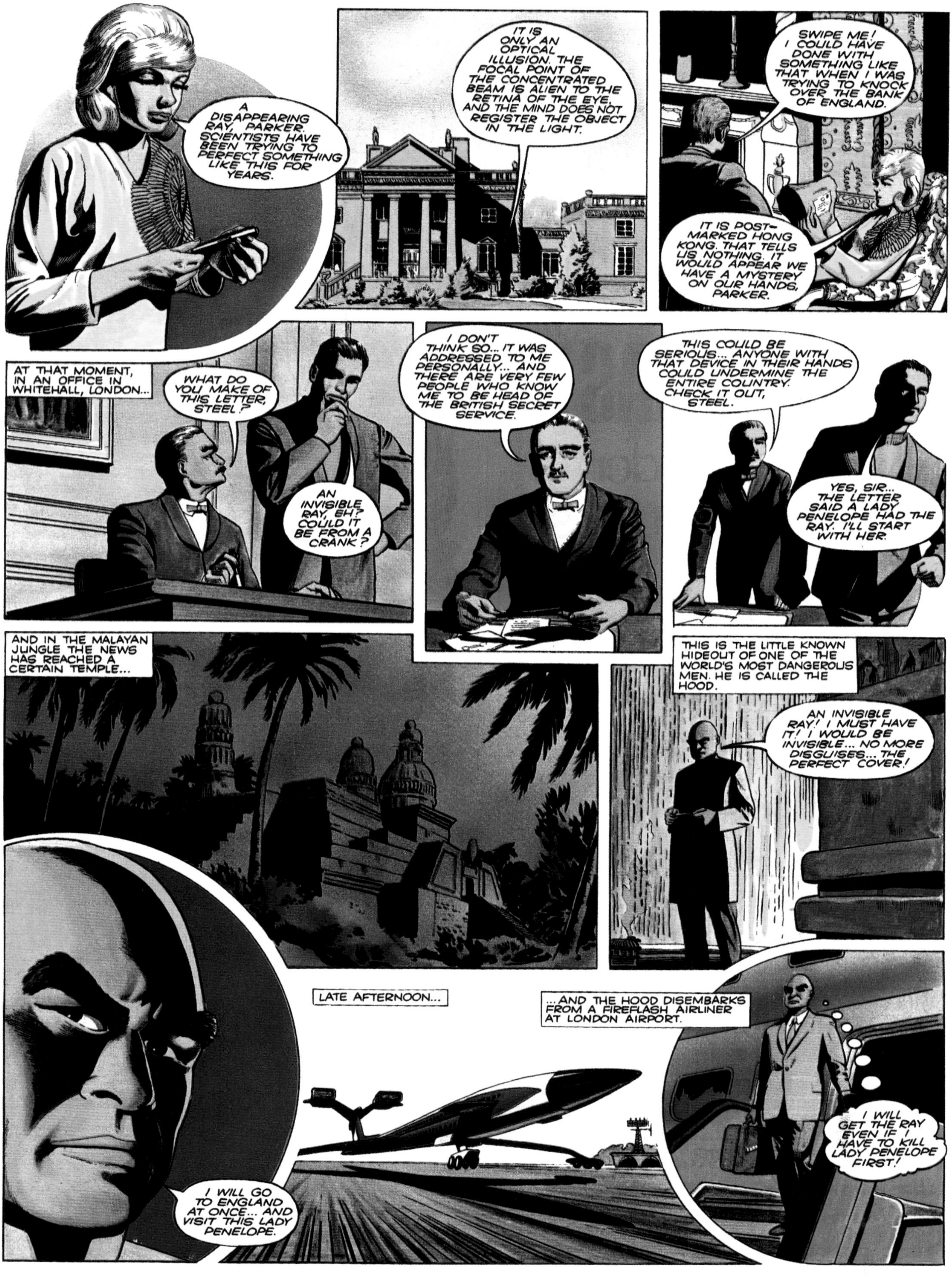
A DISAPPEARING RAY, PARKER. SCIENTISTS HAVE BEEN TRYING TO PERFECT SOMETHING LIKE THIS FOR YEARS.
IT IS ONLY AN OPTICAL ILLUSION. THE FOCAL POINT OF THE CONCENTRATED BEAM IS ALIEN TO THE RETINA OF THE EYE, AND THE MIND DOES NOT REGISTER THE OBJECT IN THE LIGHT.
SWIPE ME! I COULD HAVE DONE WITH SOMETHING LIKE THAT WHEN I WAS TRYING TO KNOCK OVER THE BANK OF ENGLAND.
IT IS POST-MARKED HONG KONG. THAT TELLS US NOTHING. IT WOULD APPEAR WE HAVE A MYSTERY ON OUR HANDS, PARKER.
AT THAT MOMENT, IN AN OFFICE IN WHITEHALL, LONDON...
WHAT DO YOU MAKE OF THIS LETTER, STEEL?
AN INVISIBLE RAY, EH? COULD IT BE FROM A CRANK?
I DON'T THINK SO... IT WAS ADDRESSED TO ME PERSONALLY... AND THERE ARE VERY FEW PEOPLE WHO KNOW ME TO BE HEAD OF THE BRITISH SECRET SERVICE.
THIS COULD BE SERIOUS... ANYONE WITH THAT DEVICE IN THEIR HANDS COULD UNDERMINE THE ENTIRE COUNTRY. CHECK IT OUT, STEEL.
YES, SIR... THE LETTER SAID A LADY PENELOPE HAD THE RAY. I'LL START WITH HER.
AND IN THE MALAYAN JUNGLE THE NEWS HAS REACHED A CERTAIN TEMPLE...
THIS IS THE LITTLE KNOWN HIDEOUT OF ONE OF THE WORLD'S MOST DANGEROUS MEN. HE IS CALLED THE HOOD.
AN INVISIBLE RAY! I MUST HAVE IT! I WOULD BE INVISIBLE... NO MORE DISGUISES... THE PERFECT COVER!
I WILL GO TO ENGLAND AT ONCE... AND VISIT THIS LADY PENELOPE.
LATE AFTERNOON...
...AND THE HOOD DISEMBARKS FROM A FIREFLASH AIRLINER AT LONDON AIRPORT.
I WILL GET THE RAY EVEN IF I HAVE TO KILL LADY PENELOPE FIRST!

Elegance Charm and Deadly Danger
Lady Penelope

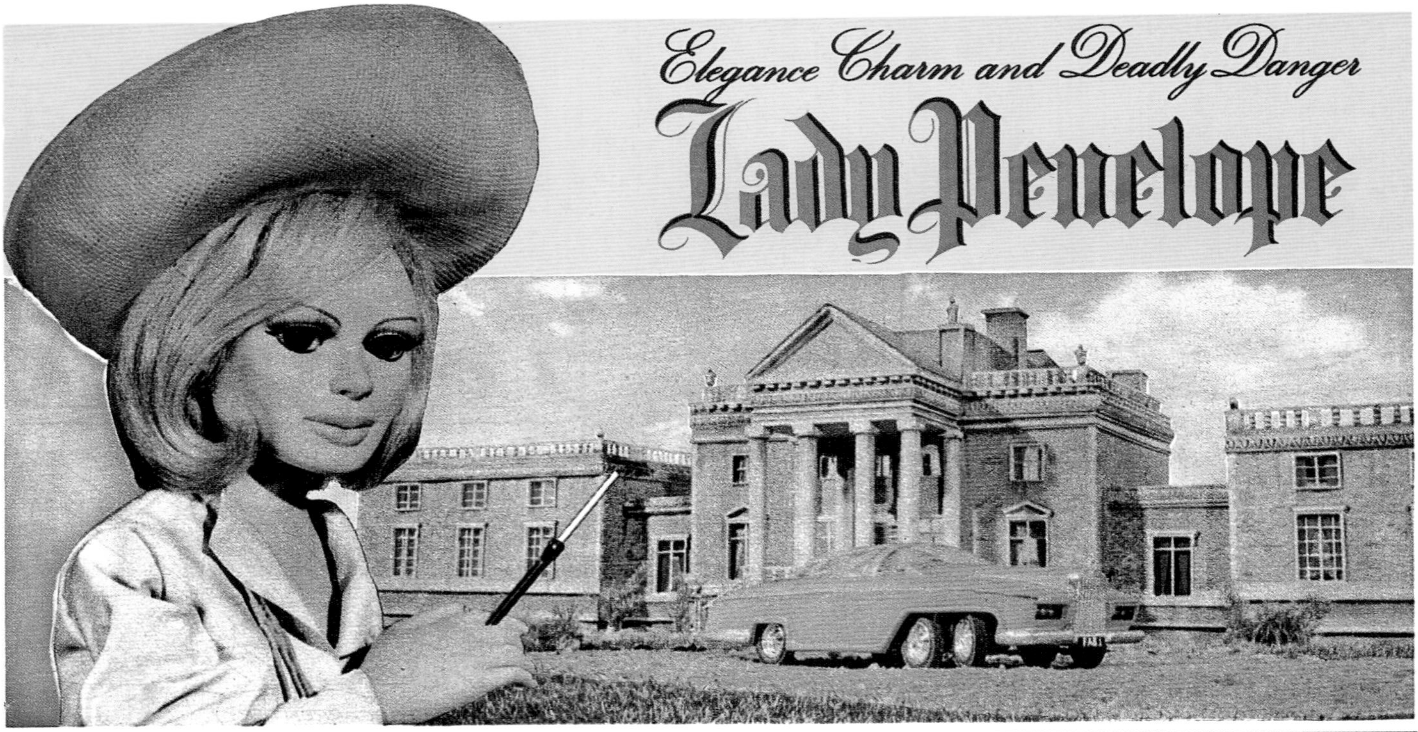

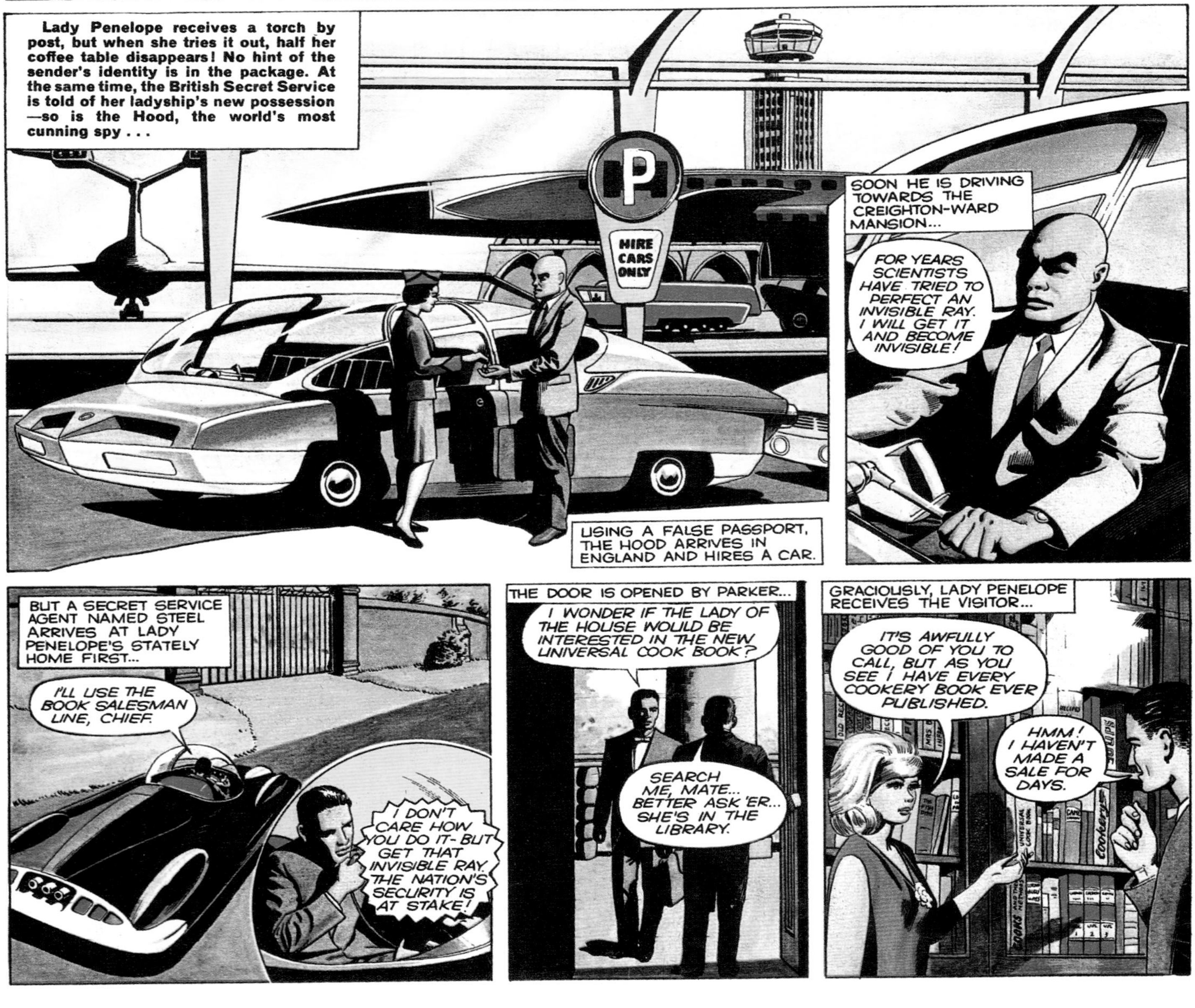

Lady Penelope receives a torch by post, but when she tries it out, half her coffee table disappears! No hint of the sender's identity is in the package. At the same time, the British Secret Service is told of her ladyship's new possession—so is the Hood, the world's most cunning spy . . .
P
HIRE CARS ONLY
USING A FALSE PASSPORT, THE HOOD ARRIVES IN ENGLAND AND HIRES A CAR.
SOON HE IS DRIVING TOWARDS THE CREIGHTON-WARD MANSION...
FOR YEARS SCIENTISTS HAVE TRIED TO PERFECT AN INVISIBLE RAY. I WILL GET IT AND BECOME INVISIBLE!
BUT A SECRET SERVICE AGENT NAMED STEEL ARRIVES AT LADY PENELOPE'S STATELY HOME FIRST...
I'LL USE THE BOOK SALESMAN LINE, CHIEF.
I DON'T CARE HOW YOU DO IT- BUT GET THAT INVISIBLE RAY. THE NATION'S SECURITY IS AT STAKE!
THE DOOR IS OPENED BY PARKER...
I WONDER IF THE LADY OF THE HOUSE WOULD BE INTERESTED IN THE NEW UNIVERSAL COOK BOOK?
SEARCH ME, MATE... BETTER ASK 'ER... SHE'S IN THE LIBRARY.
GRACIOUSLY, LADY PENELOPE RECEIVES THE VISITOR...
IT'S AWFULLY GOOD OF YOU TO CALL, BUT AS YOU SEE I HAVE EVERY COOKERY BOOK EVER PUBLISHED.
HMM! I HAVEN'T MADE A SALE FOR DAYS.

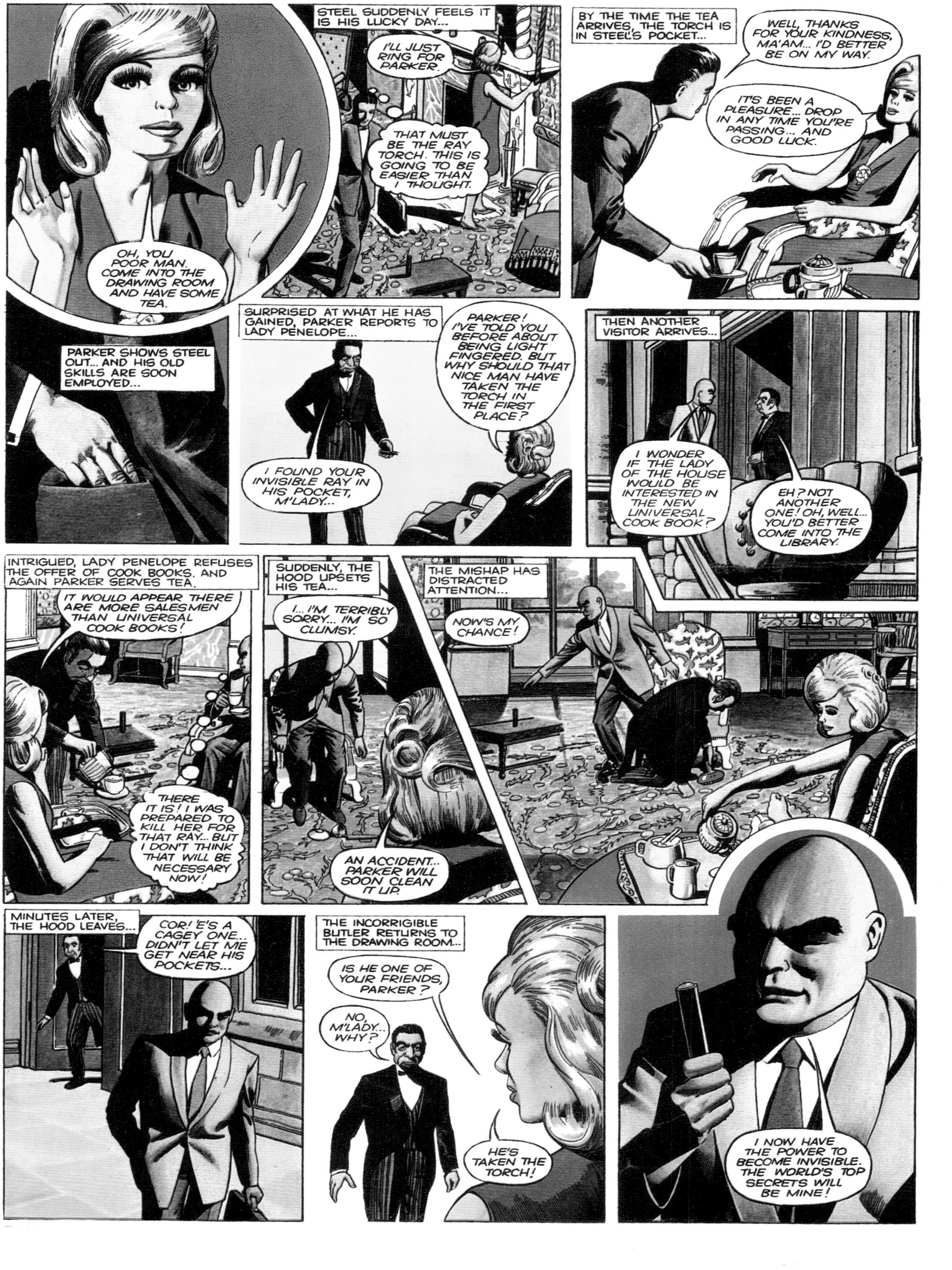
OH, YOU POOR MAN. COME INTO THE DRAWING ROOM AND HAVE SOME TEA.
STEEL SUDDENLY FEELS IT IS HIS LUCKY DAY...
I'LL JUST RING FOR PARKER.
THAT MUST BE THE RAY TORCH. THIS IS GOING TO BE EASIER THAN I THOUGHT.
BY THE TIME THE TEA ARRIVES, THE TORCH IS IN STEEL'S POCKET...
WELL, THANKS FOR YOUR KINDNESS, MA'AM... I'D BETTER BE ON MY WAY.
IT'S BEEN A PLEASURE... DROP IN ANY TIME YOU'RE PASSING... AND GOOD LUCK.
PARKER SHOWS STEEL OUT... AND HIS OLD SKILLS ARE SOON EMPLOYED...
SURPRISED AT WHAT HE HAS GAINED, PARKER REPORTS TO LADY PENELOPE...
I FOUND YOUR INVISIBLE RAY IN HIS POCKET, M'LADY...
PARKER! I'VE TOLD YOU BEFORE ABOUT BEING LIGHT FINGERED. BUT WHY SHOULD THAT NICE MAN HAVE TAKEN THE TORCH IN THE FIRST PLACE?
THEN ANOTHER VISITOR ARRIVES...
I WONDER IF THE LADY OF THE HOUSE WOULD BE INTERESTED IN THE NEW UNIVERSAL COOK BOOK?
EH? NOT ANOTHER ONE! OH, WELL... YOU'D BETTER COME INTO THE LIBRARY.
INTRIGUED, LADY PENELOPE REFUSES THE OFFER OF COOK BOOKS, AND AGAIN PARKER SERVES TEA.
IT WOULD APPEAR THERE ARE MORE SALESMEN THAN UNIVERSAL COOK BOOKS!
THERE IT IS! I WAS PREPARED TO KILL HER FOR THAT RAY... BUT I DON'T THINK THAT WILL BE NECESSARY NOW!
SUDDENLY, THE HOOD UPSETS HIS TEA...
I... I'M TERRIBLY SORRY... I'M SO CLUMSY.
AN ACCIDENT... PARKER WILL SOON CLEAN IT UP.
THE MISHAP HAS DISTRACTED ATTENTION...
NOW'S MY CHANCE!
MINUTES LATER, THE HOOD LEAVES...
COR! 'E'S A CAGEY ONE... DIDN'T LET ME GET NEAR HIS POCKETS...
THE INCORRIGIBLE BUTLER RETURNS TO THE DRAWING ROOM...
IS HE ONE OF YOUR FRIENDS, PARKER?
NO, M'LADY... WHY?
HE'S TAKEN THE TORCH!
I NOW HAVE THE POWER TO BECOME INVISIBLE. THE WORLD'S TOP SECRETS WILL BE MINE!

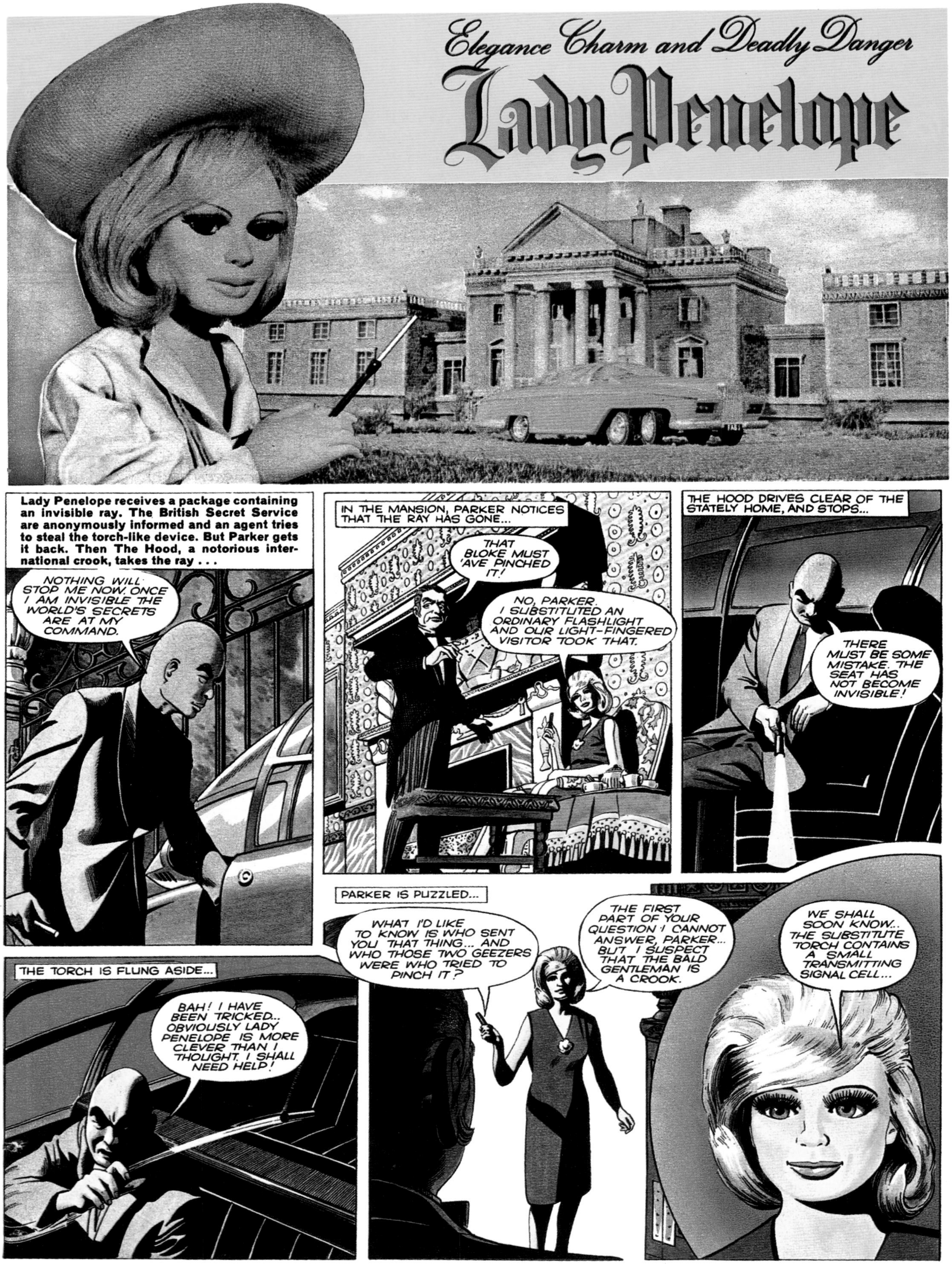
Elegance Charm and Deadly Danger
Lady Penelope
Lady Penelope receives a package containing an invisible ray. The British Secret Service are anonymously informed and an agent tries to steal the torch-like device. But Parker gets it back. Then The Hood, a notorious international crook, takes the ray . . .
NOTHING WILL STOP ME NOW. ONCE I AM INVISIBLE THE WORLD'S SECRETS ARE AT MY COMMAND.
IN THE MANSION, PARKER NOTICES THAT THE RAY HAS GONE...
THAT BLOKE MUST 'AVE PINCHED IT!
NO, PARKER. I SUBSTITUTED AN ORDINARY FLASHLIGHT AND OUR LIGHT-FINGERED VISITOR TOOK THAT.
THE HOOD DRIVES CLEAR OF THE STATELY HOME, AND STOPS...
THERE MUST BE SOME MISTAKE. THE SEAT HAS NOT BECOME INVISIBLE!
THE TORCH IS FLUNG ASIDE...
BAH! I HAVE BEEN TRICKED... OBVIOUSLY LADY PENELOPE IS MORE CLEVER THAN I THOUGHT. I SHALL NEED HELP!
PARKER IS PUZZLED...
WHAT I'D LIKE TO KNOW IS WHO SENT YOU THAT THING... AND WHO THOSE TWO GEEZERS WERE WHO TRIED TO PINCH IT?
THE FIRST PART OF YOUR QUESTION I CANNOT ANSWER, PARKER... BUT I SUSPECT THAT THE BALD GENTLEMAN IS A CROOK.
WE SHALL SOON KNOW... THE SUBSTITUTE TORCH CONTAINS A SMALL TRANSMITTING SIGNAL CELL...

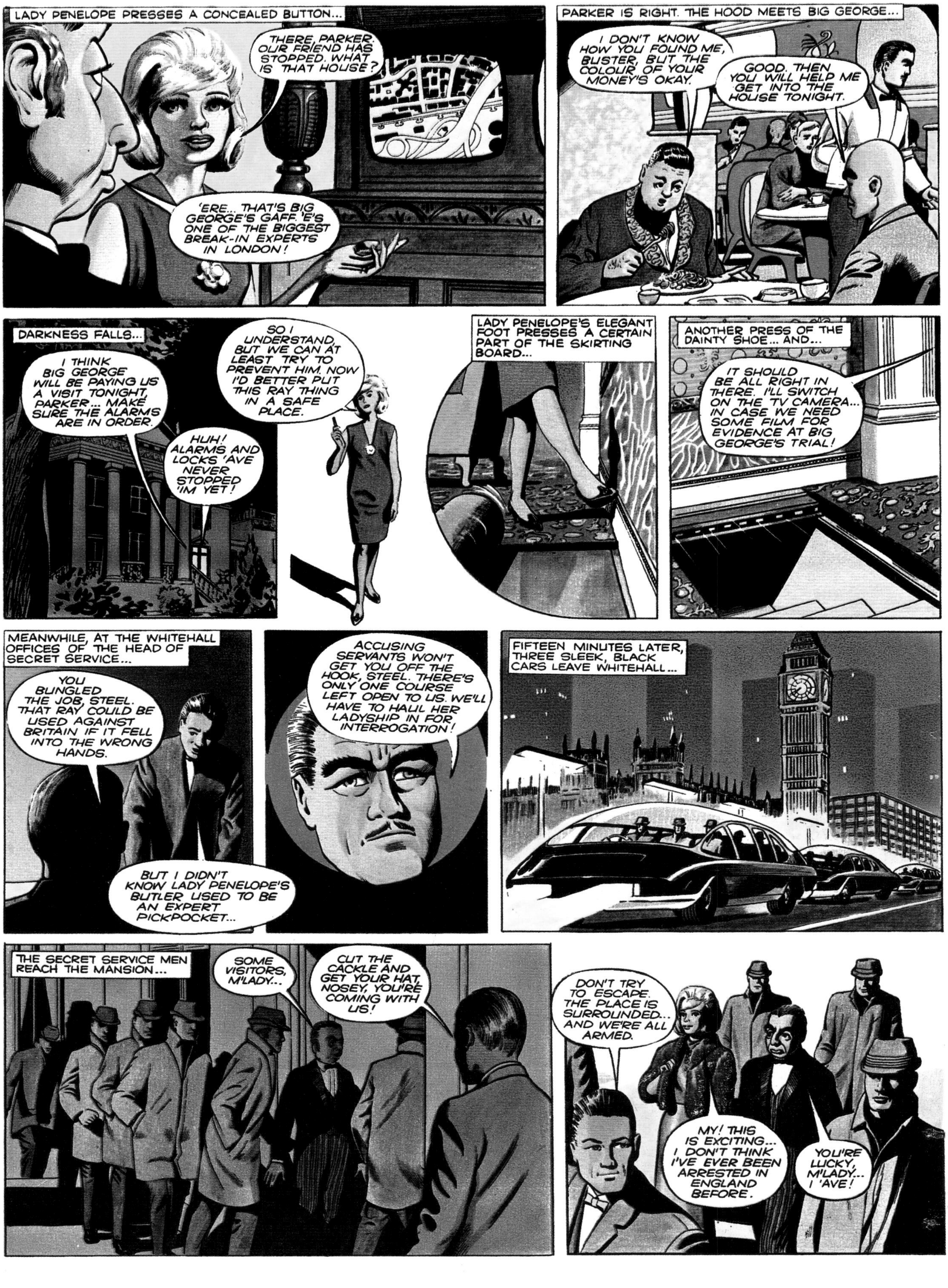

LADY PENELOPE PRESSES A CONCEALED BUTTON...
THERE, PARKER. OUR FRIEND HAS STOPPED. WHAT IS THAT HOUSE?
'ERE... THAT'S BIG GEORGE'S GAFF. 'E'S ONE OF THE BIGGEST BREAK-IN EXPERTS IN LONDON!
PARKER IS RIGHT. THE HOOD MEETS BIG GEORGE...
I DON'T KNOW HOW YOU FOUND ME, BUSTER, BUT THE COLOUR OF YOUR MONEY'S OKAY.
GOOD. THEN YOU WILL HELP ME GET INTO THE HOUSE TONIGHT.
DARKNESS FALLS...
I THINK BIG GEORGE WILL BE PAYING US A VISIT TONIGHT, PARKER... MAKE SURE THE ALARMS ARE IN ORDER.
HUH! ALARMS AND LOCKS 'AVE NEVER STOPPED 'IM YET!
SO I UNDERSTAND, BUT WE CAN AT LEAST TRY TO PREVENT HIM. NOW I'D BETTER PUT THIS RAY THING IN A SAFE PLACE.
LADY PENELOPE'S ELEGANT FOOT PRESSES A CERTAIN PART OF THE SKIRTING BOARD...
ANOTHER PRESS OF THE DAINTY SHOE... AND...
IT SHOULD BE ALL RIGHT IN THERE. I'LL SWITCH ON THE TV CAMERA... IN CASE WE NEED SOME FILM FOR EVIDENCE AT BIG GEORGE'S TRIAL!
MEANWHILE, AT THE WHITEHALL OFFICES OF THE HEAD OF SECRET SERVICE...
YOU BUNGLED THE JOB, STEEL. THAT RAY COULD BE USED AGAINST BRITAIN IF IT FELL INTO THE WRONG HANDS.
BUT I DIDN'T KNOW LADY PENELOPE'S BUTLER USED TO BE AN EXPERT PICKPOCKET...
ACCUSING SERVANTS WON'T GET YOU OFF THE HOOK, STEEL. THERE'S ONLY ONE COURSE LEFT OPEN TO US. WE'LL HAVE TO HAUL HER LADYSHIP IN FOR INTERROGATION!
FIFTEEN MINUTES LATER, THREE SLEEK, BLACK CARS LEAVE WHITEHALL...
THE SECRET SERVICE MEN REACH THE MANSION...
SOME VISITORS, M'LADY...
CUT THE CACKLE AND GET YOUR HAT, NOSEY, YOU'RE COMING WITH US!
DON'T TRY TO ESCAPE. THE PLACE IS SURROUNDED... AND WE'RE ALL ARMED.
MY! THIS IS EXCITING... I DON'T THINK I'VE EVER BEEN ARRESTED IN ENGLAND BEFORE.
YOU'RE LUCKY, M'LADY... I 'AVE!

Elegance Charm and Deadly Danger
Lady Penelope

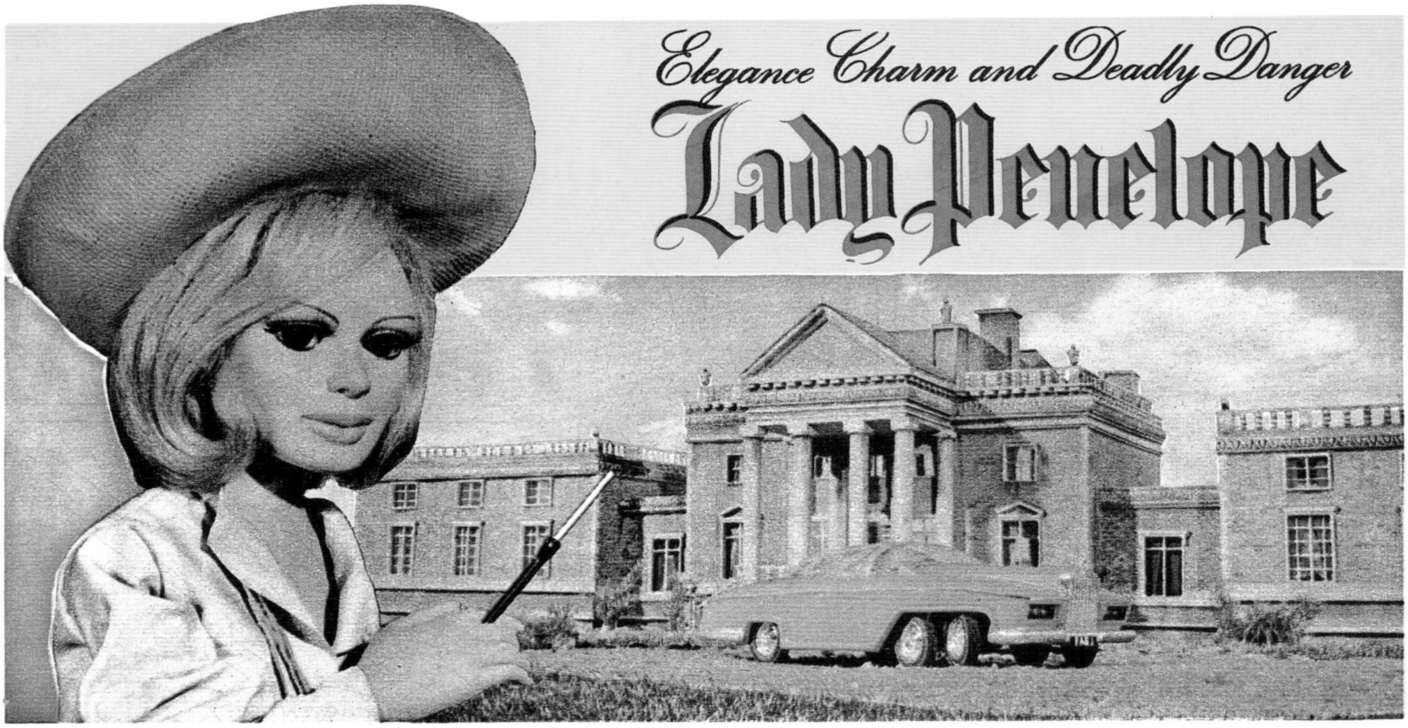

Lady Penelope receives a package containing an invisible ray torch. The Hood, an international crook, tries to steal the device and the British Secret Service also are interested for security reasons. Some M.I.5. men arrive at night and arrest Parker and her ladyship . . .

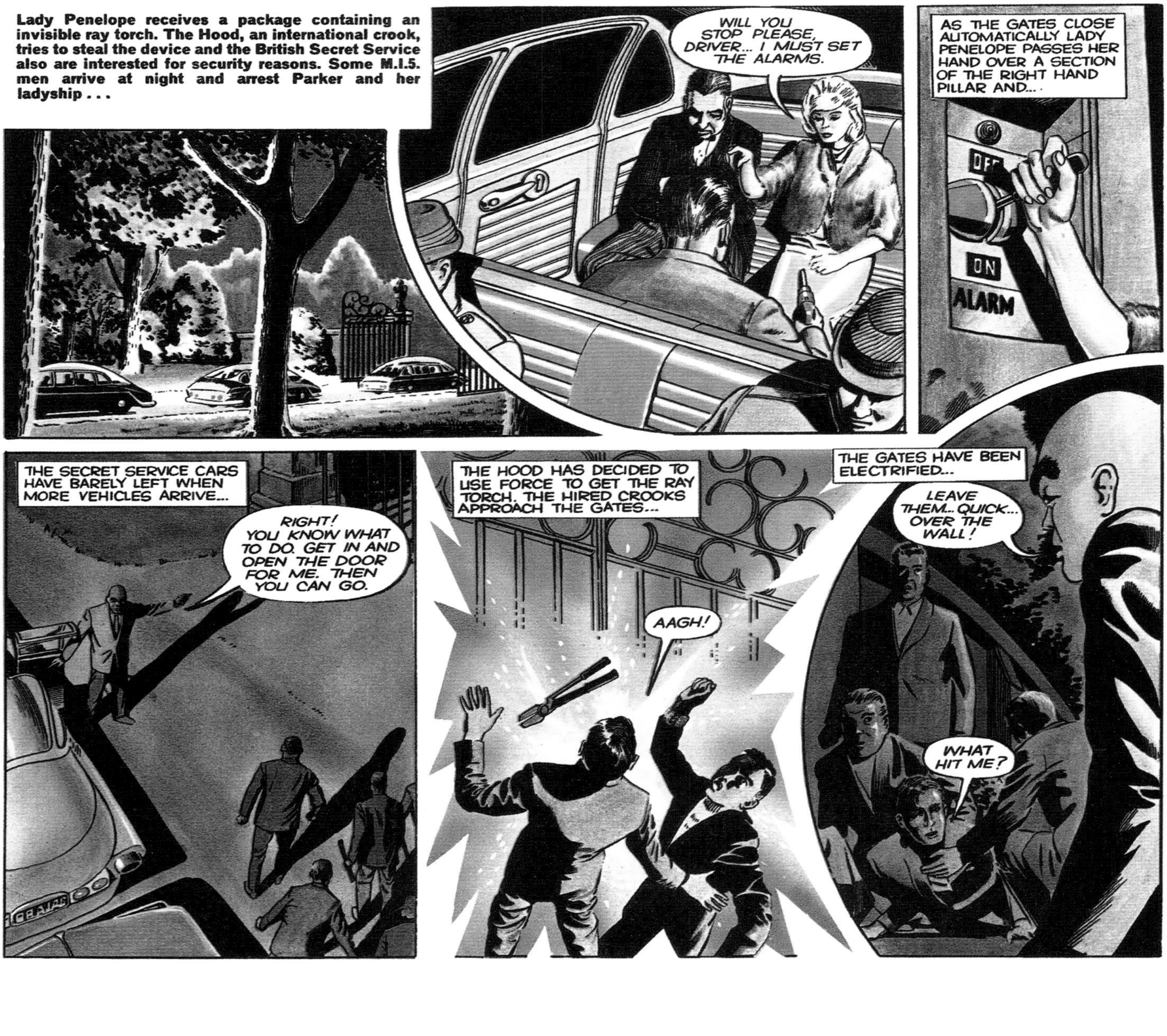

WILL YOU STOP PLEASE, DRIVER... I MUST SET THE ALARMS.
AS THE GATES CLOSE AUTOMATICALLY LADY PENELOPE PASSES HER HAND OVER A SECTION OF THE RIGHT HAND PILLAR AND...
OFF
ON
ALARM
THE SECRET SERVICE CARS HAVE BARELY LEFT WHEN MORE VEHICLES ARRIVE...
RIGHT! YOU KNOW WHAT TO DO. GET IN AND OPEN THE DOOR FOR ME. THEN YOU CAN GO.
THE HOOD HAS DECIDED TO USE FORCE TO GET THE RAY TORCH. THE HIRED CROOKS APPROACH THE GATES...
AAGH!
THE GATES HAVE BEEN ELECTRIFIED...
LEAVE THEM... QUICK... OVER THE WALL!
WHAT HIT ME?

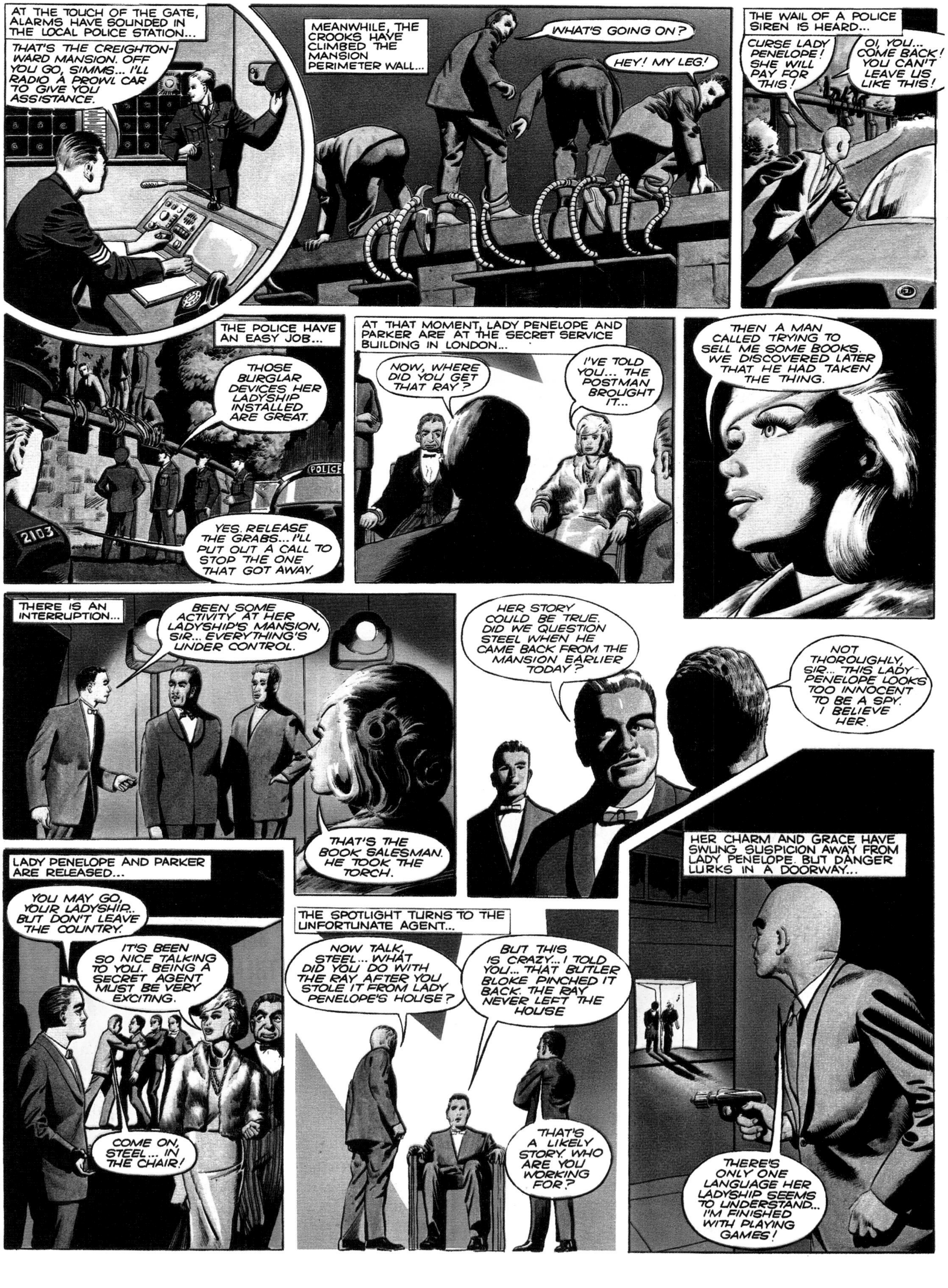

AT THE TOUCH OF THE GATE, ALARMS HAVE SOUNDED IN THE LOCAL POLICE STATION...
THAT'S THE CREIGHTON-WARD MANSION. OFF YOU GO, SIMMS... I'LL RADIO A PROWL CAR TO GIVE YOU ASSISTANCE.
MEANWHILE, THE CROOKS HAVE CLIMBED THE MANSION PERIMETER WALL...
WHAT'S GOING ON?
HEY! MY LEG!
THE WAIL OF A POLICE SIREN IS HEARD...
CURSE LADY PENELOPE! SHE WILL PAY FOR THIS!
OI, YOU... COME BACK! YOU CAN'T LEAVE US LIKE THIS!
THE POLICE HAVE AN EASY JOB...
THOSE BURGLAR DEVICES HER LADYSHIP INSTALLED ARE GREAT.
YES. RELEASE THE GRABS... I'LL PUT OUT A CALL TO STOP THE ONE THAT GOT AWAY.
POLICE
2103
AT THAT MOMENT, LADY PENELOPE AND PARKER ARE AT THE SECRET SERVICE BUILDING IN LONDON...
NOW, WHERE DID YOU GET THAT RAY?
I'VE TOLD YOU... THE POSTMAN BROUGHT IT...
THEN A MAN CALLED TRYING TO SELL ME SOME BOOKS. WE DISCOVERED LATER THAT HE HAD TAKEN THE THING.
THERE IS AN INTERRUPTION...
BEEN SOME ACTIVITY AT HER LADYSHIP'S MANSION, SIR... EVERYTHING'S UNDER CONTROL.
THAT'S THE BOOK SALESMAN. HE TOOK THE TORCH.
HER STORY COULD BE TRUE. DID WE QUESTION STEEL WHEN HE CAME BACK FROM THE MANSION EARLIER TODAY?
NOT THOROUGHLY, SIR... THIS LADY PENELOPE LOOKS TOO INNOCENT TO BE A SPY. I BELIEVE HER.
LADY PENELOPE AND PARKER ARE RELEASED...
YOU MAY GO, YOUR LADYSHIP... BUT DON'T LEAVE THE COUNTRY.
IT'S BEEN SO NICE TALKING TO YOU. BEING A SECRET AGENT MUST BE VERY EXCITING.
COME ON, STEEL... IN THE CHAIR!
THE SPOTLIGHT TURNS TO THE UNFORTUNATE AGENT...
NOW TALK, STEEL... WHAT DID YOU DO WITH THE RAY AFTER YOU STOLE IT FROM LADY PENELOPE'S HOUSE?
BUT THIS IS CRAZY... I TOLD YOU... THAT BUTLER BLOKE PINCHED IT BACK. THE RAY NEVER LEFT THE HOUSE
THAT'S A LIKELY STORY. WHO ARE YOU WORKING FOR?
HER CHARM AND GRACE HAVE SWUNG SUSPICION AWAY FROM LADY PENELOPE. BUT DANGER LURKS IN A DOORWAY...
THERE'S ONLY ONE LANGUAGE HER LADYSHIP SEEMS TO UNDERSTAND... I'M FINISHED WITH PLAYING GAMES!

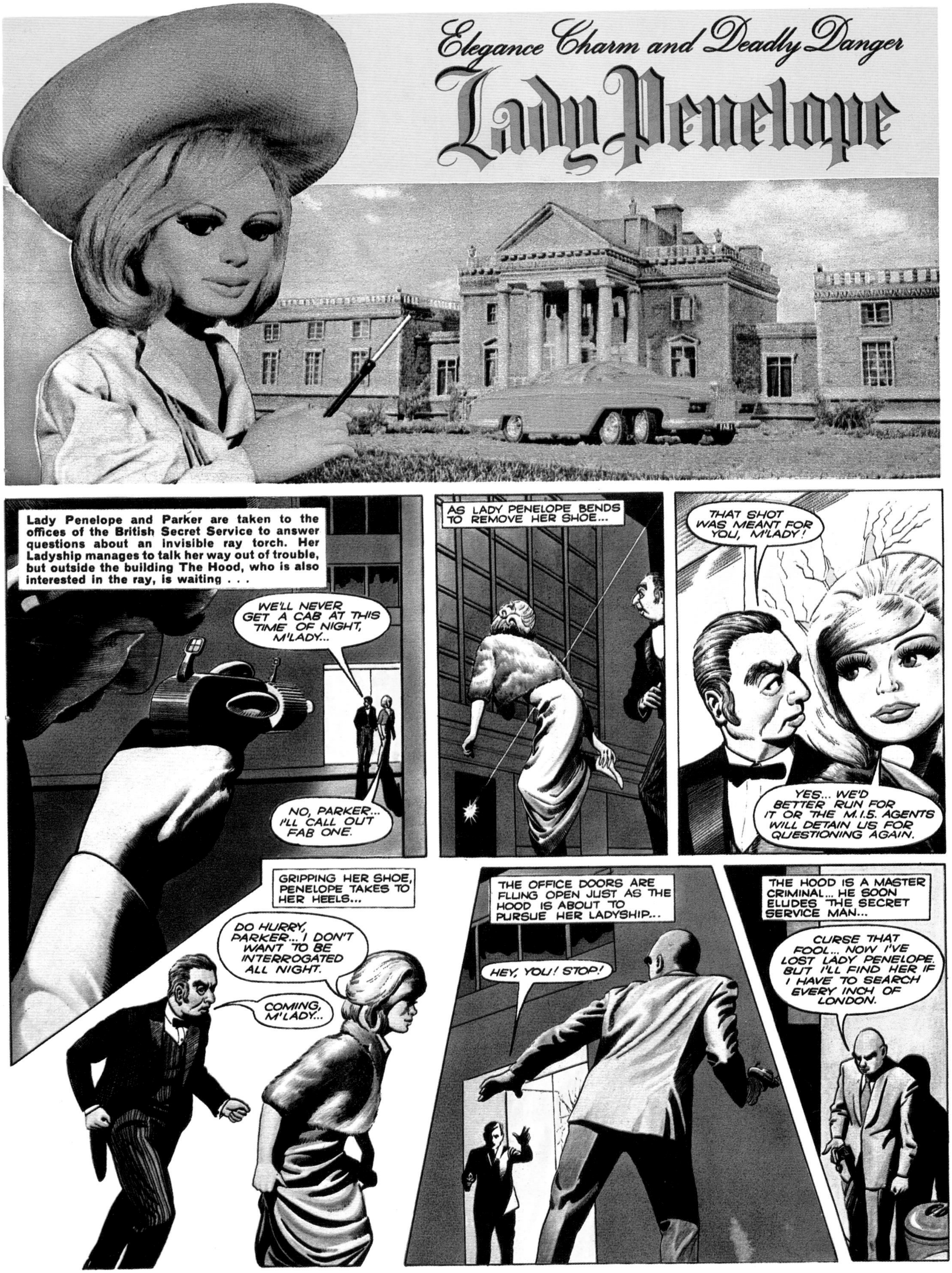

Elegance Charm and Deadly Danger
Lady Penelope
Lady Penelope and Parker are taken to the offices of the British Secret Service to answer questions about an invisible ray torch. Her Ladyship manages to talk her way out of trouble, but outside the building The Hood, who is also interested in the ray, is waiting . . .
WE'LL NEVER GET A CAB AT THIS TIME OF NIGHT, M'LADY...
NO, PARKER... I'LL CALL OUT FAB ONE.
AS LADY PENELOPE BENDS TO REMOVE HER SHOE...
THAT SHOT WAS MEANT FOR YOU, M'LADY!
YES... WE'D BETTER RUN FOR IT OR THE M.I.5. AGENTS WILL DETAIN US FOR QUESTIONING AGAIN.
GRIPPING HER SHOE, PENELOPE TAKES TO HER HEELS...
DO HURRY, PARKER... I DON'T WANT TO BE INTERROGATED ALL NIGHT.
COMING, M'LADY...
THE OFFICE DOORS ARE FLUNG OPEN JUST AS THE HOOD IS ABOUT TO PURSUE HER LADYSHIP...
HEY, YOU! STOP!
THE HOOD IS A MASTER CRIMINAL... HE SOON ELUDES THE SECRET SERVICE MAN...
CURSE THAT FOOL... NOW I'VE LOST LADY PENELOPE. BUT I'LL FIND HER IF I HAVE TO SEARCH EVERY INCH OF LONDON.

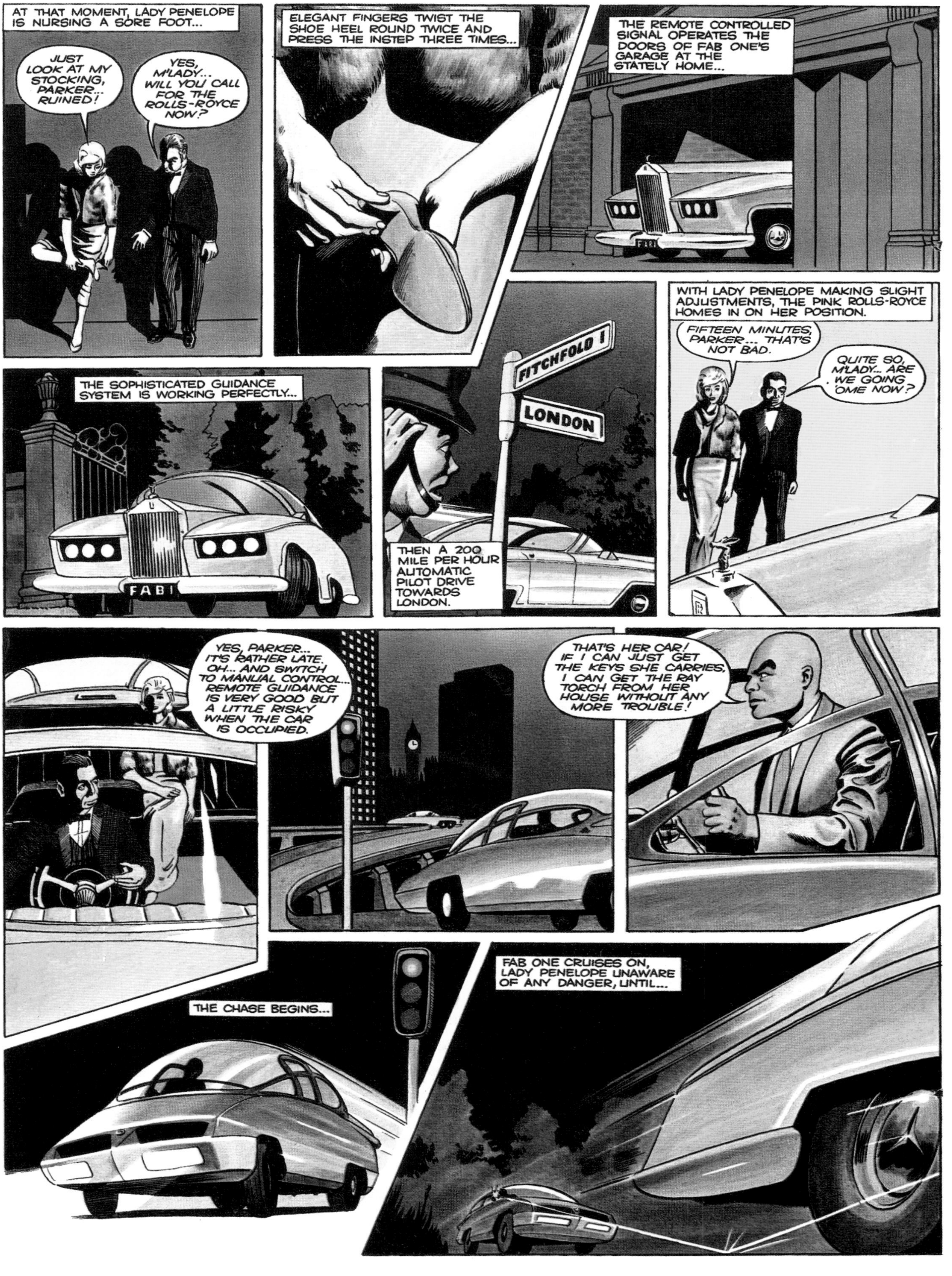
AT THAT MOMENT, LADY PENELOPE IS NURSING A SORE FOOT...
JUST LOOK AT MY STOCKING, PARKER... RUINED!
YES, M'LADY... WILL YOU CALL FOR THE ROLLS-ROYCE NOW?
ELEGANT FINGERS TWIST THE SHOE HEEL ROUND TWICE AND PRESS THE INSTEP THREE TIMES...
THE REMOTE CONTROLLED SIGNAL OPERATES THE DOORS OF FAB ONE'S GARAGE AT THE STATELY HOME...
THE SOPHISTICATED GUIDANCE SYSTEM IS WORKING PERFECTLY...
FAB 1
FITCHFOLD 1
LONDON
THEN A 200 MILE PER HOUR AUTOMATIC PILOT DRIVE TOWARDS LONDON.
WITH LADY PENELOPE MAKING SLIGHT ADJUSTMENTS, THE PINK ROLLS-ROYCE HOMES IN ON HER POSITION.
FIFTEEN MINUTES, PARKER... THAT'S NOT BAD.
QUITE SO, M'LADY... ARE WE GOING 'OME NOW?
YES, PARKER... IT'S RATHER LATE. OH... AND SWITCH TO MANUAL CONTROL... REMOTE GUIDANCE IS VERY GOOD BUT A LITTLE RISKY WHEN THE CAR IS OCCUPIED.
THAT'S HER CAR! IF I CAN JUST GET THE KEYS SHE CARRIES, I CAN GET THE RAY TORCH FROM HER HOUSE WITHOUT ANY MORE TROUBLE!
THE CHASE BEGINS...
FAB ONE CRUISES ON, LADY PENELOPE UNAWARE OF ANY DANGER, UNTIL...

Elegance Charm and Deadly Danger
Lady Penelope

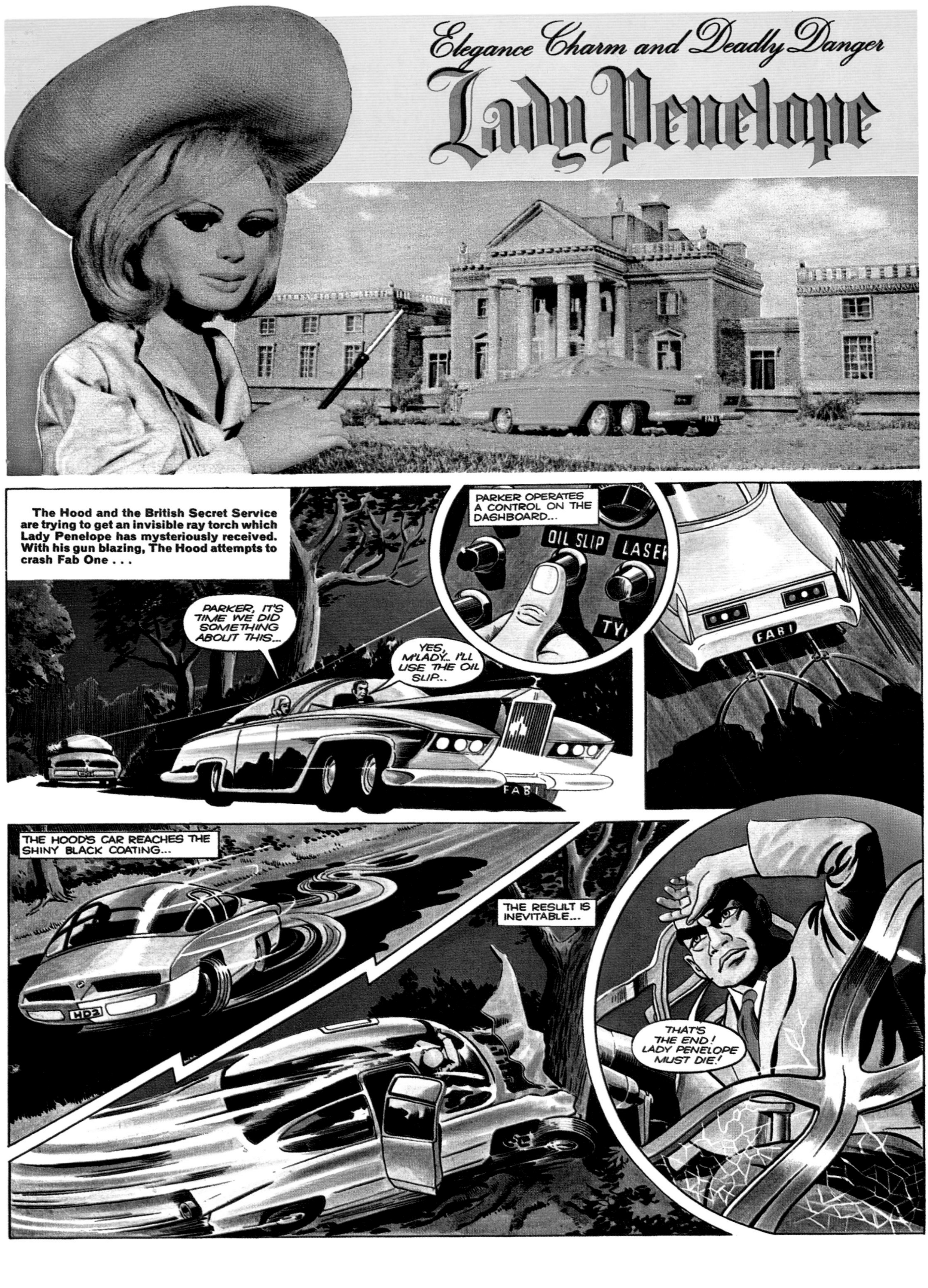

The Hood and the British Secret Service are trying to get an invisible ray torch which Lady Penelope has mysteriously received. With his gun blazing, The Hood attempts to crash Fab One . . .
PARKER, IT'S TIME WE DID SOMETHING ABOUT THIS...
YES, M'LADY... I'LL USE THE OIL SLIP...
FAB 1
PARKER OPERATES A CONTROL ON THE DASHBOARD...
OIL SLIP
FAB 1
THE HOOD'S CAR REACHES THE SHINY BLACK COATING...
HD2
THE RESULT IS INEVITABLE...
THAT'S THE END! LADY PENELOPE MUST DIE!

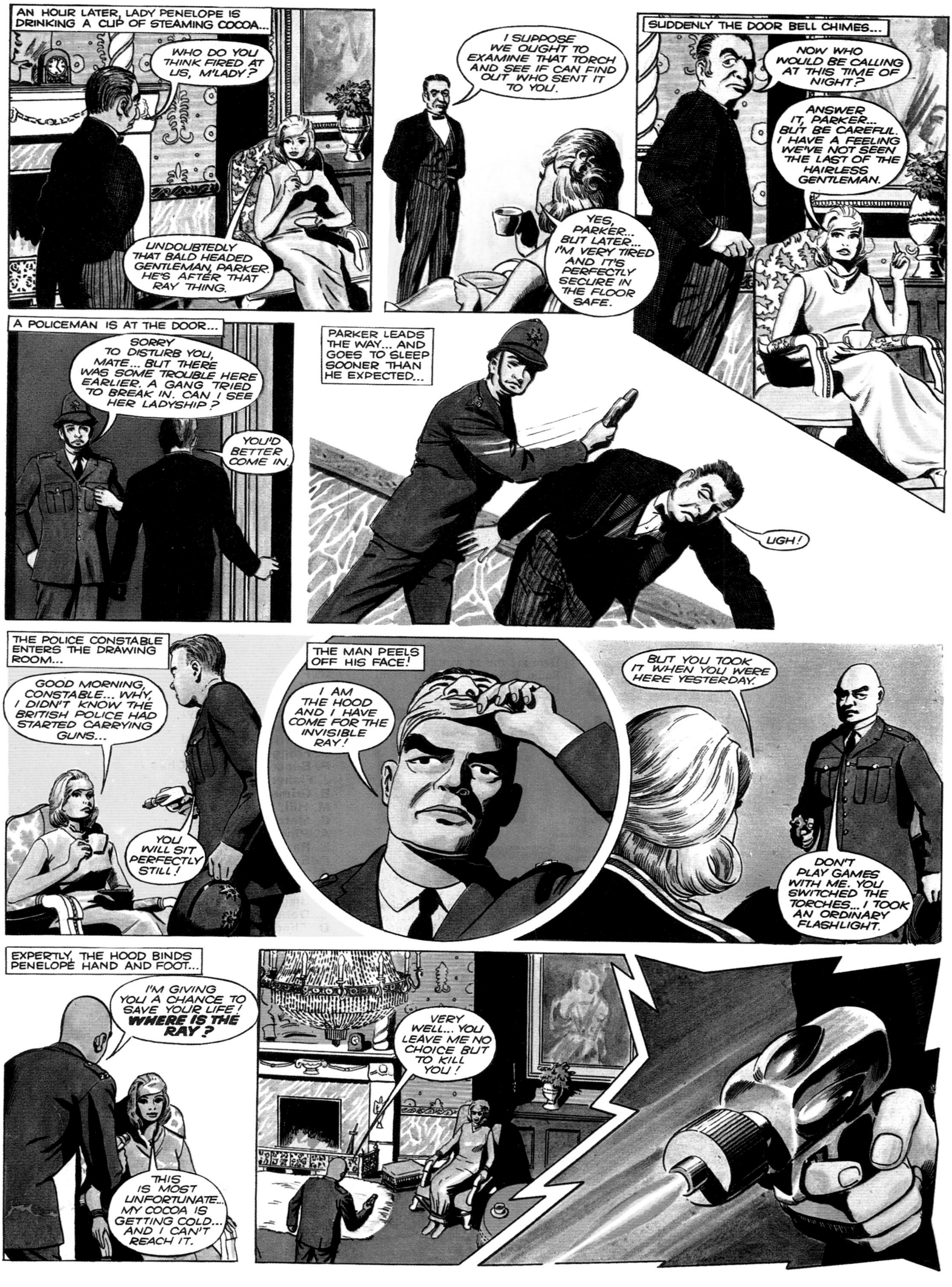

AN HOUR LATER, LADY PENELOPE IS DRINKING A CUP OF STEAMING COCOA...
WHO DO YOU THINK FIRED AT US, M'LADY?
UNDOUBTEDLY THAT BALD HEADED GENTLEMAN, PARKER. HE'S AFTER THAT RAY THING.
I SUPPOSE WE OUGHT TO EXAMINE THAT TORCH AND SEE IF CAN FIND OUT WHO SENT IT TO YOU.
YES, PARKER... BUT LATER... I'M VERY TIRED AND IT'S PERFECTLY SECURE IN THE FLOOR SAFE.
SUDDENLY THE DOOR BELL CHIMES...
NOW WHO WOULD BE CALLING AT THIS TIME OF NIGHT?
ANSWER IT, PARKER... BUT BE CAREFUL. I HAVE A FEELING WE'VE NOT SEEN THE LAST OF THE HAIRLESS GENTLEMAN.
A POLICEMAN IS AT THE DOOR...
SORRY TO DISTURB YOU, MATE... BUT THERE WAS SOME TROUBLE HERE EARLIER. A GANG TRIED TO BREAK IN. CAN I SEE HER LADYSHIP?
YOU'D BETTER COME IN.
PARKER LEADS THE WAY... AND GOES TO SLEEP SOONER THAN HE EXPECTED...
UGH!
THE POLICE CONSTABLE ENTERS THE DRAWING ROOM...
GOOD MORNING, CONSTABLE... WHY, I DIDN'T KNOW THE BRITISH POLICE HAD STARTED CARRYING GUNS...
YOU WILL SIT PERFECTLY STILL!
THE MAN PEELS OFF HIS FACE!
I AM THE HOOD AND I HAVE COME FOR THE INVISIBLE RAY!
BUT YOU TOOK IT WHEN YOU WERE HERE YESTERDAY.
DON'T PLAY GAMES WITH ME. YOU SWITCHED THE TORCHES... I TOOK AN ORDINARY FLASHLIGHT.
EXPERTLY, THE HOOD BINDS PENELOPE HAND AND FOOT...
I'M GIVING YOU A CHANCE TO SAVE YOUR LIFE! WHERE IS THE RAY?
THIS IS MOST UNFORTUNATE... MY COCOA IS GETTING COLD... AND I CAN'T REACH IT.
VERY WELL... YOU LEAVE ME NO CHOICE BUT TO KILL YOU!

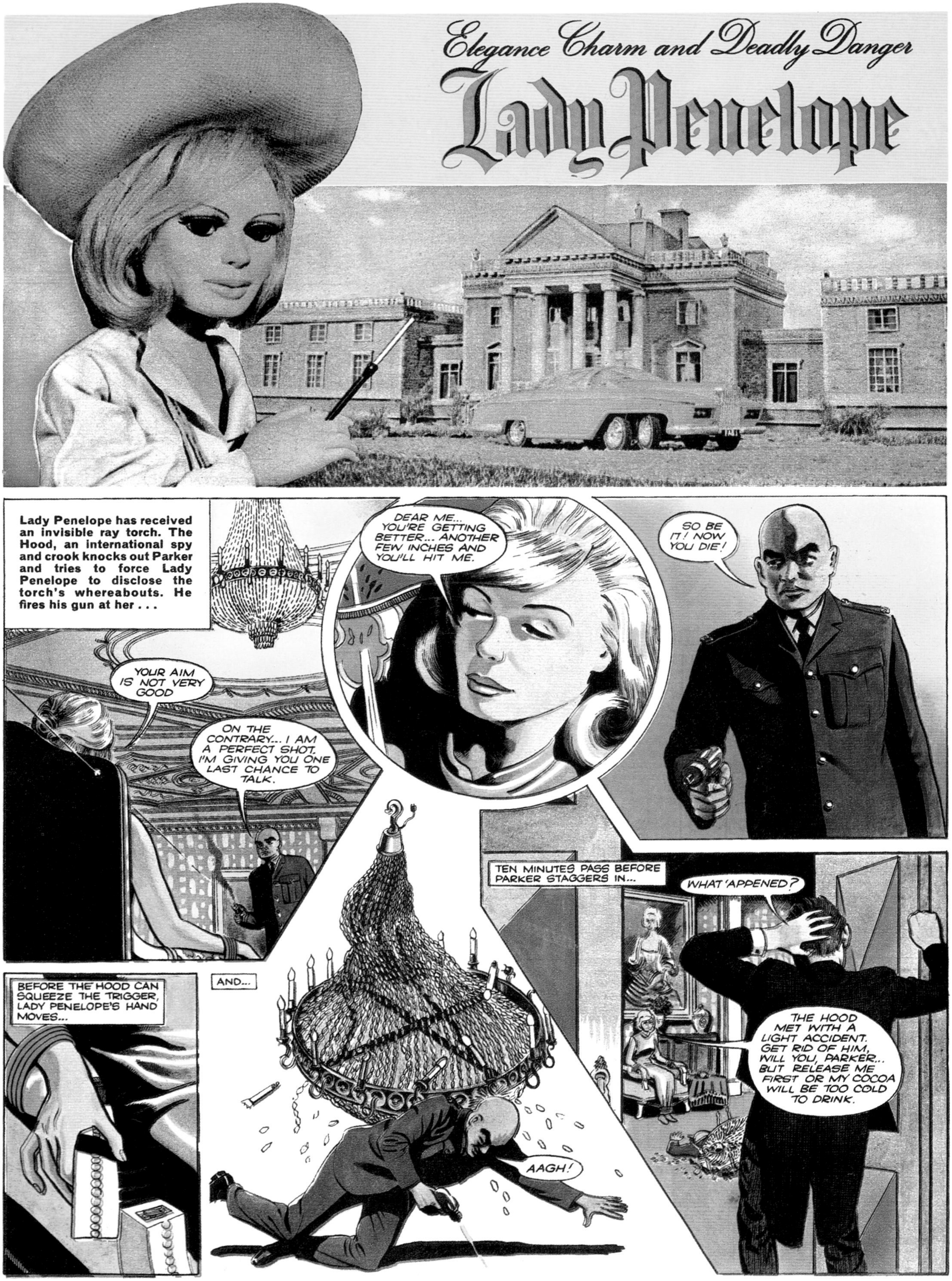

Elegance Charm and Deadly Danger
Lady Penelope
Lady Penelope has received an invisible ray torch. The Hood, an international spy and crook knocks out Parker and tries to force Lady Penelope to disclose the torch's whereabouts. He fires his gun at her . . .
YOUR AIM IS NOT VERY GOOD
ON THE CONTRARY... I AM A PERFECT SHOT. I'M GIVING YOU ONE LAST CHANCE TO TALK.
DEAR ME... YOU'RE GETTING BETTER... ANOTHER FEW INCHES AND YOU'LL HIT ME.
SO BE IT! NOW YOU DIE!
BEFORE THE HOOD CAN SQUEEZE THE TRIGGER, LADY PENELOPE'S HAND MOVES...
AND...
AAGH!
TEN MINUTES PASS BEFORE PARKER STAGGERS IN...
WHAT 'APPENED?
THE HOOD MET WITH A LIGHT ACCIDENT. GET RID OF HIM, WILL YOU, PARKER... BUT RELEASE ME FIRST OR MY COCOA WILL BE TOO COLD TO DRINK.

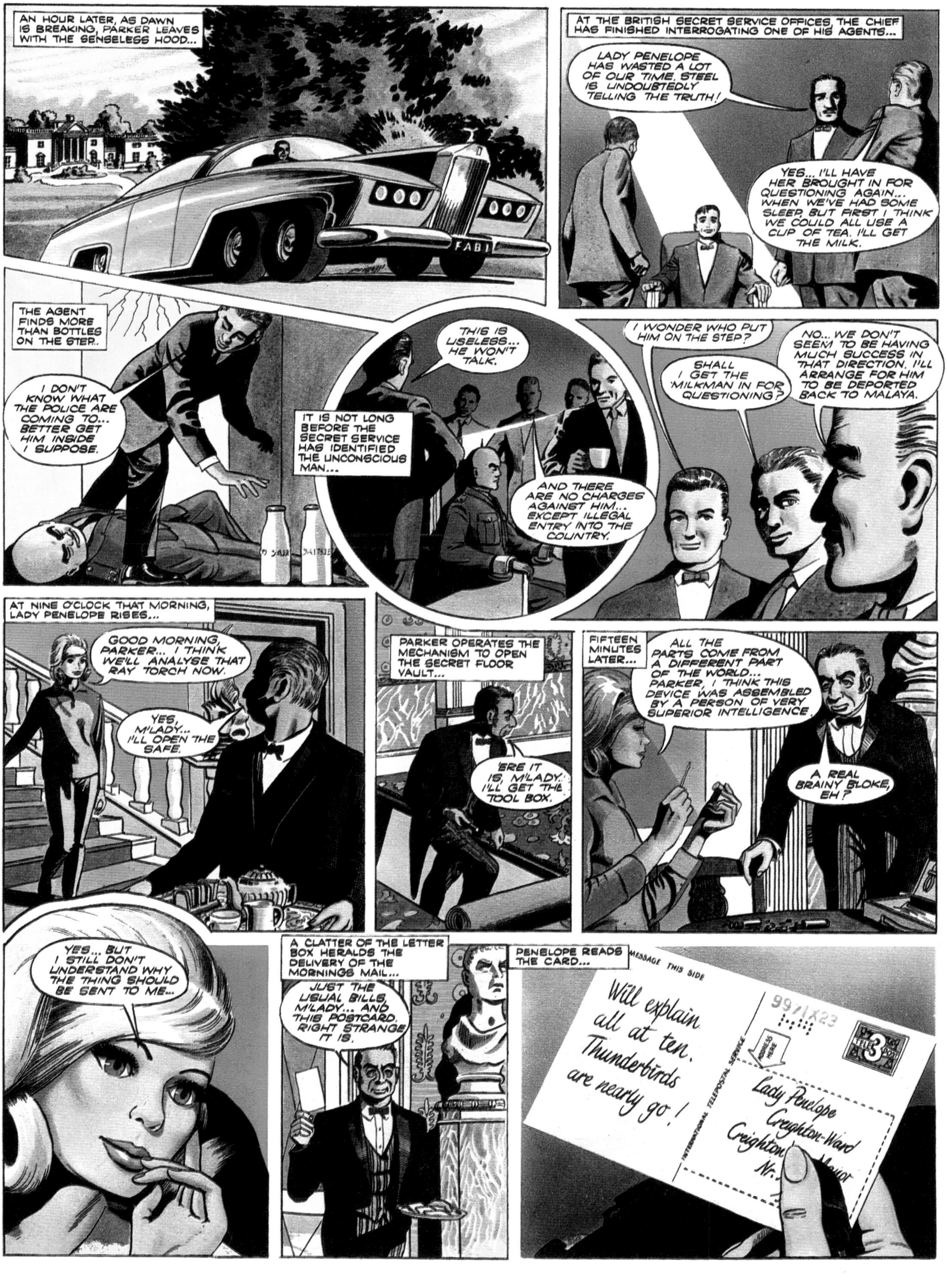
AN HOUR LATER, AS DAWN IS BREAKING, PARKER LEAVES WITH THE SENSELESS HOOD...
FAB 1
AT THE BRITISH SECRET SERVICE OFFICES, THE CHIEF HAS FINISHED INTERROGATING ONE OF HIS AGENTS...
LADY PENELOPE HAS WASTED A LOT OF OUR TIME. STEEL IS UNDOUBTEDLY TELLING THE TRUTH!
YES... I'LL HAVE HER BROUGHT IN FOR QUESTIONING AGAIN... WHEN WE'VE HAD SOME SLEEP, BUT FIRST I THINK WE COULD ALL USE A CUP OF TEA. I'LL GET THE MILK.
THE AGENT FINDS MORE THAN BOTTLES ON THE STEP..
I DON'T KNOW WHAT THE POLICE ARE COMING TO... BETTER GET HIM INSIDE I SUPPOSE.
IT IS NOT LONG BEFORE THE SECRET SERVICE HAS IDENTIFIED THE UNCONSCIOUS MAN...
THIS IS USELESS... HE WON'T TALK.
AND THERE ARE NO CHARGES AGAINST HIM... EXCEPT ILLEGAL ENTRY INTO THE COUNTRY.
I WONDER WHO PUT HIM ON THE STEP?
SHALL I GET THE MILKMAN IN FOR QUESTIONING?
NO... WE DON'T SEEM TO BE HAVING MUCH SUCCESS IN THAT DIRECTION. I'LL ARRANGE FOR HIM TO BE DEPORTED BACK TO MALAYA.
AT NINE O'CLOCK THAT MORNING, LADY PENELOPE RISES...
GOOD MORNING, PARKER... I THINK WE'LL ANALYSE THAT RAY TORCH NOW.
YES, M'LADY... I'LL OPEN THE SAFE.
PARKER OPERATES THE MECHANISM TO OPEN THE SECRET FLOOR VAULT...
'ERE IT IS, M'LADY. I'LL GET THE TOOL BOX.
FIFTEEN MINUTES LATER...
ALL THE PARTS COME FROM A DIFFERENT PART OF THE WORLD... PARKER, I THINK THIS DEVICE WAS ASSEMBLED BY A PERSON OF VERY SUPERIOR INTELLIGENCE.
A REAL BRAINY BLOKE, EH?
YES... BUT I STILL DON'T UNDERSTAND WHY THE THING SHOULD BE SENT TO ME...
A CLATTER OF THE LETTER BOX HERALDS THE DELIVERY OF THE MORNINGS MAIL...
JUST THE USUAL BILLS, M'LADY... AND THIS POSTCARD. RIGHT STRANGE IT IS.
PENELOPE READS THE CARD...
MESSAGE THIS SIDE
Will explain all at ten. Thunderbirds are nearly go!
997IX23
ADDRESS HERE
INTERNATIONAL TELEPOSTAL SERVICE
Lady Penelope Creighton-Ward
Creighton
Nr.

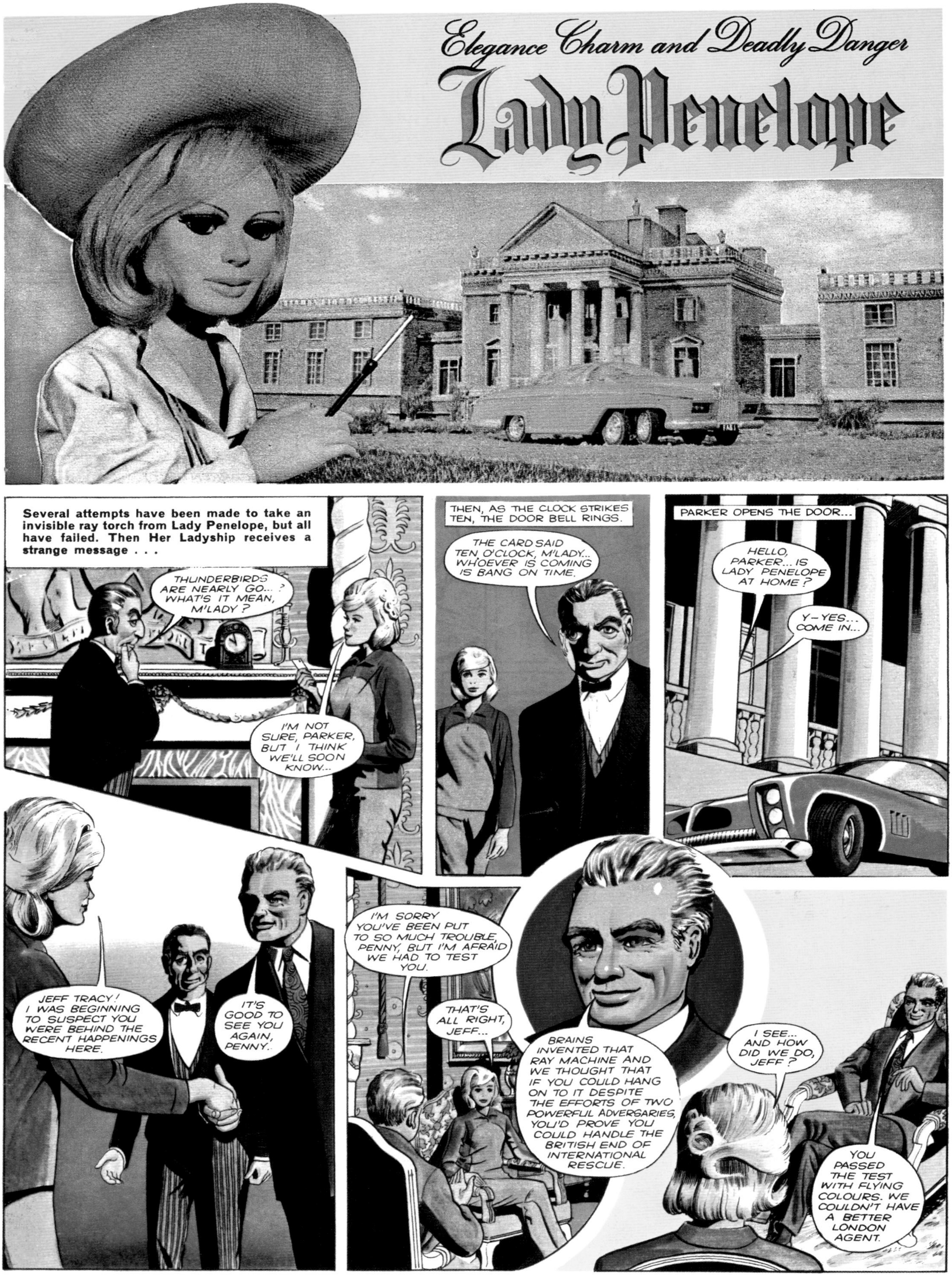
Elegance Charm and Deadly Danger
Lady Penelope
Several attempts have been made to take an invisible ray torch from Lady Penelope, but all have failed. Then Her Ladyship receives a strange message . . .
THUNDERBIRDS ARE NEARLY GO... ? WHAT'S IT MEAN, M'LADY ?
I'M NOT SURE, PARKER, BUT I THINK WE'LL SOON KNOW...
THEN, AS THE CLOCK STRIKES TEN, THE DOOR BELL RINGS.
THE CARD SAID TEN O'CLOCK, M'LADY... WHOEVER IS COMING IS BANG ON TIME.
PARKER OPENS THE DOOR...
HELLO, PARKER... IS LADY PENELOPE AT HOME ?
Y-YES... COME IN...
JEFF TRACY! I WAS BEGINNING TO SUSPECT YOU WERE BEHIND THE RECENT HAPPENINGS HERE.
IT'S GOOD TO SEE YOU AGAIN, PENNY.
I'M SORRY YOU'VE BEEN PUT TO SO MUCH TROUBLE, PENNY, BUT I'M AFRAID WE HAD TO TEST YOU.
THAT'S ALL RIGHT, JEFF...
BRAINS INVENTED THAT RAY MACHINE AND WE THOUGHT THAT IF YOU COULD HANG ON TO IT DESPITE THE EFFORTS OF TWO POWERFUL ADVERSARIES, YOU'D PROVE YOU COULD HANDLE THE BRITISH END OF INTERNATIONAL RESCUE.
I SEE... AND HOW DID WE DO, JEFF ?
YOU PASSED THE TEST WITH FLYING COLOURS. WE COULDN'T HAVE A BETTER LONDON AGENT.

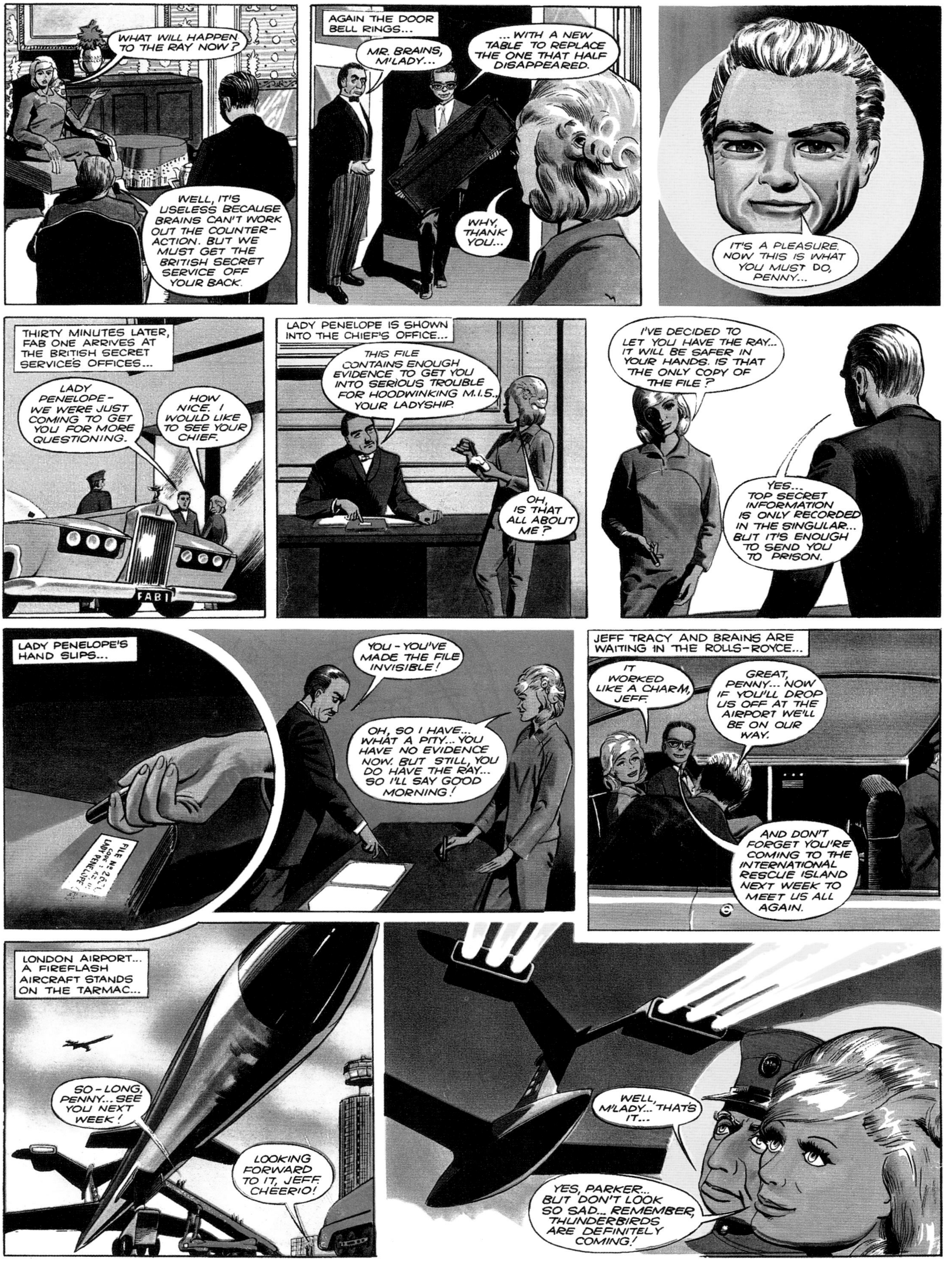
WHAT WILL HAPPEN TO THE RAY NOW?
WELL, IT'S USELESS BECAUSE BRAINS CAN'T WORK OUT THE COUNTER-ACTION. BUT WE MUST GET THE BRITISH SECRET SERVICE OFF YOUR BACK.
AGAIN THE DOOR BELL RINGS...
MR. BRAINS, M'LADY...
...WITH A NEW TABLE TO REPLACE THE ONE THAT HALF DISAPPEARED.
WHY, THANK YOU...
IT'S A PLEASURE. NOW THIS IS WHAT YOU MUST DO, PENNY...
THIRTY MINUTES LATER, FAB ONE ARRIVES AT THE BRITISH SECRET SERVICE'S OFFICES...
LADY PENELOPE - WE WERE JUST COMING TO GET YOU FOR MORE QUESTIONING.
HOW NICE. I WOULD LIKE TO SEE YOUR CHIEF.
FAB 1
LADY PENELOPE IS SHOWN INTO THE CHIEF'S OFFICE...
THIS FILE CONTAINS ENOUGH EVIDENCE TO GET YOU INTO SERIOUS TROUBLE FOR HOODWINKING M.I.5., YOUR LADYSHIP.
OH, IS THAT ALL ABOUT ME?
I'VE DECIDED TO LET YOU HAVE THE RAY... IT WILL BE SAFER IN YOUR HANDS. IS THAT THE ONLY COPY OF THE FILE?
YES... TOP SECRET INFORMATION IS ONLY RECORDED IN THE SINGULAR... BUT IT'S ENOUGH TO SEND YOU TO PRISON.
LADY PENELOPE'S HAND SLIPS...
LADY PENELOPE
YOU - YOU'VE MADE THE FILE INVISIBLE!
OH, SO I HAVE... WHAT A PITY... YOU HAVE NO EVIDENCE NOW. BUT STILL, YOU DO HAVE THE RAY... SO I'LL SAY GOOD MORNING!
JEFF TRACY AND BRAINS ARE WAITING IN THE ROLLS-ROYCE...
IT WORKED LIKE A CHARM, JEFF.
GREAT, PENNY... NOW IF YOU'LL DROP US OFF AT THE AIRPORT WE'LL BE ON OUR WAY.
AND DON'T FORGET YOU'RE COMING TO THE INTERNATIONAL RESCUE ISLAND NEXT WEEK TO MEET US ALL AGAIN.
LONDON AIRPORT... A FIREFLASH AIRCRAFT STANDS ON THE TARMAC...
SO-LONG, PENNY... SEE YOU NEXT WEEK!
LOOKING FORWARD TO IT, JEFF. CHEERIO!
WELL, M'LADY... THAT'S IT...
YES, PARKER... BUT DON'T LOOK SO SAD... REMEMBER, THUNDERBIRDS ARE DEFINITELY COMING!

FIREFLASH SAVED!

600 THANK MYSTERY ORGANISATION

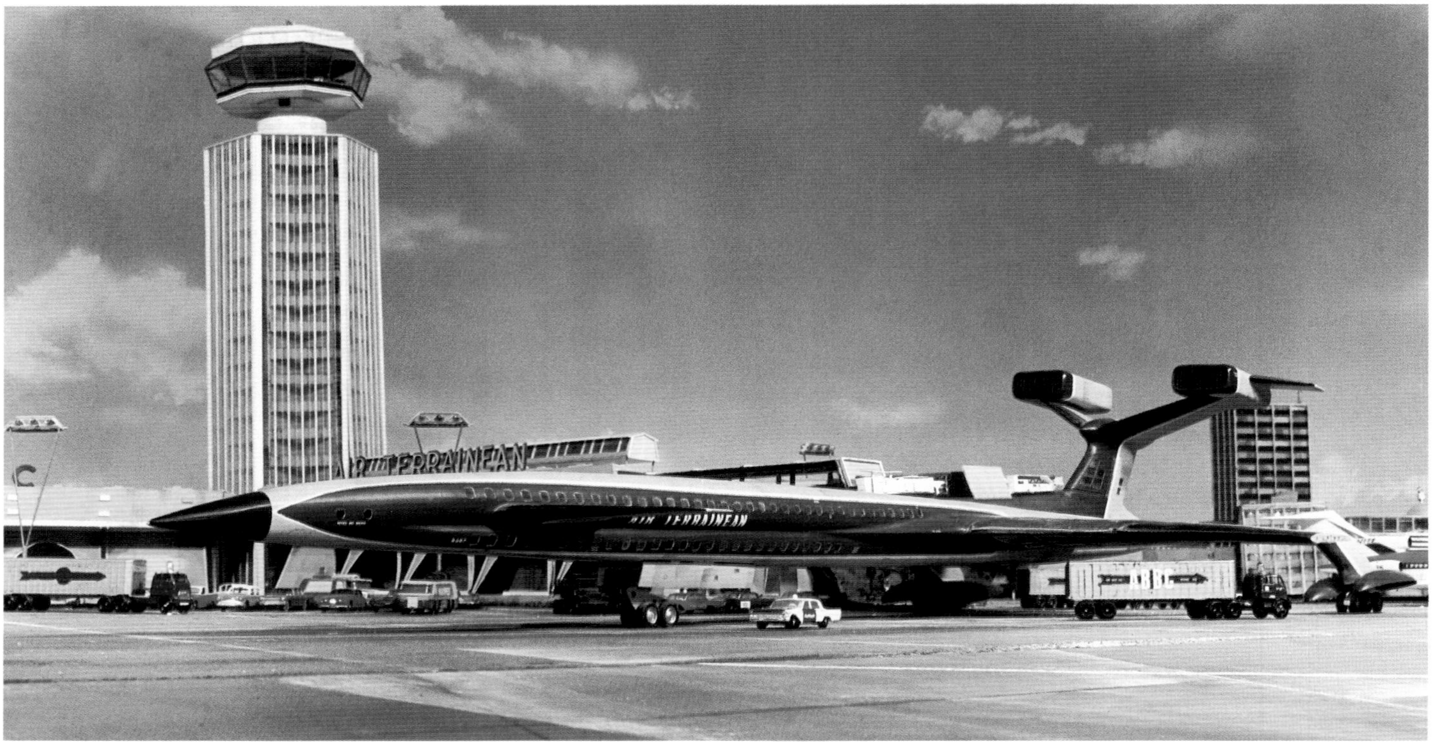
AIR TERRAINEAN

Above: The jinxed London – Tokyo Fireflash shortly before its near catastrophic flight.

Photo by TV21 photographer Len Sharpe/ Doug Luke Associates

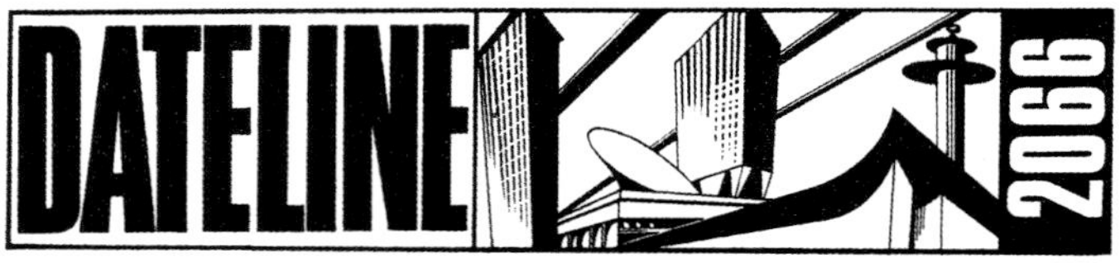
DATELINE
2066

Airport Authorities to review security arrangements

World Airlines were considering new security measures today as the 600 passengers and crew of Air Terrainean's London–Tokyo flight thanked the mystery team responsible for saving their aircraft.

In a dramatic rescue at London's International Airport, their sabotaged Fireflash was brought in to land on high speed lifting vehicles flown to the scene by a secret rescue organisation.

When questioned about the identities of the daring rescuers, Airport Controller Norman would only say, "I have been asked to respect their wishes for complete secrecy."

International Rescue: Where is their base?

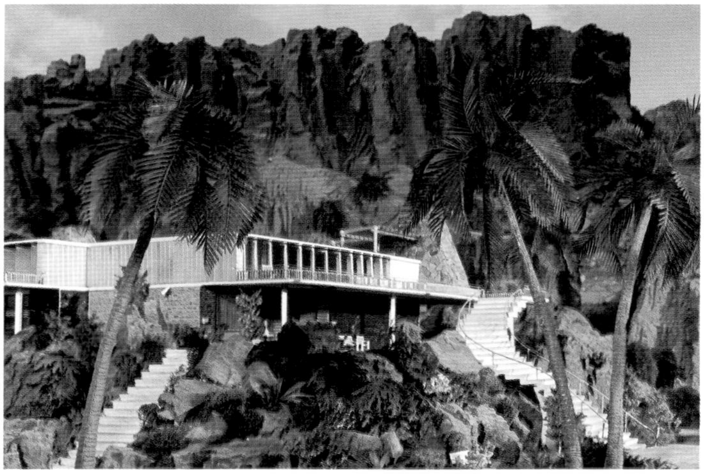

After the recent rescue drama at London Airport, the world is asking one question - "Where is the base of International Rescue?"

The location of the mystery organisation, which has requested to remain anonymous, has confounded experts. Theories include a mobile submarine, a remote jungle HQ or an isolated island.

A beautiful island in the Pacific. Could this be International Rescue's base?

FOREST INFERNO!

EMERGENCY SERVICES ALERTED IN CANADIAN FIRE DRAMA

Canadian news agency report

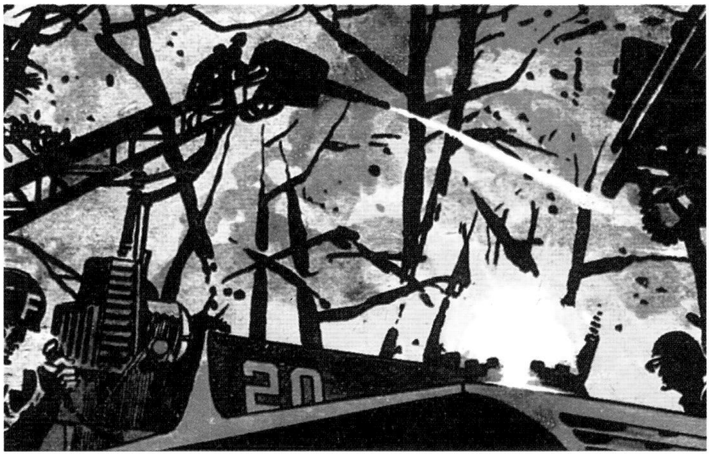

Fires raged in Northern Canada as a sudden inferno engulfed large areas of remote woodland. Rescue services raced to the scene, but all hope seems lost for two men trapped behind the wall of flames.

Jack Farrell and Sam Lincoln of the industrial giant Canada Engineering Incorporated were reported to be on a fishing trip in the area when the forest seemed to ignite without reason.

Full story page 60

Left: **Firefighters face the forest flames**
Picture courtesy Pelton-Earle Associates

Mystery aircraft sighted

WORLD AIR FORCE DENIES ALL KNOWLEDGE

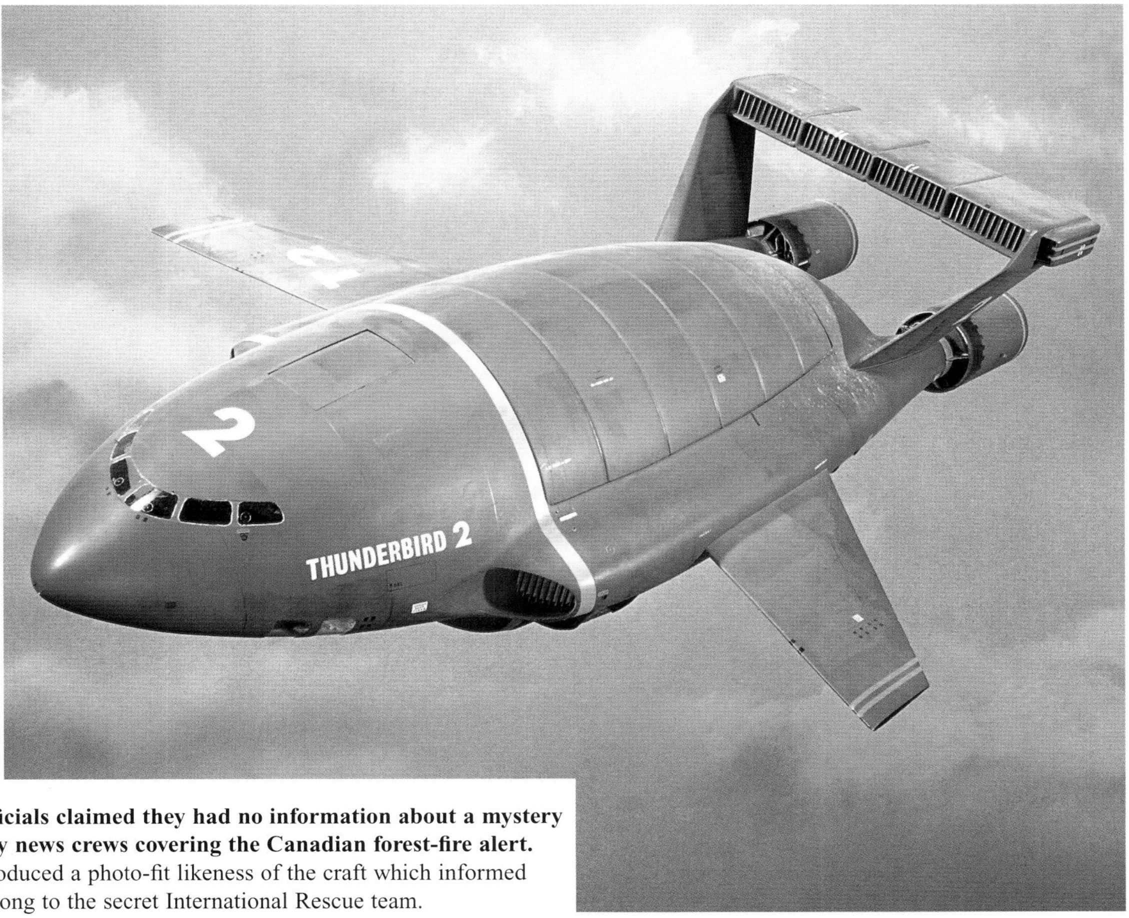
2
THUNDERBIRD 2

Photo-fit picture of mystery craft. Could this be one of International Rescue's machines?

World Air Force officials claimed they had no information about a mystery aircraft sighted by news crews covering the Canadian forest-fire alert.

Eyewitnesses later produced a photo-fit likeness of the craft which informed sources suggest could belong to the secret International Rescue team.

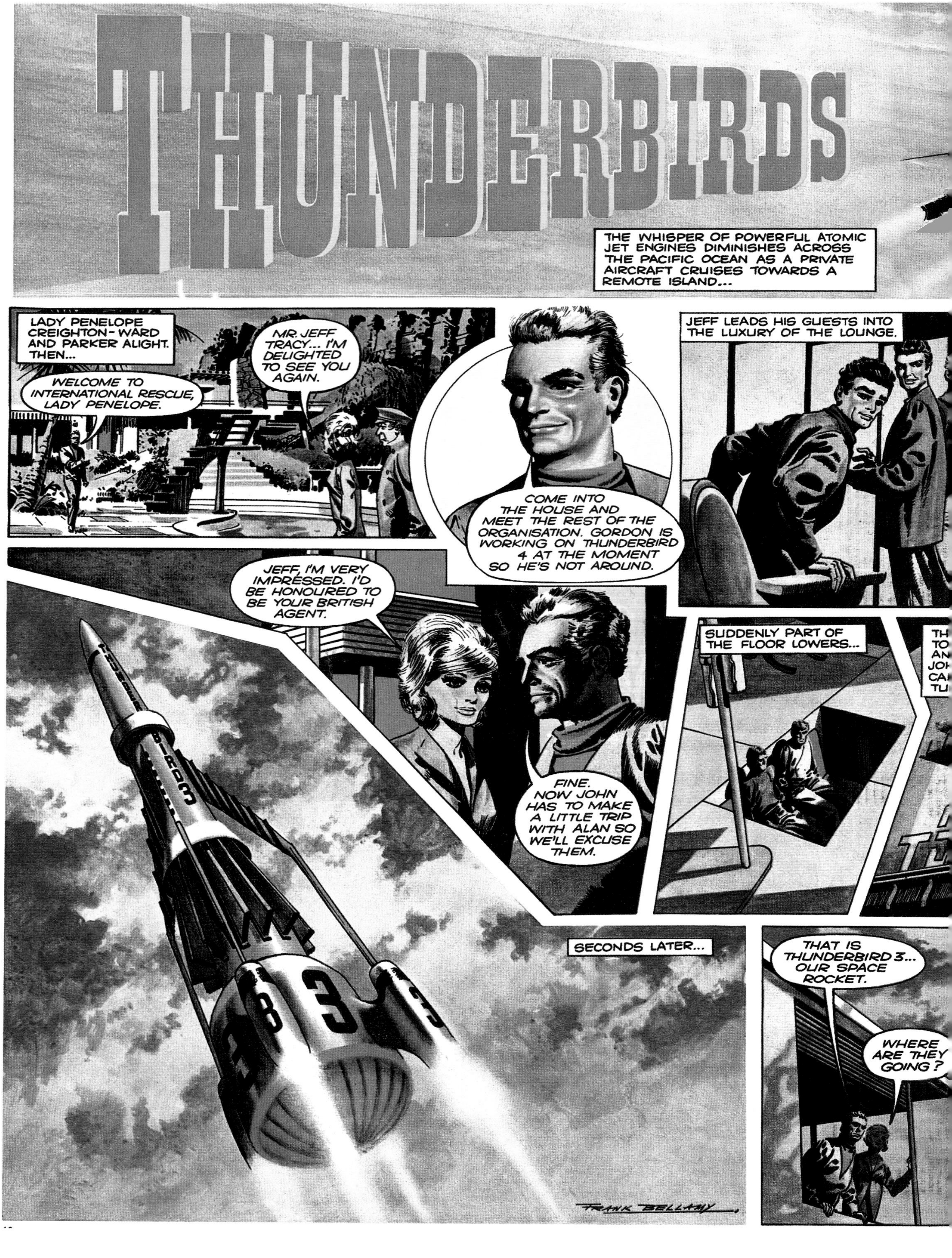
THUNDERBIRDS
THE WHISPER OF POWERFUL ATOMIC JET ENGINES DIMINISHES ACROSS THE PACIFIC OCEAN AS A PRIVATE AIRCRAFT CRUISES TOWARDS A REMOTE ISLAND...
LADY PENELOPE CREIGHTON-WARD AND PARKER ALIGHT. THEN...
WELCOME TO INTERNATIONAL RESCUE, LADY PENELOPE.
MR. JEFF TRACY... I'M DELIGHTED TO SEE YOU AGAIN.
COME INTO THE HOUSE AND MEET THE REST OF THE ORGANISATION. GORDON IS WORKING ON THUNDERBIRD 4 AT THE MOMENT SO HE'S NOT AROUND.
JEFF LEADS HIS GUESTS INTO THE LUXURY OF THE LOUNGE.
JEFF, I'M VERY IMPRESSED. I'D BE HONOURED TO BE YOUR BRITISH AGENT.
FINE. NOW JOHN HAS TO MAKE A LITTLE TRIP WITH ALAN SO WE'LL EXCUSE THEM.
SUDDENLY PART OF THE FLOOR LOWERS...
SECONDS LATER...
THUNDERBIRD 3
THAT IS THUNDERBIRD 3... OUR SPACE ROCKET.
WHERE ARE THEY GOING?
FRANK BELLAMY

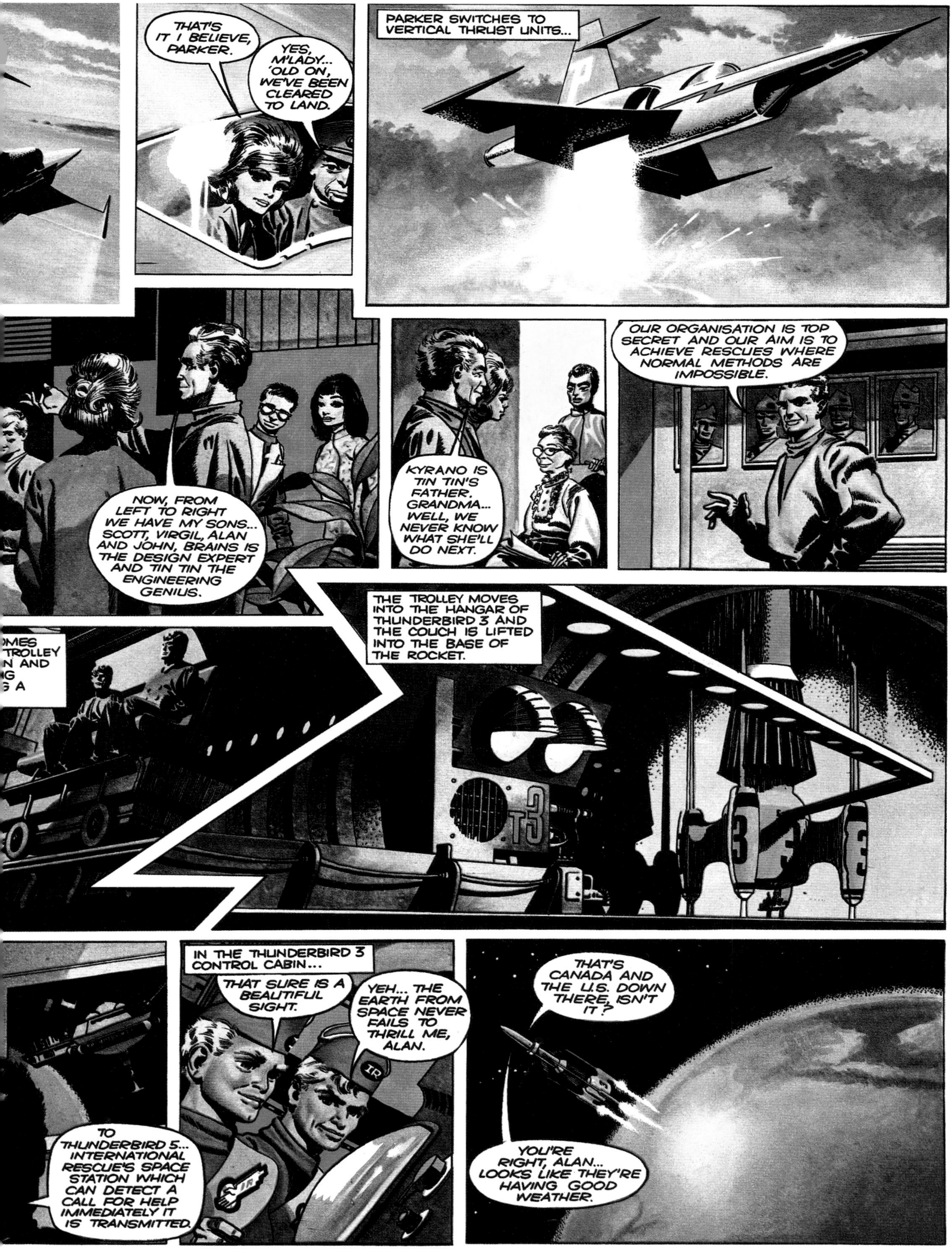
THAT'S IT I BELIEVE, PARKER.
YES, M'LADY... 'OLD ON, WE'VE BEEN CLEARED TO LAND.
PARKER SWITCHES TO VERTICAL THRUST UNITS...
NOW, FROM LEFT TO RIGHT WE HAVE MY SONS... SCOTT, VIRGIL, ALAN AND JOHN, BRAINS IS THE DESIGN EXPERT AND TIN TIN THE ENGINEERING GENIUS.
KYRANO IS TIN TIN'S FATHER. GRANDMA... WELL, WE NEVER KNOW WHAT SHE'LL DO NEXT.
OUR ORGANISATION IS TOP SECRET AND OUR AIM IS TO ACHIEVE RESCUES WHERE NORMAL METHODS ARE IMPOSSIBLE.
OMES TROLLEY N AND G G A
THE TROLLEY MOVES INTO THE HANGAR OF THUNDERBIRD 3 AND THE COUCH IS LIFTED INTO THE BASE OF THE ROCKET.
TO THUNDERBIRD 5... INTERNATIONAL RESCUE'S SPACE STATION WHICH CAN DETECT A CALL FOR HELP IMMEDIATELY IT IS TRANSMITTED.
IN THE THUNDERBIRD 3 CONTROL CABIN...
THAT SURE IS A BEAUTIFUL SIGHT.
YEH... THE EARTH FROM SPACE NEVER FAILS TO THRILL ME, ALAN.
THAT'S CANADA AND THE U.S. DOWN THERE, ISN'T IT?
YOU'RE RIGHT, ALAN... LOOKS LIKE THEY'RE HAVING GOOD WEATHER.

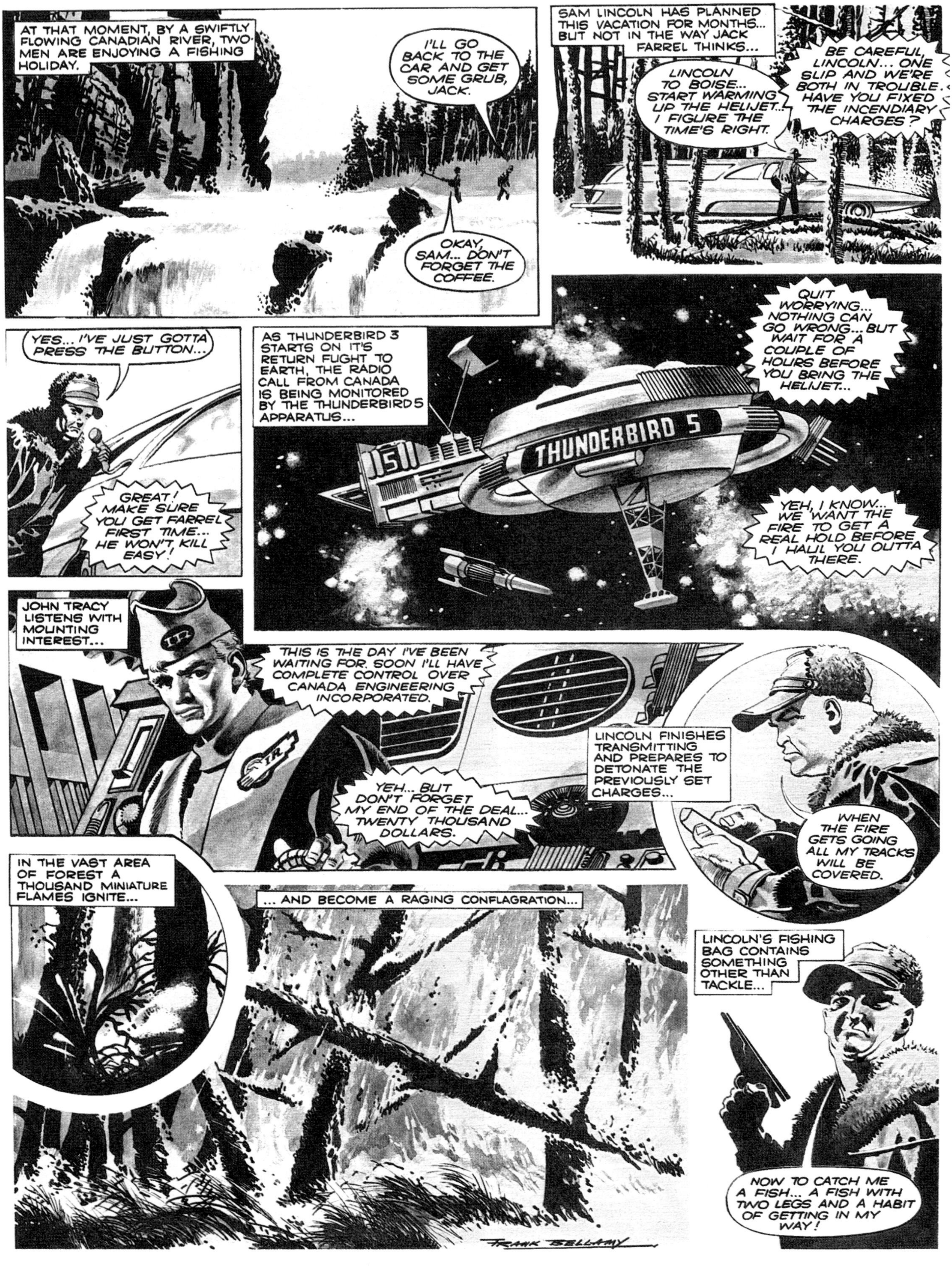

AT THAT MOMENT, BY A SWIFTLY FLOWING CANADIAN RIVER, TWO MEN ARE ENJOYING A FISHING HOLIDAY.
I'LL GO BACK TO THE CAR AND GET SOME GRUB, JACK.
OKAY, SAM... DON'T FORGET THE COFFEE.
SAM LINCOLN HAS PLANNED THIS VACATION FOR MONTHS... BUT NOT IN THE WAY JACK FARREL THINKS...
LINCOLN TO BOISE... START WARMING UP THE HELIJET... I FIGURE THE TIME'S RIGHT.
BE CAREFUL, LINCOLN... ONE SLIP AND WE'RE BOTH IN TROUBLE. HAVE YOU FIXED THE INCENDIARY CHARGES?
YES... I'VE JUST GOTTA PRESS THE BUTTON...
GREAT! MAKE SURE YOU GET FARREL FIRST TIME... HE WON'T KILL EASY!
AS THUNDERBIRD 3 STARTS ON IT'S RETURN FLIGHT TO EARTH, THE RADIO CALL FROM CANADA IS BEING MONITORED BY THE THUNDERBIRD 5 APPARATUS...
QUIT WORRYING... NOTHING CAN GO WRONG... BUT WAIT FOR A COUPLE OF HOURS BEFORE YOU BRING THE HELIJET...
THUNDERBIRD 5
5
YEH, I KNOW... WE WANT THE FIRE TO GET A REAL HOLD BEFORE I HAUL YOU OUTTA THERE.
JOHN TRACY LISTENS WITH MOUNTING INTEREST...
THIS IS THE DAY I'VE BEEN WAITING FOR. SOON I'LL HAVE COMPLETE CONTROL OVER CANADA ENGINEERING INCORPORATED.
YEH... BUT DON'T FORGET MY END OF THE DEAL... TWENTY THOUSAND DOLLARS.
LINCOLN FINISHES TRANSMITTING AND PREPARES TO DETONATE THE PREVIOUSLY SET CHARGES...
WHEN THE FIRE GETS GOING ALL MY TRACKS WILL BE COVERED.
IN THE VAST AREA OF FOREST A THOUSAND MINIATURE FLAMES IGNITE...
... AND BECOME A RAGING CONFLAGRATION...
LINCOLN'S FISHING BAG CONTAINS SOMETHING OTHER THAN TACKLE...
NOW TO CATCH ME A FISH... A FISH WITH TWO LEGS AND A HABIT OF GETTING IN MY WAY!
FRANK BELLAMY

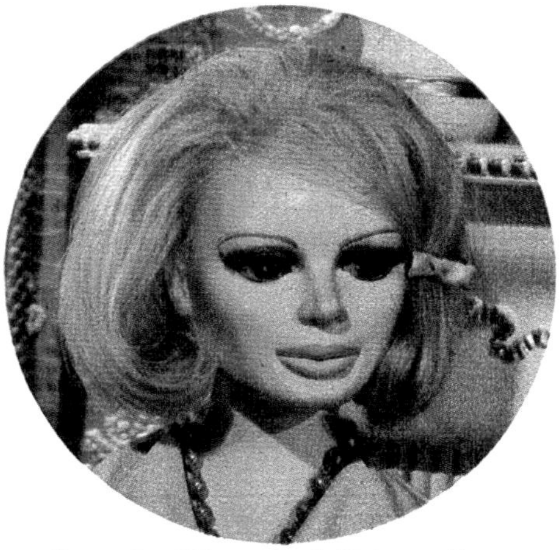

Harry O. O'Donnell of Malay writes, "Please investigate Thunderbirds."

Lady Penelope Investigates THUNDERBIRDS

THE INTERNATIONAL RESCUE ORGANISATION

"ERE, M'Lady. This letter's meant for World We Share," Parker muttered, as he handed me your letter, Harry.

"Oh, Parker," I smiled, "Thunderbirds are machines not animals. Now, prepare the jet! We have quite a journey ahead."

While Parker was busy with my aircraft, I chose my latest outfit to wear for the flight.

Later we spotted the Tracy Island nestling in the blue Pacific Ocean.

Suddenly a flash of light scarred a green mountain slope.

"Look out, M'Lady," Parker yelled at me. "They've fired a missile at us".

Banking our little jet in a tight turn, Parker fired our laser gun and the missile exploded.

"Now to find out who took a pot shot at us." Parker sounded serious.

Skilfully he brought the plane down to land by a simply fabulous swimming pool that nestled under a hillside house.

A tall grey-haired figure stepped forward to meet us.

"Lady Penelope, I do apologise. A radar missile control has developed a fault."

"Yes—and we nearly developed one, too, mate," Parker replied aggressively. It took all my diplomacy to cool him down and allow me to introduce our host, Jeff Tracy.

After I had insisted upon Jeff calling me Penny, he led us inside.

Putting on my most winning smile, I asked him about Thunderbirds, but he only grinned and said "Come and meet the boys."

I had the feeling that Jeff did not want to tell me about his machines and I'll tell you what I did about that next week.

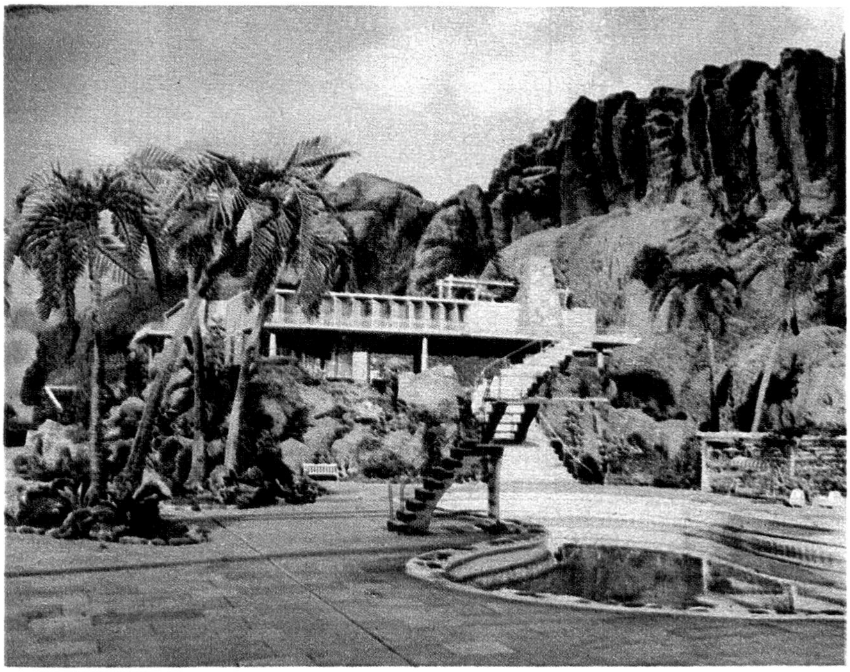

The fabulous swimming pool and hillside home of the Tracy family. I am sure that the swimming pool hides some secret or other.

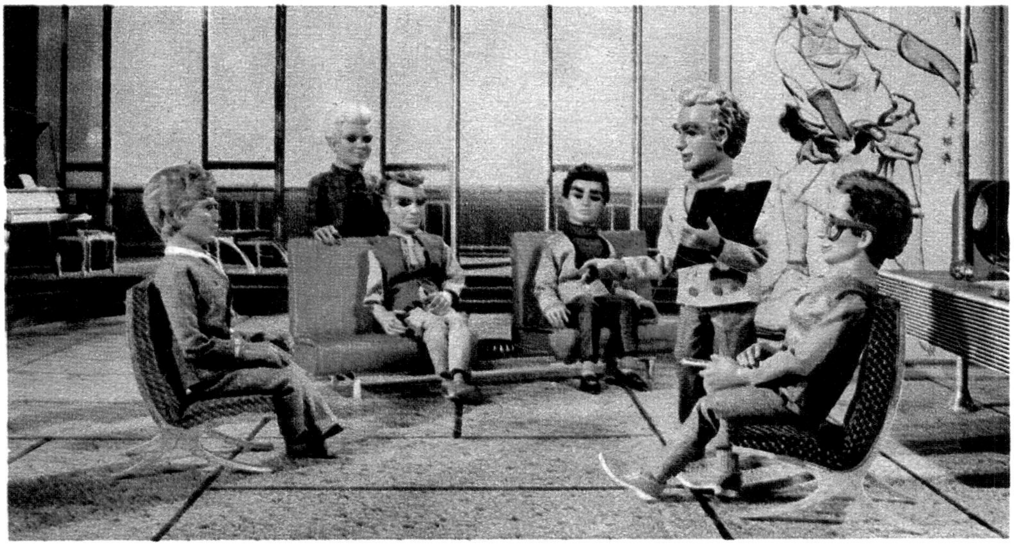

Jeff Tracy with his sons, Alan, Virgil, Scott and Gordon . . . and Brains, a quiet genius who, I think, designed the Thunderbird machines.

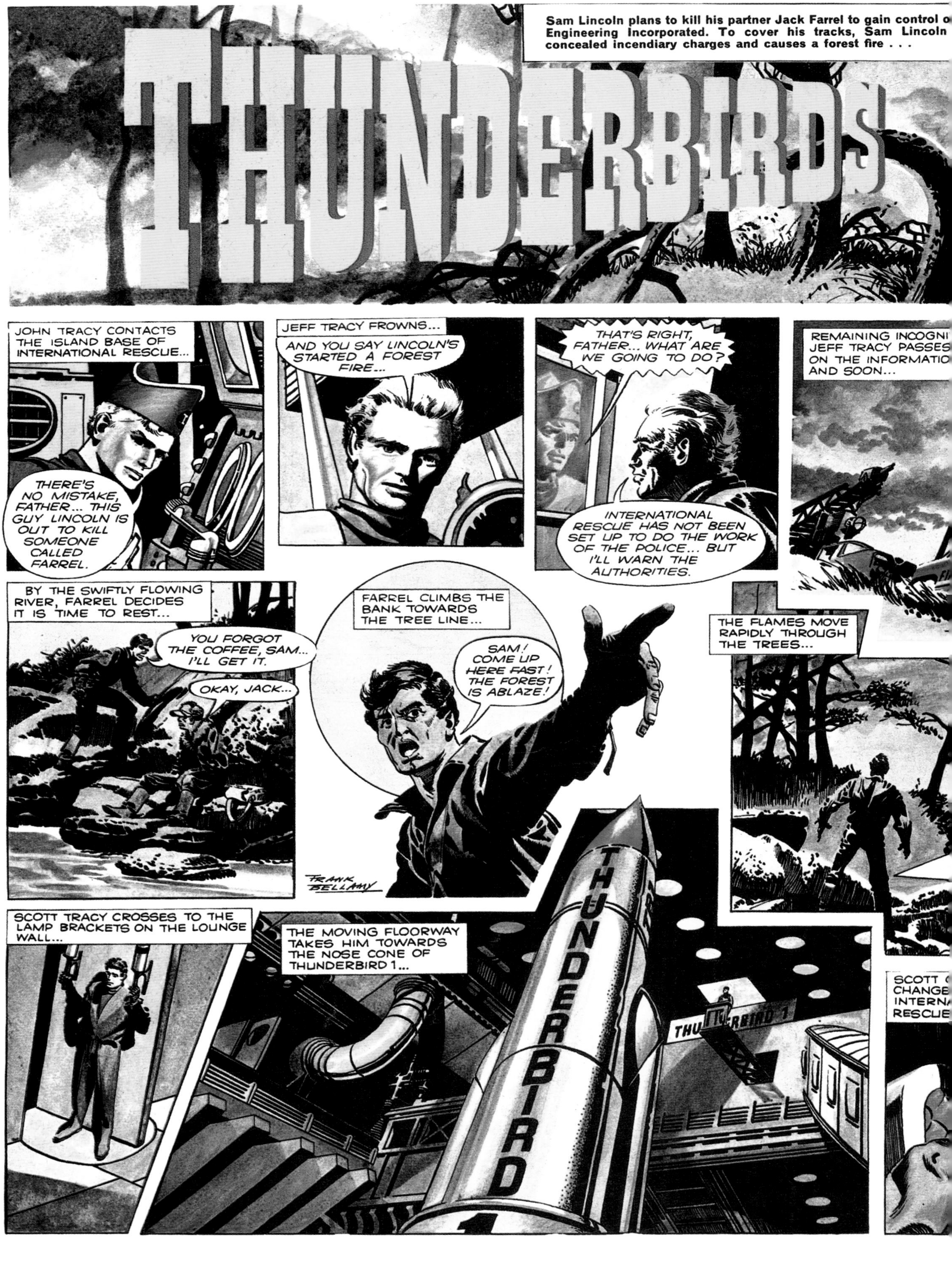

Sam Lincoln plans to kill his partner Jack Farrel to gain control o
Engineering Incorporated. To cover his tracks, Sam Lincoln
concealed incendiary charges and causes a forest fire . . .
THUNDERBIRDS
JOHN TRACY CONTACTS THE ISLAND BASE OF INTERNATIONAL RESCUE...
THERE'S NO MISTAKE, FATHER... THIS GUY LINCOLN IS OUT TO KILL SOMEONE CALLED FARREL.
JEFF TRACY FROWNS...
AND YOU SAY LINCOLN'S STARTED A FOREST FIRE...
THAT'S RIGHT, FATHER... WHAT ARE WE GOING TO DO?
INTERNATIONAL RESCUE HAS NOT BEEN SET UP TO DO THE WORK OF THE POLICE... BUT I'LL WARN THE AUTHORITIES.
REMAINING INCOGNI
JEFF TRACY PASSES
ON THE INFORMATIO
AND SOON...
BY THE SWIFTLY FLOWING RIVER, FARREL DECIDES IT IS TIME TO REST...
YOU FORGOT THE COFFEE, SAM... I'LL GET IT.
OKAY, JACK...
FARREL CLIMBS THE BANK TOWARDS THE TREE LINE...
SAM! COME UP HERE FAST! THE FOREST IS ABLAZE!
FRANK BELLAMY
THE FLAMES MOVE RAPIDLY THROUGH THE TREES...
SCOTT TRACY CROSSES TO THE LAMP BRACKETS ON THE LOUNGE WALL...
THE MOVING FLOORWAY TAKES HIM TOWARDS THE NOSE CONE OF THUNDERBIRD 1...
THUNDERBIRD
1
SCOTT
CHANGE
INTERNA
RESCUE

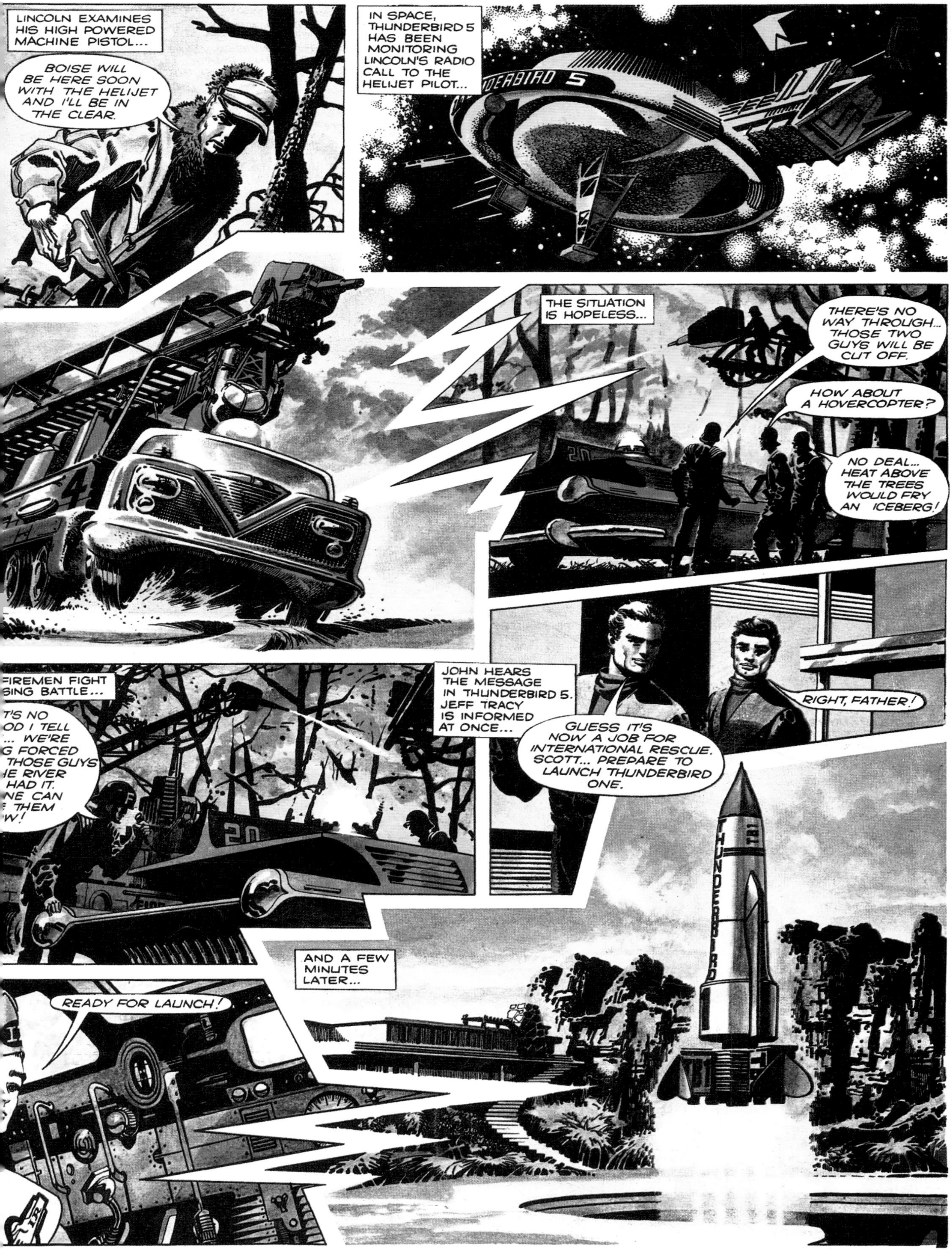
LINCOLN EXAMINES HIS HIGH POWERED MACHINE PISTOL...
BOISE WILL BE HERE SOON WITH THE HELIJET AND I'LL BE IN THE CLEAR.
IN SPACE, THUNDERBIRD 5 HAS BEEN MONITORING LINCOLN'S RADIO CALL TO THE HELIJET PILOT...
THE SITUATION IS HOPELESS...
THERE'S NO WAY THROUGH... THOSE TWO GUYS WILL BE CUT OFF.
HOW ABOUT A HOVERCOPTER?
NO DEAL... HEAT ABOVE THE TREES WOULD FRY AN ICEBERG!
FIREMEN FIGHT
SING BATTLE...
T'S NO
OD I TELL
... WE'RE
G FORCED
THOSE GUYS
HE RIVER
HAD IT.
NE CAN
THEM
W!
JOHN HEARS THE MESSAGE IN THUNDERBIRD 5. JEFF TRACY IS INFORMED AT ONCE...
GUESS IT'S NOW A JOB FOR INTERNATIONAL RESCUE. SCOTT... PREPARE TO LAUNCH THUNDERBIRD ONE.
RIGHT, FATHER!
AND A FEW MINUTES LATER...
READY FOR LAUNCH!

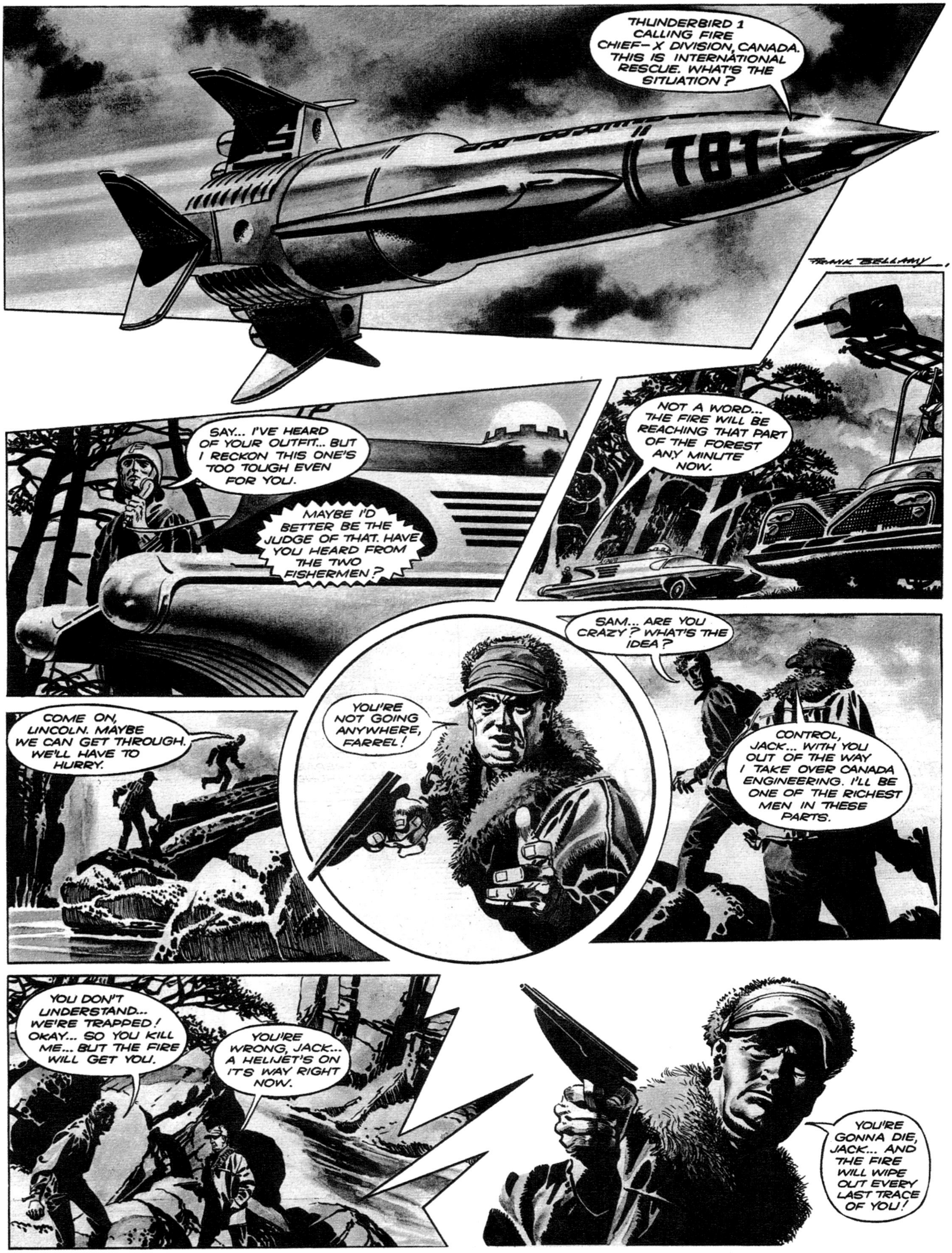
THUNDERBIRD 1 CALLING FIRE CHIEF– X DIVISION, CANADA. THIS IS INTERNATIONAL RESCUE. WHAT'S THE SITUATION?
TB1
FRANK BELLAMY
SAY... I'VE HEARD OF YOUR OUTFIT... BUT I RECKON THIS ONE'S TOO TOUGH EVEN FOR YOU.
MAYBE I'D BETTER BE THE JUDGE OF THAT. HAVE YOU HEARD FROM THE TWO FISHERMEN?
NOT A WORD... THE FIRE WILL BE REACHING THAT PART OF THE FOREST ANY MINUTE NOW.
COME ON, LINCOLN. MAYBE WE CAN GET THROUGH. WE'LL HAVE TO HURRY.
YOU'RE NOT GOING ANYWHERE, FARREL!
SAM... ARE YOU CRAZY? WHAT'S THE IDEA?
CONTROL, JACK... WITH YOU OUT OF THE WAY I TAKE OVER CANADA ENGINEERING. I'LL BE ONE OF THE RICHEST MEN IN THESE PARTS.
YOU DON'T UNDERSTAND... WE'RE TRAPPED! OKAY... SO YOU KILL ME... BUT THE FIRE WILL GET YOU.
YOU'RE WRONG, JACK... A HELIJET'S ON IT'S WAY RIGHT NOW.
YOU'RE GONNA DIE, JACK... AND THE FIRE WILL WIPE OUT EVERY LAST TRACE OF YOU!

Lady Penelope Investigates

THUNDERBIRDS

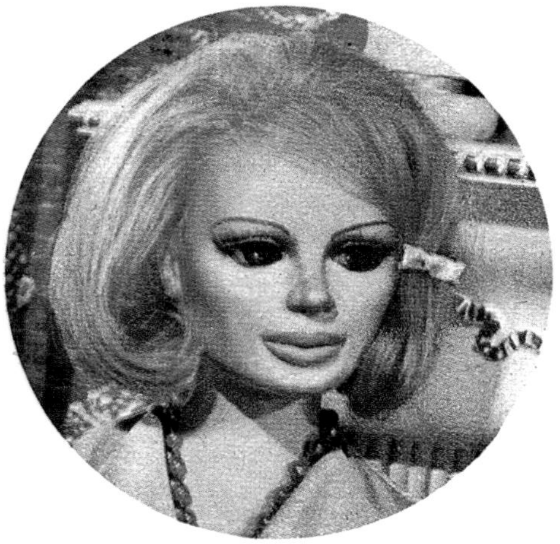

Space monitor John Tracy in the International Rescue space station Thunderbird 5. This was my first look at John, when he appeared on the photograph TV screen.

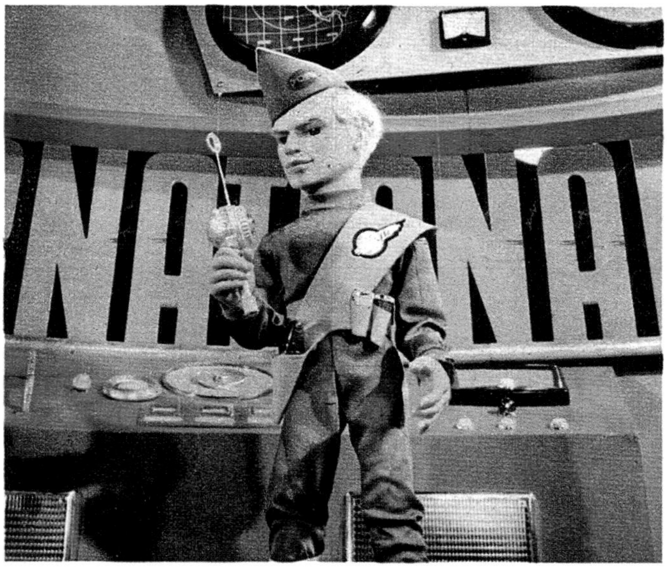

LADY PENELOPE has been asked by Harry O'Donnell to investigate Thunderbirds. She arrives at the Tracy island in the Pacific and meets Jeff Tracy and four of his sons, but none of them will tell her about the machines, so she decides to find out for herself.

I HAD arranged to meet Parker down in the lounge at half past one in the morning. At one fifteen, dressed in my black burglar's suit, I slipped from my room. The Tracy house was dark and silent and I was sure everyone was asleep.

Parker was waiting, his burglar kit ready.

"Where shall we start, M'lady?" he whispered.

"I think we'll just look around first, Parker."

Parker drew a small pencil flashlight from his pocket and swept the room.

"Hold it, Parker." I felt a surge of excitement.

"The portraits on the wall."

Parker swung the torch back to the five portraits on the wall. "So what, M'lady? They're just pictures of his five sons."

"Exactly, Parker—five sons, but we've met only four. Where is the fifth?"

As if in answer to this question, the eyes of the portrait of the Tracy we had not met lit up and the room was filled with a high pitched bleeping noise.

Immediately lights went on all over the house and doors were thrown open above.

Jeff Tracy appeared, "Penny—Parker!" He snapped.

"Allow me to explain," I answered.

"Not now, Penny, kindly wait until this is over."

He hurried to his desk and stabbed a control hidden from our view. Immediately the photograph with the flashing eyes turned to a TV screen showing the Tracy boy in a large room. An International Rescue was under way.

When Alan and Brains returned from their rescue, the family gathered in the lounge to face Parker and myself.

"We allowed you to visit us, Penny—so that you could see how International Rescue worked, in view of this and because of your unusual ability as an undercover agent, we would like you to become the London agent of International Rescue."

So Harry O'Donnell of Malaya, whom I strongly suspect is the notorious spy 'The Hood,' I cannot tell you the secrets of Thunderbirds, for I'm one of them now!

The beautiful round house, a very comfortable sun-trap, ideal for sunbathing. Unfortunately, it could be rather uncomfortable lying there when Thunderbird 3 is launched as the space ship rises from an underground silo, straight through the hollow centre of the house.

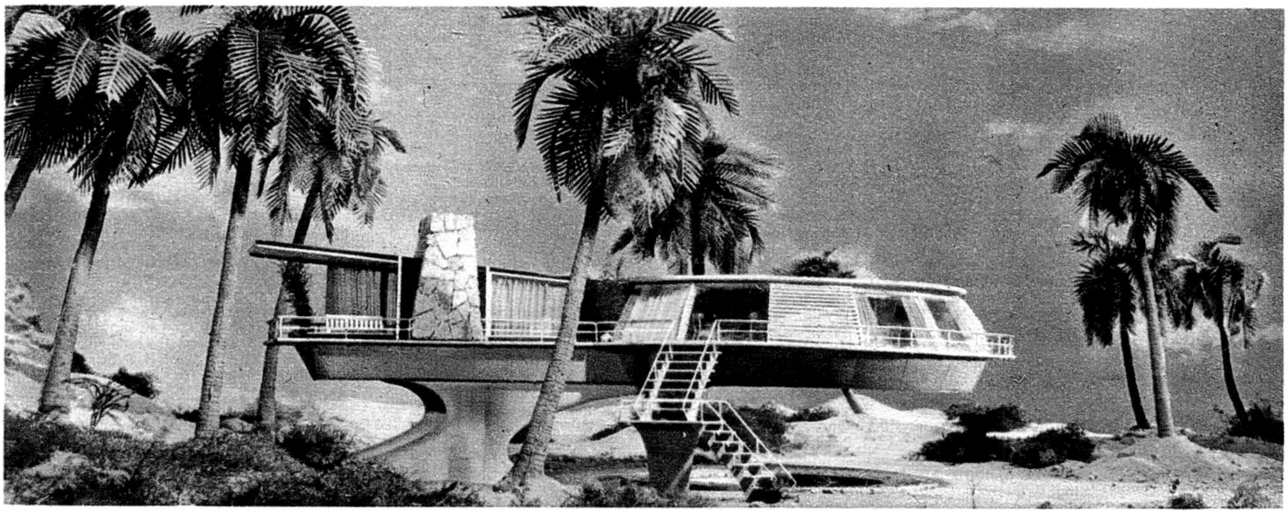

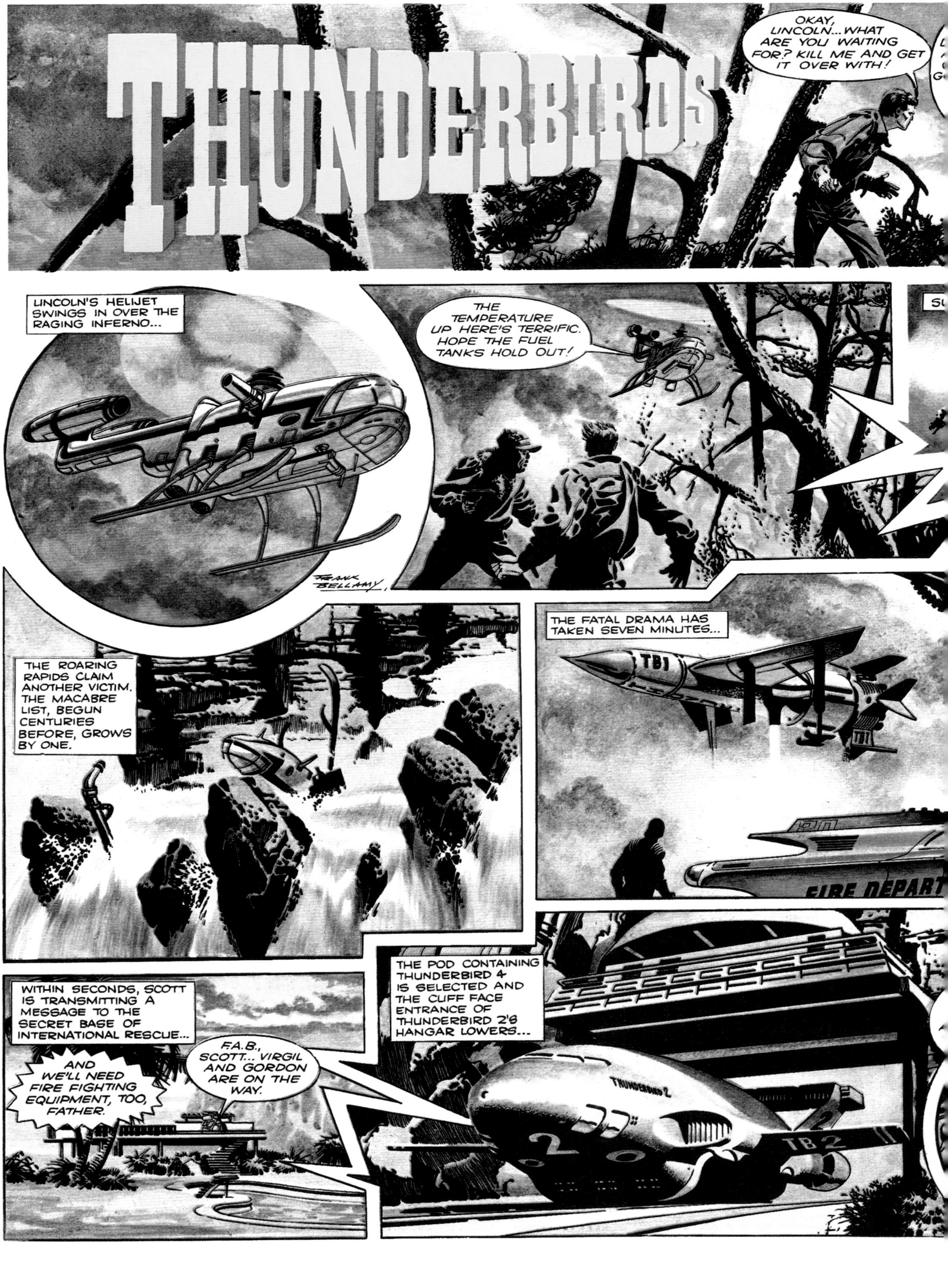
THUNDERBIRDS
OKAY, LINCOLN... WHAT ARE YOU WAITING FOR? KILL ME AND GET IT OVER WITH!
LINCOLN'S HELIJET SWINGS IN OVER THE RAGING INFERNO...
THE TEMPERATURE UP HERE'S TERRIFIC. HOPE THE FUEL TANKS HOLD OUT!
FRANK BELLAMY
THE ROARING RAPIDS CLAIM ANOTHER VICTIM. THE MACABRE LIST, BEGUN CENTURIES BEFORE, GROWS BY ONE.
THE FATAL DRAMA HAS TAKEN SEVEN MINUTES...
TB1
WITHIN SECONDS, SCOTT IS TRANSMITTING A MESSAGE TO THE SECRET BASE OF INTERNATIONAL RESCUE...
AND WE'LL NEED FIRE FIGHTING EQUIPMENT, TOO, FATHER.
F.A.B., SCOTT... VIRGIL AND GORDON ARE ON THE WAY.
THE POD CONTAINING THUNDERBIRD 4 IS SELECTED AND THE CLIFF FACE ENTRANCE OF THUNDERBIRD 2'S HANGAR LOWERS...
THUNDERBIRD 2
TB2

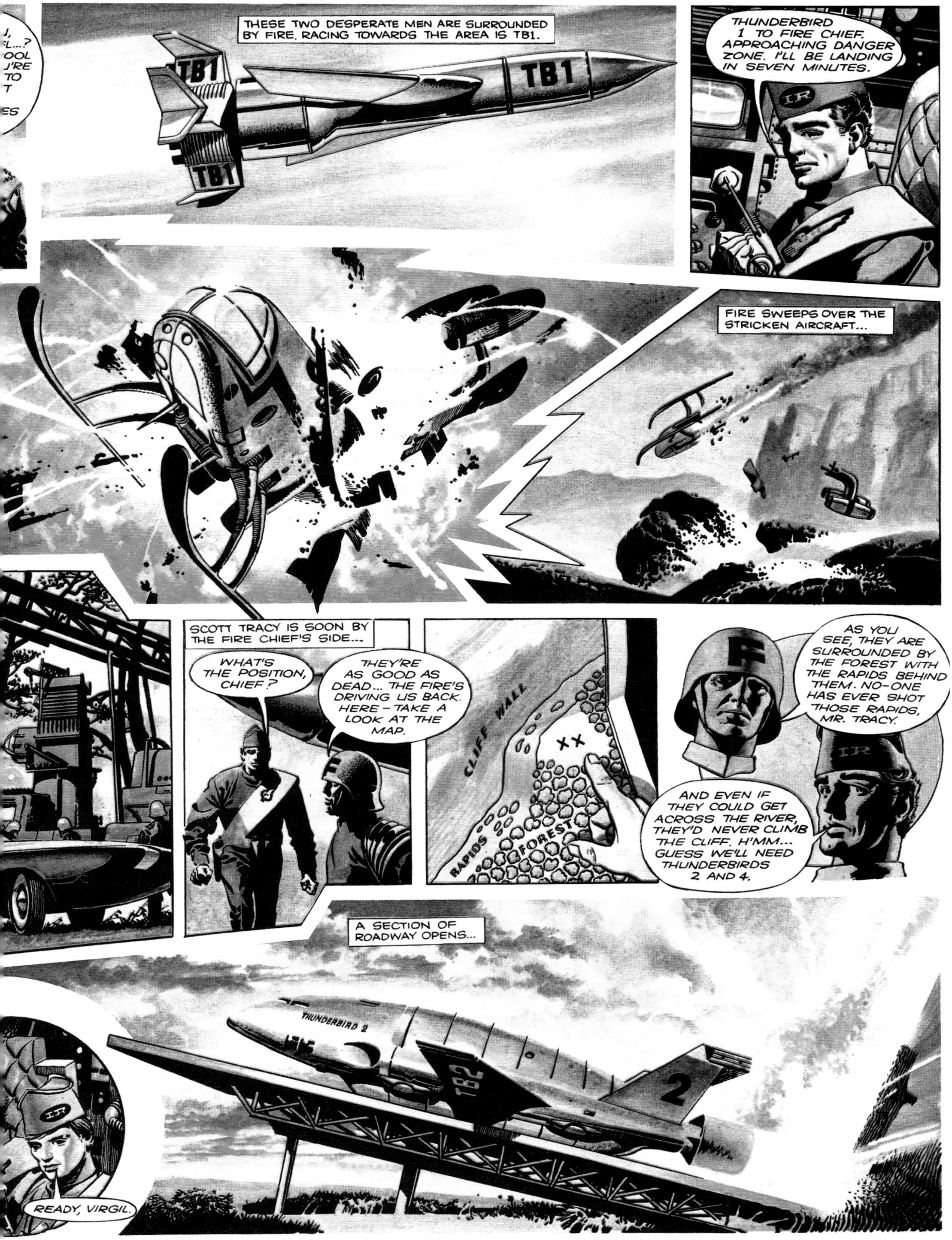
THESE TWO DESPERATE MEN ARE SURROUNDED BY FIRE. RACING TOWARDS THE AREA IS TB1.
TB1
TB1
TB1
THUNDERBIRD 1 TO FIRE CHIEF. APPROACHING DANGER ZONE. I'LL BE LANDING IN SEVEN MINUTES.
FIRE SWEEPS OVER THE STRICKEN AIRCRAFT...
SCOTT TRACY IS SOON BY THE FIRE CHIEF'S SIDE...
WHAT'S THE POSITION, CHIEF?
THEY'RE AS GOOD AS DEAD... THE FIRE'S DRIVING US BACK. HERE - TAKE A LOOK AT THE MAP.
CLIFF WALL
RAPIDS
FOREST
AS YOU SEE, THEY ARE SURROUNDED BY THE FOREST WITH THE RAPIDS BEHIND THEM. NO-ONE HAS EVER SHOT THOSE RAPIDS, MR. TRACY.
AND EVEN IF THEY COULD GET ACROSS THE RIVER, THEY'D NEVER CLIMB THE CLIFF. H'MM... GUESS WE'LL NEED THUNDERBIRDS 2 AND 4.
A SECTION OF ROADWAY OPENS...
THUNDERBIRD 2
TB2
2
READY, VIRGIL.

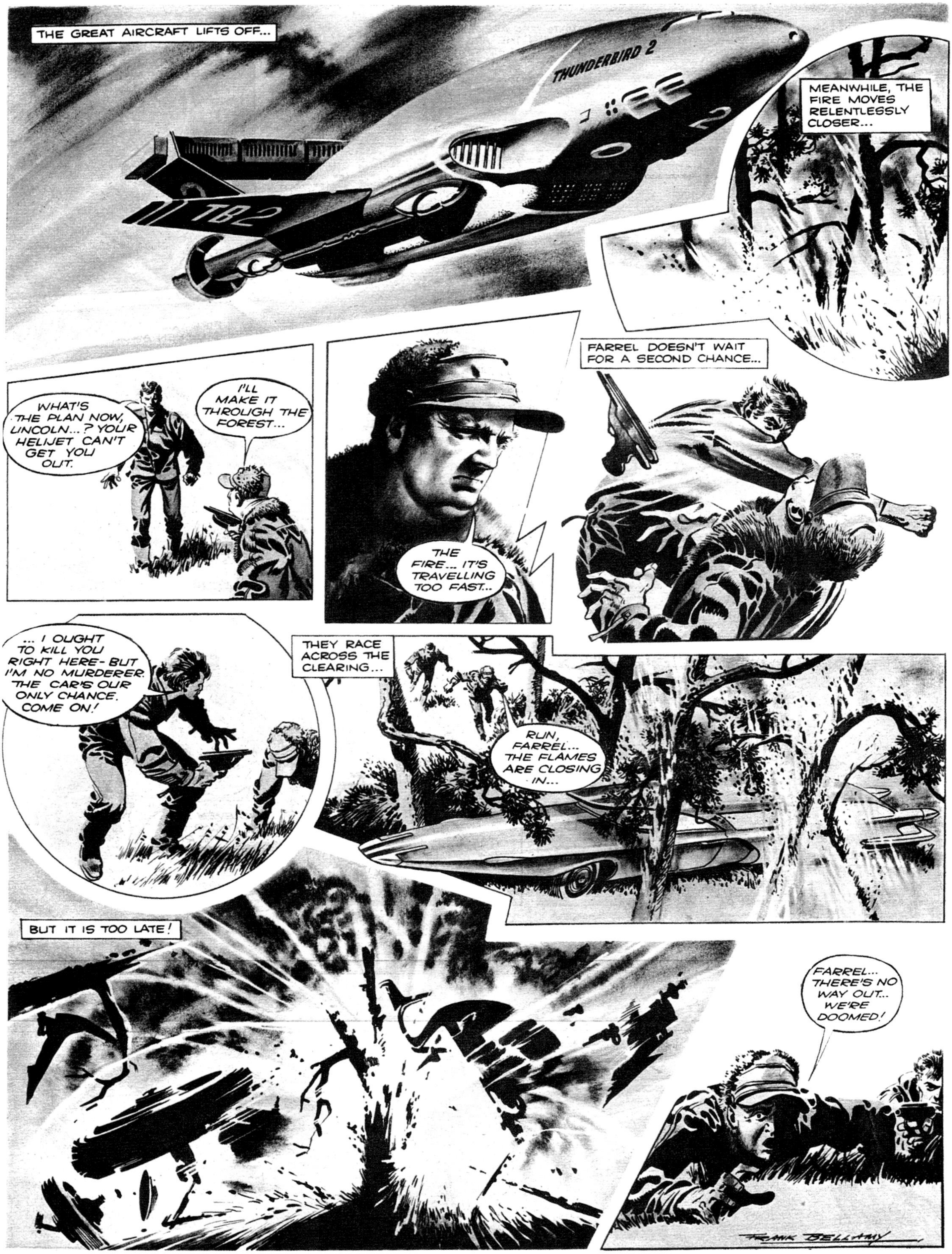

THE GREAT AIRCRAFT LIFTS OFF...
THUNDERBIRD 2
TB2
MEANWHILE, THE FIRE MOVES RELENTLESSLY CLOSER...
WHAT'S THE PLAN NOW, LINCOLN...? YOUR HELIJET CAN'T GET YOU OUT.
I'LL MAKE IT THROUGH THE FOREST...
THE FIRE... IT'S TRAVELLING TOO FAST...
FARREL DOESN'T WAIT FOR A SECOND CHANCE...
... I OUGHT TO KILL YOU RIGHT HERE- BUT I'M NO MURDERER. THE CAR'S OUR ONLY CHANCE. COME ON!
THEY RACE ACROSS THE CLEARING...
RUN, FARREL... THE FLAMES ARE CLOSING IN...
BUT IT IS TOO LATE!
FARREL... THERE'S NO WAY OUT... WE'RE DOOMED!
FRANK BELLAMY

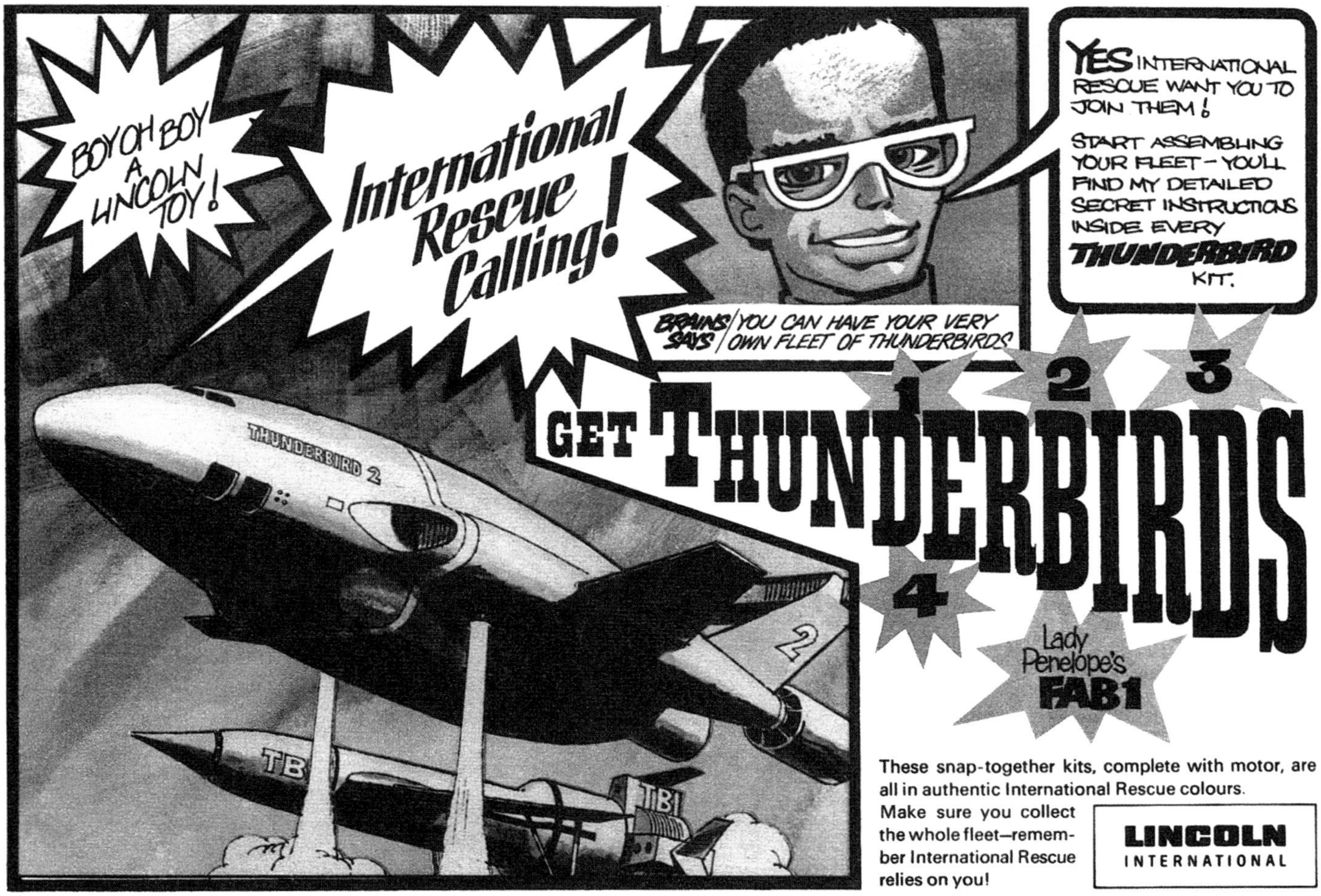

BOY OH BOY A LINCOLN TOY!
International Rescue Calling!
YES INTERNATIONAL RESCUE WANT YOU TO JOIN THEM!
START ASSEMBLING YOUR FLEET – YOU'LL FIND MY DETAILED SECRET INSTRUCTIONS INSIDE EVERY THUNDERBIRD KIT.
BRAINS SAYS YOU CAN HAVE YOUR VERY OWN FLEET OF THUNDERBIRDS
THUNDERBIRD 2
TB1
GET THUNDERBIRDS
1 2 3 4
Lady Penelope's FAB1
These snap-together kits, complete with motor, are all in authentic International Rescue colours.
Make sure you collect the whole fleet—remember International Rescue relies on you!
LINCOLN INTERNATIONAL

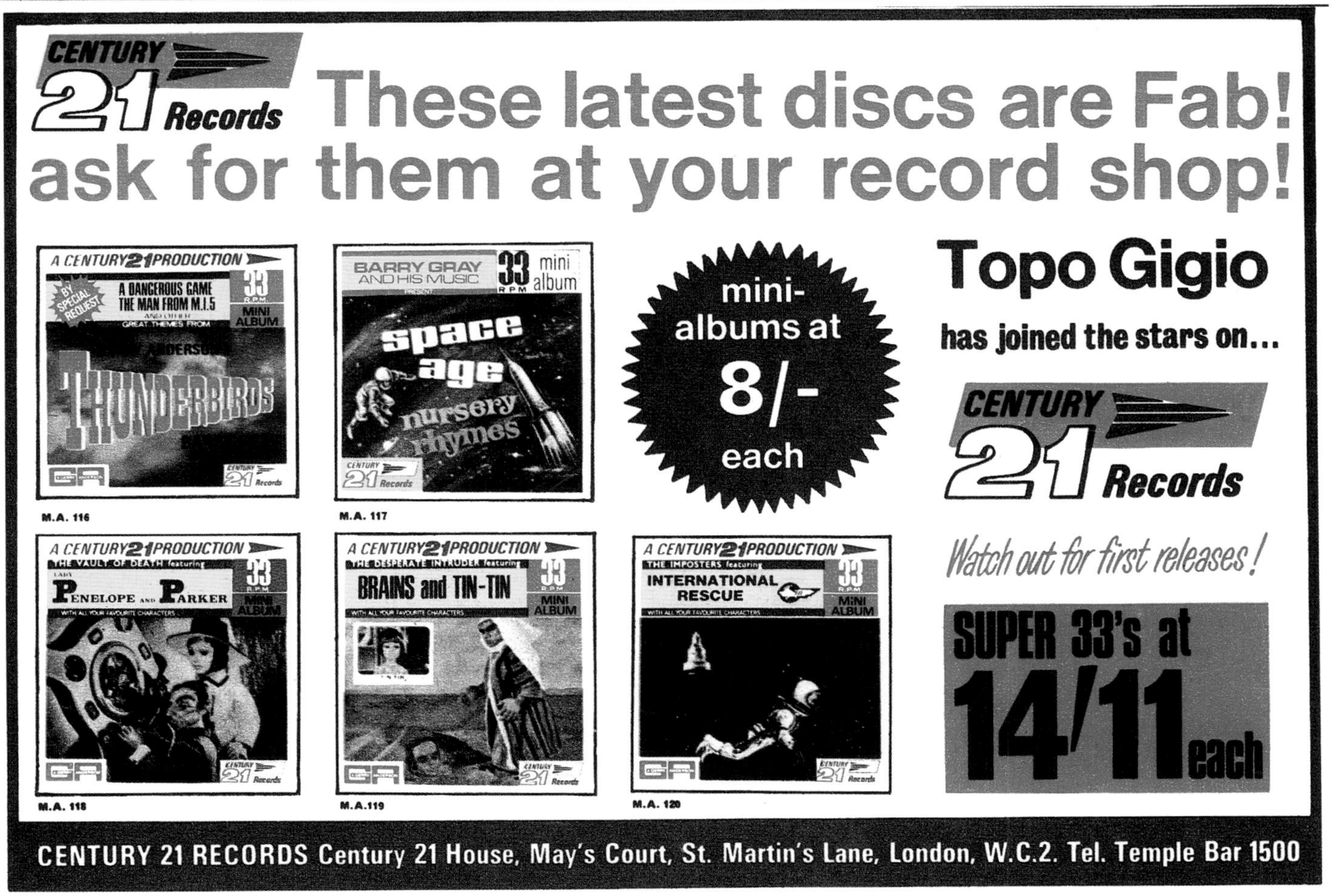

CENTURY 21 Records
These latest discs are Fab! ask for them at your record shop!
A CENTURY 21 PRODUCTION
BY SPECIAL REQUEST
A DANGEROUS GAME THE MAN FROM M.I.5 AND OTHER GREAT THEMES FROM
THUNDERBIRDS
33 R.P.M. MINI ALBUM
M.A. 116
BARRY GRAY AND HIS MUSIC
33 RPM mini album
space age nursery rhymes
M.A. 117
mini-albums at 8/- each
Topo Gigio
has joined the stars on...
CENTURY 21 Records
Watch out for first releases!
SUPER 33's at 14/11 each
THE VAULT OF DEATH featuring LADY PENELOPE AND PARKER
WITH ALL YOUR FAVOURITE CHARACTERS
M.A. 118
THE DESPERATE INTRUDER featuring BRAINS and TIN-TIN
M.A.119
THE IMPOSTERS featuring INTERNATIONAL RESCUE
M.A. 120
CENTURY 21 RECORDS Century 21 House, May's Court, St. Martin's Lane, London, W.C.2. Tel. Temple Bar 1500

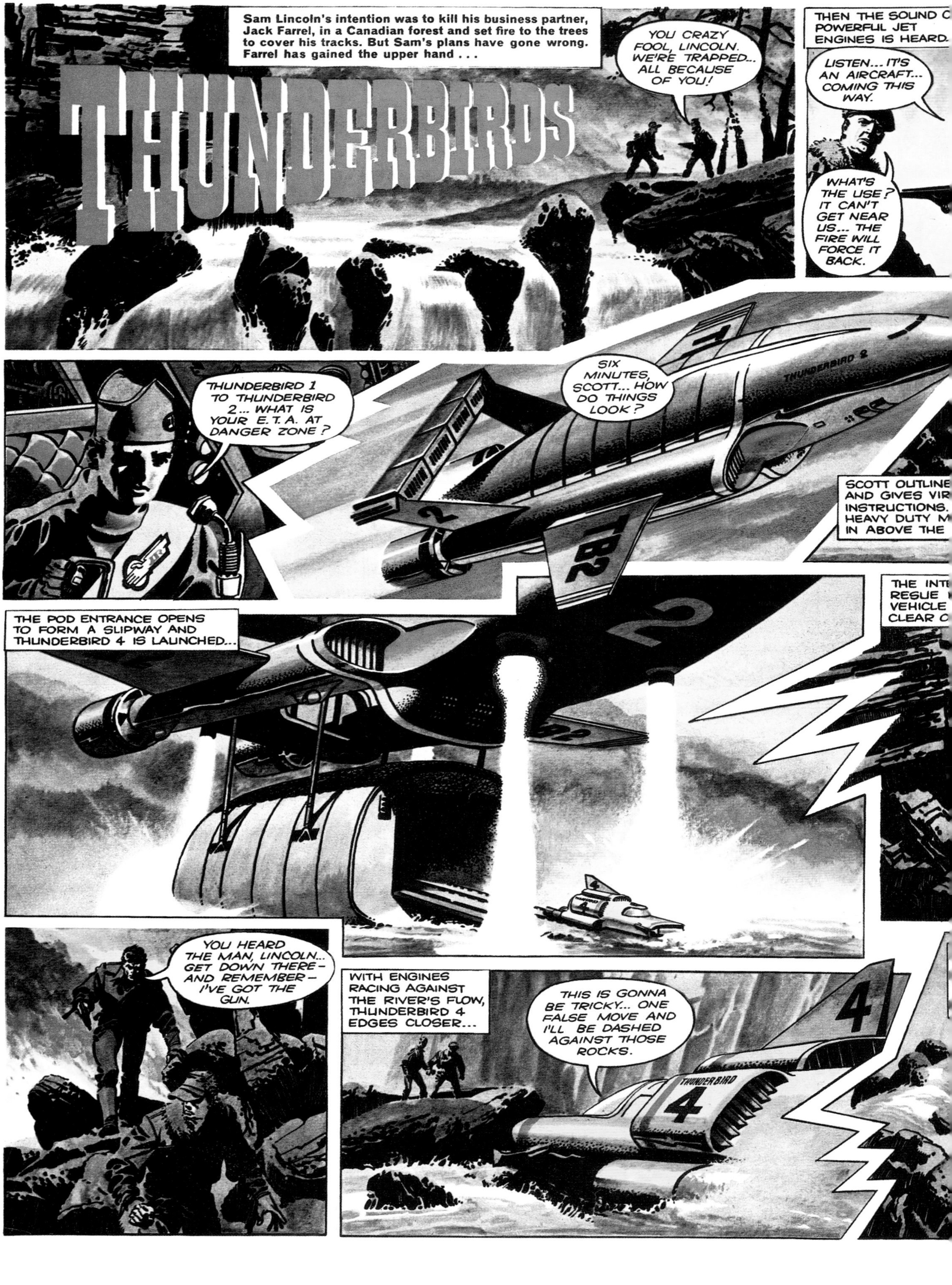

Sam Lincoln's intention was to kill his business partner, Jack Farrel, in a Canadian forest and set fire to the trees to cover his tracks. But Sam's plans have gone wrong. Farrel has gained the upper hand . . .
THUNDERBIRDS
YOU CRAZY FOOL, LINCOLN. WE'RE TRAPPED... ALL BECAUSE OF YOU!
THEN THE SOUND O
POWERFUL JET
ENGINES IS HEARD.
LISTEN... IT'S AN AIRCRAFT... COMING THIS WAY.
WHAT'S THE USE? IT CAN'T GET NEAR US... THE FIRE WILL FORCE IT BACK.
THUNDERBIRD 1 TO THUNDERBIRD 2... WHAT IS YOUR E.T.A. AT DANGER ZONE?
SIX MINUTES, SCOTT... HOW DO THINGS LOOK?
SCOTT OUTLINE
AND GIVES VIR
INSTRUCTIONS.
HEAVY DUTY M
IN ABOVE THE
THE POD ENTRANCE OPENS TO FORM A SLIPWAY AND THUNDERBIRD 4 IS LAUNCHED...
THE INT
RESUE
VEHICLE
CLEAR O
YOU HEARD THE MAN, LINCOLN... GET DOWN THERE– AND REMEMBER– I'VE GOT THE GUN.
WITH ENGINES RACING AGAINST THE RIVER'S FLOW, THUNDERBIRD 4 EDGES CLOSER...
THIS IS GONNA BE TRICKY... ONE FALSE MOVE AND I'LL BE DASHED AGAINST THOSE ROCKS.

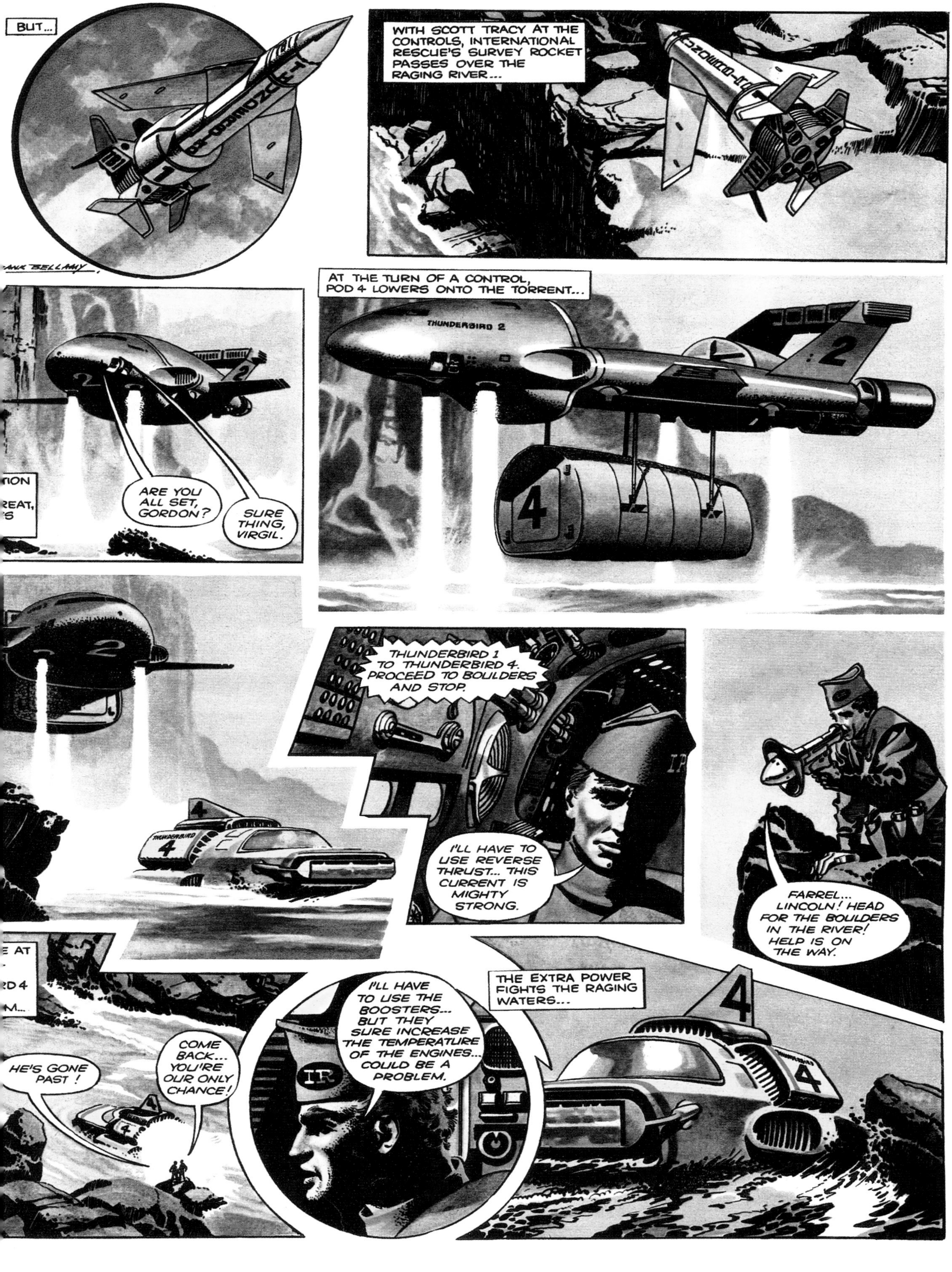
BUT...
WITH SCOTT TRACY AT THE CONTROLS, INTERNATIONAL RESCUE'S SURVEY ROCKET PASSES OVER THE RAGING RIVER...
ARE YOU ALL SET, GORDON?
SURE THING, VIRGIL.
AT THE TURN OF A CONTROL, POD 4 LOWERS ONTO THE TORRENT...
THUNDERBIRD 2
THUNDERBIRD 1 TO THUNDERBIRD 4. PROCEED TO BOULDERS AND STOP.
I'LL HAVE TO USE REVERSE THRUST... THIS CURRENT IS MIGHTY STRONG.
FARREL... LINCOLN! HEAD FOR THE BOULDERS IN THE RIVER! HELP IS ON THE WAY.
HE'S GONE PAST!
COME BACK... YOU'RE OUR ONLY CHANCE!
I'LL HAVE TO USE THE BOOSTERS... BUT THEY SURE INCREASE THE TEMPERATURE OF THE ENGINES... COULD BE A PROBLEM.
THE EXTRA POWER FIGHTS THE RAGING WATERS...

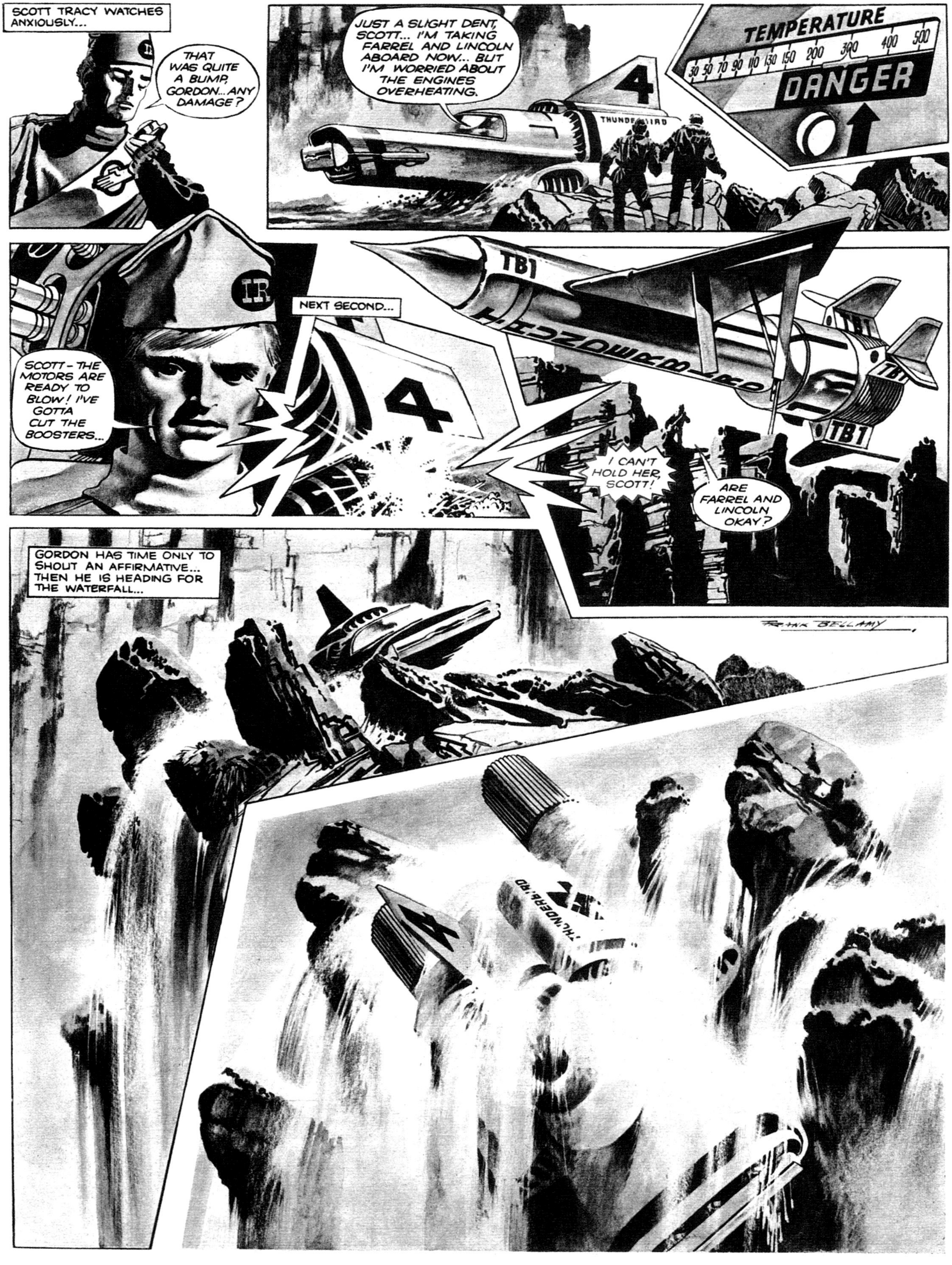
SCOTT TRACY WATCHES ANXIOUSLY...
THAT WAS QUITE A BUMP, GORDON... ANY DAMAGE?
JUST A SLIGHT DENT, SCOTT... I'M TAKING FARREL AND LINCOLN ABOARD NOW... BUT I'M WORRIED ABOUT THE ENGINES OVERHEATING.
TEMPERATURE
30 50 70 90 110 130 150 200 300 400 500
DANGER
NEXT SECOND...
SCOTT - THE MOTORS ARE READY TO BLOW! I'VE GOTTA CUT THE BOOSTERS...
TB1
I CAN'T HOLD HER, SCOTT!
ARE FARREL AND LINCOLN OKAY?
GORDON HAS TIME ONLY TO SHOUT AN AFFIRMATIVE... THEN HE IS HEADING FOR THE WATERFALL...
FRANK BELLAMY

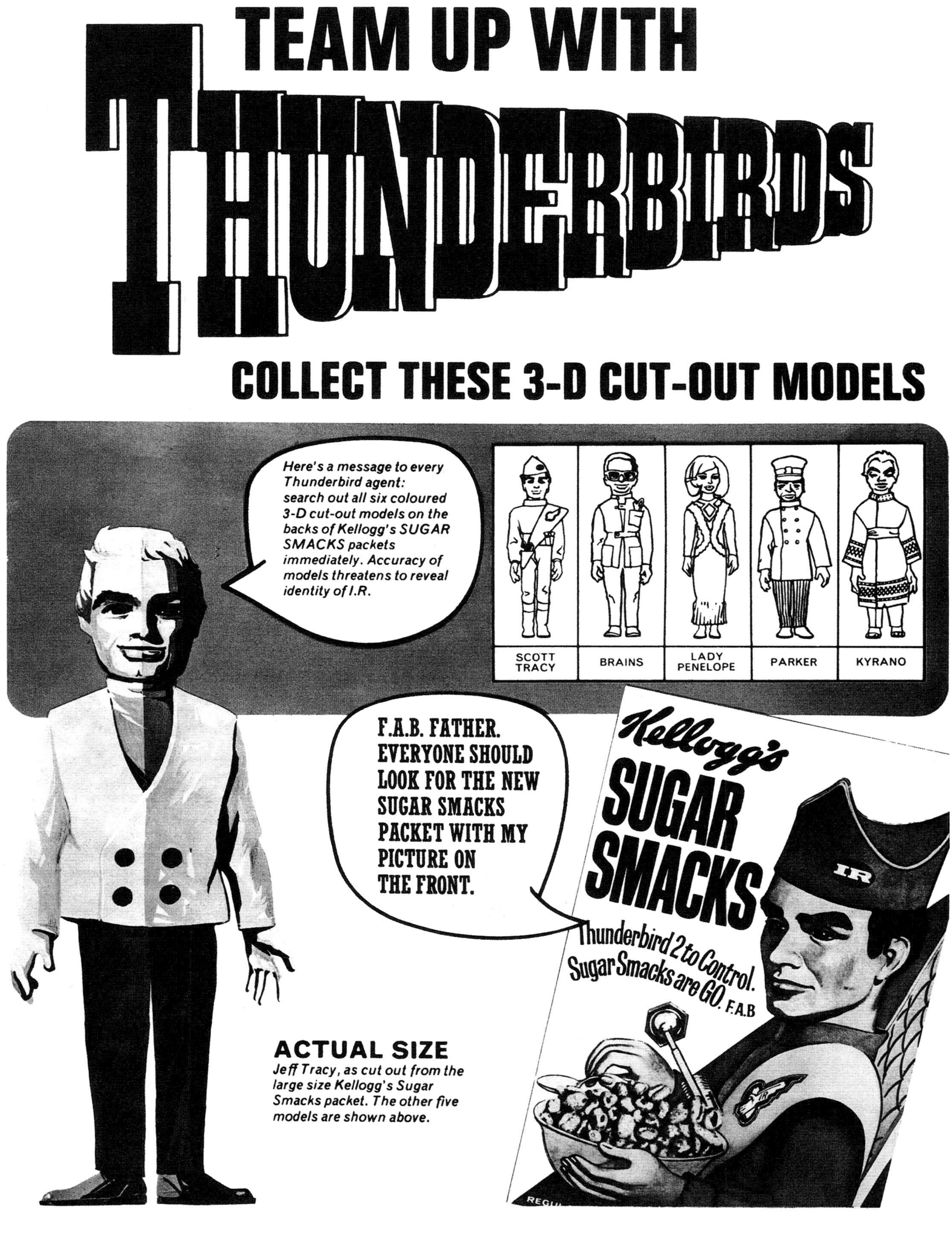
TEAM UP WITH
THUNDERBIRDS
COLLECT THESE 3-D CUT-OUT MODELS
Here's a message to every Thunderbird agent: search out all six coloured 3-D cut-out models on the backs of Kellogg's SUGAR SMACKS packets immediately. Accuracy of models threatens to reveal identity of I.R.
SCOTT TRACY
BRAINS
LADY PENELOPE
PARKER
KYRANO
F.A.B. FATHER. EVERYONE SHOULD LOOK FOR THE NEW SUGAR SMACKS PACKET WITH MY PICTURE ON THE FRONT.
Kellogg's
SUGAR SMACKS
Thunderbird 2 to Control. Sugar Smacks are GO. F.A.B
IR
ACTUAL SIZE
Jeff Tracy, as cut out from the large size Kellogg's Sugar Smacks packet. The other five models are shown above.

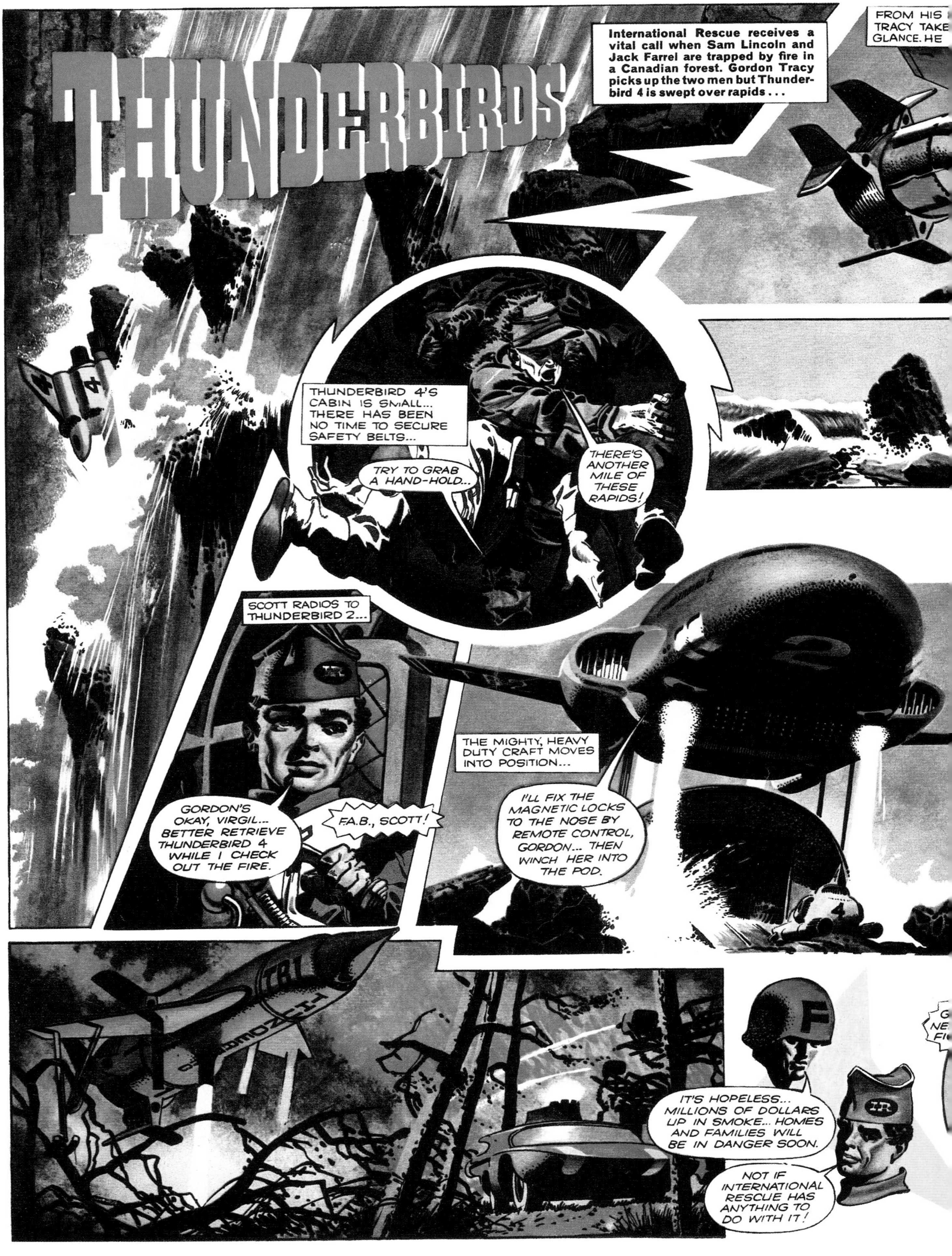
THUNDERBIRDS
International Rescue receives a vital call when Sam Lincoln and Jack Farrel are trapped by fire in a Canadian forest. Gordon Tracy picks up the two men but Thunderbird 4 is swept over rapids . . .
THUNDERBIRD 4'S CABIN IS SMALL... THERE HAS BEEN NO TIME TO SECURE SAFETY BELTS...
TRY TO GRAB A HAND-HOLD...
THERE'S ANOTHER MILE OF THESE RAPIDS!
SCOTT RADIOS TO THUNDERBIRD 2...
GORDON'S OKAY, VIRGIL... BETTER RETRIEVE THUNDERBIRD 4 WHILE I CHECK OUT THE FIRE.
F.A.B., SCOTT!
THE MIGHTY, HEAVY DUTY CRAFT MOVES INTO POSITION...
I'LL FIX THE MAGNETIC LOCKS TO THE NOSE BY REMOTE CONTROL, GORDON... THEN WINCH HER INTO THE POD.
IT'S HOPELESS... MILLIONS OF DOLLARS UP IN SMOKE... HOMES AND FAMILIES WILL BE IN DANGER SOON.
NOT IF INTERNATIONAL RESCUE HAS ANYTHING TO DO WITH IT!

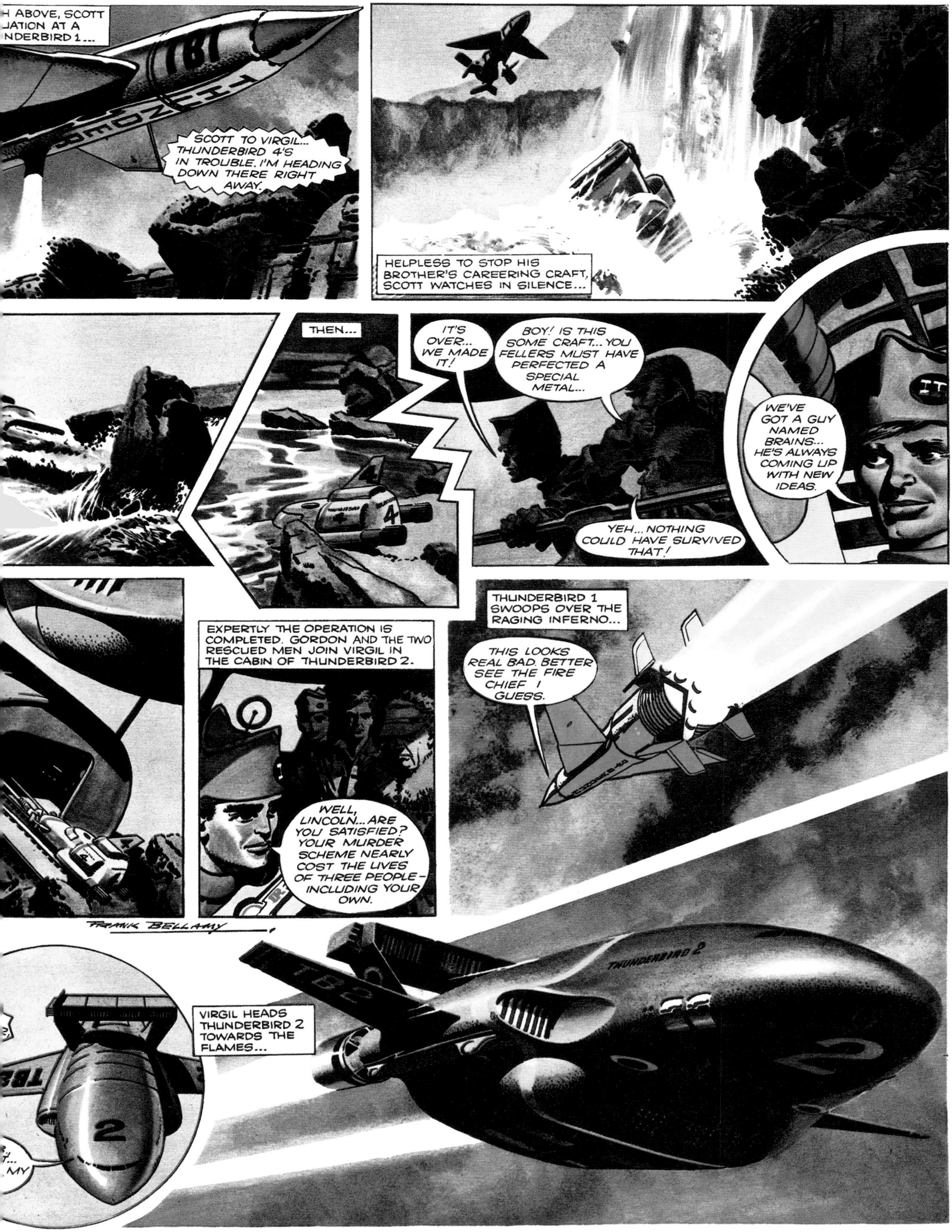

H ABOVE, SCOTT
UATION AT A
NDERBIRD 1...
SCOTT TO VIRGIL... THUNDERBIRD 4'S IN TROUBLE. I'M HEADING DOWN THERE RIGHT AWAY.
HELPLESS TO STOP HIS BROTHER'S CAREERING CRAFT, SCOTT WATCHES IN SILENCE...
THEN...
IT'S OVER... WE MADE IT!
BOY! IS THIS SOME CRAFT... YOU FELLERS MUST HAVE PERFECTED A SPECIAL METAL...
YEH... NOTHING COULD HAVE SURVIVED THAT!
WE'VE GOT A GUY NAMED BRAINS... HE'S ALWAYS COMING UP WITH NEW IDEAS.
EXPERTLY THE OPERATION IS COMPLETED. GORDON AND THE TWO RESCUED MEN JOIN VIRGIL IN THE CABIN OF THUNDERBIRD 2.
WELL, LINCOLN... ARE YOU SATISFIED? YOUR MURDER SCHEME NEARLY COST THE LIVES OF THREE PEOPLE - INCLUDING YOUR OWN.
THUNDERBIRD 1 SWOOPS OVER THE RAGING INFERNO...
THIS LOOKS REAL BAD. BETTER SEE THE FIRE CHIEF I GUESS.
FRANK BELLAMY
VIRGIL HEADS THUNDERBIRD 2 TOWARDS THE FLAMES...

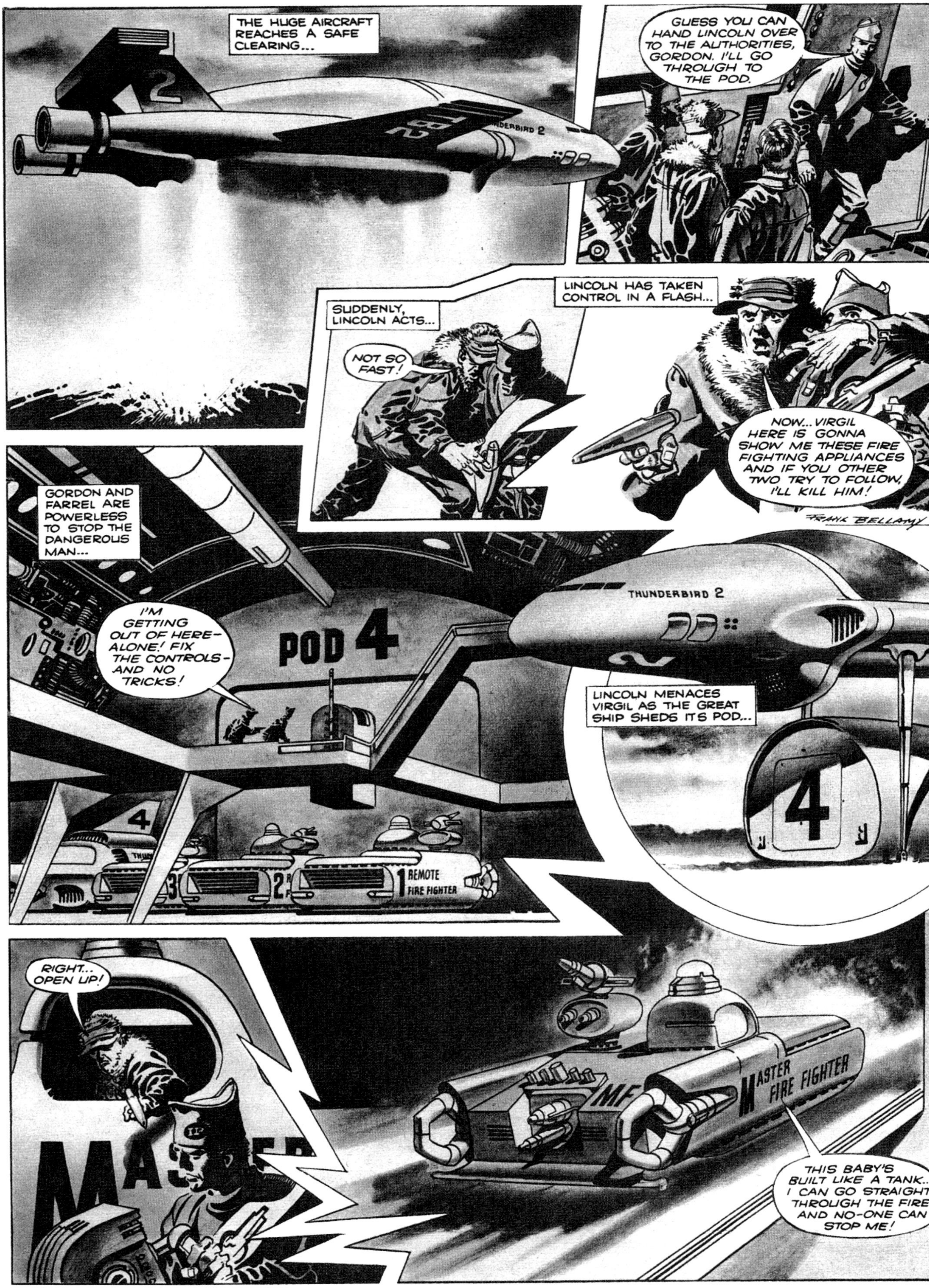

THE HUGE AIRCRAFT REACHES A SAFE CLEARING...
THUNDERBIRD 2
GUESS YOU CAN HAND LINCOLN OVER TO THE AUTHORITIES, GORDON. I'LL GO THROUGH TO THE POD.
SUDDENLY, LINCOLN ACTS...
NOT SO FAST!
LINCOLN HAS TAKEN CONTROL IN A FLASH...
NOW... VIRGIL HERE IS GONNA SHOW ME THESE FIRE FIGHTING APPLIANCES AND IF YOU OTHER TWO TRY TO FOLLOW, I'LL KILL HIM!
FRANK BELLAMY
GORDON AND FARREL ARE POWERLESS TO STOP THE DANGEROUS MAN...
POD 4
I'M GETTING OUT OF HERE– ALONE! FIX THE CONTROLS– AND NO TRICKS!
REMOTE FIRE FIGHTER
THUNDERBIRD 2
LINCOLN MENACES VIRGIL AS THE GREAT SHIP SHEDS ITS POD...
RIGHT... OPEN UP!
MASTER FIRE FIGHTER
THIS BABY'S BUILT LIKE A TANK... I CAN GO STRAIGHT THROUGH THE FIRE... AND NO-ONE CAN STOP ME!

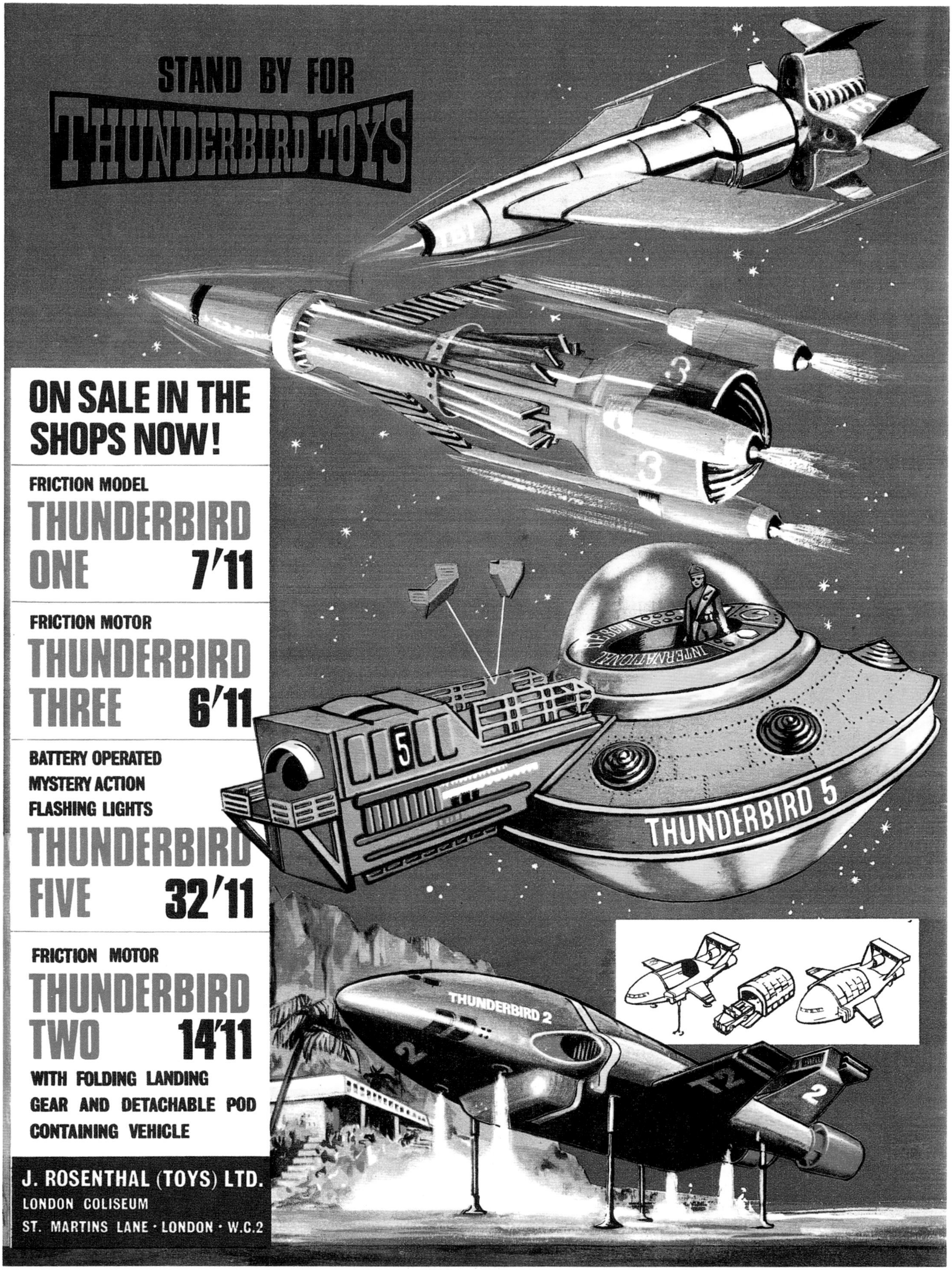

STAND BY FOR
THUNDERBIRD TOYS
ON SALE IN THE SHOPS NOW!
FRICTION MODEL
THUNDERBIRD ONE 7'11
FRICTION MOTOR
THUNDERBIRD THREE 6'11
BATTERY OPERATED
MYSTERY ACTION
FLASHING LIGHTS
THUNDERBIRD FIVE 32'11
FRICTION MOTOR
THUNDERBIRD TWO 14'11
WITH FOLDING LANDING GEAR AND DETACHABLE POD CONTAINING VEHICLE
J. ROSENTHAL (TOYS) LTD.
LONDON COLISEUM
ST. MARTINS LANE · LONDON · W.C.2
THUNDERBIRD 5
THUNDERBIRD 2

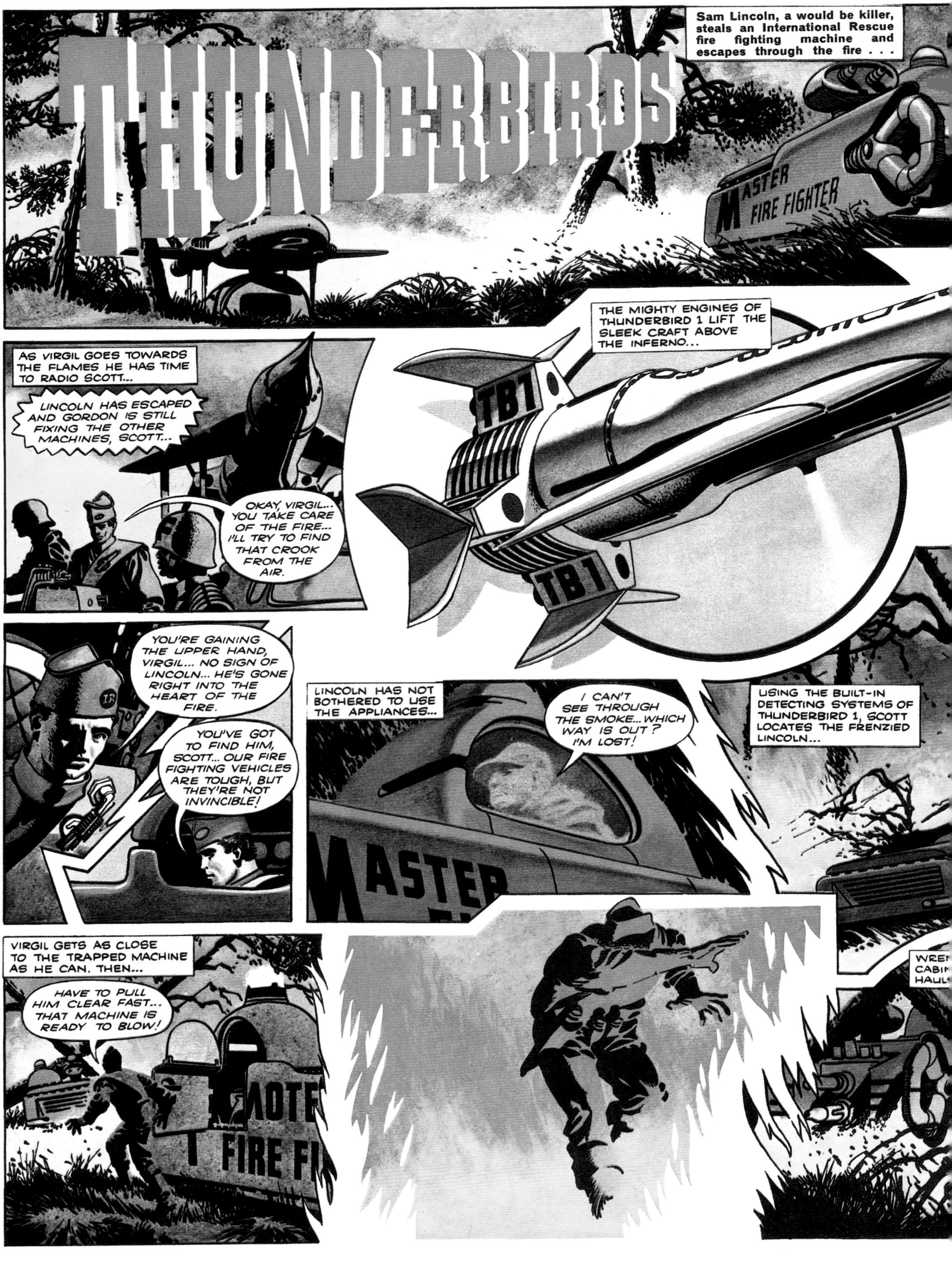

THUNDERBIRDS
Sam Lincoln, a would be killer, steals an International Rescue fire fighting machine and escapes through the fire . . .
MASTER FIRE FIGHTER
AS VIRGIL GOES TOWARDS THE FLAMES HE HAS TIME TO RADIO SCOTT...
LINCOLN HAS ESCAPED AND GORDON IS STILL FIXING THE OTHER MACHINES, SCOTT...
OKAY, VIRGIL... YOU TAKE CARE OF THE FIRE... I'LL TRY TO FIND THAT CROOK FROM THE AIR.
THE MIGHTY ENGINES OF THUNDERBIRD 1 LIFT THE SLEEK CRAFT ABOVE THE INFERNO...
TB1
TB1
YOU'RE GAINING THE UPPER HAND, VIRGIL... NO SIGN OF LINCOLN... HE'S GONE RIGHT INTO THE HEART OF THE FIRE.
YOU'VE GOT TO FIND HIM, SCOTT... OUR FIRE FIGHTING VEHICLES ARE TOUGH, BUT THEY'RE NOT INVINCIBLE!
LINCOLN HAS NOT BOTHERED TO USE THE APPLIANCES...
I CAN'T SEE THROUGH THE SMOKE... WHICH WAY IS OUT? I'M LOST!
MASTER
USING THE BUILT-IN DETECTING SYSTEMS OF THUNDERBIRD 1, SCOTT LOCATES THE FRENZIED LINCOLN...
VIRGIL GETS AS CLOSE TO THE TRAPPED MACHINE AS HE CAN. THEN...
HAVE TO PULL HIM CLEAR FAST... THAT MACHINE IS READY TO BLOW!
FIRE FI

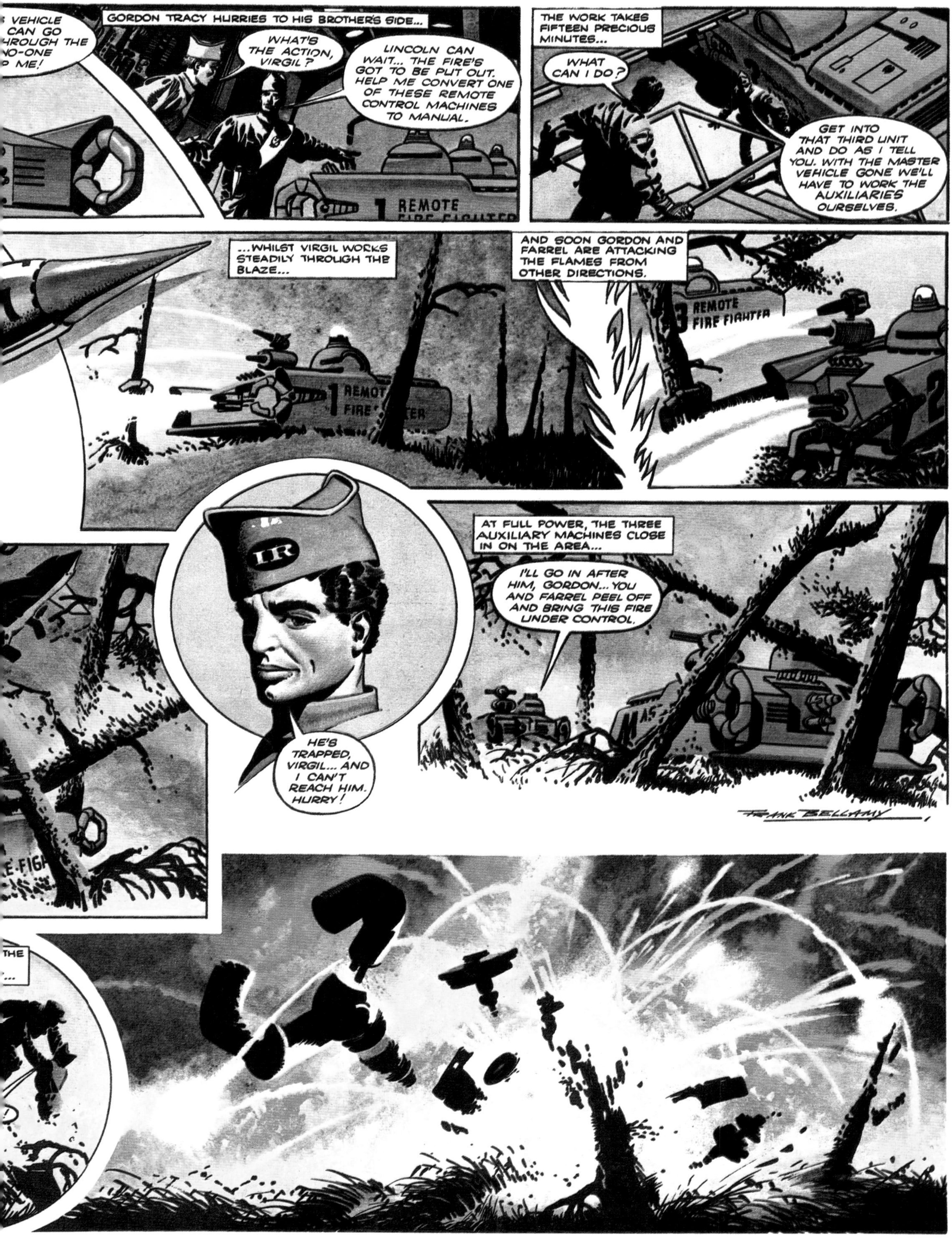

GORDON TRACY HURRIES TO HIS BROTHER'S SIDE...
WHAT'S THE ACTION, VIRGIL?
LINCOLN CAN WAIT... THE FIRE'S GOT TO BE PUT OUT. HELP ME CONVERT ONE OF THESE REMOTE CONTROL MACHINES TO MANUAL.
1 REMOTE
THE WORK TAKES FIFTEEN PRECIOUS MINUTES...
WHAT CAN I DO?
GET INTO THAT THIRD UNIT AND DO AS I TELL YOU. WITH THE MASTER VEHICLE GONE WE'LL HAVE TO WORK THE AUXILIARIES OURSELVES.
...WHILST VIRGIL WORKS STEADILY THROUGH THE BLAZE...
AND SOON GORDON AND FARREL ARE ATTACKING THE FLAMES FROM OTHER DIRECTIONS.
3 REMOTE FIRE FIGHTER
IR
HE'S TRAPPED, VIRGIL... AND I CAN'T REACH HIM. HURRY!
AT FULL POWER, THE THREE AUXILIARY MACHINES CLOSE IN ON THE AREA...
I'LL GO IN AFTER HIM, GORDON... YOU AND FARREL PEEL OFF AND BRING THIS FIRE UNDER CONTROL.
FRANK BELLAMY

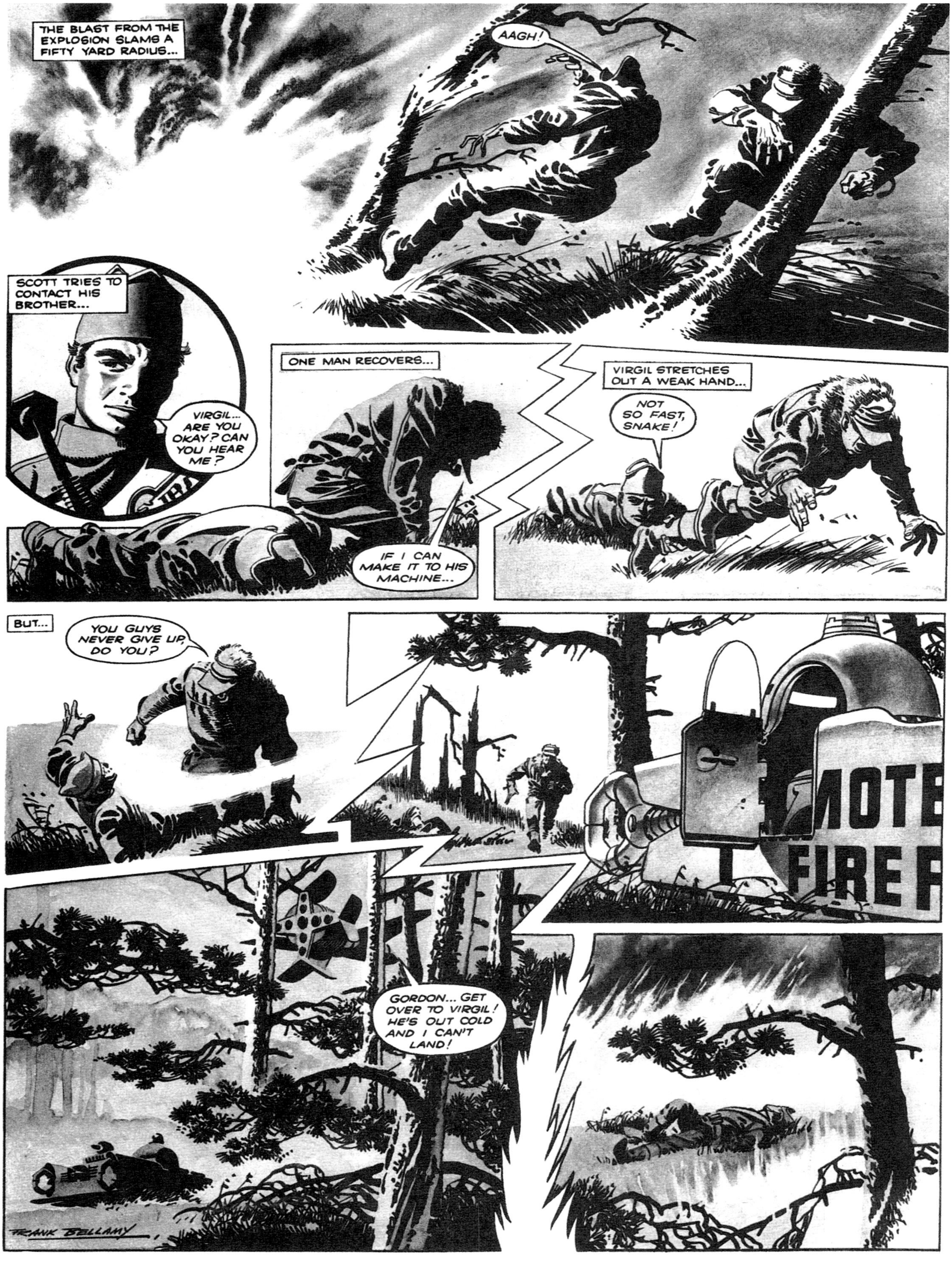
THE BLAST FROM THE EXPLOSION SLAMS A FIFTY YARD RADIUS...
AAGH!
SCOTT TRIES TO CONTACT HIS BROTHER...
VIRGIL... ARE YOU OKAY? CAN YOU HEAR ME?
ONE MAN RECOVERS...
IF I CAN MAKE IT TO HIS MACHINE...
VIRGIL STRETCHES OUT A WEAK HAND...
NOT SO FAST, SNAKE!
BUT...
YOU GUYS NEVER GIVE UP, DO YOU?
MOTE
FIRE F
GORDON... GET OVER TO VIRGIL! HE'S OUT COLD AND I CAN'T LAND!
FRANK BELLAMY

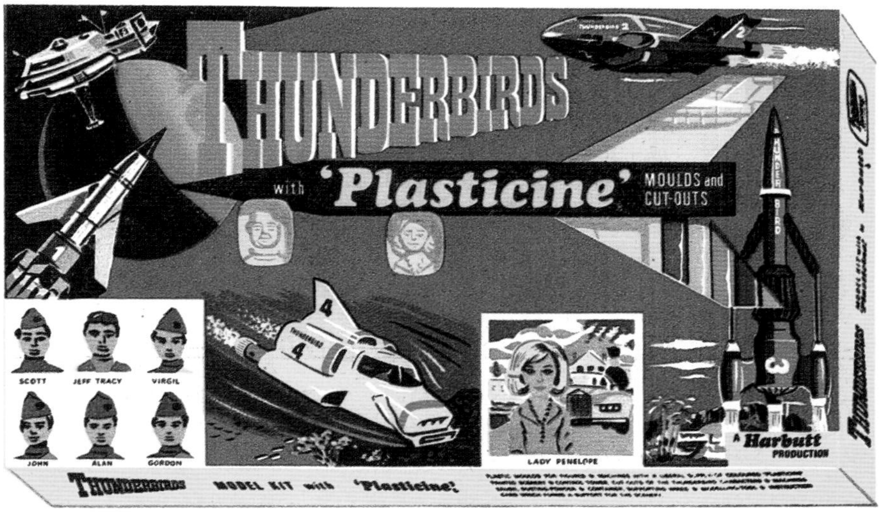
THUNDERBIRDS
with 'Plasticine' MOULDS and CUT-OUTS
SCOTT
JEFF TRACY
VIRGIL
JOHN
ALAN
GORDON
LADY PENELOPE
A Harbutt PRODUCTION
THUNDERBIRDS MODEL KIT with 'Plasticine'

MAKE YOUR OWN 'THUNDERBIRDS' IN

Plasticine®

The amazing TV exploits of 'THUNDERBIRDS' (The A.P. Films Ltd. production) can be recaptured with this entirely new model outfit. The attractive box contains 'Plasticine' the world-famous modelling material, moulds, realistic scenery and cut outs. Price 10/6 (U.K.). Obtainable at all good stores, toy shops, etc.

Sole Manufacturer **HARBUTT'S PLASTICINE LTD.**, BATHAMPTON, BATH, SOMERSET

NOW IN ORBIT!

3 GREAT NEW MINI-ALBUMS
PLUS
2 FAB SUPER 33's.

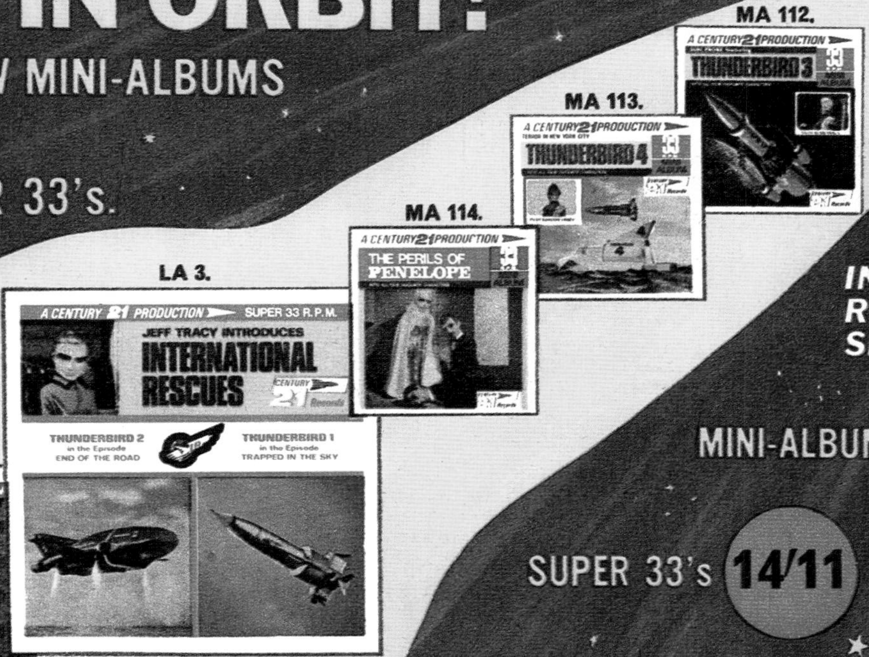
MA 112.
A CENTURY 21 PRODUCTION
THUNDERBIRD 3
MA 113.
A CENTURY 21 PRODUCTION
THUNDERBIRD 4
MA 114.
A CENTURY 21 PRODUCTION
THE PERILS OF PENELOPE
LA 3.
A CENTURY 21 PRODUCTION SUPER 33 R.P.M.
JEFF TRACY INTRODUCES
INTERNATIONAL RESCUES
THUNDERBIRD 2 in the Episode END OF THE ROAD
THUNDERBIRD 1 in the Episode TRAPPED IN THE SKY

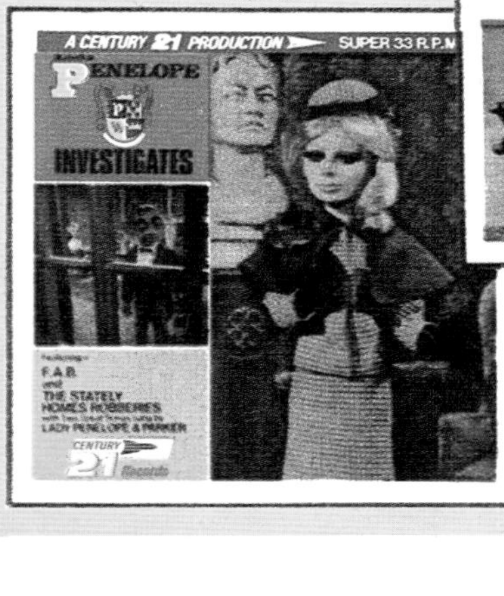
LA 4.
A CENTURY 21 PRODUCTION SUPER 33 R.P.M.
PENELOPE
INVESTIGATES

IN YOUR RECORD SHOPS NOW

MINI-ALBUMS 8/-

SUPER 33's 14/11

ADVENTURE! INTRIGUE! DRAMA!

"Watch out for new release December 2nd"

CENTURY 21 Records

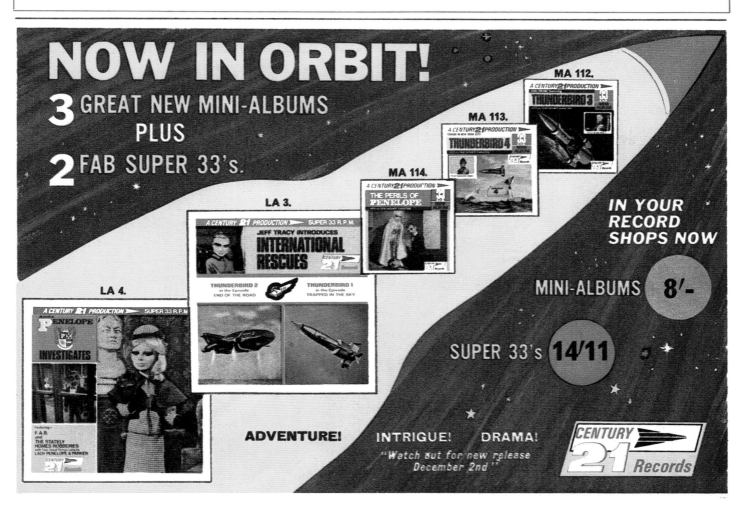

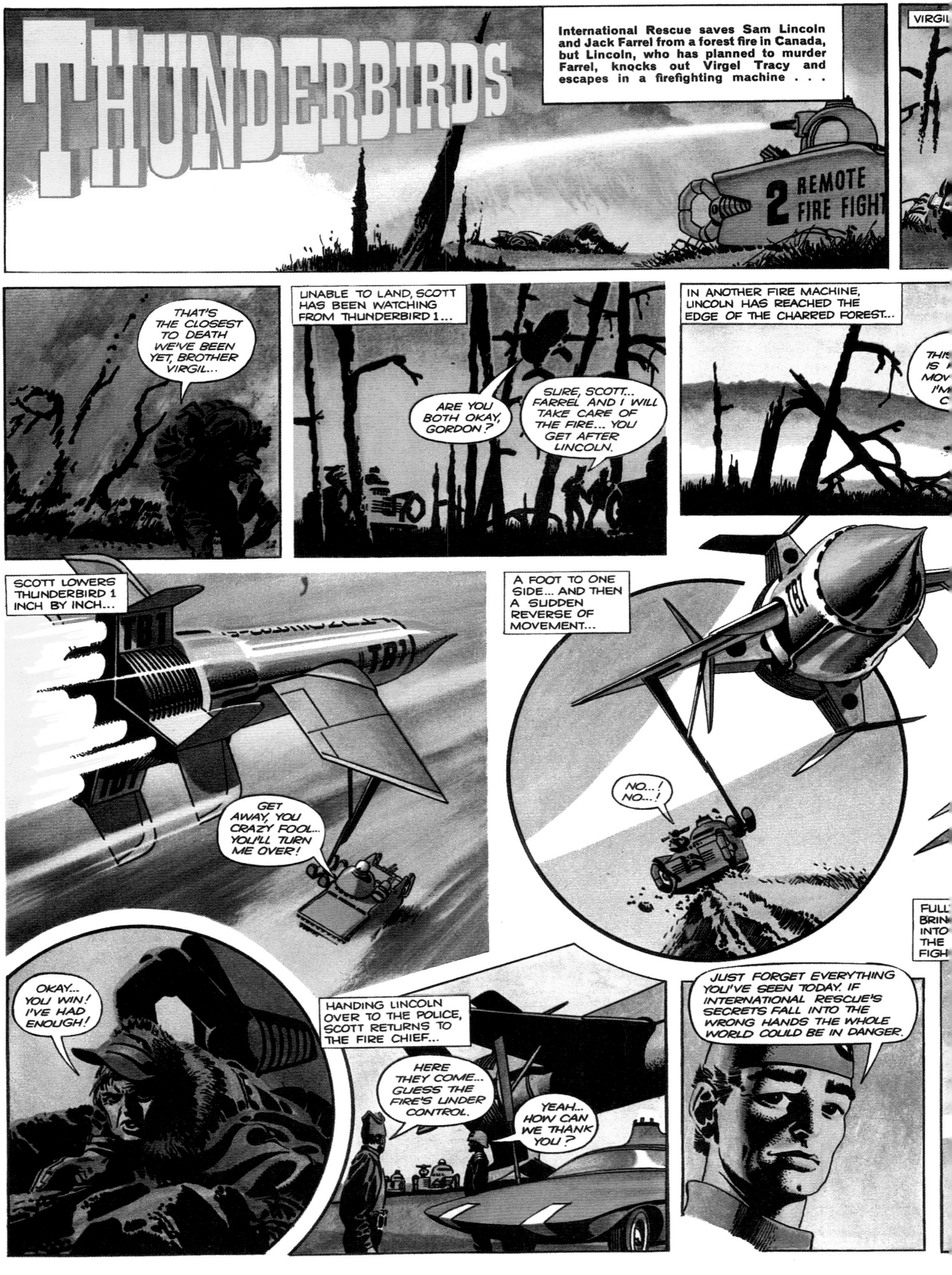
THUNDERBIRDS
International Rescue saves Sam Lincoln and Jack Farrel from a forest fire in Canada, but Lincoln, who has planned to murder Farrel, knocks out Virgel Tracy and escapes in a firefighting machine . . .
2 REMOTE FIRE FIGHT
THAT'S THE CLOSEST TO DEATH WE'VE BEEN YET, BROTHER VIRGIL...
UNABLE TO LAND, SCOTT HAS BEEN WATCHING FROM THUNDERBIRD 1...
ARE YOU BOTH OKAY, GORDON?
SURE, SCOTT... FARREL AND I WILL TAKE CARE OF THE FIRE... YOU GET AFTER LINCOLN.
IN ANOTHER FIRE MACHINE, LINCOLN HAS REACHED THE EDGE OF THE CHARRED FOREST...
SCOTT LOWERS THUNDERBIRD 1 INCH BY INCH...
GET AWAY, YOU CRAZY FOOL... YOU'LL TURN ME OVER!
A FOOT TO ONE SIDE... AND THEN A SUDDEN REVERSE OF MOVEMENT...
NO...! NO...!
OKAY... YOU WIN! I'VE HAD ENOUGH!
HANDING LINCOLN OVER TO THE POLICE, SCOTT RETURNS TO THE FIRE CHIEF...
HERE THEY COME... GUESS THE FIRE'S UNDER CONTROL.
YEAH... HOW CAN WE THANK YOU?
JUST FORGET EVERYTHING YOU'VE SEEN TODAY. IF INTERNATIONAL RESCUE'S SECRETS FALL INTO THE WRONG HANDS THE WHOLE WORLD COULD BE IN DANGER.

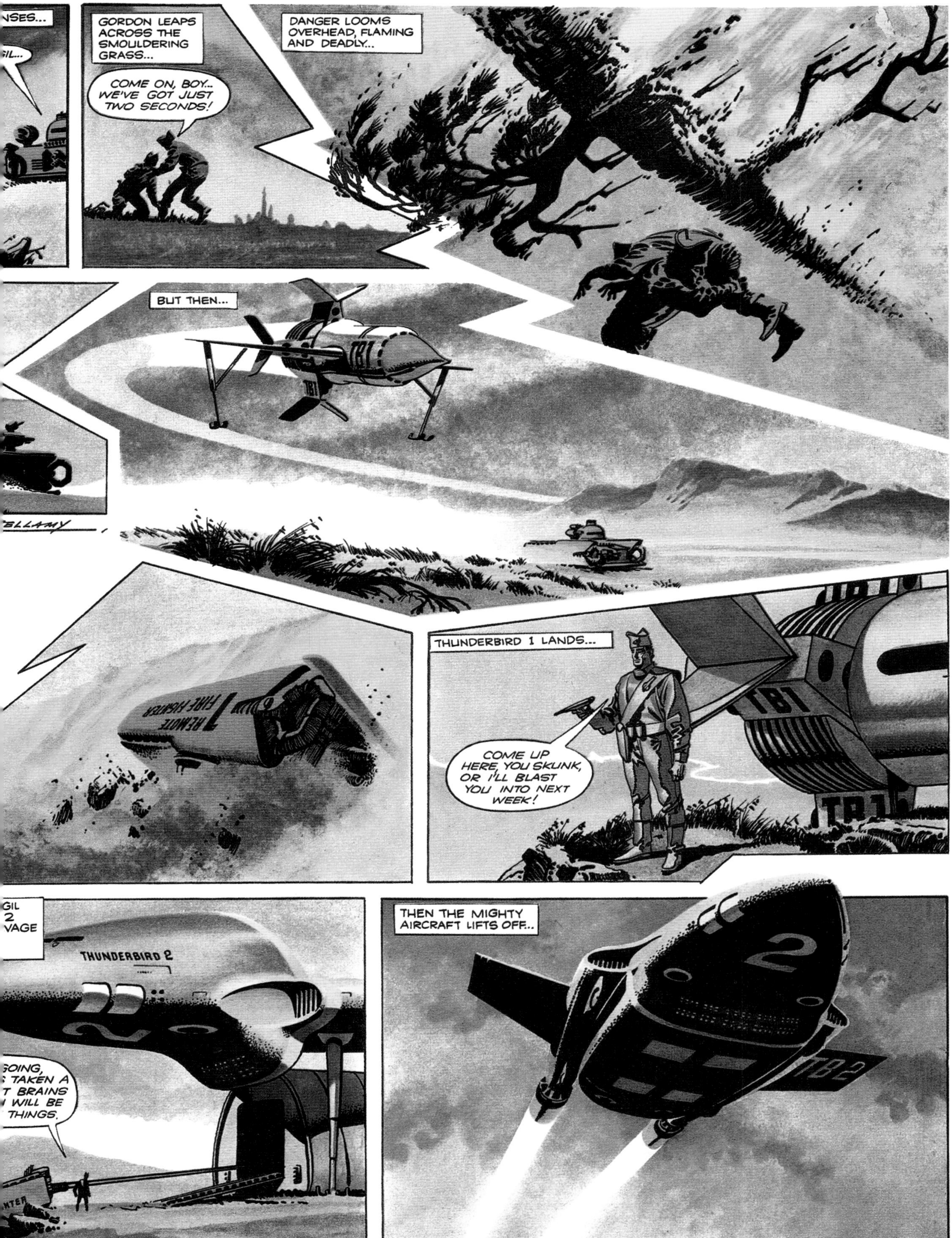
GORDON LEAPS ACROSS THE SMOULDERING GRASS...
COME ON, BOY... WE'VE GOT JUST TWO SECONDS!
DANGER LOOMS OVERHEAD, FLAMING AND DEADLY...
BUT THEN...
TB1
BELLAMY
REMOTE FIRE-FIGHTER
THUNDERBIRD 1 LANDS...
COME UP HERE, YOU SKUNK, OR I'LL BLAST YOU INTO NEXT WEEK!
THUNDERBIRD 2
THEN THE MIGHTY AIRCRAFT LIFTS OFF...
TB2

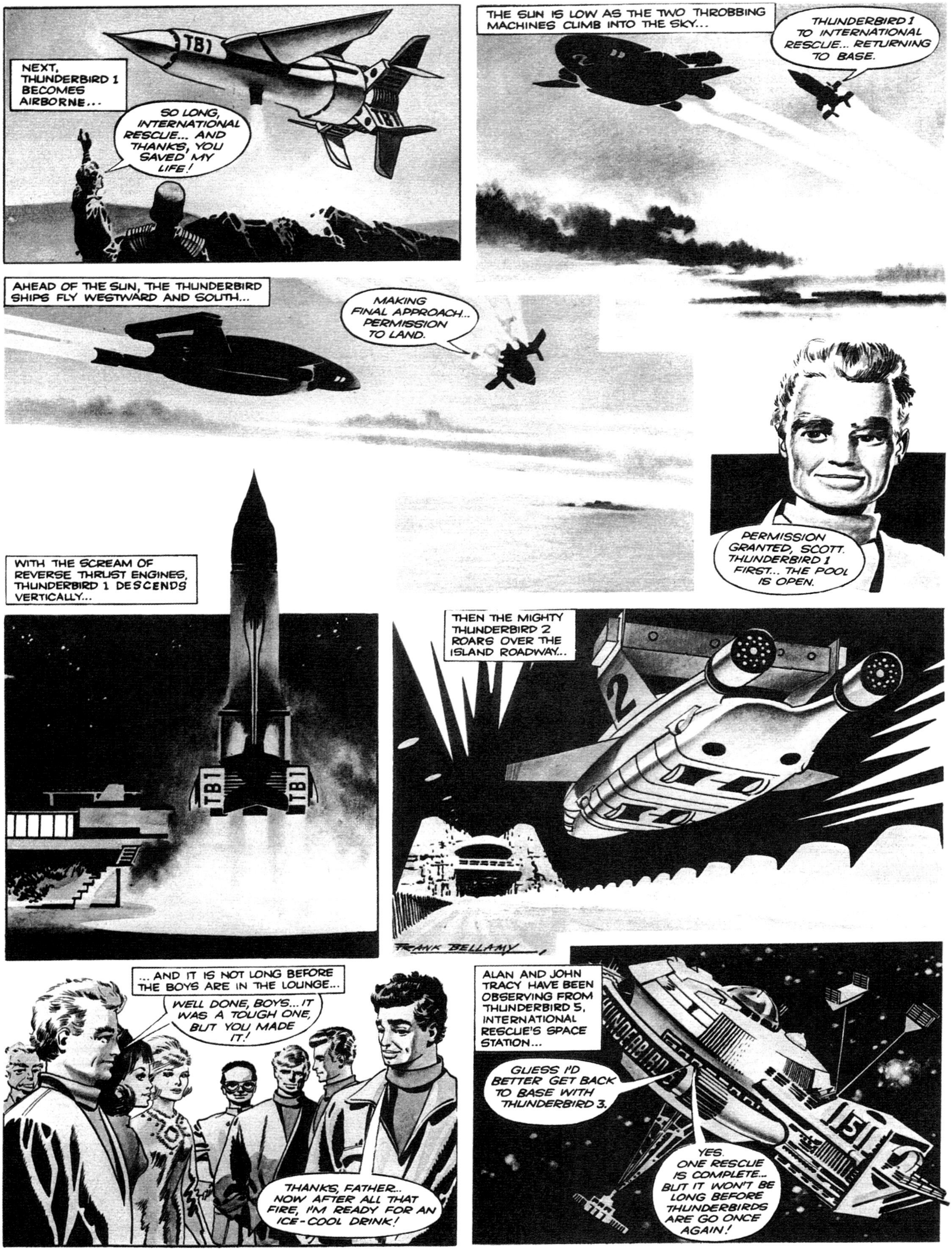

NEXT, THUNDERBIRD 1 BECOMES AIRBORNE...
SO LONG, INTERNATIONAL RESCUE... AND THANKS, YOU SAVED MY LIFE!
THE SUN IS LOW AS THE TWO THROBBING MACHINES CLIMB INTO THE SKY...
THUNDERBIRD 1 TO INTERNATIONAL RESCUE... RETURNING TO BASE.
AHEAD OF THE SUN, THE THUNDERBIRD SHIPS FLY WESTWARD AND SOUTH...
MAKING FINAL APPROACH... PERMISSION TO LAND.
PERMISSION GRANTED, SCOTT. THUNDERBIRD 1 FIRST... THE POOL IS OPEN.
WITH THE SCREAM OF REVERSE THRUST ENGINES, THUNDERBIRD 1 DESCENDS VERTICALLY...
TB1
TB1
THEN THE MIGHTY THUNDERBIRD 2 ROARS OVER THE ISLAND ROADWAY...
2
FRANK BELLAMY
...AND IT IS NOT LONG BEFORE THE BOYS ARE IN THE LOUNGE...
WELL DONE, BOYS... IT WAS A TOUGH ONE, BUT YOU MADE IT!
THANKS, FATHER... NOW AFTER ALL THAT FIRE, I'M READY FOR AN ICE-COOL DRINK!
ALAN AND JOHN TRACY HAVE BEEN OBSERVING FROM THUNDERBIRD 5, INTERNATIONAL RESCUE'S SPACE STATION...
GUESS I'D BETTER GET BACK TO BASE WITH THUNDERBIRD 3.
YES. ONE RESCUE IS COMPLETE... BUT IT WON'T BE LONG BEFORE THUNDERBIRDS ARE GO ONCE AGAIN!
THUNDERBIRD
5

MISSING IN AFRICA

Last sighting of missing medic's jet over Kenya *Nairobi News Agency Picture*

Medic in mercy dash mystery

Where is Dr Adams?

Worried officials in Madagascar report that there is still no news of missing heart specialist Dr. Adams. Last seen flying across the Kenya Game Reserve, Adams was due to carry out emergency surgery on Madagascar's General N'Mobo.

Only Adams is thought capable of saving the General thanks to his experiments with the miracle medical compound Rexsta Seven. Concern is growing that Adams' two-man atomic jet may have crash-landed following radio reports of nuclear turbine failure. In a race against time search teams have rushed to the area, but so far have found no trace of the doctor or his aircraft.

Full story page 88

EARTHSHOCK!

POISON GAS THREATENS AUSTRALIA

DATELINE 2066

World Government scientists have revealed that nitrosynatic gas build-up in oil-bearing rock cavities led to the destruction of Australia's molten energy complex earlier this week.

Only immediate action by complex operators prevented a major disaster when gas pressure on strata fissures led to massive earth tremors, and the potential release of a lethal gas cloud.

Fears are now being raised about the safety of other centre core installations, including the recently completed Zarabian complex, the only site not under World Government control.

Right: **First signs of danger at the Australian complex**

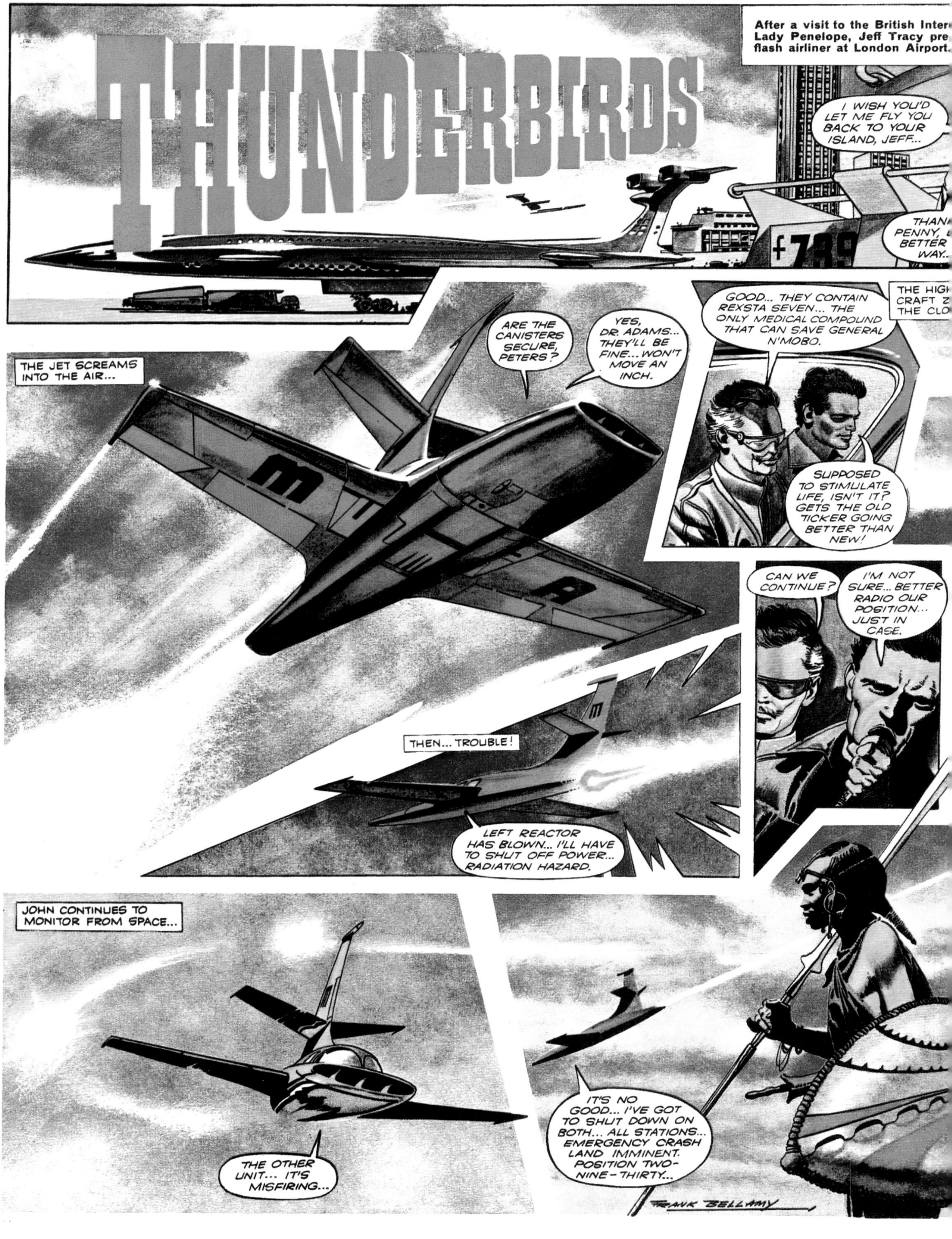
THUNDERBIRDS
After a visit to the British Inter
Lady Penelope, Jeff Tracy pre
flash airliner at London Airport.
I WISH YOU'D LET ME FLY YOU BACK TO YOUR ISLAND, JEFF...
THAN
PENNY,
BETTER
WAY..
THE JET SCREAMS INTO THE AIR...
ARE THE CANISTERS SECURE, PETERS?
YES, DR. ADAMS... THEY'LL BE FINE... WON'T MOVE AN INCH.
THE HIG
CRAFT Z
THE CLO
GOOD... THEY CONTAIN REXSTA SEVEN... THE ONLY MEDICAL COMPOUND THAT CAN SAVE GENERAL N'MOBO.
SUPPOSED TO STIMULATE LIFE, ISN'T IT? GETS THE OLD TICKER GOING BETTER THAN NEW!
THEN... TROUBLE!
LEFT REACTOR HAS BLOWN... I'LL HAVE TO SHUT OFF POWER... RADIATION HAZARD.
CAN WE CONTINUE?
I'M NOT SURE... BETTER RADIO OUR POSITION... JUST IN CASE.
JOHN CONTINUES TO MONITOR FROM SPACE...
THE OTHER UNIT... IT'S MISFIRING...
IT'S NO GOOD... I'VE GOT TO SHUT DOWN ON BOTH... ALL STATIONS... EMERGENCY CRASH LAND IMMINENT. POSITION TWO-NINE-THIRTY...
FRANK BELLAMY

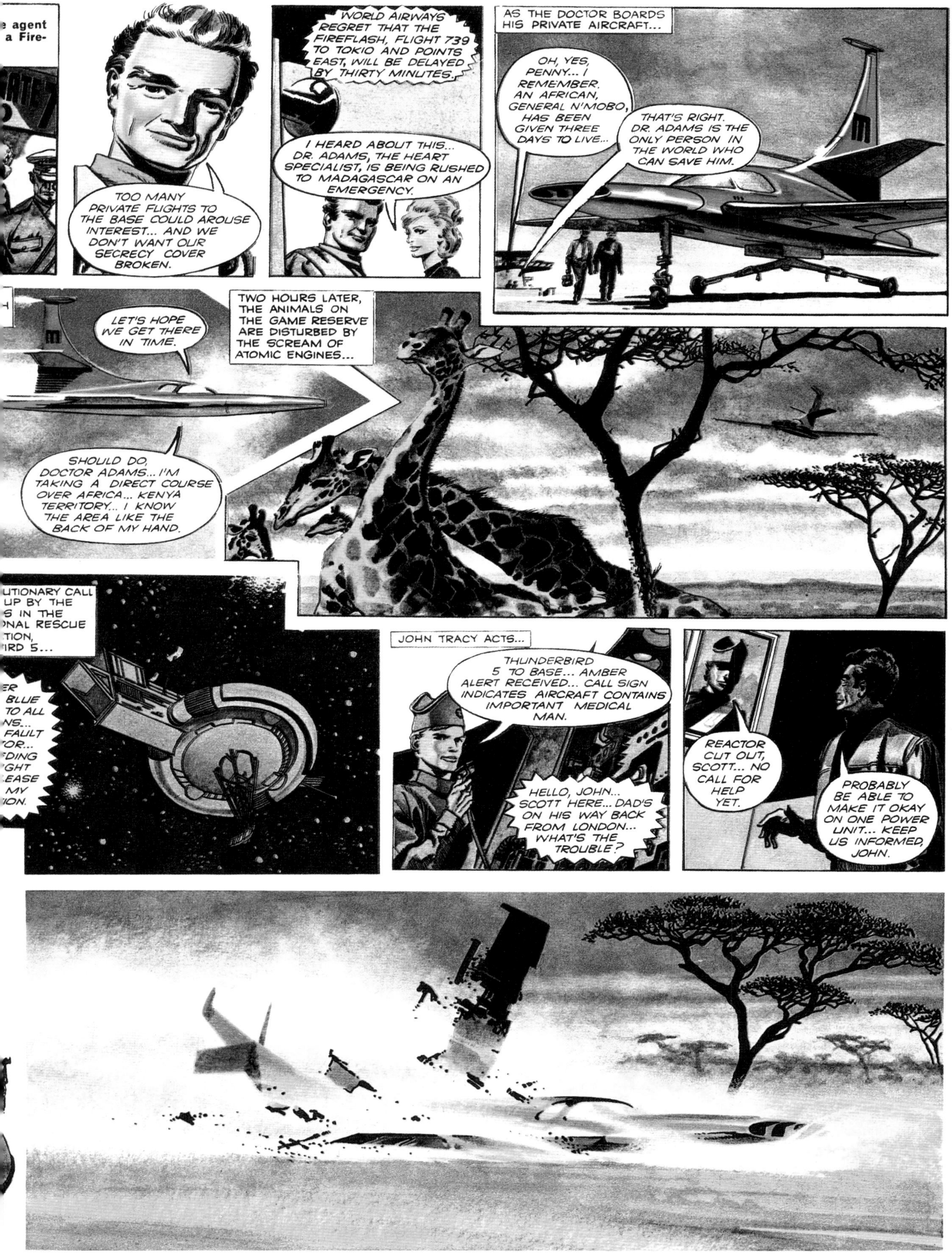

TOO MANY PRIVATE FLIGHTS TO THE BASE COULD AROUSE INTEREST... AND WE DON'T WANT OUR SECRECY COVER BROKEN.
WORLD AIRWAYS REGRET THAT THE FIREFLASH, FLIGHT 739 TO TOKIO AND POINTS EAST, WILL BE DELAYED BY THIRTY MINUTES.
I HEARD ABOUT THIS... DR. ADAMS, THE HEART SPECIALIST, IS BEING RUSHED TO MADAGASCAR ON AN EMERGENCY.
AS THE DOCTOR BOARDS HIS PRIVATE AIRCRAFT...
OH, YES, PENNY... I REMEMBER. AN AFRICAN, GENERAL N'MOBO, HAS BEEN GIVEN THREE DAYS TO LIVE...
THAT'S RIGHT. DR. ADAMS IS THE ONLY PERSON IN THE WORLD WHO CAN SAVE HIM.
LET'S HOPE WE GET THERE IN TIME.
SHOULD DO, DOCTOR ADAMS... I'M TAKING A DIRECT COURSE OVER AFRICA... KENYA TERRITORY... I KNOW THE AREA LIKE THE BACK OF MY HAND.
TWO HOURS LATER, THE ANIMALS ON THE GAME RESERVE ARE DISTURBED BY THE SCREAM OF ATOMIC ENGINES...
JOHN TRACY ACTS...
THUNDERBIRD 5 TO BASE... AMBER ALERT RECEIVED... CALL SIGN INDICATES AIRCRAFT CONTAINS IMPORTANT MEDICAL MAN.
HELLO, JOHN... SCOTT HERE... DAD'S ON HIS WAY BACK FROM LONDON... WHAT'S THE TROUBLE?
REACTOR CUT OUT, SCOTT... NO CALL FOR HELP YET.
PROBABLY BE ABLE TO MAKE IT OKAY ON ONE POWER UNIT... KEEP US INFORMED, JOHN.

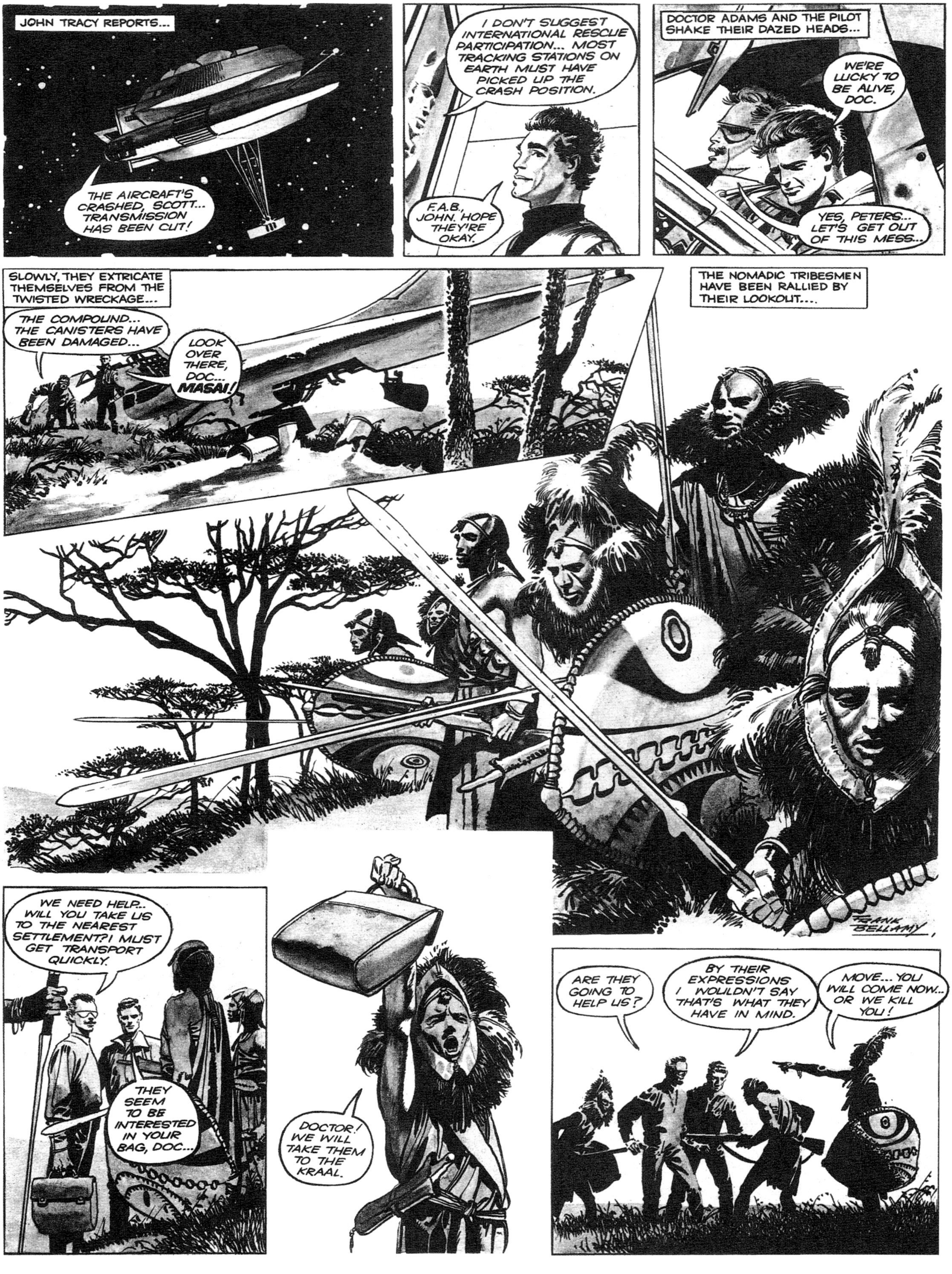
JOHN TRACY REPORTS...
THE AIRCRAFT'S CRASHED, SCOTT... TRANSMISSION HAS BEEN CUT!
I DON'T SUGGEST INTERNATIONAL RESCUE PARTICIPATION... MOST TRACKING STATIONS ON EARTH MUST HAVE PICKED UP THE CRASH POSITION.
F.A.B., JOHN. HOPE THEY'RE OKAY.
DOCTOR ADAMS AND THE PILOT SHAKE THEIR DAZED HEADS...
WE'RE LUCKY TO BE ALIVE, DOC.
YES, PETERS... LET'S GET OUT OF THIS MESS...
SLOWLY, THEY EXTRICATE THEMSELVES FROM THE TWISTED WRECKAGE...
THE COMPOUND... THE CANISTERS HAVE BEEN DAMAGED...
LOOK OVER THERE, DOC... MASAI!
THE NOMADIC TRIBESMEN HAVE BEEN RALLIED BY THEIR LOOKOUT...
FRANK BELLAMY
WE NEED HELP... WILL YOU TAKE US TO THE NEAREST SETTLEMENT? I MUST GET TRANSPORT QUICKLY.
THEY SEEM TO BE INTERESTED IN YOUR BAG, DOC...
DOCTOR! WE WILL TAKE THEM TO THE KRAAL.
ARE THEY GOING TO HELP US?
BY THEIR EXPRESSIONS I WOULDN'T SAY THAT'S WHAT THEY HAVE IN MIND.
MOVE... YOU WILL COME NOW... OR WE KILL YOU!

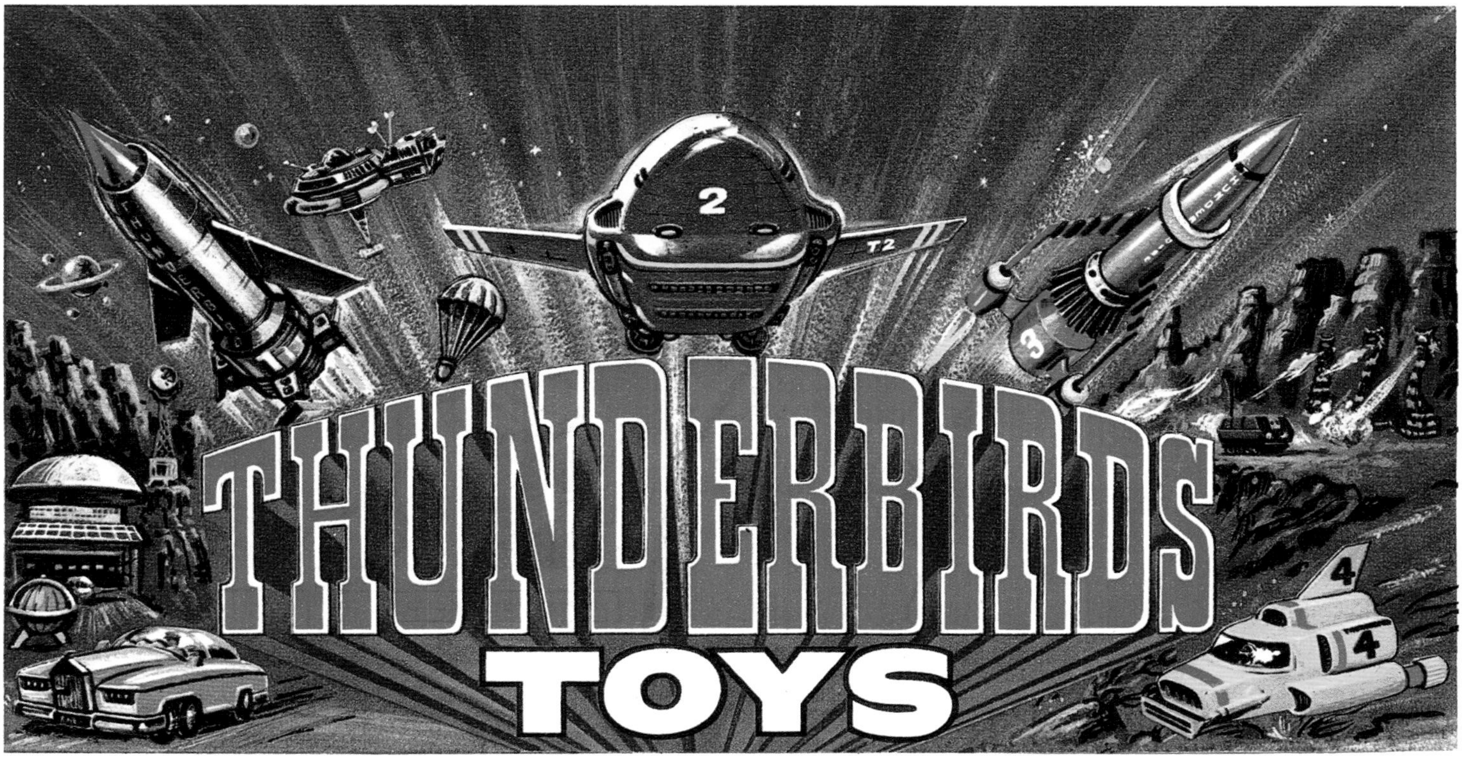
2
T2
3
4
4
THUNDERBIRDS
TOYS

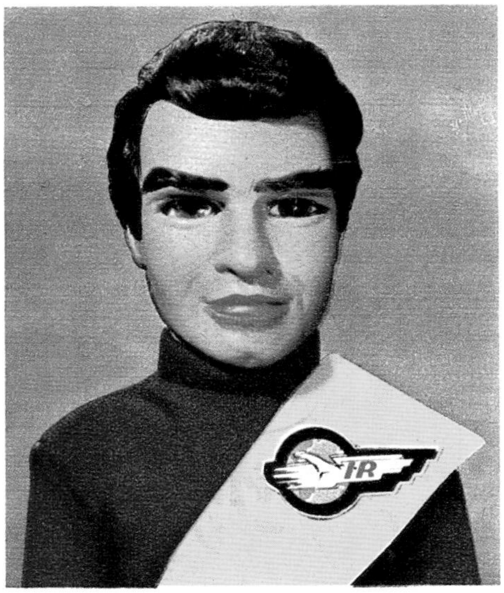

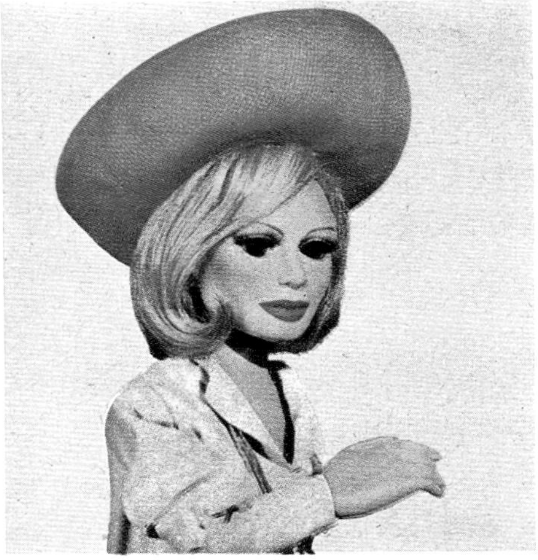

FOR GIRLS AND BOYS

THUNDERBIRD ONE
friction motor 6/11
remote control battery operated 29/11

THUNDERBIRD TWO
friction motor 14/11

THUNDERBIRD THREE
friction motor 5/11

THUNDERBIRD FOUR
battery operated amphibious 29/11

THUNDERBIRD FIVE
battery operated 29/11

CAP FIRING PISTOL 2/11

MULTI-DIRECTIONAL WATER PISTOL 2/6

LADY PENELOPE'S FAB 1
friction motor scale model 9/11
also battery operated with retractable guns, steerable front wheels, with forward and reverse steering, remote control 24/11

Lady Penelope's Tea Set 15/11

Lady Penelope's Jewellery Set 1/11

Lady Penelope's Dressing Table Set 7/11

Thunderbird's Painting Set 9/11

CENTURY 21 TOYS LTD., CENTURY 21 HOUSE, MAY'S COURT, ST. MARTIN'S LANE, LONDON W.C.2.

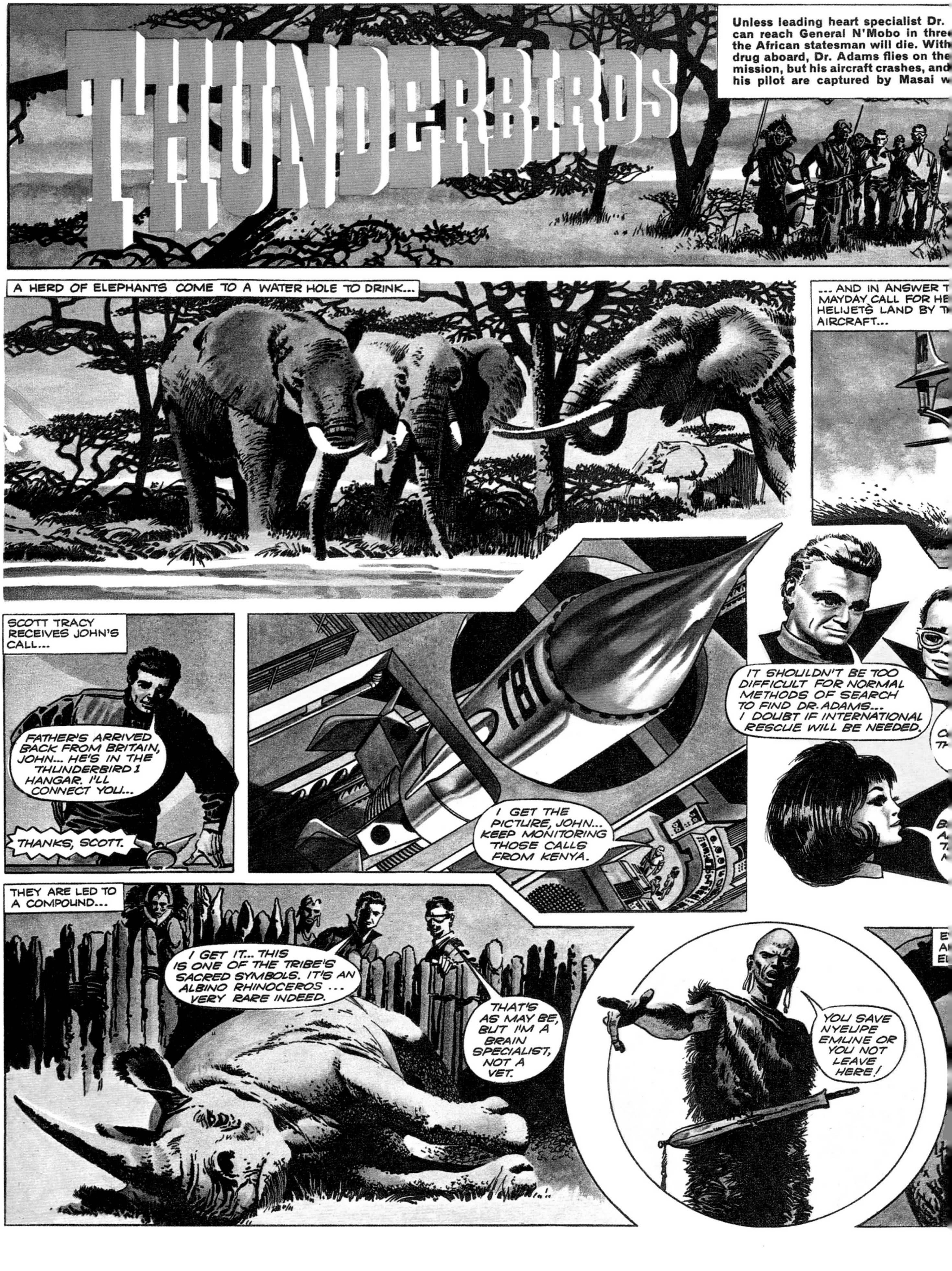
THUNDERBIRDS
Unless leading heart specialist Dr.
can reach General N'Mobo in thre
the African statesman will die. With
drug aboard, Dr. Adams flies on the
mission, but his aircraft crashes, and
his pilot are captured by Masai w
A HERD OF ELEPHANTS COME TO A WATER HOLE TO DRINK...
... AND IN ANSWER T
MAYDAY CALL FOR HE
HELIJETS LAND BY T
AIRCRAFT...
SCOTT TRACY RECEIVES JOHN'S CALL...
FATHER'S ARRIVED BACK FROM BRITAIN, JOHN... HE'S IN THE THUNDERBIRD 1 HANGAR. I'LL CONNECT YOU...
THANKS, SCOTT.
TB1
I GET THE PICTURE, JOHN... KEEP MONITORING THOSE CALLS FROM KENYA.
IT SHOULDN'T BE TOO DIFFICULT FOR NORMAL METHODS OF SEARCH TO FIND DR. ADAMS... I DOUBT IF INTERNATIONAL RESCUE WILL BE NEEDED.
THEY ARE LED TO A COMPOUND...
I GET IT... THIS IS ONE OF THE TRIBE'S SACRED SYMBOLS. IT'S AN ALBINO RHINOCEROS ... VERY RARE INDEED.
THAT'S AS MAY BE, BUT I'M A BRAIN SPECIALIST, NOT A VET.
YOU SAVE NYEUPE EMLINE OR YOU NOT LEAVE HERE!

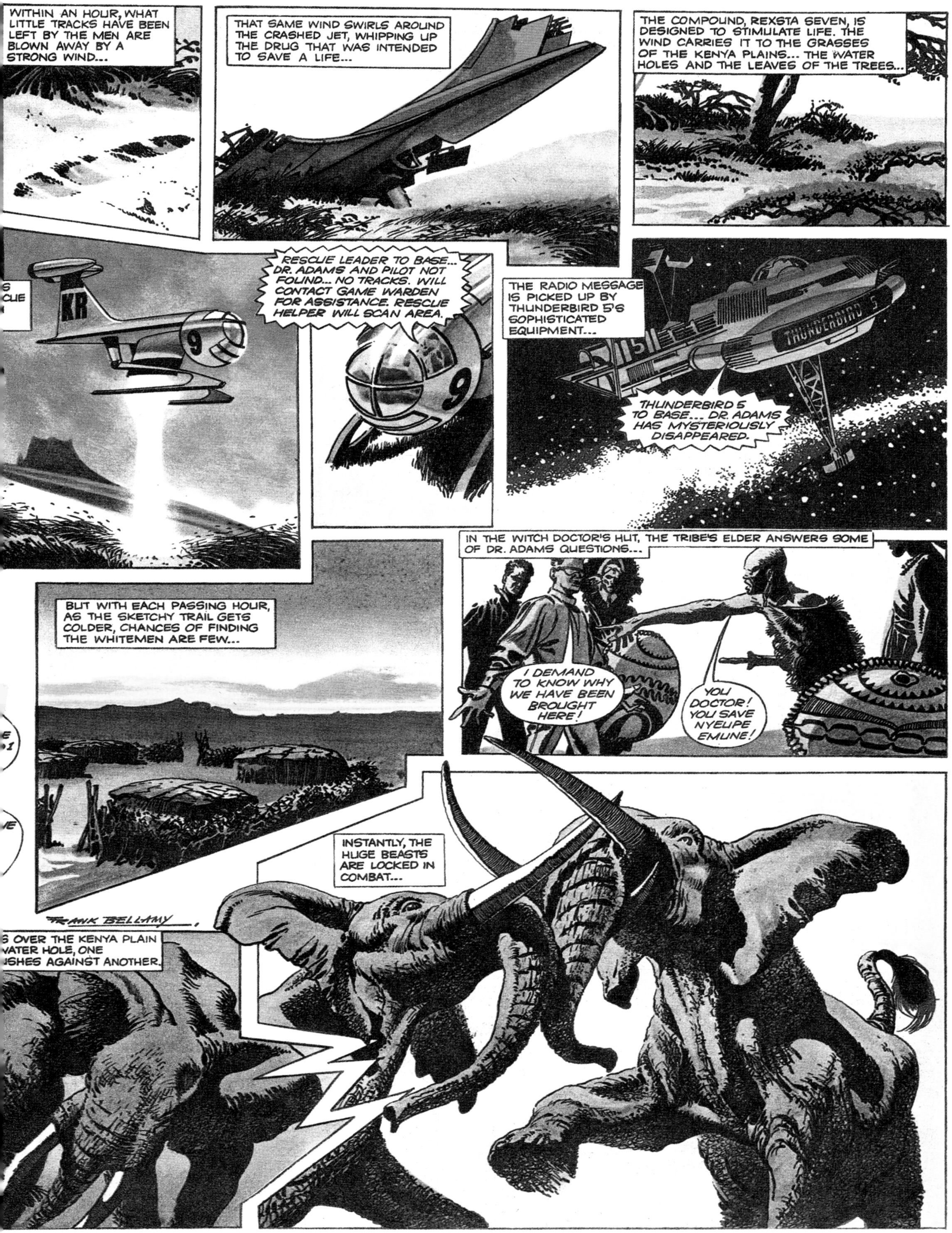
WITHIN AN HOUR, WHAT LITTLE TRACKS HAVE BEEN LEFT BY THE MEN ARE BLOWN AWAY BY A STRONG WIND...
THAT SAME WIND SWIRLS AROUND THE CRASHED JET, WHIPPING UP THE DRUG THAT WAS INTENDED TO SAVE A LIFE...
THE COMPOUND, REXSTA SEVEN, IS DESIGNED TO STIMULATE LIFE. THE WIND CARRIES IT TO THE GRASSES OF THE KENYA PLAINS... THE WATER HOLES AND THE LEAVES OF THE TREES...
KR
9
RESCUE LEADER TO BASE... DR. ADAMS AND PILOT NOT FOUND... NO TRACKS. WILL CONTACT GAME WARDEN FOR ASSISTANCE. RESCUE HELPER WILL SCAN AREA.
9
THE RADIO MESSAGE IS PICKED UP BY THUNDERBIRD 5'S SOPHISTICATED EQUIPMENT...
THUNDERBIRD 5
THUNDERBIRD 5 TO BASE... DR. ADAMS HAS MYSTERIOUSLY DISAPPEARED.
BUT WITH EACH PASSING HOUR, AS THE SKETCHY TRAIL GETS COLDER, CHANCES OF FINDING THE WHITEMEN ARE FEW...
IN THE WITCH DOCTOR'S HUT, THE TRIBE'S ELDER ANSWERS SOME OF DR. ADAMS QUESTIONS...
I DEMAND TO KNOW WHY WE HAVE BEEN BROUGHT HERE!
YOU DOCTOR! YOU SAVE NYEUPE EMUNE!
FRANK BELLAMY
S OVER THE KENYA PLAIN
WATER HOLE, ONE
USHES AGAINST ANOTHER.
INSTANTLY, THE HUGE BEASTS ARE LOCKED IN COMBAT...

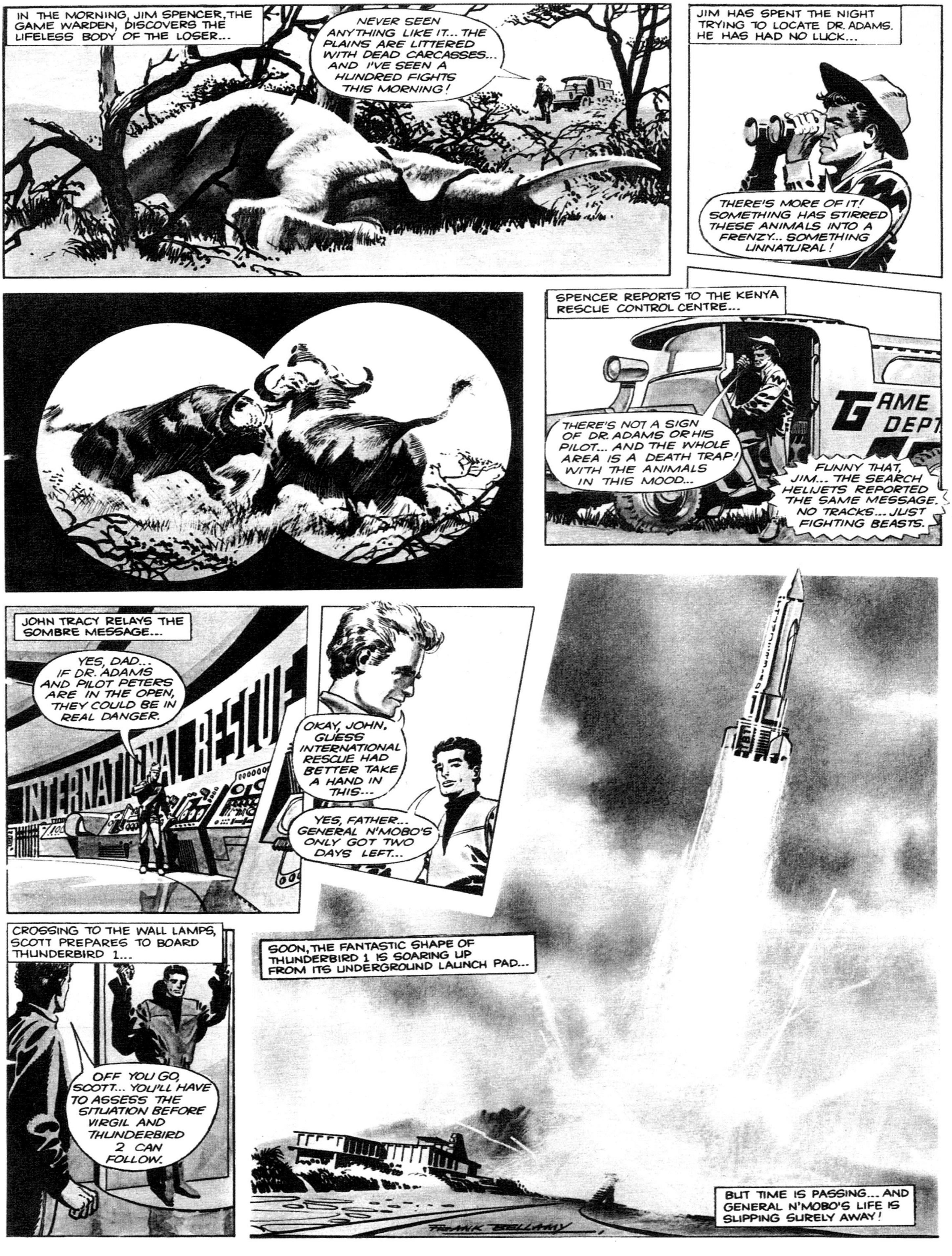

IN THE MORNING, JIM SPENCER, THE GAME WARDEN, DISCOVERS THE LIFELESS BODY OF THE LOSER...
NEVER SEEN ANYTHING LIKE IT... THE PLAINS ARE LITTERED WITH DEAD CARCASSES... AND I'VE SEEN A HUNDRED FIGHTS THIS MORNING!
JIM HAS SPENT THE NIGHT TRYING TO LOCATE DR. ADAMS. HE HAS HAD NO LUCK...
THERE'S MORE OF IT! SOMETHING HAS STIRRED THESE ANIMALS INTO A FRENZY... SOMETHING UNNATURAL!
SPENCER REPORTS TO THE KENYA RESCUE CONTROL CENTRE...
GAME DEPT
THERE'S NOT A SIGN OF DR. ADAMS OR HIS PILOT... AND THE WHOLE AREA IS A DEATH TRAP! WITH THE ANIMALS IN THIS MOOD...
FUNNY THAT, JIM... THE SEARCH HELIJETS REPORTED THE SAME MESSAGE. NO TRACKS... JUST FIGHTING BEASTS.
JOHN TRACY RELAYS THE SOMBRE MESSAGE...
YES, DAD... IF DR. ADAMS AND PILOT PETERS ARE IN THE OPEN, THEY COULD BE IN REAL DANGER.
INTERNATIONAL RESCUE
OKAY, JOHN, GUESS INTERNATIONAL RESCUE HAD BETTER TAKE A HAND IN THIS...
YES, FATHER... GENERAL N'MOBO'S ONLY GOT TWO DAYS LEFT...
CROSSING TO THE WALL LAMPS, SCOTT PREPARES TO BOARD THUNDERBIRD 1...
OFF YOU GO, SCOTT... YOU'LL HAVE TO ASSESS THE SITUATION BEFORE VIRGIL AND THUNDERBIRD 2 CAN FOLLOW.
SOON, THE FANTASTIC SHAPE OF THUNDERBIRD 1 IS SOARING UP FROM ITS UNDERGROUND LAUNCH PAD...
BUT TIME IS PASSING... AND GENERAL N'MOBO'S LIFE IS SLIPPING SURELY AWAY!
FRANK BELLAMY

smiths crisps
THUNDERBIRDS
ARE GO!!!
super space age models 1'6 each
1
2
Thunderbird 2 (4½" long)—Huge rescue vehicle, speed of 5,000 mph.
3
4
Thunderbird 4 (3" long)—Ocean-going craft for under-water rescue.
Thunderbird 1 (4½" high)—Leading rescue craft, speed of 15,000 mph.
Thunderbird 3 (4½" high)—Fast space rocket, requires crew of two.
HOW TO GET YOUR THUNDERBIRD FLEET
They're yours for only 1/6 each plus three empty Smiths Crisps bags (or one 2/6 carton top). If you'd like the whole fleet at once you can have them all for only 4/3 plus six empty bags (or one 2/6 carton top). Send your postal order and empty bags together with your name and address, stating which Thunderbird(s) you'd like, to:
SMITH'S THUNDERBIRD OFFER
Dept. A, 103 Northwold Rd., London, E.5.
Allow 14 days for delivery. Go! Go! Go!
©1966 A.P. FILMS LTD.

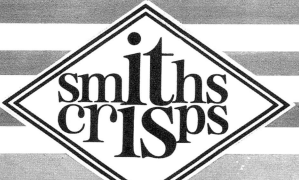

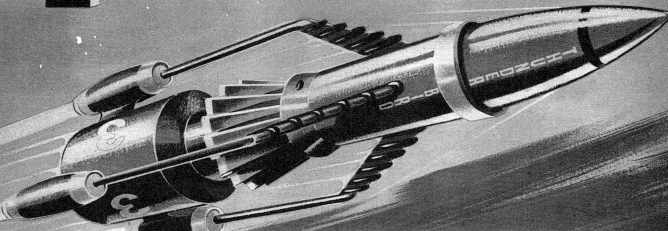

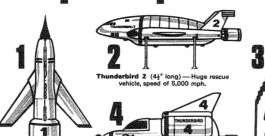

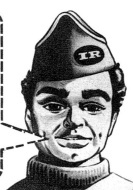

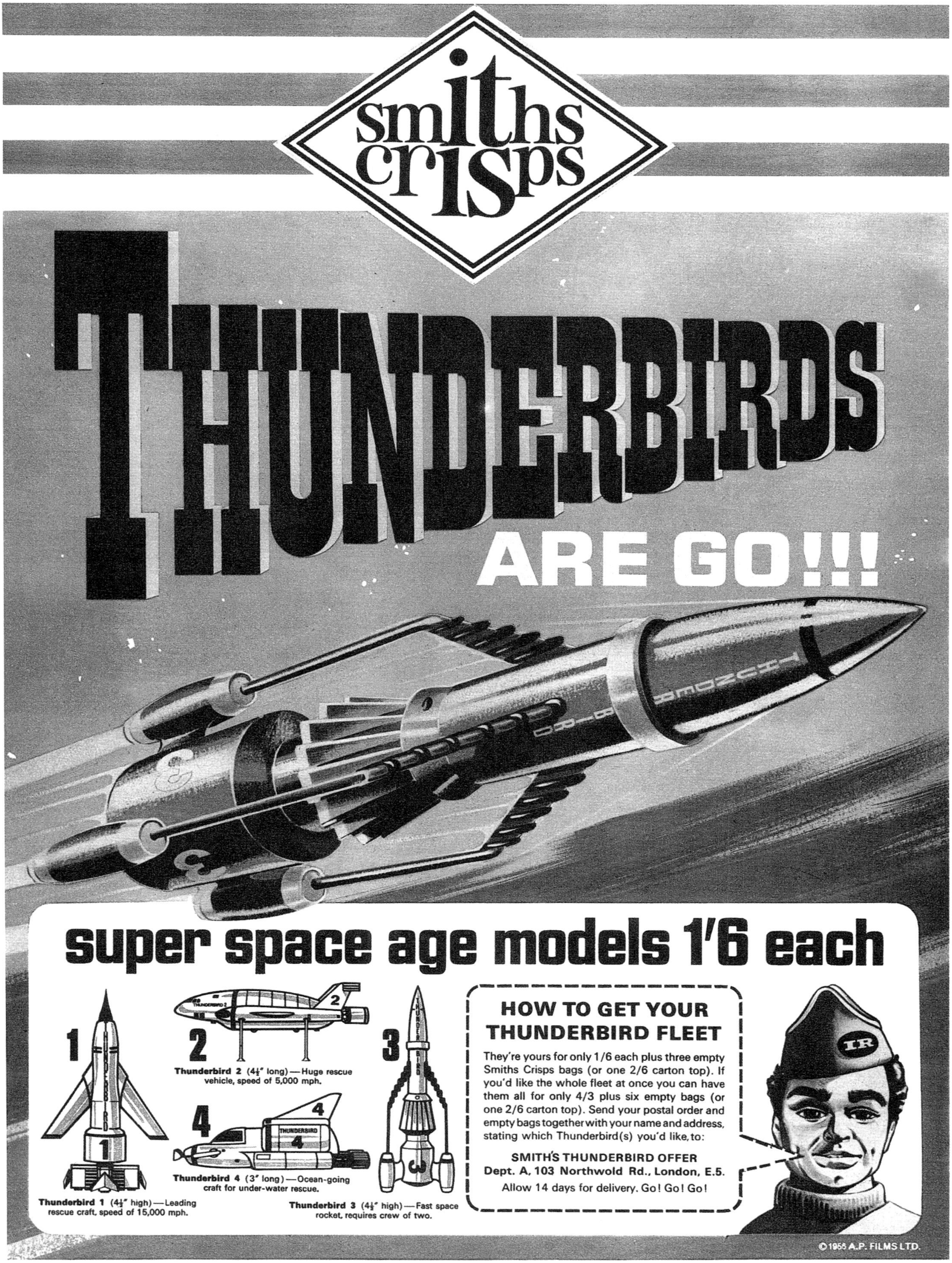

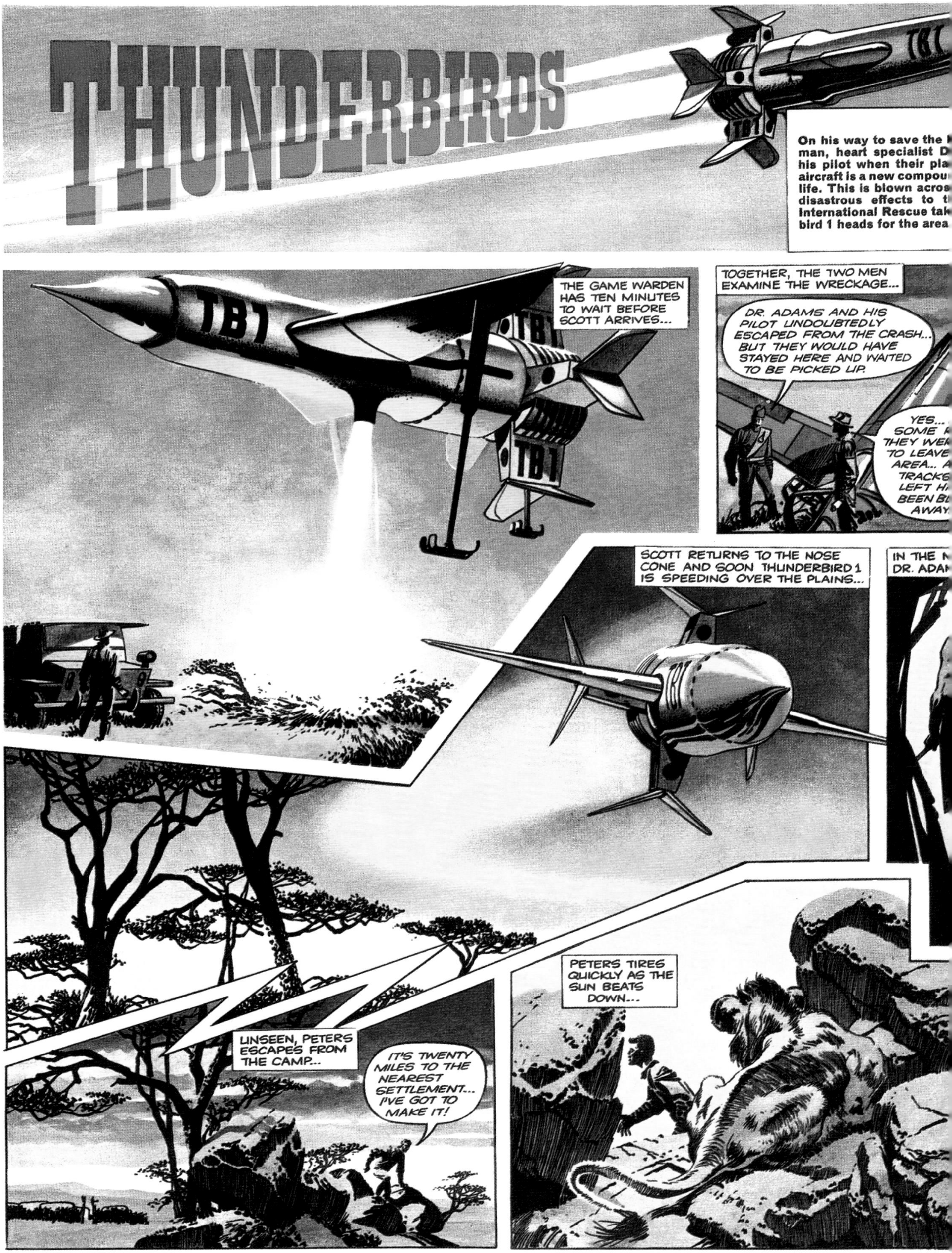
THUNDERBIRDS
TB1
On his way to save the
man, heart specialist D
his pilot when their pla
aircraft is a new compou
life. This is blown acros
disastrous effects to t
International Rescue tak
bird 1 heads for the area
THE GAME WARDEN HAS TEN MINUTES TO WAIT BEFORE SCOTT ARRIVES...
TOGETHER, THE TWO MEN EXAMINE THE WRECKAGE...
DR. ADAMS AND HIS PILOT UNDOUBTEDLY ESCAPED FROM THE CRASH... BUT THEY WOULD HAVE STAYED HERE AND WAITED TO BE PICKED UP.
SCOTT RETURNS TO THE NOSE CONE AND SOON THUNDERBIRD 1 IS SPEEDING OVER THE PLAINS...
UNSEEN, PETERS ESCAPES FROM THE CAMP...
IT'S TWENTY MILES TO THE NEAREST SETTLEMENT... I'VE GOT TO MAKE IT!
PETERS TIRES QUICKLY AS THE SUN BEATS DOWN...

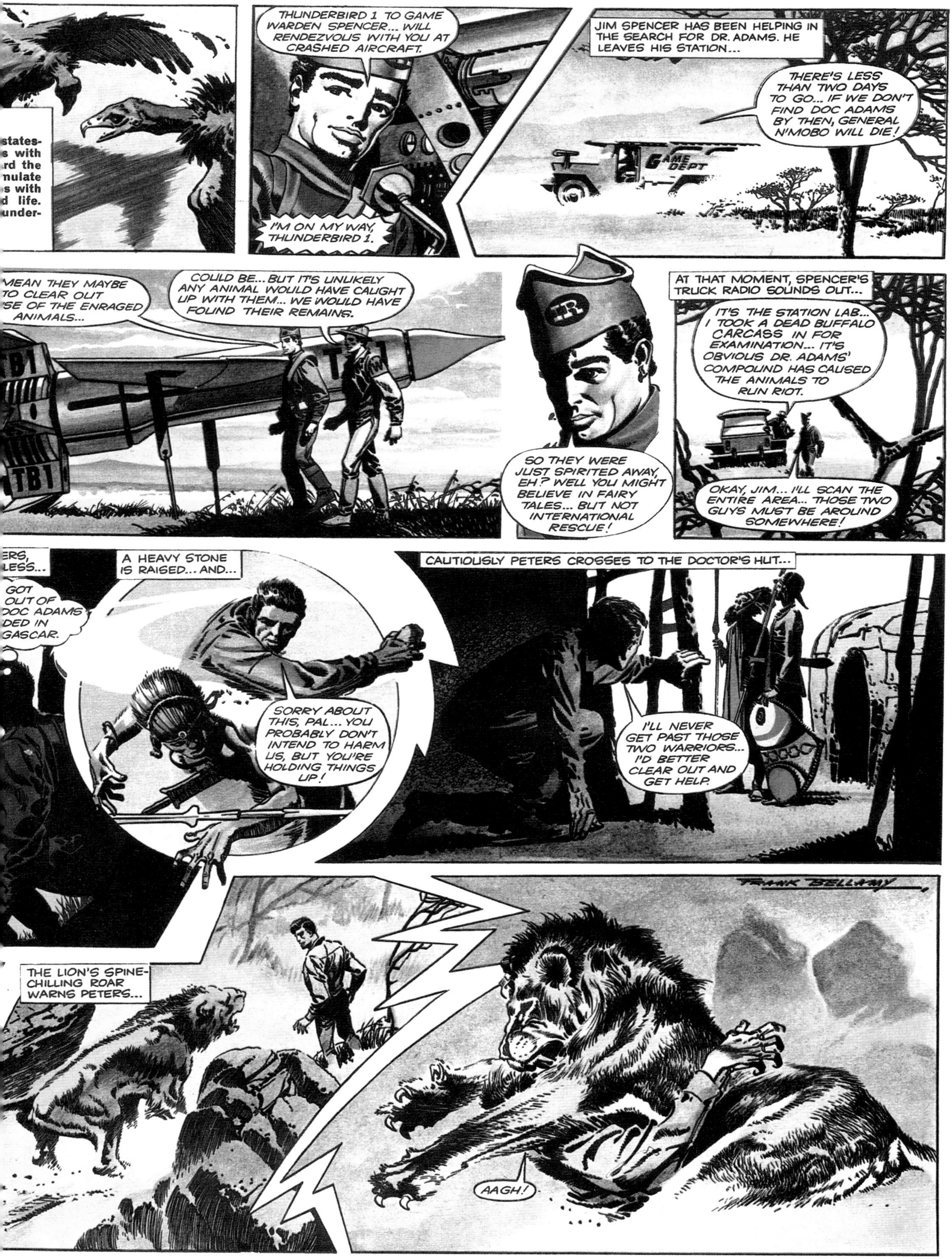
THUNDERBIRD 1 TO GAME WARDEN SPENCER... WILL RENDEZVOUS WITH YOU AT CRASHED AIRCRAFT.
I'M ON MY WAY, THUNDERBIRD 1.
JIM SPENCER HAS BEEN HELPING IN THE SEARCH FOR DR. ADAMS. HE LEAVES HIS STATION...
THERE'S LESS THAN TWO DAYS TO GO... IF WE DON'T FIND DOC ADAMS BY THEN, GENERAL N'MOBO WILL DIE!
GAME DEPT
MEAN THEY MAYBE TO CLEAR OUT SE OF THE ENRAGED ANIMALS...
COULD BE... BUT IT'S UNLIKELY ANY ANIMAL WOULD HAVE CAUGHT UP WITH THEM... WE WOULD HAVE FOUND THEIR REMAINS.
TB1
SO THEY WERE JUST SPIRITED AWAY, EH? WELL YOU MIGHT BELIEVE IN FAIRY TALES... BUT NOT INTERNATIONAL RESCUE!
AT THAT MOMENT, SPENCER'S TRUCK RADIO SOUNDS OUT...
IT'S THE STATION LAB... I TOOK A DEAD BUFFALO CARCASS IN FOR EXAMINATION... IT'S OBVIOUS DR. ADAMS' COMPOUND HAS CAUSED THE ANIMALS TO RUN RIOT.
OKAY, JIM... I'LL SCAN THE ENTIRE AREA... THOSE TWO GUYS MUST BE AROUND SOMEWHERE!
A HEAVY STONE IS RAISED... AND...
SORRY ABOUT THIS, PAL... YOU PROBABLY DON'T INTEND TO HARM US, BUT YOU'RE HOLDING THINGS UP!
CAUTIOUSLY PETERS CROSSES TO THE DOCTOR'S HUT...
I'LL NEVER GET PAST THOSE TWO WARRIORS... I'D BETTER CLEAR OUT AND GET HELP.
FRANK BELLAMY
THE LION'S SPINE-CHILLING ROAR WARNS PETERS...
AAGH!

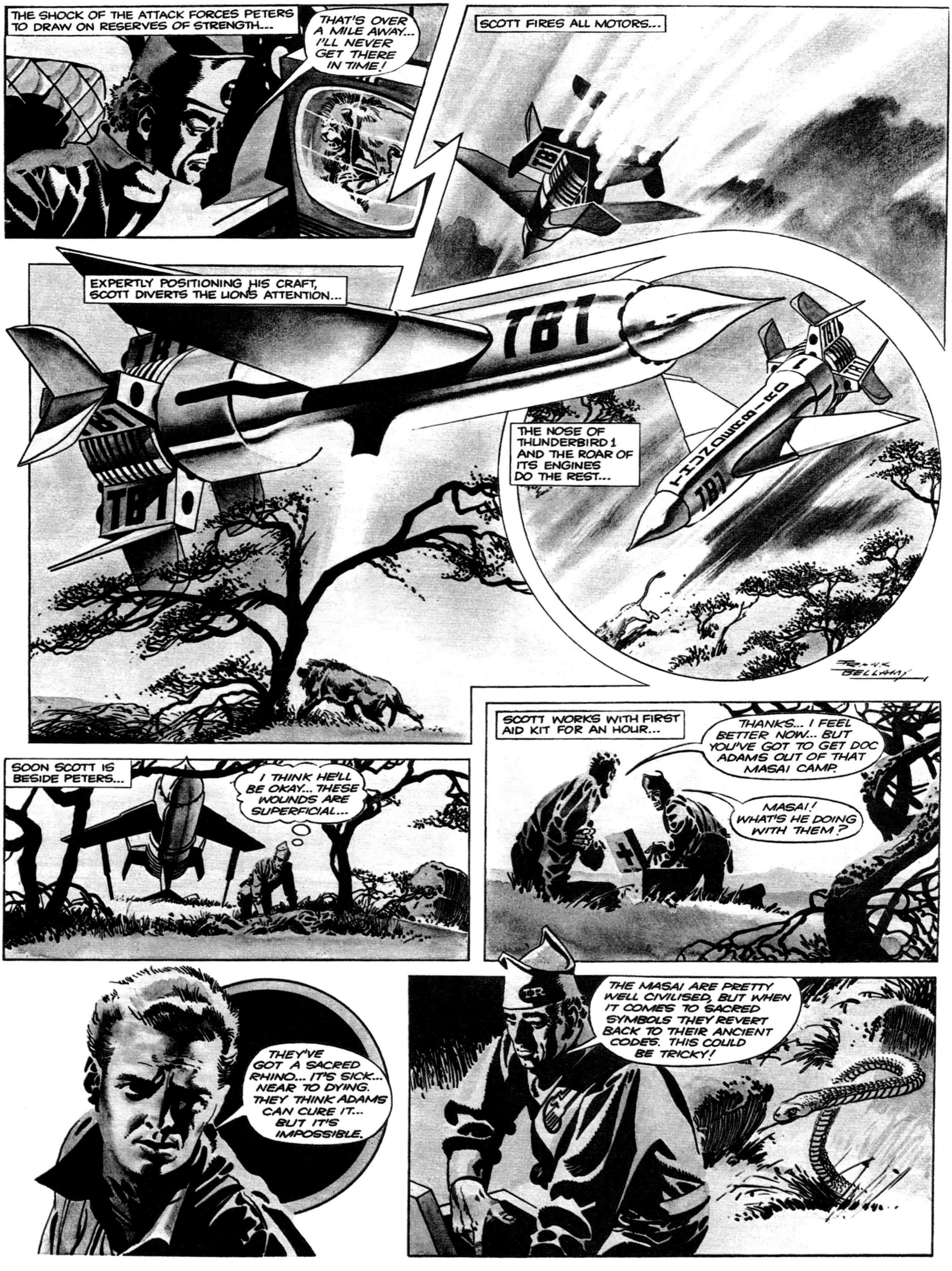
THE SHOCK OF THE ATTACK FORCES PETERS TO DRAW ON RESERVES OF STRENGTH...
THAT'S OVER A MILE AWAY... I'LL NEVER GET THERE IN TIME!
SCOTT FIRES ALL MOTORS...
TB1
EXPERTLY POSITIONING HIS CRAFT, SCOTT DIVERTS THE LION'S ATTENTION...
TB1
THE NOSE OF THUNDERBIRD 1 AND THE ROAR OF ITS ENGINES DO THE REST...
SOON SCOTT IS BESIDE PETERS...
I THINK HE'LL BE OKAY... THESE WOUNDS ARE SUPERFICIAL...
SCOTT WORKS WITH FIRST AID KIT FOR AN HOUR...
THANKS... I FEEL BETTER NOW... BUT YOU'VE GOT TO GET DOC ADAMS OUT OF THAT MASAI CAMP.
MASAI! WHAT'S HE DOING WITH THEM?
THEY'VE GOT A SACRED RHINO... IT'S SICK... NEAR TO DYING. THEY THINK ADAMS CAN CURE IT... BUT IT'S IMPOSSIBLE.
THE MASAI ARE PRETTY WELL CIVILISED, BUT WHEN IT COMES TO SACRED SYMBOLS THEY REVERT BACK TO THEIR ANCIENT CODES. THIS COULD BE TRICKY!

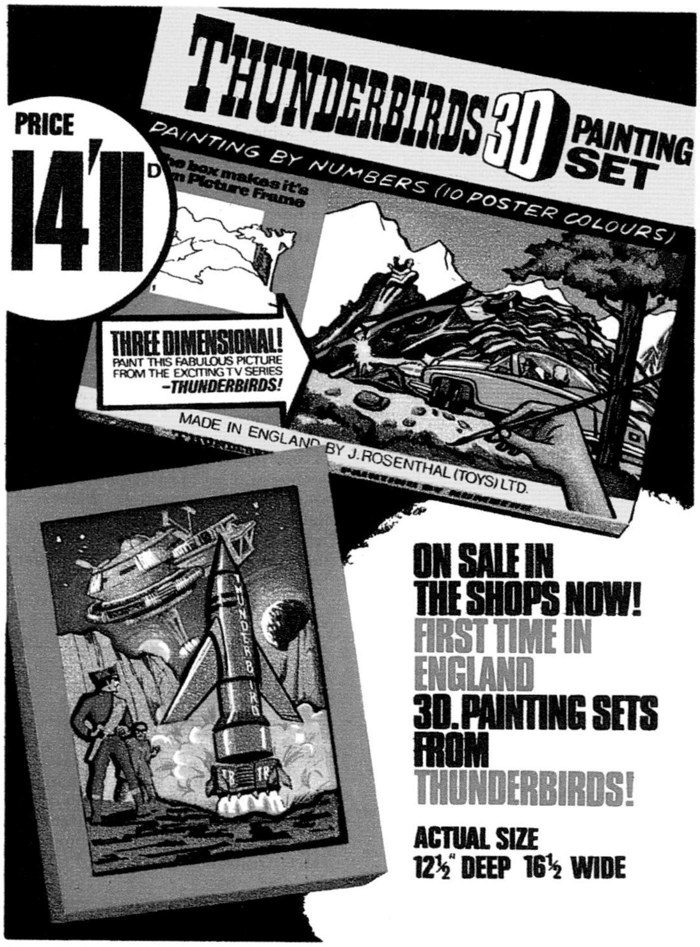
THUNDERBIRDS 3D PAINTING SET
PAINTING BY NUMBERS (10 POSTER COLOURS)
PRICE
14'11D
THREE DIMENSIONAL!
PAINT THIS FABULOUS PICTURE FROM THE EXCITING TV SERIES
-THUNDERBIRDS!
MADE IN ENGLAND BY J. ROSENTHAL (TOYS) LTD.
ON SALE IN
THE SHOPS NOW!
FIRST TIME IN
ENGLAND
3D. PAINTING SETS
FROM
THUNDERBIRDS!
ACTUAL SIZE
12½" DEEP 16½ WIDE

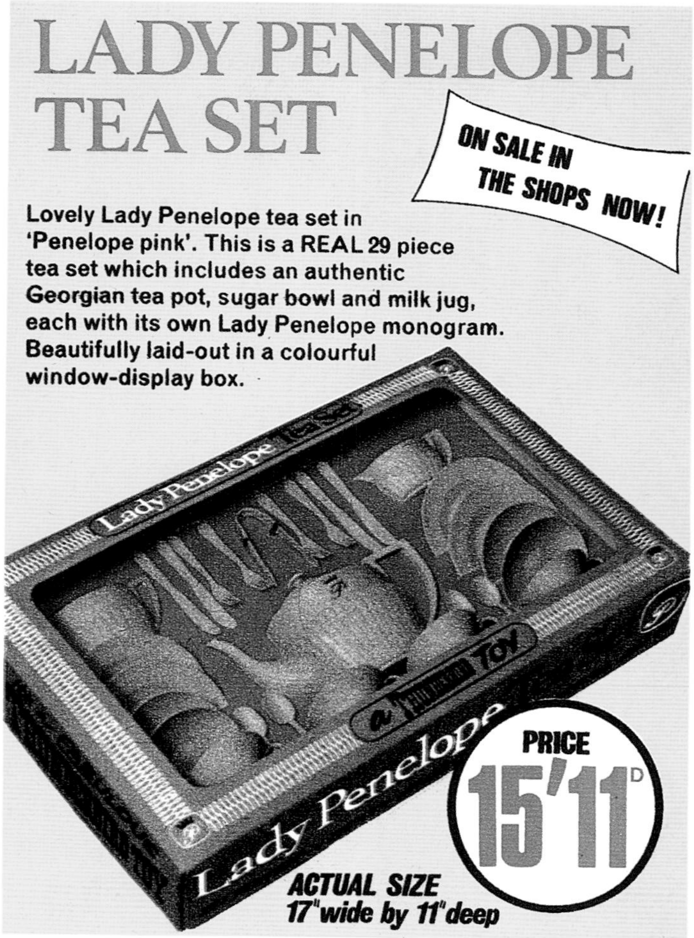
LADY PENELOPE
TEA SET
ON SALE IN
THE SHOPS NOW!
Lovely Lady Penelope tea set in 'Penelope pink'. This is a REAL 29 piece tea set which includes an authentic Georgian tea pot, sugar bowl and milk jug, each with its own Lady Penelope monogram. Beautifully laid-out in a colourful window-display box.
Lady Penelope Tea Set
Lady Penelope
PRICE
15'11D
ACTUAL SIZE
17" wide by 11" deep

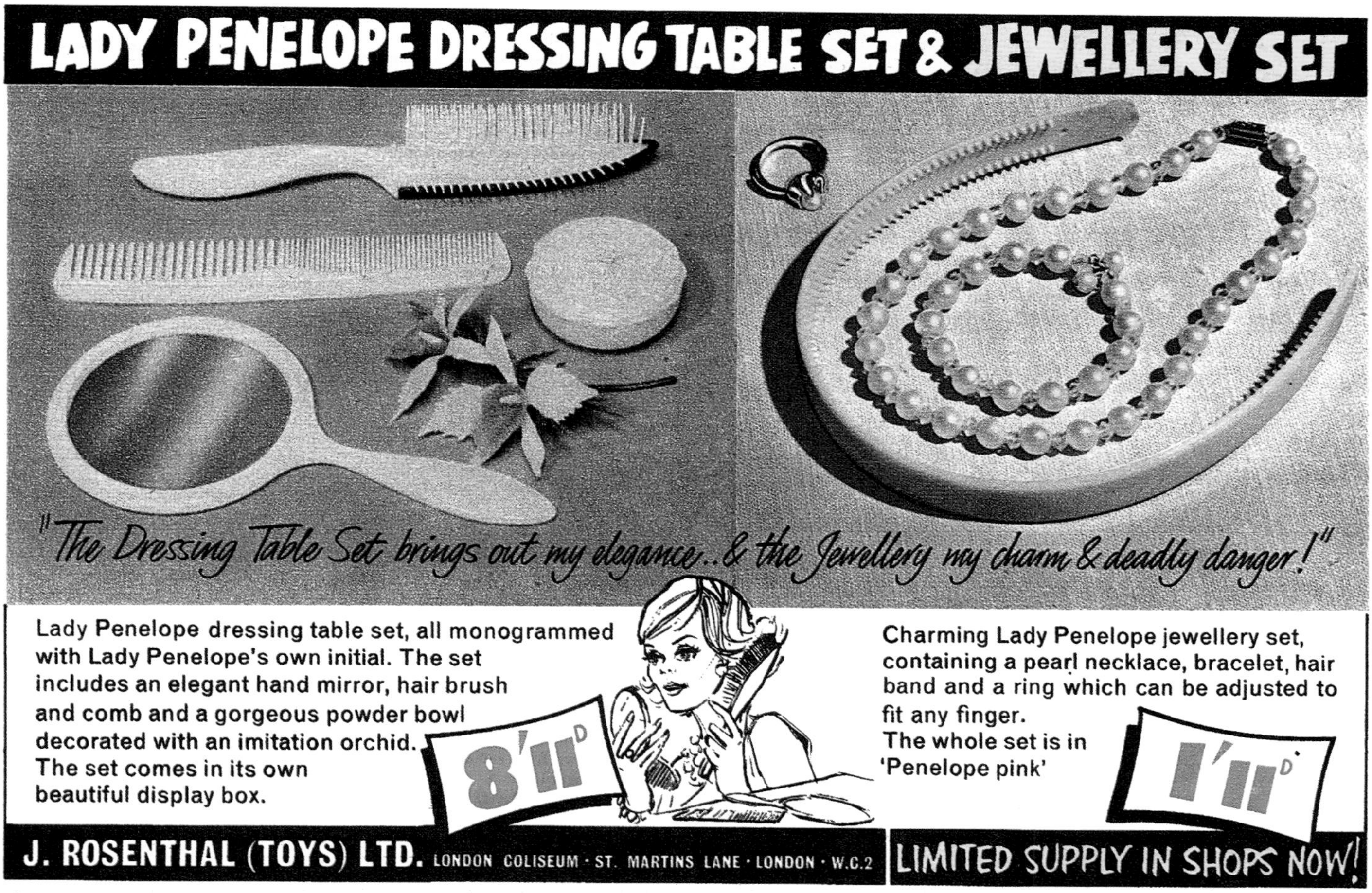
LADY PENELOPE DRESSING TABLE SET & JEWELLERY SET
"The Dressing Table Set brings out my elegance..& the Jewellery my charm & deadly danger!"
Lady Penelope dressing table set, all monogrammed with Lady Penelope's own initial. The set includes an elegant hand mirror, hair brush and comb and a gorgeous powder bowl decorated with an imitation orchid. The set comes in its own beautiful display box.
8'11D
Charming Lady Penelope jewellery set, containing a pearl necklace, bracelet, hair band and a ring which can be adjusted to fit any finger.
The whole set is in 'Penelope pink'
1'11D
J. ROSENTHAL (TOYS) LTD. LONDON COLISEUM · ST. MARTINS LANE · LONDON · W.C.2
LIMITED SUPPLY IN SHOPS NOW!

THUNDERBIRDS

Dr. Adams, a heart specialist, is captured by Masai tribesmen after his plane crashes in Kenya. International Rescue sends Thunderbird 1 to the area and Scott Tracy manages to save the doctor's pilot from an attack by a lion.

YOU SAY THE MASAI WANT THE DOC TO CURE... A DYING SACRED RHINO?

YES... LOOK O BEHIND YOU!

AT HIS ISLAND HOME, JEFF TRACY NODS SERIOUSLY...

F.A.B., SCOTT... WE'LL BE WAITING FOR YOUR NEXT REPORT. TIME IS AT A PREMIUM NOW... THAT AFRICAN STATESMAN DR. ADAMS WAS GOING TO TEND HAS THIRTY-SIX HOURS TO LIVE!

THE GAME WARDEN ARRIVES AND SCOTT TAKES OFF...

DR. ADAMS HAS JUST GOTTA BE RESCUED... HE'S THE ONLY MAN WHO CAN SAVE GENERAL N'MOBO.

IT'S NOT GOING TO BE EASY... THE MASAI WILL FIGHT TO HOLD THE DOC.

SCOTT CHOOSES A LANDING SITE HALF A MILE FROM THE CAMP...

...AND THEN APPROACHES ON FOOT...

HMM... I COULD BLAST MY WAY INTO DR. ADAMS' TENT... BUT THAT WOULD MEAN KILLING THOSE GUARDS FIRST.

I'D STIR U WHOLE MAS IF I DID THA GOT TO BE WAY.

REACHING THE SAFETY OF THUNDERBIRD 1, SCOTT RADIOS BASE...

SOMEHOW, DAD, WE'VE GOTTA GET DR. ADAMS CLEAR WITHOUT HARMING THE MASAI!

I AGREE, SCOTT... TO AS MUCH AS SCRATCH ONE OF THOSE TRIBESMEN WOULD BE AGAINST EVERY PRINCIPLE INTERNATIONAL RESCUE STANDS FOR!

YES... AS I SEE IT, THE MASAI'S SACRED RHINO IS DYING. WE HAVE TO REPLACE IT WITHOUT THE TRIBESMEN REALISING...

KEEP YOUR DISTANCE, SCOTT... LEAVE THIS TO BRAINS TO FIGURE OUT... I THINK HE'S GOT SOME ANSWERS.

I SEE... THAT WAY THEY WILL THINK THE ANIMAL HAS BEEN CURED AND THE DOCTOR WILL BE RELEASED.

BRAINS ACTIO

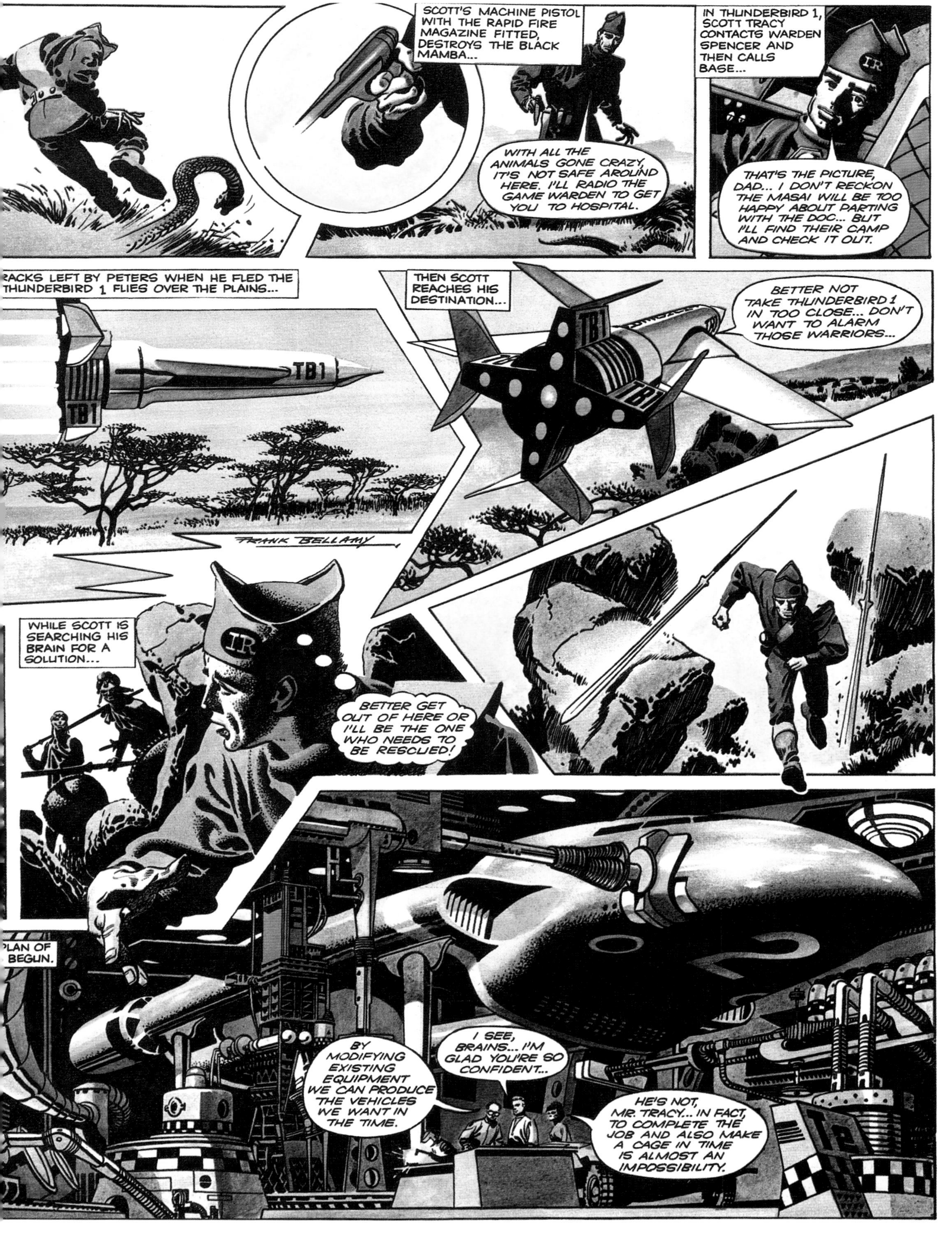
SCOTT'S MACHINE PISTOL WITH THE RAPID FIRE MAGAZINE FITTED, DESTROYS THE BLACK MAMBA...
WITH ALL THE ANIMALS GONE CRAZY, IT'S NOT SAFE AROUND HERE. I'LL RADIO THE GAME WARDEN TO GET YOU TO HOSPITAL.
IN THUNDERBIRD 1, SCOTT TRACY CONTACTS WARDEN SPENCER AND THEN CALLS BASE...
THAT'S THE PICTURE, DAD... I DON'T RECKON THE MASAI WILL BE TOO HAPPY ABOUT PARTING WITH THE DOC... BUT I'LL FIND THEIR CAMP AND CHECK IT OUT.
RACKS LEFT BY PETERS WHEN HE FLED THE THUNDERBIRD 1 FLIES OVER THE PLAINS...
TB1
TB1
FRANK BELLAMY
THEN SCOTT REACHES HIS DESTINATION...
BETTER NOT TAKE THUNDERBIRD 1 IN TOO CLOSE... DON'T WANT TO ALARM THOSE WARRIORS...
TB1
TB1
WHILE SCOTT IS SEARCHING HIS BRAIN FOR A SOLUTION...
BETTER GET OUT OF HERE OR I'LL BE THE ONE WHO NEEDS TO BE RESCUED!
IR
PLAN OF BEGUN.
BY MODIFYING EXISTING EQUIPMENT WE CAN PRODUCE THE VEHICLES WE WANT IN THE TIME.
I SEE, BRAINS... I'M GLAD YOU'RE SO CONFIDENT...
HE'S NOT, MR. TRACY... IN FACT, TO COMPLETE THE JOB AND ALSO MAKE A CAGE IN TIME IS ALMOST AN IMPOSSIBILITY.

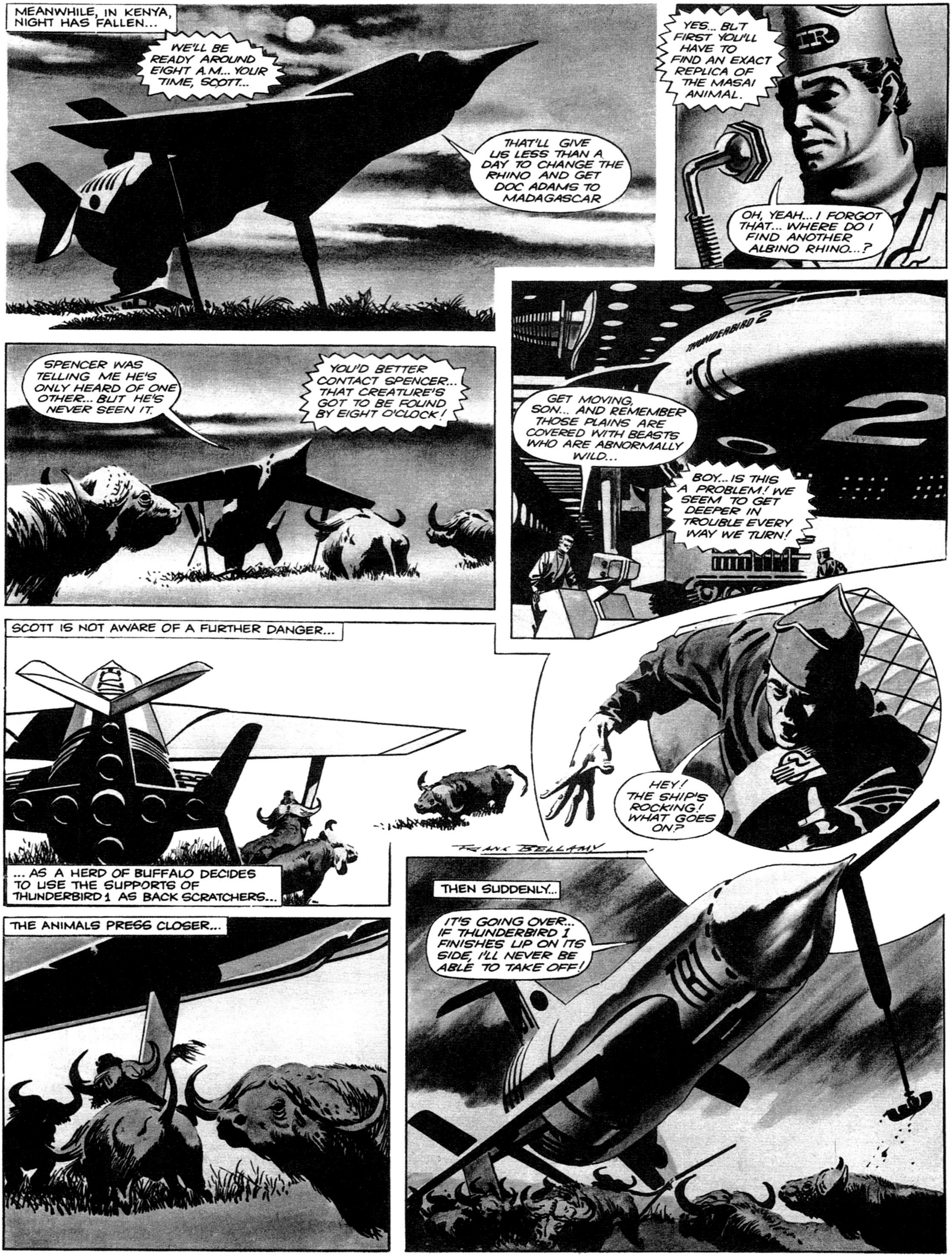
MEANWHILE, IN KENYA, NIGHT HAS FALLEN...
WE'LL BE READY AROUND EIGHT A.M... YOUR TIME, SCOTT...
THAT'LL GIVE US LESS THAN A DAY TO CHANGE THE RHINO AND GET DOC ADAMS TO MADAGASCAR
YES... BUT FIRST YOU'LL HAVE TO FIND AN EXACT REPLICA OF THE MASAI ANIMAL.
OH, YEAH... I FORGOT THAT... WHERE DO I FIND ANOTHER ALBINO RHINO...?
SPENCER WAS TELLING ME HE'S ONLY HEARD OF ONE OTHER... BUT HE'S NEVER SEEN IT.
YOU'D BETTER CONTACT SPENCER... THAT CREATURE'S GOT TO BE FOUND BY EIGHT O'CLOCK!
THUNDERBIRD 2
GET MOVING, SON... AND REMEMBER THOSE PLAINS ARE COVERED WITH BEASTS WHO ARE ABNORMALLY WILD...
BOY... IS THIS A PROBLEM! WE SEEM TO GET DEEPER IN TROUBLE EVERY WAY WE TURN!
SCOTT IS NOT AWARE OF A FURTHER DANGER...
... AS A HERD OF BUFFALO DECIDES TO USE THE SUPPORTS OF THUNDERBIRD 1 AS BACK SCRATCHERS...
HEY! THE SHIP'S ROCKING! WHAT GOES ON?
FRANK BELLAMY
THE ANIMALS PRESS CLOSER...
THEN SUDDENLY...
IT'S GOING OVER... IF THUNDERBIRD 1 FINISHES UP ON ITS SIDE, I'LL NEVER BE ABLE TO TAKE OFF!

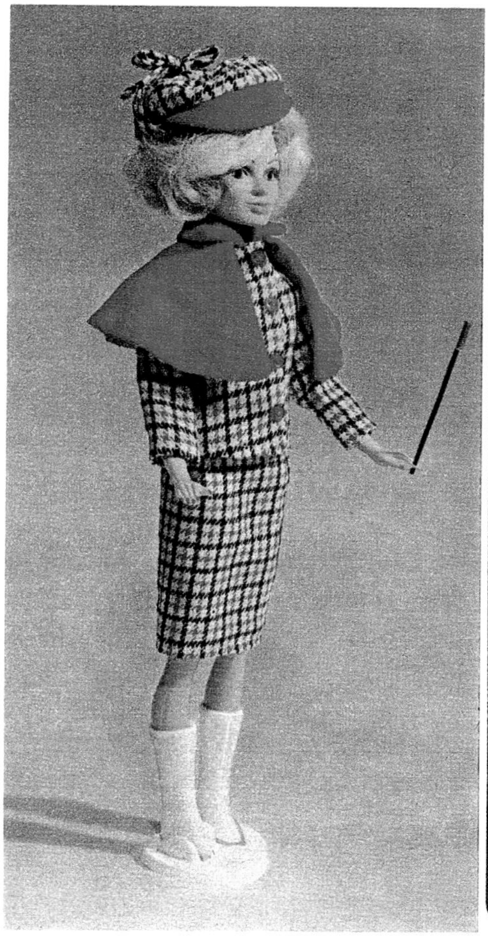

GIRLS! GIRLS! GIRLS!

Would you like to own

LADY PENELOPE–

The Doll of the YEAR!

Well, you can! It's in your local toy shop NOW.

With beautifully styled hair, this glamorous doll is 11 inches tall. Perfectly dressed—right down to the last detail—no LADY PENELOPE fan could resist her!

ALSO AVAILABLE—

a complete range of top fashion creations to dress her in

Fairylite REGD QUALITY TOYS

AND REMEMBER . . .

TIN TIN Same size! Same price!

(HURRY—Limited Supply)

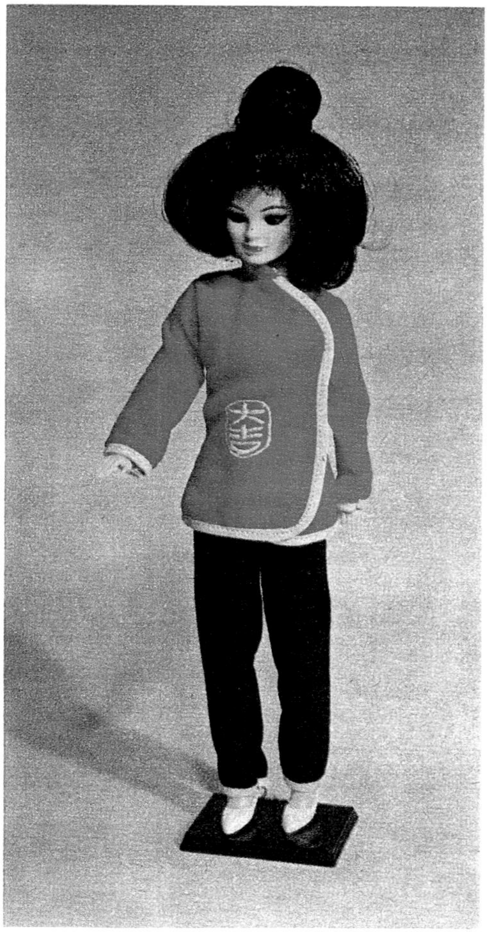

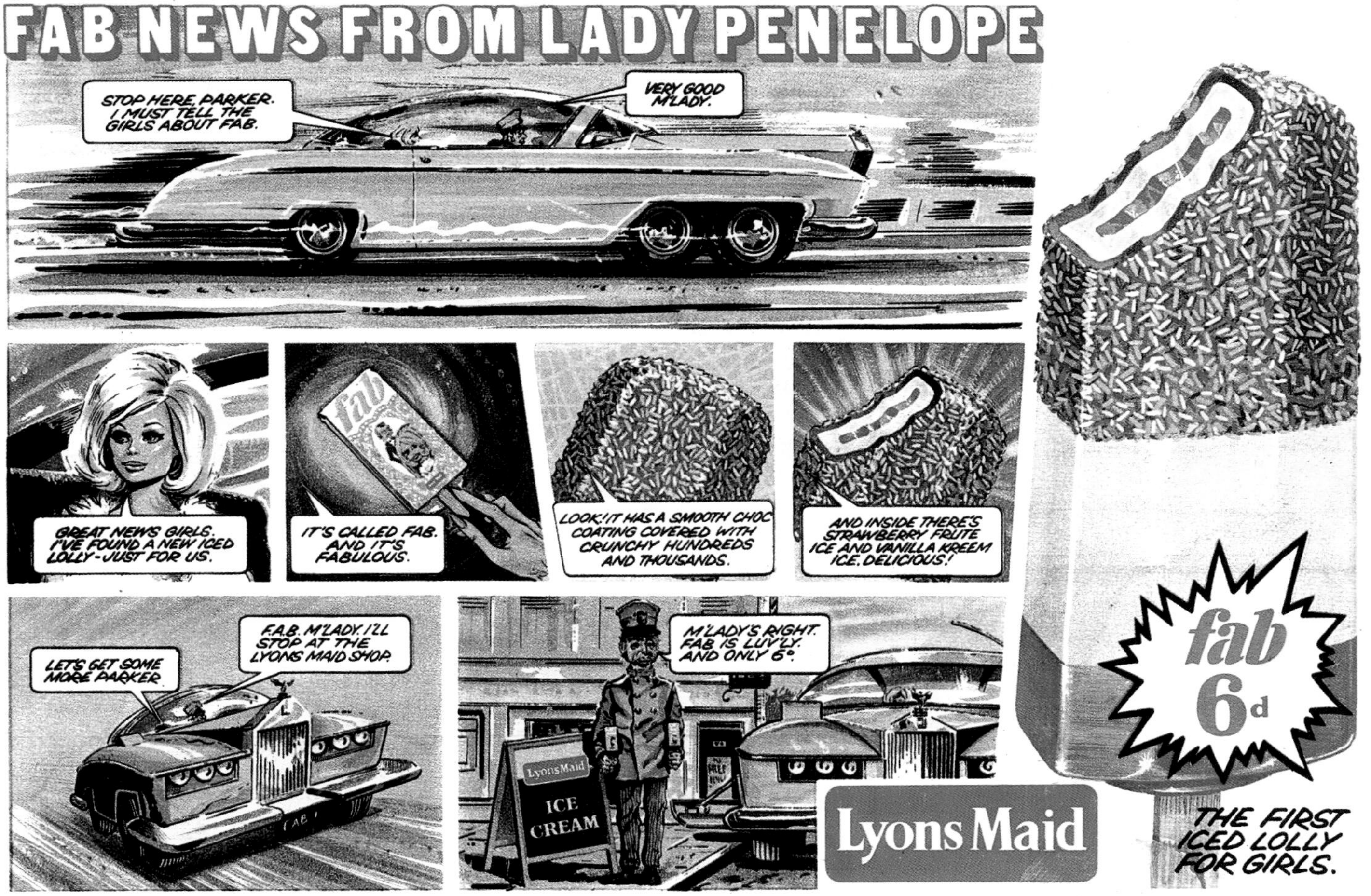
FAB NEWS FROM LADY PENELOPE
STOP HERE, PARKER. I MUST TELL THE GIRLS ABOUT FAB.
VERY GOOD M'LADY.
GREAT NEWS GIRLS. I'VE FOUND A NEW ICED LOLLY - JUST FOR US.
IT'S CALLED FAB. AND IT'S FABULOUS.
fab
LOOK! IT HAS A SMOOTH CHOC COATING COVERED WITH CRUNCHY HUNDREDS AND THOUSANDS.
AND INSIDE THERE'S STRAWBERRY FRUTE ICE AND VANILLA KREEM ICE. DELICIOUS!
LET'S GET SOME MORE PARKER
F.A.B. M'LADY. I'LL STOP AT THE LYONS MAID SHOP.
M'LADY'S RIGHT. FAB IS LUV'LY. AND ONLY 6D.
Lyons Maid
ICE CREAM
Lyons Maid
fab 6d
THE FIRST ICED LOLLY FOR GIRLS.

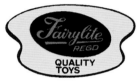

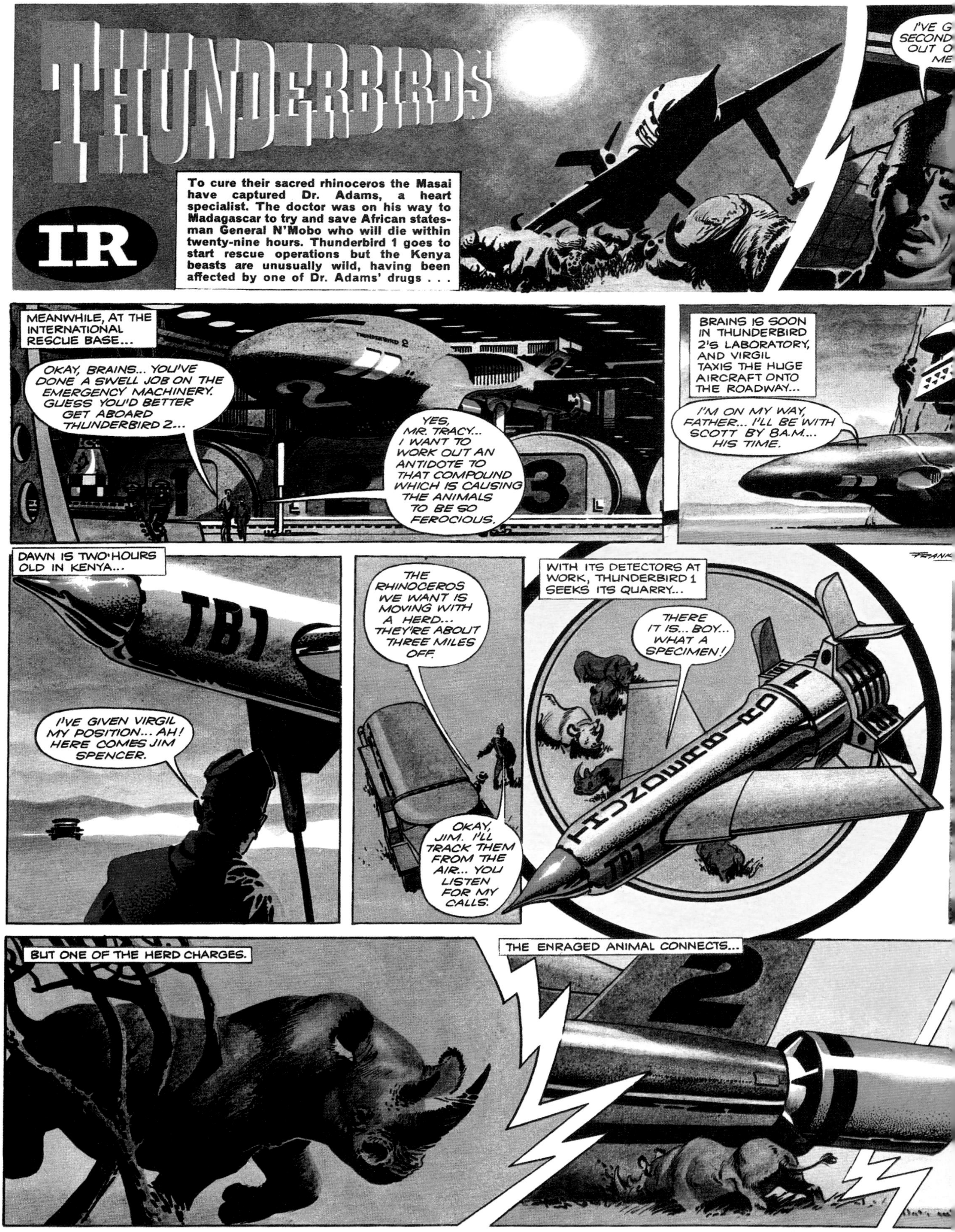
THUNDERBIRDS
IR
To cure their sacred rhinoceros the Masai have captured Dr. Adams, a heart specialist. The doctor was on his way to Madagascar to try and save African statesman General N'Mobo who will die within twenty-nine hours. Thunderbird 1 goes to start rescue operations but the Kenya beasts are unusually wild, having been affected by one of Dr. Adams' drugs . . .
MEANWHILE, AT THE INTERNATIONAL RESCUE BASE...
OKAY, BRAINS... YOU'VE DONE A SWELL JOB ON THE EMERGENCY MACHINERY. GUESS YOU'D BETTER GET ABOARD THUNDERBIRD 2...
YES, MR. TRACY... I WANT TO WORK OUT AN ANTIDOTE TO THAT COMPOUND WHICH IS CAUSING THE ANIMALS TO BE SO FEROCIOUS.
BRAINS IS SOON IN THUNDERBIRD 2'S LABORATORY, AND VIRGIL TAXIS THE HUGE AIRCRAFT ONTO THE ROADWAY...
I'M ON MY WAY, FATHER... I'LL BE WITH SCOTT BY 8A.M.... HIS TIME.
DAWN IS TWO HOURS OLD IN KENYA...
TB1
I'VE GIVEN VIRGIL MY POSITION... AH! HERE COMES JIM SPENCER.
THE RHINOCEROS WE WANT IS MOVING WITH A HERD... THEY'RE ABOUT THREE MILES OFF.
OKAY, JIM. I'LL TRACK THEM FROM THE AIR... YOU LISTEN FOR MY CALLS.
WITH ITS DETECTORS AT WORK, THUNDERBIRD 1 SEEKS ITS QUARRY...
THERE IT IS... BOY... WHAT A SPECIMEN!
BUT ONE OF THE HERD CHARGES.
THE ENRAGED ANIMAL CONNECTS...

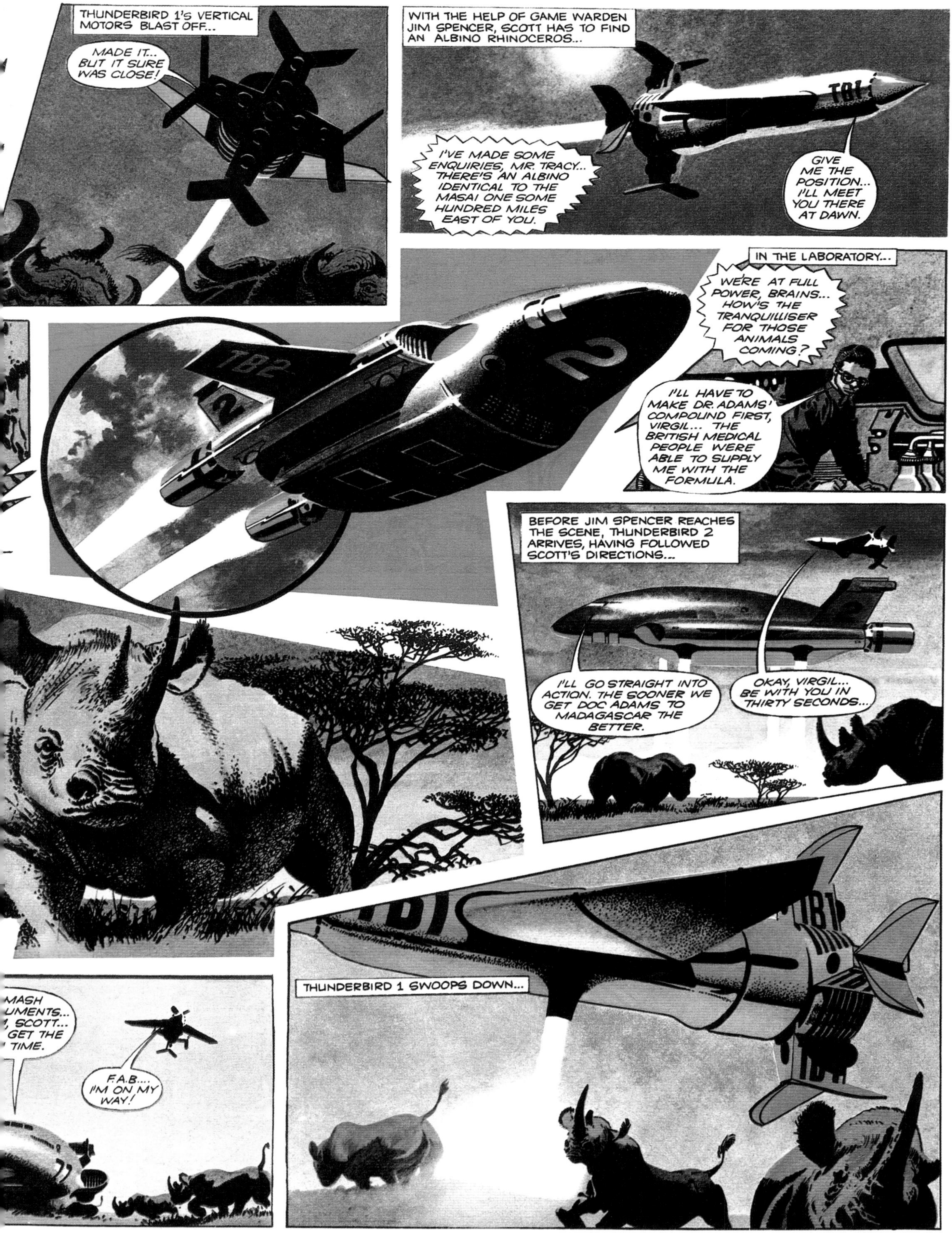

THUNDERBIRD 1'S VERTICAL MOTORS BLAST OFF...
MADE IT... BUT IT SURE WAS CLOSE!
WITH THE HELP OF GAME WARDEN JIM SPENCER, SCOTT HAS TO FIND AN ALBINO RHINOCEROS...
I'VE MADE SOME ENQUIRIES, MR. TRACY... THERE'S AN ALBINO IDENTICAL TO THE MASAI ONE SOME HUNDRED MILES EAST OF YOU.
GIVE ME THE POSITION... I'LL MEET YOU THERE AT DAWN.
IN THE LABORATORY...
WE'RE AT FULL POWER, BRAINS... HOW'S THE TRANQUILLISER FOR THOSE ANIMALS COMING?
I'LL HAVE TO MAKE DR. ADAMS' COMPOUND FIRST, VIRGIL... THE BRITISH MEDICAL PEOPLE WERE ABLE TO SUPPLY ME WITH THE FORMULA.
BEFORE JIM SPENCER REACHES THE SCENE, THUNDERBIRD 2 ARRIVES, HAVING FOLLOWED SCOTT'S DIRECTIONS...
I'LL GO STRAIGHT INTO ACTION. THE SOONER WE GET DOC ADAMS TO MADAGASCAR THE BETTER.
OKAY, VIRGIL... BE WITH YOU IN THIRTY SECONDS...
MASH UMENTS... , SCOTT... GET THE TIME.
F.A.B.... I'M ON MY WAY!
THUNDERBIRD 1 SWOOPS DOWN...

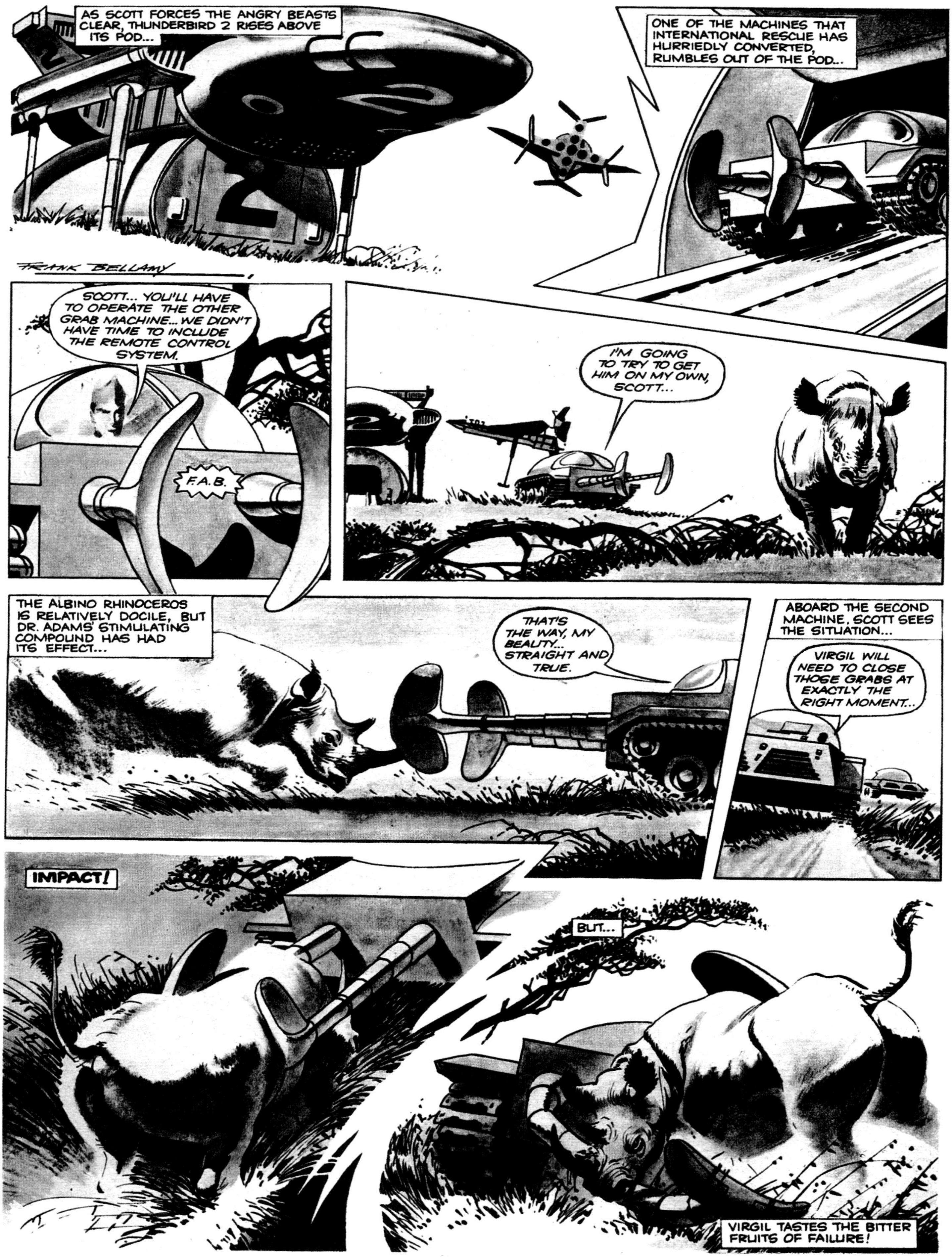
AS SCOTT FORCES THE ANGRY BEASTS CLEAR, THUNDERBIRD 2 RISES ABOVE ITS POD...
FRANK BELLAMY
ONE OF THE MACHINES THAT INTERNATIONAL RESCUE HAS HURRIEDLY CONVERTED, RUMBLES OUT OF THE POD...
SCOTT... YOU'LL HAVE TO OPERATE THE OTHER GRAB MACHINE... WE DIDN'T HAVE TIME TO INCLUDE THE REMOTE CONTROL SYSTEM.
F.A.B.
I'M GOING TO TRY TO GET HIM ON MY OWN, SCOTT...
THE ALBINO RHINOCEROS IS RELATIVELY DOCILE, BUT DR. ADAMS' STIMULATING COMPOUND HAS HAD ITS EFFECT...
THAT'S THE WAY, MY BEAUTY... STRAIGHT AND TRUE.
ABOARD THE SECOND MACHINE, SCOTT SEES THE SITUATION...
VIRGIL WILL NEED TO CLOSE THOSE GRABS AT EXACTLY THE RIGHT MOMENT...
IMPACT!
BUT...
VIRGIL TASTES THE BITTER FRUITS OF FAILURE!

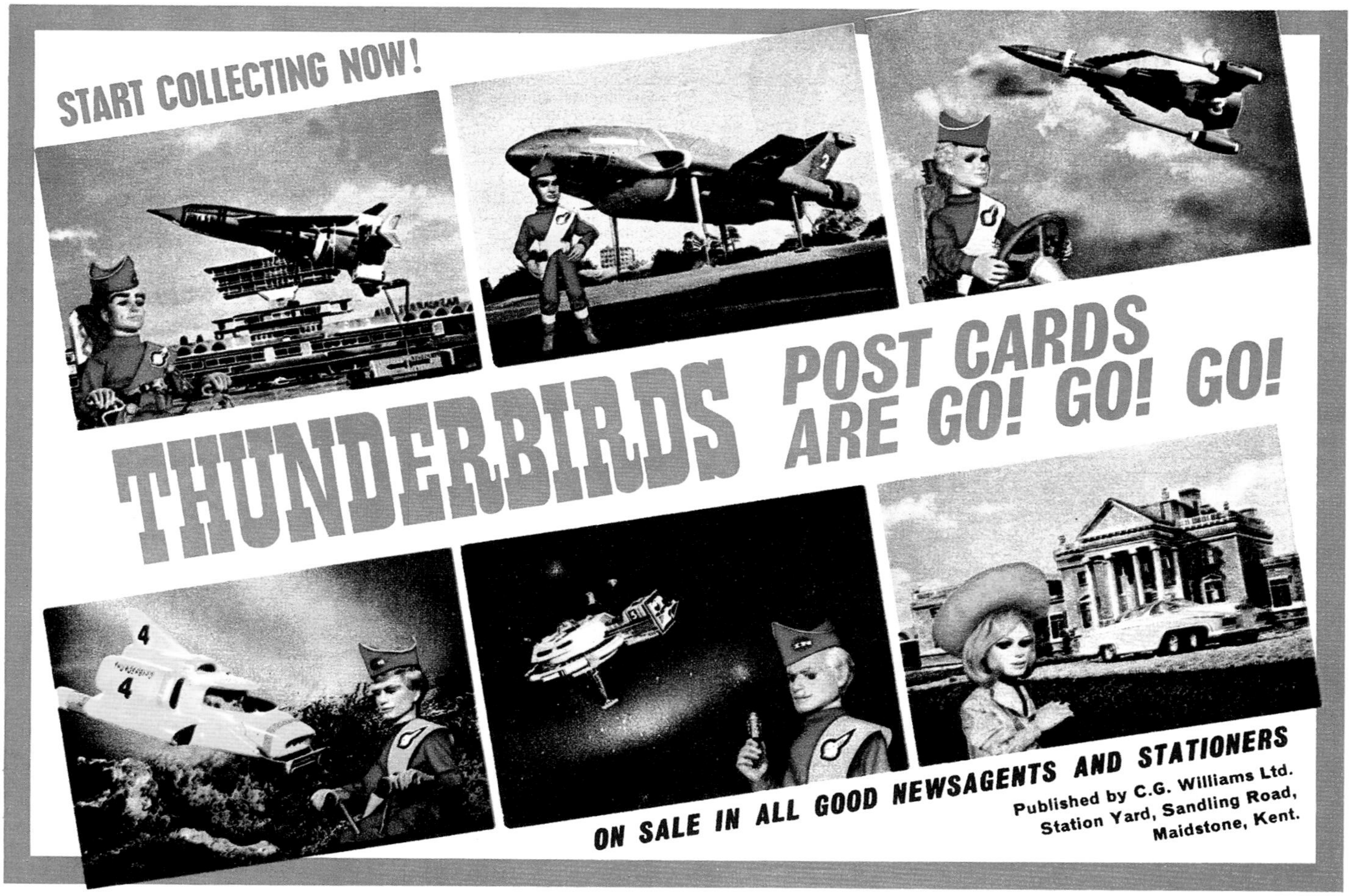

START COLLECTING NOW!
THUNDERBIRDS
POST CARDS ARE GO! GO! GO!
ON SALE IN ALL GOOD NEWSAGENTS AND STATIONERS
Published by C.G. Williams Ltd. Station Yard, Sandling Road, Maidstone, Kent.

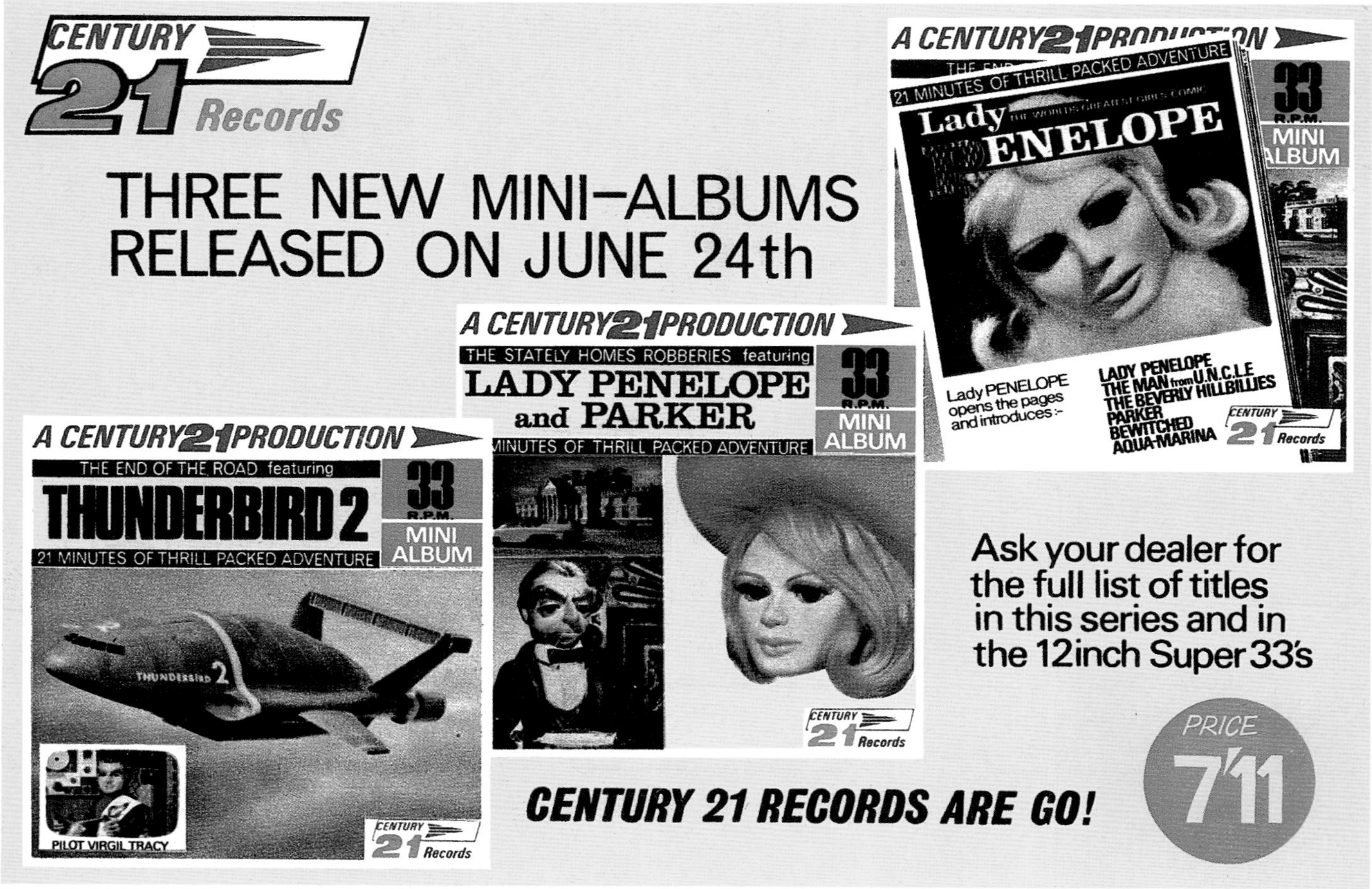

CENTURY 21 Records
THREE NEW MINI-ALBUMS
RELEASED ON JUNE 24th
A CENTURY 21 PRODUCTION
THE END OF THE ROAD featuring
THUNDERBIRD 2
21 MINUTES OF THRILL PACKED ADVENTURE
33 R.P.M.
MINI ALBUM
PILOT VIRGIL TRACY
A CENTURY 21 PRODUCTION
THE STATELY HOMES ROBBERIES featuring
LADY PENELOPE and PARKER
MINUTES OF THRILL PACKED ADVENTURE
33 R.P.M.
MINI ALBUM
21 MINUTES OF THRILL PACKED ADVENTURE
Lady PENELOPE
33 R.P.M.
MINI ALBUM
Lady PENELOPE opens the pages and introduces:-
LADY PENELOPE
THE MAN from U.N.C.L.E
THE BEVERLY HILLBILLIES
PARKER
BEWITCHED
AQUA-MARINA
Ask your dealer for the full list of titles in this series and in the 12inch Super 33's
CENTURY 21 RECORDS ARE GO!
PRICE 7'11

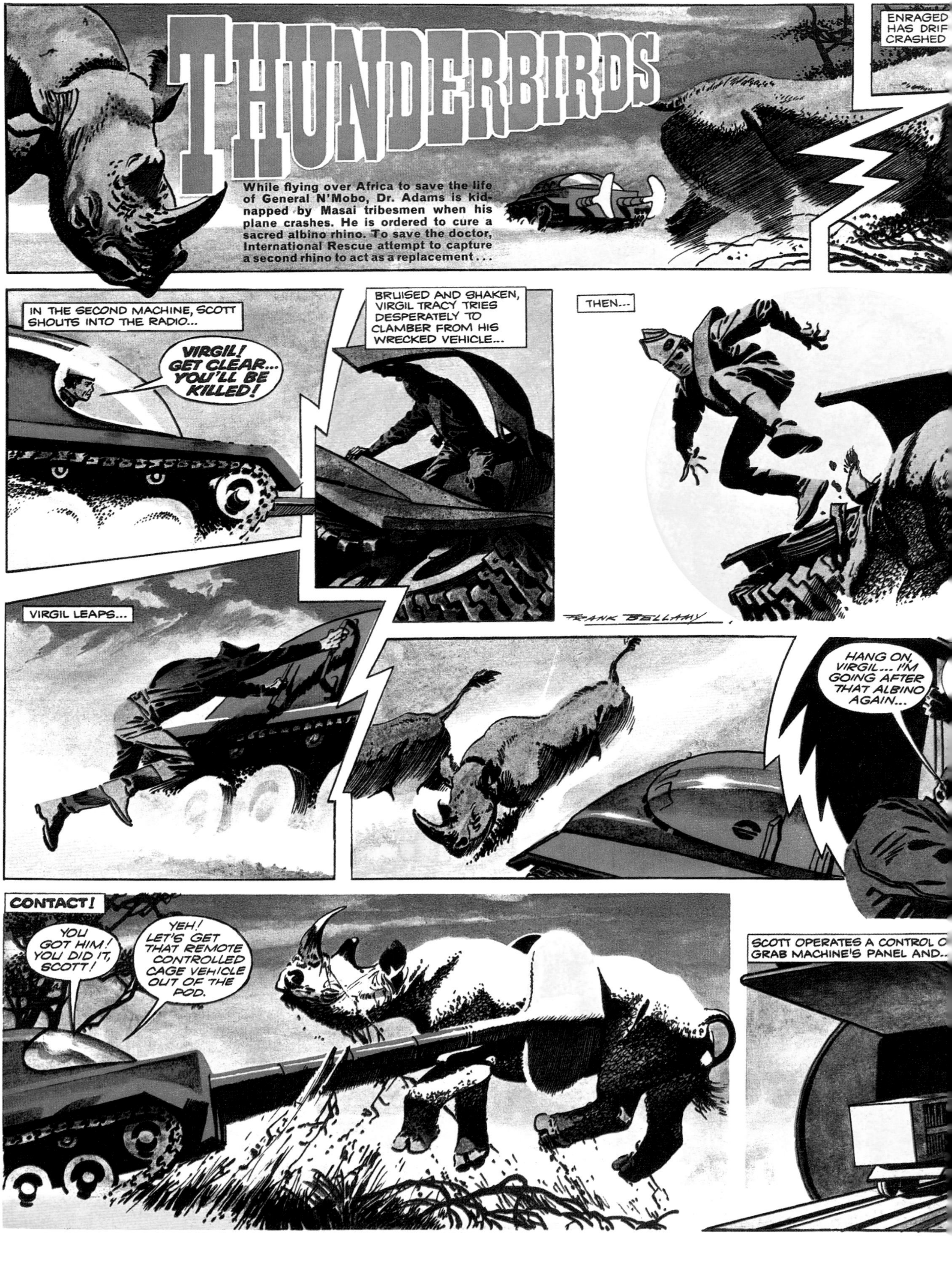
THUNDERBIRDS
While flying over Africa to save the life of General N'Mobo, Dr. Adams is kidnapped by Masai tribesmen when his plane crashes. He is ordered to cure a sacred albino rhino. To save the doctor, International Rescue attempt to capture a second rhino to act as a replacement . . .
ENRAGED HAS DRIF CRASHED
IN THE SECOND MACHINE, SCOTT SHOUTS INTO THE RADIO...
VIRGIL! GET CLEAR... YOU'LL BE KILLED!
BRUISED AND SHAKEN, VIRGIL TRACY TRIES DESPERATELY TO CLAMBER FROM HIS WRECKED VEHICLE...
THEN...
FRANK BELLAMY
VIRGIL LEAPS...
HANG ON, VIRGIL... I'M GOING AFTER THAT ALBINO AGAIN...
CONTACT!
YOU GOT HIM! YOU DID IT, SCOTT!
YEH! LET'S GET THAT REMOTE CONTROLLED CAGE VEHICLE OUT OF THE POD.
SCOTT OPERATES A CONTROL O GRAB MACHINE'S PANEL AND...

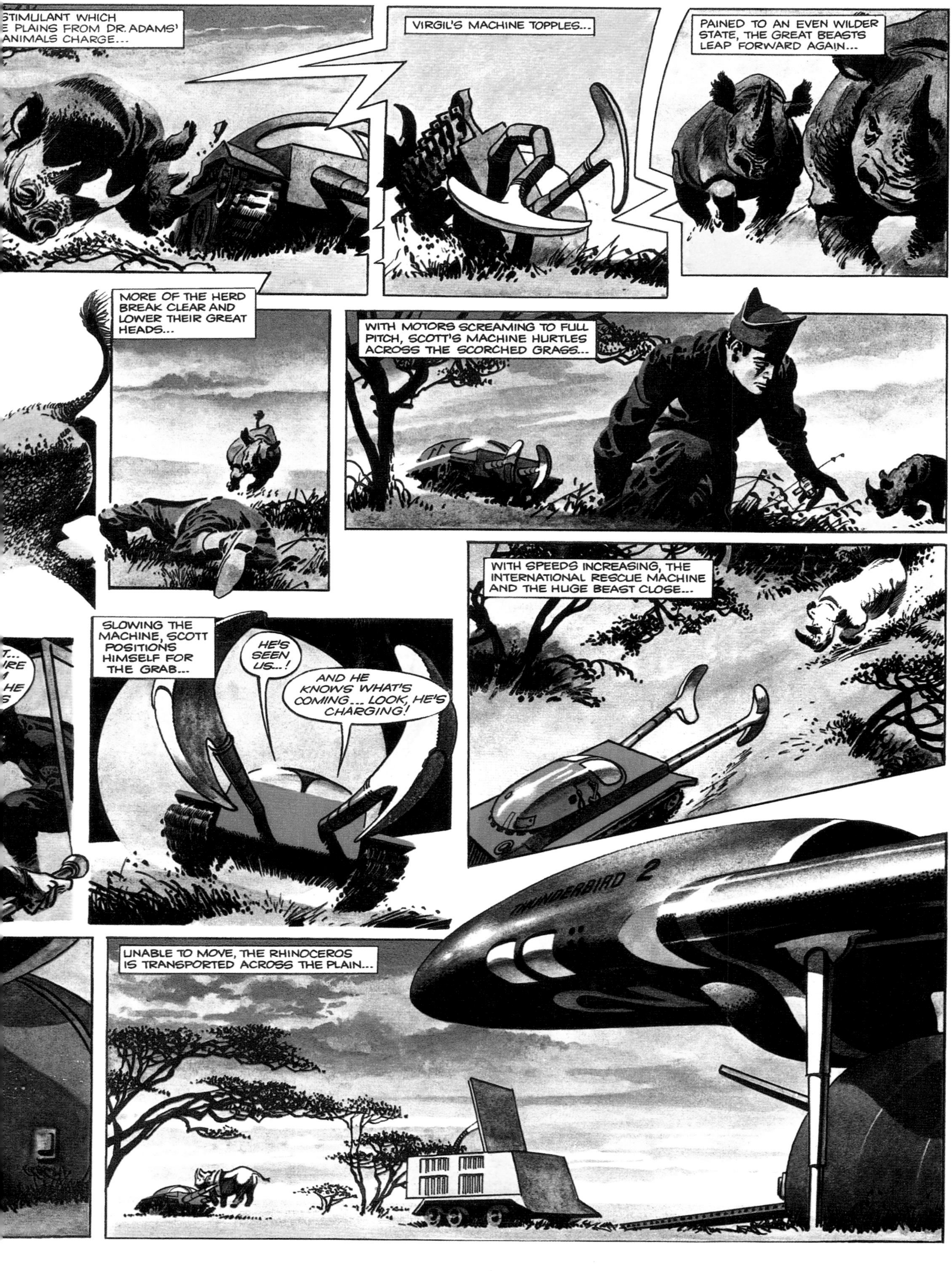
STIMULANT WHICH
E PLAINS FROM DR. ADAMS'
ANIMALS CHARGE...
VIRGIL'S MACHINE TOPPLES...
PAINED TO AN EVEN WILDER STATE, THE GREAT BEASTS LEAP FORWARD AGAIN...
MORE OF THE HERD BREAK CLEAR AND LOWER THEIR GREAT HEADS...
WITH MOTORS SCREAMING TO FULL PITCH, SCOTT'S MACHINE HURTLES ACROSS THE SCORCHED GRASS...
WITH SPEEDS INCREASING, THE INTERNATIONAL RESCUE MACHINE AND THE HUGE BEAST CLOSE...
SLOWING THE MACHINE, SCOTT POSITIONS HIMSELF FOR THE GRAB...
HE'S SEEN US...!
AND HE KNOWS WHAT'S COMING... LOOK, HE'S CHARGING!
THUNDERBIRD 2
UNABLE TO MOVE, THE RHINOCEROS IS TRANSPORTED ACROSS THE PLAIN...

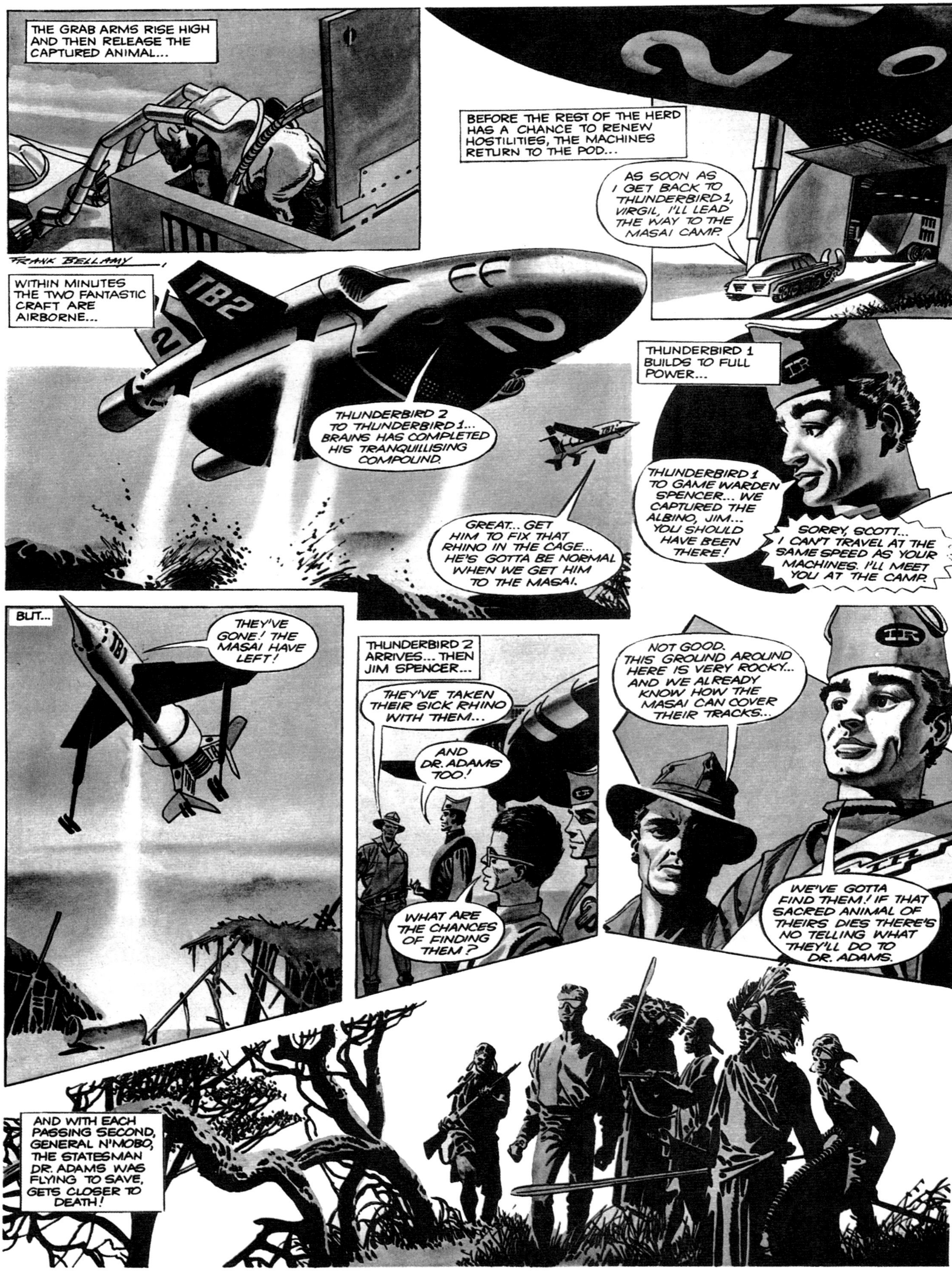
THE GRAB ARMS RISE HIGH AND THEN RELEASE THE CAPTURED ANIMAL...
BEFORE THE REST OF THE HERD HAS A CHANCE TO RENEW HOSTILITIES, THE MACHINES RETURN TO THE POD...
AS SOON AS I GET BACK TO THUNDERBIRD 1, VIRGIL, I'LL LEAD THE WAY TO THE MASAI CAMP.
FRANK BELLAMY
WITHIN MINUTES THE TWO FANTASTIC CRAFT ARE AIRBORNE...
TB2
THUNDERBIRD 2 TO THUNDERBIRD 1... BRAINS HAS COMPLETED HIS TRANQUILLISING COMPOUND.
GREAT... GET HIM TO FIX THAT RHINO IN THE CAGE... HE'S GOTTA BE NORMAL WHEN WE GET HIM TO THE MASAI.
THUNDERBIRD 1 BUILDS TO FULL POWER...
THUNDERBIRD 1 TO GAME WARDEN SPENCER... WE CAPTURED THE ALBINO, JIM... YOU SHOULD HAVE BEEN THERE!
SORRY, SCOTT... I CAN'T TRAVEL AT THE SAME SPEED AS YOUR MACHINES. I'LL MEET YOU AT THE CAMP.
BUT...
THEY'VE GONE! THE MASAI HAVE LEFT!
TB1
THUNDERBIRD 2 ARRIVES... THEN JIM SPENCER...
THEY'VE TAKEN THEIR SICK RHINO WITH THEM...
AND DR. ADAMS TOO!
WHAT ARE THE CHANCES OF FINDING THEM?
NOT GOOD. THIS GROUND AROUND HERE IS VERY ROCKY... AND WE ALREADY KNOW HOW THE MASAI CAN COVER THEIR TRACKS...
WE'VE GOTTA FIND THEM! IF THAT SACRED ANIMAL OF THEIRS DIES THERE'S NO TELLING WHAT THEY'LL DO TO DR. ADAMS.
AND WITH EACH PASSING SECOND, GENERAL N'MOBO, THE STATESMAN DR. ADAMS WAS FLYING TO SAVE, GETS CLOSER TO DEATH!

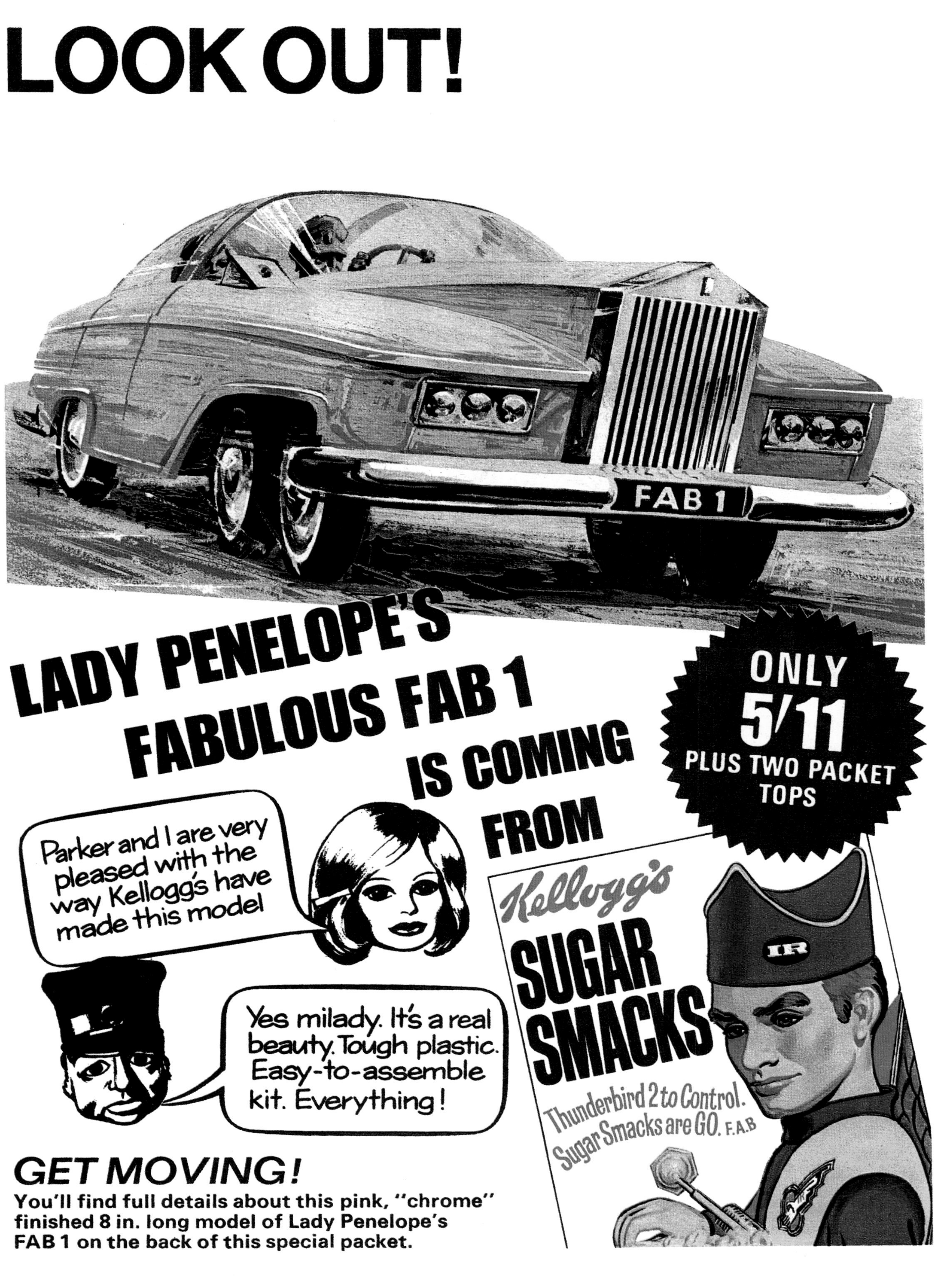
LOOK OUT!
FAB 1
LADY PENELOPE'S
FABULOUS FAB 1
IS COMING
FROM
ONLY
5/11
PLUS TWO PACKET TOPS
Parker and I are very pleased with the way Kellogg's have made this model
Yes milady. It's a real beauty. Tough plastic. Easy-to-assemble kit. Everything!
Kellogg's
SUGAR SMACKS
IR
Thunderbird 2 to Control. Sugar Smacks are GO. F.A.B
GET MOVING!
You'll find full details about this pink, "chrome" finished 8 in. long model of Lady Penelope's FAB 1 on the back of this special packet.

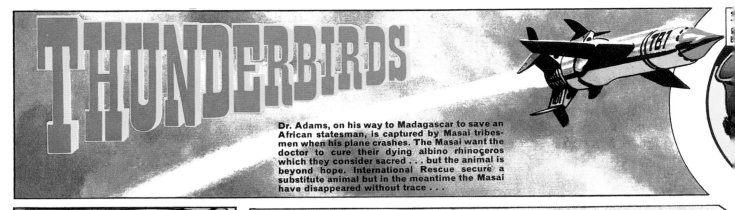

THUNDERBIRDS

Dr. Adams, on his way to Madagascar to save an African statesman, is captured by Masai tribesmen when his plane crashes. The Masai want the doctor to cure their dying albino rhinoceros which they consider sacred . . . but the animal is beyond hope. International Rescue secure a substitute animal but in the meantime the Masai have disappeared without trace . . .

I SEE, BRAINS, SO THAT THE TRIBESMEN THINK THEIR SACRED BEAST HAS BEEN CURED...

YES... THEN THEY WILL RELEASE DR. ADAMS. NOW THIS IS WHAT YOU HAVE TO DO, VIRGIL...

BRAINS EXPLAINS THAT THE MASAI HAVE MANY SACRED SYMBOLS, ONE OF WHICH IS RAIN. THUNDERBIRD 2 ALTERS COURSE, AND SCOTT CONTINUES THE SEARCH FOR THE TRIBESMEN...

THUNDERBIRD 1 TO THUNDERBIRD 2... I'VE FOUND THEM! MAP REFERENCE 7 AREA 19. HURRY, VIRGIL!

FRANK BELLAMY

INSIDE THE MACHINE IS THE TRANQUIL ALBINO RHINOCEROS CAPTURED BY SCOTT. HE GUIDES THE VEHICLE CLOSER TO THE CAMP...

THUNDERBIRD 2 LIFTS OFF...

THE CAMP BECOMES WILD WITH EXCITEMENT...

COME, WE MUST GIVE THANKS FOR THE RAIN.

SCOTT MEANWHILE HAS LANDED, AND BY REMOTE CONTROL STEERS THE CAGE VEHICLE INTO THE CAMP...

BRAINS' PLAN WORKED... NOW TO SWITCH THE RHINOS.

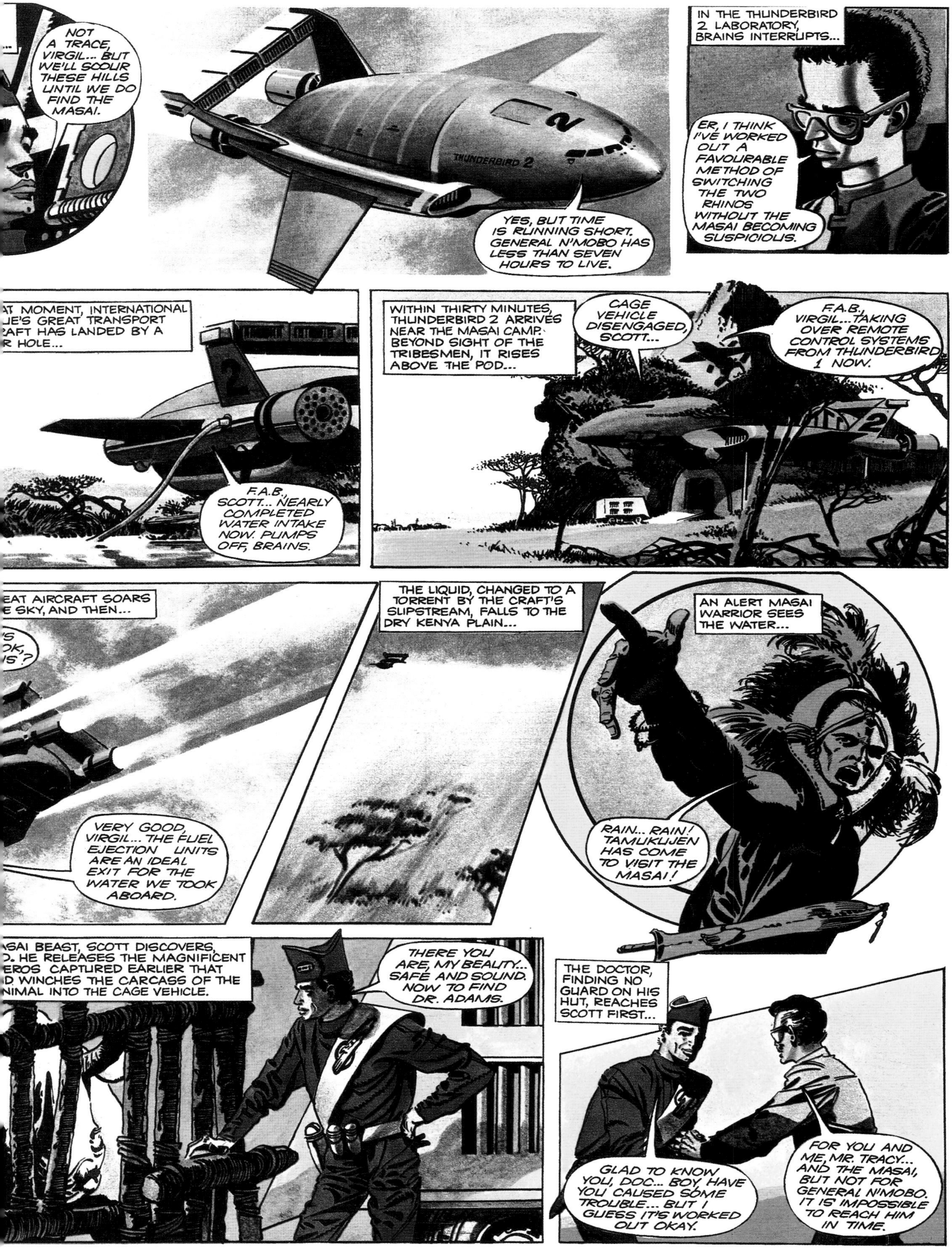

NOT A TRACE, VIRGIL... BUT WE'LL SCOUR THESE HILLS UNTIL WE DO FIND THE MASAI.
THUNDERBIRD 2
YES, BUT TIME IS RUNNING SHORT. GENERAL N'MOBO HAS LESS THAN SEVEN HOURS TO LIVE.
IN THE THUNDERBIRD 2 LABORATORY, BRAINS INTERRUPTS...
ER, I THINK I'VE WORKED OUT A FAVOURABLE METHOD OF SWITCHING THE TWO RHINOS WITHOUT THE MASAI BECOMING SUSPICIOUS.
AT MOMENT, INTERNATIONAL UE'S GREAT TRANSPORT RAFT HAS LANDED BY A R HOLE...
F.A.B., SCOTT... NEARLY COMPLETED WATER INTAKE NOW. PUMPS OFF, BRAINS.
WITHIN THIRTY MINUTES, THUNDERBIRD 2 ARRIVES NEAR THE MASAI CAMP. BEYOND SIGHT OF THE TRIBESMEN, IT RISES ABOVE THE POD...
CAGE VEHICLE DISENGAGED, SCOTT...
F.A.B., VIRGIL... TAKING OVER REMOTE CONTROL SYSTEMS FROM THUNDERBIRD 1 NOW.
EAT AIRCRAFT SOARS E SKY, AND THEN...
VERY GOOD, VIRGIL... THE FUEL EJECTION UNITS ARE AN IDEAL EXIT FOR THE WATER WE TOOK ABOARD.
THE LIQUID, CHANGED TO A TORRENT BY THE CRAFT'S SLIPSTREAM, FALLS TO THE DRY KENYA PLAIN...
AN ALERT MASAI WARRIOR SEES THE WATER...
RAIN... RAIN! TAMUKUJEN HAS COME TO VISIT THE MASAI!
ASAI BEAST, SCOTT DISCOVERS, D. HE RELEASES THE MAGNIFICENT EROS CAPTURED EARLIER THAT D WINCHES THE CARCASS OF THE NIMAL INTO THE CAGE VEHICLE.
THERE YOU ARE, MY BEAUTY... SAFE AND SOUND. NOW TO FIND DR. ADAMS.
THE DOCTOR, FINDING NO GUARD ON HIS HUT, REACHES SCOTT FIRST...
GLAD TO KNOW YOU, DOC... BOY HAVE YOU CAUSED SOME TROUBLE... BUT I GUESS IT'S WORKED OUT OKAY.
FOR YOU AND ME, MR. TRACY... AND THE MASAI, BUT NOT FOR GENERAL N'MOBO. IT IS IMPOSSIBLE TO REACH HIM IN TIME.

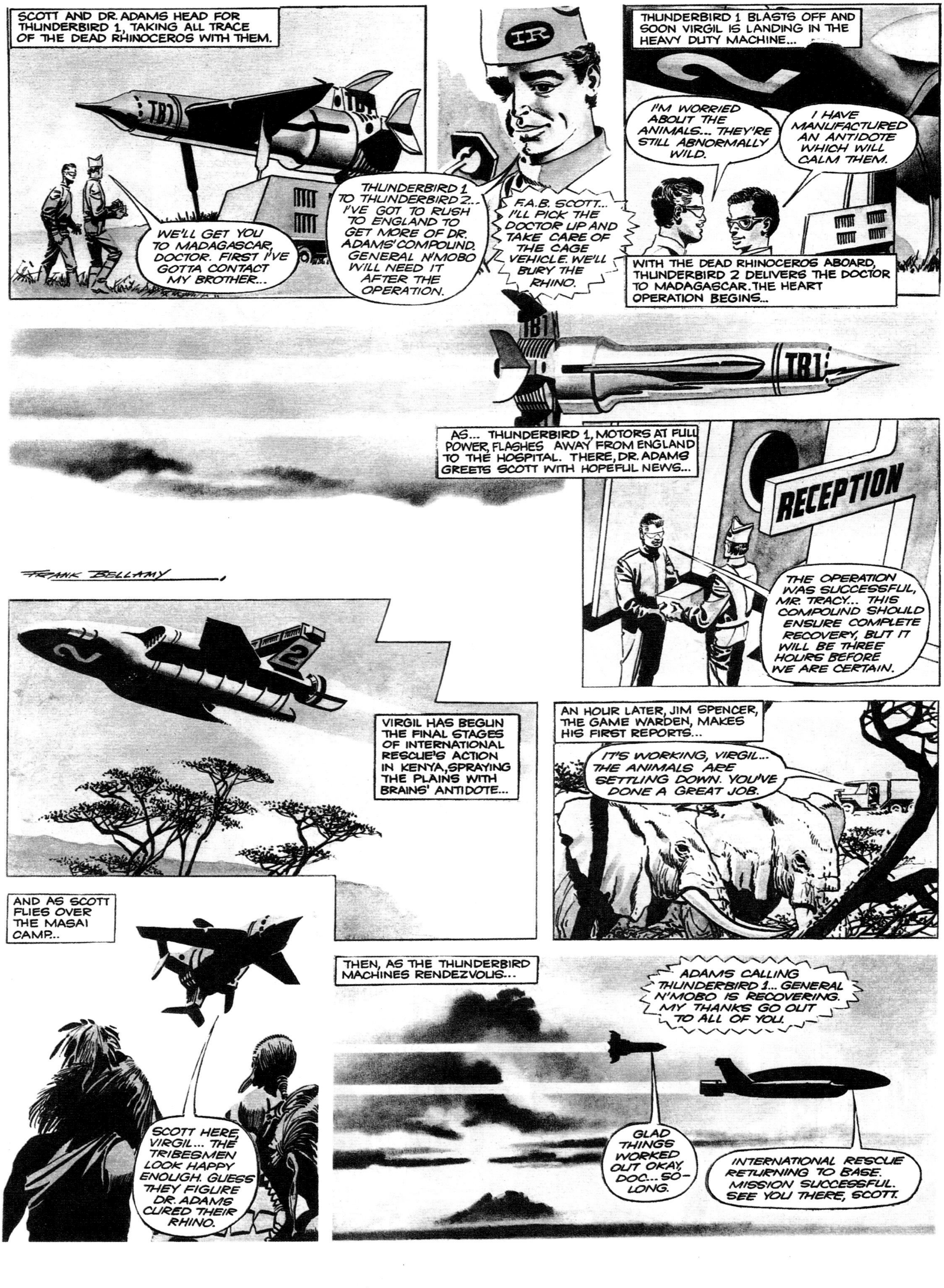
SCOTT AND DR. ADAMS HEAD FOR THUNDERBIRD 1, TAKING ALL TRACE OF THE DEAD RHINOCEROS WITH THEM.
WE'LL GET YOU TO MADAGASCAR, DOCTOR. FIRST I'VE GOTTA CONTACT MY BROTHER...
THUNDERBIRD 1 TO THUNDERBIRD 2... I'VE GOT TO RUSH TO ENGLAND TO GET MORE OF DR. ADAMS' COMPOUND. GENERAL N'MOBO WILL NEED IT AFTER THE OPERATION.
F.A.B. SCOTT... I'LL PICK THE DOCTOR UP AND TAKE CARE OF THE CAGE VEHICLE. WE'LL BURY THE RHINO.
THUNDERBIRD 1 BLASTS OFF AND SOON VIRGIL IS LANDING IN THE HEAVY DUTY MACHINE...
I'M WORRIED ABOUT THE ANIMALS... THEY'RE STILL ABNORMALLY WILD.
I HAVE MANUFACTURED AN ANTIDOTE WHICH WILL CALM THEM.
WITH THE DEAD RHINOCEROS ABOARD, THUNDERBIRD 2 DELIVERS THE DOCTOR TO MADAGASCAR. THE HEART OPERATION BEGINS...
AS... THUNDERBIRD 1, MOTORS AT FULL POWER, FLASHES AWAY FROM ENGLAND TO THE HOSPITAL. THERE, DR. ADAMS GREETS SCOTT WITH HOPEFUL NEWS...
RECEPTION
THE OPERATION WAS SUCCESSFUL, MR. TRACY... THIS COMPOUND SHOULD ENSURE COMPLETE RECOVERY, BUT IT WILL BE THREE HOURS BEFORE WE ARE CERTAIN.
FRANK BELLAMY
VIRGIL HAS BEGUN THE FINAL STAGES OF INTERNATIONAL RESCUE'S ACTION IN KENYA, SPRAYING THE PLAINS WITH BRAINS' ANTIDOTE...
AN HOUR LATER, JIM SPENCER, THE GAME WARDEN, MAKES HIS FIRST REPORTS...
IT'S WORKING, VIRGIL... THE ANIMALS ARE SETTLING DOWN. YOU'VE DONE A GREAT JOB.
AND AS SCOTT FLIES OVER THE MASAI CAMP...
SCOTT HERE, VIRGIL... THE TRIBESMEN LOOK HAPPY ENOUGH. GUESS THEY FIGURE DR. ADAMS CURED THEIR RHINO.
THEN, AS THE THUNDERBIRD MACHINES RENDEZVOUS...
ADAMS CALLING THUNDERBIRD 1... GENERAL N'MOBO IS RECOVERING. MY THANKS GO OUT TO ALL OF YOU.
GLAD THINGS WORKED OUT OKAY, DOC... SO LONG.
INTERNATIONAL RESCUE RETURNING TO BASE. MISSION SUCCESSFUL. SEE YOU THERE, SCOTT.

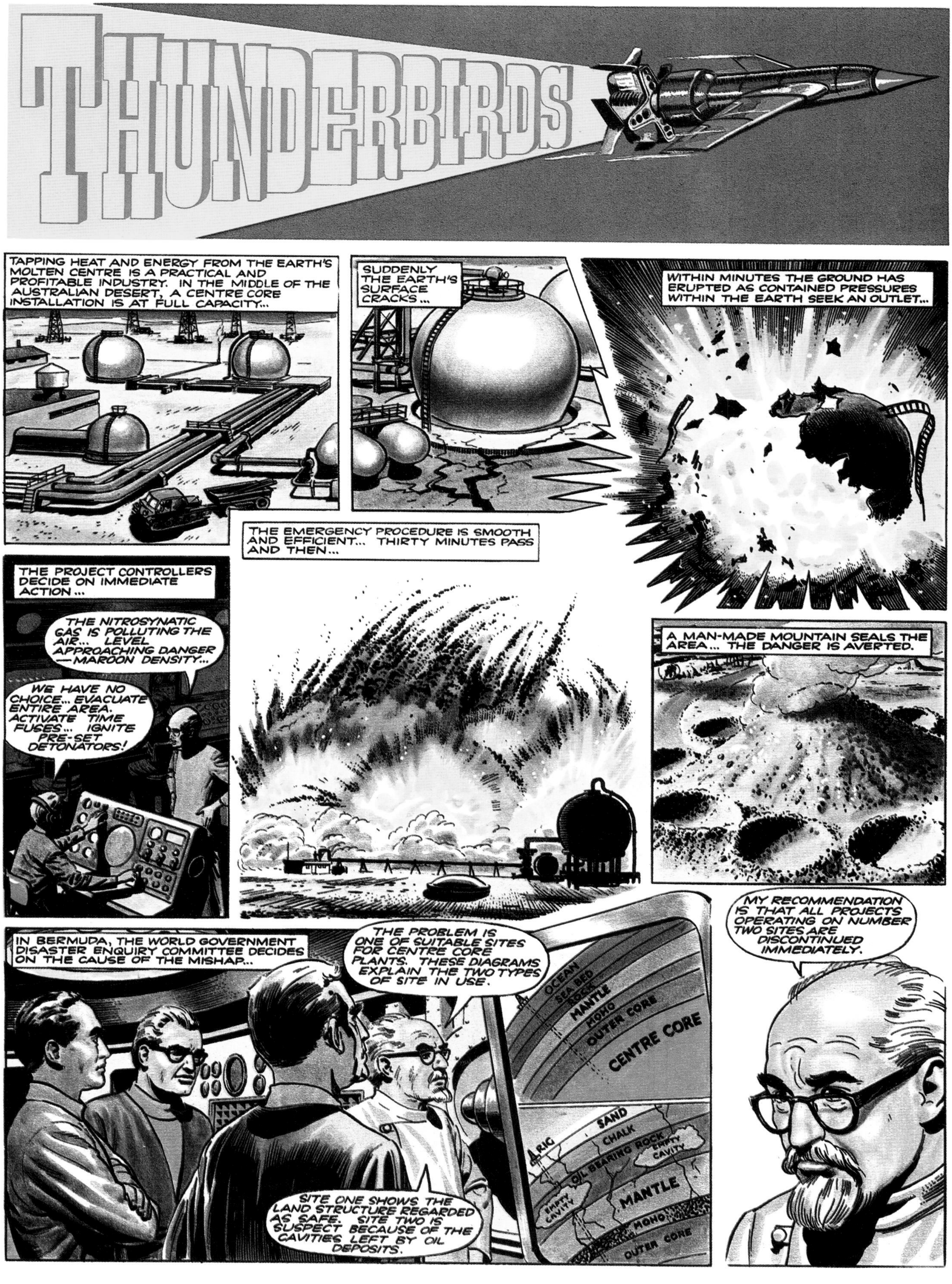
THUNDERBIRDS
TAPPING HEAT AND ENERGY FROM THE EARTH'S MOLTEN CENTRE IS A PRACTICAL AND PROFITABLE INDUSTRY. IN THE MIDDLE OF THE AUSTRALIAN DESERT, A CENTRE CORE INSTALLATION IS AT FULL CAPACITY...
SUDDENLY THE EARTH'S SURFACE CRACKS...
WITHIN MINUTES THE GROUND HAS ERUPTED AS CONTAINED PRESSURES WITHIN THE EARTH SEEK AN OUTLET...
THE EMERGENCY PROCEDURE IS SMOOTH AND EFFICIENT... THIRTY MINUTES PASS AND THEN...
THE PROJECT CONTROLLERS DECIDE ON IMMEDIATE ACTION...
THE NITROSYNATIC GAS IS POLLUTING THE AIR... LEVEL APPROACHING DANGER —MAROON DENSITY...
WE HAVE NO CHOICE... EVACUATE ENTIRE AREA. ACTIVATE TIME FUSES... IGNITE PRE-SET DETONATORS!
A MAN-MADE MOUNTAIN SEALS THE AREA... THE DANGER IS AVERTED.
IN BERMUDA, THE WORLD GOVERNMENT DISASTER ENQUIRY COMMITTEE DECIDES ON THE CAUSE OF THE MISHAP...
THE PROBLEM IS ONE OF SUITABLE SITES FOR CENTRE CORE PLANTS. THESE DIAGRAMS EXPLAIN THE TWO TYPES OF SITE IN USE.
OCEAN
SEA BED
ROCK
MANTLE
MOHO
OUTER CORE
CENTRE CORE
RIG
SAND
CHALK
OIL BEARING ROCK
EMPTY CAVITY
EMPTY CAVITY
MANTLE
MOHO
OUTER CORE
SITE ONE SHOWS THE LAND STRUCTURE REGARDED AS SAFE. SITE TWO IS SUSPECT BECAUSE OF THE CAVITIES LEFT BY OIL DEPOSITS.
MY RECOMMENDATION IS THAT ALL PROJECTS OPERATING ON NUMBER TWO SITES ARE DISCONTINUED IMMEDIATELY.

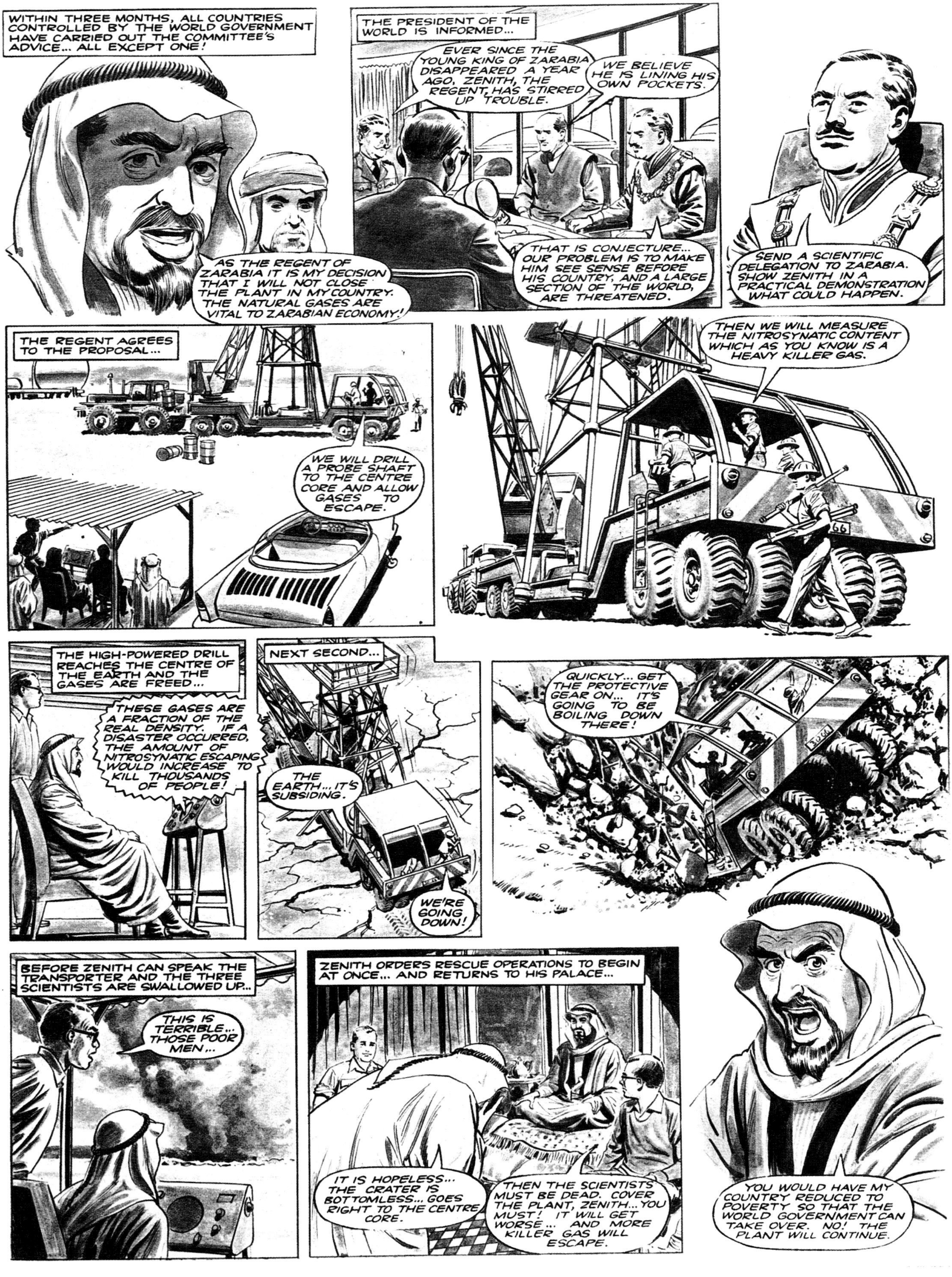

WITHIN THREE MONTHS, ALL COUNTRIES CONTROLLED BY THE WORLD GOVERNMENT HAVE CARRIED OUT THE COMMITTEE'S ADVICE... ALL EXCEPT ONE!
AS THE REGENT OF ZARABIA IT IS MY DECISION THAT I WILL NOT CLOSE THE PLANT IN MY COUNTRY. THE NATURAL GASES ARE VITAL TO ZARABIAN ECONOMY!
THE PRESIDENT OF THE WORLD IS INFORMED...
EVER SINCE THE YOUNG KING OF ZARABIA DISAPPEARED A YEAR AGO, ZENITH, THE REGENT, HAS STIRRED UP TROUBLE.
WE BELIEVE HE IS LINING HIS OWN POCKETS.
THAT IS CONJECTURE... OUR PROBLEM IS TO MAKE HIM SEE SENSE BEFORE HIS COUNTRY, AND A LARGE SECTION OF THE WORLD, ARE THREATENED.
SEND A SCIENTIFIC DELEGATION TO ZARABIA. SHOW ZENITH IN A PRACTICAL DEMONSTRATION WHAT COULD HAPPEN.
THE REGENT AGREES TO THE PROPOSAL...
WE WILL DRILL A PROBE SHAFT TO THE CENTRE CORE AND ALLOW GASES TO ESCAPE.
THEN WE WILL MEASURE THE NITROSYNATIC CONTENT WHICH AS YOU KNOW IS A HEAVY KILLER GAS.
THE HIGH-POWERED DRILL REACHES THE CENTRE OF THE EARTH AND THE GASES ARE FREED...
THESE GASES ARE A FRACTION OF THE REAL DENSITY. IF A DISASTER OCCURRED, THE AMOUNT OF NITROSYNATIC ESCAPING WOULD INCREASE TO KILL THOUSANDS OF PEOPLE!
NEXT SECOND...
THE EARTH... IT'S SUBSIDING.
WE'RE GOING DOWN!
QUICKLY... GET THE PROTECTIVE GEAR ON... IT'S GOING TO BE BOILING DOWN THERE!
BEFORE ZENITH CAN SPEAK THE TRANSPORTER AND THE THREE SCIENTISTS ARE SWALLOWED UP...
THIS IS TERRIBLE... THOSE POOR MEN...
ZENITH ORDERS RESCUE OPERATIONS TO BEGIN AT ONCE... AND RETURNS TO HIS PALACE...
IT IS HOPELESS... THE CRATER IS BOTTOMLESS... GOES RIGHT TO THE CENTRE CORE.
THEN THE SCIENTISTS MUST BE DEAD. COVER THE PLANT, ZENITH... YOU MUST! IT WILL GET WORSE... AND MORE KILLER GAS WILL ESCAPE.
YOU WOULD HAVE MY COUNTRY REDUCED TO POVERTY SO THAT THE WORLD GOVERNMENT CAN TAKE OVER. NO! THE PLANT WILL CONTINUE.

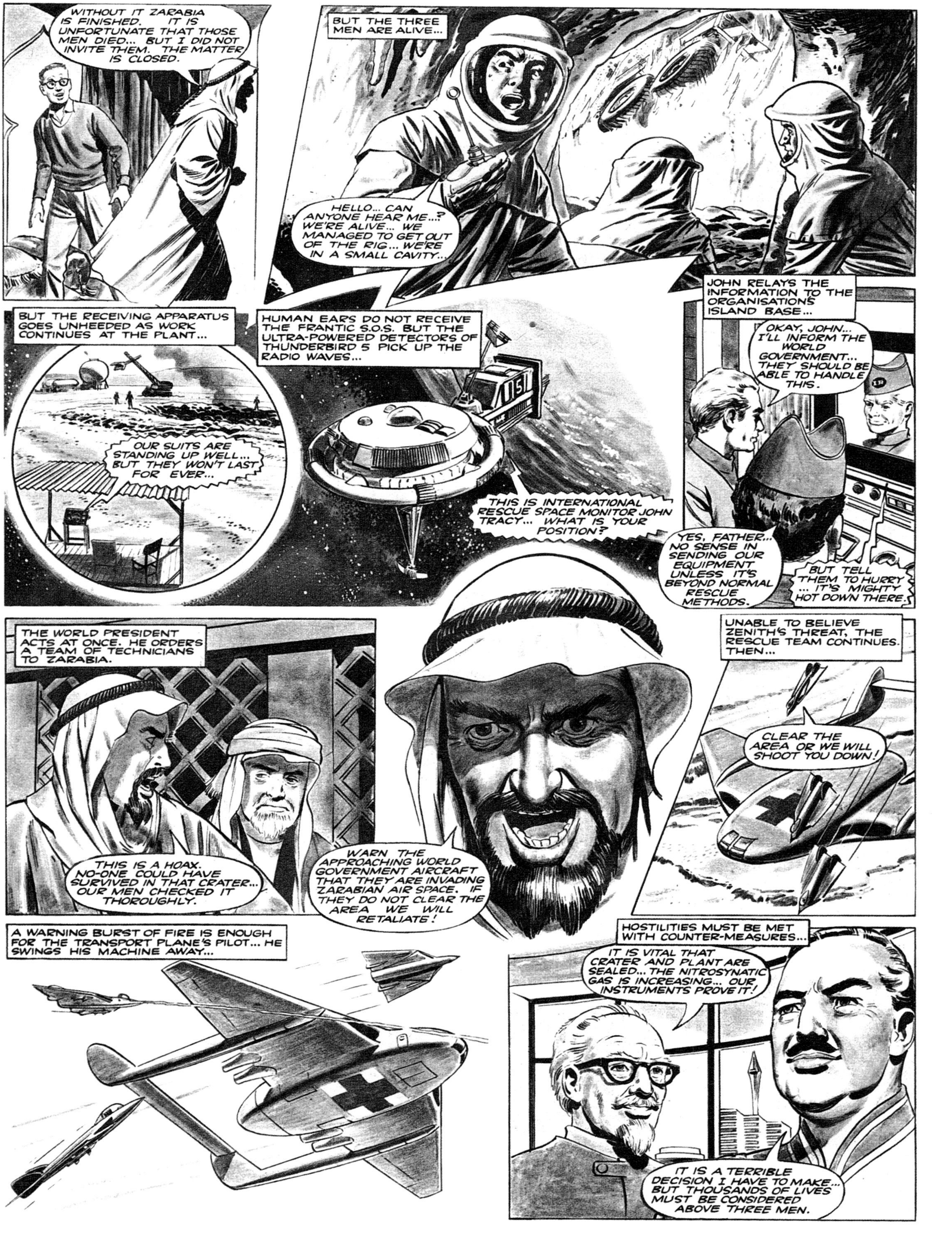
WITHOUT IT ZARABIA IS FINISHED. IT IS UNFORTUNATE THAT THOSE MEN DIED... BUT I DID NOT INVITE THEM. THE MATTER IS CLOSED.
BUT THE THREE MEN ARE ALIVE...
HELLO... CAN ANYONE HEAR ME...? WE'RE ALIVE... WE MANAGED TO GET OUT OF THE RIG... WE'RE IN A SMALL CAVITY...
BUT THE RECEIVING APPARATUS GOES UNHEEDED AS WORK CONTINUES AT THE PLANT...
OUR SUITS ARE STANDING UP WELL... BUT THEY WON'T LAST FOR EVER...
HUMAN EARS DO NOT RECEIVE THE FRANTIC S.O.S. BUT THE ULTRA-POWERED DETECTORS OF THUNDERBIRD 5 PICK UP THE RADIO WAVES...
THIS IS INTERNATIONAL RESCUE SPACE MONITOR JOHN TRACY... WHAT IS YOUR POSITION?
JOHN RELAYS THE INFORMATION TO THE ORGANISATION'S ISLAND BASE...
OKAY, JOHN... I'LL INFORM THE WORLD GOVERNMENT... THEY SHOULD BE ABLE TO HANDLE THIS.
YES, FATHER... NO SENSE IN SENDING OUR EQUIPMENT UNLESS IT'S BEYOND NORMAL RESCUE METHODS.
BUT TELL THEM TO HURRY ... IT'S MIGHTY HOT DOWN THERE.
THE WORLD PRESIDENT ACTS AT ONCE. HE ORDERS A TEAM OF TECHNICIANS TO ZARABIA.
THIS IS A HOAX. NO-ONE COULD HAVE SURVIVED IN THAT CRATER... OUR MEN CHECKED IT THOROUGHLY.
WARN THE APPROACHING WORLD GOVERNMENT AIRCRAFT THAT THEY ARE INVADING ZARABIAN AIR SPACE. IF THEY DO NOT CLEAR THE AREA WE WILL RETALIATE!
UNABLE TO BELIEVE ZENITH'S THREAT, THE RESCUE TEAM CONTINUES. THEN...
CLEAR THE AREA OR WE WILL SHOOT YOU DOWN!
A WARNING BURST OF FIRE IS ENOUGH FOR THE TRANSPORT PLANE'S PILOT... HE SWINGS HIS MACHINE AWAY...
HOSTILITIES MUST BE MET WITH COUNTER-MEASURES...
IT IS VITAL THAT CRATER AND PLANT ARE SEALED... THE NITROSYNATIC GAS IS INCREASING... OUR INSTRUMENTS PROVE IT!
IT IS A TERRIBLE DECISION I HAVE TO MAKE... BUT THOUSANDS OF LIVES MUST BE CONSIDERED ABOVE THREE MEN.

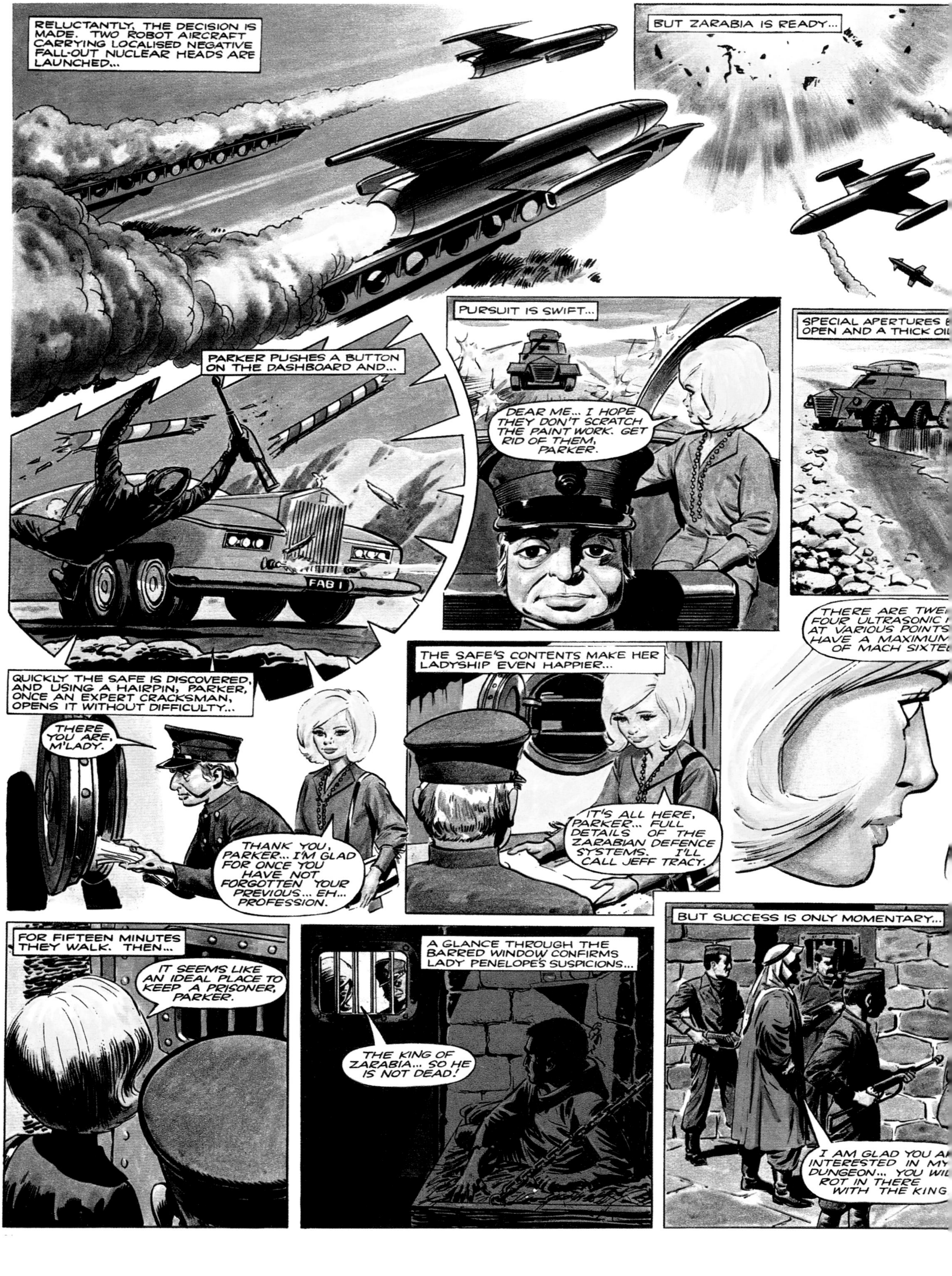

RELUCTANTLY, THE DECISION IS MADE. TWO ROBOT AIRCRAFT CARRYING LOCALISED NEGATIVE FALL-OUT NUCLEAR HEADS ARE LAUNCHED...
BUT ZARABIA IS READY...
PARKER PUSHES A BUTTON ON THE DASHBOARD AND...
FAB 1
PURSUIT IS SWIFT...
DEAR ME... I HOPE THEY DON'T SCRATCH THE PAINT WORK. GET RID OF THEM, PARKER.
SPECIAL APERTURES B
OPEN AND A THICK OIL
THERE ARE TWE
FOUR ULTRASONIC
AT VARIOUS POINTS
HAVE A MAXIMUM
OF MACH SIXTE
QUICKLY THE SAFE IS DISCOVERED, AND USING A HAIRPIN, PARKER, ONCE AN EXPERT CRACKSMAN, OPENS IT WITHOUT DIFFICULTY...
THERE YOU ARE, M'LADY.
THANK YOU, PARKER... I'M GLAD FOR ONCE YOU HAVE NOT FORGOTTEN YOUR PREVIOUS... EH... PROFESSION.
THE SAFE'S CONTENTS MAKE HER LADYSHIP EVEN HAPPIER...
IT'S ALL HERE, PARKER... FULL DETAILS OF THE ZARABIAN DEFENCE SYSTEMS. I'LL CALL JEFF TRACY.
FOR FIFTEEN MINUTES THEY WALK. THEN...
IT SEEMS LIKE AN IDEAL PLACE TO KEEP A PRISONER, PARKER.
A GLANCE THROUGH THE BARRED WINDOW CONFIRMS LADY PENELOPE'S SUSPICIONS...
THE KING OF ZARABIA... SO HE IS NOT DEAD!
BUT SUCCESS IS ONLY MOMENTARY...
I AM GLAD YOU A
INTERESTED IN MY
DUNGEON... YOU WIL
ROT IN THERE
WITH THE KING

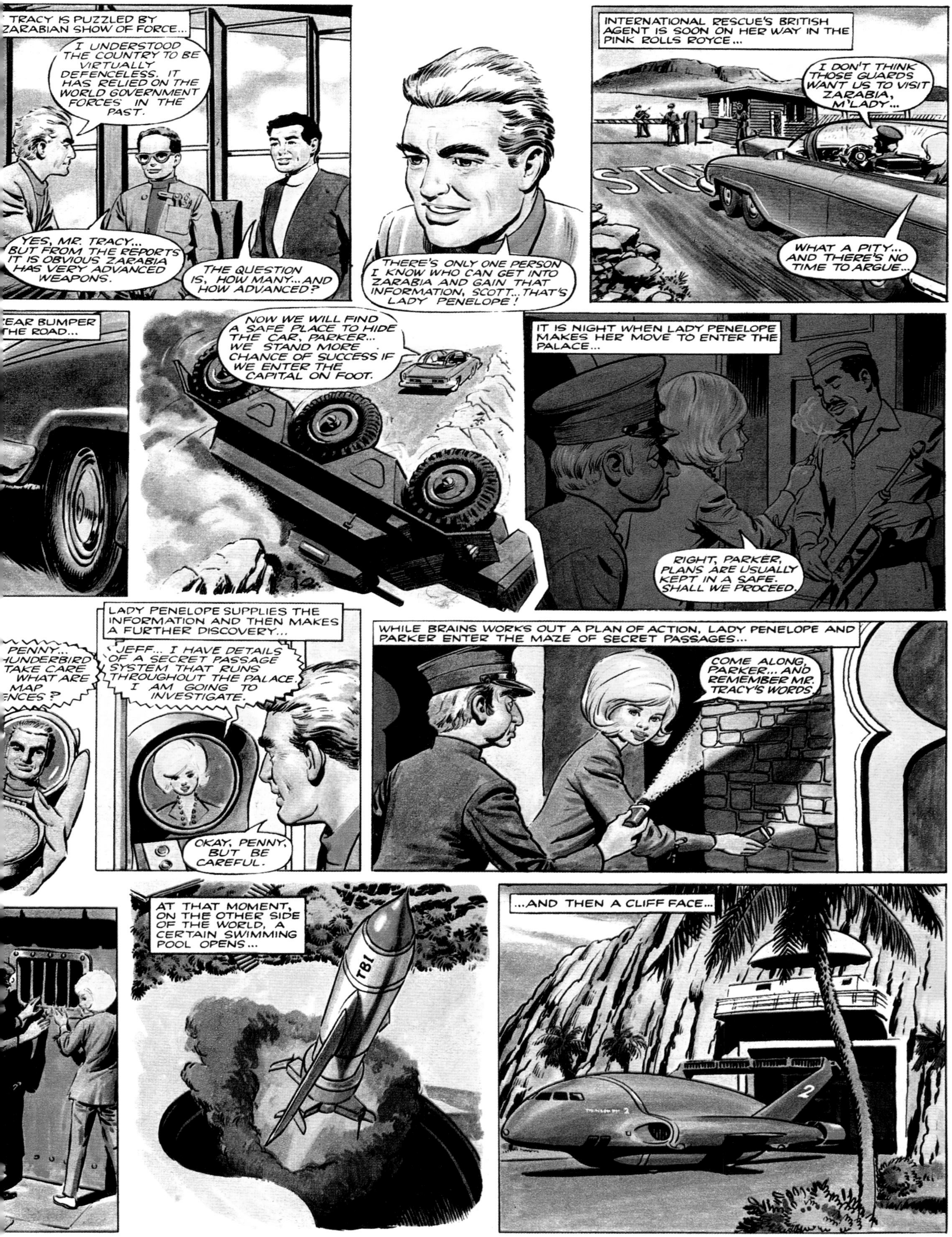

TRACY IS PUZZLED BY ZARABIAN SHOW OF FORCE...
I UNDERSTOOD THE COUNTRY TO BE VIRTUALLY DEFENCELESS. IT HAS RELIED ON THE WORLD GOVERNMENT FORCES IN THE PAST.
YES, MR. TRACY... BUT FROM THE REPORTS IT IS OBVIOUS ZARABIA HAS VERY ADVANCED WEAPONS.
THE QUESTION IS, HOW MANY... AND HOW ADVANCED?
THERE'S ONLY ONE PERSON I KNOW WHO CAN GET INTO ZARABIA AND GAIN THAT INFORMATION, SCOTT... THAT'S LADY PENELOPE!
INTERNATIONAL RESCUE'S BRITISH AGENT IS SOON ON HER WAY IN THE PINK ROLLS ROYCE...
I DON'T THINK THOSE GUARDS WANT US TO VISIT ZARABIA, M'LADY...
WHAT A PITY... AND THERE'S NO TIME TO ARGUE...
REAR BUMPER THE ROAD...
NOW WE WILL FIND A SAFE PLACE TO HIDE THE CAR, PARKER... WE STAND MORE CHANCE OF SUCCESS IF WE ENTER THE CAPITAL ON FOOT.
IT IS NIGHT WHEN LADY PENELOPE MAKES HER MOVE TO ENTER THE PALACE...
RIGHT, PARKER, PLANS ARE USUALLY KEPT IN A SAFE. SHALL WE PROCEED.
PENNY... HUNDERBIRD TAKE CARE WHAT ARE MAP ENCES?
LADY PENELOPE SUPPLIES THE INFORMATION AND THEN MAKES A FURTHER DISCOVERY...
JEFF... I HAVE DETAILS OF A SECRET PASSAGE SYSTEM THAT RUNS THROUGHOUT THE PALACE. I AM GOING TO INVESTIGATE.
OKAY, PENNY, BUT BE CAREFUL.
WHILE BRAINS WORKS OUT A PLAN OF ACTION, LADY PENELOPE AND PARKER ENTER THE MAZE OF SECRET PASSAGES...
COME ALONG, PARKER... AND REMEMBER MR. TRACY'S WORDS.
AT THAT MOMENT, ON THE OTHER SIDE OF THE WORLD, A CERTAIN SWIMMING POOL OPENS...
TB1
...AND THEN A CLIFF FACE...
2

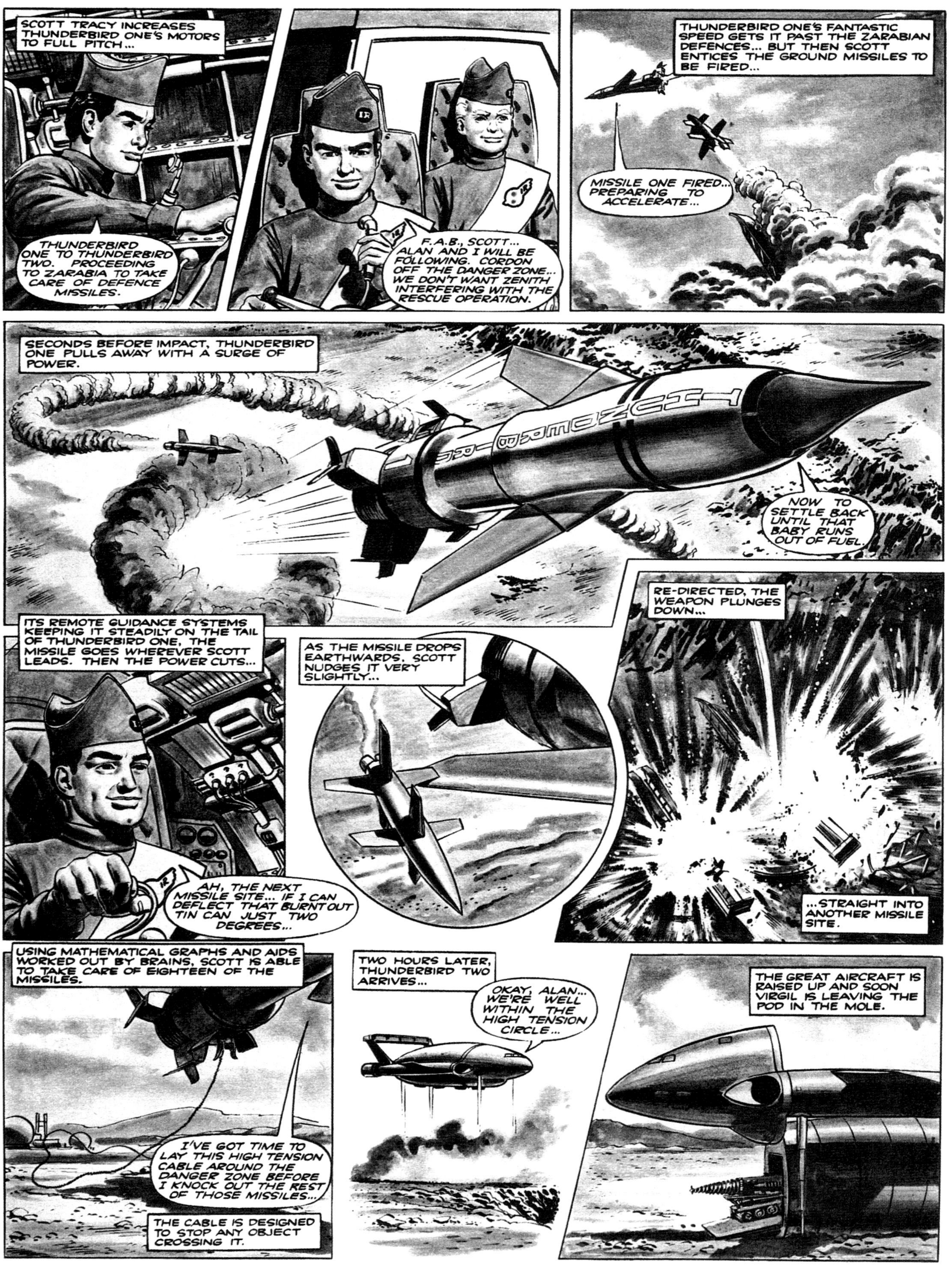
SCOTT TRACY INCREASES THUNDERBIRD ONE'S MOTORS TO FULL PITCH...
THUNDERBIRD ONE TO THUNDERBIRD TWO. PROCEEDING TO ZARABIA TO TAKE CARE OF DEFENCE MISSILES.
F.A.B., SCOTT... ALAN AND I WILL BE FOLLOWING. CORDON OFF THE DANGER ZONE... WE DON'T WANT ZENITH INTERFERING WITH THE RESCUE OPERATION.
THUNDERBIRD ONE'S FANTASTIC SPEED GETS IT PAST THE ZARABIAN DEFENCES... BUT THEN SCOTT ENTICES THE GROUND MISSILES TO BE FIRED...
MISSILE ONE FIRED... PREPARING TO ACCELERATE...
SECONDS BEFORE IMPACT, THUNDERBIRD ONE PULLS AWAY WITH A SURGE OF POWER.
THUNDERBIRD 1
NOW TO SETTLE BACK UNTIL THAT BABY RUNS OUT OF FUEL.
ITS REMOTE GUIDANCE SYSTEMS KEEPING IT STEADILY ON THE TAIL OF THUNDERBIRD ONE, THE MISSILE GOES WHEREVER SCOTT LEADS. THEN THE POWER CUTS...
AH, THE NEXT MISSILE SITE... IF I CAN DEFLECT THAT BURNT OUT TIN CAN JUST TWO DEGREES...
AS THE MISSILE DROPS EARTHWARDS, SCOTT NUDGES IT VERY SLIGHTLY...
RE-DIRECTED, THE WEAPON PLUNGES DOWN...
...STRAIGHT INTO ANOTHER MISSILE SITE.
USING MATHEMATICAL GRAPHS AND AIDS WORKED OUT BY BRAINS, SCOTT IS ABLE TO TAKE CARE OF EIGHTEEN OF THE MISSILES.
I'VE GOT TIME TO LAY THIS HIGH TENSION CABLE AROUND THE DANGER ZONE BEFORE I KNOCK OUT THE REST OF THOSE MISSILES...
THE CABLE IS DESIGNED TO STOP ANY OBJECT CROSSING IT.
TWO HOURS LATER, THUNDERBIRD TWO ARRIVES...
OKAY, ALAN... WE'RE WELL WITHIN THE HIGH TENSION CIRCLE...
THE GREAT AIRCRAFT IS RAISED UP AND SOON VIRGIL IS LEAVING THE POD IN THE MOLE.

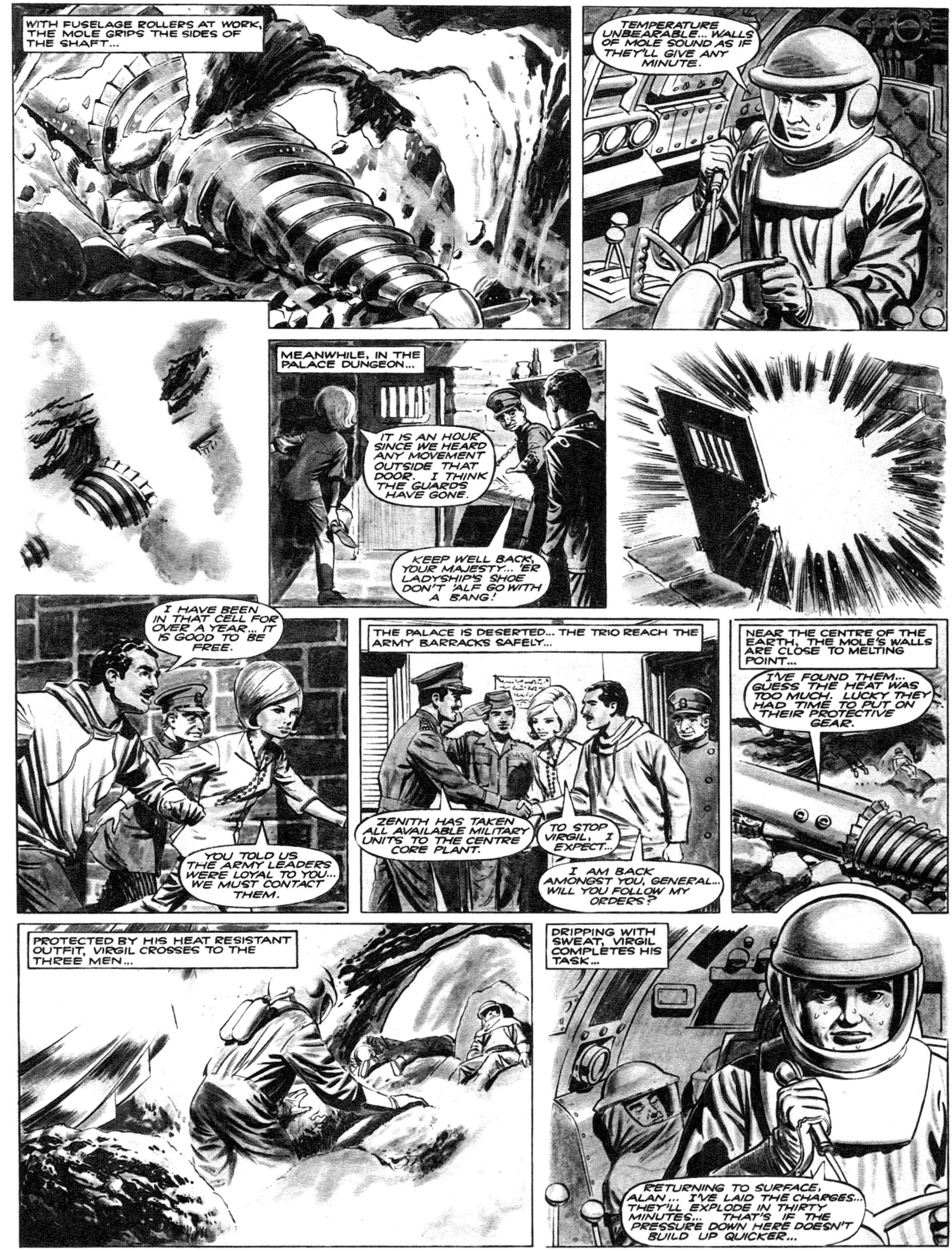

WITH FUSELAGE ROLLERS AT WORK, THE MOLE GRIPS THE SIDES OF THE SHAFT...
TEMPERATURE UNBEARABLE... WALLS OF MOLE SOUND AS IF THEY'LL GIVE ANY MINUTE.
MEANWHILE, IN THE PALACE DUNGEON...
IT IS AN HOUR SINCE WE HEARD ANY MOVEMENT OUTSIDE THAT DOOR. I THINK THE GUARDS HAVE GONE.
KEEP WELL BACK, YOUR MAJESTY... 'ER LADYSHIP'S SHOE DON'T 'ALF GO WITH A BANG!
I HAVE BEEN IN THAT CELL FOR OVER A YEAR... IT IS GOOD TO BE FREE.
YOU TOLD US THE ARMY LEADERS WERE LOYAL TO YOU... WE MUST CONTACT THEM.
THE PALACE IS DESERTED... THE TRIO REACH THE ARMY BARRACKS SAFELY...
ZENITH HAS TAKEN ALL AVAILABLE MILITARY UNITS TO THE CENTRE CORE PLANT.
TO STOP VIRGIL, I EXPECT...
I AM BACK AMONGST YOU, GENERAL... WILL YOU FOLLOW MY ORDERS?
NEAR THE CENTRE OF THE EARTH, THE MOLE'S WALLS ARE CLOSE TO MELTING POINT...
I'VE FOUND THEM... GUESS THE HEAT WAS TOO MUCH. LUCKY THEY HAD TIME TO PUT ON THEIR PROTECTIVE GEAR.
PROTECTED BY HIS HEAT RESISTANT OUTFIT, VIRGIL CROSSES TO THE THREE MEN...
DRIPPING WITH SWEAT, VIRGIL COMPLETES HIS TASK...
RETURNING TO SURFACE, ALAN... I'VE LAID THE CHARGES... THEY'LL EXPLODE IN THIRTY MINUTES... THAT'S IF THE PRESSURE DOWN HERE DOESN'T BUILD UP QUICKER...

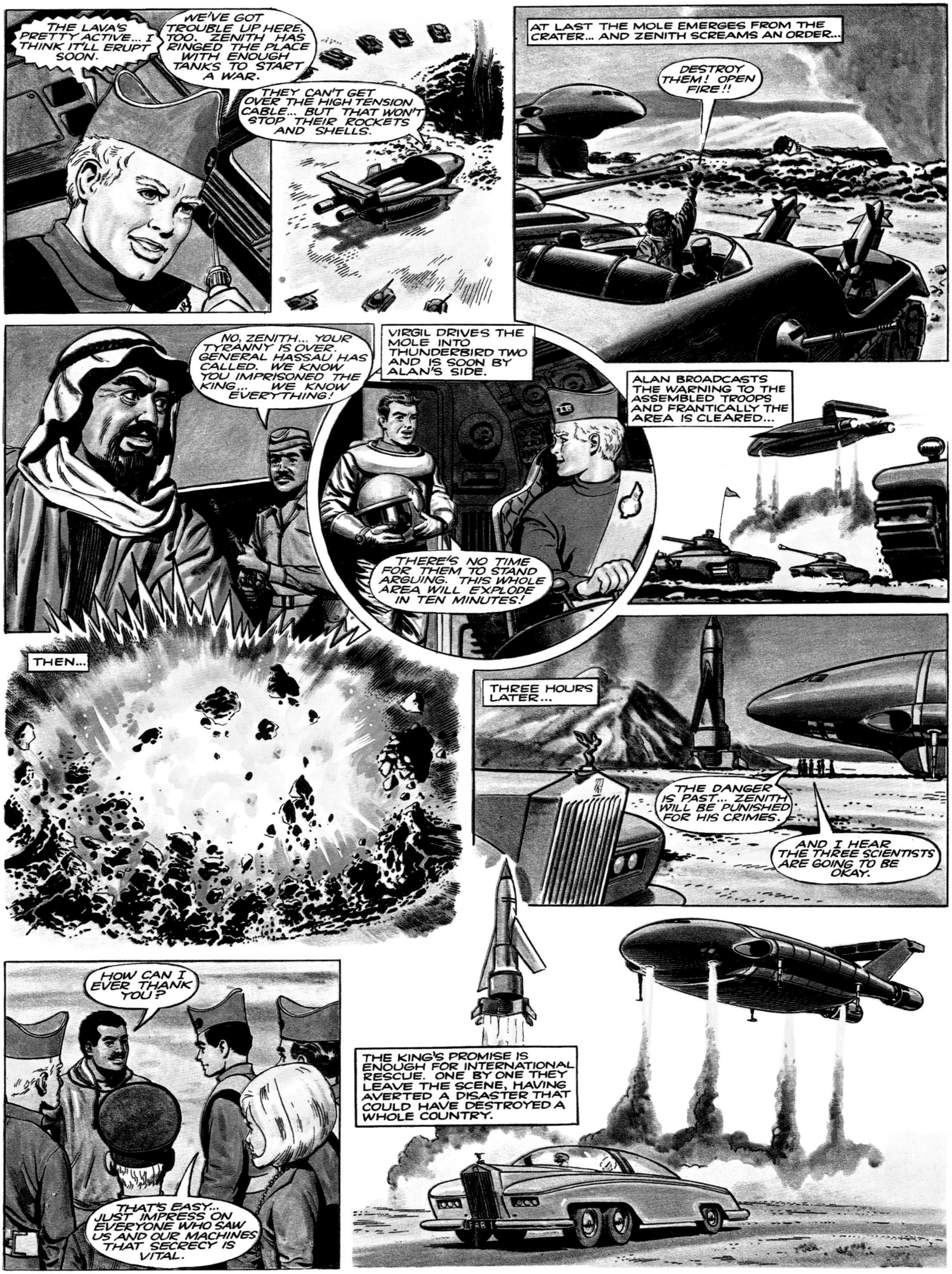
THE LAVA'S PRETTY ACTIVE... I THINK IT'LL ERUPT SOON.
WE'VE GOT TROUBLE UP HERE, TOO. ZENITH HAS RINGED THE PLACE WITH ENOUGH TANKS TO START A WAR.
THEY CAN'T GET OVER THE HIGH TENSION CABLE... BUT THAT WON'T STOP THEIR ROCKETS AND SHELLS.
AT LAST THE MOLE EMERGES FROM THE CRATER... AND ZENITH SCREAMS AN ORDER...
DESTROY THEM! OPEN FIRE!!
NO, ZENITH... YOUR TYRANNY IS OVER. GENERAL HASSAU HAS CALLED. WE KNOW YOU IMPRISONED THE KING... WE KNOW EVERYTHING!
VIRGIL DRIVES THE MOLE INTO THUNDERBIRD TWO AND IS SOON BY ALAN'S SIDE.
THERE'S NO TIME FOR THEM TO STAND ARGUING. THIS WHOLE AREA WILL EXPLODE IN TEN MINUTES!
ALAN BROADCASTS THE WARNING TO THE ASSEMBLED TROOPS AND FRANTICALLY THE AREA IS CLEARED...
THEN...
THREE HOURS LATER...
THE DANGER IS PAST... ZENITH WILL BE PUNISHED FOR HIS CRIMES.
AND I HEAR THE THREE SCIENTISTS ARE GOING TO BE OKAY.
HOW CAN I EVER THANK YOU?
THAT'S EASY... JUST IMPRESS ON EVERYONE WHO SAW US AND OUR MACHINES THAT SECRECY IS VITAL.
THE KING'S PROMISE IS ENOUGH FOR INTERNATIONAL RESCUE. ONE BY ONE THEY LEAVE THE SCENE, HAVING AVERTED A DISASTER THAT COULD HAVE DESTROYED A WHOLE COUNTRY.

LOST IN THE SKIES!

AIR FORCE CLAMPS DOWN ON MISSING PLANE PUZZLE

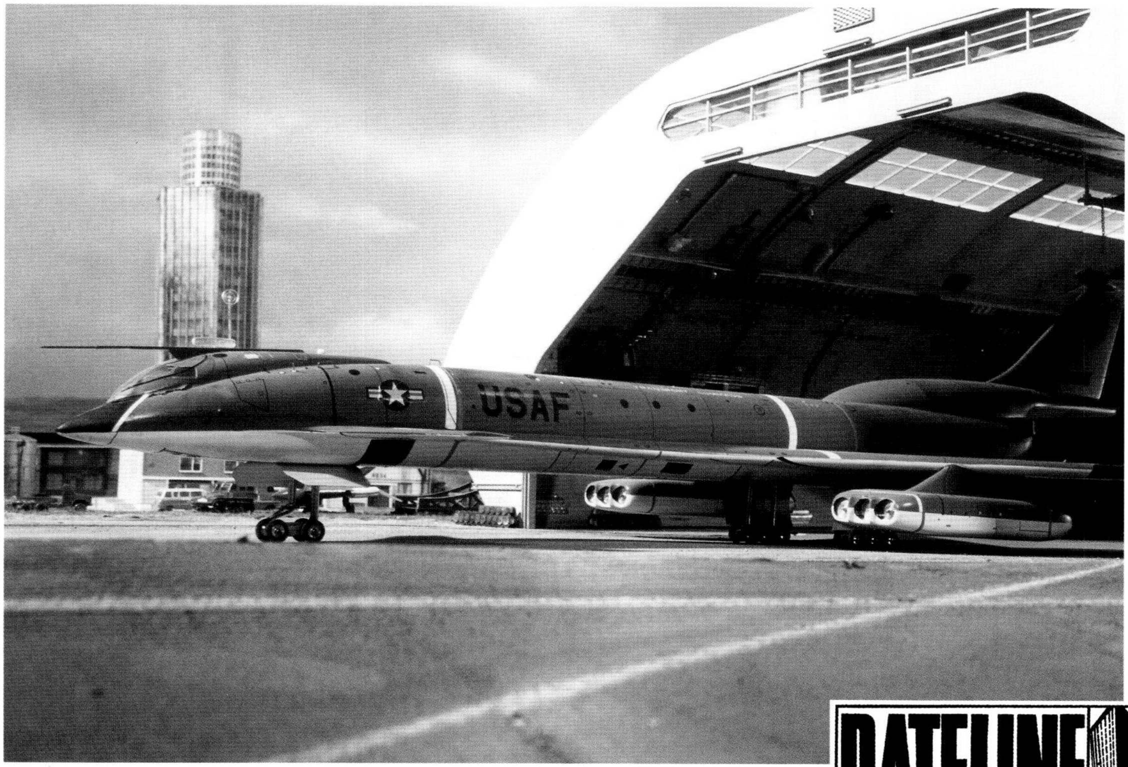

USAF

Above: The TC193 test plane leaves its Anti-blast hanger
(Photo courtesy of the United States Airforce press office)

The United Sates Air Force refused to comment on rumours that it had appealed to the World Government for help in tracing a missing top secret aircraft.

The TC193 troop carrier is believed to have vanished during a routine test flight. Reports that the pilot had mentioned an approaching rocket ship in his last video message were also unconfirmed.

Full story page 124

DATELINE 2066

UNIDENTIFIED!

The aircraft that wasn't there

Is the missing TC 193 the same craft that was engaged in a recent air battle reported by Fireflash pilot Captain J.W.Bell?

If so, the aircraft possesses a fantastic new radar jamming system, as it failed to register on the ultra-frequency Fireflash detectors. And if it is the same craft, could it have now been involved in further battles?

Below: Base 27ZX – home of the TC193 aircraft.

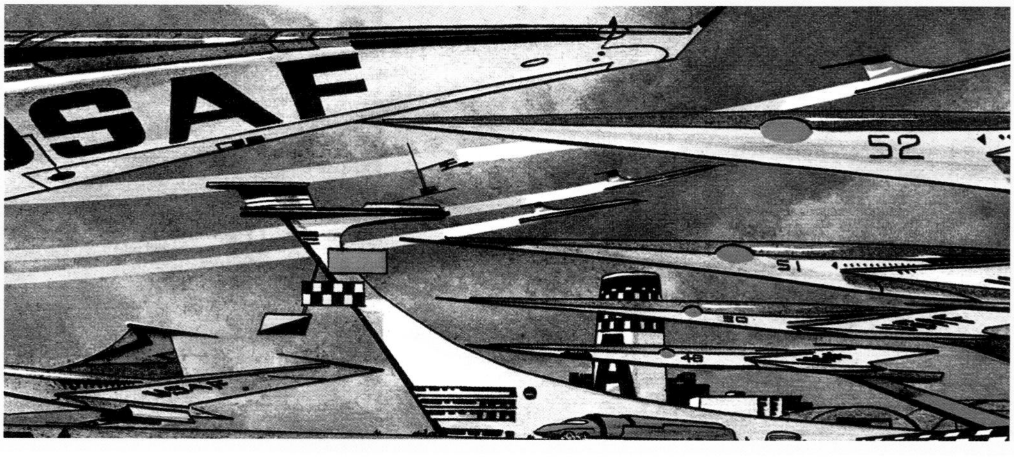

USAF
52

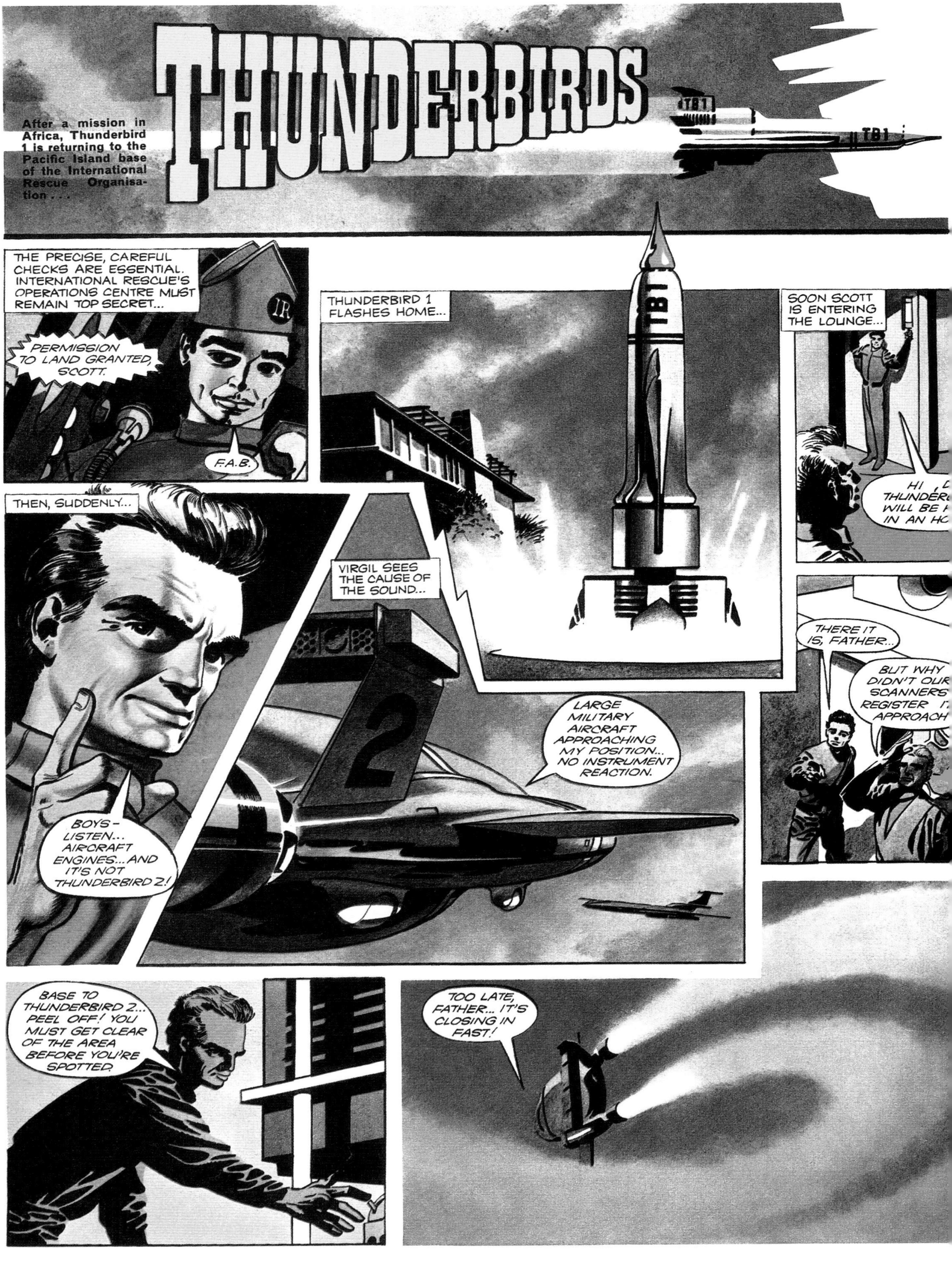
THUNDERBIRDS
After a mission in Africa, Thunderbird 1 is returning to the Pacific Island base of the International Rescue Organisation . . .
TB1
TB1
THE PRECISE, CAREFUL CHECKS ARE ESSENTIAL. INTERNATIONAL RESCUE'S OPERATIONS CENTRE MUST REMAIN TOP SECRET...
IR
PERMISSION TO LAND GRANTED, SCOTT.
F.A.B.
THUNDERBIRD 1 FLASHES HOME...
TB1
SOON SCOTT IS ENTERING THE LOUNGE...
THEN, SUDDENLY...
BOYS– LISTEN... AIRCRAFT ENGINES... AND IT'S NOT THUNDERBIRD 2!
VIRGIL SEES THE CAUSE OF THE SOUND...
2
LARGE MILITARY AIRCRAFT APPROACHING MY POSITION... NO INSTRUMENT REACTION.
THERE IT IS, FATHER...
BUT WHY
BASE TO THUNDERBIRD 2... PEEL OFF! YOU MUST GET CLEAR OF THE AREA BEFORE YOU'RE SPOTTED!
TOO LATE, FATHER... IT'S CLOSING IN FAST!

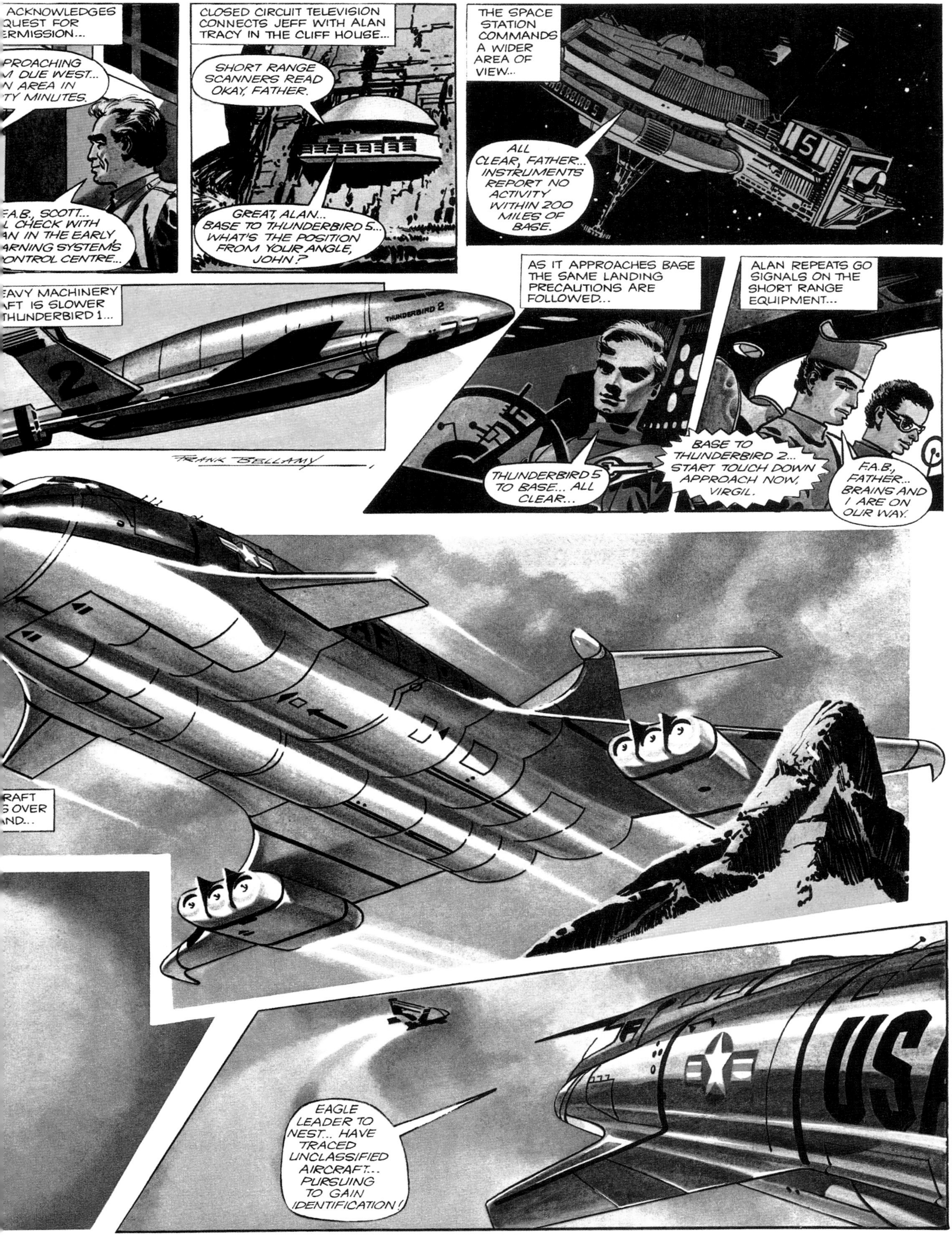

ACKNOWLEDGES
QUEST FOR
ERMISSION...
PROACHING
M DUE WEST...
N AREA IN
TY MINUTES.
F.A.B., SCOTT...
L CHECK WITH
AN IN THE EARLY
ARNING SYSTEM'S
ONTROL CENTRE...
CLOSED CIRCUIT TELEVISION CONNECTS JEFF WITH ALAN TRACY IN THE CLIFF HOUSE...
SHORT RANGE SCANNERS READ OKAY, FATHER.
GREAT, ALAN... BASE TO THUNDERBIRD 5... WHAT'S THE POSITION FROM YOUR ANGLE, JOHN?
THE SPACE STATION COMMANDS A WIDER AREA OF VIEW...
ALL CLEAR, FATHER... INSTRUMENTS REPORT NO ACTIVITY WITHIN 200 MILES OF BASE.
EAVY MACHINERY
AFT IS SLOWER
THUNDERBIRD 1...
THUNDERBIRD 2
FRANK BELLAMY
AS IT APPROACHES BASE THE SAME LANDING PRECAUTIONS ARE FOLLOWED...
THUNDERBIRD 5 TO BASE... ALL CLEAR...
ALAN REPEATS GO SIGNALS ON THE SHORT RANGE EQUIPMENT...
BASE TO THUNDERBIRD 2... START TOUCH DOWN APPROACH NOW, VIRGIL.
F.A.B., FATHER... BRAINS AND I ARE ON OUR WAY.
RAFT
S OVER
AND...
EAGLE LEADER TO NEST... HAVE TRACED UNCLASSIFIED AIRCRAFT... PURSUING TO GAIN IDENTIFICATION!

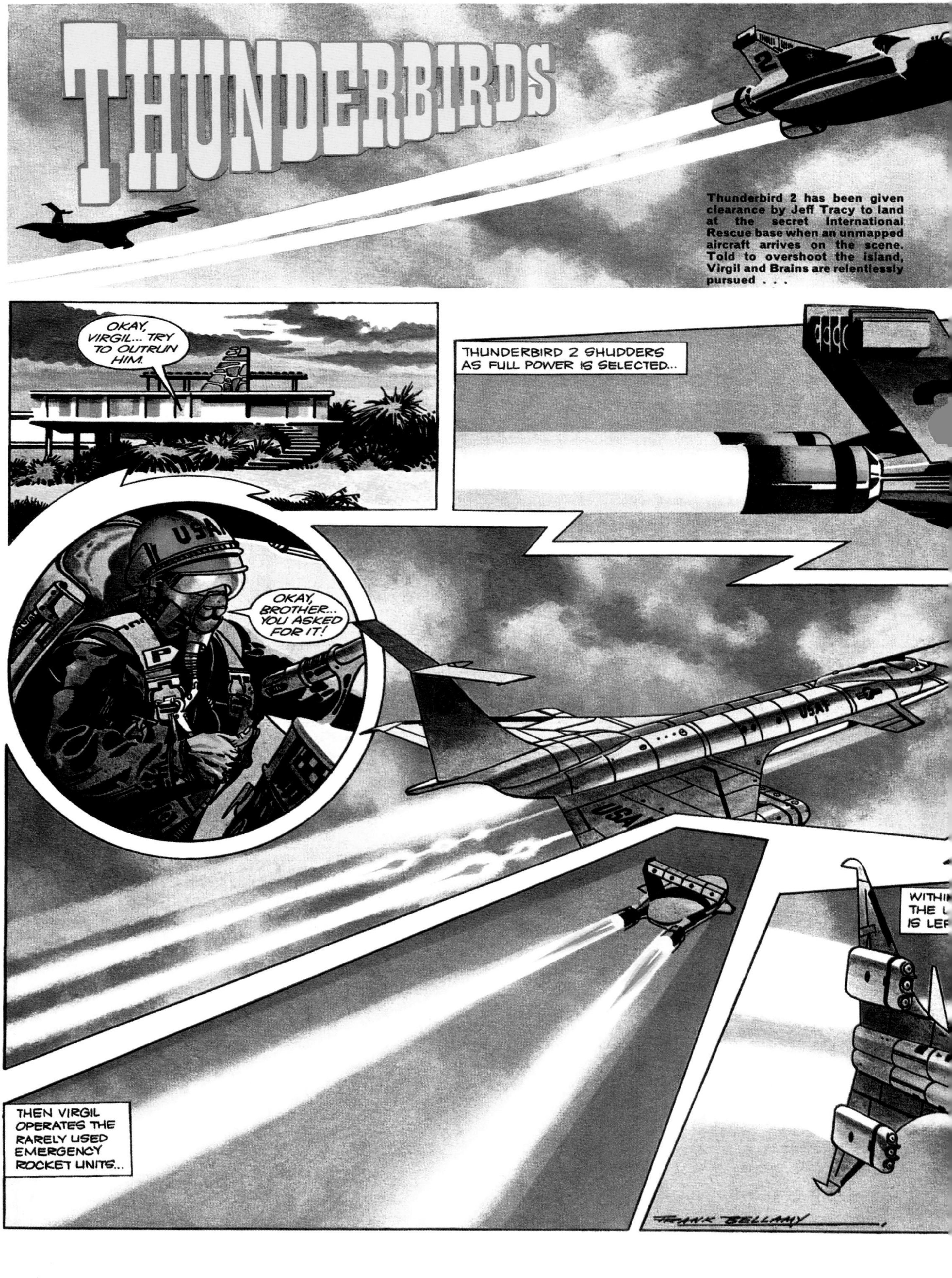
THUNDERBIRDS
Thunderbird 2 has been given clearance by Jeff Tracy to land at the secret International Rescue base when an unmapped aircraft arrives on the scene. Told to overshoot the island, Virgil and Brains are relentlessly pursued . . .
OKAY, VIRGIL... TRY TO OUTRUN HIM.
THUNDERBIRD 2 SHUDDERS AS FULL POWER IS SELECTED...
OKAY, BROTHER... YOU ASKED FOR IT!
USAF
THEN VIRGIL OPERATES THE RARELY USED EMERGENCY ROCKET UNITS...
FRANK BELLAMY

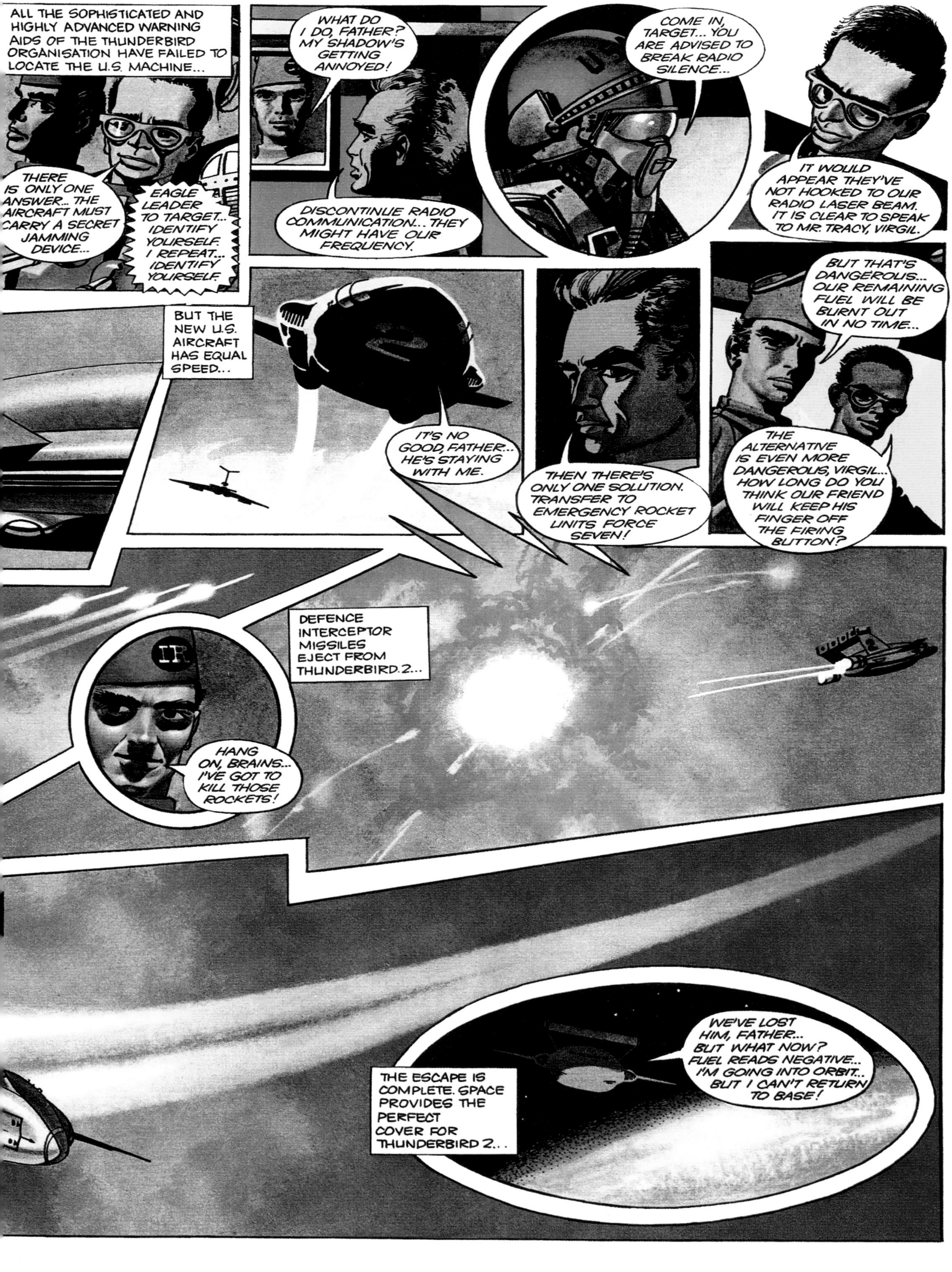

ALL THE SOPHISTICATED AND HIGHLY ADVANCED WARNING AIDS OF THE THUNDERBIRD ORGANISATION HAVE FAILED TO LOCATE THE U.S. MACHINE...
THERE IS ONLY ONE ANSWER... THE AIRCRAFT MUST CARRY A SECRET JAMMING DEVICE...
EAGLE LEADER TO TARGET... IDENTIFY YOURSELF. I REPEAT... IDENTIFY YOURSELF.
WHAT DO I DO, FATHER? MY SHADOW'S GETTING ANNOYED!
DISCONTINUE RADIO COMMUNICATION... THEY MIGHT HAVE OUR FREQUENCY.
COME IN, TARGET... YOU ARE ADVISED TO BREAK RADIO SILENCE...
IT WOULD APPEAR THEY'VE NOT HOOKED TO OUR RADIO LASER BEAM. IT IS CLEAR TO SPEAK TO MR. TRACY, VIRGIL.
BUT THE NEW U.S. AIRCRAFT HAS EQUAL SPEED...
IT'S NO GOOD, FATHER... HE'S STAYING WITH ME.
THEN THERE'S ONLY ONE SOLUTION. TRANSFER TO EMERGENCY ROCKET UNITS FORCE SEVEN!
BUT THAT'S DANGEROUS... OUR REMAINING FUEL WILL BE BURNT OUT IN NO TIME...
THE ALTERNATIVE IS EVEN MORE DANGEROUS, VIRGIL... HOW LONG DO YOU THINK OUR FRIEND WILL KEEP HIS FINGER OFF THE FIRING BUTTON?
DEFENCE INTERCEPTOR MISSILES EJECT FROM THUNDERBIRD 2...
HANG ON, BRAINS... I'VE GOT TO KILL THOSE ROCKETS!
THE ESCAPE IS COMPLETE. SPACE PROVIDES THE PERFECT COVER FOR THUNDERBIRD 2...
WE'VE LOST HIM, FATHER... BUT WHAT NOW? FUEL READS NEGATIVE... I'M GOING INTO ORBIT... BUT I CAN'T RETURN TO BASE!

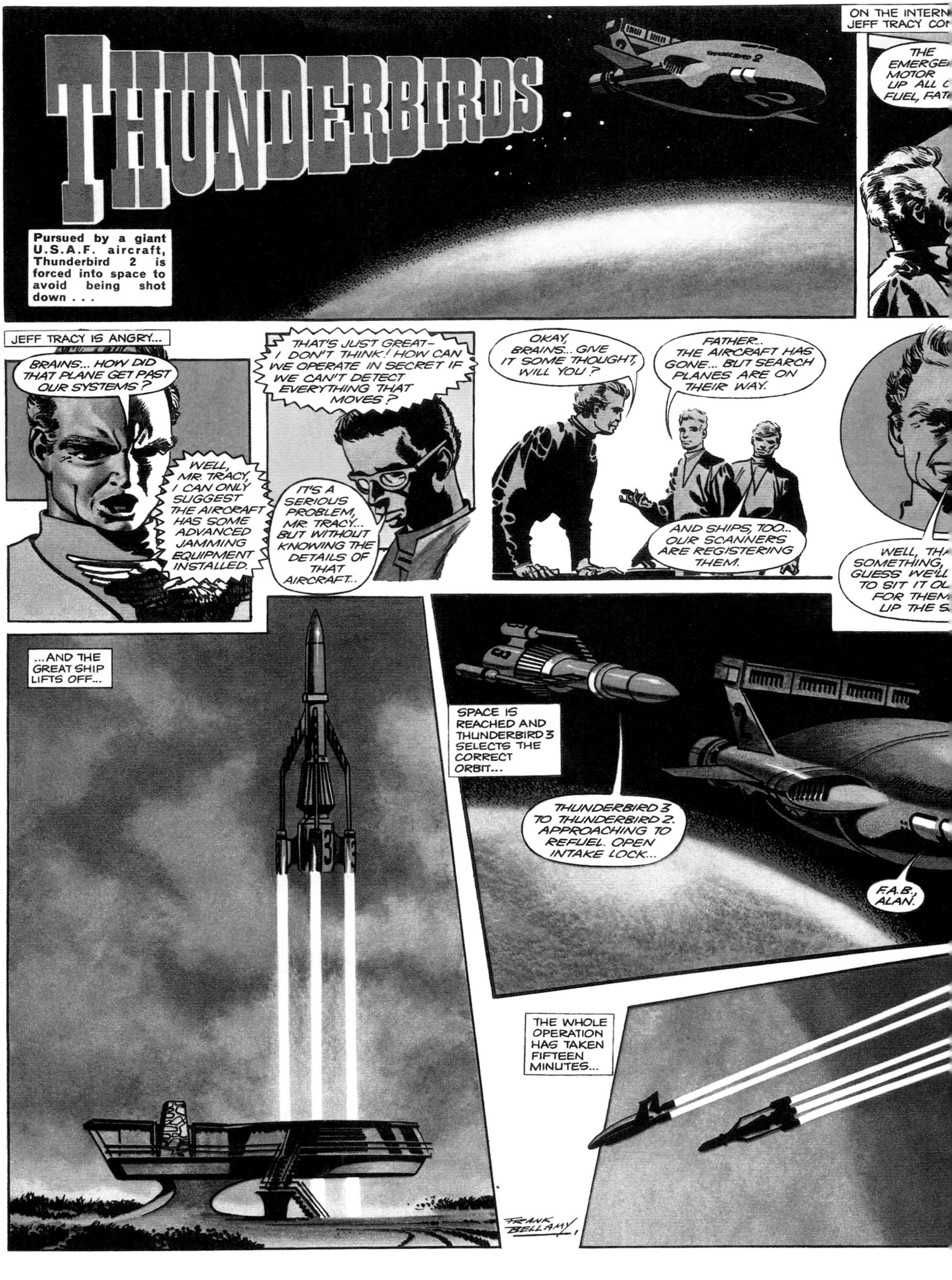

THUNDERBIRDS
Pursued by a giant U.S.A.F. aircraft, Thunderbird 2 is forced into space to avoid being shot down . . .
ON THE
JEFF TRACY
THE MOTOR UP ALL FUEL,
JEFF TRACY IS ANGRY...
BRAINS... HOW DID THAT PLANE GET PAST OUR SYSTEMS?
WELL, MR. TRACY, I CAN ONLY SUGGEST THE AIRCRAFT HAS SOME ADVANCED JAMMING EQUIPMENT INSTALLED.
THAT'S JUST GREAT– I DON'T THINK! HOW CAN WE OPERATE IN SECRET IF WE CAN'T DETECT EVERYTHING THAT MOVES?
IT'S A SERIOUS PROBLEM, MR. TRACY... BUT WITHOUT KNOWING THE DETAILS OF THAT AIRCRAFT...
OKAY, BRAINS... GIVE IT SOME THOUGHT, WILL YOU?
FATHER... THE AIRCRAFT HAS GONE... BUT SEARCH PLANES ARE ON THEIR WAY.
AND SHIPS, TOO... OUR SCANNERS ARE REGISTERING THEM.
WELL, SOMETHING, GUESS TO SIT IT FOR UP THE
...AND THE GREAT SHIP LIFTS OFF...
SPACE IS REACHED AND THUNDERBIRD 3 SELECTS THE CORRECT ORBIT...
THUNDERBIRD 3 TO THUNDERBIRD 2. APPROACHING TO REFUEL. OPEN INTAKE LOCK...
F.A.B., ALAN.
THE WHOLE OPERATION HAS TAKEN FIFTEEN MINUTES...
FRANK BELLAMY

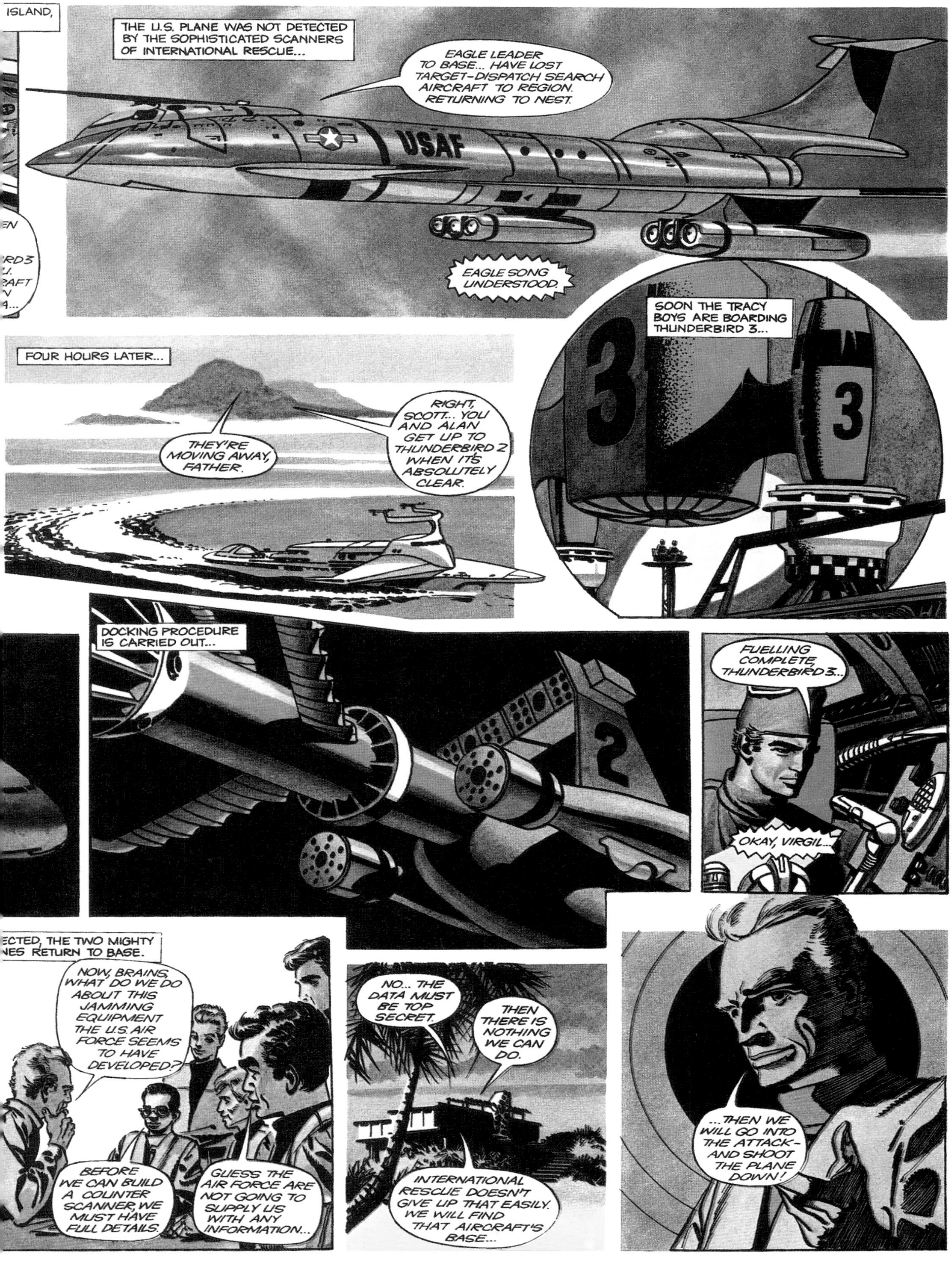
ISLAND,
THE U.S. PLANE WAS NOT DETECTED BY THE SOPHISTICATED SCANNERS OF INTERNATIONAL RESCUE...
EAGLE LEADER TO BASE... HAVE LOST TARGET-DISPATCH SEARCH AIRCRAFT TO REGION. RETURNING TO NEST.
EAGLE SONG UNDERSTOOD.
SOON THE TRACY BOYS ARE BOARDING THUNDERBIRD 3...
FOUR HOURS LATER...
THEY'RE MOVING AWAY, FATHER.
RIGHT, SCOTT... YOU AND ALAN GET UP TO THUNDERBIRD 2 WHEN IT'S ABSOLUTELY CLEAR.
DOCKING PROCEDURE IS CARRIED OUT...
FUELLING COMPLETE, THUNDERBIRD 3...
OKAY, VIRGIL...
ECTED, THE TWO MIGHTY NES RETURN TO BASE.
NOW, BRAINS, WHAT DO WE DO ABOUT THIS JAMMING EQUIPMENT THE U.S. AIR FORCE SEEMS TO HAVE DEVELOPED?
BEFORE WE CAN BUILD A COUNTER SCANNER, WE MUST HAVE FULL DETAILS.
GUESS THE AIR FORCE ARE NOT GOING TO SUPPLY US WITH ANY INFORMATION...
NO... THE DATA MUST BE TOP SECRET.
THEN THERE IS NOTHING WE CAN DO.
INTERNATIONAL RESCUE DOESN'T GIVE UP THAT EASILY. WE WILL FIND THAT AIRCRAFT'S BASE...
...THEN WE WILL GO INTO THE ATTACK- AND SHOOT THE PLANE DOWN!

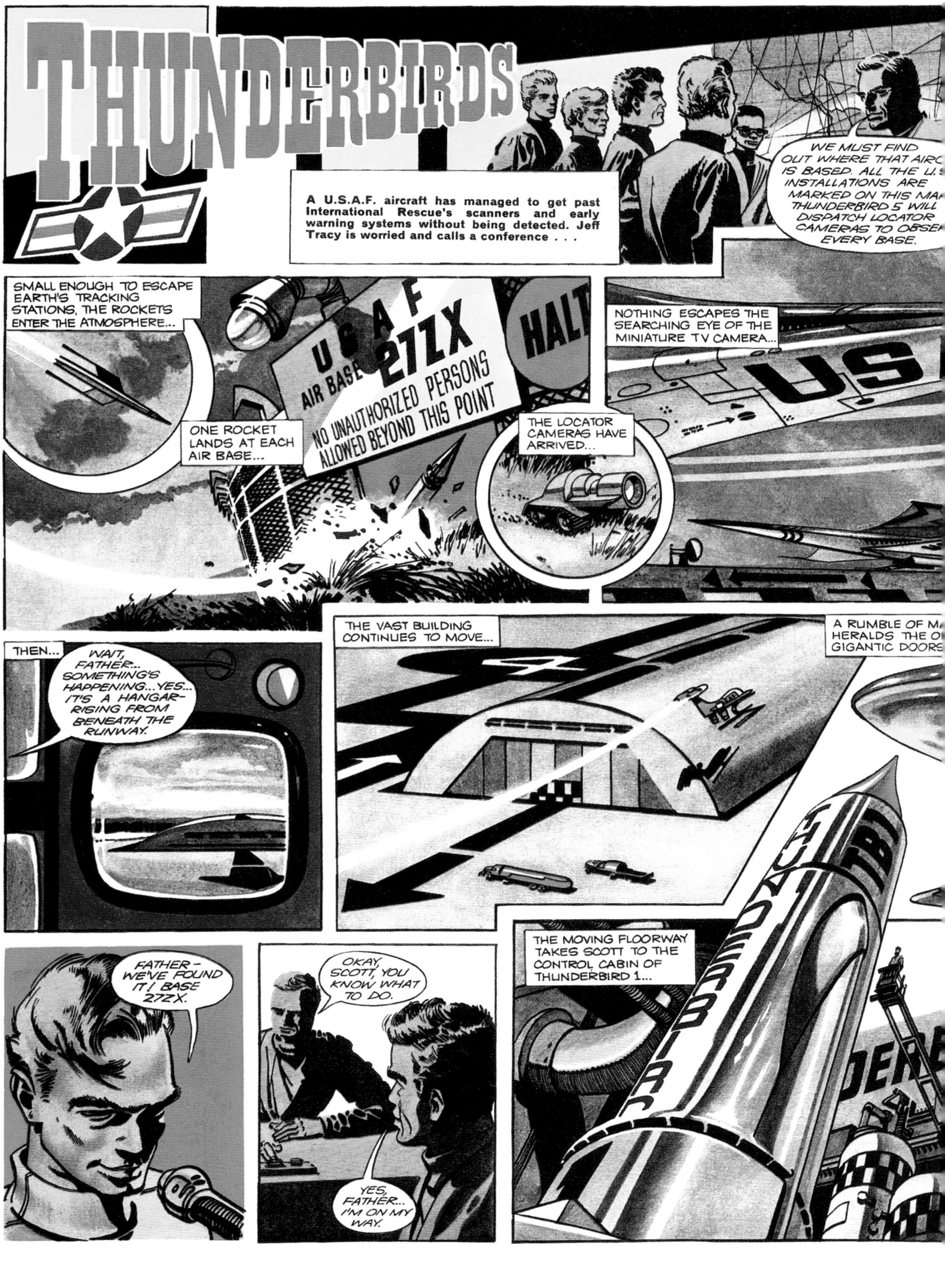
THUNDERBIRDS
A U.S.A.F. aircraft has managed to get past International Rescue's scanners and early warning systems without being detected. Jeff Tracy is worried and calls a conference . . .
WE MUST FIND OUT WHERE THAT AIRC IS BASED. ALL THE U.S INSTALLATIONS ARE MARKED ON THIS MA THUNDERBIRD 5 WILL DISPATCH LOCATOR CAMERAS TO OBSE EVERY BASE.
SMALL ENOUGH TO ESCAPE EARTH'S TRACKING STATIONS, THE ROCKETS ENTER THE ATMOSPHERE...
USAF AIR BASE 27ZX
NO UNAUTHORIZED PERSONS ALLOWED BEYOND THIS POINT
HALT
ONE ROCKET LANDS AT EACH AIR BASE...
THE LOCATOR CAMERAS HAVE ARRIVED...
NOTHING ESCAPES THE SEARCHING EYE OF THE MINIATURE TV CAMERA...
US
THEN...
WAIT, FATHER... SOMETHING'S HAPPENING... YES... IT'S A HANGAR-RISING FROM BENEATH THE RUNWAY.
THE VAST BUILDING CONTINUES TO MOVE...
A RUMBLE OF M HERALDS THE O GIGANTIC DOORS
FATHER - WE'VE FOUND IT! BASE 27ZX.
OKAY, SCOTT, YOU KNOW WHAT TO DO.
YES, FATHER... I'M ON MY WAY.
THE MOVING FLOORWAY TAKES SCOTT TO THE CONTROL CABIN OF THUNDERBIRD 1...
TB1

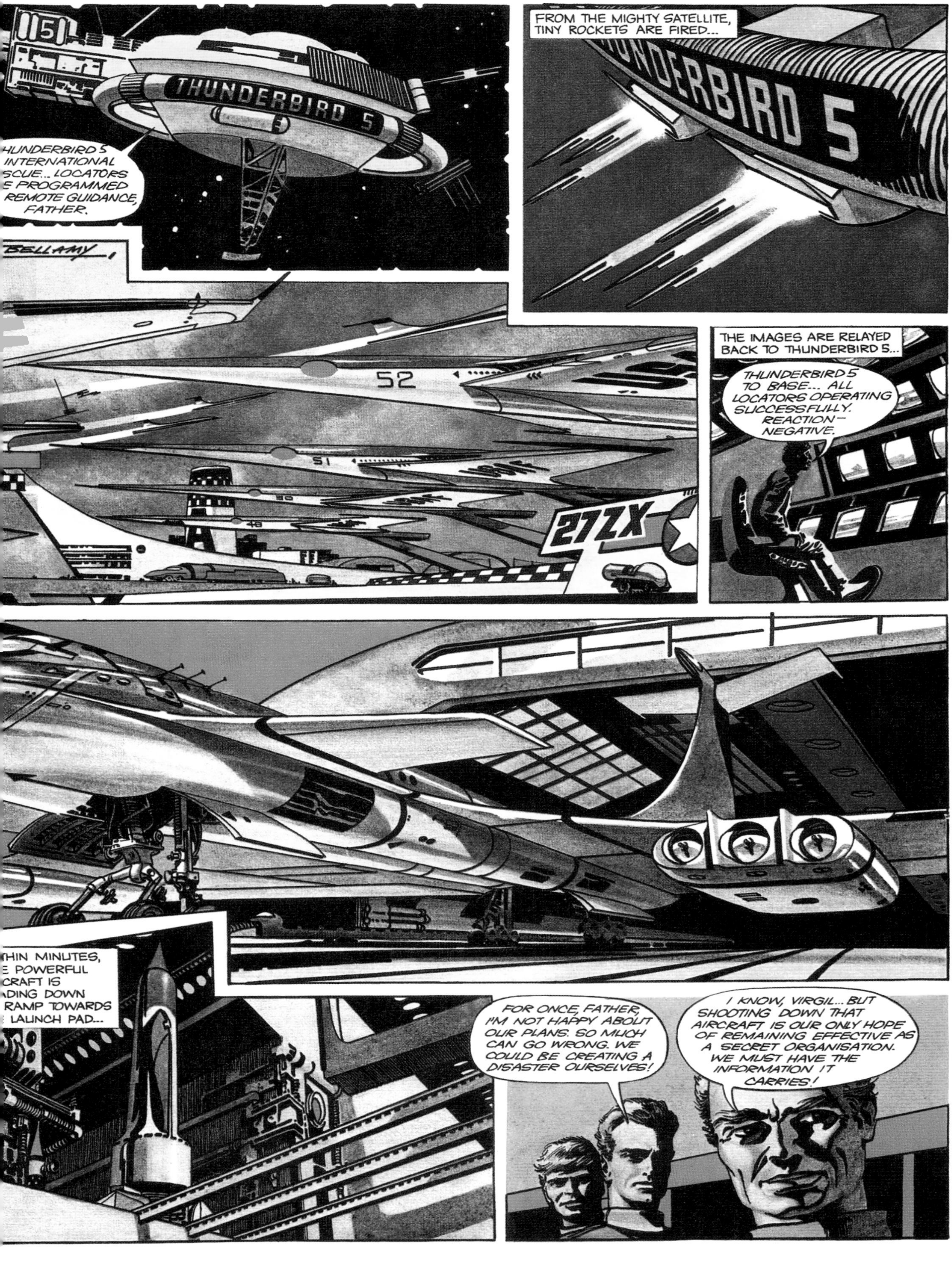

HUNDERBIRD 5 INTERNATIONAL SCUE... LOCATORS E PROGRAMMED REMOTE GUIDANCE, FATHER.
THUNDERBIRD 5
BELLAMY
FROM THE MIGHTY SATELLITE, TINY ROCKETS ARE FIRED...
THUNDERBIRD 5
52
51
27ZX
THE IMAGES ARE RELAYED BACK TO THUNDERBIRD 5...
THUNDERBIRD 5 TO BASE... ALL LOCATORS OPERATING SUCCESSFULLY. REACTION— NEGATIVE.
THIN MINUTES, E POWERFUL CRAFT IS DING DOWN RAMP TOWARDS E LAUNCH PAD...
FOR ONCE, FATHER, I'M NOT HAPPY ABOUT OUR PLANS. SO MUCH CAN GO WRONG. WE COULD BE CREATING A DISASTER OURSELVES!
I KNOW, VIRGIL... BUT SHOOTING DOWN THAT AIRCRAFT IS OUR ONLY HOPE OF REMAINING EFFECTIVE AS A SECRET ORGANISATION. WE MUST HAVE THE INFORMATION IT CARRIES!

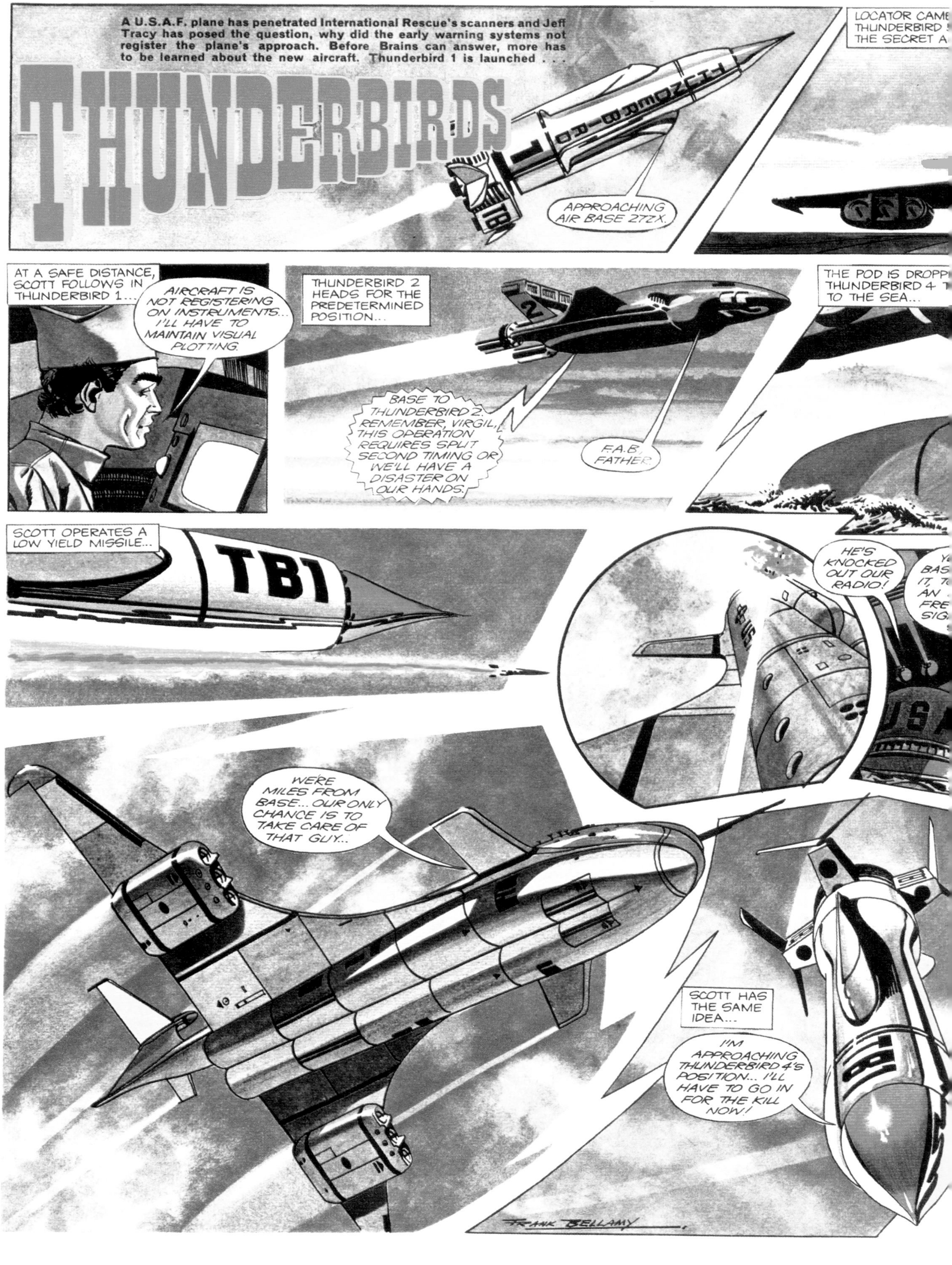

A U.S.A.F. plane has penetrated International Rescue's scanners and Jeff Tracy has posed the question, why did the early warning systems not register the plane's approach. Before Brains can answer, more has to be learned about the new aircraft. Thunderbird 1 is launched . . .
THUNDERBIRDS
APPROACHING AIR BASE 27ZX.
LOCATOR CAME
THUNDERBIRD
THE SECRET A
AT A SAFE DISTANCE, SCOTT FOLLOWS IN THUNDERBIRD 1...
AIRCRAFT IS NOT REGISTERING ON INSTRUMENTS... I'LL HAVE TO MAINTAIN VISUAL PLOTTING.
THUNDERBIRD 2 HEADS FOR THE PREDETERMINED POSITION...
BASE TO THUNDERBIRD 2. REMEMBER, VIRGIL, THIS OPERATION REQUIRES SPLIT SECOND TIMING OR WE'LL HAVE A DISASTER ON OUR HANDS.
F.A.B. FATHER.
THE POD IS DROPP
THUNDERBIRD 4
TO THE SEA...
SCOTT OPERATES A LOW YIELD MISSILE...
TB1
HE'S KNOCKED OUT OUR RADIO!
WE'RE MILES FROM BASE... OUR ONLY CHANCE IS TO TAKE CARE OF THAT GUY...
SCOTT HAS THE SAME IDEA...
I'M APPROACHING THUNDERBIRD 4'S POSITION... I'LL HAVE TO GO IN FOR THE KILL NOW!
FRANK BELLAMY

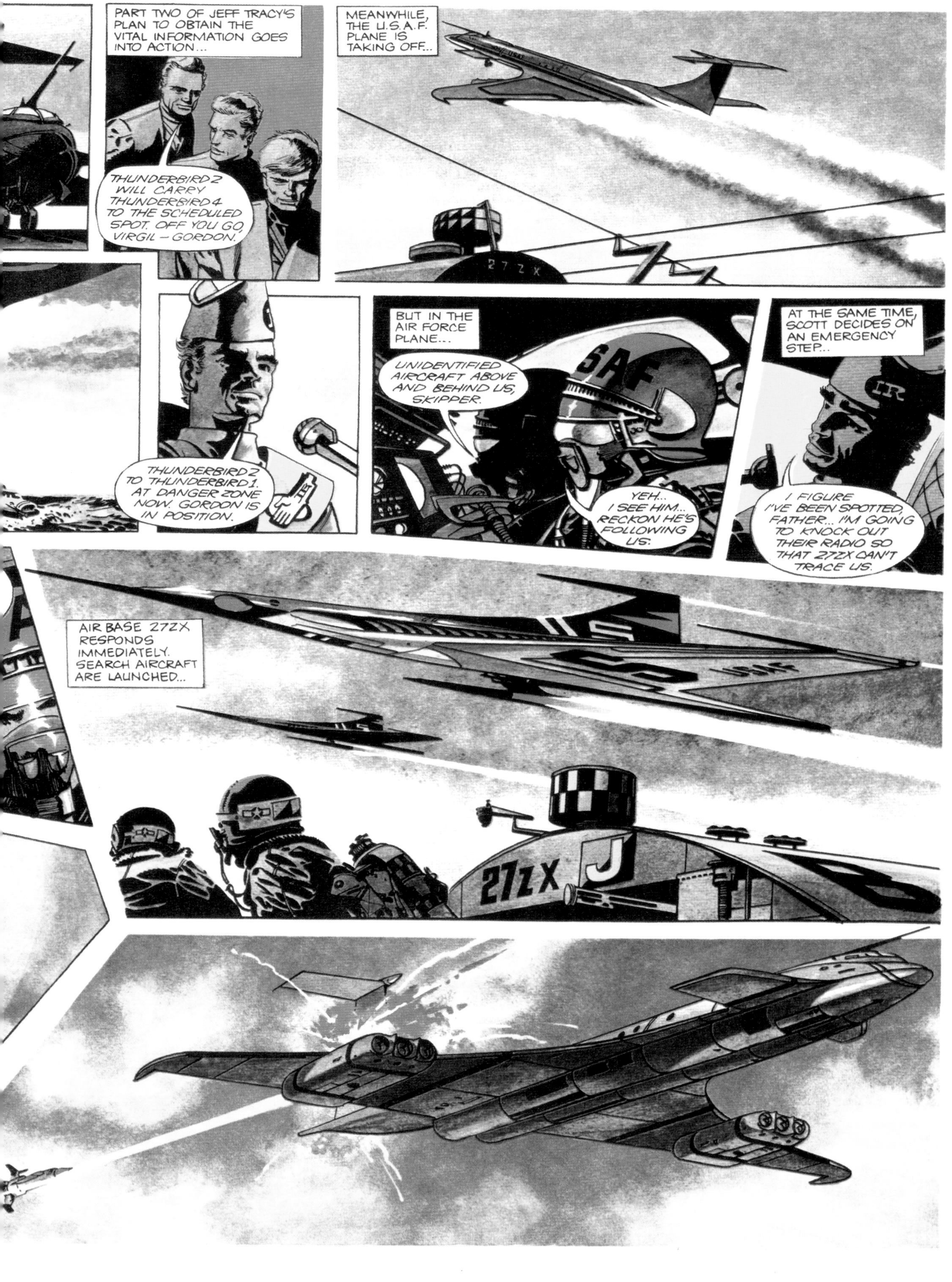

PART TWO OF JEFF TRACY'S PLAN TO OBTAIN THE VITAL INFORMATION GOES INTO ACTION...
THUNDERBIRD 2 WILL CARRY THUNDERBIRD 4 TO THE SCHEDULED SPOT. OFF YOU GO, VIRGIL — GORDON!
MEANWHILE, THE U.S.A.F. PLANE IS TAKING OFF...
27ZX
THUNDERBIRD 2 TO THUNDERBIRD 1. AT DANGER ZONE NOW. GORDON IS IN POSITION.
BUT IN THE AIR FORCE PLANE...
UNIDENTIFIED AIRCRAFT ABOVE AND BEHIND US, SKIPPER.
YEH... I SEE HIM... RECKON HE'S FOLLOWING US.
AT THE SAME TIME, SCOTT DECIDES ON AN EMERGENCY STEP...
I FIGURE I'VE BEEN SPOTTED, FATHER... I'M GOING TO KNOCK OUT THEIR RADIO SO THAT 27ZX CAN'T TRACE US.
AIR BASE 27ZX RESPONDS IMMEDIATELY. SEARCH AIRCRAFT ARE LAUNCHED...
USAF
27ZX
J

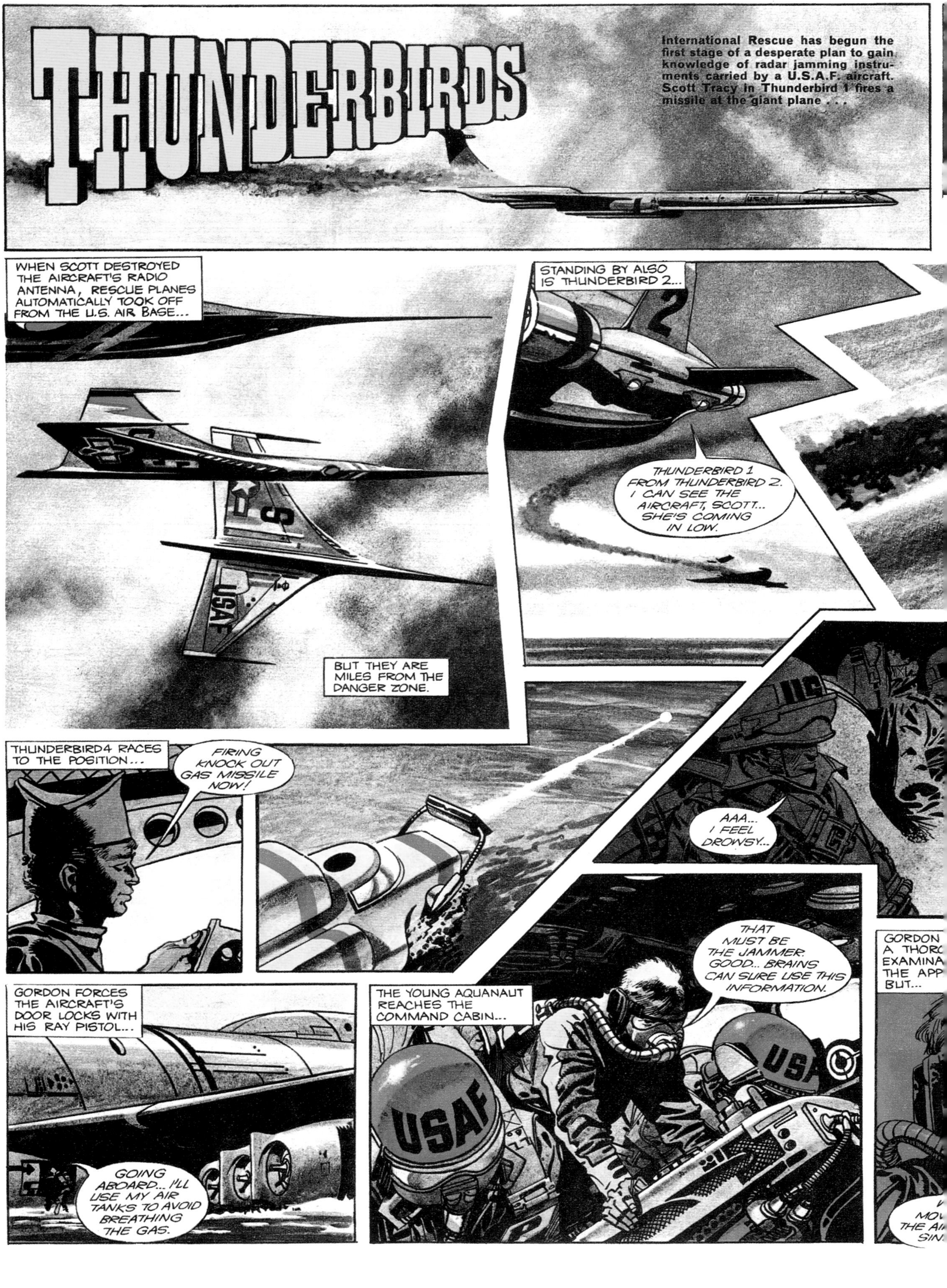
THUNDERBIRDS
International Rescue has begun the first stage of a desperate plan to gain knowledge of radar jamming instruments carried by a U.S.A.F. aircraft. Scott Tracy in Thunderbird 1 fires a missile at the giant plane . . .
WHEN SCOTT DESTROYED THE AIRCRAFT'S RADIO ANTENNA, RESCUE PLANES AUTOMATICALLY TOOK OFF FROM THE U.S. AIR BASE...
BUT THEY ARE MILES FROM THE DANGER ZONE.
STANDING BY ALSO IS THUNDERBIRD 2...
THUNDERBIRD 1 FROM THUNDERBIRD 2. I CAN SEE THE AIRCRAFT, SCOTT... SHE'S COMING IN LOW.
THUNDERBIRD 4 RACES TO THE POSITION...
FIRING KNOCK OUT GAS MISSILE NOW!
AAA... I FEEL DROWSY...
GORDON FORCES THE AIRCRAFT'S DOOR LOCKS WITH HIS RAY PISTOL...
GOING ABOARD... I'LL USE MY AIR TANKS TO AVOID BREATHING THE GAS.
THE YOUNG AQUANAUT REACHES THE COMMAND CABIN...
THAT MUST BE THE JAMMER. GOOD... BRAINS CAN SURE USE THIS INFORMATION.

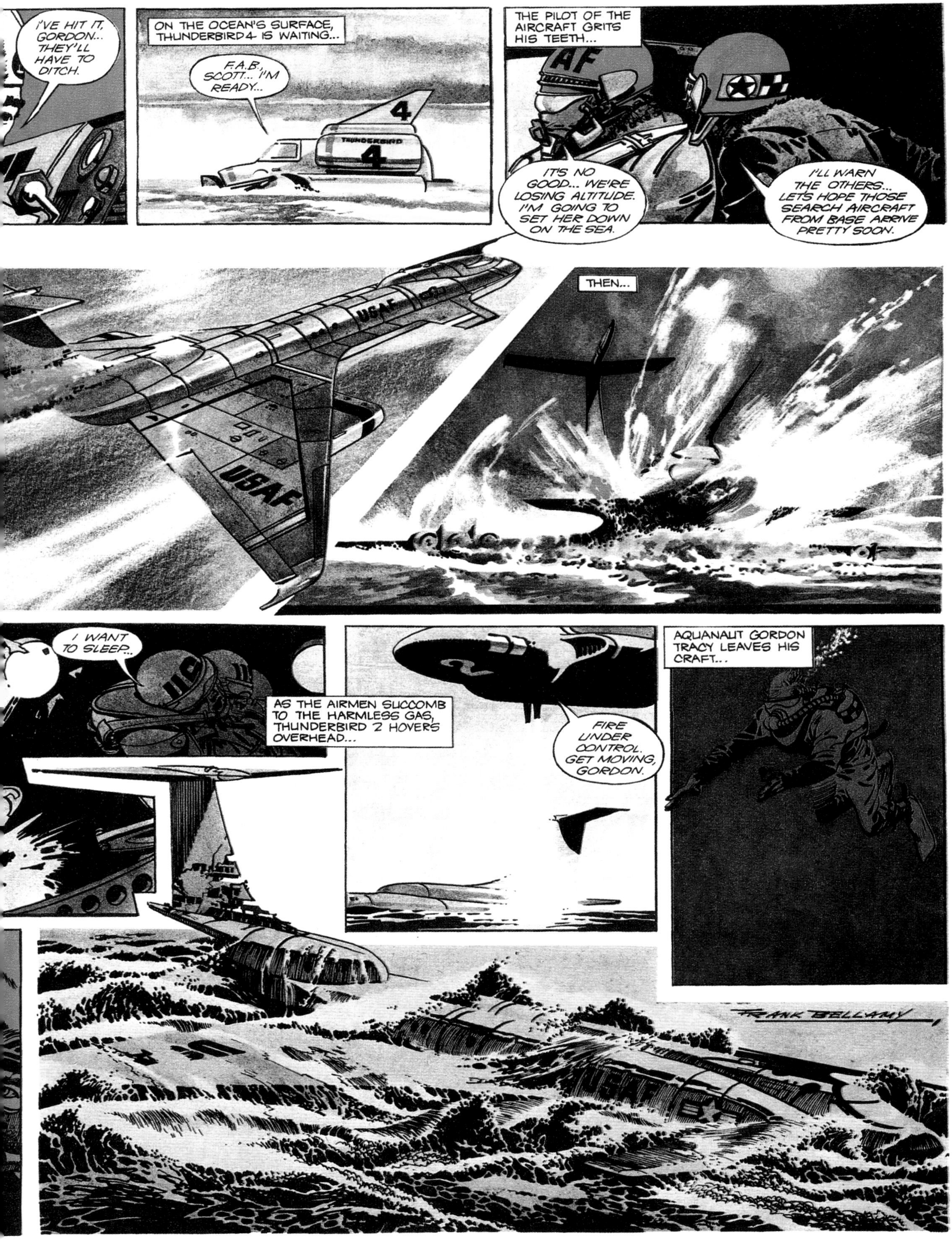
I'VE HIT IT, GORDON... THEY'LL HAVE TO DITCH.
ON THE OCEAN'S SURFACE, THUNDERBIRD 4 IS WAITING...
F.A.B., SCOTT... I'M READY...
THE PILOT OF THE AIRCRAFT GRITS HIS TEETH...
IT'S NO GOOD... WE'RE LOSING ALTITUDE. I'M GOING TO SET HER DOWN ON THE SEA.
I'LL WARN THE OTHERS... LET'S HOPE THOSE SEARCH AIRCRAFT FROM BASE ARRIVE PRETTY SOON.
THEN...
I WANT TO SLEEP...
AS THE AIRMEN SUCCOMB TO THE HARMLESS GAS, THUNDERBIRD 2 HOVERS OVERHEAD...
FIRE UNDER CONTROL. GET MOVING, GORDON.
AQUANAUT GORDON TRACY LEAVES HIS CRAFT...
FRANK BELLAMY

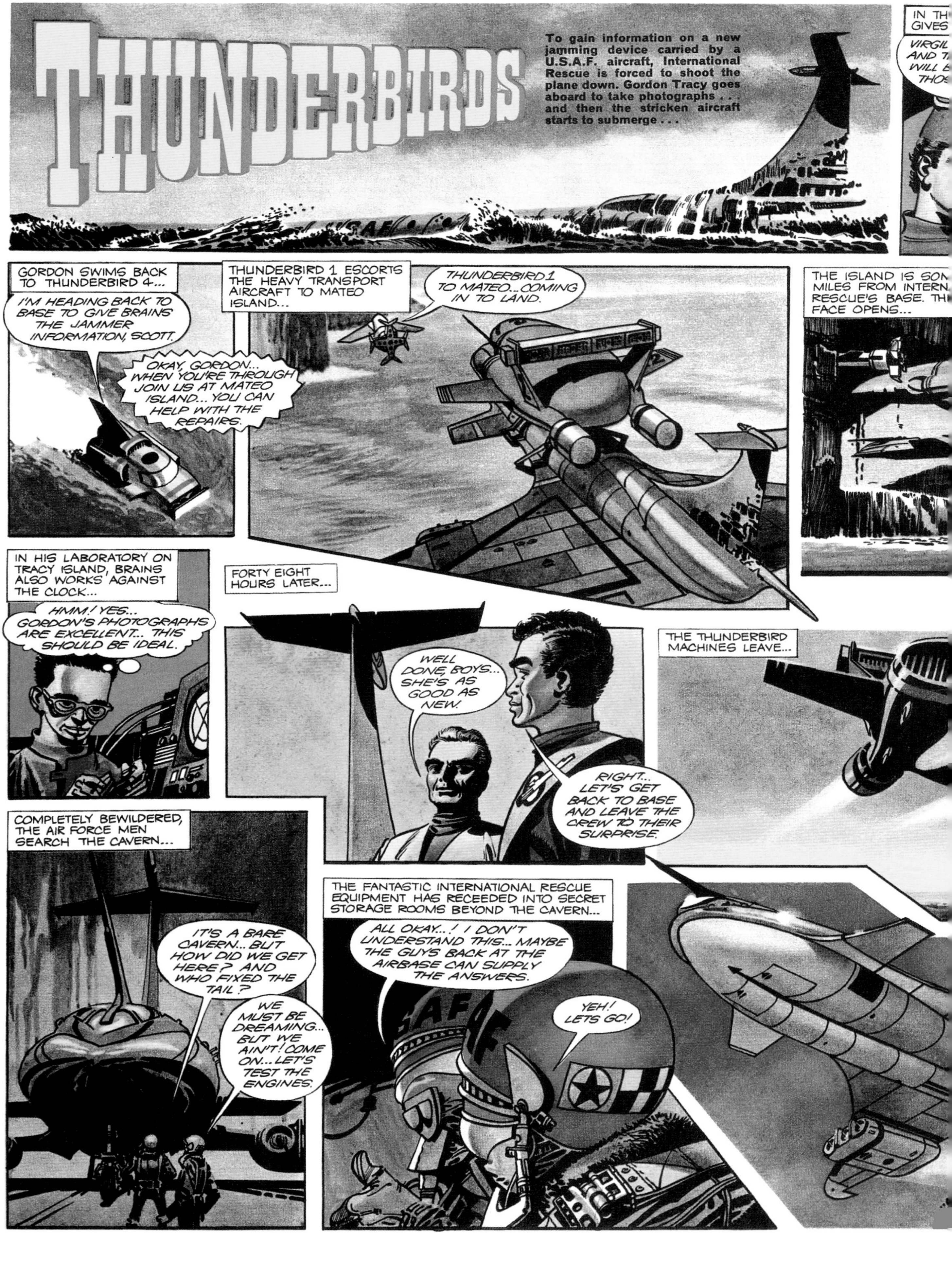
THUNDERBIRDS
To gain information on a new jamming device carried by a U.S.A.F. aircraft, International Rescue is forced to shoot the plane down. Gordon Tracy goes aboard to take photographs . . . and then the stricken aircraft starts to submerge . . .
GORDON SWIMS BACK TO THUNDERBIRD 4...
I'M HEADING BACK TO BASE TO GIVE BRAINS THE JAMMER INFORMATION, SCOTT.
OKAY, GORDON... WHEN YOU'RE THROUGH JOIN US AT MATEO ISLAND... YOU CAN HELP WITH THE REPAIRS.
THUNDERBIRD 1 ESCORTS THE HEAVY TRANSPORT AIRCRAFT TO MATEO ISLAND...
THUNDERBIRD 1 TO MATEO... COMING IN TO LAND.
IN HIS LABORATORY ON TRACY ISLAND, BRAINS ALSO WORKS AGAINST THE CLOCK...
HMM! YES... GORDON'S PHOTOGRAPHS ARE EXCELLENT... THIS SHOULD BE IDEAL.
FORTY EIGHT HOURS LATER...
WELL DONE, BOYS... SHE'S AS GOOD AS NEW.
RIGHT... LET'S GET BACK TO BASE AND LEAVE THE CREW TO THEIR SURPRISE.
THE THUNDERBIRD MACHINES LEAVE...
COMPLETELY BEWILDERED, THE AIR FORCE MEN SEARCH THE CAVERN...
IT'S A BARE CAVERN... BUT HOW DID WE GET HERE? AND WHO FIXED THE TAIL?
WE MUST BE DREAMING... BUT WE AIN'T! COME ON... LET'S TEST THE ENGINES.
THE FANTASTIC INTERNATIONAL RESCUE EQUIPMENT HAS RECEEDED INTO SECRET STORAGE ROOMS BEYOND THE CAVERN...
ALL OKAY...! I DON'T UNDERSTAND THIS... MAYBE THE GUYS BACK AT THE AIRBASE CAN SUPPLY THE ANSWERS.
YEH! LETS GO!

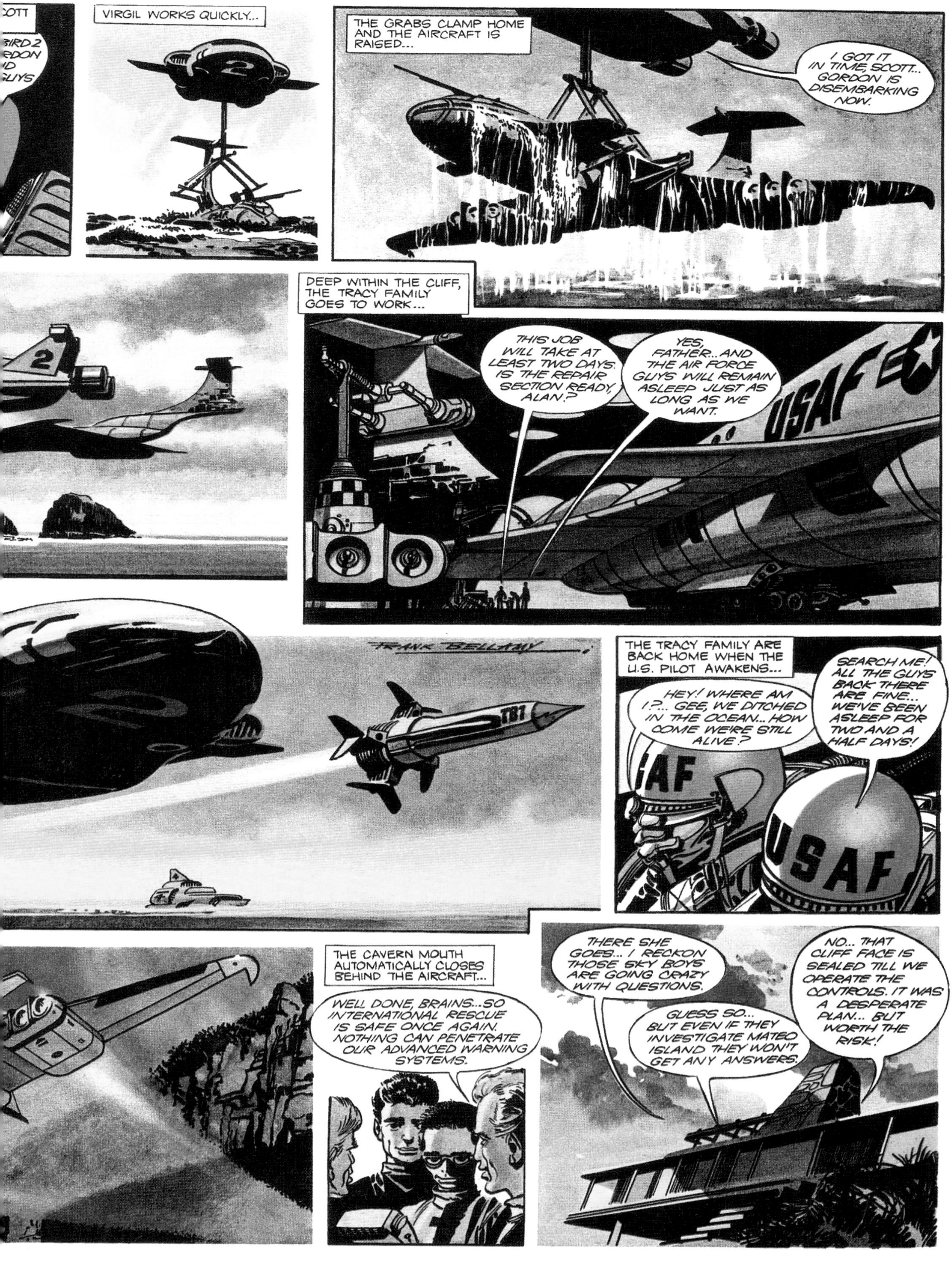
COTT
BIRD 2
EDON
D
GUYS
VIRGIL WORKS QUICKLY...
THE GRABS CLAMP HOME AND THE AIRCRAFT IS RAISED...
I GOT IT IN TIME, SCOTT... GORDON IS DISEMBARKING NOW.
DEEP WITHIN THE CLIFF, THE TRACY FAMILY GOES TO WORK...
THIS JOB WILL TAKE AT LEAST TWO DAYS. IS THE REPAIR SECTION READY, ALAN?
YES, FATHER... AND THE AIR FORCE GUYS WILL REMAIN ASLEEP JUST AS LONG AS WE WANT.
USAF
FRANK BELLAMY
TB1
THE TRACY FAMILY ARE BACK HOME WHEN THE U.S. PILOT AWAKENS...
HEY! WHERE AM I?... GEE, WE DITCHED IN THE OCEAN... HOW COME WE'RE STILL ALIVE?
SEARCH ME! ALL THE GUYS BACK THERE ARE FINE... WE'VE BEEN ASLEEP FOR TWO AND A HALF DAYS!
AF
USAF
THE CAVERN MOUTH AUTOMATICALLY CLOSES BEHIND THE AIRCRAFT...
WELL DONE, BRAINS... SO INTERNATIONAL RESCUE IS SAFE ONCE AGAIN. NOTHING CAN PENETRATE OUR ADVANCED WARNING SYSTEMS.
THERE SHE GOES... I RECKON THOSE SKY BOYS ARE GOING CRAZY WITH QUESTIONS.
GUESS SO... BUT EVEN IF THEY INVESTIGATE MATEO ISLAND THEY WON'T GET ANY ANSWERS.
NO... THAT CLIFF FACE IS SEALED TILL WE OPERATE THE CONTROLS. IT WAS A DESPERATE PLAN... BUT WORTH THE RISK!

ATLANTIC GOLD RUSH!

Millionaire stakes claim

by our business correspondent

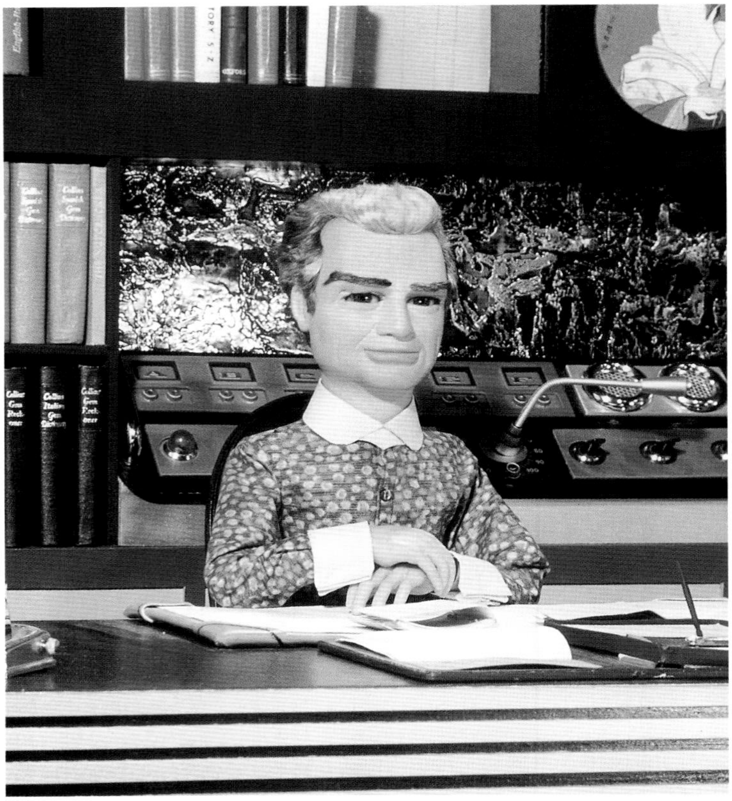

Millionaire ex-astronaut Jeff Tracy revealed he was one of the lucky bidders to be assigned a licence to mine off-shoots of the Atlantic Tunnel.

Tracy, whose Tracy Engineering company has supplied specialised equipment to the Tunnel project, commented, "This is a great opportunity to develop new mining techniques."

The mining off-shoots are believed to be rich in vast deposits of natural gas, Iron Ore, Copper, Cahelium, and if latest reports prove accurate, the ultra-rare mineral Mozatinum.

Right: **Millionaire Jeff Tracy, "Fabulous prospects."**

THE MIRACLE MACHINE

DATELINE 2066

Grinding forward at the incredible rate of five miles a day, Tunnel Unit One is the most advanced tunnelling rig ever constructed.

With blades made of toughened Cahelium, the massive tunnelling unit can slice through the hardest rock section in a matter of seconds.

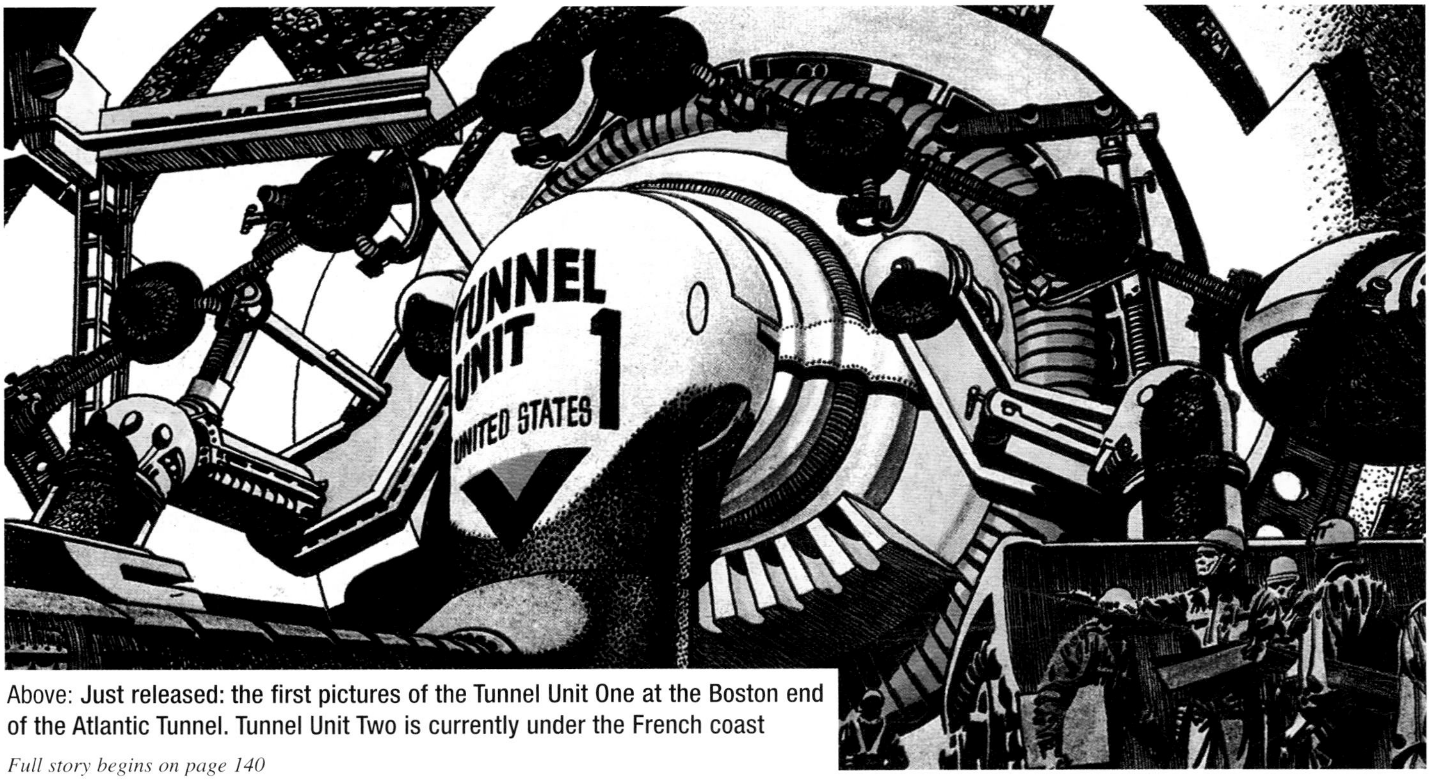
TUNNEL
UNIT 1
UNITED STATES

Above: **Just released: the first pictures of the Tunnel Unit One at the Boston end of the Atlantic Tunnel. Tunnel Unit Two is currently under the French coast**

Full story begins on page 140

HIGHWAY THROUGH THE DEEP

By our science correspondent

The Atlantic Tunnel has been planned to provide fast and efficient travel for thousands of trans-Atlantic travellers through a combination of road and pneumo-transport tubes. Journey times are calculated to be twelve hours by pneumo-tube and two days by road including compulsory overnight breaks.

FACTS ON TUNNEL TRAVEL

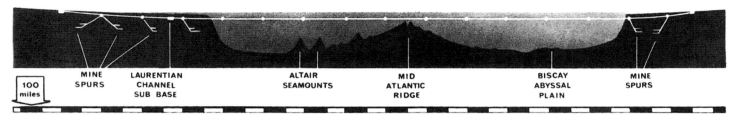

| 100 miles | MINE SPURS | LAURENTIAN CHANNEL SUB BASE | ALTAIR SEAMOUNTS | MID ATLANTIC RIDGE | BISCAY ABYSSAL PLAIN | MINE SPURS |

Above: The Atlantic Tunnel route. The central section is designed to float a mile beneath the ocean surface

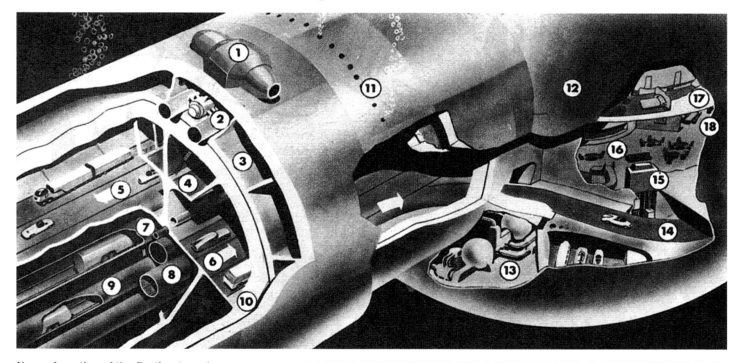

Above: A section of the floating tunnel
Below: The pneumatic powered tunnel train

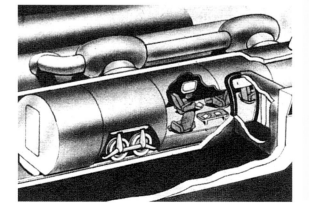

Key to tunnel cross-section

1. Lateral deviation correction turbine
2. Air pipes and pump situated in 3
3. Buoyancy correction compartments between inner core and outer pressure wall
4. Service roads used by maintenance engineers and crash wagons
5. Three lane eastbound highway
6. Three lane westbound highway
7. Central laser duct tube
8. Twin pneumo-transport tubes for passenger trains with central air-booster tube
9. Twin pneumobile freight tubes
10. Corrosion-resistant Cahelium pressure walls
11. Flood tank vents
12. Part-way station
13. Air-conditioning and pneumo-tube booster plant
14. Ramp to parking lot
15. Lifts from parking area
16. Reception lounge
17. Hotel accommodation
18. Traveller's dining room

139

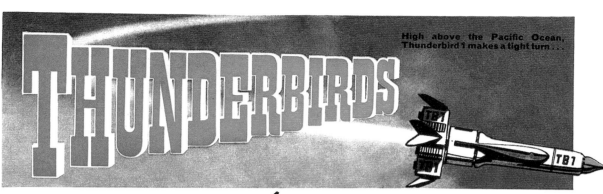

THUNDERBIRDS

High above the Pacific Ocean, Thunderbird 1 makes a tight turn...

SCOTT TRACY RADIOS RESCUE'S ISLAND BAS[E]

SCOTT OPERATES A CONTROL AND...

THE SMALL TARGET CRAFT STREAKS ABOVE THUNDERBIRD 4... AND GORDON ACTS...

THUNDERBIRD 4

A SIGNAL IS BEAMED ONTO THE TARGET CRAFT...

IN THE LOUNGE THE SMALL DART IS EXAMINED...

RIGHT, BRAINS. BRING IN THE TARGET... ALAN, CALL SCOTT AND GORDON BACK TO BASE!

SCOTT'S RIGHT, BRAINS. WHAT'S THE ANSWER?

NOW HE TELLS US! THERE'S NOT ENOUGH MOZATINUM IN THE WHOLE WORLD TO BUILD A DODGEM CAR... LET ALONE THE MACHINERY WE NEED.

THE ORE IS FOUND BENEATH THE OCEAN BED. WE MUST GET PERMITS TO SURVEY THE OFFSHOOT EXCAVATIONS OF THE ATLANTIC TUNNEL PROJECT.

I SEE... YOU'RE HOPING TO FIND DEPOSITS OF MOZATINUM THERE, EH? OKAY... I'LL CONTACT THE TUNNEL AUTHORITIES AND REGISTER A CLAIM.

E[XCUSE] ME, THE NE[W] A77[?]

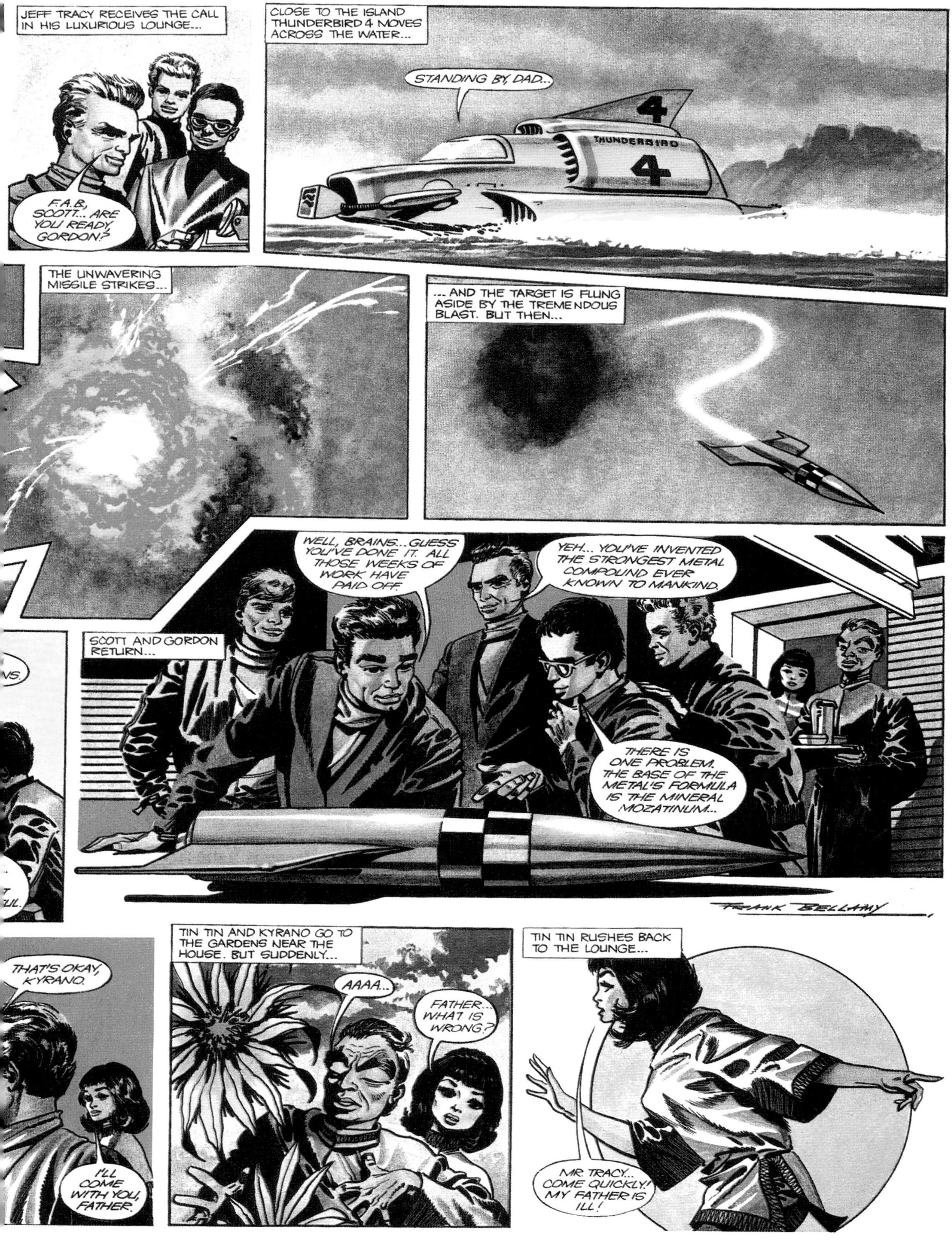

JEFF TRACY RECEIVES THE CALL IN HIS LUXURIOUS LOUNGE...
F.A.B, SCOTT... ARE YOU READY, GORDON?
CLOSE TO THE ISLAND THUNDERBIRD 4 MOVES ACROSS THE WATER...
STANDING BY, DAD...
THUNDERBIRD 4
THE UNWAVERING MISSILE STRIKES...
... AND THE TARGET IS FLUNG ASIDE BY THE TREMENDOUS BLAST. BUT THEN...
SCOTT AND GORDON RETURN...
WELL, BRAINS... GUESS YOU'VE DONE IT. ALL THOSE WEEKS OF WORK HAVE PAID OFF.
YEH... YOU'VE INVENTED THE STRONGEST METAL COMPOUND EVER KNOWN TO MANKIND.
THERE IS ONE PROBLEM. THE BASE OF THE METAL'S FORMULA IS THE MINERAL MOZATINUM...
FRANK BELLAMY
THAT'S OKAY, KYRANO.
I'LL COME WITH YOU, FATHER.
TIN TIN AND KYRANO GO TO THE GARDENS NEAR THE HOUSE. BUT SUDDENLY...
AAAA...
FATHER... WHAT IS WRONG?
TIN TIN RUSHES BACK TO THE LOUNGE...
MR. TRACY... COME QUICKLY! MY FATHER IS ILL!

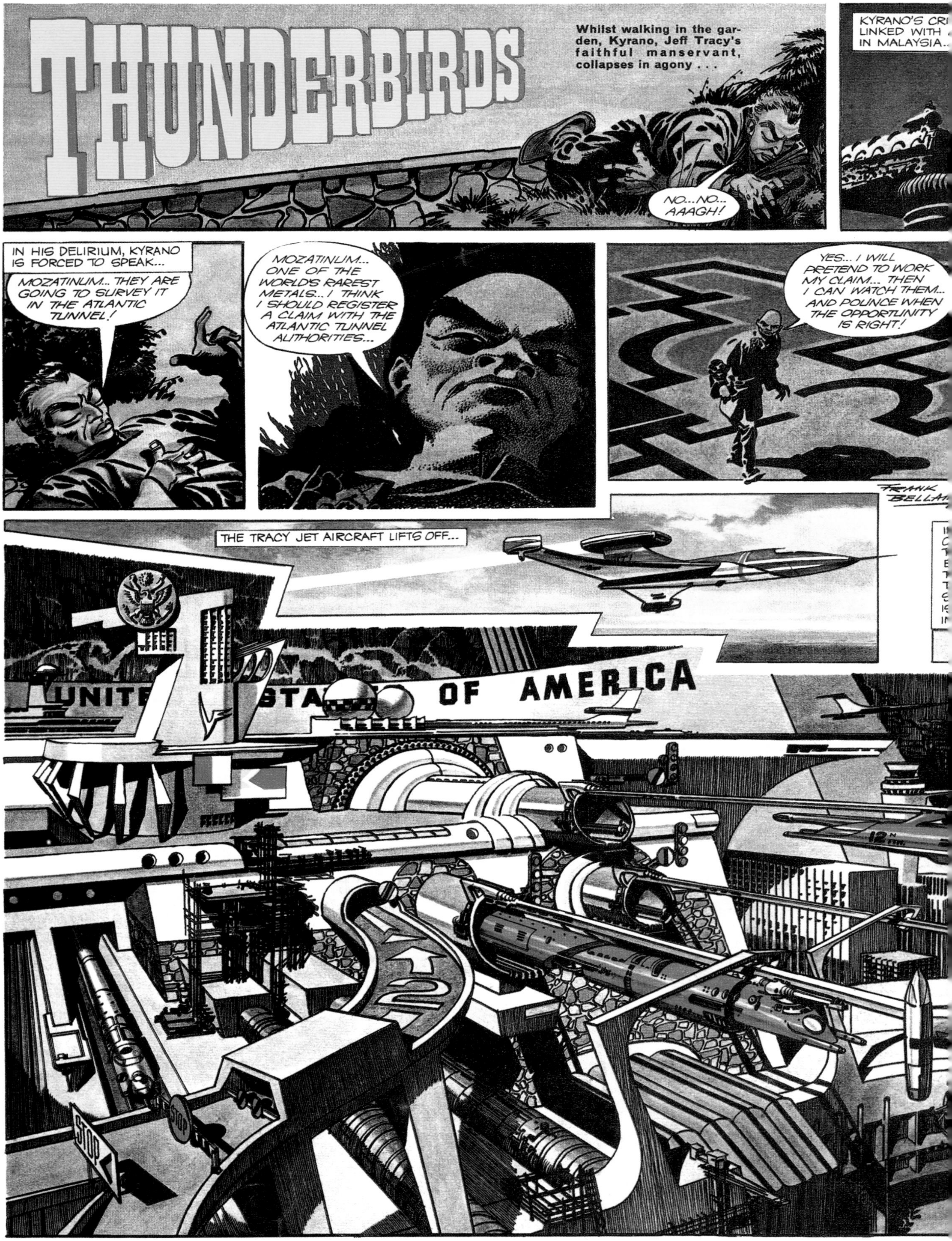
THUNDERBIRDS
Whilst walking in the garden, Kyrano, Jeff Tracy's faithful manservant, collapses in agony . . .
NO...NO... AAAGH!
KYRANO'S CRI
LINKED WITH
IN MALAYSIA...
IN HIS DELIRIUM, KYRANO IS FORCED TO SPEAK...
MOZATINUM... THEY ARE GOING TO SURVEY IT IN THE ATLANTIC TUNNEL!
MOZATINUM... ONE OF THE WORLD'S RAREST METALS... I THINK I SHOULD REGISTER A CLAIM WITH THE ATLANTIC TUNNEL AUTHORITIES...
YES... I WILL PRETEND TO WORK MY CLAIM... THEN I CAN WATCH THEM... AND POUNCE WHEN THE OPPORTUNITY IS RIGHT!
FRANK BELLA
THE TRACY JET AIRCRAFT LIFTS OFF...
UNITE
STA
OF AMERICA
STOP
STOP

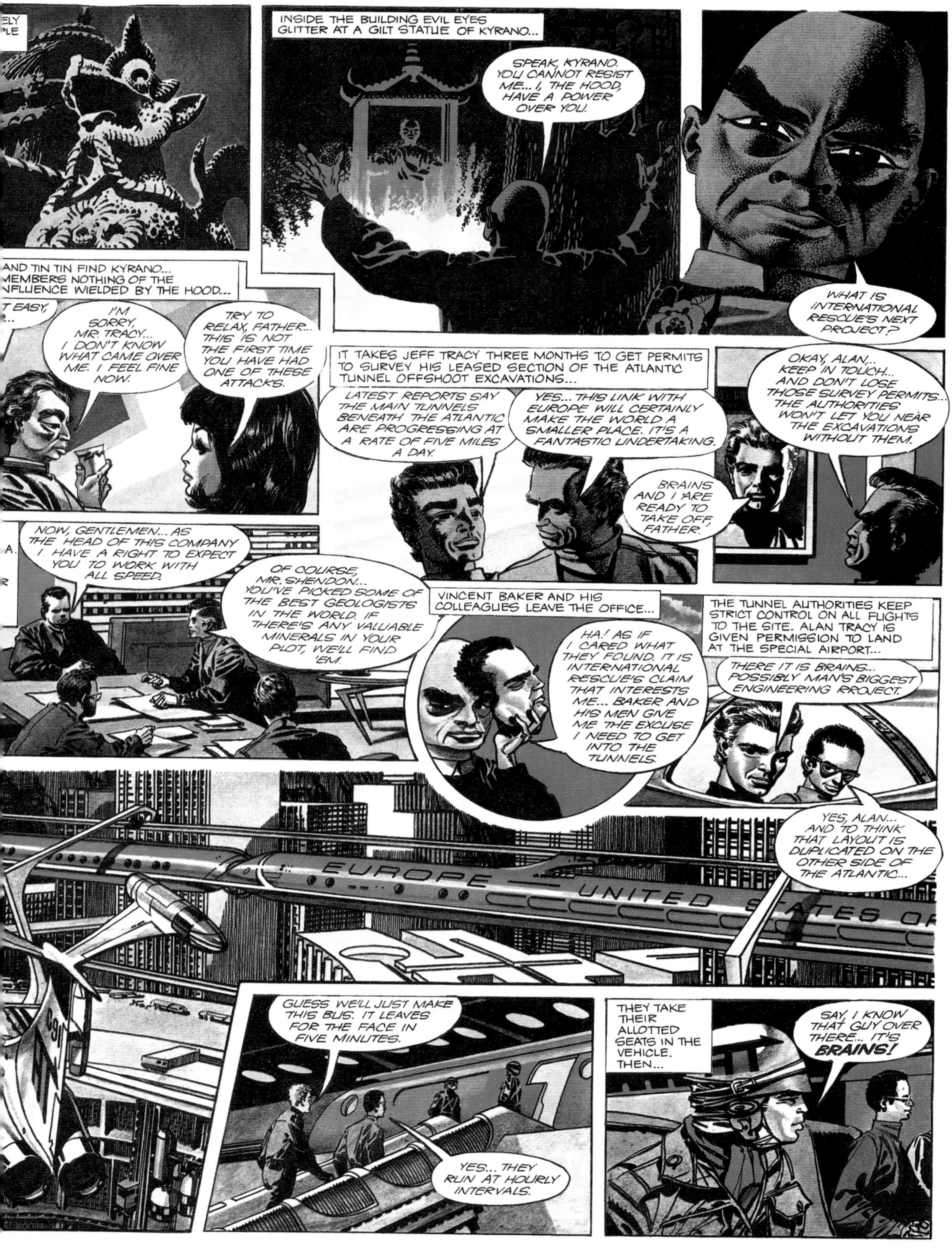

INSIDE THE BUILDING EVIL EYES GLITTER AT A GILT STATUE OF KYRANO...
SPEAK, KYRANO. YOU CANNOT RESIST ME... I, THE HOOD, HAVE A POWER OVER YOU.
WHAT IS INTERNATIONAL RESCUE'S NEXT PROJECT?
AND TIN TIN FIND KYRANO... MEMBERS NOTHING OF THE NFLUENCE WIELDED BY THE HOOD...
I'M SORRY, MR. TRACY... I DON'T KNOW WHAT CAME OVER ME. I FEEL FINE NOW.
TRY TO RELAX, FATHER... THIS IS NOT THE FIRST TIME YOU HAVE HAD ONE OF THESE ATTACKS.
IT TAKES JEFF TRACY THREE MONTHS TO GET PERMITS TO SURVEY HIS LEASED SECTION OF THE ATLANTIC TUNNEL OFFSHOOT EXCAVATIONS...
LATEST REPORTS SAY THE MAIN TUNNELS BENEATH THE ATLANTIC ARE PROGRESSING AT A RATE OF FIVE MILES A DAY.
YES... THIS LINK WITH EUROPE WILL CERTAINLY MAKE THE WORLD A SMALLER PLACE. IT'S A FANTASTIC UNDERTAKING.
BRAINS AND I ARE READY TO TAKE OFF, FATHER.
OKAY, ALAN... KEEP IN TOUCH... AND DON'T LOSE THOSE SURVEY PERMITS... THE AUTHORITIES WON'T LET YOU NEAR THE EXCAVATIONS WITHOUT THEM.
NOW, GENTLEMEN... AS THE HEAD OF THIS COMPANY I HAVE A RIGHT TO EXPECT YOU TO WORK WITH ALL SPEED.
OF COURSE, MR. SHENDON... YOU'VE PICKED SOME OF THE BEST GEOLOGISTS IN THE WORLD. IF THERE'S ANY VALUABLE MINERALS IN YOUR PLOT, WE'LL FIND 'EM.
VINCENT BAKER AND HIS COLLEAGUES LEAVE THE OFFICE...
HA! AS IF I CARED WHAT THEY FOUND. IT IS INTERNATIONAL RESCUE'S CLAIM THAT INTERESTS ME... BAKER AND HIS MEN GIVE ME THE EXCUSE I NEED TO GET INTO THE TUNNELS.
THE TUNNEL AUTHORITIES KEEP STRICT CONTROL ON ALL FLIGHTS TO THE SITE. ALAN TRACY IS GIVEN PERMISSION TO LAND AT THE SPECIAL AIRPORT...
THERE IT IS BRAINS... POSSIBLY MAN'S BIGGEST ENGINEERING RROJECT.
YES, ALAN... AND TO THINK THAT LAYOUT IS DUPLICATED ON THE OTHER SIDE OF THE ATLANTIC...
EUROPE
UNITED STATES OF
GUESS WE'LL JUST MAKE THIS BUS. IT LEAVES FOR THE FACE IN FIVE MINUTES.
YES... THEY RUN AT HOURLY INTERVALS.
THEY TAKE THEIR ALLOTTED SEATS IN THE VEHICLE. THEN...
SAY, I KNOW THAT GUY OVER THERE... IT'S **BRAINS!**

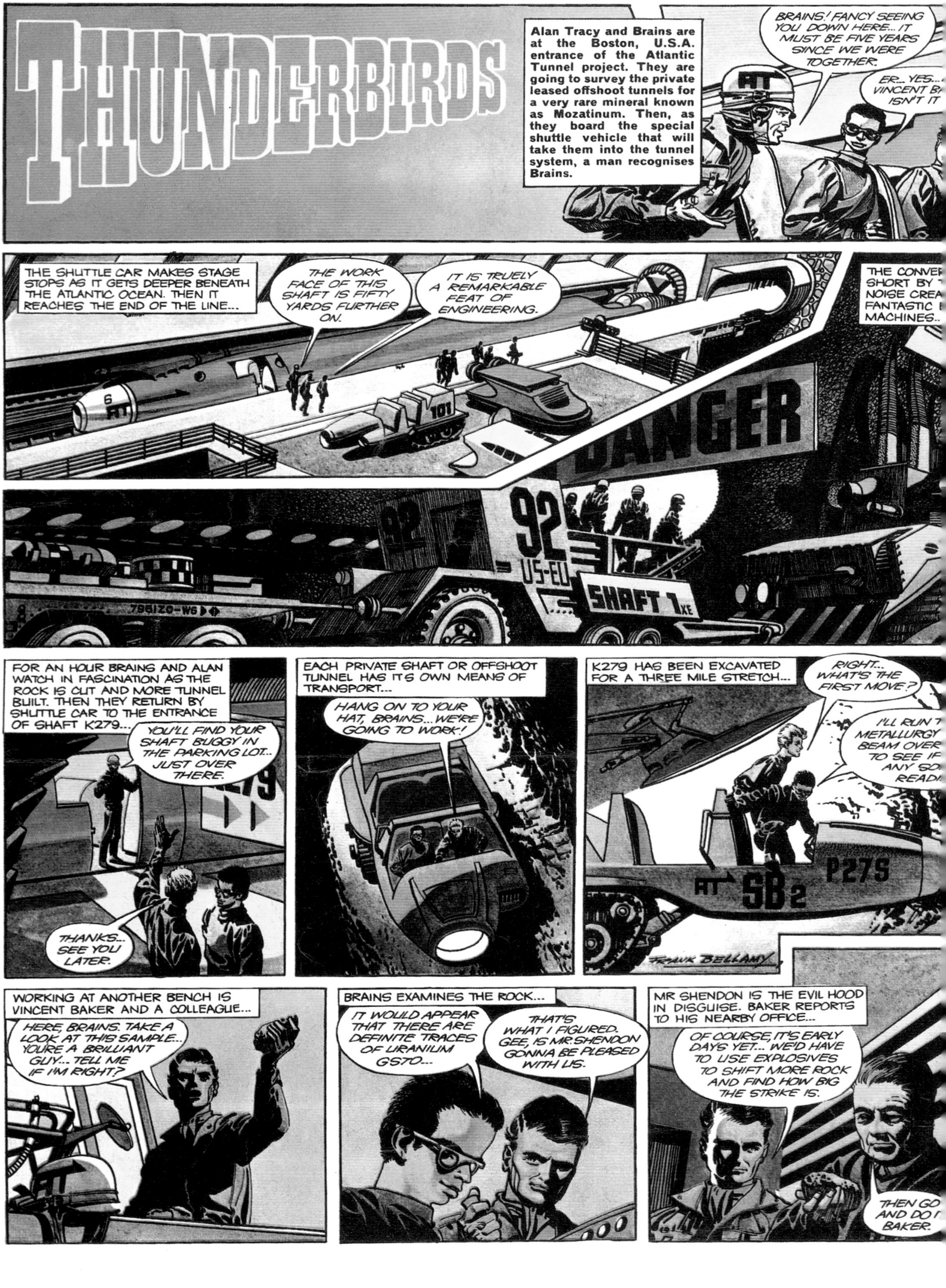
THUNDERBIRDS
Alan Tracy and Brains are at the Boston, U.S.A. entrance of the Atlantic Tunnel project. They are going to survey the private leased offshoot tunnels for a very rare mineral known as Mozatinum. Then, as they board the special shuttle vehicle that will take them into the tunnel system, a man recognises Brains.
BRAINS! FANCY SEEING YOU DOWN HERE... IT MUST BE FIVE YEARS SINCE WE WERE TOGETHER.
ER... YES... VINCENT BA ISN'T IT
THE SHUTTLE CAR MAKES STAGE STOPS AS IT GETS DEEPER BENEATH THE ATLANTIC OCEAN. THEN IT REACHES THE END OF THE LINE...
THE WORK FACE OF THIS SHAFT IS FIFTY YARDS FURTHER ON.
IT IS TRUELY A REMARKABLE FEAT OF ENGINEERING.
THE CONVER SHORT BY NOISE CREA FANTASTIC MACHINES...
DANGER
92
US-EU
SHAFT 1 XE
FOR AN HOUR BRAINS AND ALAN WATCH IN FASCINATION AS THE ROCK IS CUT AND MORE TUNNEL BUILT. THEN THEY RETURN BY SHUTTLE CAR TO THE ENTRANCE OF SHAFT K279...
YOU'LL FIND YOUR SHAFT BUGGY IN THE PARKING LOT... JUST OVER THERE.
THANKS... SEE YOU LATER.
EACH PRIVATE SHAFT OR OFFSHOOT TUNNEL HAS IT'S OWN MEANS OF TRANSPORT...
HANG ON TO YOUR HAT, BRAINS... WE'RE GOING TO WORK!
K279 HAS BEEN EXCAVATED FOR A THREE MILE STRETCH...
RIGHT... WHAT'S THE FIRST MOVE?
I'LL RUN METALLURGY BEAM OVER TO SEE IF ANY SO READ
SB 2
P27S
FRANK BELLAMY
WORKING AT ANOTHER BENCH IS VINCENT BAKER AND A COLLEAGUE...
HERE, BRAINS. TAKE A LOOK AT THIS SAMPLE... YOU'RE A BRILLIANT GUY... TELL ME IF I'M RIGHT?
BRAINS EXAMINES THE ROCK...
IT WOULD APPEAR THAT THERE ARE DEFINITE TRACES OF URANIUM G570...
THAT'S WHAT I FIGURED. GEE, IS MR. SHENDON GONNA BE PLEASED WITH US.
MR SHENDON IS THE EVIL HOOD IN DISGUISE. BAKER REPORTS TO HIS NEARBY OFFICE...
OF COURSE, IT'S EARLY DAYS YET... WE'D HAVE TO USE EXPLOSIVES TO SHIFT MORE ROCK AND FIND HOW BIG THE STRIKE IS.
THEN GO AND DO BAKER.

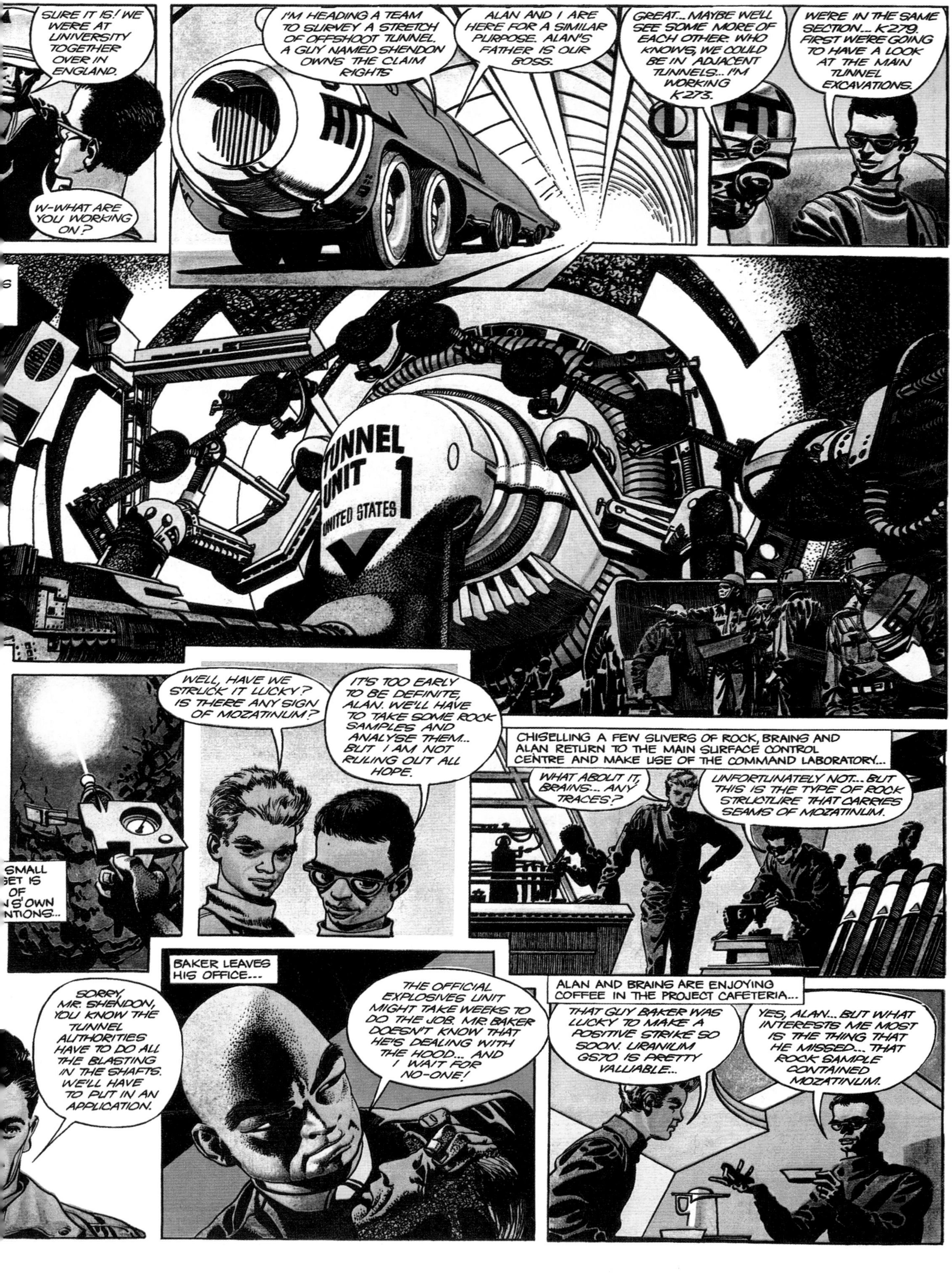

SURE IT IS! WE WERE AT UNIVERSITY TOGETHER OVER IN ENGLAND.
W-WHAT ARE YOU WORKING ON?
I'M HEADING A TEAM TO SURVEY A STRETCH OF OFFSHOOT TUNNEL. A GUY NAMED SHENDON OWNS THE CLAIM RIGHTS
ALAN AND I ARE HERE FOR A SIMILAR PURPOSE. ALAN'S FATHER IS OUR BOSS.
GREAT... MAYBE WE'LL SEE SOME MORE OF EACH OTHER. WHO KNOWS, WE COULD BE IN ADJACENT TUNNELS... I'M WORKING K273.
WE'RE IN THE SAME SECTION... K279. FIRST WE'RE GOING TO HAVE A LOOK AT THE MAIN TUNNEL EXCAVATIONS.
TUNNEL UNIT 1
UNITED STATES
SMALL
GET IS
OF
N S' OWN
NTIONS...
WELL, HAVE WE STRUCK IT LUCKY? IS THERE ANY SIGN OF MOZATINUM?
IT'S TOO EARLY TO BE DEFINITE, ALAN. WE'LL HAVE TO TAKE SOME ROCK SAMPLES AND ANALYSE THEM... BUT I AM NOT RULING OUT ALL HOPE.
CHISELLING A FEW SLIVERS OF ROCK, BRAINS AND ALAN RETURN TO THE MAIN SURFACE CONTROL CENTRE AND MAKE USE OF THE COMMAND LABORATORY...
WHAT ABOUT IT, BRAINS... ANY TRACES?
UNFORTUNATELY NOT... BUT THIS IS THE TYPE OF ROCK STRUCTURE THAT CARRIES SEAMS OF MOZATINUM.
SORRY, MR. SHENDON, YOU KNOW THE TUNNEL AUTHORITIES HAVE TO DO ALL THE BLASTING IN THE SHAFTS. WE'LL HAVE TO PUT IN AN APPLICATION.
BAKER LEAVES HIS OFFICE---
THE OFFICIAL EXPLOSIVES UNIT MIGHT TAKE WEEKS TO DO THE JOB. MR. BAKER DOESN'T KNOW THAT HE'S DEALING WITH THE HOOD... AND I WAIT FOR NO-ONE!
ALAN AND BRAINS ARE ENJOYING COFFEE IN THE PROJECT CAFETERIA...
THAT GUY BAKER WAS LUCKY TO MAKE A POSITIVE STRIKE SO SOON. URANIUM G570 IS PRETTY VALUABLE...
YES, ALAN... BUT WHAT INTERESTS ME MOST IS THE THING THAT HE MISSED... THAT ROCK SAMPLE CONTAINED MOZATINUM.

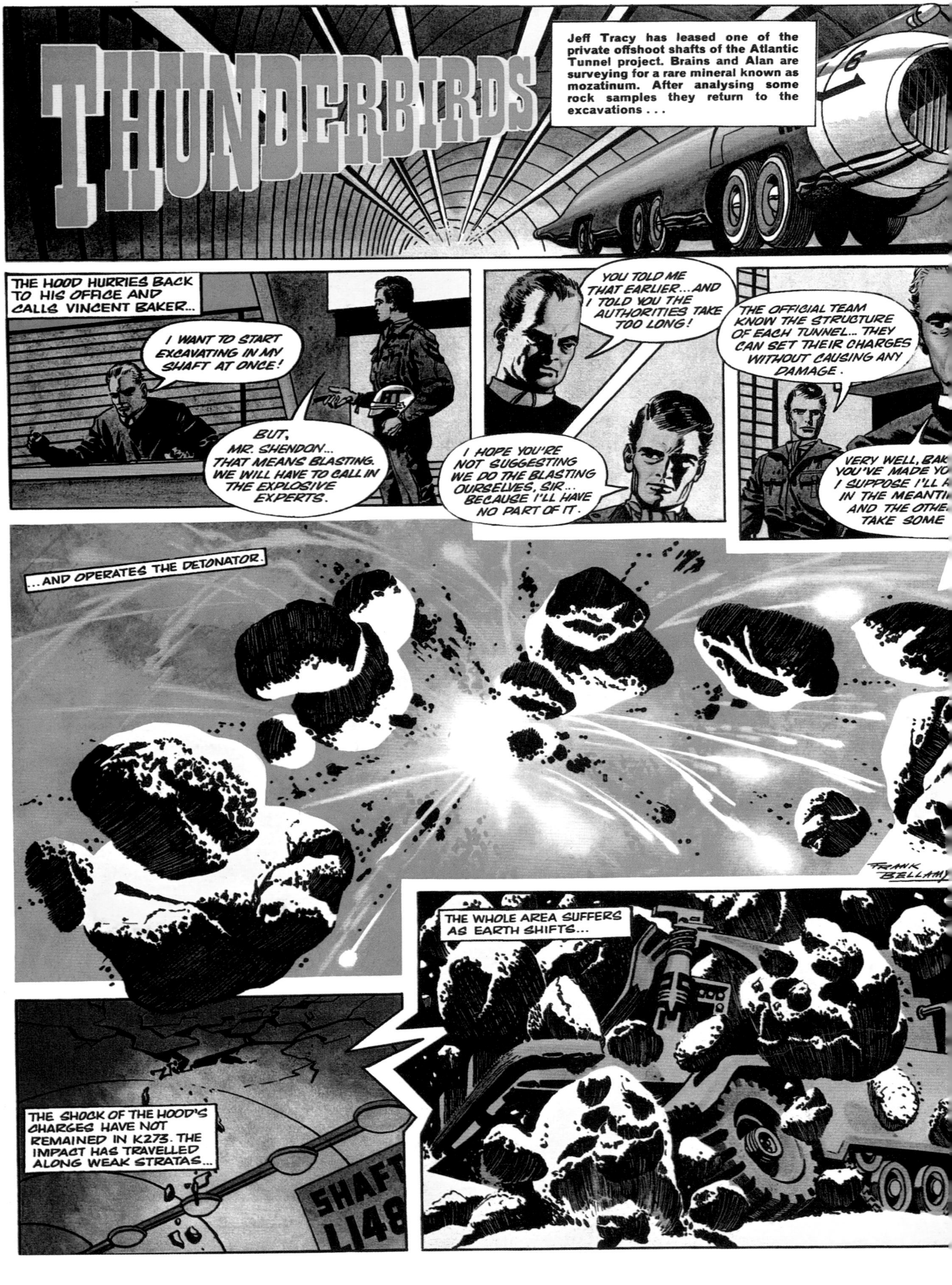
THUNDERBIRDS
Jeff Tracy has leased one of the private offshoot shafts of the Atlantic Tunnel project. Brains and Alan are surveying for a rare mineral known as mozatinum. After analysing some rock samples they return to the excavations . . .
THE HOOD HURRIES BACK TO HIS OFFICE AND CALLS VINCENT BAKER...
I WANT TO START EXCAVATING IN MY SHAFT AT ONCE!
BUT, MR. SHENDON... THAT MEANS BLASTING. WE WILL HAVE TO CALL IN THE EXPLOSIVE EXPERTS.
YOU TOLD ME THAT EARLIER... AND I TOLD YOU THE AUTHORITIES TAKE TOO LONG!
I HOPE YOU'RE NOT SUGGESTING WE DO THE BLASTING OURSELVES, SIR... BECAUSE I'LL HAVE NO PART OF IT.
THE OFFICIAL TEAM KNOW THE STRUCTURE OF EACH TUNNEL... THEY CAN SET THEIR CHARGES WITHOUT CAUSING ANY DAMAGE.
VERY WELL, BAK
YOU'VE MADE YO
I SUPPOSE I'LL A
IN THE MEANTI
AND THE OTHE
TAKE SOME
...AND OPERATES THE DETONATOR.
FRANK BELLAMY
THE WHOLE AREA SUFFERS AS EARTH SHIFTS...
THE SHOCK OF THE HOOD'S CHARGES HAVE NOT REMAINED IN K273. THE IMPACT HAS TRAVELLED ALONG WEAK STRATAS...
SHAFT L148

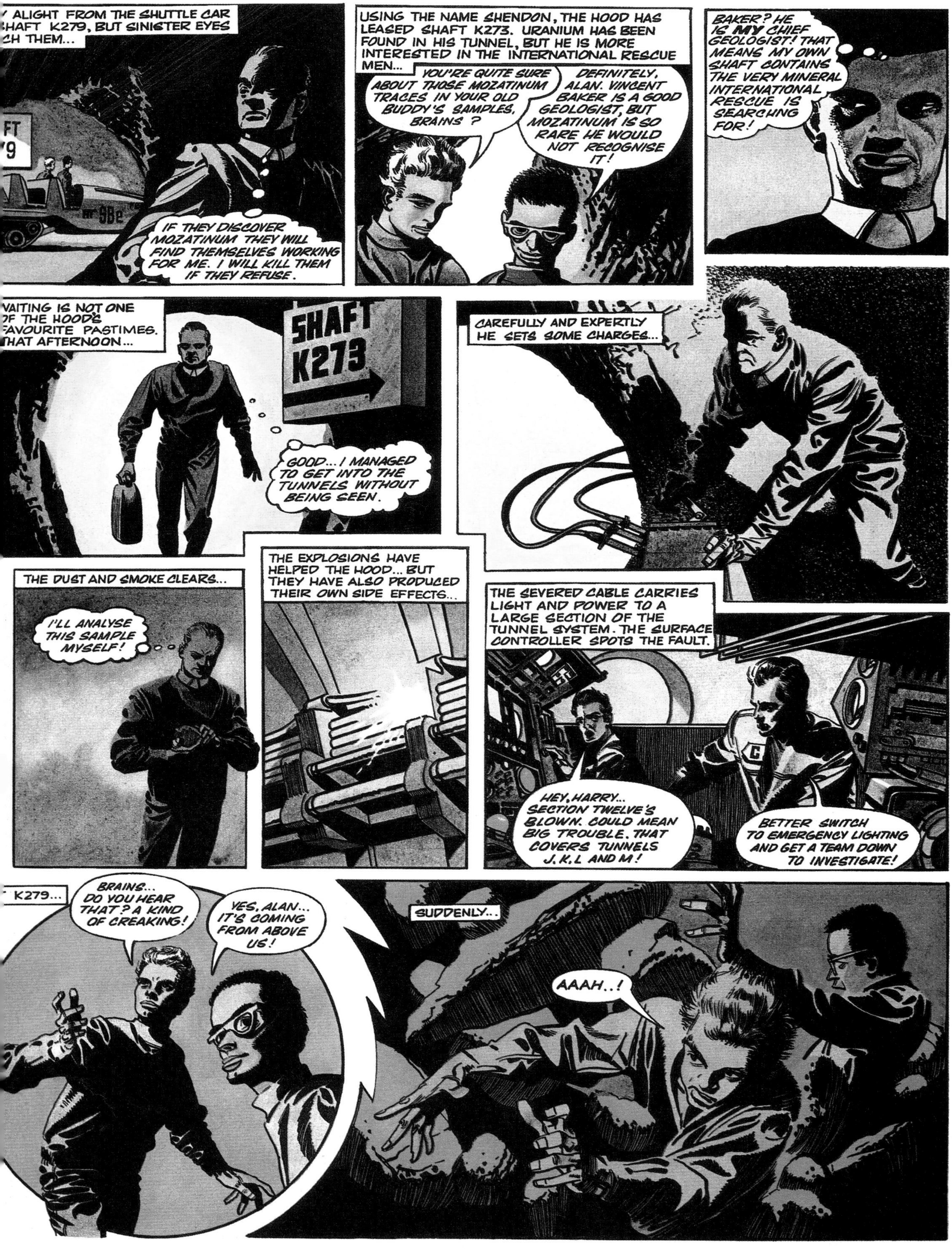

Y ALIGHT FROM THE SHUTTLE CAR SHAFT K279, BUT SINISTER EYES CH THEM...
FT 79
IF THEY DISCOVER MOZATINUM THEY WILL FIND THEMSELVES WORKING FOR ME. I WILL KILL THEM IF THEY REFUSE.
USING THE NAME SHENDON, THE HOOD HAS LEASED SHAFT K273. URANIUM HAS BEEN FOUND IN HIS TUNNEL, BUT HE IS MORE INTERESTED IN THE INTERNATIONAL RESCUE MEN...
YOU'RE QUITE SURE ABOUT THOSE MOZATINUM TRACES IN YOUR OLD BUDDY'S SAMPLES, BRAINS ?
DEFINITELY, ALAN. VINCENT BAKER IS A GOOD GEOLOGIST, BUT MOZATINUM IS SO RARE HE WOULD NOT RECOGNISE IT!
BAKER? HE IS MY CHIEF GEOLOGIST! THAT MEANS MY OWN SHAFT CONTAINS THE VERY MINERAL INTERNATIONAL RESCUE IS SEARCHING FOR!
WAITING IS NOT ONE OF THE HOOD'S FAVOURITE PASTIMES. THAT AFTERNOON...
SHAFT K273
GOOD... I MANAGED TO GET INTO THE TUNNELS WITHOUT BEING SEEN.
CAREFULLY AND EXPERTLY HE SETS SOME CHARGES...
THE DUST AND SMOKE CLEARS...
I'LL ANALYSE THIS SAMPLE MYSELF!
THE EXPLOSIONS HAVE HELPED THE HOOD... BUT THEY HAVE ALSO PRODUCED THEIR OWN SIDE EFFECTS...
THE SEVERED CABLE CARRIES LIGHT AND POWER TO A LARGE SECTION OF THE TUNNEL SYSTEM. THE SURFACE CONTROLLER SPOTS THE FAULT.
HEY, HARRY... SECTION TWELVE'S BLOWN. COULD MEAN BIG TROUBLE. THAT COVERS TUNNELS J, K, L AND M!
BETTER SWITCH TO EMERGENCY LIGHTING AND GET A TEAM DOWN TO INVESTIGATE!
K279...
BRAINS... DO YOU HEAR THAT? A KIND OF CREAKING!
YES, ALAN... IT'S COMING FROM ABOVE US!
SUDDENLY...
AAAH..!

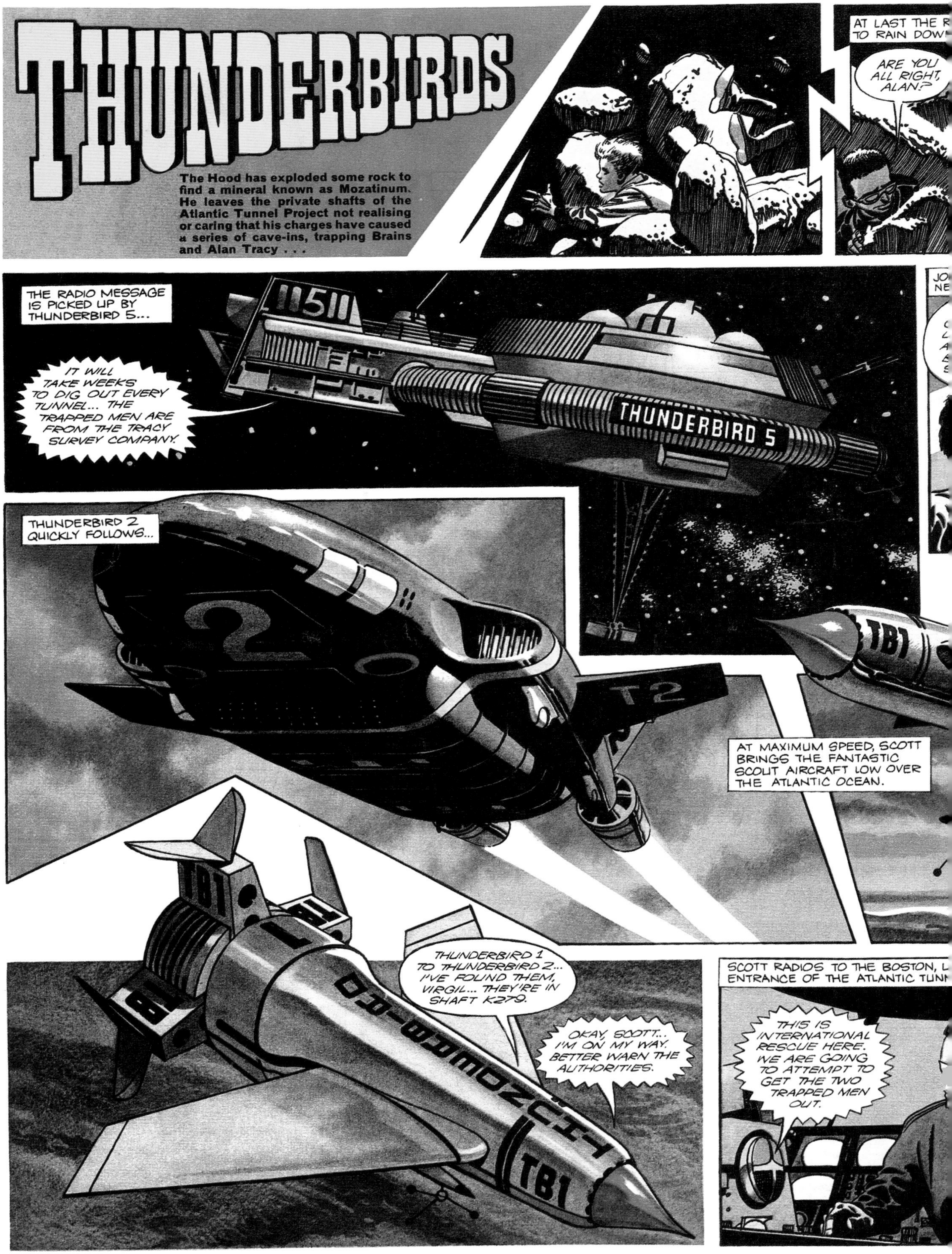
THUNDERBIRDS
The Hood has exploded some rock to find a mineral known as Mozatinum. He leaves the private shafts of the Atlantic Tunnel Project not realising or caring that his charges have caused a series of cave-ins, trapping Brains and Alan Tracy . . .
AT LAST THE
TO RAIN
ARE YOU ALL RIGHT, ALAN?
THE RADIO MESSAGE IS PICKED UP BY THUNDERBIRD 5...
IT WILL TAKE WEEKS TO DIG OUT EVERY TUNNEL... THE TRAPPED MEN ARE FROM THE TRACY SURVEY COMPANY.
THUNDERBIRD 5
THUNDERBIRD 2 QUICKLY FOLLOWS...
AT MAXIMUM SPEED, SCOTT BRINGS THE FANTASTIC SCOUT AIRCRAFT LOW OVER THE ATLANTIC OCEAN.
THUNDERBIRD 1 TO THUNDERBIRD 2... I'VE FOUND THEM, VIRGIL... THEY'RE IN SHAFT K279.
OKAY, SCOTT... I'M ON MY WAY. BETTER WARN THE AUTHORITIES.
SCOTT RADIOS TO THE BOSTON,
ENTRANCE OF THE ATLANTIC
THIS IS INTERNATIONAL RESCUE HERE. WE ARE GOING TO ATTEMPT TO GET THE TWO TRAPPED MEN OUT.

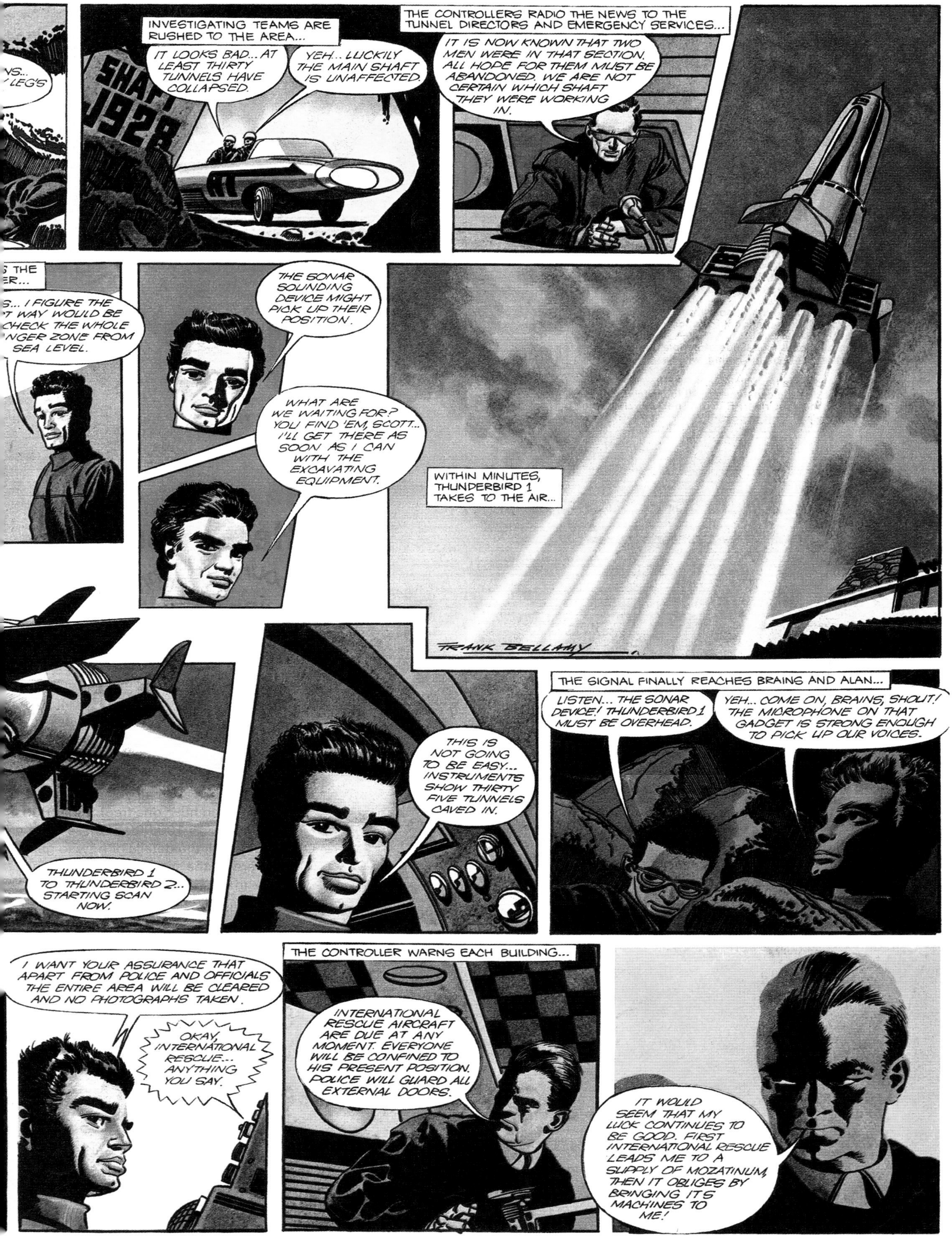

INVESTIGATING TEAMS ARE RUSHED TO THE AREA...
IT LOOKS BAD... AT LEAST THIRTY TUNNELS HAVE COLLAPSED.
YEH... LUCKILY THE MAIN SHAFT IS UNAFFECTED.
SHAFT 1928
THE CONTROLLERS RADIO THE NEWS TO THE TUNNEL DIRECTORS AND EMERGENCY SERVICES...
IT IS NOW KNOWN THAT TWO MEN WERE IN THAT SECTION. ALL HOPE FOR THEM MUST BE ABANDONED. WE ARE NOT CERTAIN WHICH SHAFT THEY WERE WORKING IN.
THE SONAR SOUNDING DEVICE MIGHT PICK UP THEIR POSITION.
WHAT ARE WE WAITING FOR? YOU FIND 'EM, SCOTT... I'LL GET THERE AS SOON AS I CAN WITH THE EXCAVATING EQUIPMENT.
WITHIN MINUTES, THUNDERBIRD 1 TAKES TO THE AIR...
FRANK BELLAMY
THUNDERBIRD 1 TO THUNDERBIRD 2... STARTING SCAN NOW.
THIS IS NOT GOING TO BE EASY... INSTRUMENTS SHOW THIRTY FIVE TUNNELS CAVED IN.
THE SIGNAL FINALLY REACHES BRAINS AND ALAN...
LISTEN... THE SONAR DEVICE! THUNDERBIRD 1 MUST BE OVERHEAD.
YEH... COME ON, BRAINS, SHOUT! THE MICROPHONE ON THAT GADGET IS STRONG ENOUGH TO PICK UP OUR VOICES.
I WANT YOUR ASSURANCE THAT APART FROM POLICE AND OFFICIALS THE ENTIRE AREA WILL BE CLEARED AND NO PHOTOGRAPHS TAKEN.
OKAY, INTERNATIONAL RESCUE... ANYTHING YOU SAY.
THE CONTROLLER WARNS EACH BUILDING...
INTERNATIONAL RESCUE AIRCRAFT ARE DUE AT ANY MOMENT. EVERYONE WILL BE CONFINED TO HIS PRESENT POSITION. POLICE WILL GUARD ALL EXTERNAL DOORS.
IT WOULD SEEM THAT MY LUCK CONTINUES TO BE GOOD. FIRST INTERNATIONAL RESCUE LEADS ME TO A SUPPLY OF MOZATINUM, THEN IT OBLIGES BY BRINGING ITS MACHINES TO ME!

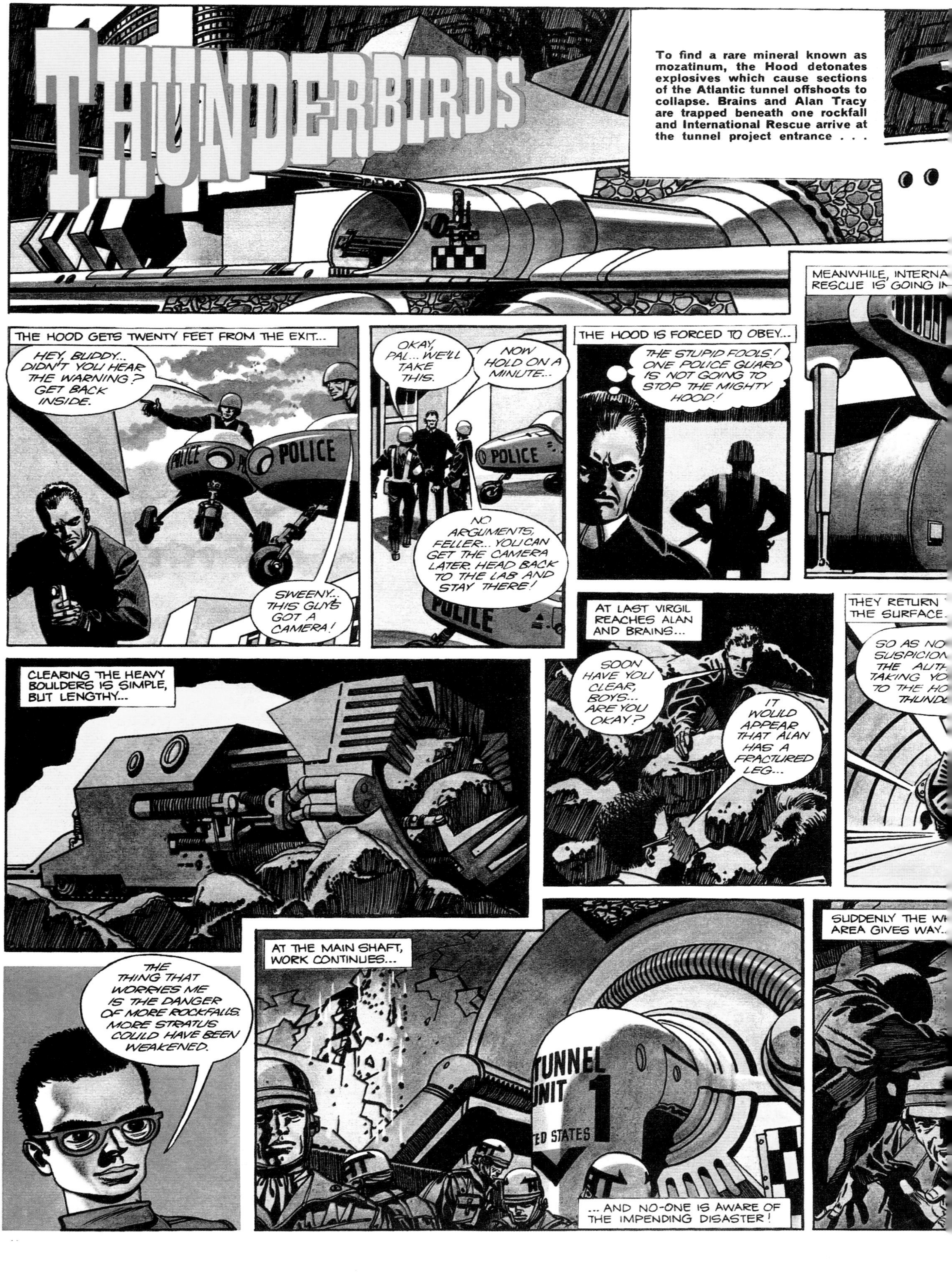
THUNDERBIRDS
To find a rare mineral known as mozatinum, the Hood detonates explosives which cause sections of the Atlantic tunnel offshoots to collapse. Brains and Alan Tracy are trapped beneath one rockfall and International Rescue arrive at the tunnel project entrance . . .
MEANWHILE, INTERNA
RESCUE IS GOING IN
THE HOOD GETS TWENTY FEET FROM THE EXIT...
HEY, BUDDY... DIDN'T YOU HEAR THE WARNING? GET BACK INSIDE.
POLICE
POLICE
SWEENY... THIS GUY'S GOT A CAMERA!
OKAY, PAL... WE'LL TAKE THIS.
NOW HOLD ON A MINUTE...
POLICE
NO ARGUMENTS, FELLER... YOU CAN GET THE CAMERA LATER. HEAD BACK TO THE LAB AND STAY THERE!
POLICE
THE HOOD IS FORCED TO OBEY...
THE STUPID FOOLS! ONE POLICE GUARD IS NOT GOING TO STOP THE MIGHTY HOOD!
THEY RETURN
THE SURFACE.
SO AS NO
SUSPICION
THE AUTH
TAKING YO
TO THE HO
THUNDE
CLEARING THE HEAVY BOULDERS IS SIMPLE, BUT LENGTHY...
AT LAST VIRGIL REACHES ALAN AND BRAINS...
SOON HAVE YOU CLEAR, BOYS... ARE YOU OKAY?
IT WOULD APPEAR THAT ALAN HAS A FRACTURED LEG...
SUDDENLY THE W
AREA GIVES WAY...
THE THING THAT WORRIES ME IS THE DANGER OF MORE ROCKFALLS. MORE STRATUS COULD HAVE BEEN WEAKENED.
AT THE MAIN SHAFT, WORK CONTINUES...
TUNNEL UNIT 1
ED STATES
... AND NO-ONE IS AWARE OF THE IMPENDING DISASTER!

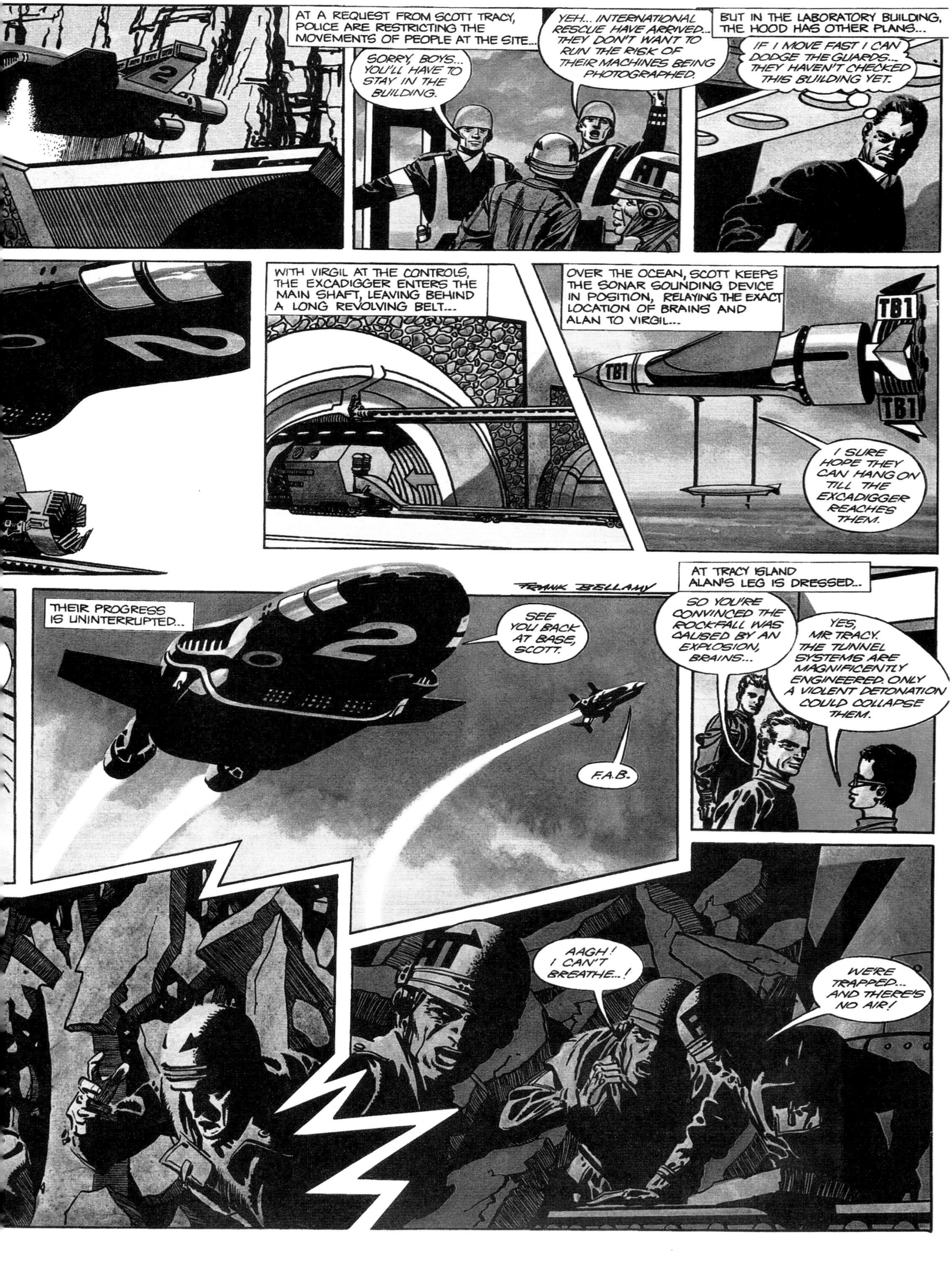

AT A REQUEST FROM SCOTT TRACY, POLICE ARE RESTRICTING THE MOVEMENTS OF PEOPLE AT THE SITE...
SORRY, BOYS... YOU'LL HAVE TO STAY IN THE BUILDING.
YEH... INTERNATIONAL RESCUE HAVE ARRIVED... THEY DON'T WANT TO RUN THE RISK OF THEIR MACHINES BEING PHOTOGRAPHED.
BUT IN THE LABORATORY BUILDING, THE HOOD HAS OTHER PLANS...
IF I MOVE FAST I CAN DODGE THE GUARDS... THEY HAVEN'T CHECKED THIS BUILDING YET.
WITH VIRGIL AT THE CONTROLS, THE EXCADIGGER ENTERS THE MAIN SHAFT, LEAVING BEHIND A LONG REVOLVING BELT...
OVER THE OCEAN, SCOTT KEEPS THE SONAR SOUNDING DEVICE IN POSITION, RELAYING THE EXACT LOCATION OF BRAINS AND ALAN TO VIRGIL...
TB1
I SURE HOPE THEY CAN HANG ON TILL THE EXCADIGGER REACHES THEM.
FRANK BELLAMY
THEIR PROGRESS IS UNINTERRUPTED...
SEE YOU BACK AT BASE, SCOTT.
F.A.B.
AT TRACY ISLAND ALAN'S LEG IS DRESSED...
SO YOU'RE CONVINCED THE ROCKFALL WAS CAUSED BY AN EXPLOSION, BRAINS...
YES, MR. TRACY. THE TUNNEL SYSTEMS ARE MAGNIFICENTLY ENGINEERED. ONLY A VIOLENT DETONATION COULD COLLAPSE THEM.
AAGH! I CAN'T BREATHE...!
WE'RE TRAPPED... AND THERE'S NO AIR!

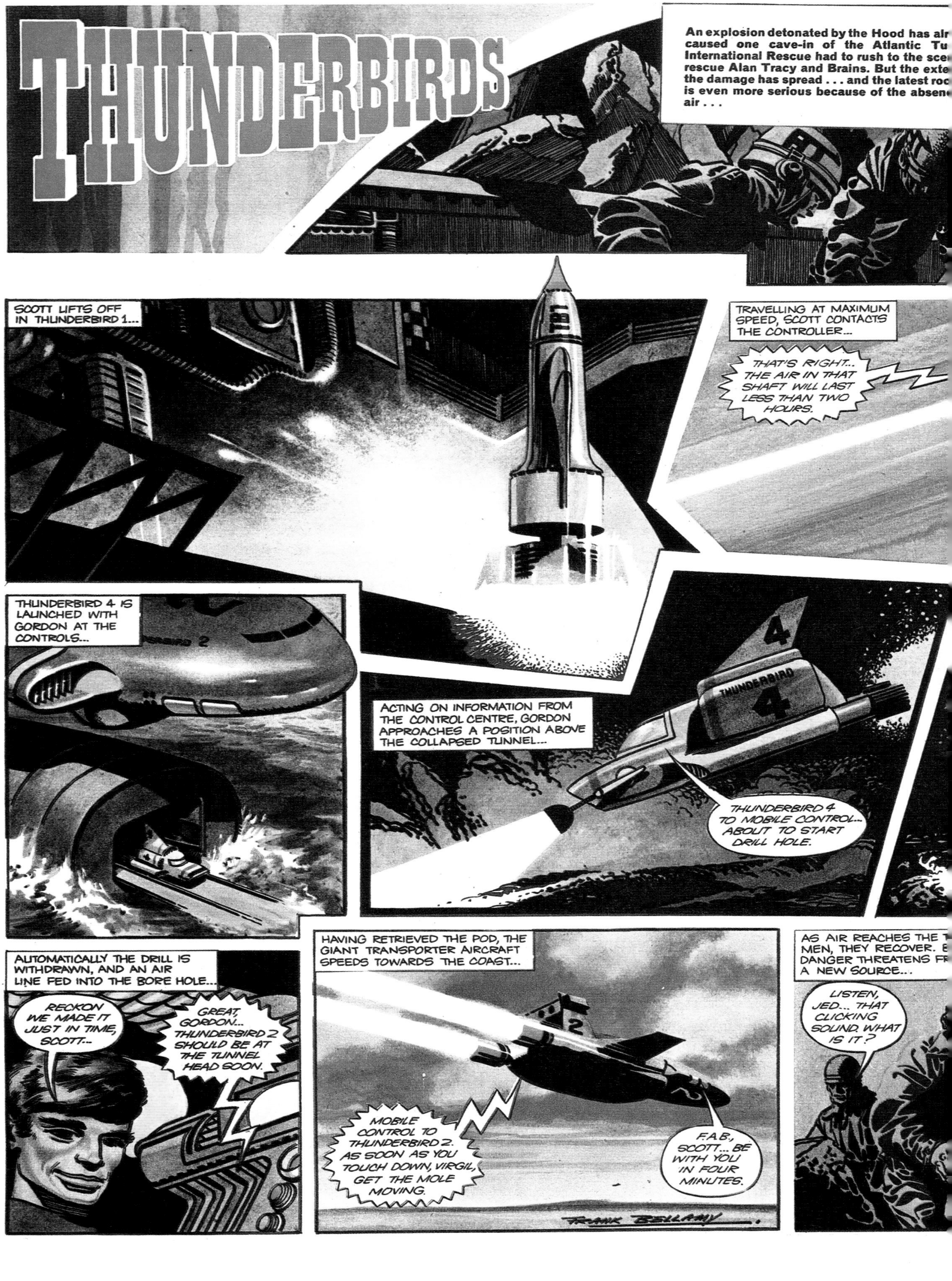

THUNDERBIRDS
An explosion detonated by the Hood has al caused one cave-in of the Atlantic Tu International Rescue had to rush to the sce rescue Alan Tracy and Brains. But the exte the damage has spread . . . and the latest roc is even more serious because of the absen air . . .
SCOTT LIFTS OFF IN THUNDERBIRD 1...
TRAVELLING AT MAXIMUM SPEED, SCOTT CONTACTS THE CONTROLLER...
THAT'S RIGHT... THE AIR IN THAT SHAFT WILL LAST LESS THAN TWO HOURS.
THUNDERBIRD 4 IS LAUNCHED WITH GORDON AT THE CONTROLS...
ACTING ON INFORMATION FROM THE CONTROL CENTRE, GORDON APPROACHES A POSITION ABOVE THE COLLAPSED TUNNEL...
THUNDERBIRD 4
THUNDERBIRD 4 TO MOBILE CONTROL... ABOUT TO START DRILL HOLE.
AUTOMATICALLY THE DRILL IS WITHDRAWN, AND AN AIR LINE FED INTO THE BORE HOLE...
RECKON WE MADE IT JUST IN TIME, SCOTT...
GREAT, GORDON... THUNDERBIRD 2 SHOULD BE AT THE TUNNEL HEAD SOON.
HAVING RETRIEVED THE POD, THE GIANT TRANSPORTER AIRCRAFT SPEEDS TOWARDS THE COAST...
MOBILE CONTROL TO THUNDERBIRD 2. AS SOON AS YOU TOUCH DOWN, VIRGIL, GET THE MOLE MOVING.
F.A.B., SCOTT... BE WITH YOU IN FOUR MINUTES.
FRANK BELLAMY
AS AIR REACHES THE MEN, THEY RECOVER. DANGER THREATENS F A NEW SOURCE...
LISTEN, JED... THAT CLICKING SOUND. WHAT IS IT?

LINKED TO THE DISASTER AREA BY NORMAL RADIO TRANSMITTER, THE CONTROLLER IS ABLE TO ASSESS THE SITUATION...

THEY CAN'T BREATHE... THIS TIME WE KNOW EXACTLY WHERE THEY ARE—BUT THERE'S NO TIME FOR OUR MACHINES TO GET THROUGH.

THOSE INTERNATIONAL RESCUE GUYS DID A FAST JOB LAST TIME. TRY TO CALL THEM.

JOHN TRACY, IN THUNDERBIRD 5, PICKS UP THE EMERGENCY CALL AND RELAYS IT TO TRACY ISLAND...

THIS IS A REAL HOT ONE, BOYS. GET MOVING, SCOTT.

OKAY, FATHER... SEE YOU THERE, VIRGIL.

YOU'LL NEED THUNDERBIRD 4 AND THE MOLE, VIRGIL...

COME ON, BIG BROTHER... LET'S GO!

THUNDERBIRD 1 TO THUNDERBIRD 2. YOU'LL HAVE TO LAUNCH GORDON SO THAT HE CAN GET AIR TO THOSE GUYS.

F.A.B., SCOTT... LEAVE IT TO US. YOU WARN THE AUTHORITIES TO GUARD THE AREA.

FIFTEEN MINUTES ARE LEFT AS THUNDERBIRD 2 STARTS ITS DESCENT ABOVE THE OCEAN...

...E GET ...E THROUGH ...M IN

...PECIAL DRILL ...S THE BORE ...DESCENDS, ...NTS THROUGH ...CK...

HEY... THEY'RE DRILLING THROUGH TO US...

YEH... BUT IF WE DON'T GET AIR SOON, THEY'LL BE SAVING CORPSES!

DANGER

...E ...ER... IT'S ...TERING ...TION ...RD!

THE ROCK CUTTER... THE ATOMIC REACTOR HAS BEEN DAMAGED!

ATOMIC REACTOR
AUTHORITY SEAL MUST NOT BE BROKEN

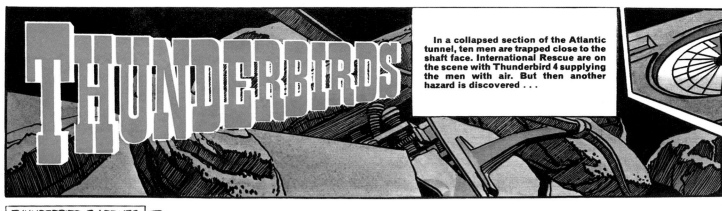

THUNDERBIRDS

In a collapsed section of the Atlantic tunnel, ten men are trapped close to the shaft face. International Rescue are on the scene with Thunderbird 4 supplying the men with air. But then another hazard is discovered . . .

THUNDERBIRD 2 ARRIVES...

BUT THE HOOD — CAUSE OF THE DISASTER — INTE TO TAKE NO NOTICE OF THE RESTRICTIONS...

EVERYONE BEEN ORDERE REMAIN EXACTL PRESENT POSIT THE POLICE GU GOOD THAT I PHOTOGRAPH

IT MOVES ALONG THE MAIN SHAFT AND BEGINS ITS VITAL WORK...

MOLE

UNSEEN, THE HOOD MANAGES TO LOCATE THE POLICE GUARD WHO IS SO VIVID IN HIS MEMORY...

THE RADIATION HAZARD INCREASES WITH EACH SECOND...

TWENTY MINUTES AND WE'LL ALL BE DEAD! CAN'T THAT DRILL OF YOURS GO ANY FASTER?

YOU'VE GOT TO SPEED THINGS UP, VIRGIL... EVEN NOW THOSE GUYS COULD HAVE SERIOUS AFTER EFFECTS.

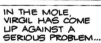

PHOTO ALERT

IN THE MOLE, VIRGIL HAS COME UP AGAINST A SERIOUS PROBLEM...

MOLE TO MOBILE CONTROL... THERE'S A STRATA OF SOLID GRANITE IMMEDIATELY AHEAD. IT COULD TAKE LONGER TO CUT THROUGH THAN WE FIGURED.

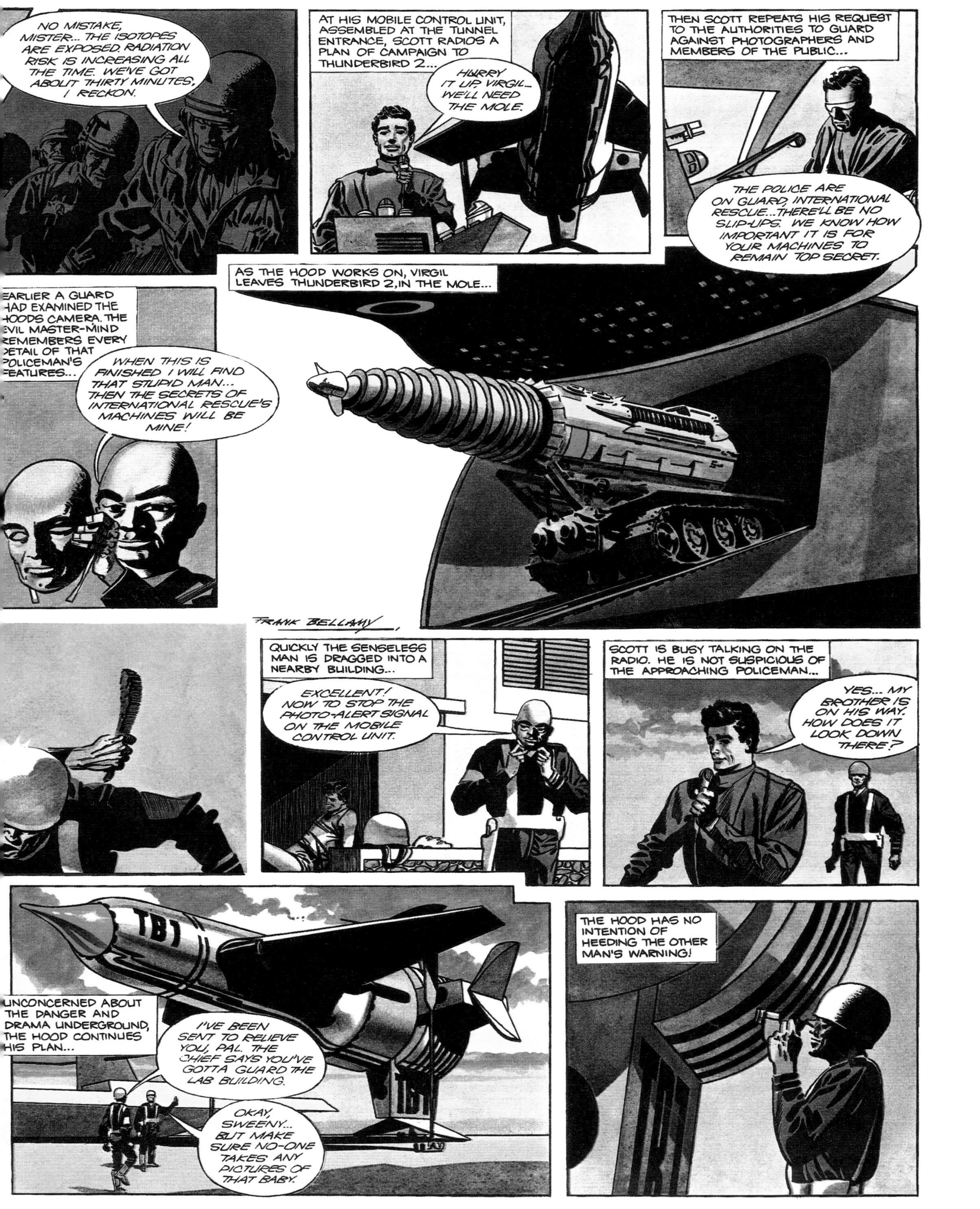

NO MISTAKE, MISTER... THE ISOTOPES ARE EXPOSED. RADIATION RISK IS INCREASING ALL THE TIME. WE'VE GOT ABOUT THIRTY MINUTES, I RECKON.
AT HIS MOBILE CONTROL UNIT, ASSEMBLED AT THE TUNNEL ENTRANCE, SCOTT RADIOS A PLAN OF CAMPAIGN TO THUNDERBIRD 2...
HURRY IT UP, VIRGIL... WE'LL NEED THE MOLE.
THEN SCOTT REPEATS HIS REQUEST TO THE AUTHORITIES TO GUARD AGAINST PHOTOGRAPHERS AND MEMBERS OF THE PUBLIC...
THE POLICE ARE ON GUARD, INTERNATIONAL RESCUE...THERE'LL BE NO SLIP-UPS. WE KNOW HOW IMPORTANT IT IS FOR YOUR MACHINES TO REMAIN TOP SECRET.
EARLIER A GUARD HAD EXAMINED THE HOODS CAMERA. THE EVIL MASTER-MIND REMEMBERS EVERY DETAIL OF THAT POLICEMAN'S FEATURES...
WHEN THIS IS FINISHED I WILL FIND THAT STUPID MAN... THEN THE SECRETS OF INTERNATIONAL RESCUE'S MACHINES WILL BE MINE!
AS THE HOOD WORKS ON, VIRGIL LEAVES THUNDERBIRD 2, IN THE MOLE...
FRANK BELLAMY
QUICKLY THE SENSELESS MAN IS DRAGGED INTO A NEARBY BUILDING...
EXCELLENT! NOW TO STOP THE PHOTO-ALERT SIGNAL ON THE MOBILE CONTROL UNIT.
SCOTT IS BUSY TALKING ON THE RADIO. HE IS NOT SUSPICIOUS OF THE APPROACHING POLICEMAN...
YES... MY BROTHER IS ON HIS WAY. HOW DOES IT LOOK DOWN THERE?
TB1
UNCONCERNED ABOUT THE DANGER AND DRAMA UNDERGROUND, THE HOOD CONTINUES HIS PLAN...
I'VE BEEN SENT TO RELIEVE YOU, PAL. THE CHIEF SAYS YOU'VE GOTTA GUARD THE LAB BUILDING.
OKAY, SWEENY... BUT MAKE SURE NO-ONE TAKES ANY PICTURES OF THAT BABY.
THE HOOD HAS NO INTENTION OF HEEDING THE OTHER MAN'S WARNING!

THUNDERBIRDS

Ten men are trapped in a collapsed shaft of the Atlantic Tunnel. One of the atomic excavating machines is damaged and radiation hazard is critical. Virgil Tracy, in International Rescue's machine The Mole, is up against tunnelling difficulties of the worst kind . . .

SCOTT CHECKS HIS ELECTRONIC SPEAKERS...

THERE'S BEEN A RADIO FAILURE ON THE LINK WITH THE DANGER ZONE. MAYBE GORDON CAN RAISE THEM.

THUNDERBIRD 4 IS ON THE SEA BED SUPPLYING AIR TO THE TRAPPED MEN...

I CAN HEAR THEM, SCOTT, OVER THE SONIC MICROPHONE. THEY ESTIMATE FIFTEEN MINUTES TO DISASTER.

AS THE DRAMA C... THE HOOD, IN TH... GUARD, IS COMP...

I THINK I SUFFICIEN... PICTURES ONE OF T... POWERFUL... THE W...

DRESSED IN HIS ANTI-RADIATION SUIT, VIRGIL MOVES PAST THE TRAPPED MEN...

I'VE GOT TO SEAL THE ISOTOPES... THESE MEN LOOK PRETTY BAD.

VIRGIL CLAMBERS INTO THE EXCAVATING MACHINE...

I CAN'T SHIFT THE ATOMIC MOTOR HATCH COVER!

FIGHTING AGAINST TIME, VIRGIL AT LAST FREES THE COVER...

HERE GOES... HOPE THERE ARE NO DEFECTS IN THIS SUIT.

HE SWEA... DANGERO... TASK BE...

AS THE HOOD MAKES HIS GETAWAY...

HEY! YOU'RE THE GUY WHO STOLE MY UNIFORM!

GET OUT OF MY WAY!

BUT THE POLICE GUARD HANGS ON...

LET'S HAVE A GOOD LOOK AT YOU... I'LL TEACH YOU TO IMPERSONATE ME!

DESPERATELY THE HOOD REACHES INTO HIS POCKET...

YOU ASKED FOR IT!

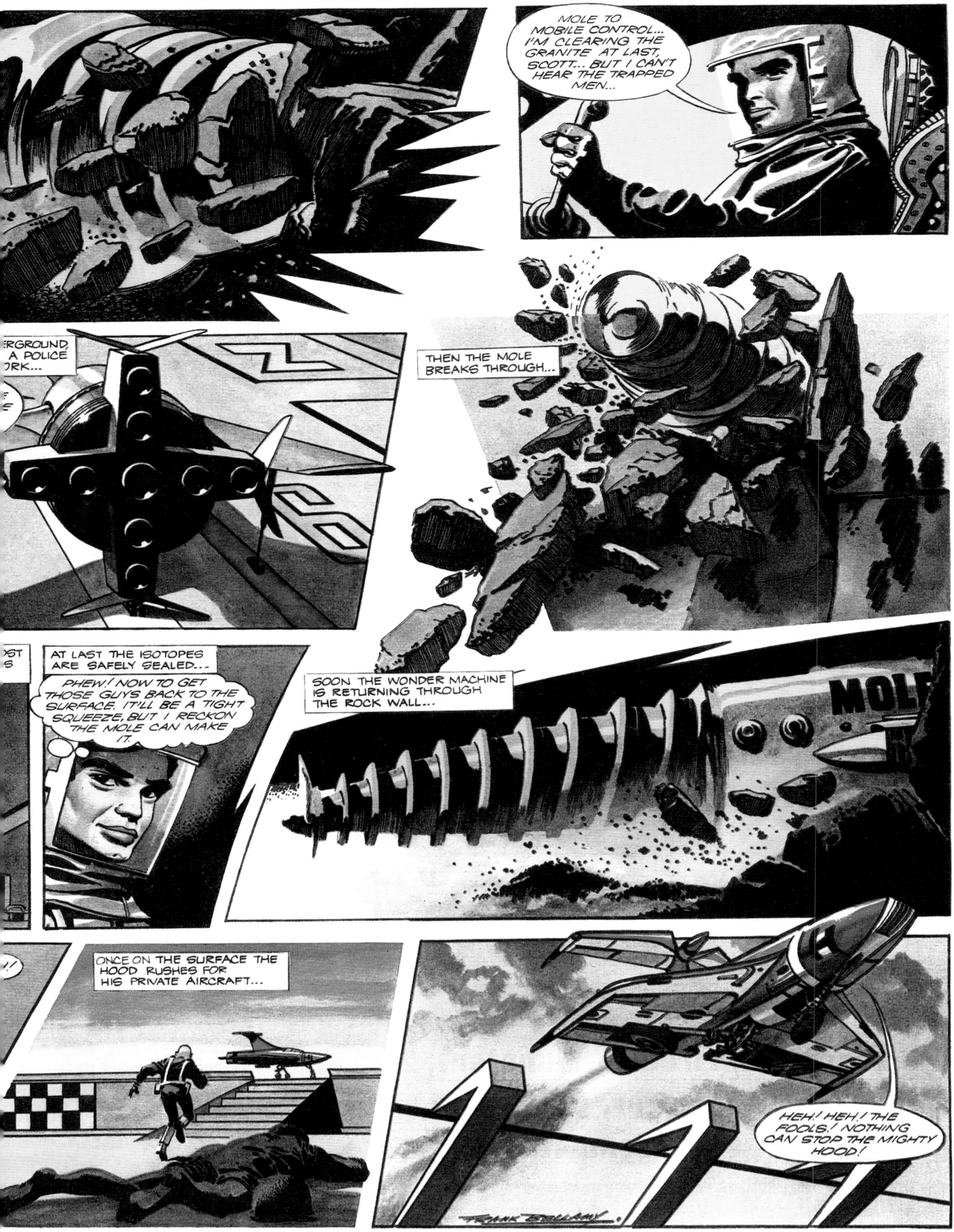
MOLE TO MOBILE CONTROL... I'M CLEARING THE GRANITE AT LAST, SCOTT... BUT I CAN'T HEAR THE TRAPPED MEN...
ERGROUND, A POLICE ORK...
THEN THE MOLE BREAKS THROUGH...
AT LAST THE ISOTOPES ARE SAFELY SEALED...
PHEW! NOW TO GET THOSE GUYS BACK TO THE SURFACE. IT'LL BE A TIGHT SQUEEZE, BUT I RECKON THE MOLE CAN MAKE IT.
SOON THE WONDER MACHINE IS RETURNING THROUGH THE ROCK WALL...
MOL
ONCE ON THE SURFACE THE HOOD RUSHES FOR HIS PRIVATE AIRCRAFT...
HEH! HEH! THE FOOLS! NOTHING CAN STOP THE MIGHTY HOOD!
FRANK BELLAMY

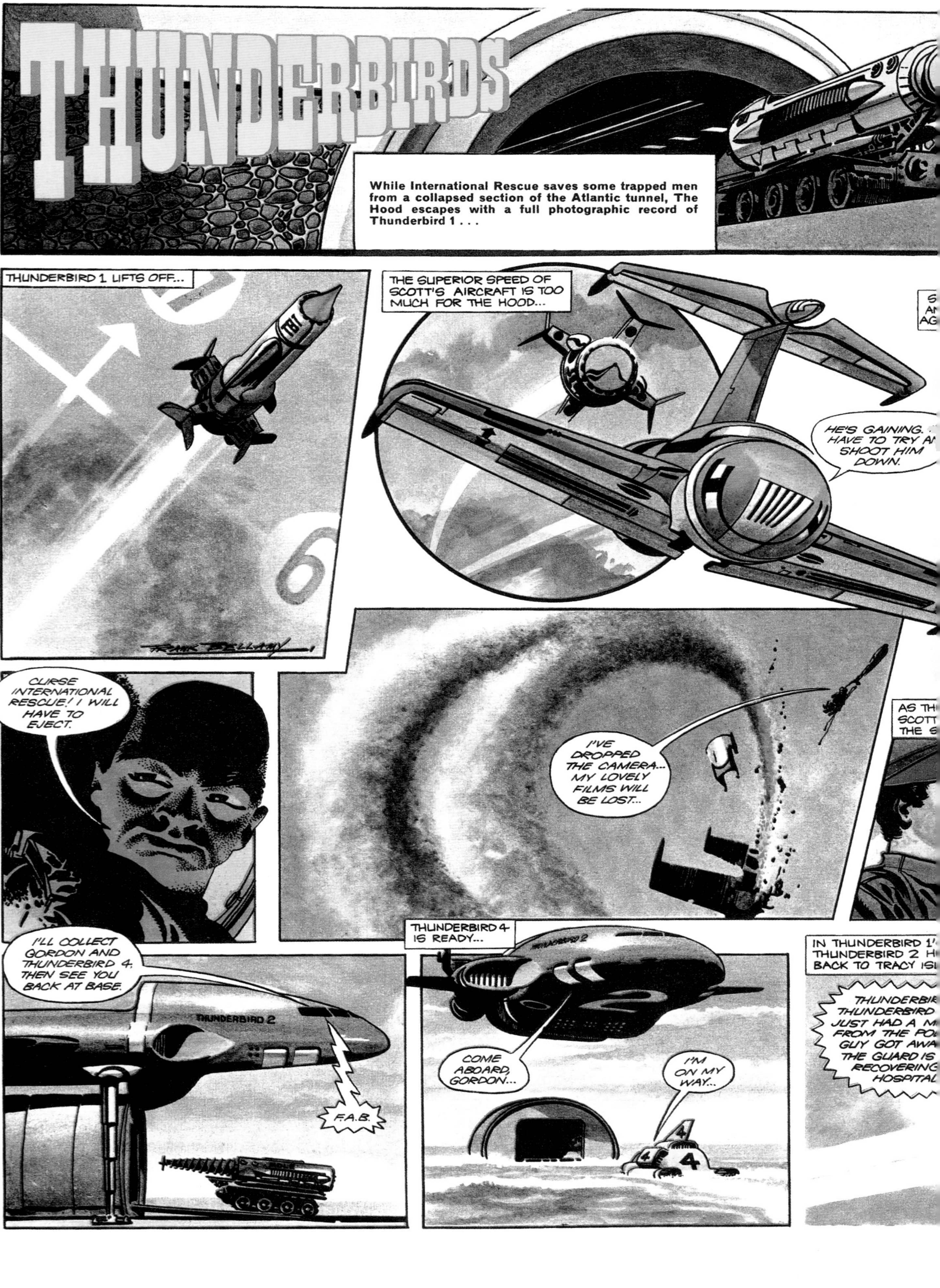
THUNDERBIRDS
While International Rescue saves some trapped men from a collapsed section of the Atlantic tunnel, The Hood escapes with a full photographic record of Thunderbird 1 . . .
THUNDERBIRD 1 LIFTS OFF...
TB1
FRANK BELLAMY
THE SUPERIOR SPEED OF SCOTT'S AIRCRAFT IS TOO MUCH FOR THE HOOD...
HE'S GAINING.
SHOOT HIM DOWN.
CURSE INTERNATIONAL RESCUE! I WILL HAVE TO EJECT.
I'VE DROPPED THE CAMERA... MY LOVELY FILMS WILL BE LOST...
I'LL COLLECT GORDON AND THUNDERBIRD 4. THEN SEE YOU BACK AT BASE.
THUNDERBIRD 2
F.A.B.
THUNDERBIRD 4 IS READY...
COME ABOARD, GORDON...
I'M ON MY WAY...

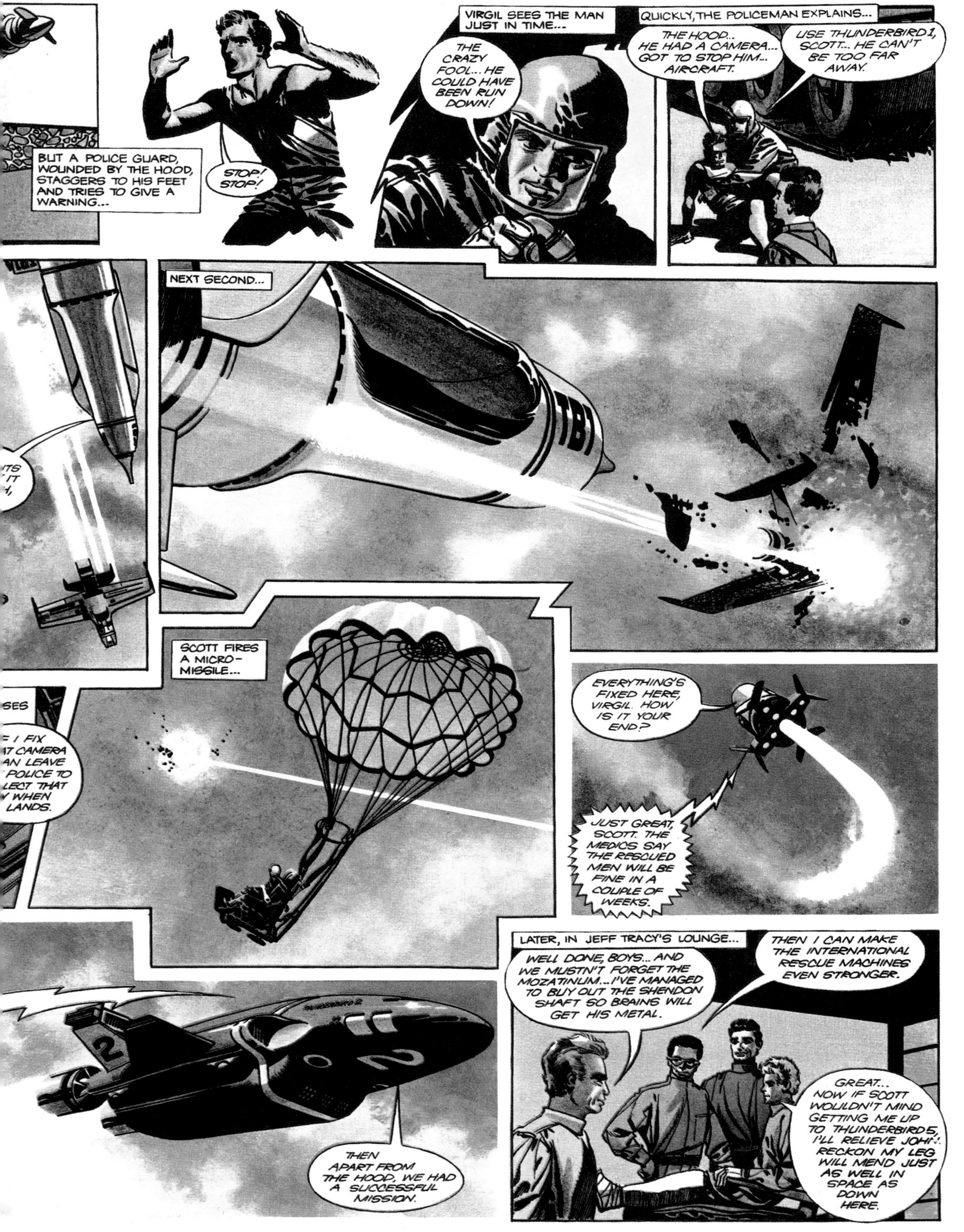
BUT A POLICE GUARD, WOUNDED BY THE HOOD, STAGGERS TO HIS FEET AND TRIES TO GIVE A WARNING...
STOP! STOP!
VIRGIL SEES THE MAN JUST IN TIME...
THE CRAZY FOOL... HE COULD HAVE BEEN RUN DOWN!
QUICKLY, THE POLICEMAN EXPLAINS...
THE HOOD... HE HAD A CAMERA... GOT TO STOP HIM... AIRCRAFT.
USE THUNDERBIRD 1, SCOTT... HE CAN'T BE TOO FAR AWAY.
NEXT SECOND...
SCOTT FIRES A MICRO-MISSILE...
LANDS.
EVERYTHING'S FIXED HERE, VIRGIL. HOW IS IT YOUR END?
JUST GREAT, SCOTT. THE MEDICS SAY THE RESCUED MEN WILL BE FINE IN A COUPLE OF WEEKS.
THEN APART FROM THE HOOD, WE HAD A SUCCESSFUL MISSION.
LATER, IN JEFF TRACY'S LOUNGE...
WELL DONE, BOYS... AND WE MUSTN'T FORGET THE MOZATINUM... I'VE MANAGED TO BUY OUT THE SHENDON SHAFT SO BRAINS WILL GET HIS METAL.
THEN I CAN MAKE THE INTERNATIONAL RESCUE MACHINES EVEN STRONGER.
GREAT... NOW IF SCOTT WOULDN'T MIND GETTING ME UP TO THUNDERBIRD 5, I'LL RELIEVE JOHN. RECKON MY LEG WILL MEND JUST AS WELL IN SPACE AS DOWN HERE.

Acknowledgements

The authors would like to thank the following for their help and support on this book:
Graeme Bassett, Milton Finesilver, Katie Bleathman, Alex Summersby, Steve Cambden, the *Salisbury Journal*, Keith Ansell.

Select Bibliography

Speakeasy, issue 100 (July 1989), "*The Unseen Frank Bellamy*" by Alan Woollcombe

Fraser of Africa (Hawk Books 1990) by Mike Higgs

Timescreen: British Telefantasy in Comics (Engale Marketing 1995) by Andrew Pixley

Fantasy Advertiser International vol 3, no. 50, November 1973: Frank Bellamy Interview, conducted by Dez Skinn and Dave Gibbons

Century 21, issue 10 Autumn 1992. "Frank Bellamy" by Richard Farrell

The Man Who Drew Tomorrow (Who Dares Publishing 1985) Alastair Crompton

Timeview: the Complete Doctor Who Illustrations of Frank Bellamy (Who Dares Publishing, 1985) by David Bellamy

Gopherville Argus (Bellamy Fanzine) 1993: Bill Stone, editor

Portal 31: Adventures in the 21st Century, Graeme Bassett, editor

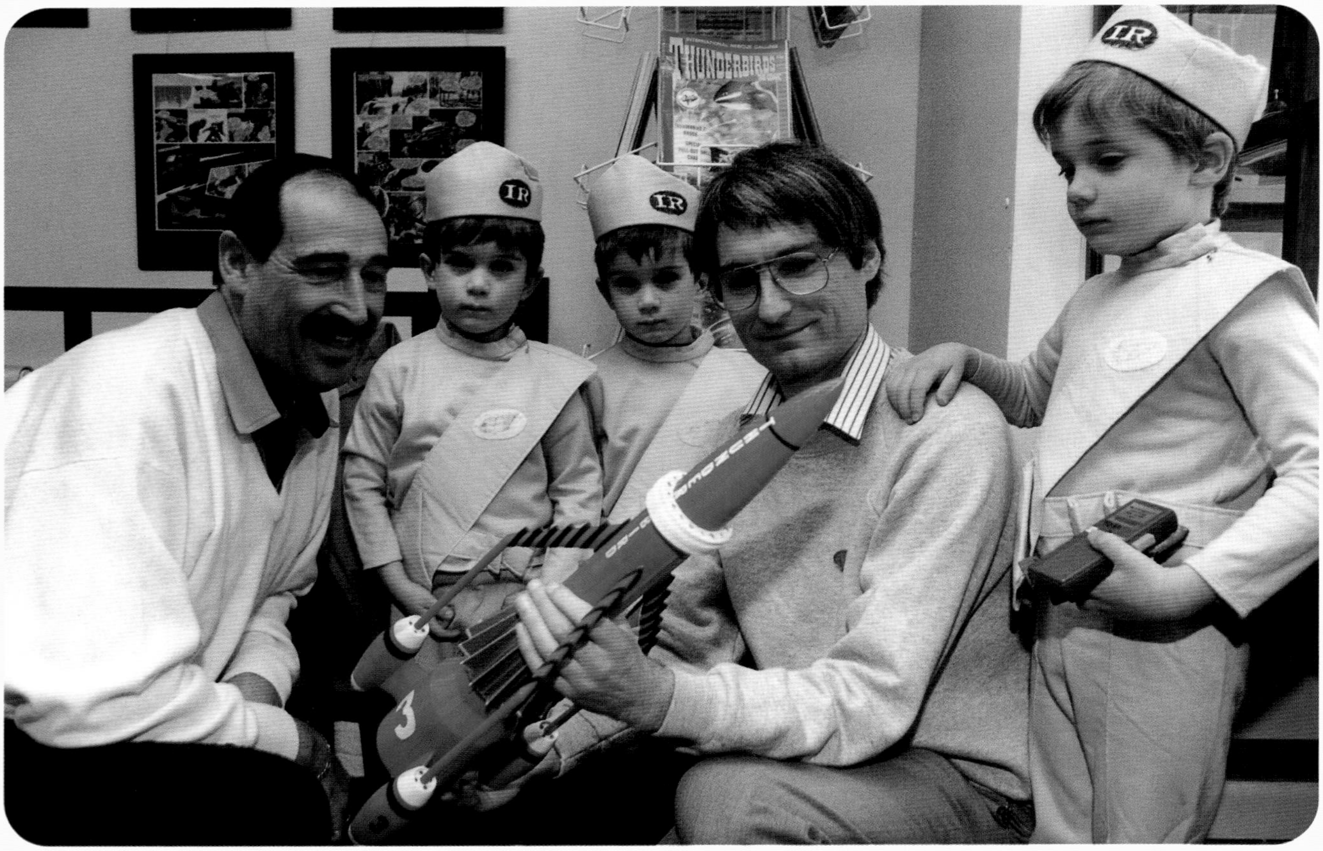
THUNDERBIRDS

Photo by Roger Elliott, *Salisbury Journal*

Alan Fennell with illustrator Graham Bleathman and local children at a signing in Salisbury for *Thunderbirds: The Comic* in 1992.

"It was a privilege to work for Alan during the 1990s. Drawing cross-sections on a regular basis for Thunderbirds: The Comic almost seemed like working on TV Century 21 itself."

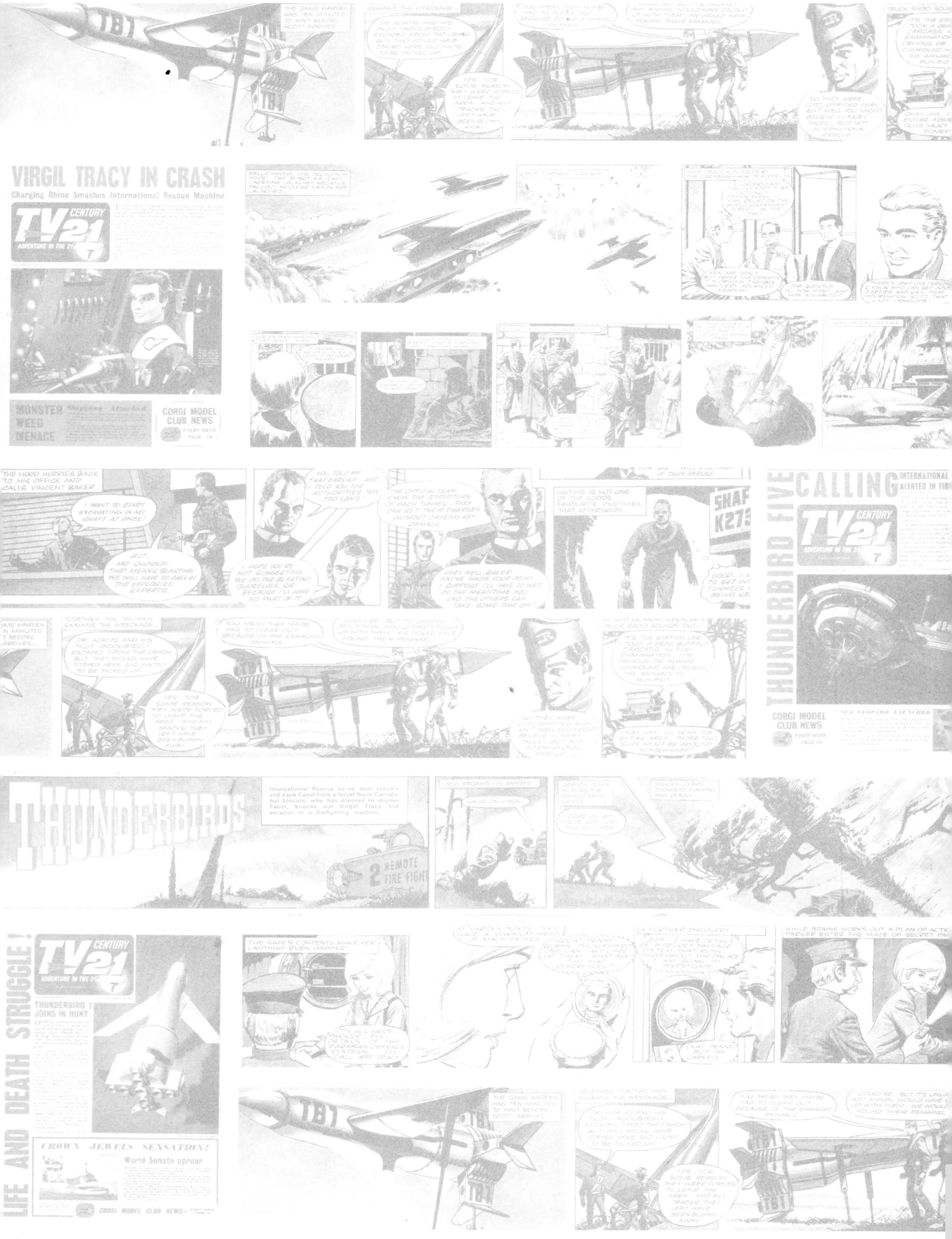

THE GAME WARDEN HAS TEN MINUTES TO WAIT BEFORE SCOTT ARRIVES.
VIRGIL TRACY IN CRASH
Charging Rhino Smashes International Rescue Machine
TV CENTURY 21
MONSTER WEED MENACE
CORGI MODEL CLUB NEWS
EVERY WEEK PAGE 19
BUT ZARABIA IS READY...
THE QUESTION IS, HOW MANY AND HOW ADVANCED?
THE HOOD HURRIES BACK TO HIS OFFICE AND CALLS VINCENT BAKER
I WANT TO START EXCAVATING IN MY SHAFT AT ONCE!
BUT, MR SHENDON THAT MEANS BLASTING. WE WILL HAVE TO CALL IN THE EXPLOSIVE EXPERTS.
YOU TOLD ME THAT EARLIER AND I TOLD YOU THE AUTHORITIES TAKE TOO LONG!
I HOPE YOU'RE NOT SUGGESTING WE DO THE BLASTING OURSELVES, SIR. BECAUSE I'LL HAVE NO PART OF IT.
THE OFFICIAL TEAM KNOW THE STRUCTURE OF EACH TUNNEL. THEY CAN SET THEIR CHARGES WITHOUT CAUSING ANY DAMAGE.
VERY WELL, BAKER. YOU'VE MADE YOUR POINT. I SUPPOSE I'LL HAVE TO WAIT. IN THE MEANTIME YOU AND THE OTHERS CAN TAKE SOME TIME OFF.
WAITING IS NOT ONE OF THE HOOD'S FAVOURITE PASTIMES THAT AFTERNOON.
THUNDERBIRD FIVE CALLING
TOGETHER THE TWO MEN EXAMINE THE WRECKAGE...
DR ADAMS AND HIS PILOT UNDOUBTEDLY ESCAPED FROM THE CRASH BUT THEY WOULD HAVE STAYED HERE AND WAITED TO BE PICKED UP.
YES. FOR SOME REASON THEY WERE FORCED TO LEAVE THE AREA... AND ANY TRACKS THEY LEFT HAVE BEEN BLOWN AWAY.
YOU MEAN THEY MAYBE HAD TO CLEAR OUT BECAUSE OF THE ENRAGED ANIMALS
COULD BE... BUT IT'S UNLIKELY ANY ANIMAL WOULD HAVE CAUGHT UP WITH THEM... WE WOULD HAVE FOUND THEIR REMAINS.
SO THEY WERE JUST SPIRITED AWAY. EH? WELL YOU MIGHT BELIEVE IN FAIRY TALES... BUT NOT INTERNATIONAL RESCUE.
AT THAT MOMENT, SPENCER'S TRUCK RADIO SOUNDS OUT...
IT'S THE STATION LAB. I TOOK A DEAD BUFFALO CARCASS IN FOR EXAMINATION. IT'S OBVIOUS DR ADAMS' COMPOUND HAS CAUSED THE ANIMALS TO RUN RIOT.
OKAY, JIM... I'LL SCAN THE ENTIRE AREA. THOSE TWO GUYS MUST BE AROUND SOMEWHERE!
THUNDERBIRDS
International Rescue saves Sam Lincoln and Jack Farrel from a forest fire in Canada, but Lincoln, who has planned to murder Farrel, knocks out Virgel Tracy and escapes in a firefighting machine
VIRGIL REGAINS HIS SENSES...
HANG ON, VIRGIL
LIFE AND DEATH STRUGGLE!
THUNDERBIRD 1 JOINS IN HUNT
THE SAFE'S CONTENTS MAKE HER LADYSHIP EVEN HAPPIER
A FURTHER DISCOVERY...
OKAY, PENNY... BUT BE CAREFUL.
CROWN JEWELS SENSATION!
World Senate uproar
CORGI MODEL CLUB NEWS

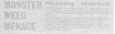

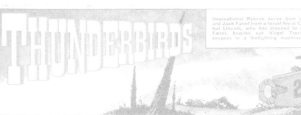

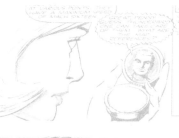

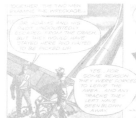